THE
THOMPSON
SISTERS
RACHEL'S PERIL
TRILOGY

GIRL OF LIES

GIRL OF RAGE

GIRL OF VENGEANCE

Books by Charles Sheehan-Miles

Thompson Sisters
A Song for Julia
Falling Stars
A View From Forever
Just Remember to Breathe
The Last Hour

Thompson Sisters / Rachel's Peril
Girl of Lies
Girl of Rage
Girl of Vengeance

America's Future
Republic
Insurgent

Nocturne (with Andrea Randall)

Prayer at Rumayla
A Novel of the Gulf War

Saving the World on Thirty Dollars a Day: An Activist's Guide to
Starting, Organizing and Running a Non-Profit Organization

Become A Full-Time Author (with Andrea Randall)

GIRL OF LIES
GIRL OF RAGE
GIRL OF VENGEANCE

www.sheehanmiles.com

Published by Cincinnatus Press
PO Box 814
South Hadley, Massachusetts
United States of America

ISBN: 978-1-63202-122-9

v04152015

GIRL
OF
LIES

Dedication

for Andrea

Acknowledgements

Thank you to Andrea. For your heart, your courage, your love.

Lori Sabin, you've been a wonderful editor for most of the Thompson Sisters books and Nocturne. Thank you.

Thank you to my fantastic beta reader team: Brett Lewis, Jackie Yeadon, Tanya Spence Hall, Kristen Teaff, Emma Corcoran, Kathy Harshaw Baker, Wendy Neuman Wilken, Dimitra Fleissner, Laura Wilson, Bryan James, Michelle Kannan, Sarah Griffin, Amy Burt, Jennifer Mirabelli, Stacy McDowell Grice, Kirsten Papi, Beth Suit, Rita Jenkins Post, Kelly Moorhouse, Kirsty Lander and Sally Bouley.

Thank you to Ashley Wilcox and ACS Tours for organizing the blog tour.

Jillian Dodd, Tiffany King, Tara Sivec, Michelle Pace, Les Pace, Maggi Myers, Jenn Sterling, Melissa Perea, Michelle Warren and Priscilla Glenn form part of my professional network of authors: all gave advice and suggestions regarding the cover, blurb and more through this process. Thank you.

Cast of Characters

The Thompson Family

Richard Thompson
Adelina Thompson
Julia Wilson (Thompson)
— Crank Wilson
Carrie Thompson-Sherman
— Ray Sherman
— Rachel Sherman
Alexandra Paris (Thompson)
— Dylan Paris
Sarah Thompson
Jessica Thompson
Andrea Thompson

The Wakhan File

Roshan al Saud
Leslie Collins
Mitch Filner
Vasily Karatygin
Senator Chuck Rainsley

The British

George-Phillip Patrick Nicholas, Duke of Kent
Duncan Howard, Prime Minister
Oswald O'Leary
Stephen Easton, Ambassador to the United States

Diplomatic Security

John "Bear" Wyden
Leah Simpson
Scott Kelly

The Washington Post

Anthony Walker

The Investigation

Rory Armitage, Special Prosecutor
Wolfram Schmidt, Internal Revenue Service
Emma Smith, Internal Revenue Service

Prologue

Andrea Thompson

Andrea Thompson shivered as Javier's hands slid up the back of her shirt, his fingers curled, raising goose bumps and sensation as they ran down her spine. She gasped a little as his lips touched her, his stubble rough against her neck.

"*Te quiero*," he said as her back arched, pressing her chest against him. I want you.

"No," she replied. "*Abuelita* expects me home."

He sighed, lifting his head. His eyes were dark, too dark, easy to get lost in. "You know you're the only girl I want, ever."

She put her lips to his ear, the faint, aquatic smell of his cologne gratifying her senses. "You say that because your *verga* is hard and I'm in the car with you. You want every girl you see, Javier. Take me home."

He smiled, his full lips curving up a little more on the right side, and said, "*Sí*, Andrea."

One second later, she felt the buzzing of her phone in her pocket, and then the ringtone that represented her sisters.

He sighed, and broke away from her, his smile wistful. She returned the smile as she dug in her jacket pocket for her phone. As Javier started the car, she got the phone out. *Mierda!* She wasn't in time.

"Which one of your sisters is it?"

"Carrie," she said as she unlocked the phone. "She lives in Washington, DC."

As Andrea dialed the phone, she counted the hours back. It was close to ten pm in Calella, so that would make it about four in the afternoon in Washington. She hadn't expected to hear from Carrie. Truthfully, she hadn't expected to hear from any of her sisters. Julia, the oldest of her sisters at thirty-two years old, was the only one who called her regularly.

"Hello?" Carrie's voice. A little breathy.

"Carrie? It's Andrea."

"Andrea! Thank you so much for calling back so quickly! Your number didn't show up on my phone."

Andrea shrugged. International calls could be weird sometimes. "How are you? How's the baby?"

Silence. Just long enough that Andrea sat up straight in her seat, her eyebrows scrunching together, and then she said, "Carrie? What's going on? How's the baby?"

Andrea felt a shiver down her spine at the sound of a sniffle from Carrie. Carrie, the foundation of her family, the daughter who'd always taken care of all of them. Carrie, who lost her husband to murder and tragedy less than a year ago.

"Andrea...I need help. Rachel needs help."

"Anything," Andrea said without thinking.

"Can you come? To Washington?"

Andrea swallowed. "I have school..."

"Andrea. Rachel is very sick...she needs a bone marrow transplant. And I'm not a close enough match. I just...will you come get tested? *Please?*"

Andrea had seen little Rachel's pictures on Facebook. A beautiful, tiny, five-week-old baby. Carrie and Ray's daughter, who would never know her father.

Carrie couldn't take any more pain.

"Of course I'll come."

Andrea shivered at the sound of a sob on the other line. She looked up and met Javier's eyes. He raised his eyebrows, and she mouthed the words *llévame a casa.* Take me home.

Javier nodded and put the car in gear. A moment later, he was driving through the narrow streets of Calella. "I'm going home now, Carrie. I'll talk with *Abuelita* and get a flight home right away, okay? I promise." As she spoke the words, she couldn't help but see in her mind how much of a mess her sister had been eight months ago. Everything had been a disaster. Her husband Ray was in the hospital alongside their sister Sarah, both of them badly injured in a car accident that turned out to be intentional.

Murder. That's what it had been. Ray, her brother-in-law who she barely knew, had been brutally murdered. And now his daughter was sick.

Andrea sighed. She would figure out something for school. Right now she needed to make arrangements to get back to the United States.

Javier turned the car onto Carrer Diputatio, the tiny one lane street two blocks from the beach. Abuelita, her grandmother, had her flat here, a third floor apartment above the don Panini snack bar. The snack bar was still open when Javier pulled the car to a stop in front of it, and patrons were crowded into the open restaurant and spilling out onto the sidewalk. Bared midriffs, short skirts, coverall dresses, sweat and carnal intentions. Loud music blasted out of the Isard restaurant and pizzeria across the narrow lane. A car came to a stop behind Javier's and the driver immediately honked the horn as more traffic backed up behind it.

"You're going away?" Javier asked, ignoring the honking.

She signed. Then nodded. "I have to go to the United States."

"You'll be careful?"

She thought the question seemed odd. Of course she'd be careful. "I'll be back soon. My niece needs a bone marrow transplant. I'm probably not even a match. But I have to go to my sister."

The driver behind them honked his horn again, shouting obscenities out the open window. The street was too narrow for him to drive around unless he went onto the sidewalk in front of the *Gaviota* bar, which had a crowd of twenty or more people crowded outside.

"I have to go," she said.

"*Te amo,*" he said softly.

Andrea shivered, even though she knew he didn't mean it. Because...what if he did? She leaned forward and kissed him goodbye.

"*Despedida,*" she said. *Farewell.* Then she slipped out of the car, shutting the door behind her.

The driver behind Javier, an angry, frustrated man in his mid thirties with a remarkable mustache, had laid on the horn, letting it continuously sound. She gave mustache-man a scornful look, slapped her left bicep with her right hand and raised her left fist in an obscene gesture. Then she slipped into her grandmother's apartment building.

CHAPTER ONE
Hairy Chest

1. Andrea. April 28. 11:30 am EST

"**Is** Washington your final destination?" the man asked. He wore a black suit with a white shirt, the collar open. Medium brown skin with a hairy chest, Andrea thought he looked Arab, possibly from Egypt or Saudi Arabia. His eyes danced a little, from her face to the swell of her breasts, and he spoke too loud, even over the whine of the jets. A creeper, probably. He wore cologne, too much of it, and Andrea was disturbed to notice that it was the same scent as Javier's, but not *exactly* the same. The man next to her smelled earthier, almost musky. Disturbing.

She shifted in her seat, hoping the questions were friendly, but not too friendly. She didn't relish an eight-hour flight with someone hoping to get lucky.

"It is," she said.

"Business? Vacation?"

"Personal," Andrea answered, looking him straight in the eye. "I don't have any business, I'm sixteen. My father's an American diplomat and I'm flying home."

The creeper swallowed. "I'm headed that way for business," he said. Then his eyes darted to her legs.

Damn it. Her sister Julia had made her travel arrangements, and she was flying first class. So far as she could see there weren't any other first-class seats, and as much as she didn't want to ride all the way to the United States with this guy checking her out, she also didn't want to ride in the back of the plane, jammed in like commuters on a Tokyo subway.

She reached into her purse and took out a paperback guide to backpacking in Italy, which she was planning to do that summer. More importantly, the book would act as a shield, hopefully fending off a too friendly conversationalist. Once the flight was in the air, she would switch to her laptop. She wanted to research *beta thalassemia major*, a rare genetically linked condition that could result in severe anemia. Failure to thrive. Bone malformation. Early death.

Rachel had it.

How was that even possible?

She certainly didn't know of anyone in the family with thalassemia. What little she'd had time to read while waiting for the cab to take her to the airport hadn't reassured her. The lifetime prognosis wasn't good unless they could find a matching donor.

She tried to bend her mind away from her niece's health condition and back to the book. Her creeper kept his distance while she read. Or pretended to. Her mind wasn't really focused on the intricacies of the youth hostels of Italy, and what she really wanted to do once the plane was in the air was put her seat back and take a nap. She'd barely made the last non-stop out of Barcelona and would arrive in Baltimore late in the afternoon. But if she caught a short nap now, she'd be able to stay up most of the flight. Or…something. Jetlag was hell.

In any event, within half an hour the flight was in the air, the seat belt signs were off, she had cup of tea and her laptop was open, earbuds plugged into her phone and music playing.

Her first stop was Wikipedia, where she began reading about genetic blood disorders. She found it interesting that Queen Victoria of England had apparently spontaneously carried hemophilia as a mutation, which she'd then passed on to her children and ultimately several European royal houses in Russia, Spain and Germany. *The Royal Disease*, it had been called. Thanks to all the inbreeding. But thalassemia was primarily seen in people with Mediterranean and Asian backgrounds, which of course the sisters shared through their mother Adelina. And while it didn't have the immediate life-threatening properties of hemophilia, the longterm effects were just as severe.

She pressed pause on her music, shifting in her seat. Time to make a stop in the facilities.

"Excuse me."

Andrea jerked in her seat, looking up from the computer. It was her next door neighbor in first class, Mister Hairy Chest.

"Yes?"

"I couldn't help but noticing you were researching medical conditions. Are you a medical student?"

That was just…strange. Why would he ask that? She'd already told him she was only sixteen. She didn't want to be a giant bitch. But something about him set off all her alarms. "No," she replied. "I'm in secondary school. I'm reading… actually my niece has a genetic blood disease…I'm going to Washington to help my sister."

"Ahhh," he said. "I see. I only ask because I've considered going to med school."

Andrea let a breath out. Something about this guy rubbed her completely the wrong way. But Abuelita hadn't raised her to be impolite to anyone.

"Are you a student?" she asked.

"I am...*Universidad Autònoma de Madrid.*"

"I see. And you study...?" One of the several schools she'd looked into had been UAM.

His teeth gleamed in a broad grin. "Mechanical engineer. I'm in my third year."

She swallowed, feeling an odd tightness in her chest. "Well. That's nice. Excuse me just a moment."

She slid her laptop into the leather pocket of the seat in front of her and folded back the table, then slipped out of her seat. Heart thudding a little, she made her way to the restroom at the front of the cabin, stepped inside and closed and locked the door.

Something was wrong. She'd spent two days touring the University and had met with the science and engineering faculty there. He was a lot older than his twenties. And UAM didn't have a major in mechanical engineering. Which meant Hairy Chest was lying.

Why?

2. George-Phillip. April 28

"**S**ir? A moment please?"

George-Phillip looked up from his desk, raising his ample eyebrows. There were only two people in the Special Intelligence Service...four people in the entire country...who could walk into his exquisitely decorated office and interrupt him without an appointment. As the Chief of the SIS he controlled the British government's foreign intelligence service. Thousands upon thousands of people and billions of pounds dedicated to tracking the enemies of the Queen. And friends, of course.

George-Phillip—formally known as *Prince* George-Phillip, Duke of Kent—had served in the SIS since 1986. Unlike his father, who had been content to waste the family's fortune on fast cars, drunken parties and inappropriate women, George-Phillip had decided immediately on his father's death that he would spend his life in service to his country. And he had done so, for more than thirty years. One could almost say he had his position in spite of his heritage—members of the Royal family, even those so far removed from the throne that assuming it would be inconceivable, simply did not rise to high ranks in the *civil* service.

George-Phillip, however, ended up with a fairly unique career. Starting with a brief stint as a special aide to the ambassador in Washington, DC, he'd attended Sandhurst, the Royal Military Academy, and then entered the SIS. That career had taken him to places as diverse as Afghanistan and China, Istanbul and Paris and finally here, at the nerve center of the intelligence world.

George-Phillip's role in the intelligence world was well known by the public—after all, he often appeared in testimony before Parliament or in meetings. He was clearly recognizable in public by his unusual height and his bushy, over expressive eyebrows. George-Phillip had eyebrows that were unruly, often out of control, acting out their own soliloquy regardless of his audience or his desires. It was his eyebrows that kept George-Phillip honest. It was his eyebrows (or, as the *Times* always said, his *unibrow*) that provided the media with plenty of entertainment fodder.

SIS Chief Raises Eyebrow Over Improprieties, said one headline on the front page of the *Mirror*. He was still convinced, two years later, the picture had been manipulated in Photoshop.

George-Phillip took such things in stride. His job didn't require that he be popular with the British public, nor did it require a movie-star reputation. It *did* require credibility, and that George-Phillip had. His credibility had led him unerringly to the job of Ambassador to the United Nations, followed by his current position as Chief of the Special Intelligence Service.

At the door was Oswald O'Leary. O'Leary was as unlikely an aide as one could ever expect the Chief of Intelligence to have. He was Irish, for one thing. Small, with beady eyes and the flattened nose and hanging jowls of a pug, O'Leary always looked as if he wanted to grab the nearest person and just *shake* them.

He was also brilliant, incredibly loyal, and therefore the recipient of some of the most unusual assignments George-Phillip could hand out.

"Sir, I have some information on the Wakhan file."

George-Phillip winced inwardly. Then he beckoned O'Leary forward.

"What is it?"

O'Leary laid the file on his desk and George-Phillip opened it. His eyes widened.

"Andrea Thompson," O'Leary said. "This is the youngest daughter of Ambassador Thompson."

There was no mistaking who she was, even though she was much older now. A much younger twin to Carrie Thompson, her older sister. Dark hair, pale bluegreen eyes, fair skin, remarkable height.

"What's the situation with the Thompson children?"

O'Leary shifted. "It seems she lives in Spain with Ambassador Thompson's mother-in-law, and has little contact with the family. She did briefly visit the United States last summer during the Dega Payan court-martial, then returned home."

"So what takes her home now?"

"It seems that she's to be tested as a possible donor match."

George-Phillip raised his hand to his mouth, covering it. He closed his eyes and sat, motionless, for several seconds. Finally, his eyes opened and darted to O'Leary. "It is imperative you keep me informed, O'Leary. This is a matter of the highest national security. You understand?"

O'Leary looked back at George-Phillip with grim eyes. "I understand, sir."

3. Andrea. April 28. 4:35 pm

As always, Baltimore-Washington International airport was a chaotic mess of people. Andrea moved through the crowds, grateful that she finally shook Hairy Chest at Customs. Her U.S. passport took her into a separate line, and that was all it took. Now, as she walked to the ground transportation area to catch her ride, she also kept an eye out for his return. Her backpack was slung over her shoulder and she wheeled a larger suitcase behind her.

The terminal smelled like machine oil and body odor, and every few minutes overhead speakers burst out in mechanical sounding voices, making announcements in half a dozen languages. Finally she found her way to the baggage carousel. Her last two flights into Washington, DC had taken her through Dulles airport, and her unfamiliarity with this one made everything just a little bit more difficult.

On top of that, her mobile wouldn't boot back up. The black screen mocked her repeated attempts to turn it on. She supposed the battery was dead, but now, once she found her luggage, she was going to have to find a pay phone. If such a thing even still existed.

Finally. Ahead, near the taxi entrance, a man stood holding an iPad with the name "Andrea Thompson"displayed with glowing white letters.

"Hello!" she called, waving to the man. He was tall, in his mid-thirties, with a blonde crew-cut and blue eyes. He didn't look like a limo driver...he looked like a bodyguard.

Of course, if Julia had sent him, he might well be a bodyguard.

"I'm Andrea," she said.

He flashed a mouthful of glowing white teeth at her. "Nice to meet ya, Miss Thompson. I'm Dan. This way to the car...you got any luggage? Just that?"

He reached out a hand and took her suitcase. She turned to follow him, then said, "Wait…" and walked, slowly toward the newspaper stand next to the exit.

The *Washington Post* was displayed prominently, and caught her eye, because her father's photograph was splashed across the cover. The headline was a shock. *Ambassador Thompson tapped for Defense Secretary.*

She didn't realize her father was planning to come out of retirement. And Secretary of Defense?

The driver—Dan—paused, failing to hide his irritation. Andrea shrugged. That didn't matter to her. And what was the idea of sending a driver to pick her up anyway? She wasn't close to her family, but it felt awfully impersonal to send a hired driver.

Then again, her mother was probably there, and Adelina Thompson was Queen of the impersonal.

Andrea pulled the top paper off the stack and handed over her debit card, hoping it would work in the United States. She held her breath for a moment. It did. Then she turned and followed Dan to a black Lincoln Town Car. He opened the back door and she slid inside. The back seat was wide, leather. Cool and comfortable. A moment later the car shuddered as he tossed her bag into the trunk and closed it.

As he slid into his seat, she said, "Do you have a USB phone charger? Mine's dead."

Dan grunted, then leaned over and dug in the glove box. "I've got one, but the only plug is up here."

"Do you mind plugging this in?" she asked, and then passed her phone forward.

"Sure."

A horn honked somewhere behind them. Dan glanced in the rearview mirror. For a second she thought she saw a flash of worry in his eyes, but it was gone as quick as it came. Then he looked away and put the car in gear.

Where the car sat now, it was dim, one or more layers of road and parking deck above them. Taxicabs and shuttle buses surrounded them, the sound of horns and engines overriding everything except the occasional jet engine, the smell of diesel fumes heavy in the air. She was glad the window was up as she leaned back in her seat and said, "How long will it take to get to Bethesda from here?"

The driver shrugged. "Depends on traffic." He turned away from her and began to drive, turning the radio on and flooding the car with the sound of too-loud and too-excited disk jockeys.

Andrea felt tension tighten the muscles in her neck and shoulders. At the very end of the ground transportation area stood Hairy Chest. His eyes scanned the traffic, looking for his ride. He didn't have any bags, just a small backpack. Odd for an international flight. At least she was done with him. She leaned forward in her seat a little to look at her phone, laying on the dashboard. It hadn't taken enough of a charge to start yet.

Dan muttered, "Can you sit back please?" Then she jerked in her seat as he suddenly swing the car over to the curb, directly in front of Hairy Chest.

Before she could speak or say anything, Hairy Chest opened the door and jumped into the front passenger seat. "What the hell?" she cried, reaching for the door handle.

It pulled, but the door didn't open. She yanked at the handle again, as Hairy Chest shouted, "Go! Go!"

Dan, the driver, hit the gas, the car accelerating rapidly away from the airport.

CHAPTER TWO
AMBER Alert

1. Sarah. April 28. 4:50 pm

Sarah Thompson leaned her head against the steering wheel, trying to contain her frustration. The sound of cars and shuttle buses echoed off the roof above her, and she could smell gasoline and diesel fumes in the air. The text message from her little sister Andrea was clear enough. She was waiting at the Terminal C, near ground transportation, at the first exit from the terminal.

That's where Sarah was. That's where the cop waving her on was. But Andrea was nowhere in sight.

She double-checked her phone, and then sent a reply.

I'm here … where are you?

This time there was no response at all. *What now?*

Sarah had turned eighteen years old just a few weeks before, and she was a bundle of walking contradictions. Dressed in grey and black, her hair was cut off in jagged, rough edges at her collar, died black with bleached white highlights shifting as her head moved. Dark eyeliner and mascara set off pale blue eyes that scanned the terminal for her sister.

The cop waved her on again. His face was growing tense.

She checked her phone again. Still no answer. Had Andrea's battery died? What the hell?

A loud rap on the window. She jerked in her seat.

"You can't sit here." The cop...actually TSA...looked cranky. His face was a little round, a little red in the cheeks. Late forties, balding, a good-sized paunch. But the gun on his hip and the badge he wore were real enough.

Sarah rolled down the window. "I'm picking up my little sister."

"Go back around, and wait at the cell phone lot until she calls you." The cop's demeanor was agitated.

Feeling her face flush, "She *did* call me. I'm confused, she says she's at Terminal C at the first exit."

The cop frowned. "Well, is she?"

Sarah shrugged. "No! I don't understand, look, here's the text from her." She showed him the phone, with Andrea's message. **I am Terminal C, next to first exit.**

The cop shook his head. "She must be confused. How old is your sister?"

"Sixteen," Sarah responded.

The cop frowned, looking at the text. "And when did she send you this text?"

"Five minutes ago? I tried to call her back and she's not answering now."

He stood there for a moment, as if undecided whether or not to take this seriously. Then he looked back at Sarah. "All right, I want you to pull ahead, down there to the end of the terminal so you aren't blocking traffic. I'll meet you there in two minutes."

Sarah nodded, her pulse throbbing in the arteries in her neck. She knew it was nothing. Andrea was in one of the other terminals, and her battery had died, or something else. Andrea was fine.

But sometimes, even when you thought things were fine, they weren't. She'd learned that the hard way. It still felt like yesterday. She'd been sitting in the back seat of Carrie's Mercedes, arguing with Jessica, when a jeep came out of nowhere, slamming into the car. Instantly her life had changed. Everything changed. When she woke, her brother-in-law Ray was dead, killed in the accident.

Not accident. It was murder. It took away the life of her sister's husband. Sarah herself had nearly died, and undergone major surgeries leaving her left leg scarred with what looked like huge shoe laces running up the outside of her calf up to her thigh. She spent weeks in the hospital, months in a wheelchair, and still went to physical therapy twice a week.

That wasn't the worst part. The worst part was the panic.

It snuck up on her, always. She'd think about Carrie and the pregnancy, or Rachel after she was born, or her twin Jessica, and a tiny tendril of fear would work its way into her chest. Her muscles would tighten up, her breath quickening, and soon she felt as if her throat were closing and she couldn't breathe.

She hadn't told anyone about the panic attacks. She hadn't told anyone that sometimes she thought she was going to die. But moments like this, her muscles would tense, and the pain in her chest would bloom like some hideous flower, and the tears would be just below the surface ready to burst. Sometimes she felt a tingling in her fingertips and in her throat, as if she'd been electrified.

Now, she swallowed the rock in her throat as she pulled the car up to the sidewalk just past the terminal. The cop jogged over to her, then leaned in to her.

Sarah tried to slow her breathing.

"All right...by the way, I'm Officer Harmon. Let me get some details from you, and we'll find your sister, okay? First, what's her name?"

"Andrea Thompson."

"Age?"

"Sixteen."

"Traveling alone?"

"Yes...she flew in on, um...American Airlines flight 3663 from Madrid."

"Spain?"

"Yes..."

"Why was she traveling alone?"

"She lives there with our grandmother...she flew in because our niece is sick...and may need bone marrow transplants. We're all being tested."

The cop nodded. "I see. Description?"

"Um...I haven't seen her in a few months." She felt a sharp pain in her chest as she said the words. The last time she'd seen Andrea, Sarah was still in the hospital, out of her mind with grief and morphine. "She's um...tall. Six feet. Dark brown hair. Green eyes. Not sure what she's wearing."

"All right. And she definitely got off the plane from Madrid."

"You saw the text," she replied.

Officer Harmon grimaced. "Yeah. All right, hold still, I'm calling this in. The airport will page her, and we'll alert TSA and the police to look out for her. She's in the airport somewhere, all right? She's probably in the bathroom or something, and you guys will get a big laugh out of this in a few minutes. You got a picture of your sister? On your phone?"

Sarah nodded, trying to contain the panicky feeling bubbling up in her chest. She flipped through her photos as quickly as she could, but she couldn't find any recent pictures of Andrea. *Wait.* She went online. Andrea had updated her profile picture just a few days ago.

"I've got it."

"Can you text that to me?" Officer Harmon gave her the number.

A moment later, Harmon stepped away and began speaking rapidly into the microphone at his shoulder. She barely heard the words through the rushing sound in her ears. "White female…sixteen years old…unaccompanied minor…did not meet sister at ground transportation…"

Sarah stared at the steering wheel. Her chest was twisting tighter and tighter, so much that she felt a sharp pain in her sternum. She put a fist to her chest, trying to breathe.

"You all right, miss?"

She tried to answer, but couldn't, just nodded her head, tears welling up. In her head, the thoughts kept running through her mind. *Please be okay. Please be okay. Don't let her be hurt too.*

Hands shaking, she picked up her phone and sent another text message to Andrea.

Call. Me. Please.

No reply.

Flashes of her hospitalization ran through her mind. The bizarre dreams she'd had of walking through the ghostly hospital with Ray. Waking up to find her leg cut open from ankle to thigh, swollen to triple its normal diameter, shoelace-sized sutures crisscrossed over the surgical wound, her brain fuzzy from heavy doses of morphine.

In her dream she'd made a promise to someone. Ray? Her sisters? She couldn't remember what the promise was, and it terrified her.

"Miss?"

Jerked back to the present, she looked up at Officer Harmon. "Can you come with me? One of the other officers will keep an eye on your car."

"Yeah," she said. The shaking threatened to burst into the open, and the one thing she would not do, the one thing she *refused* to do, was give in to the slightest weakness in front of anyone else. There would be no fucking tears. No fucking shaking. No panic. No *nothing.*

She opened the car door and stepped out. The cop got his first good look at her and his eyes went a little wide. She wore a grey t-shirt with the *Yellowcard* logo emblazoned across it. Whenever it wasn't too cold she stuck with shorts and miniskirts, hiding none of the extensive scarring on her left leg. Right now she wore black shorts, and the crisscrossed pattern of scars on her leg stood out above her black leather combat boots.

With one look at Sarah's leg, Officer Harmon was thrown way off balance. In some ways, that helped her regain her own. She said, "Where to?"

Harmon didn't kid around. Taking long strides, he led her through the clean, well-lit terminal. She had to run to keep up, and a moment later he stopped at an unmarked door and swiped an access card.

Behind the door was a hallway. It was utilitarian, the walls the dull beige of a public school or hospital, the floor scuffed and cracked tile. Outside was the public area, brushed with veneer of polished wood and glass, an exfoliated and cosmetic covered skin disguising an aging, sickly infrastructure the public never viewed. Inside, the debilitated condition lasted right up to the door of the security suite.

Security, here as everywhere in the United States, was well funded, portly, even corpulent. Inside, the equipment was new and expensive, the product of more than a decade of continuous budget priority. Half a dozen uniformed TSA officers sat at desks with security camera feeds in front of them. Three large displays on the wall cycled through various security camera feeds all over the airport, and the security center as a whole had a high-tech, well funded appearance.

A tall African American man approached her. "You're Miss Thompson?"

"Sarah."

"Lieutenant Aaron Miller. I'm with the Transportation Security Administration. I understand your sister texted you a few minutes ago?"

Sarah nodded, fumbling with her phone, then handed it over to Miller.

His brow furrowed, and he said, "Your sister lives in Spain? Is her English okay?"

"Yeah, of course," Sarah responded.

"This text…it's oddly worded." He passed the phone back to her, and she read it. **I am Terminal C, next to first exit.** Miller was right. It was strangely worded. Not like teenaged text-speak, but like someone who didn't know the language. She slowly nodded. "What's going on?"

"Just one second…we've got an image of her coming through Customs, can you verify it's actually her?"

Miller nodded to one of the cops. An image appeared on the leftmost screen. She expected the stereotypical grainy security camera image, but this was digital, in focus, and very clear.

The image was of Andrea standing in a Customs lane, holding her passport out to the inspector. She was smiling, wearing a knit sweater that revealed one shoulder, her hair slightly longer than shoulder length. She was taller than the Customs inspector.

"That's her."

"What about this…do you recognize either of these two men?"

On the other two screens, images appeared. In the center was a tall, well built man with short blond hair. The image was slightly blurry, but it was clear enough. He carried an iPad with her name on it, and was smiling directly at Andrea, who walked directly toward him in the photo.

The other picture showed a man in his thirties, dark hair, shirt open halfway down his chest with extensive chest hair, getting into a black Lincoln Town Car.

"No," Sarah said, panic suddenly rising in her voice. "I don't recognize those men. And I was supposed to pick her up, not some random driver."

Officer Harmon and Lieutenant Miller met each other's eyes.

"Miss Thompson, can I get your parents' phone number?"

"Yes," she said. Her father would be at the Pentagon right now, or maybe on Capitol Hill, but he was at least in the same time zone. She quickly gave his number to the police, and then sank into a chair, the rushing in her ears too loud to hear much of anything else. But some words came through. *AMBER Alert. Possible abduction. FBI.*

She exhaled forcefully. She had to keep it together. She scanned the room. Miller stood there, giving orders. An officer was talking into a phone, reading the license plate of the Town Car to someone on the other end. Officer Harmon was on another phone. With her father? Maybe. She took another breath. She needed to make some calls.

2. Andrea. April 28. 4:52 pm

"**W**ho are you? Where are you taking me?"

"Shut up," said Crew Cut. "I told you to keep your mouth shut." *Dan*, he'd said. Whatever his real name was. Deep furrows on either side of his mouth marked a lifelong frown, and sweat dampened his crewcut, demonstrated his current worry.

The clock on the dashboard showed 4:52 pm. 32 minutes had passed since they'd picked her up. *Kidnapped* her. Crew Cut had passed an automatic pistol to Hairy Chest moments after they left the airport. And then he held another pistol up in his right hand, displaying it for her appreciation.

"Don't try anything funny. I don't much care whether you survive this or not."

The words sent chills down her spine, but not as much as moments later when Hairy Chest said, "Give me your purse. And your passport."

She had no choice. What was this? Who were these people? Terror twisted her guts when she passed the purse, with her identification and passport, over to the man in the front passenger seat. Last year she'd done a report on sex trafficking for school. And too often it happened like this. Passports and documents seized, young women carried off from airports or bus stations.

The back door latch didn't work; she'd tried that at the airport. Surreptitiously, she'd tried the power windows. They didn't work either. Child-safety locks? She didn't know. Whatever the mechanism, she was trapped in the spacious leather back seat, with two armed men in the front, in a car moving at high speed down the highway.

She swallowed, keeping her fear in check. She needed to stay alert and pay attention to her surroundings. She'd been watching the road, a circuitous route that had taken them around Baltimore and now onto Interstate 70 West. She needed details. If she managed to get to a phone, she'd send a text message, anything. She watched the road closely.

A sign. Exit 80, for Sykesville Road in Clarkesville, Maryland.

4:56 pm. She was getting further by the minute from the airport, further from her family, further from safety.

She took a deep breath. Maybe she could try negotiation. She leaned forward in her seat slightly then said, "My father is wealthy. He'll pay a big ransom."

Crew Cut rolled his head to the left for just a second, his jaw tightening, the powerful muscles in his neck going tense. She didn't anticipate the sudden violence, as he lashed out with his right fist. Her vision went white as his fist connected and she cried out, her mouth flooding with blood. She'd bit her tongue, hard.

Hairy Chest shook his head and chuckled. He glanced over his shoulder at her, and then said, "Don't mess her face up too much. I want to break her in before we get rid of her."

Andrea's entire body shuddered. She'd taken self-defense. More than one course, in fact. *Abuelita* had always been insistent that Andrea be able to defend herself in any situation. She knew how to fight, how to draw blood, how to run away. But fighting in real life was a completely different undertaking than in the control of the classroom, or even kneeing an obnoxious drunk in the balls. Plus, there were two of them. And they had guns.

"Yeah, well right now, every second fucking counts," the driver said. "We need to get off the road."

"How far?"

"Twenty minutes. No way they'll have an alert out that fast, but we can't kid around. Keep her fucking quiet back there."

She sniffled then ground her teeth. She wasn't giving up. No matter what. Hairy Chest met her eyes, then said in a conversational tone, "I fuck you so hard you scream."

The words froze her in place, all panic and fear gone. She was ice cold. And if she'd held a knife in her hand at that moment, she wouldn't have hesitated to slide it right between his ribs.

As it was, she needed to think, and quickly.

There was nothing in the backseat she could use as a weapon. Normally she carried a can of mace, but she couldn't take that on an airplane. *Fuckers.* Heavy floor mats lined the backseat floor. They wouldn't make much of a weapon, though she might be able to use one to blind the driver for a moment. And cause the car to crash. At the moment the speedometer rested at 74 miles per hour. She might be killed if they crashed, but she thought her odds would be better in a high speed collision than whatever else these two had in mind.

Her eyes moved back to Hairy Chest, still watching her, and she intentionally breathed in deeply and made her lower lip tremble. "I'll cooperate. Please don't hurt me."

She said it in as meek a voice as she could muster. But she was going to fucking hurt him if she got the chance.

And that's when she saw it. The driver braked a little, as a state patrolman pulled out onto the highway three lanes over.

Without thought or preparation or hesitation, she reached down with her left hand and grabbed the floor mat.

Hairy Chest shouted. "What the—"

He was too late. The floor mat swung wide and caught Crew Cut right in the face. The car lurched to the left, away from the police car, and skidded onto the median. The ride suddenly went rough as the car ran partly onto the gravel and grass, bumping this way and that, and then hitting a pothole with a wrenching thud that jarred her brain in her skull.

"Fucking bitch!" shouted the driver as he fought to get the vehicle back under control.

She reached both hands forward and grabbed Hairy Chest from behind, digging her nails into his face. He let out a scream and forced his way out of her grip, then spun around and lunged blindly, just missing her with his fist as she scrunched back as far in the seat as she could get.

That got the response she wanted. The squeal of a siren, then a flash of blue light, as the cops responded to the highly visible fight inside the Lincoln.

"Motherfucker!" shouted the driver. Hairy Chest reached for his gun, and she grabbed at his arm, but screamed as the driver punched her in the head. Once. Twice. Her vision narrowed to black and she lost her grip on Hairy Chest's arm. The driver accelerated, and Hairy Chest moved in nightmare slow motion as he raised his pistol. She dived down behind the seat as far as she could go, and then heard an explosion of sound.

Hairy Chest leaned out the window and fired his pistol at the pursuing police car.

3. Sarah. April 28. 4:58 pm

"**W****hat** the hell?" shouted Lieutenant Miller into a phone. "Can someone please tell me how the daughter of the Secretary of Defense came through my airport...and was abducted...and I wasn't notified? What the hell is wrong with you people?" A long pause. "I don't give a damn if he hasn't been confirmed yet. You people dropped the ball, and now there's a sixteen-year-old girl who's been kidnapped!"

Sarah groaned and stayed low in her seat. She didn't want to remind them she was here, because right now, she had some clue what was going on. If they made her leave, she'd lose that. For the last ten minutes she'd been sending text updates to her sisters: Carrie in Maryland, Alexandra in New York, Julia in Los Angeles and Jessica in San Francisco. Jessica hadn't responded, but then again, she didn't much lately.

Carrie had reminded her in a message that their father, recently called out of retirement by the President, was on Capitol Hill today preparing for his confirmation hearings. He wouldn't take any phone calls, but Carrie thought she could reach him through the Pentagon.

"Lieutenant!" one of the cops called. "State patrol spotted the vehicle. They're in pursuit."

Miller covered the receiver of the phone he'd been shouting into. "Any visual?"

The cop shook his head. "Audio only."

"Put it up."

Sarah shook. She couldn't breathe. She couldn't think. She started to send another text message to her sisters.

The room filled with sounds from the state patrol dispatchers. A lot of unrelated radio chatter. Then a loud, strong voice calling, "Shots fired, four-four-four, shots fired."

More voices, calling in locations, more cars responding.

Miller hung up on whoever he was talking with, and Sarah dropped her phone. The glass front of the phone shattered.

4. Andrea. April 28. 5:02 pm

Andrea felt her stomach lurch as the car swerved left, right, left again. Hairy Chest was yelling now, cursing in Arabic at the following cars. She stayed hunched down as tightly as possible, ignoring the rushing wind, the stomach churning swaying of the car, the sound of the tires screeching—she was focused only on survival. Terror threatened to paralyze her as she thought of never being able to see Javier again, the thought of losing her sisters, of not being there for them.

Then it happened. Hairy Chest's body jerked, then spasmed. Blood splattered on the windshield in a splotchy pattern, and he fell awkwardly against Crew Cut, who swerved again, shoving him away. Hairy Chest's face was dark with blood, his lips swollen, as he fell between the seats. Hairy Chest's head came to rest right next to Andrea, who let out a scream as blood poured from his mouth.

The scream was cut short a second later when the driver fired a shot, unaimed, a wild shot, right through the seat. At her.

She jerked up behind the seat, powered by adrenaline and fear, grabbing his gun hand from behind and covering his eyes with the other. He screamed and she did too as he lost control of the car and then he pulled the trigger once, twice, three more times. The bullets flew randomly, all of them missing her. The sickening screech of tires grew lower in pitch, the car moving sideways now, threatening to roll. As the car reached a stop she realized her mistake. The police were behind them, but there was nothing to prevent the son of a bitch from shooting her right now.

In desperation, she leaned forward, over his shoulder, and sank her teeth into his cheek. She felt her teeth break the skin, salty, copper tasting blood spurting into her mouth as he jerked and howled in pain, and then it happened. His hand released the pistol.

Instantly, she grabbed it, diving into the back seat.

And then the driver was gone, running, the front door of the car swinging open.

She sagged into the seat, spitting out her kidnapper's blood, and dropped the gun. Her eyes went to Hairy Chest. His bloodshot, dead eyes stared up at the roof of the car. Did he wonder what had happened? Did he wonder how two armed men managed to lose control of their prisoner, a sixteen-year-old girl?

Well, fuck him.

She flinched at the sound of gunshots outside. A lot of shots, followed by silence.

A few seconds later, a police officer appeared in the window, shouting, "Step out of the car now!"

She exhaled slowly, exhaustion sinking fast into her bones. Then she called out, "I can't open the back door!"

She *didn't* say that there was no way in hell she was crawling over the body of Hairy Chest to get to the front door. They could figure that out on their own.

Seconds later, the door opened, and she staggered out of the vehicle.

CHAPTER THREE
Bear

1. Andrea. April 28. 5:20 pm

"**It's** just a precaution," the police officer said. "We've got orders to make sure you get to the hospital safely and get checked out."

Andrea sighed. She knew it was necessary, especially since she'd gotten an unfortunate amount of blood in her mouth from the driver. But a helicopter?

Whatever her objections, the bright red air ambulance was coming in for a landing, the rotors throwing up a wash of dirt and dust all over the highway. Westbound traffic on Interstate 70 was stopped, and police directed frustrated and angry commuters to alternate routes. Half a dozen police cars, two ambulances, a fire truck and a swat team truck had converged on the site.

The need for that level of force had already come to an end. Fifteen seconds after exiting the car, Crew Cut, or *Dan*, or whatever his name was, opened fire on the police, then died from half a dozen gunshot wounds. The police were quite thorough making sure he wasn't getting back up.

The police had refused to allow her to retrieve her phone or purse. *Evidence*, they said. It might be evidence, but her passport was in there. Her frustration about that situation lasted right up until the moment she stood up to walk to the helicopter. After a brief argument with an EMT who wanted her to be strapped down on a stretcher, she squeezed herself into a crew seat and they buckled her in.

She stared out the windows as the twin engines roared to a high pitch and the helicopter lifted into the sky. To the east stood Baltimore, a city she'd never actually been in other than passing through the airport. Toy buildings, tiny cars, the hazy horizon, all contributed to her sense of unreality and isolation. Was it only two days ago she'd said goodbye to Javier? To her grandmother?

She wanted to go back home. She shivered, looking out at the harbor on the right side of the helicopter as it sped toward its destination.

Damn it. She didn't even know Javier's number. Or any of her friends from school. And if she got a replacement phone, it wouldn't do any good, because her backup was on her laptop, in the trunk of the stupid car.

Who the hell were they? What did they want? It didn't make any sense. Sure, her father had been nominated for some job with the US Defense ministry or whatever they called it. But that had nothing to do with her. And her attempt at negotiation wasn't exactly honest. For all she knew, her parents wouldn't lift a finger to ransom her. She barely knew them, and had been raised primarily by her grandmother. Her mother and father were remote figures on another continent.

The only one of her sisters she was close to was Julia, the oldest. At thirty-two, she was double Andrea's age. But she'd also been the one sister who consistently visited her in Spain. She was the sister she could count on.

It had been eight months since she'd seen Julia. That was a long time. They'd sat in the park together near Carrie's condo in Bethesda, Maryland, the day after Ray Sherman's funeral.

"Why don't they want me home, Julia?"

She had asked the question, not really expecting an answer. What possible answer could there be when your parents don't want you there?

"Of course they want you, sis," Julia said.

Andrea shook her head. "No...they don't. When I told Mom I wasn't coming home for Christmas last year, she didn't even argue."

Julia flinched. "Mother and I...I've never understood her."

Andrea said, "There's nothing to understand. They're both awful. She's crazy and he's an icebox. I'm *glad* Abuelita raised me. At least I know I'm loved."

Julia sniffed. "They love you...our parents are just screwed up. They don't know how to show it. And...we love you. Your sisters."

"You say that, but you know as well as I do that except for you, I barely know the others. Carrie might as well be a stranger."

Julia shook her head. "That's not true. She practically raised you."

"Until I was what...six? I don't even remember."

"I feel like we failed you."

Andrea sighed and sniffed. "I'm sorry. I didn't mean to…I just…sometimes I'm so lonely, you know?"

She'd cried that day, and Julia held her. Two days later, she flew back to Spain. She and Julia talked on the phone twice a week, whether they had anything to say or not. She called once every two weeks to check on Sarah and Carrie. Sarah was recovering from her injuries and Carrie was going through her pregnancy.

Her mother rarely asked to speak to her during those calls. That loneliness pervaded her.

The helicopter circled the hospital, a low bass vibration rising up through the soles of her feet. Bright light sparked out in the harbor, sunlight reflecting off the waves.

The crew chief sat across from her. "We're going to land in a minute…they're going to want to do the full VIP work-up on you. Keep your chin up, okay? I know it's going to suck, but they just want to cover their asses and look out for your best interests, okay?"

The unexpected kindness caught her off guard. Andrea nodded. The crew chief touched her shoulder and said, "Did you get any of *his* blood on you?"

"Yeah," she said at a whisper. He couldn't hear her, but he could see her shudder.

"You're gonna be all right, kid. This is just about the best hospital in the country. They're gonna do all the tests and make sure you're good to go. You got nothing to be worried about."

She sniffed. She wasn't used to being called *kid* and having someone reassure her. She wasn't used to needing other people. But something about the crew chief reminded her of her Uncle Luis, and before she could stop herself, she said it. "I'm scared."

She hated herself for saying it. He smiled kindly then squeezed her shoulder.

"Here we go," he said. He stretched up a little, wrapping his hand around a handle mounted above the door. The helicopter landed gently.

"You ready, kid?"

She nodded. "Thanks."

2. George-Phillip. April 28

"**D**addy, I love you."

"And I love you, darling."

George-Phillip leaned close to his daughter and kissed her on the forehead, then tucked her in. Jane was six years old, raven haired with green eyes. Creative. Mischievous.

Trouble.

His lips turned up in a half smile at the thought.

"I'm turning out the light, Jane."

"No…" she said.

He said, "I'll leave the door cracked?"

"Thank you, Daddy."

He smiled, switched the light out and stepped out into the hall, leaving the door open six inches.

Adriana Poole, Jane's nanny, sat reading a book in the room down the hall. "She's down," he said.

"For now," Adriana replied. "I'll be here, sir."

"Thank you."

He sighed, walking down the hall. He left the overhead lamp off in the study, choosing to only turn on the small desk lamp that lit one spot in the center of his desk. He turned on his computer and looked out at Belgrave Square.

Department security had warned him repeatedly about the wisdom of having his study facing the square. But Dukes of Kent had occupied this home for more than a hundred years. Princess Alexandra had been born in this house in 1936. Grudgingly, SIS security had installed additional equipment, bulletproof glass and a twenty-four hour security detail on the premises. And George-Phillip kept his study where he could see into the square.

The Wakhan file had been troubling him ever since O'Leary brought him the news of Andrea Thompson's travel to the United States. It was one of the oldest files he'd worked on. One of the most explosive, on a personal and international level.

It haunted him. He unlocked his desk and slid the top drawer open, taking out the file marked with seals labeled *CONFIDENTIAL* and *EYES ONLY*. He opened the file.

As always, it was the photos that caught him first. The bodies, laying where they'd fallen, twisted, bloated.

Many of them had been children.

He closed the file. He wouldn't find any answers in there tonight, any more than he did ten years ago or twenty years ago.

Thirty years since the photos had been taken. *Thirty years.*

He sighed then slid the folder back into his locked drawer. In the morning, he would instruct O'Leary to increase the surveillance on everyone related to the Wakhan file. But for now, he needed to get some sleep.

That, of course, was when the phone rang. Not his personal phone. The official phone.

He lifted it to his ear. "This is the Chief," he said.

"O'Leary, sir."

"What is it?"

"Wakhan file, sir. It's heating up."

"Tell me."

"Andrea Thompson was abducted on arrival at Baltimore Washington airport."

George-Phillip stood up, suddenly, his chair rolling back on its casters.

"What?" he cried.

"That's right, sir. We didn't have any assets on the scene, unfortunately. She was able to overpower her abductors, though. Both of them are dead, and she's en route to Johns Hopkins Hospital in Baltimore."

"How serious were her injuries? Any idea who they were?"

"Not serious, sir, and we've got a lead on one from the surveillance video. This one's getting massive attention from the Yanks though, so I've not put anyone too close to the investigation. One of the kidnappers looks like Tariq Koury. Saudi born, he's been around ISI and CIA and a bunch of other three letter agencies for decades."

"Three letter agencies...like SIS?"

"He did a couple jobs for us in the early 90s. Nothing since then that I can tell. He works for the highest bidder...not reliable. But he's a killer. He spent most of the last five years working for Blackwater."

George-Phillip shook his head. "And a sixteen-year-old girl *escaped* from him?"

"Not just escaped. As best as I can find out, she killed him. I'll get more info as soon as I can."

"We need to know who hired him, O'Leary."

"Working on it, sir."

"Put some serious assets on it. I want to know who was behind the abduction, O'Leary."

They hung up, and he stared out the window. George-Phillip thought about what he knew of Andrea Thompson, which amounted to virtually nothing. The idea that a sixteen year old girl had fought—and killed—two trained intelligence agents simply defied credibility. But then, nothing about this case, from the very beginning, had made sense. Especially not the contents of the file, which he didn't need to have open to see its contents. The twisted and darkened bodies. They haunted his every thought.

3. Bear. April 28. 6:30 pm

It was long past six o'clock when John "Bear" Wyden closed the briefing folder and walked it down the hall to the Classified Materials Officer, who signed for the documents and gave Bear a receipt. Temporarily, Bear occupied a desk on the sixth floor at Main State. For the last three years, he'd been assigned as the deputy Regional Security Officer in Pakistan for the Diplomatic Security Service. An insanely challenging job, where he'd supervised dozens of agents in one of the largest and most strategic field offices.

In two weeks he'd be taking over as an assistant deputy at the FBI's National Joint Terrorism Task Force. Bear was forty-three years old, with dark hair starting to turn grey. But he was fit, weighing in at little more than the one hundred eighty pounds he'd carried the day he entered Diplomatic Security twenty years ago. Back then he'd been called Bear because of the thick hair covering his arms, legs and chest, a fact which had embarrassed him for years.

For now, he had a couple of weeks to kill, and Tom Cantwell, the head of Diplomatic Security, had given him several ongoing files to work with. Busywork, really, reviewing findings of existing investigations and raising questions and holes. He didn't mind. Bear Wyden liked to stay busy.

For now, though, it was time to go home.

Bear had rented a studio apartment not far from DuPont Circle and walking distance from the office. He didn't have many needs these days. Leah left with their two dogs and three kids and everything he'd owned two years before. He couldn't blame her. They'd often worked together, and as colleagues, they were good to go. Not so much as husband and wife. So now he had his apartment and his books, a laptop computer, and way too much time on his hands, and she had a new husband, a new house, and had cut back her hours.

He locked his temporary desk, and put on his jacket, preparing to leave the office. There were no personal touches—no point, considering he'd be leaving soon anyway.

The phone rang, and for five seconds he considered ignoring it.

It was Cantwell.

"Bear Wyden," he answered.

"Cantwell. Can you come up for a few minutes, Wyden? We've got a hot one."

Bear raised his eyebrows. Cantwell was normally dull, tired, uninterested. He described potential crises as "synergistic opportunities," not as "hot ones." Something was definitely odd here.

"I'll be right there."

Five minutes later he'd ridden the temperamental old elevators up to the seventh floor, the inner sanctum. Secretary Kerry had his office here, as had predecessors throughout his career: Hillary Clinton, Madeleine Albright, Colin Powell, Condoleezza Rice. It might be a little old fashioned and hokey, but Bear was a believer. He was a believer in democracy. He was a believer in his country. And sometimes he was a little bit in awe of the stature of the place he worked, when he wasn't overwhelmed by the bullshit. Whenever his work took him to the seventh floor at Main State—not very often—he felt that sense of awe.

Cantwell did not awe him. A political functionary, appointed to the job after the shakeup following the Benghazi attack, Cantwell did little to offend and little to inspire. He occupied his desk, let the department work underneath him, and periodically testified on Capitol Hill.

Bear supposed there could be worse people sitting in this chair.

"Bear. Good, I'm glad you were still in the building. I need to brief you in on a case, and it's one with potentially serious implications."

"Yes, sir."

"All right. Do you happen to know Ambassador Richard Thompson?"

"The new Sec Def? Of course. I ran the security detail for the Embassy in Brussels when he was there. We had to provide protection for the entire family, along with some of the other high profile people, if I remember correctly."

"What's your impression?"

Bear tilted his head. His impression had always been that Richard Thompson was a cold fish, and a dangerous one, and that his wife...*what was her name?* Something Spanish, he thought. She was way too young for Thompson, way too passionate. It was a bad match, he thought. But Diplomatic Security agents weren't paid to have personal opinions about their charges.

"I can't really give one, sir. That was more than twenty years ago. I knew the Ambassador and his wife, and I arranged for their security detail."

"Anything unusual?"

Bear shrugged his shoulders. "Not really. There were some specific threats against his family, if I remember correctly. They had two...no, three little girls. I think the oldest was ten or so at the time."

"What sort of threats against the family?"

Bear shrugged. "The usual. It was all stuff out of the Middle East...remember this was about a year after the Gulf War. What's all this about?"

Cantwell sat back in his seat. "Ambassador Thompson ended up having six daughters. The youngest was abducted this afternoon."

"Son of a bitch," Bear muttered.

"Exactly. Sixteen years old. She escaped. But we've already got indications there may have been a foreign power involved."

"What? Who?"

"Tariq Koury was one of the kidnappers. We've got a positive ID, though he came through with fake papers. He flew to the States right next to her in first class, and then they grabbed her plain as day. It was dumb luck and quick thinking on her part that got her free."

Tariq Koury. That was...odd. He was a low life, a mercenary, and an opportunist. Bear had encountered him a number of times in the course of his work in Pakistan. Koury wasn't driven by ideology or religion or political loyalties; his only desire was money. But he typically didn't get involved in serious wet-work, and kidnapping the daughter of an American cabinet member was as serious as it got.

"Who else was involved?"

"We're still trying to identify the other perp."

"All right. Who's running the show?"

"Who isn't? Fucking Pentagon wants a piece of this. FBI, maybe Secret Service. But the Secretary talked to the President and Ambassador Thompson half an hour ago. DSS is running the show. I want you to head the investigation. I'll get Joyce Brown or someone to run the back office stuff. You get out there while things are hot and find out what's what."

"I want to talk to the girl, if I can."

"They're flying her to Johns Hopkins."

"Is she seriously hurt?"

"No, just a precaution, from what I understand. Everybody wants to close the barn door now the horses have escaped."

Right. Just like Cantwell. He grimaced and checked his watch. It could easily take two hours to drive to Baltimore from downtown DC at this time of day. He'd requisition a uniformed officer and official car with lights and sirens, and hopefully that would shorten the trip. In the meantime, he'd scramble Leah and have her get a protective detail organized. She'd be just thrilled.

"All right. I'm on it."

Twenty minutes later, Bear Wyden was in a car, speeding up the Baltimore-Washington Parkway.

CHAPTER FOUR
Talk to your therapist

1. Andrea. April 28. 8:00 pm

Andrea Thompson was losing her patience. For nearly two hours she'd been poked, prodded, examined, and exhausted. She'd been questioned by the police, subjected to a host of blood tests, x-rays and a CT scan. "Just as a precaution." She'd drawn the line at a rape kit, finally threatening to call the police if they touched her any more.

Finally the first round of doctors backed off, replaced by a trauma therapist. Dirty Blonde drifting to grey, with a salt and pepper beard, he shoved his way past the other doctors, nurses, hospital administrators and the morbidly curious, then forced them all out with a few well chosen obscene comments.

Against her will, Andrea immediately warmed to the man, if only for running off the med students who had been gawking at her. She breathed a sigh of relief as the room cleared out.

"I'm Will Fisher," he said.

"Andrea Thompson," she replied. "Thanks for…clearing them out."

"It won't last," he said. "The police are outside clamoring to get in, too. For now I've got you on restricted access."

She scrunched her eyebrows close to her nose. "My family?"

"Of course your family can come in. And I expect you'll be out of here in a couple more hours."

"What's left?"

"Let's just talk for a moment."

"About?"

Will gave her a warm, crooked smile, his teeth flashing white behind the beard. "How are you *feeling?*"

"Are you a priest?"

He coughed. "I'm a psychiatrist."

"I don't need a psychiatrist."

"I'm sure you don't," he said. "You're a resourceful young lady. But this is part of what we have to do. It's kind of like getting a chest x-ray, but for your brain."

She blinked. "No. It's not. You can see the results of an x-ray. Your examination consists of nothing but supposition and your own biases."

Will's eyes widened and he grinned. "Humor me, then. Because in order to get you out of here quickly, I have to reassure the hospital administration that you're fit to go and you aren't a danger to yourself."

Andrea crossed her arms over her chest and said, "All right, then. Psychoanalyze me if you must."

Will laughed and gave her a sideways grin. "Tell me about your mother, then."

Eye roll. "My mother sent me off to Spain when I was six, and I see her on holidays whether I like it or not."

He frowned. "I was actually joking, but...you've really lived in Spain since you were six? Who with?"

"My grandmother," Andrea replied. "We have a flat in Calella...it's a small town on the beach, about half an hour from Barcelona."

"What brings you to the States?"

"My sister Carrie...her daughter needs a bone marrow transplant. I'm supposed to be tested to see if I'm a match."

He grimaced. "Leukemia?"

She shook her head. "Thalassemia."

He frowned. "It's been a while since my straight med school days, but my recollection is thalassemia isn't life threatening, at least not in the short term."

She shrugged. "It can be. Depends. If she can't find a donor, she'll be dependent on blood transfusions the rest of her life. The typical prognosis is pretty poor."

"You're a pretty smart girl for sixteen."

She shrugged her shoulder. "I'm a freak."

"I wouldn't say that."

"How else do you explain it? Why didn't my parents come pick me up from the airport, then? Why do they pack me off to live in Spain? The only reason I'm here is for my sister. The minute we know if I'm a donor or not, I'm on a plane back home."

Will nodded. "Tell me about your sister and her daughter."

Andrea shrugged. "I barely know her." Her tone was sharp-edged, bitter.

He raised his eyebrows. "But you fly thousands of miles to undergo a potentially painful medical procedure to help her daughter."

Andrea blinked. Then she said, "I didn't have much a mother as a child. But what mothering I got was from Carrie." She choked up a little, and then said, "I'd do anything for her. And she's had an awful time."

"How so?"

Andrea shrugged. "Husband murdered last summer. Surely you read about it in the papers."

He sat back and studied her. She could almost see the wheels working in his brain, as he put together the names Carrie Thompson, the fact of Ray's murder and her mention of the papers. Then his eyes widened just a little bit. Yep. He got it. Ray Sherman, Carrie's husband, had been falsely accused and brought before a war crimes court last summer. Exonerated by the court, he was murdered by another soldier.

Will thought that through, then said, "Your brother-in-law was murdered. Is there any possibility that the kidnapping attempt was related to that?"

She shrugged.

"Did your kidnappers say anything to you? Were you scared?"

She swallowed and thought of Hairy Chest, staring her in the eye as he said, "*I fuck you so hard you scream.*" She closed her eyes, her mind resting on the death in his eyes. It was terrifying. But it was also oddly impersonal. Hairy Chest and the driver—the best way she could put it was, they didn't seem to be emotionally engaged in their work. This was just that. They'd been hired or ordered to kidnap her. It wasn't personal for them.

But it was damn personal for her, and for that reason, she was glad they were dead.

There. She'd settled on her answer. "I'm glad they're both dead," she replied.

Will nodded. "How do you feel about that?"

"About the fact they are dead?"

"Yes."

She gave him an ironic grin. "I'm delighted. It's like someone bought me an iPhone for Christmas, I'm so excited."

"You don't sound excited."

"You don't sound very intelligent."

He rubbed a hand along his forehead, briefly massaging the bridge of his nose. "Andrea, I'm here to help you."

"Then sign whatever papers it is you need to sign, and let me go. I didn't commit the crime here. I didn't kidnap anyone. I didn't hurt anyone. I didn't threaten to rape anyone. I didn't assault anyone. All I did was fly to help my sister. So there is absolutely no reason for me to be here anymore. If you wish to have me arrested, call the police. Otherwise, I'm leaving."

Andrea stood.

"Andrea, please. I'm very concerned about trauma."

She stared at him for a solid thirty seconds. Then she blinked her eyes, and said, "You should talk to your therapist about that."

She ostentatiously stepped around him and opened the door.

The first thing she saw was two Maryland state troopers blocking the door. They wore crisply pressed khaki shirts and matching hats, and both of them had the look of too many cases of beer in between lifting weights.

Beyond them, to the right, stood a large man grey suit that looked as if it had been used for a pillow. A leather folder, folded outward, displayed a badge at his pocket. She looked close enough to see he was from the Diplomatic Security Service.

To the left stood two of her sisters.

Carrie Thompson-Sherman might have been an older twin to Andrea. Dark brown hair, cut almost savagely short, framed a pert face with blue green eyes. Like Andrea, she was more than six feet tall, with narrow features, high cheekbones and unusually pale skin. Andrea did the math in her head…Carrie was born in 1985, so she must be 29 now. She didn't look close to thirty, but she didn't have the fresh look of eighteen anymore either. Worry and strain had given her new lines around her eyes and in the center of her forehead.

Next to her…and considerably shorter than either of them…was their pixie-like sister Sarah. She was a few inches over five feet, and since Andrea saw her last, Sarah's leg had healed into a permanent and startling network of scars running up her calf to her thigh. The scarring looked like shoelaces. Sarah had dark hair, dyed black with white streaks, and strikingly pale blue eyes and a nose ring that matched her eyes perfectly. She was still the same girl Andrea had last scene in a hospital bed in August, but something inside of her had changed. Her eyes were cold and distant, as if she'd seen too much.

Andrea pushed her way past the police and walked to her sisters, silently pulling them both into an embrace.

"Oh my God, Andrea," Carrie whispered, her tone fierce. Sarah, almost comically, put her arms around both of them, like a child around both parents.

"Are you okay?" Sarah asked.

"Yeah," Andrea replied. "I'm all right. Just…can we get out of here?"

"Miss Thompson." The voice was deep, unpleasant.

Andrea looked up. It was the large man in suit that desperately needed dry-cleaning. She sighed.

"I'm Bear Wyden. Diplomatic Security Service. Before you go, I need a few minutes of your time."

For just a second, Andrea wanted to cry. She just wanted to get out of this hospital, get away from all these people, and curl up under a blanket.

Carrie saw her reaction and said, "Mr. Wyden, is this necessary right now? I think she's exhausted."

"It is, unfortunately," he said. "At this point we don't know who was behind the kidnapping, so there are significant concerns about your security."

Andrea said, "The kidnappers are dead." But then she thought back to her earlier conclusion that the kidnappers were hired. She swayed a little on her feet. It was long past midnight at home, and she'd had little sleep the night before.

Wyden said, "We'll make this quick."

"Fine."

He led the way down the hall. "In here, please, the hospital's provided a meeting room."

"We're staying with our sister," Carrie said.

"No problem." He held the door open and waved them forward. Then he said, "Are you Julia or Carrie?"

Carrie jumped a little. "What?"

"You won't remember me, you were too young. But I was in charge of your family's security detail in Brussels in the early 90s."

"Oh... I'm Carrie."

He frowned quickly. "I'm sorry for your loss. I didn't have much of a chance to brush up on the files before I drove up here, but I did read the *Post's* coverage of Sergeant Sherman's court martial."

Carrie was never off balance. Poised. Intelligent. Brave. But now she recoiled almost, and Andrea felt a flash of rage. *How dare he?*

"We're done here." Andrea said it at the exact same moment Sarah said, "Will you just leave her alone?" Sarah's face was flushed and angry.

Bear looked between the three sisters and froze in place. Then he looked at Carrie and said, "My apologies. I...I'm very sorry."

Carrie sighed then said, "It's okay. It's just...very fresh."

"I understand." His voice was soothing. "Please. Have a seat."

The three sisters sat, Andrea and Sarah flanking Carrie.

"Let's start over. And again, my apologies. My name's Bear Wyden, and I'm a special investigator for the Diplomatic Security Service. Until three weeks ago I was assistant regional security officer at the Embassy in Pakistan."

"Three weeks ago?" Sarah said. "Were you fired for insensitivity?"

Bear smiled wryly. "Maybe I should have been. In fact, I'm moving on to the Joint Terrorism Task Force. But in the meantime, I'm heading the investigation into your kidnapping, Andrea."

She shrugged. "I don't know if there's much to investigate. They gave the impression it was some kind of human trafficking ring?"

"Oh?" he said. "What gave you that idea?"

She thought back. Then said, "At some point one of them...the hairy one... said he was going to rape me before they...disposed of me."

Carrie reached out and gripped Andrea's hand.

"I see," Bear said. "Why don't we start at the beginning, then? Just tell me everything you remember. When did you first see the kidnappers?"

"Well, the hairy one, he was on the plane."

Bear nodded. "Tariq Koury."

"That's his name? He claimed he was a student."

He shook his head. "He's no student. I can't really say anything more."

"Koury…he's middle eastern?"

"Saudi," Bear answered. "Had you ever met him before this flight?"

Andrea shook her head. "No. Neither of them."

Bear asked her a series of questions. When did she first see him on the flight? He took her through everything Koury said on the plane, then back through it a second and then a third time. Then they moved on. The car. She described how she'd passed her phone up to the front of the car.

"Wait," Sarah said. "I got text messages from you when you got off the plane. I was waiting at Terminal C."

"You didn't get any text messages from me," Andrea said. "My phone was dead. In fact…" She froze. How could she be so *stupid?* "Wait. I went off to the bathroom pretty early on the flight. And left my phone in the seat. It was dead when I got back."

Bear made some notes. "It sounds like Koury may have switched batteries or SIM cards, then sent the texts to Sarah to keep her unaware of what was happening."

"This was all planned, then," Carrie said.

Bear met Carrie's eyes. Then he nodded. "I think it best that we assign a security detail for now."

Andrea's eyes widened. She didn't need or want that. "I'm only going to be here a few days. It's not necessary."

"I think it is," Bear said. "And I'm certain your father will agree."

This provoked nothing more than a sneer from Andrea. "I'm not terribly concerned about my father's opinion. May I go?"

Bear sat back. "Fine. Let me ride along behind, for now, until we've got the security detail in place."

Carrie gave him the address, while Andrea stood there rolling her eyes and wishing she could just go back to Calella.

2. Carrie. April 28. 8:50 pm

Carrie Thompson-Sherman looked in the rearview mirror at her much younger sister Andrea. Andrea sat in the middle row of seats, staring vacantly out the window. Her mouth was slightly open, as if she were suffering from exhaustion and shock. Which she probably was.

Carrie understood shock and exhaustion. She put the Suburban in reverse, slowly backing out of the too small parking space and into the main area of the parking deck. Up until last summer, for years she'd driven a restored 1976 Mercedes 280S. Gleaming black, fully restored, she'd loved that car until it was destroyed in the same collision that killed her husband and nearly crippled her sister Sarah.

When she finally got back on the road, her newfound fear of accidents drove part of her buying decisions. She'd purchased a new black Chevy Suburban. It felt like it weighed five thousand pounds. She felt safe behind the wheel, and it wasn't often these days that Carrie felt safe.

The clock on the dashboard said 8:55 pm. She glanced back at Andrea again. The poor girl was traumatized and exhausted. To Carrie's right, Sarah didn't seem to be in much better shape. Sarah liked to push herself and act like she could do anything, and, in fact, she could. But sometimes she pushed herself too much. Her injuries in the accident that killed Ray were severe, and it had taken months before she was even able to walk again. Today had been a very long day for her.

"Tomorrow can you give me a ride back out to the airport to pick up my car?" Sarah asked.

"Sure. Or we can send someone to get it." Carrie didn't want to say that she thought Sarah was much too tired to make the drive in the morning.

"So..." Sarah turned to Andrea. In a completely deadpan voice, she said, "How was your flight?"

Carrie held her breath for a moment, as silence descended on the car for just a moment. She swallowed. Then she looked in the rearview mirror. Andrea stared at Sarah in shock, her eyes wide. Then Andrea's eyes darted over to Carrie. One second of eye contact was all it took. Andrea burst into laughter, and then all three of them were laughing.

"Oh my fucking God," Andrea said. Carrie bent over in her seat, resting her head against the steering wheel. Then a loud belly laugh burst out, uncontrollably.

Gasping for air, she said, "Andrea, I was so worried about you."

"I was scared," Andrea said, sobering a little. Then, in a mock-serious tone, she raised her left eyebrow. "Tell me, please. How was your flight?"

All three of them rocked with laughter again. Carrie felt tears running down her face, at first slow ones, then quickly. She hiccoughed then laughed again.

"Carrie?" Sarah had stopped laughing, and was leaning toward her now.

"I'm okay," Carrie replied, waving a hand in the air. "I just...it's been a long time since I laughed." She sniffed then chuckled again, at the same time as she fiercely wiped away tears. "Sometimes I just...I needed to laugh, okay?"

She felt a slender hand touch her shoulder as she put the Suburban back in gear. "It'll be okay, Carrie. Rachel will be okay."

Andrea's voice was soothing. But Carrie knew the dangers of soothing voices, the dangers of putting faith in anything you couldn't see, the dangers of believing miracles could happen. Miracles didn't happen. Not in a world where your husband could be exonerated the same day you told the doctors to pull the plug and let him die.

So she got them out of Baltimore and onto 95 South headed for Washington. It was late enough they'd likely make it to the condo in forty minutes. And then Carrie could deal with the next big question of the day.

Where the fuck was their father? And why hadn't he come out to Baltimore the moment he learned of the kidnapping?

3. Andrea. April 28. 9:05 pm

Carrie, who sat in the seat in front of Andrea, gripped the steering wheel so hard that her knuckles were white. Her hands shook every time she let go of the wheel, the occasional traffic light catching off her wedding ring with tiny tremulous sparkles. She was bordering so close to hysterical that Andrea almost wished Sarah would take the wheel. But Sarah herself wasn't in the best of condition.

The last time Andrea saw Sarah was the day after the funeral. Andrea went to the hospital and spent half an hour with her. At the time she'd been laid up in the intensive care unit. Her left leg had been crushed in the accident, and the doctors had performed a fasciotomy to prevent tissue death. But leaving an open and draining wound for days at a time had its own dangers, and she'd fought a days-long battle with an antibiotic-resistant staph infection that kept her in the hospital for nearly two months after the accident. It was a miracle, really, that she was up and around.

Andrea knew for sure she wasn't capable of driving. She'd been awake far too long and had one too many shocks. Right now it was all she could do to keep her eyes open, and the longer they drove, the more she had to fight the heaviness of her eyelids.

She lost that battle. She didn't know how long she was out, or when she fell asleep, but when she woke up, they were sitting at a red light in Bethesda, Maryland, and their parents' condo was straight ahead of them. Andrea was groggy, her head still cloudy from confusing, messy dreams. Dreams featuring her father and Hairy Chest, dreams where she was being choked.

She shook as Carrie pulled the Suburban to a stop in front of the doorman.

It took Andrea's brain several seconds to register that half a dozen news vans were parked in front, a line of reporters along the sidewalk.

Carrie looked around, and Andrea followed her eyes. Several police officers were blocking the sidewalk, preventing the reporters from coming any closer. But that didn't stop Bear Wyden, who had pulled up behind them, from approaching the vehicle. One of the county police ran to him, but Bear held up a badge. After a few words, the cop turned away and Bear knocked on the window.

Carrie slid her window down.

"I'll escort you up, and the cops will keep the reporters from coming any further. All right?"

Sarah looked a little panicked.

"Don't worry," Carrie said. She put a hand on Sarah's. "You'll be fine. Andrea? You okay?"

Her eyes met Andrea's in the rearview mirror. Andrea felt panicked. She didn't want to deal with reporters. That was never in the plan. But there was nothing she could do about it now.

"I'm good," Andrea replied.

"Come on, then," Bear said.

The three of them burst out of the vehicle. Andrea and Carrie moving at a very fast pace. Sarah, who had to come around from the passenger side, and who was so tired she'd begun to move with a painful limp, was slower. The reporters began to shoot pictures of her, one of them shouting, and Bear quickly moved to her.

"Put your arm on my shoulder," he said, wrapping a sizeable arm around her waist.

With his assistance, they crossed the ground to the doorman quickly.

"Upstairs," he said.

"Let me be clear, Mr. Wyden," Carrie said. "This is my home. I appreciate your concern, but I'm not sure we're going to accept security guards from the State Department."

"Doctor Sherman," he replied. "You're a smart woman. We don't know who tried to kidnap your sister or why, but I know Koury. He doesn't come cheap. Whoever wanted her kidnapped or dead still does."

Carrie swallowed and took a deep breath. "Very well."

She turned and walked to the elevator, her sisters following.

The four of them rode up the elevators in silence. Andrea felt her eyes wanting to close again, and she had to force them open. Finally, the bell rang and the door opened to the eighteenth floor and they were moving down the hallway.

She remembered the condo, of course. Her earliest memories were here, when she was three, maybe four years old, before they went to Moscow for a year. Over the years she'd come back a few times, when the family had visited Washington, and most recently she'd slept here during the two weeks she'd been in Washington last summer. When Ray and Sarah were injured, and Ray died.

So it didn't come entirely as a shock when they walked in the door and she saw her father standing at the mantel, his eyes apparently resting on an ancient copper head. He turned around as they came in, and then he closed his eyes and said, "Andrea. Thank God."

A confused rush of emotions overcame her. For one thing, where was Jessica? Sarah's twin. Or their mother?

She looked at Sarah and asked, "Where's Jessica?"

Sarah shrugged, but her face guarded something, and Andrea didn't know what it was. "California with Mom."

"She's not coming?"

Carrie looked sad and Sarah rolled her eyes. "I don't know," Carrie replied.

Andrea looked back at her father. It was so confusing. To find him here, with his arms out like he meant it. To find their mother just...*gone?* It didn't make any sense. She had thought Jessica and her father had gone back to California together. Everything was mixed up, and no one had told her anything.

Richard Thompson stood for a moment more, then put his arms out stiffly in front of him. "Come here, my daughter. Welcome home."

She shook her head and gave him a look of disdain. Then she brushed past

him and down the hallway.

CHAPTER FIVE
Home is Calella

1. Andrea. April 29. 12:10 pm

Andrea Thompson was awakened by a shout, and she didn't know if it was real or a dream.

She lay in the unfamiliar, too-soft bed, eyes open and fixed on the ceiling. Her heart was thumping, adrenaline flooding her system, her pulse urgent at her throat.

From the angle of the sun in the brightly lit room, it was nearly noon. She lay there, letting her heart calm down, listening. Listening. A murmur of voices from beyond the bedroom door, but no shouting. Whoever it was, sounded calm. Engaged.

A dream, then.

She sat up, eyes falling to the clock at her bedside. Noon or so. Six in the morning back home. She generally didn't have problems with jetlag—Andrea traveled far too frequently for that. But given what she'd had waiting for her on her arrival in the United States this time, it was no wonder she'd slept so long.

Foggy, she stood, eyes scanning for her bag, before she remembered that her bag was in the custody of the police. She'd have to go shopping today, because she couldn't wear the same clothes every day. In the meantime, she'd ask Carrie for something to wear. They were close enough to the same size.

When she walked out of the bedroom and down the hall, she immediately identified the voices. Carrie. Sarah. And another voice, a woman, clipped and professional.

Andrea listened for just a second, then walked out into the living room.

Carrie and Sarah sat on a couch, facing the mantel and fireplace. Carrie looked serious and attentive. She was a scientist, a systems ecologist working on infectious diseases at the National Institutes of Health. She hadn't gone back to work yet after her pregnancy, but she always dressed elegantly and professionally.

Sarah, on the other hand, was busy outlining the crosshatch scars on her legs with black eyeliner. She'd already outlined her eyes in the heavy black eyeliner curling up in cat's eyes. The very pale blue of her eyes was startling against the dark circles around them. Her clothes were all black: a torn t-shirt, black Dockers shorts and combat boots. The scars on her left leg stood out in stark relief underneath the black outlines.

The woman was across from them in another chair. Khakis, combat boots which ironically matched Sarah's, and a black t-shirt with the logo DSS in gold letters across the left breast. Her tanned face was framed by dirty blonde hair. Somewhere in her early forties, she looked competent and probably deadly. Her wedding ring was a plain gold band. She stood up when Andrea entered the room.

Andrea came to a stop, and the woman said, "Good morning. I'm Leah Simpson, with Diplomatic Security Services."

"Andrea Thompson."

"I'm in charge of your family's security detail."

"Not Bear?"

Simpson smiled at the use of the nickname. "Bear…uh…Mr. Wyden's overall in charge of the investigation, among other things. You'll be seeing a lot of both of us, I'm afraid."

Andrea nodded unhappily. Right now she wanted nothing more than to get on a plane and fly back to Spain. Instead, she had to deal with investigations into her *kidnappers*, parents who seemed to be missing—*at least that was normal*—and everything seemed to be out of control. She closed her eyes and said, "How long does this go on? When will I be able to go home?"

Leah looked over to Carrie. Then she said, "I don't know how long your family business will take, but unless we receive orders otherwise, a protective detail will accompany you back to Spain until we're sure the danger is past."

Andrea closed her eyes. She tried to imagine Abuelita's response to a bunch of armed agents in her flat. Then she snickered a little. Federal agents or not, Abuelita was a fierce old woman. She'd tear them to pieces.

"Let me get some coffee," Andrea said. "Then we can discuss all this?"

"Of course," Leah said.

As gracefully as she could, Andrea made her way to the kitchen. A pot of coffee was already on the counter, still half-full. As she poured it, Carrie walked in.

"Sorry we couldn't warn you first. I figured you needed the sleep."

"I did." Andrea mixed sugar into her coffee as she spoke. "It's okay, this isn't your fault."

Carrie smiled uncertainly. Then her eyes darted away at the sound of crying.

"Rachel's awake." Carrie hesitated a moment, as if she needed to stay and reassure Andrea.

"Go, I'm fine," Andrea said. She opened up the refrigerator in search of milk for her coffee as Carrie slipped out. Carrie looked tired...exhausted really. The good news was she had help—a full time nanny their father paid for. Undoubtedly that helped. But it didn't take away the worry gnawing away at her soul. It didn't take away the trauma of her husband being murdered.

Andrea didn't want to be here. She didn't want to be dealing with the police, the feds, and whoever it was who had attempted to abduct her. But no matter what, she'd be there for her sister.

She stepped back into the living room. Sarah was still intently drawing a detailed outline around the lines of the scarring on her left leg. Andrea walked over, sipping her coffee and watched her sister. Hair draped over Sarah's face, almost hiding it. Her eyebrows were scrunched together, a vertical line of concentration centered in between them.

"Is it getting better?" Andrea asked.

"I can walk again. That took months."

Andrea swallowed. "What about the scarring?"

Sarah leaned her head back and met Andrea's eyes. "Mom wants me to see a plastic surgeon next month to start talking about repairing it. For a while they thought I was going to lose the leg."

Leah Simpson sat forward in her seat. "This happened when Sergeant Sherman was killed last summer?"

Sarah nodded. "Ray."

"You were in the back seat?"

"Yes," Sarah said. "I woke up two days after the accident. Ray died a few hours later."

Andrea lowered herself into her seat and sipped her coffee. Her emotions were roiling, confused. She had only met Ray Sherman once while he was alive. She'd flown to New York last summer for Alexandra's wedding to Dylan Paris. Alexandra, the third eldest sister of six, had fallen in love with a boy who eventually ended up in the Army. Dylan and Ray were best friends and had married sisters in ceremonies two days apart.

She thought back to that ceremony, and the reception that followed. Alexandra standing up, hand on her sister's shoulder, and saying words that spoke of loyalty and love and intense, passionate sisterhood. Andrea suddenly wondered how Alexandra was doing. They hadn't spoken in months. Nor had Andrea talked with Jessica, currently at their childhood home in San Francisco finishing her senior year in high school. She didn't know how either of them was doing. She found herself wishing she'd talked with Jessica more. They'd been close once.

Sitting here now, watching Sarah outlining her scars in black, she wished she knew them. All of them. She wished she'd been there to comfort Carrie after Ray died. She wished she'd been there for the thousands of big things and small things that had happened in their lives, and she wondered, for the ten thousandth time, why her parents had taken that away from her.

Leah's eyes shifted to Andrea like a pair of searchlights. "And you live with your grandmother? In Spain?"

Mind your own business.

Instead of vocalizing the thought, she said, "Yes."

"It must be beautiful."

Andrea shrugged, a short gesture devoid of any meaning.

"Why do you live there?"

The eyeliner pencil froze in Sarah's hand, and her eyes swiveled up toward Leah. Andrea shook her head. "I don't know. I used to go for summers, then they got longer and longer. When I was about six or seven, my mom sent me to live there permanently, and then I visited here on the holidays."

Leah Simpson looked troubled, her face reflecting ill-formed emotions. Andrea looked away. She didn't need or want anyone's pity. The one thing she was grateful for was Abuelita. Her grandmother didn't just raise her. She filled her life with love. Abuelita made sure, every day, that Andrea knew she was loved, no matter what was wrong with her parents.

"When was the last time you came home?"

"Home is Calella. Spain."

Simpson nodded. "Of course. I meant to say, when was the last time you visited the United States?"

"Last summer. After the accident."

"Not the holidays?"

Andrea rolled her eyes, but not quick enough to hide the sting.

She remembered the phone call. A week before Thanksgiving, last fall.

"Hello?" her mother had said.

"Mother, it's Andrea."

"Andrea, dear, how are you?"

Andrea had leaned back at the question, staring at the ceiling, and said, "Bueno, mother. And you?"

"I miss you, darling."

"I'm sure." Her mother didn't react to the sarcasm.

"Mother…" she said.

"Yes, dear?"

"I think I want to stay in Spain for the holidays this year. Carrie is still grieving and I have final exams in January. I think I just need some down time."

Silence at the other end of the line. Her mother didn't react. She didn't say, *no, you have to come home,* or even *no, please come home.* She didn't say that she'd miss Andrea. She didn't say *anything.*

"Mother?" Andrea had said.

Adelina Thompson's tone of voice had been uninterpretable. "I see. Well, then." She had fallen silent again.

A few weeks later, Christmas had come. Andrea spent Christmas Eve with her grandmother and two of her cousins in the old town centre, walking around the *Nacimiento,* a massive Nativity scene spreading over nearly the entire square. The town centre was heavily decorated with colorful fruit and flowers, candles in windowsills, Christmas trees and along the edge of the town centre, a bustling Christmas market. Across from the market, the *Hogueras,* a Christmas bonfire celebrated the shortest day of the year. Shortly after sunset the bonfire was lit. Later, some daring young people would jump over the bonfire. Javier would be among them, laughing and strutting.

As the stars rose that night, families all over town lit oil lamps in their windows, leaving the entire town sparkling with the lights. She'd ended up spotting Javier that night, kissing a girl in the alley. She wasn't jealous—Javier was someone to have fun with, and a good friend. But he wasn't boyfriend material, no matter what he thought.

At midnight, Abuelita served a Christmas turkey with truffles and a variety of other dishes. Both of Andrea's uncles were there. Miguel—forty years old, married to the flighty and vain Maria Carmen. Their two children, both preteens, threw fits when Andrea wouldn't let them play in her closet. Luis, her younger uncle, was thirty-five. Single, nattily dressed, he wore an easy smile and had a confident gaze as he talked of building his advertising business in Barcelona. They all talked and laughed until the early hours of the morning.

Christmas morning was spent primarily at the parish church of Santa Maria in old town. The front of the building, with its rounded arches and tower, was faced with old tan and brown brick, and dominated the intersection of three narrow streets. The three alleys were decorated with lights and candles, creating a magical scene.

Later, she spoke on the phone with Carrie, still silent and wounded from the loss of her husband, saving strength for the coming birth of their child. Sarah, on the phone, had been snappy and irritable, and her parents distant. Julia had been in Boston, and Jessica sounded stoned. In the end, Andrea decided that the magical Christmas she'd experienced was far preferable to the cold, often quiet holidays she'd grown up with in San Francisco with her parents.

Staying in Spain for the holidays had been the right decision. Increasingly as she'd come closer to finishing secondary school, she'd felt that Calella was home and the United States just a place she visited sometimes. Last Christmas hadn't just reinforced it…it had solidified it. After discussion with Abuelita, she'd struck the American colleges off her list, confining her search to universities in Spain, Paris and London.

Now, answering Leah Simpson's questions, she felt awkward, unsure of herself. How do you explain to a stranger the hurts and rejections that you can barely even admit to yourself? Somehow she had the feeling this self-confident, mature woman who wore a sidearm wouldn't be sympathetic to the sometimes overpowering sense of loneliness and grief Andrea felt.

Whatever she felt, Simpson at least mimicked feeling some empathy. Her eyes softened, and she said, "As I'm sure you're aware, Bear and his team are working to investigate your kidnappers. But…can you remember anything about them that might give us a clue what they were after? Is there anyone you've angered? Anyone have a reason to hurt you?"

Andrea shook her head. "No…I…I don't have any enemies. Nothing like that."

"When did Tariq Koury first approach you?"

"He was in the seat next to me on the flight. He was…creepy. I knew something was wrong because he lied to me about where he was going to school, and he was too old for that anyway. But I figured he was just a creep…not a kidnapper or whatever."

"Koury was much more than a kidnapper." Simpson shifted in her seat, as if debating how much to say.

"Don't hesitate," Sarah said. "Andrea needs to know what she's up against. *We* need to know what we're up against."

Andrea flashed a grateful look at her sister.

Simpson said, "Koury's fairly well known. He's Saudi born. Not religious, he's been involved in various sorts of intelligence work for a long time."

"Spy stuff?" Sarah raised her eyebrows.

Andrea frowned. What did that kind of thing have to do with her?

Simpson nodded unhappily. "More often mercenary. Koury did some contract work in Iraq, Afghanistan, plenty of other places not all that safe for Americans. We're not sure who he was working for in this case."

"But you're certain he was working for someone?" The words came from Carrie, who had returned to the room with a baby clutched to her chest.

Andrea's eyes were drawn instantly to the small figure in Carrie's arms. Tiny. She stood up and moved to Carrie in deliberate motions.

Carrie met her eyes and smiled. "Andrea, this is Rachel."

Andrea swallowed. Her chest was tight, stomach clenched, throat closed up to the point she felt as if she was going to have difficulty breathing. She whispered. "May I...may I hold her?"

"Very carefully. Have you held a baby before? Cradle her head."

"I have," Andrea replied. Carrie wouldn't know, of course, but Andrea had spent much of the last four years babysitting for two young couples in her building. She knew how to handle babies.

But this was different.

She took baby Rachel in her arms, sliding her left hand up behind Rachel's head. For just a second, Rachel's face began to go red, and her toothless mouth opened. Andrea pulled her a little closer then rocked on her feet.

Rachel quieted. Her skin was very pale, like Carrie and Andrea's, and her eyes were a faint blue. A diaphanous fringe of hair showed on her head.

"She's beautiful." Andrea said it in a reserved voice, not demonstrating any of the storm of emotions she felt. Inside, it was as if a gale had been unleashed. Her emotions on holding the infant were confused, conflicted. More than once she'd sat at home in Calella and felt a cold knot of resentment in her stomach. Not for her parents, who she knew were shits. But for her sisters, who knew it too, but who didn't seek her out. Except for Julia, she knew about the rest of her sisters' lives through Facebook, or in Carrie's case, through the newspapers.

She didn't want to feel that way. And this infant drew her in. Instead of disdain, or separation, or anger, what she felt was fierce protectiveness. She looked in those eyes and knew that if it came down to it, she'd give her life to protect that baby. It was a difficult, confusing emotion, and her eyes flooded with tears as she thought about it. She looked up at Carrie, and saw in Carrie's expression the mirror of what she felt. Except that Carrie wasn't looking at the baby. Carrie was looking at *Andrea*.

She swallowed. That naked protectiveness and love felt raw and dangerous. She held Rachel out to Carrie, her hands suddenly shaking.

Carrie took the baby without hesitation. "Are you all right?" she asked. Her eyes dropped to Andrea's shaking hands.

Andrea nodded. In her peripheral vision, she saw Leah Simpson stand.

"I'll be going. For the time being, until we have more permanent arrangements made, two uniformed officers are stationed in the lobby and one at your door twenty-four hours a day. If you need to go anywhere, please talk with the officer outside so you'll have an escort."

Andrea nodded, desperately wanting to get out of that room.

"Here's my card," Simpson said. Andrea reached out and wordlessly snatched it. She needed this woman to leave. She needed to step out of this room.

Sarah was staring at her frankly now, eyes filled with curiosity.

"I…I need to…I'll be back."

Clutching the card in her hand, she ran down the hallway to the bathroom and slammed the door behind her. She barely made it to the toilet before the nausea forced her to her knees.

2. Leslie Collins. April 29. 12:30 pm

Leslie Collins looked around the relative darkness of Assaggi's on Bethesda Avenue and took a bite of his tortelli di zucca. Organic whole grain fresh pasta filled with pumpkin and glazed with a butter sage sauce, it was surprisingly good. Despite the fact that his job frequently forced him to eat in sometimes inconvenient and occasionally downright awful locations, Collins preferred to eat at home, with his wife.

Today that wasn't an option. For one thing, the planned topic of discussion would ruin her appetite.

Filner was late. Again. Collins would have preferred to have met somewhere more discreet, or not at all. Or that he'd never been forced into his uneasy business relationship with Mitch Filner in the first place. He often wished none of this had ever happened.

But since it had, he had no choice but to see it to the bitter end. He took a sip of his Dewar's and Soda, breaking yet another of his own informal rules. He didn't drink in the middle of the day. But then again, he'd never ordered the kidnap and murder of a teenage girl before, either. No matter what most Americans thought—especially the liberals and conspiracy theorists—his agency was scrupulous about law virtually all of the time. Unfortunately, this was one of those times when extraordinary measures became necessary.

Filner seethed as he scanned the headlines on his tablet. *Daughter of Secretary of Defense escapes abduction attempt.* That was the front page of the Washington Post. The New York Times said *Police Identify Suspect in Kidnap Attempt.* This was a real shit-show, one that had been turning Collins's stomach all morning. It took the feds no more than an hour to identify Tariq Koury. One hour. His identification was bound to lead to plenty of uncomfortable questions to several agencies in Washington Koury had freelanced for at one time or another. Not to mention the private military contractor where he'd found a home.

Collins was relatively sure nothing would find its way back to him. But relatively sure wasn't good enough. Too much rested on Wakhan staying buried forever. Anything threatening to bring it out in the open needed to be dealt with.

Mitch Filner arrived fifteen minutes late. Collins spotted him walking up the street from the direction of the Apple Store, then crossing Bethesda Avenue behind a gaggle of mothers with drooling and bubbling children in their strollers. When Filner crossed the street, he was hidden from view for a moment, but Collins knew he would reappear.

Collins mentally catalogued once again the people who knew about Wakhan. Thompson...soon to be Secretary of Defense. Roshan al Saud, the head of the Saudi Arabian Intelligence Agency and brother to the King. George-Phillip Windsor, the appallingly nosy busybody who saw himself as an intelligence professional and found himself in a game he couldn't have imagined. Windsor was a dilettante, a distant cousin of Queen Elizabeth who owed his position as Chief of the Special Intelligence Service to his family name. Senator Chuck Rainsley, retired Marine Corps Colonel and now Senior Senator from Texas. Before the Marines had their heads handed to them in Beirut in 1983, he'd been a nobody, an obscure man assigned to an obscure position. Somehow he'd turned the massacre of his own troops into political capital that fueled his powerful career in Washington. Finally, there was Vasily Karatygin, who had disappeared for much of the 90s, only to turn up as a prominent "businessman" after the Northern Alliance swept the Taliban out of Kabul.

Karatygin could be eliminated without anyone knowing or caring. But the rest were prominent in their own countries and agencies. With the exception of George-Phillip, they all owed their careers to maintaining their secrecy. And Windsor knew the consequences of letting the secret out would be especially dire.

Another variable he couldn't control was Thompson's children. The moment Collins received the report that all of the children were getting genetic testing to find a match for the baby, he scrambled. The results of those genetic tests were going to raise questions that might fuck everything up. If Collins could have gone back in time and retroactively sterilized Thompson's slut of a wife, he would have done so without hesitation.

Filner appeared in the doorway and made his way through the restaurant, scanning everyone in the crowd. An Army veteran, he'd been with the CIA Directorate of Operations through most of the 90s and into the early part of the 2000s. Filner was a bit of a roughneck and didn't fit in well with the buttoned-down Ivy League culture at CIA's headquarters in Langley, Virginia. But he'd been an ace at some of the ugliest operations, until a rape accusation in Singapore ended his agency career.

Collins had been forced to personally break the news in 2008. Filner had been quietly booted from the agency. Since then, Filner had transitioned into a world even more shadowy than the Agency. He was a private contractor, sometimes providing services via contacting outfits like Blackwater, but sometimes directly.

Right now he was on a private assignment. Off the books.

"Collins."

"Filner."

Filner's eyes scanned the room again then looked at Collins's half-finished plate. "Sorry I'm late."

Collins's eyebrows pulled together. He leaned forward and said, "I'm not concerned that you're late, Filner. I'm concerned about the situation with Richard Thompson."

Filner shrugged. "It was unexpected."

"It's a disaster. I give you the job of quietly making that girl disappear. Instead, we've got a massive media fiasco. How the hell did Koury end up dead?"

"Dumb luck, Collins. You know that happens sometimes. The cops saw something they didn't like and pursued them."

"You sent two seasoned killers to pick up a sixteen-year-old girl, and somehow she not only gets away, but also kills both of them."

"She didn't kill them. The cops did."

Collins waved his hand. "Semantics. And here's the thing. She's under the eye of the media now, and Diplomatic Security is lining up to give protection to the entire family. You fucked up, Filner. You blew it."

"We can still take her out."

Collins shook his head. "Too late. It was one thing for her to disappear. It's another thing for something to happen now with the entire world watching. We're going to have to wait and see. I expect you to pull together whatever assets you need. Every member of that family needs to be watched. Where the fuck is the mother?"

Filner shrugged. "Don't know. Nobody seems to. Wherever she is, she hasn't used her credit cards in the last few days."

Collins muttered. "And the other twin is with her?"

"We assume so."

"Has MI-6 moved on this?"

"Not that I'm aware of. My source there says there's nothing he knows of related to this. But you know how it is. It's all compartmentalized. England probably has more spies in the U.S. than Russia."

"We need someone closer to Windsor. He's the one person who could blow everything."

Filner nodded. "Normal rates still apply?"

Collins leaned forward, spearing another fork of pasta and turning it over, examining it before he placed it in his mouth. He chewed for a few seconds before answering. "Emergency. I don't care what assets. I don't care how many hours. Your mission in life is to make sure Richard Thompson's secrets never come to light, Filner. At all costs. This was all supposed to be nice and quiet, and now it's not, and it's your fault. I want it fixed. I want it to go away. Am I clear? If this problem doesn't go away, then *you* will."

"You're clear, Collins. But let *me* be clear. You better have some contingency plans in place. If you'd taken care of this problem fifteen years ago, no one would have noticed. A simple house fire would have wiped them all out. Now you've got Thompson up as the next Secretary of Defense and one of his daughters is married to a rock star. Anything happens to them and it's visible."

Collins shook his head. "I can manage Thompson. And rock stars die in plane crashes all the time. You worry about the rest."

CHAPTER SIX
Classified

1. Andrea. April 29

It took Andrea several minutes to compose herself, rinse her mouth and wash her face. Her heart was racing, and she felt tension in her chest, but she forced herself to calm down and focus.

Once she was calm, she opened the medicine chest in hopes of finding a hairbrush. Instead, she was faced with a shelf of medications. Zoloft. Andrea felt a morbid fascination and didn't want to touch it or look, because it was none of her business. But she couldn't stop herself, and she turned the bottle. The prescription was two weeks old and was written for her sister Carrie.

She tried to imagine what it must be like for Carrie. Andrea hadn't known Ray well, but she'd been impressed with him. A handsome and tall soldier, he'd been brave, incredibly brave, and that courage had directly resulted in his death.

When Andrea flew into Washington last summer, she'd had little opportunity to speak with the devastated Carrie, lost in the debris of a life Andrea knew nothing about. They'd barely spoken half a dozen words, Carrie overwhelmed by the stress of the accident and the court martial. It was all just too much. Way too much.

Was this stuff even safe to take during a pregnancy? Andrea didn't know, but presumably the doctor did.

Whatever the answer was, Andrea wasn't going to second-guess or judge. She took out the hairbrush and carefully brushed her hair, then put it away, the brush and the medicine now out of sight.

Finally composed, she stepped out of the bathroom and walked back toward the family room. As she walked down the hall, she heard a phone ringing in the kitchen. She stopped in place and sagged against the wall, overcome by a wave of exhaustion. It hadn't even been a day since she landed in the United States. Not even twenty-four hours since two men had attempted to kidnap and possibly murder her. She didn't know why. But, despite the presence of federal security guards at the door, she felt afraid like she'd never felt before.

The phone stopped ringing, and she heard Carrie's voice. Quiet. Words, then more words, unclear, out of focus. Then, "Andrea! Phone!"

Andrea swallowed. Was it one of her sisters? Her mother? Julia and Crank were in Los Angeles this week, she knew that. Crank's band, *Morbid Obesity*, was recording a new album. She had no idea what was going on with Alexandra or Jessica.

She walked into the kitchen and promised herself one thing. She was going to get to know all of her sisters. She was fed up with secrets and isolation.

Carrie had the baby on one shoulder and the phone at her ear. "Sí," she said nodding. "Sí." Then in terribly accented Spanish, she said, "Adios." Grinning, she passed the phone to Andrea.

"Hello?"

"Andrea! Como estas?"

"Luis!" she replied, delighted. Uncle Luis owned a growing marketing design firm in Barcelona, and often visited with his mother, and therefore Andrea. Over the last three years he'd become a trusted figure in her life. A father in many ways.

"Andrea, why didn't you call me? I wake up this morning to the news that thugs kidnapped you? Mother will have a heart attack when she watches the news."

Andrea whispered, "Does she know yet?"

"No," he said. "She thinks her television is broken, no thanks to your resourceful uncle. I should be at work today, but the minute I saw the news I got on the road to Calella."

Andrea breathed a sigh of relief. Then she said, "It was scary, Luis. But it's over. I'm all right. There's no need to tell Abuelita."

"I see how it is, Andrea. You want the old women at Church to tell her, and then she'll say, *Luis, why do you keep secrets from me?* No. No. Who were these thugs?"

"The police here are investigating. And they've given me bodyguards."

"It's because of your father? I saw in the paper he's to be the new Defense Minister."

"It might be that," Andrea said. "I don't know."

"You should come home," he said.

Andrea swallowed. "I will soon, Uncle, I promise."

"Okay. And next time you tell me when you're leaving the country, and if you're planning to mix it up with kidnappers. You understand?"

She giggled, feeling tears forming at the edge of her eyes. "I promise."

"Okay, *Muñequita*. Let me talk to my sister, por favor."

Andrea blinked and said, "She's not here."

"What? Your mother isn't there? Where is she?"

"I...I don't..."

Luis muttered a series of curses, and then in an angry voice, said, "What about your father? No doubt he's off saving the government instead of taking care of you."

She didn't want to lose it. She didn't want to respond that way. She didn't want to do anything. But involuntarily, Andrea burst into tears. "I don't know!" she cried. "He was here last night, but not this morning. I don't know where he is."

"*Muñequita*," he said in a quiet voice. "I'm sorry. I didn't mean to upset you."

"It's not *your* fault," she replied.

"No, it is. Maybe not my fault your parents are no-good, but it's my fault I lost my temper. Andrea, just...I know your parents are loco, but they love you in their own way. And more importantly, I love you, little doll."

She sniffed back tears. Then said, "Thank you, Luis."

After she said goodbye, she stood there, looking at the counter, a growing rage spreading in her chest. *Where was her mother?* Why the hell had she left her to be cared for by her brokenhearted and injured sisters? She didn't care if Carrie were thirty or fifty. She'd lost her husband and had a sick daughter. Sarah was technically an adult now, but she'd only been eighteen for four weeks.

All of which took Andrea back to the same question again. Where the hell was her mother?

She walked out of the kitchen into the living room. Sarah was still sitting, staring out the glass at the balcony, arms wrapped around her legs. Carrie rocked the baby in her arms, a nursing cloth draped over her shoulder.

The phone rang again. Carrie stirred, and Andrea said, "I'll get it."

Carrie gave her a relieved smile, and Andrea picked up the phone. "Hello?"

"Hello, this is Sergeant Gorman, with the security detail. We have a couple of people here to visit. Dylan and Alexandra Paris. Okay to clear them in?"

"Yes!" Andrea cried.

2. Carrie. April 29

Oh, *thank God*, Carrie thought.

The minute the AMBER Alert went out the night before, Carrie had called Alexandra and Julia, and kept them updated during the terrorizing ninety minutes before Andrea was found again. Both had agreed to come as soon as possible. Alexandra and Dylan were coming in on the train from New York, and Julia on a flight from Los Angeles later in the day.

"I didn't know they were coming," Andrea said.

Carrie frowned. "Of course they are. We're your sisters."

Andrea gave her a weak smile. A doubtful smile. "I just assumed they were all busy."

Carrie sighed. She couldn't stand up easily, Rachel was still breastfeeding, but as she shifted in frustration, Sarah unfolded herself and stood. She looked almost comical as she reached her arms up to her much taller sister. But her expression was fierce. "We take care of each other, Andrea."

Andrea looked doubtful. And really, why shouldn't she? It's not like they'd done anything to seek her out. Carrie had planned to last summer. She'd even talked with Ray about it. Then everything in her life went horribly wrong. And it was just exhausting, because she *wanted* to watch out for Andrea. She wanted to know why she'd spent most of the last years in Europe. She wanted to be there for her. But she couldn't be *everywhere*. She couldn't be the only one. Especially not now, when she had a young daughter to care for. She'd been a surrogate mother at one time or another to every single one of her sisters but Julia.

It was time for someone else to pick up that mantle. She was a real mother now, to a helpless little girl—Ray's daughter—and she'd be damned if she'd let *anything* interfere with that.

Sarah and Andrea both walked to the door of the condominium when they heard the knock. Then, a moment later, Sarah opened the door.

Outside, in the hall, stood twenty-two-year-old Alexandra and her husband Dylan Paris. Alexandra looked weary. Her honey-brown hair was windblown, a little tangled, and she had circles under her green eyes. Carrie sat up a little at the sight of her. This wasn't a night's lost sleep. Alexandra looked like she'd been going without rest for a while.

Dylan was in worse condition. His eyes were bloodshot, hair unkempt, several days' growth of beard on his chin and neck.

The worst part was that Dylan and Alex weren't touching anywhere. A solid inch of space divided them, but it might as well have been a mile. Neither of them seemed conscious of it.

Alexandra's eyes teared up at the sight of Andrea, and then they were embracing.

Dylan gave a wry smile to Sarah. She returned the smile, then said, "Hey Dylan, show me your scars later?"

He shrugged. "Only if you show me yours."

They hugged, then all four of them moved back into the apartment.

Objectively, Dylan looked awful. Carrie had a sinking, dreadful feeling tied up in her throat. Dylan had been a heavy drinker in high school, but he quit. But the last couple years had been tough on him. Wounded in Afghanistan, then his best friend murdered. She watched him closely, worried. She'd never seen him looking this disheveled.

Dylan approached Carrie. She studied him. She was assuming too much. Exams at Columbia would be in another week or two. Dylan and Alexandra were probably just tired. This was Alexandra's last term at Columbia—she would be graduating in a few weeks.

Rachel had fallen asleep. Carrie smiled then whispered, "Give me just a second to put her down." Very carefully she unlatched the baby, covered herself, then stood and carried Rachel into the bedroom and lay her in the crib.

She felt Dylan's presence behind her. He was silent, as was she, but his eyes were on Rachel. Carrie looked over at him. He was somber. Dark circles under his eyes were accentuated by the growth of stubble all over his face. It had been several months since she'd seen him. His hair had grown down well past his collar, and she couldn't help but wonder if he'd had a haircut since Ray died.

She swallowed. Ray had loved Dylan. Brothers, in so many ways.

He whispered, "She looks like both of you. She'll be like ninety feet tall when she grows up."

She gave him a crooked smile, and then backed out of the room, switching out the light. "She'll stay out for a couple hours," she said.

Dylan followed her back down the hall. "How is she doing?"

She shrugged, moving down the hall. As she passed by the living room, she saw Andrea, Sarah and Alexandra huddled near each other on the couch talking. She paused for just a second. Even there, on the couch, she could see the separation. Sarah and Alexandra sat close to each other. Andrea was a few inches away…just enough that they didn't accidentally touch.

Carrie sighed. She couldn't fix everything. But she'd keep trying. She kept on going into the kitchen.

"Coffee?" she asked, taking down a mug for herself.

"Please."

She took down a second mug and busied herself pouring coffee. Dylan knew where the sugar and cream were. He'd been here often, both before and after Ray's death.

Dylan repeated his question. "How is she doing?"

Carrie shrugged. "Rachel? Or Andrea."

He gave her a gentle smile. "Both, I guess. Rachel first."

Carrie crossed her arms over her chest, the coffee mug in her left hand. "She's not in any immediate danger. We have a blood transfusion scheduled for next week…she'll have to get them weekly for now."

"And…finding a donor?"

Carrie shook her head. "I've been tested and I'm not a match. But I'm close. Neither is Sarah. We should have Julia's and Alexandra's results back today, and Andrea gets blood drawn tomorrow."

"I'm surprised she didn't get the testing done in Spain," he said.

Carrie shrugged. "I asked her to come. And then…well, you know what happened."

"No one could have predicted that, Carrie. Give yourself a fucking break."

She bit her lip and looked away. Abruptly, she set the coffee cup down, spilling a little on the counter. "*Damn it,*" she said. She reached for the paper towels, but Dylan grabbed her wrist.

"Carrie. You don't have to shoulder everything, okay?"

Horrified at herself, a sound escaped from her throat, somewhere between a hiccough and a scream. She covered her mouth, but said through her fingers, "I have to stay strong for Rachel."

"Christ," he muttered. Then he pulled her to him, wrapping his arms around her in a warm hug that locked her in like a vice.

She kept her arms across her chest, in between her and Dylan, shielding herself somehow. "I can't. If I let go of control I'll never get it back together."

"I know," he said, his voice raw. "It's okay. I miss him too. But you gotta know he's out there somewhere looking out for you and Rachel."

She sobbed. "*Stop,*" she said.

"Carrie, we're here. I'm here, and Alex, and your other sisters, and we won't let you fall."

Carrie nodded viciously. And then dropped her arms and wrapped them around him. "Thank you," she whispered. "I miss him so much sometimes."

And then she felt other arms on her shoulders. Andrea had squeezed beside her, wrapping an arm around her. She whispered in Carrie's ear, "We'll take care of you, Carrie. I promise."

3. Bear. April 29

Bear Wyden had spent his entire career in the Department of State, and had always thought the large four-winged building at Foggy Bottom was a huge, messy maze.

It had nothing on the Pentagon. He'd shown up fifteen minutes early, and needed that much time just to clear security. It troubled the Pentagon employees mightily that an investigator from the Department of the State would actually have a sidearm. After all, interagency cooperation only went so far, and arming diplomatic personnel was akin to arming the enemy. Several phone calls to increasing levels of seniority later, he'd finally been cleared into the building, and provided an escort to get him through the maze to the Secretary's office.

Forty-five minutes after his arrival, he was escorted into the office of the Secretary of Defense. It was a large office, nearly fifty feet along one wall, with plush blue carpeting. A nine foot long teak desk faced the room. Behind it, an equally ornate and large credenza was the Secretary's workspace. Two computers, three separate phones, and a scattering of papers. Above the desk, huge portraits dominated the room. On the left, General Dwight Eisenhower, on the right General George Marshall. In between, a family portrait showed Richard and Adelina Thompson, surrounded by their six daughters. To the left and right, the desk area was flanked by an American flag and the flag of the Department of Defense.

Bear wanted to study the portrait—he had experience with all kinds of families, including broken ones. A good look at the portrait might have shown him something—they often did. Sometimes, when he looked at the photo he and Leah had taken about six months before the divorce, he could see it. The disappointment and anger had been right there in her eyes. But, back then, he'd been too blind to see it.

So Bear tried to get a good look at the Thompson family portrait. But he didn't get a chance. Richard Thompson approached him, hand out, a smile on his face.

"Mr. Wyden, a pleasure to meet you." Bear snorted internally. Thompson wasn't one to forget a face—much less the face of the man who had once provided the protective detail for his own family. This was nothing more than a display of how important Thompson had become.

"Mr. Secretary."

"Come in, please."

Thompson led him to a round, highly polished round table with four seats near the desk. Wyden understood that Thompson was a career diplomat. A politician, really. But the smile seemed off. His youngest daughter had been kidnapped. The wide smile somehow seemed inappropriate.

The two of them took seats at the table. It was mahogany, with ornate carvings around the edge, and polished so much Bear could have safely shaved in the reflection.

"What can I do for you Mr. Wyden?"

Bear shifted uncomfortably in his seat. "Sir, as you know, I'm the lead investigator in the kidnapping of your daughter. I need to ask you some questions."

"Please, however I can assist the investigation. Can you tell me what you've found so far?"

"We're still early in the investigation."

"I know that. But I do know the identify of one of the suspects is known. A Saudi named Koury?"

Bear nodded. "There are some things I obviously can't discuss as of yet, Mr. Secretary."

"I'm sure you are aware I have security clearance, Mr. Wyden."

"Of course, sir. But this is an ongoing investigation. That said, you are correct, Koury was involved in your daughter's kidnapping."

"Who was behind it?"

Bear swallowed. "We don't know that yet."

Thompson leaned forward. Any traces of a political smile were gone. "Why the hell not?"

"Mr. Secretary, I'm sure you're aware both suspects died. It takes time—"

"Don't talk to me about time!"

Bear shook his head. "Sir, I need to ask you some questions. If you want us to resolve this, then you need to answer them."

"Fine. What do you need to know?"

"First, why does your youngest daughter live in Spain?"

Thompson waved his hand, as if swatting away a fly. "Her mother felt it was best."

Bear was stunned. That was it? "And you had no opinion?"

"Of *course* I had an opinion. What relevance does this have to the investigation?"

"Koury flew over here from Spain, sir. In the seat next to her. This was a sophisticated operation, launched on a moment's notice, with people involved from multiple countries. Who do you know who has the resources to pull off something like that?"

"Not many criminals," Thompson replied.

"That's right. Now, is there *anyone* you can think of on a personal level that might be involved? Enemies?"

Thompson shook his head. "Of course not. I'm a career diplomat, of course, and I've dealt with some unsavory characters over the years. We did, after all, require a protective detail for some time."

"I remember," Bear said. Interesting that Thompson thought he needed to remind Bear about the protective detail. Was it some kind of subtle one-up-manship? Thompson pointing out that he was so important that he didn't even remember who had been in charge of protecting his family?

Something was very wrong here.

"Mr. Thompson," Bear began. Thompson didn't respond, even though Bear deliberately violated protocol by not addressing him with his title. "Where were you last night? When your daughter was at the hospital?"

"I was on Capitol Hill all yesterday afternoon. My daughter Carrie went to pick up her sister because she could get there quicker than I could. And we agreed to meet back at the condo."

"I see. And your wife? Why wasn't she there?"

Thompson rolled his eyes. "You're asking a lot of irrelevant questions, Mr. Wyden."

"Wives are never irrelevant, sir, mine would have told you that, at least before she left me. Where is Mrs. Thompson?"

"If you must know, our daughter Jessica has been...problematic of late. My wife is in San Francisco with her."

Bear sat back in his seat. *What?* That just didn't make any sense. "Problematic how?"

Thompson coughed. Then muttered, "Drugs. Teenage issues. Nothing life threatening, but Adelina felt it necessary to take her on some...prayer retreat, some days ago. I really can't tell you any more, except that she's out of touch."

"You have no way of getting in touch with her?"

"That's correct."

"Sir...that's...don't you think that's a little odd?"

Thompson raised an eyebrow. "How so?"

Bear sat forward, finding himself unable to control the tone of his voice. "Sir, don't you think it a little odd that your wife and one of your daughters is somewhere you don't know and out of touch? Don't you think it's odd that your youngest daughter was *kidnapped* and you didn't even bother to go to the hospital to check on her?"

Thompson glared at Bear. "How dare you? Are you here to investigate a crime or not?"

"Mr. Thompson, have you ever encountered Mr. Koury before?"

Thompson frowned.

Bear sat back in his seat. "You have, haven't you?"

Thompson sighed. "It's classified, unfortunately."

What the hell is wrong with this man? "Mr. Thompson, I have the clearance."

Thompson sighed. "Well, then. You may or may not be aware that following my retirement I did a significant amount of consulting, including a diplomatic mission to Iraq in late 2002. It was a last minute attempt to get Iraq to back down and reveal their weapons of mass destruction to avert war. Mr. Koury was part of the security team for our mission in Iraq."

Bear held his breath. "He was part of the security team?"

"Yes. I believe he was the second in command? Possibly."

Bear thought through the implications of this. "Did you personally have dealings with Mr. Koury?"

"The mission was three weeks. Of course I had dealings with him."

"What do you remember about him?"

Thompson's lips curled unpleasantly. "He was an uncouth man. Barbaric really. Fond of pornography. He routinely used foul language."

"Did you ever suspect any criminal activity?"

"I wouldn't doubt it."

Bear sighed. He'd been involved in investigations for many years. He'd dealt with criminals and terrorists. He'd dealt with distraught parents and panicky corrupt officials. But he'd never held an interview as frustrating as this one. He actually found himself wondering if Thompson was a sociopath. No one was this dispassionate about his daughter's kidnapping. He knew Thompson was a cold fish, but no one was *this* cold. Thompson was hiding something.

"Mr. Thompson...when was the last time you had any contact with Tariq Koury?"

Thompson thought for a moment then said, "Koury held a contract for the coalition provisional authority in Iraq from 2003 to 2005. I dealt with him on a fairly routine basis then."

"I wasn't aware you were in government at the time, Mr. Thompson."

"I was officially retired. But I took on occasional contracts."

"And some of those contracts took you to Iraq?"

"Among other places."

Bear nodded. "Were these places classified?"

"They were."

So Koury knew Thompson. That was unexpected, and in some ways might change the direction of the investigation. But he didn't really know how. Bear studied the man, eyebrows pressing together.

Thompson looked at his watch.

"I'm aware we're running short of time, Mr. Secretary. But I have a few more questions."

"Please proceed."

"When did you learn Andrea would be coming to the United States?"

Thompson answered the softball question immediately. "Two nights ago. Right after Carrie made the call to Spain."

"I see," Bear said. "And...your wife is in California right now. How tall is she?"

Thompson's eyes widened. At 5 feet 10 inches, he was the average height for a man. The anger on his face was unmistakable. "She is five foot three inches, Mr. Wyden."

Carrie and Andrea were both taller than six feet. They looked very similar to each other...and significantly different from the rest of their sisters.

Bear could only come to one conclusion. He stared at the Secretary of Defense and said, "Sir...who is Carrie and Andrea's father?"

CHAPTER SEVEN
Play Nice

1. Bear. April 29

Sir...who *is Carrie and Andrea's father?*

Bear Wyden felt the temperature drop in the room when he asked the question. It was the sort of question that could infuriate people. The sort of question that could end careers. After all, he wasn't asking some deadbeat in Chicago this question. He was asking the Secretary of Defense.

The second the words left Bear's mouth, Secretary Thompson's eyes narrowed and he stiffened in his seat. His face went slightly red and Bear thought Thompson was going to show his teeth. "How dare you?"

"Sir, where is your wife?"

"This interview is over."

"Mr. Thompson, this is a federal investigation into your own daughter's kidnapping, and you seem more concerned—"

"Mr. Wyden, you won't be concerned with this investigation or any other for very much longer. Now get out of my office."

Thompson stood and walked toward his desk. Wyden stood too, ignoring the feeling that he'd just stuck his bare hand into a wasps' nest. "Mr. Thompson. Your daughter was kidnapped. I need answers to my questions."

Richard Thompson wasn't answering any further questions. He lifted a phone to his ear.

"Sir—"

"Colonel Richardson, please have armed guards remove this...*person*...from my office immediately."

Bear leaned over the desk, right arm extended, index finger pointing at the photo of Thompson and his family. He knew he wasn't acting rationally. He knew his behavior was neither professional nor was it really accomplishing anything. But when he thought about that girl, kidnapped and alone, and then when she got out of it neither one of her parents could be bothered to show up at the hospital? He didn't give a shit if you were the President of the United States or a local janitor...you went to your kid in that kind of situation.

The thought of her all alone filled him with rage. "Is all that a sham, then? You don't give a shit about her, do you? That's why you weren't at the hospital."

"Mr. Wyden, I've asked you twice now to get out of my office."

"And I've asked you, Mr. Secretary. Who is Andrea's father?"

The office door opened. Two men stepped inside. Bear couldn't tell if they were soldiers or not. Neither wore a standard uniform—instead, they wore black unlabeled fatigues, combat boots, and wore sidearms. Close cropped hair, tan skin, pistols at the ready. They could be military or police or private contractors. He had no way of knowing.

He did know that there were two of them, and they were armed.

Wyden threw his hands in the air. "Fine, then. I'm gone."

One of them, a blonde haired, blue-eyed former football player who was probably from Texas, pushed forward while the other stood back to cover him. "Lay down on the floor!"

Two more black-dressed quasi soldiers came into the room as he shouted.

"I'm with Diplomatic Security," Wyden said. "Can I reach in my left pocket for my credentials?"

"On the floor!" Blondie shouted.

Wyden rolled his eyes. "Look at my credentials, please." He reached to open his jacket. Unfortunately, that brought attention to the 10mm Sig-Sauer in the shoulder holster on his right side.

The blonde quasi-soldier shouted, "Gun! He's got a gun!"

That changed everything. In fifteen seconds, the four men had Bear on the floor, arms out to his side. Blondie knelt on his back, knee digging into Bear's spine. He'd been disarmed.

In a disgusted tone, Thompson said, "When you've finished removing him, please have someone inform me. I'll be in the JCS conference room."

Once they removed the Sig Sauer from his jacket, Blondie reached around the front and took out the small folder from Bear's breast pocket that contained his State Department ID and Diplomatic Security badge.

"DSS, huh?" Blondie said. "I dealt with enough of your pals before. Here's the deal. We're gonna get up nice and slow, and you're going to cooperate, and then with any luck you can leave today without handcuffs or any holes drilled through you. Got it?"

"Yeah. Play nice. Gotcha. Let me the fuck up, all right?"

Wary, sidearms still out, the four security guards let Bear to his feet, and then escorted him out of the office. Blondie kept a hand on his arm the entire time. Bear shook his head. Sometimes he regretted the fact that he still worked with his ex-wife. Once she got wind of this, he'd never hear the end of it.

2. Dylan. April 29

**ive** me one of those." Sarah was slumped back in a cast iron chair as she said the words, her injured leg tucked up in front of her.

"Hell, no," Dylan said as he lit his cigarette, shielding the lighter from the wind. He took a long drag from the cigarette, the coal lighting up, the faint sound of the tobacco burning audibly in his ears.

"I'm eighteen now."

He raised an eyebrow, glancing over at her. After the too intense discussion with Carrie, he'd stepped outside for a smoke, planning on a little solitude. Sarah had followed him out onto the balcony. Twenty stories up, he could see most of Bethesda and parts of northwest Washington, DC spread out below his feet.

"I don't give a shit if you're thirty," Dylan said. "I'm not giving you a cigarette. If you want one that bad, buy your own."

"You're kidding, right? I don't leave the house. I'm a cripple, didn't you know that?"

He slumped into the seat across from her. "You're no more a cripple than I am. Actually your injuries weren't as bad as mine."

She shrugged. "I'm not a soldier."

"Better toughen up, then. What's this about you being a cripple?"

She sneered. "It's nothing. Mom and Dad basically laid down the rule I couldn't ever leave without an escort."

"Alex said you home schooled this year?"

"Tutors, mostly. I can't imagine what it cost. But it's changed everything."

"How?"

She raised her eyebrows. "You went to high school. You know what I'm talking about."

Dylan shrugged and took a drag off his cigarette. "I don't really. My high schooling wasn't exactly normal."

Her eyes widened a little, then she said, "Oh, that's right. I forgot. I remember the night Alexandra told Dad you'd dropped out of school. He was overjoyed."

"I'm sure he was."

Unexpectedly she leaned forward, tilting her head slightly to the right, a serious expression in her eyes.

"You're drinking again, aren't you?"

Dylan froze. For nearly fifteen seconds he didn't move. Then his eyes darted to the sliding glass door.

"What makes you say that?" The question was unnecessary. He knew why she asked. Everything about his appearance made people wonder. Alex wondered. Everyone who knew him did.

"Common sense," she replied. "You lost your two closest friends in two years. You've got no one to talk to. You're up there in New York married to my uptight as hell sister and you're all alone. You look like shit."

"You don't know what the fuck you're talking about, Sarah."

She leaned forward, raising a knowing eyebrow. "I know *exactly* what I'm talking about, Dylan."

"I'm not going to tell Alexandra," she said. "That's your deal. But you need to."

Dylan grimaced. "It's not drinking a *lot*, Sarah. But like you said, I lost my two closest friends. A drink every once in a while is okay."

Sarah's eyes dropped to the floor. "I was afraid of that," she said.

Even though she wasn't looking at him any more, Dylan still felt defensive. Sarah was Alex's younger sister by several years, but she always seemed to see right through him. And somehow the experience of the accident last summer formed some kind of bond for her with Ray. It didn't make any sense. It didn't have to. But when she looked at him with sad, knowing eyes, Dylan felt like Ray was looking at him.

He didn't like the way that felt.

Dylan looked at Sarah. "Listen, Sarah. We're not discussing this any more. I've got it under control, and Alex is already freaked out enough about Ray and you and Andrea and the baby...she doesn't need this on her plate, all right? In the greater scheme of things, me grabbing a drink every now and then is not that big of a deal. But freaking out Alex is."

Sarah shook her head. "You're fooling yourself, Dylan."

He closed his eyes and sighed, then took another drag off his cigarette. The breeze up here felt cool. Calming. He remembered the first time he'd been on this balcony. Just over a year ago, after he and Alex had rushed to take an overnight train to DC in response to Carrie's call. Staff Sergeant Martin had testified at the preliminary hearing, and then called Ray that night, threatening suicide. Then he shot himself while still on the phone with Ray.

They stood outside, right here on this balcony, Ray's eyes still red, dark circles under his haunted eyes. *They're talking bridesmaid's dresses,* he had said. *Thank God you woke up.*

I'm not so good at asking for help, Ray had said.

Sometimes you have to, Dylan had responded. *You're the one who taught me that.*

The problem was, you could know something, and you could tell other people, but still not believe it in your soul. And sometimes Dylan just couldn't get his mind around the fact that his two best friends were dead in two years.

He looked back at Sarah. "Sarah, thanks for your concern. I promise, I'll be okay." The words felt hollow, brittle as he said them.

3. Andrea. April 29

Andrea looked out the sliding glass door. Dylan was slumped in his seat, smoking a cigarette. Sarah was out there with him, gesticulating as she spoke. It was a beautiful spring day. She could tell a breeze was blowing outside, because every few seconds Sarah and Dylan's hair blew in the wind.

She turned. Alexandra looked unhappy as she and Carrie exchanged small talk. *Small talk.* Final exams. Train and plane schedules. What was Columbia University like now versus ten years ago. Pretty soon they were going to start talking about the weather or something.

Their voices were like *buzz buzz buzz* in her ear, and for a second Andrea wanted to just throw some heavy object across the room. Something serious was obviously going on between Dylan and Alexandra—normally they were two of the most affectionate people she'd ever seen. Now they didn't look at each other? They didn't touch? Carrie was on the verge of falling apart every moment, and the help she got from a part-time nanny was wholly inadequate. Their mother and father were among the missing, Jessica was who-knew-where and there were armed guards right outside the condo to *protect them* from terrorists or kidnappers or whatever.

Yet, they sat here engaged in small talk.

She wanted to scream just to get their attention. Instead, she sat down on the couch across from them. Back straight, shoulders back, and legs crossed at the ankle, just as their bitchy mother taught her all those years ago before outsourcing Andrea's upbringing. Then she stared at Carrie. She didn't say a word. She just stared.

It took about 40 seconds before Carrie broke off her sentence and looked from Alexandra to Andrea.

"Are you all right?"

Andrea shrugged. She tilted her head, looked toward Alexandra, and took a deep breath. Even though she'd brought on the question, she felt suddenly frozen. A tightness in her chest, her throat closed up.

Alexandra's eyebrows pushed together, and she sat forward in her seat, leaning toward Andrea. "Hey...are you okay, hun?"

Andrea started to speak, and found her hands suddenly flapping, the words colliding in her mouth like a ten car pileup on a two-lane highway.

"Breathe," Carrie said, reaching out and taking her hand.

"When do I get tested?" Andrea blurted.

"Tomorrow morning," Carrie replied.

"Why..." She stared at her sisters, her face going pale. Then she said, "Never mind," and started to pull away.

"Whoa," Carrie said. "Wait."

"No, really, never mind," Andrea said.

"Stop," Alexandra replied. "Tell us. Whatever it is. You're safe here. We're your sisters."

Andrea stood up, her eyes swiveling back and forth between the two of them. Then she voiced the words. The words she'd never said out loud, the words that expressed every doubt and fear and insecurity she'd ever had.

"Are we?"

"What?" Alexandra asked.

"Are we sisters?"

Alexandra visibly recoiled a few inches. "Of course we are," she said.

Andrea shook her head. "I know *we* are," she said, gesturing between herself and Carrie. "That's obvious to anyone. But…why else would they send me away? Why?"

Carrie said, "I thought you wanted to go."

"*What?*" Andrea said.

Dylan and Sarah, both sitting on the balcony outside, slid open the sliding glass door. "Is everything okay?" Dylan asked.

"I said, I always thought you wanted to live with Abuelita. I mean…you started spending summers over there when I was at Columbia…and…I don't know…I guess I assumed…"

She assumed. That's what you did when you didn't even really care. But then Andrea felt her heart almost stop.

"Mom said, *Andrea doesn't want to come home.*" Carrie frowned as she spoke. "I asked her why, and she said not to pry. She said…I didn't want to get into it. That you'd be happier if I didn't dig into it…and…she said there was nothing but grief there."

Andrea sank into her seat. "I don't know how she could possibly know that. We've barely spoken a word to each other in the last five years. She won't even speak with Abuelita or Luis." She thought back. Trying to remember. Anything. Details.

She shook her head. "I kind of took it for granted. I mean, I started spending summers there when I was five? Six?"

"Something like that. It was the summer after Julia left for Harvard."

"That far back?" Andrea asked. "I don't remember Julia living with us."

"She finished high school in 2000 I think…you'd have been…two? Anyway…you didn't go to Spain for the first time until June 2002."

"You remember the timing pretty well," Andrea said.

"That's because I went with you."

Andrea's eyes widened. "You went with me the first time? I don't remember that."

"I'm not surprised, you were only four."

Sarah approached closely. Her eyes were on Andrea. "Carrie, do you have any pictures from that trip?"

Alexandra shook her head. "This is *bullshit.* We are sisters. Andrea, I'm sorry I haven't been in touch much the last year or two…college has just been…insane. And…well, you know. But we're *sisters.*"

Sarah said, "Get the photos, Carrie."

Carrie nodded. Andrea sat and watched her go, feeling dread in her stomach. Why would it be her and Carrie alone who went to Spain? The two sisters who looked different. The two of them who were more than six feet tall and looked almost like twins and *nothing* like their father?

Why did they go to Spain?

Carrie returned to the room a few minutes later. She had a well worn photo album. It had a canvas cover decorated with the word *Spain* in purple letters. Framed on the front cover was a photo.

She flushed a little when she put the book in front of them, and said, "I was a little more girly when I was seventeen."

Andrea felt a chill looking at it. The photograph, taken nearly twelve years before, looked exactly like Andrea, holding hands with a four year old. Except, of course, it was Carrie, holding hands with her. Both of them had smiles on their faces, huge smiles. Andrea's four-year-old face was smeared with what looked like chocolate ice cream.

Andrea, of course, recognized the location. They were standing on Calella Beach...unmistakable, because of the lighthouse above their shoulders and the word CALELLA in twelve-foot high rock letters on the hillside behind them. That would be near the Hotel Esplai. Javier worked there as a busboy in the summer time.

Carrie slid into the seat next to Andrea.

Andrea took a deep breath. "Was this the only time you went?" she asked.

Carrie nodded. "Mother wanted me to go in 2003, after I graduated high school, but we had a huge fight about it, because I was planning on spending my summer with my friends here."

"What happened?"

"I won the argument. I remember Dad was never around much that summer, and at the end, I drove to Columbia."

"You drove?" Andrea said.

"Yeah, with Julia and Crank and Sean. It was fun. I started college a few weeks later. And...well...I think you started first grade in September."

Andrea couldn't keep her eyes off the album. She didn't have many memories of their home in San Francisco when she was younger. She knew she'd attended her first few years of school in San Francisco, but with the exception of a few early memories, everything before ten years old was hazy. By then, she was spending her summers in California and the school year in Spain.

She reached out and touched the book. The fabric felt well used. Loved, even. She almost felt guilty. She loved Luis and Abuelita. Her family. Somehow, wanting to open that album, wanting to open that can of worms of her past, made her feel disloyal.

But Abuelita would understand. Luis would understand. And even if they didn't...she needed to know, didn't she? She needed to know. She needed to know her history. She needed to know who she was. Who her family was. She needed to know *why*.

Andrea reached out and took the album in her hands and flipped it open to the first page.

CHAPTER EIGHT
What makes you tick

1. Andrea. April 29

The first photo in the album showed two sisters, one seventeen, and the other four, flanking their mother. Carrie was frozen in time in that photo. She had braces on her teeth and wore a vintage blue dress with matching heels. She wore a huge smile on her face, and towered over Adelina Thompson.

"You look so happy," Andrea said.

"We were just leaving for the airport. It was my first trip without Mom and Dad."

"Do you remember how the trip came about? Why it was just the two of us?"

Carrie nodded. "Sort of. I had sort of hinted for a long time that I was hoping to take a trip to Europe sometime. I mean, it's not like we hadn't traveled. I remember living in Brussels, more or less, and I was in middle school most of the time we were in China. You were born there."

"In China," Andrea said. She knew that. But somehow hearing it, now, felt different.

"Right. The twins too."

A cloud fell over Carrie's face. Then she said, "Julia knows more about China, of course. She was in high school then."

Andrea sighed. She flipped the page. The first inside pages showed Carrie and Andrea arriving at the airport in Barcelona. Hugs with family members who must have been unfamiliar to Carrie at the time, but who looked very familiar to Andrea: Abuelita, Miguel and Maria Carmen, Luis. Her *family*, or at least the part of her family that had been a significant part of her life the last several years.

Carrie looked at her for a few seconds, and then she moved, wordlessly, onto the couch next to Andrea.

Andrea shifted position just a little. She knew she should be more open to her sister. Carrie, of all people. But something held her back. She shifted so that their bodies weren't touching.

Carrie said nothing about the shift. Instead, she pointed at the album. "How are Luis and Miguel?"

Andrea shrugged. "Miguel constantly complains about how his wife nags him to death. But you can tell he loves her."

Carrie smiled, nodding. "That sounds right."

"Luis started his own advertising firm in Barcelona...three years ago? Four? He loves it. Lately he's busy all the time, I don't get to see him very often."

Andrea flipped the page slowly. A smile spread across her face. The photograph showed Carrie, lying on the beach sunbathing. Luis was in the photo, lying on a towel a few feet away from Carrie, and his eyes were on her. "Oh, my God," Andrea said, laughter in her voice. "He is *so* checking you out in that picture."

Carrie chuckled. "He's not *that* much older than me. Six or seven years? That's still kind of creepy."

Not far from Luis and Carrie, half covered in sand, holding a shovel in one hand and a pair of goggles in the other, was Andrea. Four years old. Huge smile on her face.

Andrea swallowed. In the photo she looked so happy. No sign of the empty gaping loneliness she'd felt in later years.

After that, a series of beach photos. *Abuelita* in a bathing suit! Andrea gasped and laughed. A photo of a crowd of family members around a picnic table. In the foreground, Andrea played with two other children, three or four or five years old. Carrie sat on a picnic table, in avid conversation with a boy who looked remarkably like Javier. His older brother? Andrea supposed it was possible. Aunts and uncles and cousins were in the photo. In the background, near the edge of a picture, stood two men. One of them dark skinned, Spanish. The other, pale skinned, towered over him. Andrea didn't recognize either of the men.

The next several pages showed Andrea and Carrie out and about in Calella. She recognized the front of the Chapel of Santa Maria in one of the photos and smiled. In the photo, Miguel and his wife Maria Carmen were exiting the chapel. He wore a tuxedo, and she wore a garish wedding dress with entirely too much cleavage.

Andrea shook her head. "We were at Miguel and Maria Carmen's wedding?"

Carrie nodded. "Yes. It was a beautiful ceremony."

"She's a complete witch," Andrea whispered.

Carrie snickered. "Yeah. She is."

And that's when Andrea froze. She picked the album up and held it closer to her face.

In the wedding photo, a large crowd was near the plaza and the chapel. The beginning of the market was right there, and hundreds of people shopped there throughout the week.

Standing in the shade, barely visible in the photo, was a very tall, pale man. He stood next to a shorter, darker skinned man. Both of them were maddeningly out of focus. But it was the same man, she was sure of it.

"Andrea?" Carrie said.

"Wait…" Andrea whispered.

She set the album down, and flipped back to the beach photo. She studied the too fuzzy features on the man's face. Then she flipped forward to the wedding picture.

It was the same man, she thought.

From the photo, he was probably six foot five. Dark hair. Pale eyes, possibly green. Long, aquiline nose, she thought, but it was impossibly difficult to tell with the photo out of focus. But if she squinted her eyes enough, she imagined that the man might just resemble Carrie.

She reached out and pointed one shaking finger at the photo.

"Do you recognize that man?"

Carrie shook her head. "No…should I?"

"What about…" She flipped the album back to the beach photo. "Here."

"That's odd," Carrie said. Her eyebrows scrunched together. She flipped back and forth between one photo and the other.

Andrea looked up and met Carrie's eyes. Both of them stopped breathing.

"Do you think it's possible?" Carrie asked.

Andrea swallowed. "It would explain…a lot."

"But…Dad would have said something. When I started to get blood tests."

"If he knew," Andrea said.

Carrie swallowed. "But Mom…"

"Where *is* she?"

"Mom? Well…it's a long story."

Alexandra said, "I can't wait to hear this."

Sarah rolled her eyes. "It's not that long a story. Mom thinks Jessica's gay or something and took her off to a rehab camp."

"*What?*" Andrea said.

Carrie shook her head. "I don't think so. Andrea, you didn't see Jessica at Christmas this year. She was stoned out of her mind. That's why Mom decided to go back to San Francisco."

Sarah shrugged. "I can't figure Mom out."

"No one can," Carrie said. "She's never treated any of us decently. Especially Julia."

Andrea followed the discussion with a peculiar sense of confusion. For reasons she couldn't fathom, she felt the urge to defend her mother. Because even though over the years Andrea had spent increasing amounts of time overseas, even though she'd seen less and less of her parents, what memories she did have of her mother were warm.

That was part of what made her rejection hurt so much.

"So no one actually knows where she is?" Andrea asked.

She looked at her sisters. Carrie. Alexandra. Sarah. They looked mystified.

"Okay, does anyone know where *Jessica* is?"

Carrie shook her head. She swallowed and said, "Between you and her, sometimes I feel like such a failure."

Andrea and the other sisters sat there, stunned. Finally, Andrea jumped in and said, "What? What the hell are you talking about?"

Carrie closed her eyes. Then she said, "It was...ten years ago? Longer? Julia and I made a pact. That...our mom couldn't take care of us. She was too crazy. But we agreed that none of you would ever feel that loneliness. That we'd take care of you."

A tear ran down Carrie's face. Then another. She sniffed then said, "But we didn't. I couldn't."

"You did!" Sarah said. "You took care of us. Even after you left for college, you called me every week, and I always knew I could call you."

Confusion roiled through Andrea. She remembered the weekly calls from Julia. Every single week, without fail. The visits, every time Julia was in Europe, and sometimes just for the hell of it.

Had they been watching out for her all along, and she just didn't know?

"I couldn't though, after I left. I tried, but I wasn't enough."

Alexandra looked mortified. She stared at Carrie, an oddly resentful expression on her face, but she said nothing. Andrea saw it and took note.

"Oh, all of you be quiet," Sarah said. "Nobody's perfect. But you know what? The biggest hero I ever knew would have said we all do the best we can, and we have to live with that best. So don't beat yourselves up for not being perfect."

Carrie gasped at Sarah's words, and Andrea sat there. Who was she talking about? Ray, Carrie's husband? Dylan, who had remained silent throughout the long exchange between the sisters, swayed on his feet a little, then said, "He said something like that to me more than once."

Sarah continued. "So just, everybody stop. Andrea's right. Where the hell is Jessica? Can we stop with the psychobabble for thirty seconds and track down our sister?"

Carrie nodded. "I think I just took it for granted she was safe and with Mother."

Andrea nodded and then said, "I think what happened to me yesterday means we can't take anything for granted."

"Right," Carrie said. She took out her phone and dialed. "I'll try Jessica, then Mom."

"Who was the last person who talked with her?"

"Dad. A week ago. He told me when I started calling about getting blood tests. That she's at some kind of retreat or campground or something."

Sarah snorted. "What did I tell you?"

Alexandra said, "If Dad says she's at a retreat, then why—"

Andrea cut her off. "I don't have any reason to believe anything he says."

The other sisters were silenced. Not a word. No agreement. No disagreement.

Carrie took the phone away from her ear. "Jess doesn't answer." She dialed the phone again, and said, "If Mom doesn't answer, I'll try Julia. They're leaving Los Angeles tomorrow. Maybe they can make a stop in San Francisco."

2. Anthony Walker. April 29

When Anthony Walker stepped off the elevator, accompanied by a giant masquerading as a security guard, he was automatically inclined to be judgmental. People who rented the top floor suites of Los Angeles luxury hotels didn't get the benefit of the doubt in his book. Not in a world where millions starved or died prematurely of disease. Not in a world where war destroyed lives.

Never mind that he knew that Julia Wilson was an active philanthropist. He'd done his homework, and knew she served on the boards of half a dozen nonprofits, the largest of which was the Cristina Center in Detroit, a shelter for young girls who had been trafficked and forced into prostitution.

But this...palace. It was unconscionable. Appalling. Marble floors and crystal chandeliers. A dozen security guards so far.

What he *didn't* understand was where Wilson got her money. During his research for the interview, a friend had managed to pull her tax returns as well as her father's. Richard Thompson was rich, of course. Old money, lots of assets, some of them less savory than others.

But the father had nothing on daughter Julia. If the story he'd been led to believe was true, she'd taken the money earned from her husband's band and invested it in a wide range of businesses all over the globe, and made appalling sums of money. With a net worth well in excess of forty million, she could afford to fund a place like the Cristina Center and not notice the difference.

In Anthony's experience, people didn't make that kind of money unless someone was getting screwed somewhere.

Still, he didn't want to prejudge her. He followed the security guard down the hallway of the suite...*the hallway*...and stopped when the guard indicated. A knock on the door, and then the guard said, "Through here, sir."

Anthony gave the guard a weak smile, then stepped into the office.

He was met at the door by Julia Wilson. Professionally dressed in a dark blue suit and skirt with tasteful heels, she wore pearls at her neck and wrists, and smaller pearls in both ears. Rich brown, curly hair framed a face that highlighted blue-green eyes and full lips. Born December 16, 1981. She was three months older than Anthony, but looked easily five years younger.

That said, she wouldn't look out of place in any executive office in the world. He reminded himself that this woman controlled a company far bigger than the rock band that had started it—she'd built it into a multi-million dollar international business.

"Mr. Walker," she said. "I'm Julia Wilson."

"It's a pleasure to meet you, Mrs. Wilson."

She gave him an insincere smile. "Julia, please. Have a seat."

"Okay, Julia. Call me Anthony."

He took the proffered chair, positioning a digital audio recorder on the desk and taking out the small pocket sized notebook he carried everywhere with him. Anthony had a strong verbal memory and could often recall conversations with near perfect accuracy. Unfortunately he was a disaster with other types of facts: dates, locations, and sometimes even people's faces.

She took a seat behind the desk, across from him. Nice that this hotel suite had a built-in office with an imposing desk: dark stained cherry, green desk lamp, dark paneling throughout the office. It was classic east coast WASP. On the top floor of a LA hotel. He half-expected to see a balding man in a top hat with a cigar walk into the room. Anthony had interviewed enough politicians and bankers, weapons dealers and Senators to recognize the type.

"Drinks will be served in a moment," she said. "In the meantime, why don't we get started?"

"Thank you." He was happy to get to business. This was uncomfortable enough. "Yes, I'd like to get started. Will Mr. Wilson be joining us?"

"Crank may be by in a little while."

Anthony wasn't happy about that. Despite the fact that Julia was infinitely more interesting than her husband, his assignment was Crank Wilson, the lead singer and guitarist of the obnoxiously popular alt-rock band *Morbid Obesity*. Julia was the band's manager.

"I see. Well, then. I guess we'll start with you."

"Actually," she replied. "I'd like to start with *you.*"

"Excuse me?"

"I think you understood me perfectly, Mr. Walker. Surely you're aware that I've spent my entire life around the Foreign Service? And that I run a large multinational business? I'm very familiar with your work."

He blinked. "You are?"

"Of course. Which is why I find it difficult to believe that you're here to interview Crank. You're not an entertainment reporter, and I can't see any reason a foreign correspondent would want to interview him. Unless you're digging for information about something else."

Anthony exhaled. She was absolutely correct, of course. He'd made his career covering wars, peace talks and international conflict. He'd covered stories in Afghanistan and Iraq, in Liberia and London. So finding himself suddenly assigned to the *entertainment* section of the *Washington Post* wasn't exactly in his career path. "The short answer, if you must know, Mrs. Wilson, is that I'm in the doghouse."

"Julia, please," she replied, a prim smile on her face. "I'm guessing that's because you went...um...off the reservation...with regard to the sale of the paper?"

He smiled sardonically. That was a mild way to put it. In the summer of 2013, when the *Post* was purchased by rich media mogul, Walker had published a series of editorials criticizing the sale, then gone on television to do the same.

It made for nice headlines. Pulitzer Prize winning reporter criticizes the sale of his own newspaper. On the second day, he'd been suspended.

There the shock began. Anthony, at first, wanted to thumb his nose at all of them. He was a veteran reporter with a national reputation. He'd covered some of the most celebrated stories of the last fifteen years, from the invasion of Iraq to earthquakes in Pakistan. He could work anywhere.

It turned out he couldn't. The *New York Times* politely said no. Chicago and Los Angeles, the same response. Cox Enterprises, which owned a number of newspapers including the Atlanta Constitution, didn't even return his call.

Even the *Washington Times,* founded and owned by the Rev. Sun Myung Moon, only gave him the barest courtesy interview. It didn't help that Anthony had written a lengthy series of articles exploring the relationship between the self-appointed Messiah's religious and corporate holdings and how they affected the news and editorial direction of the *Times.*

Effectively he was blacklisted.

It was verified when his friend Bill Lieby took him out for lunch. Lieby, also a foreign correspondent, bought him a beer, and told him the facts of life. The new owners of the *Post* weren't happy and they made it clear. In an industry where little loyalty existed, Anthony had still managed to cross a line by going public against his own newspaper.

After four months Anthony went back to the editors of the *Post* and asked what it would take to get back to work.

The answer was not a happy one, but it was one he accepted, because he needed to work. Anthony went back to work, but his punishment was ignominy. He would spend the next several months on the entertainment desk covering for a reporter out on maternity leave.

"It's a chance to expand your horizons," Bill had said.

"It's a chance for them to humiliate me," Anthony had replied.

So here he was, faced off with the manager of a rock band, when a year ago he'd been facing off dictators. He looked at her and gave a straight, direct answer.

"I'm in exile on the entertainment desk for six months. As punishment."

"You're not here to sneak information about the court-martial last summer?"

"I'm not. And that story has pretty much played itself out, I think. I won't lie. I find your sister Carrie infinitely more interesting than…Crank. No offense, that's just what I do."

"Carrie is off limits."

He shrugged. "Like I said, there's no story there, now. And my assignment is *Morbid Obesity's* new album. Though I would love to write about you and your growing little empire."

Julia grinned. "I'm just a believer in putting my assets to work. And…I might be willing to work with you on that. But if you touch Carrie, I'll put everything to work against you."

"Mrs. Wilson, you may be rich and run a big company, but even you can't take on the *Washington Post.*"

She gave him a wicked grin then said, "Apparently, neither can you."

Anthony chuckled. "All right. Fine. Just let me get one question out of my system."

"I won't answer."

"Fine. Tell me about your sister's kidnapping."

"My official answer is *no comment.*"

"And your unofficial one?" he asked.

"*No comment.* In fact, I don't really know anything yet. I'm flying to Washington tomorrow afternoon. But she's in good hands with Carrie and our other sisters, for now. So, why don't we get started?"

Anthony nodded. "All right. So let me make sure I understand. Rules are, I can't ask about the kidnapping, or the court-martial. Are those the only restrictions?"

Julia raised an eyebrow. "That's it, but I may refuse to answer other questions as we hit them. And I want to know more about what angle you're pursuing with this piece."

"I don't know yet. But I don't want to just cover the album. Everything I've heard, you've been essential to the success of the band."

She shook her head. "Not exactly. Crank and Serena write the music, and they're magic on stage. That's where the success of the band comes from. What I do is logistics and run the business side of things. I make sure they're where they need to be when they need to be there. I make sure their investments keep growing, that the taxes are paid, and that the business keeps growing no matter what happens in the music industry."

"I'd like to start there. I want to know how you built this into such a big business. I want to know what makes *you* tick."

Julia sighed. "All right, then."

CHAPTER NINE
Change of plans

1. Julia. April 29

Julia Wilson couldn't decide what she thought of Anthony Walker.

Even though she was most often described in the media as either an "entertainment mogul" or occasionally simply as a "business savvy band manager," Julia's background was in international relations. She grew up around the Foreign Service, lived in half a dozen countries by the time she was eighteen, and had majored in international business at Harvard University. Her father—former Ambassador, now Secretary of Defense-designee—had been appalled when she chose to forego graduate school and the Foreign Service and instead take up managing her boyfriend's alternative rock band as a career. But Richard Thompson's objections had waned over the years as Crank's musical talent and Julia's business acumen built a multi-million dollar business.

In short, Julia followed international news, both foreign policy and business. She read the *Washington Post* and *New York Times* nearly every day, and consequently, Anthony Walker's name was very familiar to her. Both of his books—one covering the buildup to the Iraq War, and the other covering the savage Iraqi civil war of 2004-2006—sat on the shelves in her South Boston townhouse. She'd read with interest his editorials bashing the decision to sell the *Washington Post* in the summer of 2013. So it was with some trepidation that she'd agreed to this interview in the first place.

The phone call had come via the band's publicist, Mike DeMint.

"This guy's the real deal," Mike said.

"I know who he is," Julia replied.

"I think you should talk to him."

"But what does he *want?*" Julia had asked. "He's not a celebrity reporter. The only thing I know that might interest him is my brother-in-law's murder. And there's no way in hell I'm talking about that."

"I'll set ground rules with him before the meeting."

"All right," she had agreed.

Now she sat across the desk from a reporter who she'd admired. And her main priority was to protect her sister Carrie, which meant keeping him interested in other things. She knew most people would react by simply ignoring him. Refusing to do the interview. Refusing to have any interaction with him at all. But Julia knew better. Anthony Walker might be in the doghouse with the *Washington Post*, but he remained one of the most celebrated reporters of their generation. If she refused to talk to him, he'd dig in their trash, spy on Ray's court-martial board, hire phone hackers, or God only knew what else.

Far better to keep him close.

"Okay, then," Anthony said. "Let's start with your background. I understand you're the oldest of six daughters?"

"That's right."

"Carrie—Ray Sherman's widow—is the next youngest?"

Julia's eyebrows narrowed in warning.

Anthony's next statement was defensive. "I'm not planning on doing a story about them, all right? But it's important context."

"She's a few years younger than me," she responded.

"Right. And she's a NIH researcher."

"I don't know all the details. She's doing work on infectious diseases and animal vectors."

"Okay. And the next youngest is…" Anthony's voice trailed off.

"Alexandra. She's graduating from Columbia next month."

"Okay. And then…the next two were twins?"

"Sarah and Jessica."

"Sarah was injured when Ray Sherman was murdered."

"Right."

Anthony continued. "And the youngest is Andrea, who is all over the news right now."

"Right," Julia said. "But, as we discussed, Andrea and what happened yesterday are off limits. And I don't know anything anyway."

He held up a hand. "It's fine. Tell me a little about your background."

"Well…I went to Harvard. Majored in international relations and business. My dad kind of wanted me to go into the Foreign Service."

"But you had other plans."

Julia nodded. "I met Crank. We got involved. The band needed a manager, and I needed a new direction. It was a good fit."

"So you took on managing the band."

As he asked questions, he scribbled notes in his pocket notebook. She didn't know exactly what he was writing, but it was *loud,* the point of the pen digging into the paper.

"I did. And never looked back."

Anthony looked up at the last words. His expression, eyes widened slightly, seemed to register surprise. "Tell me why?" he asked.

She shrugged. "Not many people get to build a huge enterprise from the ground up. Every dollar we made in the first three years got reinvested into the band. Into promotion. Better instruments. Honing their skills. We got out there on MySpace when it was brand new and built a major following. The band worked hard, I worked hard. I love this work."

"You started buying unrelated businesses in 2007."

She snorted. "If Crank had his way, I'd have just bought more and more expensive guitars. But this is a big business. We started going into commercial real estate, medical devices, software. My goal was to diversify the business so it could survive anything."

The truth was, there was a lot more to it than that. Her goal wasn't to build stability, or to prove her hand at business, or to diversify the band, or anything so pedestrian. Her goal was to erase the stain of shame her mother stamped on her heart at fourteen years old. Her goal was to use the band, the business, to create wings of success that would carry her out of the abyss of her mother's abhorrence.

In the end, she'd been successful beyond her wildest dreams. Successful enough to eclipse her father's impressive (but inherited) fortune. Richard Thompson knew how to spend money. Julia knew how to *make* it.

But sometime around the time she turned thirty, she realized it was all emptiness. She'd looked around in the fall of 2012, ten years after she and Crank fell in love. In those ten years she'd made millionaires of the band several times over. She'd built a large international business. She'd far surpassed the ambitions of her parents. But it hadn't made any difference. She still felt empty inside sometimes at night when she thought of the things her mother had once said to her. She still felt like she wasn't good enough. Sometimes she still felt like that eighteen-year-old girl sneaking through the halls of Bethesda Chevy-Chase High School as the word *slut* hung in the air, pregnant with contempt.

As Anthony finished taking his notes, she tried to steer the conversation away. But he promptly said, "I'd like to go back a bit. And you can tell me to buzz off if you want. This is old news, and it's not necessarily germane to the story, and if you don't want it mentioned, then I won't mention it. Okay?"

She felt a chill as he spoke. Because she knew what he was about to say.

"When I was doing background research on the story, I came across the series of blog posts by Maria Clawson."

2. Bear. April 29

"**In** my office. Now."

That was unambiguous. Bear hadn't made it back to his desk yet after returning to Main State from the five-sided puzzle palace across the river. As he walked through the double doors into the Diplomatic Security suite, signed in with the guard, and swiped his access card at the inner doors, Tom Cantwell appeared on the other side of the door.

Bear followed Cantwell into the large corner office. Facing 23rd and C Street, Cantwell's fourth floor office was prime real estate in the State Department headquarters. From the window, the United States Institute of Peace—underfunded, largely useless in terms of real policy—occupied its brand new building overlooking the Lincoln Memorial on one side and the Kennedy Center on the other. Bear would have loved an office like this, but he knew he'd never occupy it.

Cantwell's face was red, and his eye had a slight twitch. He didn't sit down, instead walking around to the far side of his excessively large desk and turning to face Bear. He took a breath and stared, opened his mouth, then closed it.

Finally, he said, "Have you lost your mind?"

Bear blinked. "I don't believe so, sir."

The response, apparently, wasn't what Cantwell wanted to hear. He slammed a bony little fist on his desk and said, "Mr. Wyden, please explain why you had to be escorted out of the Secretary of Defense's office by armed guards!"

"He didn't want to answer questions about—" Bear didn't get a chance to finish the sentence. The door opened, and Mary Bradley, Cantwell's administrative assistant stuck her head inside.

"Sir? The Secretary wants to see...both of you."

Bear grimaced. He met Mary's eyes. They were baleful, wide, sympathetic. That lasted less than a second, and then she looked back to her boss, expressionless.

For the hundredth time, Bear thought Mary just might accept a dinner invitation. She was unattached, always polite, and she'd given him her phone number a year before.

A year ago he was still wound up tight in his divorce, and not ready to even talk with another woman.

Now was not the time for this internal discussion. Cantwell's mouth puckered up as if he'd just drunk spoiled milk. "Well, then, Mr. Wyden. It's on your head. We're going to see Mr. Perry, and there's nothing I can do to help you now."

Well, then, Bear thought. He'd known intuitively that Cantwell was a spineless weasel, but having it proved under this circumstance was unfortunate.

Silently, Bear followed Cantwell down the wide hallways to the bank of elevators.

At the elevator, Bear reached for the button at the same moment Cantwell did. Cantwell jerked his hand back, an annoyed expression on his face. Bear pushed the up button.

"I would appreciate it if you would remain quiet unless asked a direct question."

Bear raised an eyebrow. Then he said, "I presume we're being asked to see the Secretary to deal with my questioning of the Secretary of Defense?"

Cantwell was, for the first time in Bear's experience, speechless. The elevator doors opened, eliminating the need for Bear to talk with his boss for a few seconds, at least.

As he turned around, facing the elevator door, two other people walked into the elevator behind them. Good thing because it delayed, for a little while, open warfare with his boss.

Five minutes later, Bear walked behind Cantwell into the expansive office of the Secretary of State.

Bear had never been in the office. Wide paneled hardwood floors stained a deep reddish brown, stretched across the spacious office. Most of the office was white, with elegant wainscoting, detailed molding and lavish Persian carpets. The room smelled of expensive cigars, gin and privilege. Forty feet away, Secretary of State James Perry sat behind his desk, talking on the phone. He looked up at their entry and waved them toward an ornate couch, covered in sky-blue fabric and gold brocade. Bear followed Cantwell toward the couch. As they reached it, Secretary Perry hung up the phone and stood.

As he approached, Bear's first impression of the man was shock at how very tall he was. At six feet, Bear wasn't short. But the Secretary of State towered over him in his dark blue suit and red tie. His face was gaunt; hollow cheeks below sunken eyes and jowls suggestive of decades of sleep deprivation. Even though the Secretary was a Democrat, Bear had considerable respect for the man who, prior to his career in the Senate and now the State department, had once commanded naval riverboats in the Mekong Delta.

"James Perry," the Secretary said in a bold voice as he approached. He held out a hand toward Bear.

"Bear Wyden, sir," Bear replied. Perry had a confident handshake. Dry and firm, but he didn't engage in a squeezing contest like many less confident men.

Perry nodded toward Cantwell. It wasn't friendly. "Mr. Cantwell."

Cantwell swallowed. "Mr. Secretary."

"Please have a seat, both of you."

Bear took a seat to Cantwell's left on the couch. Secretary Perry sat on a similarly appointed red chair, oriented perpendicularly to the couch.

"I'll get to the point, gentlemen. I had an…unfortunate phone call from the Secretary of Defense this afternoon."

Cantwell literally squirmed in his seat and began speaking in a hurry. "Sir, my sincere apologies. I'm afraid our investigator may have gotten a little bit ahead of himself this afternoon—"

Secretary Perry narrowed his eyes at Cantwell's torrent of words, then held up a hand and cut him off. "Mr. Cantwell, that won't be necessary."

"Sir, if I could clarify."

Perry leaned forward in his seat, just slightly. "I'd prefer you didn't."

Holy shit. Bear was stunned by the exchange. If anything was clear, it was that Perry did not like Cantwell at all. Of course, now that he thought about it, it didn't surprise him that much. Cantwell was brought in after the wholesale and somewhat random firing of top DSS personnel by Secretary Clinton as a result of the deaths in Benghazi. Bear didn't like him either.

Perry turned his attention to Bear. "Perhaps you could explain the direction of your investigation at this point."

Bear coughed a little then said, "Sir, I was asked to take charge of the investigation late last night. Joyce Brown is coordinating the team and I'm lead investigator."

Perry nodded. "Go on."

Bear described his trip to the hospital the previous night and his discussions with the Thompson daughters, and his visit today with Richard Thompson.

"At this point sir, we're still trying to establish the identity of our second kidnapper. I'm particularly concerned because we've run DNA and fingerprints and not established his identity. Nothing. But based on Andrea Thompson's description, he had a clear Midwestern United States accent. Corn husker. There should be some record of this guy. So I went over to the Pentagon to interview the father."

Perry leaned a little, resting his gangly right arm on the arm of his chair, rangy fingers covering his chin.

"I may have been a little aggressive in my questioning, sir."

The Secretary's fingers shifted to cover his mouth. Bear coughed, then continued. "Anyway, sir. I'll be blunt. I'm concerned. Secretary Thompson…did not react like a concerned father. He didn't meet his daughter at the hospital. He didn't pick her up. He didn't stay home with her today. He's spent all of ten minutes with his sixteen-year-old daughter on the day when she was kidnapped by at least one known mercenary. Something is seriously wrong there, sir."

Perry nodded. Then he said, "You're aware Acting Secretary Thompson has been nominated by the President of the United States."

Bear froze a little at the words. Cantwell, the little weasel, chimed in. "Sir, Mr. Wyden's opinions are not the official opinions of this investigation. In fact, I'm questioning—"

"That will be enough, Mr. Cantwell. You may go."

"Excuse me, sir?" Cantwell looked stunned.

"You heard me, sir. But please, let me clarify. I don't wish to hear another word out of you, and I would strongly urge you to start polishing your resume, because your time in this department just became limited. If there is anything I learned about leadership in Vietnam, it's that leaders don't throw their subordinates into the line of fire."

Bear sat up in his seat. All the blood had run out of Cantwell's face, leaving him looking like a pasty-faced reflection of his already pale face.

Cantwell stood, tugging on his jacket and his dignity. "Sir, I hope you will reconsider, I'm merely looking out for the interests of the Department and Diplomatic Security."

"You may go," Perry said.

Cantwell left in a hurry. Bear held his breath.

Perry looked closely at Bear. "Mr. Wyden…Bear. May I call you Bear?"

Letting a breath loose again, he replied, "Yes sir."

"Bear. I'm aware of your suspicions and concerns about Secretary Thompson."

Bear blinked. "You *are?*"

Perry stood and walked to his desk. Then he picked up an inch-thick brown envelope. He laid it on the table.

The envelope was labeled, TOP SECRET-COMPARTMENTALIZED. Below that, in bold letters, PERSONNEL FILE/CLASSIFIED. Handwritten below that, *R. Thompson. FN 542-1342.*

"You'll need to sign for this. Sign along the flap and tear it off. This is a numbered copy. And it will answer some of your questions. Once you've read it, I want you to go see Senator Rainsley."

If a lightning bolt had struck Secretary Perry in his office, Bear wouldn't have been more surprised. "Excuse me, sir?"

Perry handed the file over. "Read it. Go see Senator Rainsley. Get your investigation underway, Bear. And don't cross paths with Richard Thompson again.

If you need answers from him, call my secretary and come see me. Am I clear? There are things you don't know."

Bear held up the file. "Are the answers in here?"

Perry raised his eyebrows. Then he said, "No. But maybe it's a step in the right direction."

3. Julia. April 29

"**When** *I was doing background research on the story, I came across the series of blog posts by Maria Clawson.*"

When Anthony said the words, Julia immediately interrupted. "I'm familiar with them. That was before she was sued for libel."

Anthony nodded. "I'm aware of that. And again, I don't want you to throw me out. But given the stuff she published about you...there had to have been some fallout. From what I understand, that was the reason Senator Rainsley put a hold on your father's appointment as Ambassador to Russia."

Julia grasped the edge of her desk, forcing herself to not stand up and march out of the room. This was all ancient history. But she knew the moment the President announced her father's nomination that it would come up. It was inevitable. He'd been nominated as head of the largest department of the United States government, in charge of trillions of dollars of assets, hundreds of thousands of people and responsibility for defense of the United States. The Senate, and the media, would be all over it.

Senator Rainsley was still in office, and he was the senior Republican on the Senate Armed Services Committee, which meant he would be in the lead with questioning and objections to her father's nomination. For the second time in her father's career, he'd be faced off with Senator Rainsley, and she couldn't help having the sinking feeling that her own past would have some bearing on what happened next.

She needed an ally, quickly. Regardless of what happened with her father's nomination, she didn't need an old scandal dragging her through the mud. Plenty of bad stuff had been written in the press about her and Crank before, but that, at least, hadn't come up in years. She didn't need it to start.

"Yes," she finally said. "It *was* Senator Rainsley who put the nomination on hold. He never stated a reason why."

"But Maria Clawson spread it far and wide that it had something to do with you."

"Not exactly," Julia replied. "I wasn't even eighteen at the time. She never printed my name."

His response made her stomach twist. "She did publish a photograph."

Her response came out in a hiss. "She did. A photograph that would probably land her in jail for child pornography if she ran it today."

Anthony nodded. "That must have been tough for you."

"Tough isn't the word, Mr. Walker. I went through some very difficult times in high school. Not the party girl Maria Clawson implied, but someone who was ill-used by a much older boy. Clawson's blog ruined my life. I know you've heard all about online bullying these days. We didn't have Facebook back then, but having a national gossip columnist attack you day after day when you're still a teenager...I ended up attempting suicide."

Anthony winced. A hint of both anger and empathy in his voice, he said, "Are you fucking serious?"

"I was a teenager. I wasn't equipped to deal with that back then."

He nodded. Then he said, "You know, I talked with Sylvia Drake. She told me you funded her lawsuit."

Julia nodded. And then she smiled. Because she remembered Sylvia Drake.

Sylvia was a 19-year-old nursing student when she was raped on campus following a football game at the University of Alabama. The suspect? A 21-year-old football player. When Sylvia went on record with her accusation, the vultures descended. Radio commentators and sports newscasters publicly speculated she was aiming for a big financial settlement from Alabama. Bloggers and newscasters alike lambasted her, but an old enemy of Julia's led the charge: Maria Clawson, whose society blog was still the terror of Washington, DC.

Julia took the opportunity to settle an old score. She discreetly donated a quarter of a million dollars to fund Sylvia Drake's lawsuit against Maria Clawson. The result? Clawson went down in personal bankruptcy and shut down the longest running gossip blog on the Internet. Julia counted that as a victory well worth winning.

"Yes," she told Anthony now. "I funded it. I'd do it again, too. Maria Clawson is a snake who makes her living off destroying other people's lives."

"Was," Anthony replied. "She mostly makes her living fending off lawsuits now."

Julia raised her eyebrows and shrugged. She knew she shouldn't be so smug about it, even as her lips curled up in a satisfied half-smile. Her youngest sister Andrea wouldn't have hesitated to lecture her about the need to keep forgiveness in her heart.

It was a lot easier to forgive someone when they no longer represented a threat.

Her phone, laying face down on the desk, rang, vibrating on the desk. She reached forward and flipped it over. A photograph of one of her sisters in the New

York City Clerk's office in the arms of a tall Army sergeant in dress blues appeared on the screen of her phone, underneath the name "Carrie."

She picked up the phone. "I have to take this, sorry."

Anthony sat back, a little annoyed. She didn't care. She unlocked the phone and said, "Hello? Carrie?" As she spoke the words, she stood and walked to the window, looking outside and keeping her back to Anthony.

"Julia? Hey, you! It's not just me…I've got Alexandra and Sarah and Andrea here too."

Julia closed her eyes. She badly wanted to be in Washington with her sisters. She'd left a message that morning on Jessica's cell phone, and on her mother's, inviting them to fly east with her. If Jessica flew east with her, it would be the first time the six of them were in the same room since the summer of 2013. All of them were present for Carrie and Alexandra's weddings, but there'd been little opportunity to talk. And technically all of them were in the same city in August after the accident, but Sarah had been hospitalized and Carrie utterly devastated by the loss of her husband.

Julia badly wanted to bring her sisters together. If nothing else, so they could wrap their arms around Carrie and Andrea and love them.

"Julia, listen, when are you planning to fly to DC. Still tomorrow?"

"Yes, tomorrow afternoon was the plan. Though if necessary we can leave in the morning." As she said the words, she studied Anthony's pale reflection in the window. He shifted uncomfortably at the words they might be leaving early. Interesting, she thought. He badly wanted a story with some meat here. She was considering giving it to him, in a way that would keep a grip on the inevitable release of her own secrets and also protect her sisters.

"Well…"

Julia frowned at the long pause.

Finally, Carrie spoke again. "We're worried about Jessica. And Mom. Neither of them have answered their phones in days."

"Well, of course they have," Julia said impatiently. "I just spoke with Mother on…oh. Friday."

She'd spoken with her mother right before lunch. They spoke *every* Friday. It hadn't always been the case. From 2002 until 2005, she'd barely spoken at all with her mother. Holidays and birthdays, and not always even then. But all that time, the thought kept percolating in her head. A statement really, made by Crank's brother Sean after the first time he met her mother. *She loves you,* Sean had said a few days later, when Sean, Carrie, Crank and Julia were in Washington, DC. Followed by the completely inexplicable statement, *She has secrets.*

Carrie hadn't been willing to accept his answer and demanded clarification.

"*Come on, Sean,*" Carrie needled. "*There has to be something behind what you said. Some evidence? Anything?*"

He sat up. "*They never touched each other. Or even looked at each other.*"

"*Who?*" Carrie replied.

"*Your parents.*"

And of course, when Julia thought it through later, Sean was exactly right. *She* couldn't remember her parents touching. At least only on the rarest of occasions, when she was very young. She had few memories of her early childhood, but some of the earliest were of eating meals with both of her parents when Carrie was still a baby. But even then, they'd never been affectionate with each other.

In any event, Sean's comment had worn on her mind, an ongoing nagging worry.

Finally, in 2005, she'd called her mother and invited herself to San Francisco for a week. A week she and her mother spent together. Talking. In a few cases, *screaming* at each other.

Adelina Thompson never divulged her secrets, but Julia came away from that week believing Sean was right. More importantly, she came away from that week believing in forgiveness. She didn't have it yet. She hadn't forgiven her mother, nor forgotten those horrible years in China and right after. But she at least believed it might be *possible.*

Since that week, they'd talked on the phone every single week without fail, with only two exceptions. The first, the week of March 11, 2011. *Morbid Obesity* was in Tokyo for a concert when a tsunami hit the coast of Japan, wiping out entire towns and setting off a nuclear disaster. For several days power in the country was unreliable, along with cell service. For the first few days after the disaster, air travel was also disrupted, and they'd been unable to get clearance to depart until five days after the tsunami. She hadn't spoken with her mother that week.

The second time was the week after Ray Sherman died. For the first time in their lives, Adelina Thompson went into overdrive as a mother, taking care of Carrie and Sarah at a time when both of them needed her. All of the sisters were stunned, most of all Julia, who had borne the brunt of her mother's bizarre behavior over the years.

Those weekly Friday calls had become a mainstay of their relationship. Sometimes she and her mother went through periods of hostility, sometimes through periods where they were cold; but no matter what, they spoke. No matter what.

This past Friday's call had been normal. Julia talked with her about the new album and the process of getting it recorded. They talked about Carrie's week-old baby Rachel, and the diagnosis, which had come as a shock to all of them. Julia had made the arrangements for Andrea's flight to Washington.

Mother and Jessica were supposed to fly east on Wednesday morning. Julia had taken that for granted, until now.

"When was the last time you talked with her?" she asked Carrie.

"A…a week ago?"

Julia made a snap decision. "I'll fly to San Francisco in the morning. But I think we need to consider having someone local go take a look." She held the phone away from her head. "It's almost 5 o'clock…let me see if I can get Bill Lemke to go take a look, just to see if they're home and not answering the phone or whatever."

Sarah, still on the speakerphone, said, "Dad said Mom was taking Jessica off to some religious retreat."

Julia scrunched her eyebrows. Their mother was a devout Catholic, but this seemed…out of character. "I'm not sure I buy that. Either way, I'll check it out in the morning."

They ended the conversation, and she turned her attention back to Anthony Walker. For just a second she studied him. Trying to decide. Could she trust him? The idea of trusting a reporter struck her as foolhardy.

Something told her this was the time.

"Anthony, I've got a chance of plans. I have to fly to San Francisco in the morning then back to Washington, DC. If you want to pursue this, you'll have to fly with us."

"Commercial?"

"No, we've got a jet. You travel as much as we do, it starts to make sense."

"I'm in."

CHAPTER TEN
Something weird going on

1. Leslie Collins. April 29. 5:50 pm

Six pm in downtown Washington and traffic was predictably snarled. Leslie Collins sat in the back of a large Chevy Suburban, papers spread across the folding worktable. The SUV was still new, the smell of leather and bulletproof glass. His driver laid on the horn and said, "You want me to go to lights and sirens, sir?"

Leslie Collins looked at his watch, an antique wind-up aviator's watch with a badly scratched glass cover. "Yes, we need to be there in twenty minutes." Even with the flashing lights and sirens it might take another fifteen minutes to navigate to their destination. Collins sometimes thought that certain roads in Washington needed to be reserved for official traffic.

Inside his jacket pocket, he felt his phone buzzing. He reached in and pulled the phone out.

Mitch Filner.

About time. Collins answered the phone brusquely.

"What is it?"

Filner, as always, sounded out of breath. "Calling to report on progress."

The large black Chevy Suburban inched forward in the traffic. The driver leaned forward, gesticulating at what looked to be a thirty-year old lobbyist at the wheel of a Cooper Mini who blocked the intersection at Massachusetts and 30th. Amazing that poor excuse for a car, which could fit in the cargo space of the Suburban, could block three lanes of traffic. The driver jerked back from the noise of the Suburban's siren and horn.

Seconds later the Mini unsnarled itself and traffic began to flow again. For a block or two.

"All right. Go."

Filner coughed in the phone. Bastard needed to quit smoking and maybe he wouldn't sound like such an invalid. "Okay, first of all, the family here in Washington has Diplomatic Security protection now. Three uniformed officers at the Bethesda condo at all times. Secretary Thompson also has protection, but not DSS—his are private contractors."

"Is Thompson still living by himself?"

"Base housing at Fort Myers. From what I understand, he booted some two-star out of his house."

Collins shook his head. "That'll make him popular with the troops."

"Yeah, well, bottom line is, I don't have any assets close to him."

Collins looked to his left. Across the street was the *Islamic Center*. Built of white stone with an ochre tiled roof and crenellations along the top wall, the building had a minaret. A fucking minaret, in Washington DC, fifteen blocks from the White House. Letters in blue lined Arabic covered the front of the building in a line about five archways into an interior courtyard. The entire building, a remarkable piece of architecture if it had been in Cairo or Baghdad, was a giant middle finger erected against the American people. Luckily for the inhabitants, the building had an eight-foot cast iron fence surrounding it.

He focused his attention back on the moment. "What about the daughters?"

"One of the DSS agents is ours," Filner replied.

"All right. Keep them in place, but don't *do* anything yet."

"Right. As I understand it, the sisters here in DC are headed out to a restaurant shortly. Our agent is with the escort."

2. Andrea. April 29. 6:00 pm

"**I**'m ready," Andrea said, walking back into the living room.

All of her clothes—along with her phone and laptop—were still in the custody of the police. Luckily, Carrie had lent her a dress, linen with a blue herringbone pattern. It wasn't something Andrea would have chosen to wear on her own—Carrie was a bit too fashionable for her taste—but it fit her.

"Ready?" It was Leah Simpson. Like the others in the security detail, she'd changed from her semi-uniform into nondescript civilian clothing, in her case jeans and a sweater that was probably too heavy for the April weather. It was just heavy enough to cover her sidearm, which was no longer visible at her hip. Her blonde hair, previously tied up in a simple ponytail, was now braided. It looked professional, but not the sort of thing you would wear out on the town.

Sarah and Alexandra were playing gin at the kitchen table, and Dylan stood on the porch smoking again. Carrie was in the nursery giving instructions to her nanny.

"I'm ready," Andrea said. "But it looks like I'm the only one."

Sarah smirked. "Soon as Carrie comes out we can go. Everything takes twice as long when you've got a baby."

Andrea shrugged. She wasn't planning on having any babies. She looked at Leah.

"You're coming with us?"

Leah nodded. "For the foreseeable future, you'll have a Diplomatic Security escort wherever you go."

"When do you go home to your family?" Andrea asked.

"We'll have a rotation in place by late tonight. But my primary concern is your safety."

She sounded like a robot. Andrea thought that Leah Simpson's primary concern was probably her family, her own safety, her career first. Which was completely normal. She didn't particularly care for misdirection.

"Are you married?" Andrea asked.

Leah raised an eyebrow. "I am."

"Kids?"

"Two." She smiled, then slid a well-worn men's wallet out of her pocket. She opened it up. "My son Jim and my daughter Rebecca."

The boy in the photo was four years old or so. If she was completely objective, Andrea thought the boy was pretty ugly. He had too small eyes and a pug nose and uneven teeth that only a mother could love. But the thing was, his mother obviously *did* love him. And that mattered more than anything. Beside him in the photo was a younger girl, maybe two years old. She wore a yellow and red Washington Redskins cheerleading outfit, complete with pompoms and an Indian head logo on the skirt.

Andrea smiled. Then she said, "I think your *first* priority is them."

Leah returned the smile. "True. But your safety is my professional responsibility, and I take that seriously. Jim and Rebecca are with their step-dad tonight. Once we get you settled we'll be on a fairly normal routine."

Andrea nodded. "You…it must be kind of scary, doing this for a living. When you have kids."

Leah shook her head. "Most of the time I do paperwork and stand around. Or we provide security details for boring old dowager countesses."

Sarah and Alexandra looked up, and Sarah stood as Carrie walked into the room. She'd changed into a knee length pleated dress, dark purple with brass buttons down the chest and flat sandals.

"Sorry about that," Carrie said. "Rachel's asleep. Why don't we get going?"

3. Bear. April 29. 6:03 pm

The studio apartment was simple. At three hundred square feet, Bear had enough room for a twin bed, a tiny couch and television, a kitchen table that doubled as a desk, and a small dresser containing most of his clothes. He owned little else.

The folder on his kitchen table, next to the laptop, was a serious enough security violation that he could expect a reprimand in his file if it was discovered. Not because he had it—after all, the Secretary of State himself handed him the file. But the fact that it was on his kitchen table, instead of secured at the office, was a problem. The tall glass of bourbon and Coke next to it also presented a problem, though not as serious as the bringing of classified documents home.

Regardless, he sat down at the table and took a sip of his drink. He felt the pungent liquor slide down his throat and breathed a sigh of relief. Bear was glad he hadn't stayed in the office, where Tom Cantwell was undoubtedly scheming to bring an end to Bear's career.

Sometimes Bear was ready to pack it in anyway. His career hadn't been perfect, but it had been solid, marked by steady promotions and steps up in seniority. But the further he moved up the ladder, the more political his job became. Sometimes it paid to keep your nose down, do your job and not get noticed.

He sighed. Then broke the seal on the envelope and slid the documents out of it.

The first document at the top of a small stack was an application for federal employment. This was a copy of course, showing the original document filled out in 1973. Richard Isaiah Thompson. Born in San Francisco, California, April 23, 1949. Attended Exeter Academy, followed by Harvard University. Exeter, of course, was an exclusive boys' preparatory school on the East Coast, far from his birthplace.

Bear began to make notes. Because the first question had already been raised. Thompson graduated from Harvard in 1971. What did he do the two years in between graduation and applying to work at State? Nothing in the personal file gave a clue, and the application itself was oddly pro forma. Not everything was filled out on the application, but the cover letter was clear enough. In May 1973, Thompson had enough pull to get a personal recommendation from then National-al Security Advisor Henry Kissinger. No wonder he hadn't filled out the entire application. He didn't need to.

Bear let his mind wander, not entirely focused on the file, letting his eyes scan over the documents as he free-associated.

Behind the federal application for employment was his initial security investigation, marked SECRET and never declassified. Bear began to page through it. Interviews with his college professors and fellow students were included. One interview with his father, Cyrus Thompson.

Still nothing in the file regarding the years from his college graduation in 1971 to his beginning of employment at State in 1973. It made no sense at all. His eyebrows began to work uncontrollably, a line appearing down his forehead. He took another drink, then scanned through the background investigation again.

Thompson was granted top-secret clearance based on a report which including *nothing* of the last two years of his life. It made no sense at all. None.

The phone rang. Bear jerked in his seat, then glanced at the phone and picked it up.

"Bear."

"Bear, it's Leah."

He winced. But he kept his tone professional, as always. "Hey, Leah. What's the low-down?"

"We're en route with the Thompson sisters to Benihanas in Bethesda. But there's something weird going on."

"What?"

"Bear, I think someone has the sisters under surveillance. And it's professional."

Crap. Who? "Professional. You mean like intelligence professionals?"

"I don't know. I haven't pinned it down yet."

Bear turned the report to the last page and froze. He narrowed his eyebrows, for just a second tuning out Leah.

Richard Thompson's background investigation was signed by William Colby.

He shook his head. That didn't make any sense. Diplomatic Security Services conducted the background investigations for State Department personnel.

William Colby, in 1973, was director of covert operations for the Central Intelligence Agency. In September of the same year he took over as Director of Central Intelligence, just a few weeks before Kissinger took over the State Department.

"Bear?"

"I'm here."

"What do you want us to do?"

Bear's heart was thumping. Richard Thompson…suddenly he began to wonder. What was Thompson doing from 1971 to 1973? And why had Henry Kissinger, then the National Security Advisor, written a letter of recommendation for him? Why had a CIA official signed off on his background investigation?

Was Thompson originally CIA? Was he still?

"Bear?" Leah sounded impatient.

"Sorry!" he shouted into the phone. "Listen. Keep an eye out. Don't approach or attempt to apprehend the followers, all right? Don't let them know you've seen them. Try to get pictures. I want to know who the hell they are. Understand?"

"There's only three of us here. We're going to need more backup."

"All right," he said. Yeah. If he was right, backup might be needed right away. "Let me make some calls."

4. Leslie Collins. April 29. 6:16 pm

Collins answered the phone again, annoyed this time. They were now two blocks away from his destination. The downtown traffic along Pennsylvania Avenue was a nightmare and he was tempted to just get out and walk.

"What?" Collins said.

It was Filner. Of course.

"Sir, we've got a problem."

"What is it?"

"The Thompson Sisters…they've got a tail."

"Your people, right?"

"No, sir. I've got two teams following them. But we've got more followers. I'm certain it's surveillance."

Collins rolled his eyes. "Who is it? The Saudis?"

"No. British, maybe."

Collins was angry now. "Give me some goddamn detail, Filner!"

"Sir. Right now the Thompson family…or four of the sisters, plus one of their husbands, are walking together down Bethesda Avenue. They're accompanied by three DSS agents in plain clothes. I've got a positive ID on all three agents. One of them works for us too."

"Okay…"

"We've also got two men, following on the other side of the street."

"You're certain they aren't just pedestrians?"

"Yeah."

"Our guys are anonymous? Run off the pursuers. Then fill me in later. I can't talk on the phone any more."

"What the fuck are you talking about, Collins? You can't stop talking to me *right now*." Filner's voice had an edge.

"Use your best judgment," Collins replied. Some things superseded even a crisis. This meeting was one of them.

The uniformed secret service agent at the gate of 1600 Pennsylvania Avenue approached the Suburban as it rolled to a stop. Collins' driver leaned out to speak with him and displayed ID.

"I'm going into a meeting that can't be interrupted," Collins said, his eyes on the White House.

"Go ahead to the West entrance, sir," the secret service guard said.

Collins' driver pulled forward onto the grounds.

5. Dylan. April 29. 6:16 pm

Dylan Paris had been walking slightly behind the four sisters. Something had set him on edge, and even though they were only walking four blocks to the restaurant, he felt as naked as if he were on patrol in Fayzabad again. A cold breeze, just a slight remnant of winter, blew up the street as they turned onto Norfolk Avenue. The restaurant was two blocks away. It was a few minutes before six-thirty, and the sky was just beginning to dim. Full sunset wouldn't be for another hour.

He scanned the street again. Across from them and slightly behind, two men were walking. Normally it wouldn't have bothered Dylan, but one of them kept eyeing the sisters. Too many times for comfort. Both of them wore nondescript grey suits and one of them spoke on a telephone. Of course the street was crowded with other people: workers leaving their offices, a few scattered soldiers from Walter Reed, men and women headed to rendezvous and happy hours.

He turned and walked backward for a second. He caught Leah Simpson's eye and discreetly pointed toward the men across the street.

She nodded. "Already on it," she said in a conversational tone. "We need to get you guys inside. But slowly. Let's not alert them, all right?"

"Alert who?" Alexandra asked.

The other sisters stalled, and Dylan spoke in a low, even and tense voice, "Keep walking, relax. Don't. Panic. Andrea, can you tell us something funny? Have any good stories?"

Andrea looked frightened for just a moment, and Dylan thought she wasn't going to be able to hold up. But she clenched a fist and began speaking. Her voice started out shaky.

"When I was fourteen, Uncle Luis took me to Rome. That week changed my life. Abuelita always took me to church. But it was different. Rome was *different*."

She paused for just a second. They kept walking as she tried to formulate her words. Dylan found himself scanning everyone on the street. A man in a t-shirt and jeans stood in the doorway of a shuttered Thai restaurant near the Starbucks.

He was smoking a cigarette and talking on a phone, running his left hand across the stubble of a buzz cut. Was he a potential kidnapper? Who was it that went after Andrea in the first place? Why were the guys across the street following them? Or were they, even? Maybe they were just checking out the four Thompson sisters—all of them highly attractive—across the street. After all, they stood out. Andrea and Carrie were both six plus feet tall, and Sarah had those bizarre black markings outlining her scars. And Alex…Alex was still the most beautiful thing he'd ever seen in his life.

And right now, Alex and her sisters were potentially in danger. Without even realizing it, Dylan was walking and thinking like a soldier again. Despite his injuries more than two years before, despite the fact that he was long out of the military, now he walked along, his eyes scanning everywhere, ready to act, ready to *move*, when he saw it coming.

Andrea was still speaking. "When I looked up at the ceiling in the chapel… you can't believe how beautiful it is. This was the work…the work people built to raise up to God. To praise him." As she spoke, the enthusiasm clearly shone through her words. This wasn't just a story—she believed in what she was talking about.

The two men across the street. One of them broke off, approaching the guy in the doorway with the buzz cut and the phone.

Buzzcut dropped his phone. He didn't close it, or switch it off—he just dropped it. And his hands kept moving.

Without a moment's thought, Dylan shouted, "Get *down*," then grabbed Alex and Carrie's arms, pulling them low behind a car parallel parked beside the street. Leah Simpson did the same with Sarah and Andrea. As Dylan lowered himself behind the car, Buzzcut appeared to drive something into the stomach of the approaching man.

Gunshots rang out.

CHAPTER ELEVEN
He's down, isn't he?

1. Bear. April 29. 6:17 ppm

Bear Wyden hung up the phone. Tension filled his body, a need to get up and move. After Leah's call, he'd immediately contacted the DSS offices and dispatched additional agents to Bethesda. But it was highly unlikely they would have anyone on site in time to affect the situation. Whatever the situation was.

Right now he had to wait.

He didn't want to fucking wait. Bear was a cop, not a desk jockey. And that was his ex-wife out there. And whether he liked it or not, he had to sit here and wait. He needed to calm down and focus, not go charging into the situation.

So he turned back to the Richard Thompson file, with new questions. Was Thompson CIA? Or had he been? Had his work at State somehow been cover for something else? He'd retired from the Foreign Service twelve years before. So it seemed likely that he was pursuing a dead end looking through ancient documents, when the most likely reason for all this attention was his appointment as Secretary of Defense.

On the other hand…Secretary Perry had personally handed him these documents. And he wasn't known for doing things on a whim.

So he reviewed the file and immediately saw an unusual pattern.

In Indonesia, Richard Thompson was detailed as a protocol officer for five years—an exceptionally long assignment. Then he was back at Main State for three years, followed by an assignment to Spain that barely lasted eleven months. That was highly unusual, but might be related to the fact that he'd apparently met and married a woman there.

A quick review of her file from 1981 revealed nothing terribly interesting. Adelina Ramos was young when they got married, the daughter of a florist in Madrid.

Thompson had no performance evaluation for his posting to Spain. The next move in his career was a surprise, given that he had a new wife and child. In 1982 he was posted to Pakistan. For...slightly less than two years.

Bear rubbed his forehead. He'd reviewed a lot of personnel files over the years. And he'd almost never seen a pattern like this. Foreign Service assignments were typically three years, exactly. But it fit the theory that Thompson was CIA. During the early 80s, the US Embassy in Pakistan had more intelligence officers than diplomats. Which meant he probably spent most of his time off doing classified work in Afghanistan or God only knew where else. Those years were some of the bloodiest following the Soviet invasion of Afghanistan.

He thought back to the early 90s, when he knew the Thompson family. Ironic that Richard Thompson hadn't recognized Bear, but not that surprising given what he knew about the character of the man. In 1992 Richard Thompson had been a remote figure: arrogant and dismissive. He'd been argumentative too, insisting he knew more about the security arrangements than was normal for diplomats. His wife had been a pain in the ass too, but in a different way, demanding to know intimate details of the security operation. She struck Bear as anxiety prone, worried unnecessarily about details far beyond her purview.

He remembered the oldest daughter, Julia. At the time she was ten years old. Curly brown hair. The loneliest little girl he'd ever seen. When he made the security arrangements, he'd assigned the youngest Marine in the detail to her. The two became fiercely attached, and Bear remembered all too well seeing her tagging along around the Embassy with him, usually in the garage where he'd somehow wrangled the space for three classic cars that he was always working on when off duty. It was an embarrassing waste of manpower to have a US Marine effectively babysitting a ten-year-old girl, but it was also important. The younger daughter, Carrie, also had her own guard.

When the assignment started, Adelina Thompson had insisted on interviewing the personal guards, an hour long ordeal for each of them that left the Marines sweating. She might have been a tiny, young and inexperienced woman, but she'd been fiercely protective of her daughters and made sure the bodyguards knew it.

In retrospect, it was interesting. The order to provide a protective detail to Thompson's family had come from Main State, but Bear couldn't recall the circumstances. It wasn't exactly normal, and Leah had asked him about it. Years before their marriage, she'd been assigned to the protective detail. It was unusual enough she'd asked about it. *Orders from Washington.*

She'd been right to wonder. Security details were routine, but dedicated security details for a specific family? That was unusual indeed. He made a note to look into it.

The phone rang. Bear snatched it up. "Bear."

"Bear, it's Leah!" The words came at a fast-pitched shout and he shot out of his seat. "Shots fired here. We're moving the family back to the condo now."

"Wait. What happened?"

2. Carrie. April 29. 6:17 pm

Carrie didn't, at first, pay much attention to Dylan when he suddenly became alert, walking backwards, scanning the street.

At the time, she was too busy. Too busy listening very closely to her sister Andrea, who was describing her experience in Rome, and specifically the awakening of her faith, in a way that Carrie found almost shocking. Shocking and…attractive?

Carrie was not quite thirty. She was a mother and a widow. She was a scientist. A pragmatist. She'd grown up attending Roman Catholic services when necessity or family obligations required, but that was it. But Andrea…her youngest sister, barely half her age, had a glow in her eyes when she described how she found herself in awe and wonder in the cathedrals of Rome.

So she paid only the barest attention when Dylan said, "Keep walking, don't panic."

But that oblivious stance came to a sudden crashing halt when Dylan shouted, "Get *down!*" and yanked at her arm, pulling her to the ground behind a car.

"What?" she started to ask then froze in place, at the sound of gunshots. First one, a low intense sound, so loud she felt it in her chest. That was followed by a succession of shots, two, then four, then more.

Dylan, her brother-in-law, Alex's husband, *Ray's* best friend…kneeled behind the car, one hand on her back and one on Alex's, holding them down. He muttered, "Motherfuckers!"

A knife shaped icicle pressed in Carrie's chest, as her mind circled around her daughter, Rachel. What if something happened to Carrie? Who would take care of her daughter? She'd promised Ray. She *promised* him. But he died anyway, and now there was no one, and who the hell was shooting and what did they want and *pleasekeepmydaughtersafe* and she felt herself begin to hyperventilate.

"Stay down," Dylan commanded. His eyes scanned the street as he spoke, his face a rictus, a savage mask. For just a second Carrie expected war paint. Ray Sherman—who had, after all, been Dylan's sergeant—was the love of her life. But she'd never seen him with a warlike expression, she'd never seen him threatened in a physical way like going into battle, and the sight of Dylan with that expression raised a clamor of loss and rage of grief all over again.

And then he was *gone*.

"Dylan!" Alexandra shouted as he stepped, suddenly, out from behind the car and ran. Across the street. Toward the shooting.

Alexandra cried out after her husband, and her legs started to straighten, as if she'd lost her mind too and was about to run out into the street after him. Carrie grabbed her arm and said, *"No!"* and a moment later Leah Simpson had her arm on Alexandra.

"Stay the fuck down," the woman said, an expression of rage on her face.

Another gunshot, and Alexandra screamed, and then there was a scuffle followed by a loud thud, and Leah Simpson was up and running too.

"Just stay," Carrie said to her sister, wrapping her arms around her. But for once, Carrie wasn't protecting anyone else but her and her daughter. She grabbed Alexandra selfishly, urgently, because no matter what happened, they needed to take care of each other, no matter what happened. *Rachel* was going to need them both, and Alexandra running after her fool of a husband to protect him from gunshots wasn't going to do any good at all.

Carrie had lost all the family she was willing to lose.

Alexandra struggled more, until finally Leah was standing over them again a minute or a hundred years later, her dirty blonde hair bedraggled and slick with sweat.

"You can let her up," Leah said, but Carrie didn't believe her, and she held on, and then Dylan was back. His face was a mask of concern, but Carrie couldn't see it. What she saw was the violence underneath. The violence they'd committed in Afghanistan, the violence that kept going and going, destroying more lives, the violence that killed her husband.

For the first time in her life, for just a second, Carrie hated soldiers and everything they stood for.

"Carrie, it's okay," Dylan said. "Let her go."

Just the sound of his voice was enough to set Leah Simpson off.

"What the *hell* is wrong with you, Paris?"

Dylan did a double take. Carrie eased her arms off of Alexandra, who finally got to her feet and threw her arms around him.

"You heard me," Leah said. "What the hell were you thinking?"

Dylan only half paid attention to Alexandra's stranglehold as he turned toward the Diplomatic Security office. "What I was thinking," he said, "was that I saw a threat to my family, and no one was doing anything about it."

Leah's mouth dropped open. "So you just charge someone with a gun?"

Dylan shrugged. "He's down, isn't he?"

Leah's nostrils were flared, her eyes two pinholes of fury, as she said, "My job is to *protect* you. We had DSS agents to take care of that."

"Yeah, well I wasn't waiting around for them to get their act together."

At this point Alexandra broke off from Dylan, growing confusion and anger on her face.

Leah pointed at Dylan. "You interfere with anything like that ever again and I'll see to it you spend the night in a jail cell."

He shrugged. "Wouldn't be the first time, lady. Threaten me with something worthwhile, why don't you?"

Leah's shoulders slumped. Then she marched off, her only parting word, "Stay right here."

Carrie watched as she stomped off, veering toward the far side of the street. There, two men were lying in a growing puddle of blood. A third had his hands tied behind his back with zip ties. He muttered and cursed. Two armed men stood over him, their pistols out as they scanned the street for threats.

Less than a minute later, she was back at their side. "We've got more officers on the way. In the meantime, I want you all back at the condo."

Carrie looked at her sisters. Andrea had her eyes closed, her lips moving. Was she praying? Impossible to tell, but that's what it looked like. Sarah was sitting on the ground, leaning against the car. Her eyes stared off into space, expression not that different from the way she'd looked in the hospital those weeks after she was injured and Ray killed.

Alexandra was saying something urgently to Dylan, her eyes boring into him.

"No," he said. "I won't. I did exactly what needed to be done."

"You could have been killed."

"I could have been killed anyway, Alex. I could have been run over on the way here. I could have been killed in Afghanistan. It's my job to protect you, and that's what I'm going to do."

Her response had an edge of hysteria. "Even if I end up a widow like Carrie?"

Carrie took a step back from the two of them, feeling as if she'd been punched in the gut. A hard, ruthless punch, delivered cold and with precision by someone who loved her.

Dylan's expression said much the same thing. But Carrie didn't wait around to find out what his response was. She turned to her youngest sisters, Andrea and Sarah, and said, "Come on."

She knew they followed her. Because that's what happened when Carrie gave orders. And because seconds later, she heard Sarah's voice, in a hiss. "That was a shitty thing to say, Alex."

Armed escort at their flanks with pistols out, Carrie led her family back toward the condominium.

3. George-Phillip. April 29

It was 11:54 pm, but a low buzz still filled the card room of White's on St. James' Street in London.

White's was a gentlemen's club. Not the modern definition of the word, with women swinging on poles, though George-Phillip had been given to understand that a similarly named *White's Gentlemen's Club* in London was exactly that. This White's, however, was considerably more reserved. Founded in 1693, it was an extremely exclusive club. For more than three centuries it had been men only, a private reserve for the extremely powerful and wealthy. One did not just request membership in the club: White's was invitation only, and often the only way onto its membership roles was proximity to royalty.

George-Phillip, at last count 46th in line for the throne, was still close enough to rate membership in the club. George-Phillip had been sponsored for club membership by the Prince of Wales in 1983. That sponsorship was a result of his father's death in a car accident when George-Phillip was seventeen, leaving him the Duke of Kent at far too young an age.

Sadly, it was an issue of membership that was on everyone's lips right now. In 2008 the Prime Minister had publicly resigned from the club. Others had actually turned down their offers of membership. All because of the fact that White's—a gentlemen's club, after all—did not count women among its members.

George-Phillip, egalitarian though he was about most issues, saw no difficulty with a men's only club. Nor would he have concerns with a women's only club. Sometimes one needed a place to be undisturbed by members of the opposite sex.

"The problem is the liberal newspapers," said Rory Wheeler, the *gentleman* currently sitting across the table from George-Phillip. "They print these libelous stories about the club and it generates hostility. I shouldn't be surprised if it were sponsored by foreign spies, George-Phillip. You really should have your MI-6 people look into it."

George-Phillip didn't bother to correct that his agency was no longer known as MI-6. He also never discussed his work as head of the Secret Intelligence Service with anyone, especially newspaper owners such as Rory. He felt a moment of pain as profound as midnight. Anne, his wife, would have appreciated this story. He and Anne had never been passionate—that was reserved for George-Phillip's first love—but they'd been partners. They had enjoyed each other's company, they had loved, and they had laughed. She would have spent an unreasonable amount of time chuckling over Rory Wheeler's bizarre opinions.

It was a blessing, really. Jane was only 13 months old when Anne passed away on Christmas Eve of 2008 after a very short, painful battle with pancreatic cancer. Jane had no memory of her mother.

He shook his head to clear it. Intrusive memories. Lovely memories, but now was not the time.

"Rory, I'm sure you know my agency is primarily concerned with disrupting terrorists and nuclear proliferation. We don't monitor what is happening with the newspapers."

Rory took a sip of his whiskey, then whispered, "Come now, Georgie."

George-Phillip winced at the overfamiliarity.

The old gasbag continued, his face seeming to expand from the alcohol fumes. "Think about it, George. It's Labour at the center of it. First they'll let women in the club, and next thing you know one of them will be leading the country."

"Like Mrs. Thatcher?" George-Phillip asked.

Wheeler waved a hand dismissively. "An aberration."

A nervous looking steward entered the room. He stood on his tiptoes and waved at George-Phillip.

George-Phillip raised his eyebrows and waved the man over. "Yes?"

"Your Grace, I'm very sorry, but there is a man here to see you. A Mr. O'Leary." He leaned close. "If you'd prefer, I can get rid of him."

O'Leary was *here?* That was unusual in the extreme. A phone call, certainly. But he could only remember two occasions when O'Leary had sought him out here at the club, and the last time had been at the behest of the Prime Minister.

"I'll see him, of course. Actually, O'Leary should be on the pre-cleared list."

George-Phillip knew he was blowing smoke. None of the staff ever paid attention to the standing pre-cleared list unless the visitors were royalty—in which case they were likely a member of the club in the first place.

He quickly moved out into the hall, saying, "Please make one of the private rooms available immediately. I'll retrieve Mr. O'Leary."

He checked his watch as he strode to the front door of the club. 12:34 am. Unusual indeed.

The steward had, of course, left O'Leary on the front step of the club in the slight drizzle and fog. George-Phillip quickly invited him in and led him down the hall to a small sitting room. Inside, he moved to the small bar and poured a drink for himself and one for O'Leary. The table was mahogany, sumptuous, excessive. It had likely sat in this room for two hundred years. This wasn't the first time he'd sat here: George-Phillip had met with the Prince of Wales here in 1984, at this very table. Even then, one leg was too short, and the table rocked just slightly, disturbing both of their drinks. But tradition said the table was not to be replaced—or, apparently, repaired—because one did not meddle with tradition. Not in a club like White's.

"I presume this is urgent?"

"Yes, sir," O'Leary said.

"Tell me."

"Charlie Frazer, sir. He was shot in Washington."

"Dear God. Who?"

"We don't have a positive ID yet."

"Details, please."

"Frazer and Linden were trailing the Thompson sisters, sir. They're in Bethesda, outside Washington, DC."

George-Phillip felt unreasonably irritated by this. "I know where Bethesda is, O'Leary."

"Of course, sir. Several of the sisters were walking to a local restaurant, accompanied by Diplomatic Security agents."

"All right."

"Frazer reported that he felt there were others watching them, but we don't know who."

"Saudis, maybe. Or CIA," George-Phillip mused.

"Regardless, sir, there was an altercation, and Frazer was shot. He's being treated at a local hospital, his prognosis is good."

"Any other injuries? The Thompson sisters?"

"They're fine, sir. No injuries."

George-Phillip closed his eyes, a sense of relief flooding him.

"How are the local police treating it?"

"Mugging. Frazer and Linden both had diplomatic ID. But Frazer's cover is likely blown."

"We'll recall him from Washington, I think. Switch to a different team. And O'Leary..."

"Yes, sir?"

"Have an armed covering team. I want contingency plans. Including one to evacuate the sisters."

O'Leary's overactive eyebrows bunched together. "Sir?"

George-Phillip leaned close. "Get me options, O'Leary. Right now that bastard Thompson holds all the cards. We need to get control of this situation."

"Yes, sir," O'Leary said.

George-Phillip stood. It was long past midnight now, and long past time to get home.

4. Andrea. April 29. 6:18 pm

That *was a shitty thing to say, Alex.*

Sarah's words echoed in Andrea's head as they hurried back to the condo at a near-run, Diplomatic Security agents clearing the way through the crowd on the sidewalk. Her words. The sound of gunshots. The sight of Dylan, face red, mouth open as he yelled a screaming challenge, running directly at an armed man.

A pool of blood spreading on the sidewalk.

She came to a sudden stop behind Carrie, police blocking the sidewalk. She heard the word *witnesses* and someone said *can't leave the scene* but then Leah Simpson was waving her badge and ordering the local police back. Then they were moving again, into the building, up the elevator, and she felt lightheaded and confused.

Why was any of this happening? None of it made any sense. Shock upon shock had been piled on her, starting with the call from Carrie only a few days ago, the flight to the United States and her sudden kidnapping *yesterday*, then this? As they stumbled down the hall, escorted by Leah Simpson and the other two agents, she found herself shaking, hard.

She didn't even really look as they entered the condo. Carrie immediately rushed to the back room to check on Rachel, while Sarah sank into the couch, haphazardly throwing her combat-boot encased feet onto the coffee table with a loud thump that caused both Dylan and Alexandra to jump.

Andrea stood there shaking for just a moment as Alexandra said, "You could have been *killed*."

"Alex, just let it go." Dylan's reply was sharp. He kept walking toward the sliding glass doors as he spoke.

"*No*, I'm not letting it go. You can't just put yourself in danger like that."

Dylan's response was swift. He spun around and pointed a finger at her face, anger written across his features like a map with driving directions to hell. "That's enough."

He turned, slid the door open, and then walked out, slamming it shut behind him.

Alexandra sagged a little, watching him light a cigarette and lean against the wall.

Sarah said, offhand, "Why don't you just cut his balls off?"

Andrea's eyes widened as Alexandra gasped.

"What did you just say?"

Sarah began methodically untying the laces of her boots. "I said, why don't you just cut his balls off? Isn't that your purpose here?"

"Shut up, Sarah. You don't know what you're talking about."

"I know your man there just acted to try to save our lives. That makes him a hero in my book. You should lay off him, maybe hug him or something instead of trying to emasculate him. And just in case you missed the message, what you said to Carrie was unforgivable."

"Can you all just stop fighting?" Andrea asked. "Things are bad enough."

Alexandra sank into the chair across from Sarah. "I'm sorry," she said, her voice shaking.

Sarah nodded her head toward Dylan, who stood, pensive, smoking on the porch, looking out at the darkening sky. "Not me you need to apologize to."

"I'm just so worried, Sarah. He's not been himself since Ray died."

"Who has been?" The question came from Carrie, who stood in the doorway to the hall. "Everything's been upside down since then."

Sarah shook her head. "Not just since then. Since...always."

Andrea sighed and slid into a chair. She looked at her sisters and whispered, "I don't get it. I don't get *any* of this."

Carrie nodded. "That's it. There's...things we don't know. A *lot* we don't know."

Andrea looked at her older sister. "Does Mom?"

Carrie looked thoughtful for a moment. Then she said, "I think so."

"Then we have to find her. And talk with her."

CHAPTER TWELVE
It's not personal

1. Sarah. April 30. 8:54 am

"You're going to be fine," Sarah said. "And Carrie would be here too, if she could."

Andrea shrugged. "I know I'll be fine...it's just...I don't know how to explain it..."

Sarah reached up to put a hand on her shoulder. "You're afraid. Not because of the donor match, but..."

Andrea nodded. "Look at us. You're practically a midget compared to me. We don't look at all alike."

"You look a lot like Mom. At least your eyes."

"Right. But who is my father?"

Sarah thought: probably not that son of a bitch Richard Thompson (*her* father, she was sure), who was so busy *preparing for his confirmation hearings* that he couldn't be bothered with his sixteen-year-old daughter. That was for sure.

But if her father wasn't Andrea's father—what did that mean? How did it happen? And Andrea and Carrie looked like twins. None of it made any sense at all! She tried to remind herself that, first of all, it had only been two days now since Andrea came home. Not even two full days. If it hadn't been urgent for Rachel's sake, Sarah would have thrown a fit. Andrea needed more time. But according to Rachel's doctors, the longer they went before a bone marrow transplant, the more transfusions she would need, and the more damage her body would sustain.

Andrea shook her head. "It doesn't matter. I'm sorry. Even if he is my father, he isn't."

Sarah winced.

Andrea looked her in the eye. "Tell me I'm wrong."

Sarah's mouth curled up in a half grimace. "I can't."

"Can we take this inside?" asked one of the Diplomatic Security agents. Terry Segal, his name was. Mid-to-late twenties and buff. Andrea had the feeling he was armed to the teeth, and that was kind of hot. On the other hand, every time he gave her his toothy grin, she noticed the bottom row of his teeth were stained badly. Chewing tobacco, she suspected, which was quite possibly the grossest thing in the world.

"Sure," Sarah said. She took Andrea's arm and they began walking in step toward the clinic. The Children's National Medical Center was an ultramodern glass structure with windows jutting out at odd angles, trees and grass surrounding a lake. It all seemed silent, pristine, calm and professional. It all seemed designed to calm. It all seemed incredibly fake.

"Where exactly is Carrie?" Andrea asked just before they reached the entry doors.

Sarah shook her head. "She said she had an appointment. Her nanny's coming at ten. I think she said she'd be back early afternoon."

Alexandra had stayed at the condo. That morning she had mumbled a barely coherent apology to Carrie. Predictably, Carrie forgave her on the spot and hugged her.

Sarah had her doubts. Because *no one* was that good and strong. No one kept their shit together under that much pressure. No one was that kind. But being the caretaker was Carrie's identity, and she wasn't going to give that up for anything. Sarah thought one day Carrie would explode from her own self-imposed sainthood.

Segal, the diplomatic security guard, jumped ahead of them and opened the door. Andrea led, with Sarah right behind.

"This way," Segal said. "We already have security in the lab suite, and they're expecting you upstairs."

Andrea's eyes were round. "That's...reassuring."

Sarah knew it wasn't reassuring at all. What sixteen-year-old wants a battalion of security guards accompanying her to get blood tests? But there was no going back. Since the shooting in Bethesda last night, the security presence had dramatically increased. Their guards were in uniform now, with visible sidearms and driving escort vehicles. She couldn't even imagine what all this was costing.

Her father had retired from the Foreign Service when she was still young, and the family's last overseas posting to Moscow she'd been very young indeed. So she'd never experienced this kind of intense security.

She didn't like it. It made her want to get on Eddie's Harley and just ride out of town as fast and as far as she could go.

Speaking of Eddie. She'd received several urgent texts from him already this morning asking for updates.

Everything is fine, she sent back.

As they stepped on the elevator, Andrea said, "You've been texting a lot. Boyfriend?"

"Sort of," Sarah replied.

The elevator door closed. The two DSS agents stood near the doors, their backs to the sisters. Sarah continued. "Eddie's a med student. He was part of the ambulance crew that...he pulled me out of the accident last summer."

"Oh my God," Andrea said. "That's so sweet! And he's your boyfriend now?"

"Not exactly." In fact they'd only been on four dates. She remembered her mother's red face and caustic words vividly when Eddie had shown up at their place.

Not until my daughter is eighteen.

The rules were set. Eddie could visit at the condo. He ate dinner with them every fourth Sunday. But until her eighteenth birthday, she was never once in a room alone with him.

The early months, that had been fine with her. Her leg had been swollen and ripped open like an overcooked sausage, and the pain was indescribable. There were days when she'd done nothing but scream, Carrie had done nothing more than weep, and Adelina, their mother, had done little more than stare at them in hollow-eyed shock as she tried to care for her daughters.

She knew Julia and Carrie would never trust their mother. She knew Andrea had left home and wanted nothing to do with her.

But Sarah would never in her life forget the nights when the morphine just wasn't enough, the nights when she'd whimpered and wept in the most awful, unimaginable hell. And it was her mother's arms around her that brought her through those nights. It was Adelina's voice in her ear, whispering, "You can do this, Sarah. Only another hour, then we can get another shot. You can make it. You're strong enough. All my daughters are strong enough."

Sarah knew her mother was crazy. She knew her mother had some fucked up past, though she didn't have a clue what it was all about. But she knew that when push came to shove, that woman dropped everything, left her home and lived with her and Carrie through the worst months of their lives.

By December, the pain was mostly dull aches, and she was dealing with the pangs of coming off the painkillers. But from what she'd seen during her twin sister Jessica's rendition of "grace" during Christmas dinner, that was an even bigger issue for her twin. As a result, their mother had gone home after Christmas, returning to San Francisco with Sarah's twin sister Jessica—exchanging places with their prick of a father, who promptly decided the condo was too small and found his own place.

That was fine. Sarah stayed and took care of Carrie. They took care of each other.

Oddly enough though—those months of her mother whispering soothing words in her ear—they changed something. Even when her mother was gone, she waited, and didn't go out with Eddie, until her eighteen birthday, just a few weeks ago on April 1st.

Her first date with Eddie was her present to herself. And it was a doozy. The hulking Puerto Rican medical student took her to a play at the Kennedy Center, followed by a late dinner at the Roof Terrace, overlooking the National Mall on one side and Arlington National Cemetery on the other.

As they rode up the elevator, Sarah found herself telling Andrea a little about Eddie. He came from a wealthy family, but for reasons he'd refused to explain, his father had disowned him during his third year of pre-med at George Washington University. Eddie kept going, getting a job as an EMT to help pay some of the bills and praying to cover the rest.

"Are you dating anyone?" Sarah asked Andrea as they reached the third floor.

"Javier," Andrea said. "But he just wants to have sex. I keep him distracted, but he's no boyfriend."

Sarah laughed. "I bet you run circles around him."

Andrea smiled mysteriously.

"This way, ladies," said Segal, their security guard. He was the only one now—the other one stayed at the elevator doors as they followed Segal down the hall. Another guard was barring the door to the lab.

Segal stopped at the door to the lab, spoke with the guard at the door, and opened the door.

Sarah and Andrea stepped into the lab.

Andrea walked up to the reception counter. "Miss Thompson?" asked a lab tech, a woman in her mid-thirties.

"Yes, ma'am."

"We've had the lab closed until you're finished. Please come this way and we'll get you taken care of."

Andrea nodded and followed. Sarah followed.

Sarah overheard one of the other hospital staffers mutter, "And then maybe we can get back to business…" She froze and gave a cold look to the woman, then sneered and kept going.

Two minutes later, a rubber band was wrapped around Andrea's arm and the lab tech had inserted a needle.

"How long will it take before we know the results?" Andrea asked.

The lab tech shrugged and responded in a brusque tone. "Normally I'd say two or three days, though rush transplant matches sometimes are the same day. I'm certain they'll rush yours, what with all the attention."

Sarah glanced back toward the door, and said, "It's not her fault she was kidnapped, you know."

The lab tech froze and blushed. "Of course."

"So maybe we can get on with this? So your coworkers aren't *inconvenienced* any more?"

"Sarah…" Andrea said. "It's okay…"

Sarah took a deep breath. "Sorry," she whispered. "Let's just finish this up and get out of here." What she wanted to say was: it didn't matter what the blood test was for. They were sisters no matter what. The blood test was to find out if Andrea was a donor match. Not to determine her parentage.

Somehow it felt like they'd both lost sight of that.

2. Mitch Filner. April 30. 9:15 am

Mitch Filner said into the phone. "Just in case you forgot, we lost one of our guys last night because of your stupid orders."

As he said the words, Mitch scanned the balcony of the highrise directly across the street through his binoculars. The former soldier—Dylan Paris—was pacing on the balcony, smoking a cigarette. Mitch would have loved to have put a bullet right between his fucking eyes for interfering the night before. Now, Joe Paretski was in the custody of federal agents, and if they didn't find him soon, this whole operation could come crashing down.

Not that it wasn't all bullshit to begin with. Leslie Collins thought he could drop a few hundred thousand here and a few hundred thousand there and contain a major disaster, but it didn't work that way. Mitch knew that much, and he was working as fast as he could to make his own insurance, even as he followed Collins' orders.

Kidnapping a teenager? Seriously? That was bullshit. They weren't in some Third World shithole, nor was Andrea Thompson some anonymous girl who could be snatched off the street without anyone noticing. She was the daughter of the fucking *Secretary of Defense.* Yeah, asshole hadn't bothered to tell him that until after it was international headlines.

That was okay. Mitch had been recording his conversations with Collins. Because one thing was for sure, Leslie Collins wasn't acting within the bounds of any approved intelligence op. No matter how much he thought he was in charge, no matter how often he had fucking cocktails at the White House, there was no way in hell the President had authorized the kidnapping of the daughter of a cabinet member. Collins was playing his own fucking game. Mitch didn't know what it was, but he was putting away plenty of information to put Leslie Collins away in prison forever.

Right now the family was split all over the place. Mitch had agents tailing the oldest daughter, Julia Wilson, spoiled rich girl husband of a fucking rock star, out in Los Angeles. He had two more tracking Carrie Thompson, the next oldest sister, currently en route to the Pentagon to have lunch with her father. That ought to be a barrel of fucking laughs. The two youngest, including the bitch who had killed two of his contractors, were at Children's Hospital. Getting blood tests, which Collins had ordered him to procure and destroy.

He ought to just put a bullet through her head rather than steal her blood tests.

Collins spoke, his voice a slow clip. "I didn't ask your opinion, Filner. I gave you instructions."

"Collins, you're losing your grip."

"Just get the blood tests and do it quietly. Switch them out with somebody's. I don't care what you do."

Filner rolled his eyes. Fine. He'd follow instructions. But it was a waste of time. They'd just get another blood test.

He eyed the former soldier on the balcony again.

Earlier that morning he'd run into a familiar face. Jackie Prince. Or at least that was the name she'd gone by when they met four years ago. Jackie had been lounging with a paperback at the Starbucks, a hundred yards away from the condo.

Filner had slipped into the seat across from her.

"Well, hullo there, Mitch," Jackie said. Her clipped London accent was as annoying as always.

"Jackie," Filner had responded. He raised an eyebrow. "Doing a little vacation reading? A little tourism here?"

"Well, of course," Jackie replied. "What else would I be doing in the United States?"

"Not a little bit of spying? Interesting place you chose here."

Jackie had smiled and leaned close to him, her nose inches from his. "I'm no more involved in intelligence operations than you are, Mitch."

Filner wiggled his eyebrows up and down; an expression he'd come to believe was somehow seductive. "You should come join me, then," he said.

She smiled. "Perhaps you should come join me," she had replied. "I've got a friend, his name's George? He's looking for some American employees."

Mitch snorted. "It's hard to beat self-employment."

She smiled and leaned close. Then she whispered, "Security's worth a lot, Mitch. Think about it. It would be a shame if you got involved in something that was going to be trouble. And just between you and me? There's trouble coming. Big trouble."

She slid a card across the table at him. He stared at the card in surprise. It listed the name and address of a comic book shop in London.

"Comics?" he had asked.

"I've got a weakness for superheroes," she had replied.

Mitch memorized the number. Then he had gotten up and walked away, leaving the card behind.

Now, with Leslie Collins droning on in his ear over the phone, all Mitch could think about was the relative security if he took her up on her offer. He knew SIS would be good for it: he had enough information to bring down Richard Thompson *and* Leslie Collins.

"Filner? Did you fucking hear me?"

Filner sighed. He thought about the operations of the last five days. Installing bombs in houses. Kidnapping teenagers. He didn't want to do this crap any more. He wanted to sit in a lounge chair on the beach in France or Spain or some place and fucking retire from this crap.

"I heard you, Collins. Let me make sure I'm hearing you. You want me to steal her blood tests."

"Yes!"

"And then?"

"We're going to contain this thing, Filner. I want contingency plans. To wipe out all of them. Am I clear?"

That was it.

"You're perfectly clear." He hung up the phone. Then he checked to make sure it had been recorded properly. *Yes.*

He stood up. He was done. Done with this bullshit. Done. Done. Done. He dialed Jackie's comic book shop from memory.

"James Street Comics," said a male voice.

"I'd like to speak with Jackie. My name's Filner."

A pause. Then a voice said, "Jackie's not in. But I'm authorized to speak on her behalf. She told me that you might be calling. Is this about the job opening?"

"Yeah. Um...you guys offering any relocation assistance?"

His phone started beeping. An incoming call. Probably Collins.

"That's doable provided we get the right employee. With the right...skills."

"All right...see, the thing is, I don't feel really secure in my current job."

"Security, we can offer, sir. But it's not a one-way street."

"I need to move right away."

A pause. Mitch felt his heart beating faster. He waited for almost three full minutes. Then someone came back on the line. "Sir? One of our recruiters would like to meet you. I understand you're in Bethesda right now? Can you get to the metro and meet our man at DuPont Circle?"

"Yeah. How will I know him?"

"He'll know you."

Mitch nodded, then hung up the phone, just in time for it to ring again. Leslie Collins. He ignored the call and quickly tossed a few things in his pockets, then walked to the door and yanked it open.

Then he stepped back in shock, a hand at his midsection, covering the sudden sharp pain. He felt hot liquid begin to pour out onto his hand and he gasped.

Danny McMillan was standing in the doorway. "Sorry, Mitch. It's not personal. Collins heard you were looking for another job."

"Fuck, Danny." *What the fuck? Was Danny here as a backup all along?*

"Yeah…that's the breaks, man." Then he reached out and with a swift jab, stabbed Mitch again, this time between ribs. Mitch gasped and fell to his knees, his vision wavering.

"I'll take that," Danny said the words as he pulled Mitch's phone out of his hands.

Mitch fell to the floor.

Danny said, "Sorry about this, buddy."

Then Mitch felt a cold line against his throat. A second later, everything went black.

CHAPTER THIRTEEN
Secret wars

1. Bear. April 30. 9:45 am

By the time Bear made it to the Russell Senate Office Building on Wednesday morning, he was exhausted. And with good reason. Following the shooting in Bethesda, a jurisdictional battle took place between the Montgomery County Police, Diplomatic Security, and the FBI.

Montgomery County had a good case. The shooter had no identification and was refusing to talk. From their perspective, he'd shot a British citizen who was in town on a tourist visa and had no diplomatic connections. But when the shooter was booked, his fingerprints hit on the National Crime Information System database. Ronald Sanderson. 32 years old. Army veteran, former Airborne, former Special Forces. He'd been thrown out of the Army with a medical discharge for a personality disorder. In Bear's experience, that usually meant improperly diagnosed post traumatic stress. Sanderson had disappeared for three years after his discharge, but attracted the FBI's attention in a bank fraud investigation. No one, however, could find him. Until yesterday.

Diplomatic Security wanted him, of course, because of the connection to the Andrea Thompson kidnapping. Unfortunately, for now at least, Sanderson was in the Montgomery County jail while the different jurisdictional arguments got worked out.

It was well after midnight before Bear had dealt with the custody issue, then beefed up security assignments for the Thompson family. At 1:30 in the morning he'd stumbled back into his studio apartment near DuPont Circle and crawled into the bed.

He was up early, and at 5:30 walked into the Starbucks around the corner from his apartment to sit, read the rest of the Thompson file, and wake up.

Bear was intrigued still by the complete lack of information in the file about Thompson's postings to Spain and Pakistan in the early 80s. No performance evaluations, no official reports, no photographs. *Nothing.* It was as if the assignments simply hadn't existed. In January 1984 Thompson was reassigned to the State Department in Washington, DC for what appeared to be a normal three-year assignment. The next three years in his file were perfectly normal. Official reports. Commendations letters, including one signed by Ronald Reagan.

The commendations were very vague, however. *For exemplary service during the period of June 1985 to July 1985.* With no specifics or description of what the assignment was.

Again...everything in his file was slightly off.

A photograph from early 1984. Bear recognized the condo currently occupied by Carrie Thompson-Sherman. In the photo, Richard Thompson sat at the large dining table with his wife Adelina and several other people. A quasi-official dinner party. On the back of the photo, someone had labeled the names in now faded, uneven type.

Richard and Adelina Thompson
Prince Roshan and Myriam al-Saud
Leslie Collins
Prince George-Phillip, Duke of Kent
LTC Chuck Rainsley and Brianna Rainsley

Bear stared at the photograph in shock. Then he took a sip of his coffee, wishing he had some whiskey to top it off.

Roshan al Saud, a member of the royal house of Saudi Arabia, was now the director general of al Mukhabarat Al A'amah...the Saudi Arabian intelligence agency.

Leslie Collins was the Director of Operations—the second-highest level executive—of the Central Intelligence Agency. In the photograph, he sat with his arm on Richard Thompson's shoulder, a sly grin on his face as he stared at the camera.

George-Phillip Windsor was a cousin of Queen Elizabeth and currently the head of the Secret Intelligence Service of the United Kingdom. He looked no older than twenty in the photo, but was clearly recognizable with his dark features and long aquiline nose.

Chuck Rainsley—then a Marine Lieutenant Colonel—was now the senior senator from Texas and head of the Senate Armed Services Committee. He wore his uniform in the photo, medals looking resplendent as he stood behind the others at the table. Bear remembered that Rainsley, an exceptionally tall man, had been one of the commanders of the Marine task force that had been so devastated by the truck bomb in Beirut that killed more than two hundred Marines.

Bear didn't understand what this was all about. But he knew that something was seriously wrong. In this photograph, they looked young, Thompson and Collins and Prince Roshan all in their early thirties, Prince George-Phillip not even twenty-five. But now, these men were some of the most powerful in the world.

And now he was on his way to face one of them. After looking at the photo, Bear had returned to his apartment, where he'd reviewed all the biographical information he could find on Senator Chuck Rainsley.

Rainsley was a conservative and one of the most powerful men in the Senate. Bear's recollection had been correct. A Vietnam veteran, Rainsley was a senior commander of the peacekeeping force deployed by President Reagan to Lebanon. In October 1983 suicide bombers attacked the Marine barracks with truck bombs, killing 241 US service members. Bear reviewed the reports—they were brutal. Unusually restrictive rules of engagement prevented sentries from responding effectively to the attack, and a political and intelligence rift in the White House and between the Pentagon and State Department prevented an effective response. In the photograph, early in 1984, Rainsley was still in uniform. But Bear knew that by March 1984, Rainsley had resigned his commission and announced he was running for Congress.

Bear felt a little better prepared, then, as he walked into the Russell Building. He didn't know the connection between Senator Rainsley and Richard Thompson, but he knew that at least as far back as 1984, the two men knew each other. He knew that on at least one occasion, Senator Rainsley sat in the same room as Thompson and the future heads or deputy heads of intelligence of three different nations.

There was no longer any question in Bear's mind that Richard Thompson had been CIA.

What did the new Secretary of State, Perry, have to do with all of this? He'd also been on the Armed Services and Foreign Relations committees in the Senate, and was known to be a good friend of Rainsley's, despite the fact they sat on opposite sides of the political aisle. Perry was a Democrat and had served in the Senate from Massachusetts for twenty years. Rainsley was a Republican from Texas. But the two of them had worked together for decades. So what would Rainsley have to say that Perry couldn't tell him?

Bear was annoyed he had to turn in his weapons at the entrance to the building. But he needed to get upstairs. He made his way down the gleaming white hallway toward the stairs, watching as men and women, legislators, aides, lobbyists, and tourists wandered the halls.

It was quieter on the third floor—only those people who had actual business came here. His shoes echoed off the marble floor as he walked down the hall, and he felt an urge to whisper.

Halfway down the quarter mile long hallway, he found the seal of the state of Texas: a lone star, circled by olive and oak branches. The door itself was thick polished wood and had gleaming brass handles. Bear reached out and opened the door.

Inside, it took his eyes a moment to adjust from the bright white marble hallway to the dark wood paneling inside the office. A receptionist sat at a desk—young, pretty and earnest. She smiled at him and said, "May I help you?"

"Jim Wyden, Diplomatic Security. I have an appointment with Senator Rainsley."

"Yes, sir. If you can wait right here, Senator Rainsley will be right with you."

It wasn't a long wait. Less than a minute later, Senator Chuck Rainsley appeared in the doorway of the anteroom. Bear's first impression: Rainsley would make a good candidate for the father of Carrie and Andrea Thompson. At six foot six, he towered over Bear. A good looking affable man with an easy smile and a broad hand, he clasped Bear's hand and said, "Mr. Wyden, it's a pleasure to meet you. Secretary Perry told me to expect you. Please come in."

Bear followed Rainsley into the office, his thoughts racing. *Could* Rainsley be the father? He'd have to look at dates. He muttered a curse at himself. He should have checked their birth dates. But it didn't make any sense, really. It didn't explain why Andrea Thompson was kidnapped. It didn't explain anything really.

"Have a seat," Rainsley said, gesturing toward a leather chair in front of a huge, highly polished desk. Bear's shoes sank into the thick carpeting of the office as he walked to the chair and sat down.

Rainsley's office was spacious. Memorabilia and photographs covered the walls. Rainsley in his Marine Corps uniform, as a young Lieutenant in Vietnam, on an aircraft carrier, at an Embassy, in Lebanon. Later photos of him in the Washington uniform, a dark suit and tie, or on the campaign trail in Texas. On the wall, a mix of items. A Bronze Star medal. A plaque from the city of Dallas. A photograph, black and white, of a twenty-year-old Chuck Rainsley in a basketball uniform with the letters USNA. Naval Academy.

Rainsley slid into the seat across from Bear. Even seated he was an imposing, impressive man.

"What can I do for you, Mr. Wyden?"

"Bear, sir."

"Right. Bear. What can I do for you?"

"Sir, you're probably aware that the night before last, the daughter of the Secretary of Defense was kidnapped at BWI airport. A foreign national with known intelligence ties was involved in the kidnapping."

Rainsley nodded. "I've been following the story. Please don't take this as nit-picking, but just a reminder, Thompson's confirmation hearings aren't until next week. He isn't the Secretary of Defense yet."

Bear nodded. "I stand corrected, Senator. I'm running the investigation into Andrea Thompson's kidnapping. And—to put it bluntly—I've got some unanswered questions that don't make sense, and Secretary Thompson is being less than cooperative."

Rainsley grimaced. "That's no surprise."

"Sir, what can you tell me about Richard Thompson?"

Rainsley grimaced. "First of all, I want to make it clear, this is not on the record."

"Fine, Senator."

"All right, then. Richard Thompson is a snake and a liar. He's one of the most dangerous men in government, and if the President thinks Thompson's nomination as Secretary of Defense is going to fly he is out of his mind."

Well, that was clear enough, Bear thought. "Can you be, um…a little more specific, Senator?"

"All right. First of all—you know Thompson's not really State Department, right? He's CIA, through and through."

"You're certain of that?"

"We held closed hearings in 2001 when he became ambassador to Russia. His CIA assignments were the reason for the closed hearings."

"I see. I understand you were responsible for the delay in that appointment?"

Rainsley grimaced. "I tried to stop it entirely. We held the nomination up for two years, and it cost me a lot of political capital."

"Tell me why."

Rainsley leaned across the desk. He held up one finger. "First…early 80s, when Thompson was in Afghanistan, he got up to some very shady stuff. *Criminal* stuff. And then he did everything he could to prevent any oversight or control from Congress."

"He was officially assigned to Pakistan, I believe."

Rainsley sneered. "So was half the Central Intelligence Agency. The Russians were in Afghanistan, and we had a lot of operatives in there. Secret little wars. Crazy stuff."

"Okay. What else?"

"All right. Second… and this you can't quote me on. But Thompson had a cruel streak. Power games in his personal and professional life."

"What sort of…power games?"

Rainsley looked disgusted. "Let's just say I feel sorry for Adelina Thompson."

"You know her." It wasn't a question.

Rainsley gave a vague answer. "We've met a few times. She's a lot younger than Richard Thompson."

"They've been married since...1981?"

"That's right."

"I thought it was unusual. His assignment to Spain was only a few months."

Rainsley leaned close. "The agency ordered him to marry her to prevent an international incident."

That didn't make any sense. Unless..."Was she raped?"

The Senator shrugged. "I don't know all the details. But they married them off and got him the hell out of there."

Bear sighed. "Sir, this is all interesting, but it doesn't really tell me anything. Did you know...there's a photograph of you with Thompson? And his wife?"

"I'm not surprised."

"The picture also has some interesting people in it. Prince Roshan from Saudi Arabia. Leslie Collins. Prince George-Phillip."

Senator Rainsley nodded. "That's right."

"All three of them ended up very high in their intelligence establishments."

"What does that tell you?"

"That I've got unanswered questions. That none of this makes sense."

Rainsley smiled. "That's all I'm going to say for now."

"Senator, one last question."

"Yes?"

"Who is Carrie and Andrea Thompson's real father?"

Rainsley raised his eyebrows. Then he said, "That's not a question for me to answer. Have a good afternoon, Mr. Wyden."

2. Carrie. April 30. Noon

The Army Sergeant who led Carrie down the hallway wore dress blues like Ray had worn to their wedding. He'd been in the Army a *lot* longer than Ray had, though. Three strips on top, three on the bottom, a dozen diagonal yellow hash marks on his sleeve and dozens upon dozens of ribbons. She recognized the Combat Infantryman's badge. Of all Ray's decorations, that one had been the most important to him.

"In here, ma'am," the Sergeant said.

The door opened into a small anteroom. A woman in her forties sat behind a desk. Two younger sergeants sat in chairs across from the woman. One read on a Kindle, while the other played a handheld video game. She wondered what they were doing. At a second desk, an Army Colonel sat. He stood up as Carrie entered the room and said, "Miss Thompson-Sherman? I'm Colonel Billingsgate, your father's aide-de-camp. He'll be available in just a few moments, ma'am."

"Thank you," Carrie said.

The secretary, still behind her desk, said, "Can I get you a drink? Coffee?"

"No, thanks."

"Please feel free to have a seat."

Carrie sat down. She was uncomfortable. Beyond uncomfortable. Her father was a lifelong diplomat, and while his appointment as the new Secretary of Defense might make sense in some political sense she didn't know about, what she did know was that her experience with the Army as an institution was not good. Not good at all. Ray had been practically persecuted, called back up by the military on a pretext because of a crime someone else had committed. He'd been put on trial, dragged through the mud, and then murdered.

She'd just as soon not spend a day here, in the Pentagon, where her husband's death had effectively been engineered.

So while she waited, she played solitaire on her phone and tried to calm her nerves. Carrie was protective of her daughter—obsessively so. And leaving her in the hands of the nanny, even for a few hours, was excruciating. She'd had to do that several times in the last couple of days.

The main door to the office opened. She looked up. Her father stood in the doorway, a politician's smile on his face. Something was wrong. Her father had always been distant. He'd always been...baffling. A little cold. But his recent behavior had been almost bizarre. She didn't understand it, and it seemed to have started right around the time they figured out that Rachel was sick.

"Carrie, darling. Please, come in."

Her father put his hand on her arm as he led her into the office.

"Have a seat. Lunch will be served in just a moment."

She walked to the indicated seat, a small table not far from the desk. White tablecloth and lunch settings. Was he kidding? She'd asked to meet her *father* for lunch. Instead, she was getting the *Secretary of Defense*.

A steward—an Army sergeant—in a white uniform entered the room and filled the water glasses at the table.

"Something to drink, ma'am?"

"Thanks, just water, please."

"And you, Mr. Secretary?"

"I'll have a vodka-tonic, please. Light."

The steward disappeared.

"How are Andrea and baby Rachel?"

Carrie winced a little. Something was really wrong here. She'd never been close to her father—but of all of his daughters, she'd been the closest. But right now she didn't feel close at all. His question seemed as superficial as possible. *How are Andrea and baby Rachel?*

She blinked at her father and said, "Andrea is terrified. She was kidnapped at the airport, and neither one of her parents could be bothered to be there for her."

"Carrie, surely you're aware that my confirmation hearings begin next week."

She leaned forward and said, "Father. What in God's name is *wrong* with you? How could you treat her like this?"

"You don't understand how—"

Her father's mouth closed suddenly when the side door to the office opened. The steward returned, with two enlisted men behind him. One carried a tray with two covered dishes, and the other brought drinks. Quickly, lunch and drinks were arrayed on the table in front of them. Carrie sat uncomfortably as the soldiers bustled around arranging the table.

Lunch was roast lamb.

As the stewards left, her father coughed into his napkin. "Carrie...there are things you don't understand."

"Right," she said. "I don't understand how you can be so cold to your own daughter."

He closed his eyes, visibly trying to contain his patience.

"Please relay to your sister my love, and let her know that the moment my confirmation hearings are complete, I'll be available."

God, she missed Ray. The grief that ran through her at that thought was over-powering, almost as if she'd been run over. "Do you know what she thinks?"

Her father leaned forward, spreading his napkin across his lap. Then, with careful motions, he cut a piece of lamb and speared it on his fork, bringing it to his mouth. Only after he'd chewed and swallowed did he say, "What does she think?"

Carrie felt a tightening in her chest, knowing that once she said it, she wouldn't be able to recall the words. Knowing—believing—for the first time, that Andrea's suspicion might be true. Believing that everything she'd ever been told by her own father was a lie.

"Andrea believes that she and I are sisters. But that you aren't our father."

He raised his eyebrows then wiped his napkin across his lips. "She does?"

Carrie nodded once.

He sighed. His face looked closed off. No emotion. No...nothing. He looked like someone about to walk into court, not her father.

Carrie pressed forward. "Is that why she's spent most of her life in Spain?"

"You'll have to discuss that with your mother," he said. His tone of voice was irritated, clipped.

"Why did Andrea get sent off and not me?"

"Again, you'll have to speak to your mother about that."

She shook her head. "Is it true?"

He didn't answer. *He didn't answer.* Something in her was cut adrift. She'd lost her husband already. Now she had to lose her father too?

Her voice ragged, Carrie asked, "Who...who is my father, then?"

Her father—no, Richard Thompson—closed his eyes. Then he shrugged, as if to say it was of little importance to him. His tone of voice was disgusted when he spoke. "Unfortunately, your birth father is Senator Chuck Rainsley."

CHAPTER FOURTEEN
The best I could

1. Carrie. April 30

Unfortunately, *your birth father is Senator Chuck Rainsley.*

The sentence rolled around in her head, a wildfire destroying everything in its path, a flood of sludge and lies clogging her ears and thoughts. Thirty years of memories. She thought of holidays in San Francisco, of birthdays, of her father's isolation in his work, of the gifts he gave her over the years. All of them lies.

Senator Chuck Rainsley.

She thought about what she knew about the man—the man Richard Thompson claimed was her actual father. Nothing really. Senator from Texas. She was under the impression he was married. He'd been the primary opposition on the Senate Foreign Relations committee to her father's nomination as Ambassador to Russia. She vaguely remembered the news, hearings, and Rainsley banging his fist on a table on television. She remembered Julia's suicidal depression, and learning years later that her parents blamed *Julia* for the stalled nomination.

Rage gripped her. *Was it true?* Had Rainsley blocked the nomination out of spite? Had he somehow used Julia to hit back at her...not her father.

"I don't even know what to call you," she said.

"I'm still your father, Carrie."

"A father is the person who gave you life. *Or* it's the person who gave you love. Or both. But you gave neither."

He winced under the onslaught of words. "Carrie, darling, that's not true."

She slowly stood up. "But it is. You may have showered me with gifts and cash...but..." She shook her head. "What kind of man are you? What kind of woman is..."

"I did the best I could. I didn't even know until..."

"You didn't know until when?"

"You were five."

"How did you find out?"

He gave a grim smile. "Your blood type is A positive. Your mother's is O positive. Therefore, your biological father can't be type B. I am. Simple really."

He leaned back in his chair, rubbing his hand across the bridge of his nose. "Your mother and I had a lot of trouble. A *lot*. But I was never unfaithful. Unfortunately, your mother was. But even so, I forgave her. She was young, and I'd spent so much of our married life away. Virtually all of it. She was a young mother alone with her daughter while I was off on assignments. I forgave her."

He nodded at her as he spoke, his expression grave. "Truly that would have been the end of it. And you can't tell me I treated you any differently than your sisters. I'm not the warmest parent in the world. But I've done my best."

Carrie stared back. "You found out in, what...1990? And you still had Alexandra that year."

"I told you I forgave her."

"What about Andrea?" she hissed.

"What about her?"

"What about her? How can you ask that, Dad? I was *twelve* when she was born! And we have the same father? How did that happen? How did the twins and Alexandra...I don't *get* it."

"I began to suspect while she was still pregnant with Andrea. And blood tests at birth confirmed it. Rainsley was briefly in China in 1996 on a political junket. I presume that's what happened."

Carrie shook her head. Trying to figure out the timeline. Julia was a freshman in high school in 1996. The year she'd struggled with an abusive, much older boyfriend. The year her mother had done nothing to help her. Carrie remembered when Julia had confronted her mother about it, years later. Winter of 2002? 2003?

"That was the year Julia…" she whispered. But she froze. Julia had accused her mother of having an affair with someone named *George Lansing*. Not Senator Rainsley. Why did she say that? It didn't make any sense. *None of this* made any sense. She *almost* interrupted and asked her fath—

She didn't know how to think of him.

Thompson leaned forward and said, "Carrie…I'm sorry. But…there's something seriously wrong with your mother psychologically. She loves you in her own way. But I don't believe she can help herself."

"I don't see how you stayed married to her," Carrie said. "She betrayed you. *Twice.*"

He sighed and shook his head. "We don't touch each other. Ever. But…you don't blame someone who has cancer, do you? She's sick. So I do what I can to take care of her." He leaned his forehead on his hand. "In truth, it's why I was so opposed to your marriage, and Alexandra's. It's not that I didn't like Ray—he was a man to be proud of. But I've spent my life married to someone who was mentally ill. I was worried about the trauma from the war—"

"Stop." Carrie said the word before she consciously thought about it.

"I'm just trying to explain—"

"Just *stop*," she said. "Don't you dare compare Ray to…all of…*that*." She couldn't say the words. Not out loud. She couldn't bear to have his name mentioned in the same breath as her mother. All her mother's lies, and spitefulness and infidelity.

Rage swept over her when she realized she was starting to cry. She stood up. "I have to go."

"Darling…"

"Stay away from me."

"Carrie, it's not my…"

"You lied to me. You lied to all of us. You've lied to me for thirty years."

She reached in her purse for a tissue and blew her nose, loud. "Seriously. I have to go. I've got a daughter to take care of."

She backed away from the table, and her father stood, taking a step around the table, closer to her. Involuntarily, she stepped away from him. His eyes narrowed, and he said, "Look, you need to calm down a little, Carrie."

"You've just told me you aren't actually my father, and you want me to calm down?"

"It appears to me that you came here expecting that answer."

"And what am I supposed to do with this information?"

"Nothing, Carrie. You keep raising your daughter. You keep doing what you've always done. Nothing changes."

She sighed. "Everything's changing. Dad…*what* happened with Andrea?"

"I told you. Your mother knows the answer to that."

"You didn't send me away. Why did you send her?"

He shook his head, muttered, "Jesus," and turned away from her. His back to her, he said, "Can you imagine what it's like *knowing* you've been betrayed? Lied to? The only thing I ever asked of Adelina was loyalty. So when I knew at birth that Andrea belonged to another man I just..." His head bowed toward the floor.

Bile flooded Carrie's throat.

"What about *me?*"

He raised an eyebrow. "You were five before I knew. We'd already...bonded."

Carrie swayed. *They'd already bonded?* In other words, if he'd known, he would have turned her away too? Sent her off to live in a foreign country with the in-laws he never saw? Abandoned her like he'd done to her sister.

"I hate you," she whispered. "I've spent my life cleaning up your and mother's messes. Loving your daughters because you couldn't. As far as I'm concerned you and mother can both go to hell."

She turned to march away from him.

He grabbed her arm. "Carrie."

"Don't *touch* me." She jerked her arm away from him.

She backed away and he stared at her, his face red with chagrin. "Carrie, please don't react this way. I'm your father."

She shook her head. "No. No, you're not."

Back out of the office, and through the anteroom, and then into the wide, confusing hallway of the Pentagon. She made it about fifty feet before one of the young soldiers from her father's office caught up with her.

"Mrs. Thompson-Sherman, let me escort you, please."

"Just Sherman, please," she replied. She'd use a name she could still be proud of.

"Yes, ma'am," the soldier said, neither understanding nor caring.

As she walked, she thought back over a million interactions with her father. He'd always been free with cash. No problem paying for college. Buying her a car. Giving her a ridiculous trust fund, with an allowance in the tens of thousands a year while she was still in college.

But he didn't touch. He didn't embrace his children, or kiss them. Especially her and Andrea. He was a father only in name, preferring the isolation of his office, the intrigue of diplomacy, the draw of politics and power. Family life evaded her father as if it were an ancient foreign language with no Rosetta stone, the complicated rituals of a mystery religion to the uninitiated.

Which left Carrie and her sisters at the mercy of Adelina Thompson. Erratic. Anxious. Vicious sometimes. Her mother was *literally* crazy, and Carrie and Julia had absorbed the worst of that crazy over the years. And their father did nothing to protect them. Nothing to help. He just…went to work. And left them to fend for themselves when the most powerful person in their lives was a disaster.

She thought about the holidays last year. What it was like to walk into Thanksgiving dinner with Ray's death still a raw, bleeding wound. The holiday dinner had been even more stilted and silent than usual, if that were even possible. Alexandra and Dylan were in Atlanta. Sarah only lasted half the meal before she had to be wheeled back to bed, her leg swollen and red from the effort of being upright for longer than thirty minutes. Carrie sat there, staring into space, mechanically going through the motions, barely noticing as her father mechanically presided over a catered meal.

He never asked her how she was doing. He flew into town from San Francisco with Jessica in tow—Jessica, grey skinned, eyes confused and lost. He should have been taking care of her, but Carrie guessed he'd not come out of his office in months except for basic functions like eating and sleeping. Jessica was on her own, and from the looks of it, she was suffering.

At the time, Carrie had no strength or bandwidth to think of it. And so she just—didn't. She moved on, didn't think about it, and didn't give a second's thought to how distant her father was.

Because that was *normal.*

Because he wasn't actually her father.

Christmas had been worse, if that was even possible. Her father had asked Jessica to say grace, because she was the youngest, by five minutes. Jessica hadn't hesitated.

Lord, thank you for this food, given to us by minimum wage caterers, Jessica had started. Mother had gasped, and Dylan started almost out of his chair. Then she continued, *Lord, we thank you for giving us this cold family, with a psychotic mother and an icebox of a father.*

The family Christmas meal came to an early end.

Of course he was an icebox. Of course. It all made sense now.

Carrie didn't realize she was crying. Maybe that's because she'd done so much crying in the last year. Maybe it was because the nerves in her face, the nerves that would normally feel the wet slide of a tear down her cheek—those nerves were dead. Numb. Too much sensation, too much grief, too much pain. But even though she couldn't *feel* it, her body responded.

The Army Sergeant who escorted her back to the main Pentagon entrance and the vast surrounding parking lots tactfully ignored the tears that streamed down her face. Others in the hallway did much the same. The Pentagon, with its thirty thousand daily inhabitants, was a small city, complete with its own police force. Like many large cities, it turned a blind eye to the pain of transients. Carrie and her tears received little more than curious looks as she finally made her way to the exit.

There, her escort broke his professionalism. He spoke in hesitant tones. "I...I hope everything's okay, ma'am."

She gave him an ungainly smile. Fuck Richard Thompson. And fuck Chuck Rainsley, her birth father who had never done a damn thing for her or her sisters. Right now, she had one focus. Getting help for her daughter. And nobody was getting in the way of that.

"Thank you, Sergeant. It's not okay now, but it will be."

2. Andrea. April 30

"**A** nd that was it. I got home as quickly as I could."

As Carrie spoke, she sat back in her cushioned chair, the one that didn't match any of the other furniture in the room, nursing Rachel. Andrea shook her head. The revelations had come hard and fast. They weren't surprises. Not really. That Richard Thompson wasn't her father. That he wasn't even related to her.

But that just raised the question.

Where the fuck was her mother?

Andrea couldn't bring herself to resent Carrie. Unlike Carrie, she'd never had any expectations that her parents loved her or cared about her. Or at least she hadn't in a long time. This revelation might be a surprise, but it wasn't devastating. It wasn't a loss. You can't lose what you never had in the first place. So on the one hand, Carrie had the love her father for a while. Whatever that was worth. But that also meant she was hurting now in a way Andrea had long since moved on from.

So she reached out, leaning toward Carrie, and put a hand on her knee.

"We need to know more," she said.

Carrie shook her head. Her eyes were wide, confused. "What else is there to know? Our parents are liars. Our *parent*. The other one is just some guy."

"For one thing, we need to know if Senator Rainsley...our father...is a donor match. Just in case I'm not."

Carrie froze. Then she took a breath, and said, "You're right. I'm going to call his office right now. Let me just put Rachel down."

Sarah, who sat across the room from them, paperback novel open in front of her, said, "Are you sure—"

"Yes," Carrie interrupted.

Rachel was asleep, latched on. Carrie shifted the baby's position, very careful, never moving her eyes from Rachel. From her daughter. Andrea watched her… watched that fierce look of love she gave her daughter. Andrea swallowed. The emotion was too powerful.

A few moments later Carrie put the baby down in her room then slowly returned to the living room.

"Shall we?" she said, then picked up her phone and dialed directory information. "Hello? Yes. Washington, DC. United States Senate…um…I'm not sure…is there a main operator? Yes, that will work."

A fifteen second wait, then Carrie spoke into the phone again. "Senator Rainsley's office, please."

Another wait, as the main switchboard transferred her to the Texas Senator's office. Then she spoke again. "Hello. Yes, this is Doctor Carrie Sherman. I'm calling to request an appointment for tomorrow afternoon with Senator Rainsley?"

Another wait. Then she said, "Yes, I'm well aware of that. You can tell his Chief of Staff that this is a personal matter, that it involves the Secretary of Defense and Adelina Thompson, and that the Senator will know *exactly* what it's about. And…please tell the Chief of Staff that if I don't have an answer by 4 pm, my next phone call will be to the press."

Damn, Andrea thought. She doesn't kid around. Of course, for Carrie this wasn't an academic exercise. It wasn't about reconnecting with their long lost father. It was about getting a blood test. It was about her daughter's health.

After another wait, this one much longer, Carrie sat up. "Hello? Yes, this is Carrie Sherman. You're the Senator's Chief of Staff? Oh…yes…no, I don't think the Senator would thank you if I were to tell you what it was about. It has to do with Adelina Thompson, my mother, and it's a potential scandal, and I think the Senator will want to hear from me, and that's all I'm going to say…" She smiled, then said, "Yes. I'll be happy to."

Another long wait. Then, Carrie was giving them her phone number.

"Do you think they'll actually call back?" Sarah asked.

"It all depends on whether or not the staffers took me seriously enough to mention it to the Senator. If they do, he'll make sure we get a meeting. I'm certain of that."

"In the meantime, I've got a lot of questions," Andrea said.

"Me too," Carrie said. "And I think the only people who can answer them are the Senator…and our mother."

"Try her again?"

"Yeah," Carrie replied. She began dialing her cell phone again. She put it on speaker, and the three of them heard the ringing…two, three, four, then five rings. Finally, their mother's voice, unusually calm. "This is Adelina Thompson. Please leave a message."

"Mother, this is Andrea, Sarah and Carrie. We're calling…because Dad told us about Senator Rainsley. And…we…just…please call."

She disconnected the phone.

"When did you talk with her last?" Andrea asked.

"A few days ago. The thing is…you know she stayed with us, after…" Carrie looked at the floor. "After the accident. And honestly, it was…so strange. Mother's never been…I don't know. Close? Touchy? She's always been distant. A little crazy."

"Not always," Sarah said.

"True. Not always. She was there for me after the accident." Carrie's voice came out rough. "Anyway…after the accident last year, she stayed here through the fall. Dad went home to San Francisco with Jessica, so she could finish her senior year of high school."

"I got to home school," Sarah said.

"Right. Screaming and bitching all the way," Carrie said. The words had sting, but the loving tone of voice smoothed out the rough edges. "Anyway… when Dad and Jessica got here for Christmas, it was obvious something was wrong. Jessica was…a mess."

Sarah leaned forward and said, "She was all strung out. Drunk, drugs, I don't know what."

"*Madre de dios,*" Andrea said. "Drugs?"

Sarah nodded, but it was Carrie who continued the story. "Yes. Mom was pissed at Dad…really pissed. It was the first time I ever heard her really launch into him. So right before New Year's, Mom came and talked to me. She said…" Carrie swallowed, hard.

Sarah continued the story. "She said something like, we were strong enough to pick up from here, and that Jessica needed her more now."

"Right," Carrie said. "And so she went back to San Francisco with Jessica. Dad moved back east a few weeks later, when the administration started talking about asking him to come out of retirement."

Andrea shrugged. This was all interesting, but it didn't really answer anything. "So where is she *now?*"

Carrie said, "I don't know. But… I'm worried.

CHAPTER FIFTEEN
Want a beer?

1. Dylan. Last fall.

In any kind of a decent world, you would only lose your best friend once.

But Dylan Paris had known for a long time that decent was a relative thing. Some days he woke up and stared at the ceiling and saw dead bodies. The bodies of his friends, the bodies of the people they killed. Because he lost two best friends. The first, Roberts, shredded by a bomb buried in dirt road. Roberts had probably lobbed a hundred thousand prayers in his lifetime, but they weren't enough to save him. Eighteen months later, when Dylan had finally healed, Ray was murdered by a fellow soldier.

Most of the time he was afraid to admit it to Alex, or even to himself. But—occasionally, in times of stress, in times of emotional upheaval, he saw other dead bodies. Of the people he *wanted* to hurt, but wouldn't. Because when Dylan Paris thought about Roberts being blown up in Afghanistan, when he thought of Kowalski's death saving a life in Dega Payan, when he thought of the closest friend he'd ever known, Ray Sherman, being run down by a fellow soldier, it filled Dylan with unspeakable rage. The kind of rage that can spontaneously combust. The kind of rage that could take a soul and twist it, turn it black and brittle, the kind of rage that could destroy a life.

The worst part was that Dylan couldn't tell anyone. He couldn't talk about it. He couldn't look his wife in the eyes and say, "Remember how I dealt with all that stuff and moved on? Just kidding." He didn't know where to turn. Once upon a time he would have turned to Ray. Ray was his sergeant, his leader, his best friend. Ray was his hero. Ray was the man who had inspired Dylan to heal.

Ray was gone.

After the funeral, Dylan moved on, because he had to. He cried in Alex's arms. But he didn't reveal the rage. He didn't tell her, because giving voice to that anger meant he might act on it. Giving voice to that anger meant he'd failed. A week after Ray's death, Dylan was back in classes at Columbia, buried in his schoolwork even as Ray had been buried under the ground. He went from class to class, physically healed from his injures in the Army, but internally isolated.

He knew other students talked about it. Even the other veterans. Sometimes he would hear whispers when he limped into class and slid into his seat in the back of the room. A buddy approached from the Milvets group on campus, and Dylan told him to leave him alone.

The hard part was, he knew his behavior and his isolation were hurting Alex. They'd only been married a couple of months when Ray was killed, and nothing had been right since. Every week she looked a little more haggard, a little more frustrated.

The third week in September, they took the train to DC, catching the 2 pm train out of Penn Station on Friday afternoon, both of them skipping their final class of the day. They leaned on each other the entire ride down. Sarah had been scheduled to go home that Friday, but a staph infection prevented that.

When asked how serious it was, Carrie didn't mince words. "It's serious. Very serious."

Dylan remembered the train ride down. Alex had been a mess of worry. Dylan stayed wrapped up tight, his arms around her but his emotions a million miles away. They'd taken this same nightmare train ride down just a few weeks prior, a trip that ended with his best friend's funeral.

"She'll be okay," he'd whispered to her, over and over again, as Alex fell apart. Inside, Dylan felt increasingly claustrophobic and angry. At one point he closed his eyes and imagined that he had somehow found Sergeant Hicks right before he pressed the gas pedal, right before he launched his jeep into a murderous downhill drive that ended with broken glass and dreams on a street in Washington, DC. He imagined that he reached over with a knife and cut Hicks's throat, the blood spattering everywhere.

Even that vision did nothing to ease his anger. It felt cold, almost clinical.

Nothing could bring Ray back. Nothing could change anything.

They spent that weekend in Washington, holding hands with Carrie, talking with Sarah, who lay desperately in an isolation room in the intensive care unit, harboring an antibiotic-resistant infection that could easily kill her.

Alex cried the whole way home, and Dylan held her. But his heart wasn't in it. At one point, she whispered into his neck, "You feel like you're a million miles away, Dylan."

Not quite a million. Kabul, Afghanistan was seven thousand miles from New York. Seven thousand miles of heartbreak. Seven thousand miles of loss.

Sarah pulled through. Dylan spent untold hours on the phone with her. After all, he'd been nearly crippled when his leg was severely injured in a bomb blast. As she began to struggle to recover and finally got out of bed, beginning physical therapy, Dylan stayed in touch on the phone almost every day. Encouraging her, because the fact was, recovery from that kind of injury was a bitter, awful process.

Finally, just before Columbus Day, Sarah went home. Not back to San Francisco, where she'd grown up, but to Carrie's condo in downtown Bethesda, Maryland.

That weekend, Dylan and Alex returned to Bethesda. They'd settled into a new equilibrium. Not distant, but not as close as they'd once been. Dylan loved Alex. He'd do anything for her, up to and including stopping a bullet if that's what it took.

But he couldn't tell her the truth. Because, by October, Dylan had a secret.

It happened almost by accident. On a Friday night at the end of September, he'd dropped in at a friend's dorm after class to go over an assignment.

"Want a beer?"

The question was casual, unintentionally deadly. Conrad Barstow had no clue Dylan had struggled with drugs as a teenager. He had no clue Dylan's dad was an alcoholic. So when he handed Dylan that beer, it was completely unexpected. Dylan popped the tab and took a long drink.

He had sighed. Relief flooded through his bones. Dylan had been subsisting on rage for weeks. The drink didn't fix that. It didn't get him drunk. But it took the edge of the rage off in a way that made Dylan close his eyes and nearly weep. "Thanks, man," he'd said.

It was that simple.

Dylan didn't run out and become a raging alcoholic. For one thing he was newly married, and he loved his wife. For Dylan, control mattered more than anything. Control over his life. Control over himself. Control over the alcohol. Because no matter what, he was never going to hurt her. He was never going to do what his father had done.

No matter what.

Alex knew something was wrong, but she didn't know what.

His mother, on the other hand, saw right through him. In November they flew to Atlanta to spend Thanksgiving with Dylan's mom. She met them just outside the security gate at Hartsfield Atlanta Airport, running forward and crying at the sight of her son. Dylan staggered under her weight as she caromed into him.

Linda Carlin was 42 years old. An active alcoholic until well into her thirties, her already greying hair and sagging skin made her look older. Her face was the contradictory tale of a gambler who was born again, a lifelong sinner who found God. In Linda's case, she hit bottom when she woke up lying beside a dumpster behind one of the city of Atlanta's many bars, her dress pushed up around her ears, sore all over her body and with no recollection of what had happened to her. Her alcoholic husband was nowhere to be found, and her twelve-year-old son was at home alone. That night she went to her first AA meeting.

Dylan only knew the barest outline of her story. But he knew that when she told others about it, her face glowed. She'd overcome the terror of that night, the shame of her drinking, the horror of its consequences. She'd learned to take care of herself, to lean on her God, and finally, in halting, difficult steps, to become the mother Dylan needed.

"Welcome home," she said to him. Then she turned to embrace her daughter in law. Alex clutched her as if she were a life preserver.

As they walked out of the terminal, Dylan lit a cigarette. His mother said, "We won't go until you finish—I finally quit, I don't really want the smoke in the car."

"You quit?" Dylan asked.

"Two months ago."

"Jesus. Congratulations, I had no idea."

She gave him a compassionate look. "You've had a lot on your mind."

What was that supposed to mean? Dylan thought. Did she somehow guess he was drinking again? He didn't know how to gauge her reactions, because he knew she was watching him very closely. Linda Carlin knew her alcohol and she knew her alcoholics. And, while Dylan never counted himself as a fullblown alcoholic like his parents, he knew it was in his blood. He knew that it wouldn't take much to push him over that edge, and he'd sworn he'd never go there.

But that didn't mean he couldn't drink at all. That didn't mean he had to completely restrict his life. Complete abstinence made sense for someone like his mom, who had completely wrecked her life. That's not who Dylan was.

So he rode in the backseat of her late 80s Ford Escort station wagon, complete with cracked dashboard, fuzzy dice on the rearview mirror and a One Day at a Time bumper sticker. Dylan stared off into space in silence as his mother drove them back to her place. Alex sat up front, making awkward conversation.

His mother and his wife couldn't have more disparity in their backgrounds. Alex came from the wealthy Thompson family. Daughter to an Ambassador. She'd lived in Belgium and China and Russia and spoke flawless French. Like all of her sisters, she'd trained on a classical instrument (the violin) from a young age and was an accomplished musician, yet she didn't judge his amateurish, self-taught guitar playing. Alex was so far out of Dylan's league that some days he was still astonished he'd won her over.

Linda Carlin—she'd gone back to her maiden name after giving Dylan's father the boot—was from a dirt-poor north Georgia family. Her father occasionally found work as a short-order cook, but usually couldn't hold a job long. Her mother was killed by a drunk driver who ran across the lane on a winding two-lane blacktop in the North Georgia mountains in 1988, Linda's junior year in high school. His mom didn't graduate high school—Jimmy Paris—the charmer with a lopsided grin, broad shoulders and too-quick fists—got her pregnant the summer before her senior year.

Despite the dramatic differences in their backgrounds, Alex and Linda got along amazingly well. They had little in common besides their love for Dylan, but that was enough to create a powerful common bond. So as they chatted on the way to her apartment in Stone Mountain, Dylan just stared out the window at the passing cars. In the front seat, Alex and his mom talked about school, about their tiny studio apartment on 102nd Street in Manhattan, and finally about the events that had rocked their lives: Ray Sherman's death.

That caught Dylan's attention, his eyes darting back up to the front of the car. He didn't say anything. Just listened. But that strategy wasn't going to work, because his mom asked him directly, "How are you holding up, Dylan?"

He shrugged. "I'm good."

"That sounds like a crock of shit to me, Dylan."

Dylan winced. Not that his language was any better. But Alex came from a much more refined background. "Mom, come on…"

"Don't you 'Mom' me, Dylan. I was worried about you before, and now even more so."

"I'm doing all right."

"You talking to your therapist?"

Christ on a crutch. He *had* been, right up until July. When Dylan had arrived in New York in the fall of 2012, he didn't kid around. Focused on healing from his injuries, he'd spent five mornings a week at the VA hospital in Manhattan. Three days for physical therapy, two for post-traumatic stress. His psychologist was a fully qualified mental health practitioner, but more important for Dylan, he was also a combat veteran with two tours in Iraq under his belt. When Dylan talked about digging entire families out of the snow, when he talked about people being blown to bits by grenades, his therapist knew *exactly* what he was talking about.

Until July, right before Sherman was killed. Then, his doctor was replaced by a twenty-three-year-old intern, Heather Katz. Heather was cute, perky, and clueless. Dylan missed two appointments, then two more, and pretty soon he was only going to his now weekly physical therapy appointments. He'd leave the apartment early in the morning, take the subway downtown, then sit on a park bench reading. It was calming and peaceful, but he didn't like that he found himself telling more and more lies to Alex.

He finally answered his mother. "Yeah, I'm talking to my therapist. It's just grief, Mom. Everybody goes through it."

"I'm worried about you," she said, eyeing him in the rearview mirror.

"Mom, leave it alone, will you?"

The rest of the awkward ride continued. Finally, they pulled up to his mom's house. A one-story, two-bedroom ranch house with brick facing on the front and 70s style wood paneling throughout the interior. The last time he and Alex had been there was mid-summer, two weeks after their wedding. His mom had done a considerable amount of landscaping in the months since, planting fall perennials.

When she parked, Dylan lagged behind and got the bags out while his mom unlocked the door. Alex hung back, leaned close, and said, "Why are you being so rude to your mom?"

His eyes widened. "What?"

"You're being mean, Dylan."

"Shit. Sorry. I'm just grumpy today."

She sighed then touched his arm. "You're always grumpy, lately."

Dylan swallowed, then said, "Sorry, sweetheart. I'll try." He turned and picked up the bags and began to carry them toward the house.

Inside, Dylan's mother's house had made progress. Growing up, he'd lived in whatever shitty apartment his parents could afford. A couple of times—when he was younger—that meant fairly nice apartment complexes. But by the time he was a preteen, they mostly lived in weekly rooms and tiny roach-infested apartments. But after six years clean, during Dylan's senior year in high school, his mother had announced a surprise. She was buying a house. It was tiny, in a depressed area well outside the city of Atlanta. But it was hers. During the months after he got out of Walter Reed and before leaving for Columbia, Dylan had stayed here. Every day she'd kept herself busy: painting, refinishing floors, and patching walls. What had been a crappy, terrible house was now a showpiece on the inside.

Along the mantelpiece were photographs. The display and the silver frames were all new, part of his mother's ongoing rehabilitation of both her living quarters and her life. Alex approached the photos eagerly when they entered the house. Dylan was a little more wary.

"This is new," Alex said, smiling.

His mom gave Alex a proud look. "I bought the frames at an estate sale for a dollar each."

"They're beautiful," Alex replied.

The frames were, indeed beautiful—silver filigreed with costume gems. The photos were something else entirely. His grandparents, before his grandmother died in the accident. His mother's older brother, crouched on the front slope of an Abrams tank in Iraq in 1991. Jay Carlin was an Army Master Sergeant now, and he'd encouraged Dylan to think about the military. The largest photo made Alex and Dylan gasp. In the center, Alex was in her white wedding dress, Dylan's arm around her waist. They were flanked by their unnaturally tall best man and maid of honor—Carrie and Ray Sherman, who had secretly married the day before. Ray looked sharp in his dress blues.

Dylan felt his eyes go wet, and he sniffed.

"I love that picture." Alex slid a hand up his arm.

"I miss him," Dylan whispered.

"Me too," she replied.

He tried to shake it off. "Come on," he said. "Let's get this stuff put away."

When Dylan awoke on Thanksgiving morning, he was disoriented. His neck hurt and his back was sore, and he was curled up on his side on the edge of a none-too-comfortable mattress in his mother's house.

In the kitchen, his mother bustled about, preparing a Thanksgiving meal as she and Alex talked. Dylan could easily hear them from the room—his mother's house was tiny, after all. So he lay there on the bed, his eyes closed. He wanted a cigarette and a cup of coffee, as soon as possible. But for the moment, he lay on his side listening.

They were talking about *him.*

"I don't know," Alex said. "He's been through an awful lot."

"Dylan's stronger than you may think," his mother said. "Even before he went into the Army, he'd lived more than a lot of adults twice his age."

"I know. But the one person who doesn't believe in him is himself. Ray used to be able to shake him out of his moods. But I don't know how to."

He heard his mother sigh. "It's a tough road. He loved Ray."

"I loved him too," Alex replied. "But I'm not dropping out of life. I'm worried about him, Linda."

His mother said something, he couldn't tell what, and Alex replied, "I don't know how to help him."

Fuck.

He rolled out of bed and threw clothes on. He didn't care what. He needed to get a cigarette and a cup of coffee. He stumbled out of the room, and both of them went quiet. Alex looked guilty. He murmured, "Morning," as he walked by, then poured himself a cup of coffee. In silence, he prepared his coffee with his back to Alex and his mom, then went and sat outside on the porch.

He lit a cigarette and stared up at the sky, grateful that it wasn't gray or raining.

Four hours later the first guest arrived—his mother's sponsor in AA. Mary Lou Sorensen was a conservatively dressed sixty-five-year-old woman, so tiny and frail Dylan was afraid a stiff breeze might carry her away. As Mary Lou got out of her car and headed slowly up the walk, she teetered a little on her heels. She wore a red and white suit, with a long string of pearls around her neck and bracelets at her wrist. Her hair was teased and poufed in a style that was probably popular in the decade before Dylan was born.

"Is that little Dylan? Well, I'll be...I haven't seen you since you was in high school."

"Hey, Mary Lou, happy Thanksgiving."

As she approached, he saw the signs of age. More wrinkles underneath the makeup around her eyes, her hair now fully grey. Dylan took her arm and led her toward the house.

"How is Columbia, Dylan?"

"It's going well," he said. "I love the classes. How about you? You still teaching at the pen?"

"I am," she replied, smiling. Mary Lou spent most of the 1970s as an *inmate* in the Atlanta Women's Prison, following her 1972 conviction for murder. While there, she'd gotten sober, found God, and begun a new life. Now she went back to the Metro State Prison, a women's maximum security prison, three times a week to lead AA meetings and teach classes.

Dylan opened the door and led her in. Alex met them as she came out of the kitchen.

"Alex, this is Miss Mary Lou. May Lou, this is my wife, Alexandra."

"Oh, Lordy," Mary Lou said, her face flushing red. "I'm so excited to meet you, Alexandra. What a beautiful name."

"I mostly just go by Alex."

"Some names shouldn't be shortened," Mary Lou replied. "And yours is one of them. That's a name that says royalty. I love it. Come sit and talk to me, dear."

Just like that, Mary Lou had Alex by the arm and was leading her off to the living room. Dylan chuckled a little as he walked into the kitchen.

His mother was still bustling around.

"Hey, Mom, Mary Lou is here."

His mother said, "Oh, can you keep her company—"

"Don't worry." He cut her off. "She and Alex are chatting."

His mother smiled. "Well, then, that's good. Maybe you and I could talk for a minute then?"

She didn't wait for an answer. Instead, she turned back into the kitchen, expecting him to follow.

He did, of course, automatically reaching to help as she stooped to pull a huge turkey out of the oven.

His mother didn't pussyfoot around. "Your wife is worried about you, Dylan. So am I."

Shit, he thought. "Mom, you gotta give it a rest—"

"No. Listen to me. I know you've had a rough couple of years. I know it's been much harder than you ever expected. You just have to stop trying to do it all on your own. You've got a lovely woman there who wants to help you."

"Ma, I'm all right—"

"You're drinking again, aren't you?"

He froze. She nodded her head. "I thought so. How much?"

"Not much. Just every once in a while. Mom, I'm not like you and Dad, I don't fall apart every time I have a drink, okay? That was your issue, not mine."

She shook her head. "You're fooling yourself. You're not out drinking at parties or social occasions."

"No, just one every once in a while to take the edge off."

"If you're drinking to *take the edge off,* you're going to turn into a drunk, Dylan. That's the way it works."

He shook his head. "Not everybody's like you, Mom."

"No. But you are. You're my son, and I'm worried about you. You haven't told her, have you?"

"No," he replied. "And I don't want you to. I'll talk to her when it's time."

"Oh, Dylan. I can't promise you that. It's not just about you."

"I don't know what that's supposed to mean."

She shook her head. "She's your wife. You need to talk with her. You need to ask her for help."

Dylan stared at his mother. "Are you seriously going to do this? You ruined my entire childhood, and now you're going to ruin my marriage?"

His mother gave him a long, sad look. "Dylan, you're making your own choices. You need to get help."

2. Alexandra. Last fall.

A**lexandra** Thompson was probably the least experienced and least cynical of the Thompson sisters. But that didn't make her an idiot. She'd been through heartache. She'd been through sexual assault. Step by step, she'd helped the man she loved rebuild his life. And then she'd gone through the heartache of seeing Dylan's best friend, her sister's husband, killed.

What Alexandra learned in the weeks following Ray's death were lessons she wished she'd never had to think about. She'd never minimize or underestimate the incredible pain Carrie went through with the loss of her husband. The two of them had been passionate lovers, and Ray's loss was a staggering blow to Carrie.

But Alexandra also saw what it did to Dylan. Because he had walked into that hospital room last August to say goodbye, and he shambled out a dead man. Cold. Isolated. His eyes a thousand miles away. He didn't speak. He didn't cry. He walked to the waiting room chairs and slumped into his seat, staring straight ahead, eyes unfocused. He broke Alexandra's heart, because she knew right then that the grief he felt was going to take a long time to deal with. She knew right then that Dylan Paris wasn't going to be healed in an hour or a day or a week or a year—this was going to be a lifetime effort.

She struggled the first few days. In the past, faced with such an emotional gut punch, she would have instinctively called her big sister Carrie. Carrie, who had taken care of all of them. Carrie, who'd been a shoulder for Julia to cry on, a protective shield for Alexandra and the younger girls. Carrie, who had been stripped of everything that mattered. She *couldn't* go to Carrie and burden her with even more problems, especially problems rooted in the same loss she'd suffered. One night she found herself picking up her phone not long after dinner. She dialed Julia without really paying attention.

Julia had just left a lunch meeting in Canberra. Alexandra didn't kid around, quickly briefing her.

"Do you think he's drinking again?" Julia had asked.

The question haunted Alexandra. Less because of any inherent concern about alcohol—she'd never known or had to live with a practicing alcoholic—but more because of the implication that Dylan might be keeping secrets from her. Because if he was hiding that from her, then she had no idea what he might be doing.

So she kept an eye out. She paid attention. When he came home late from class, she watched him. She surreptitiously smelled his breath, and sometimes her eyes fell on a receipt in the trash that she wouldn't have noticed or paid any attention to. Without being consciously aware of it, she'd slipped into the role of the suspicious or concerned wife. And she hated that. She hated even the idea of that role. For her entire life she'd seen her mother and father manipulate each other to the point where it was impossible to know what was truth and what was a lie.

Sometimes, even though she loved Dylan with all her heart, she asked herself if she'd really screwed up by marrying someone with an admitted drinking problem, someone with post-traumatic stress, someone who was the child of alcoholics. She loved Dylan. But sometimes, when he was sitting and looking out the window a million miles away from her, she was scared of him.

The one thing she never did was ask him directly if he was drinking. She wanted him to come clean on his own. She wanted him to ask for help. She wanted him to finally do what he needed to take care of himself and of her. So she didn't put him in a position where he'd lie. And, at this point, she knew if she pressed him on it, he would lie to her.

So they went to Atlanta for Thanksgiving to see his mother, and she let things slide. One night in early December he stumbled home. Not drunk, but not sober either. And his breath smelled of fresh mouthwash.

She let it go. She held him, even when he pushed away. She loved him.

But it was hard.

On December 23rd they took the train from Penn Station to Washington, DC for their third trip to the city after Ray's death. This time they'd be crowded in—the entire Thompson clan would be in town, with the exception of Andrea.

"Why isn't Andrea coming?" she'd asked Julia.

Julia just sighed. "I tried to persuade her. But can you blame her? She doesn't believe Mom and Dad want her."

Alexandra had difficulty fathoming that. She knew her father was cold and her mother difficult, but so were a million other parents. She never quite understood the level of drama Julia brought to the table when it came to their mother, even though she did remember some horrible confrontations between the two when she was younger. *Of course* Mom and Dad wanted Andrea.

Except...did they?

One day in the summer of 2002 Carrie had sat down with her. They'd taken the trolley to the waterfront and walked along the beach next to the Hyde Street Pier, both of them licking ice cream.

You know I'm leaving for college in a few weeks, Carrie had said.

Of course I do, Alexandra replied.

"I've always kind of tried to be...sort of a big sister to you and the twins and Andrea. Almost like a mom when I could. You know, for when Mom's all crazy."

Alexandra shrugged.

"The thing is," Carrie said. "Me and Julia, we made a pact. That we'd always watch out for you guys. That we'd always watch out for each other. Sisters."

The words were intense, dripping with heavy meaning that Alexandra didn't completely get. Finally she said, "What about Mom?"

"She's...not always the best mom she could be. You know? I'm just saying... with me gone...it's up to you, Alexandra. To watch out for the twins and Andrea. Just to make sure they're okay, you know?"

Alexandra nodded. "Of course, I'll watch out for them."

Carrie had stopped and looked her in the eye.

"Promise me," she said.

"I promise."

The thing was, you can't keep promises like that. You can try, you can do everything you can, but Alexandra was only thirteen years old when Carrie left for college.

Thirteen year olds can try to keep promises, but they can't keep their younger sisters from being sent away.

She did everything she could. But in the end, it wasn't enough. Andrea *did* go away, first for a few weeks, then a summer, then eventually for the school year. By the time she was a pre-teen, Andrea only came home for the holidays.

This year, not even that.

Nobody said anything to her. Julia and Carrie didn't look her in the eye and say, *You failed her.* They didn't say out loud that they blamed her for not protecting Andrea. But she knew. She'd heard about their promise to each other, to the family, for years. That's *all* she'd heard about was their sacred fucking promise.

The promise she couldn't keep. Julia and Carrie had cared for each other, and they'd cared for her. But Alexandra couldn't manage to watch out for her sisters. She'd left behind a rebellious punk rocker, a pill popping preppie and the sister who went away and wouldn't even return her phone calls.

Alex's legacy was failure, but she didn't intend to keep it that way. She wasn't going to fail Dylan. No matter what.

So she kept him close. She talked to him every day. She *tried*.

When they arrived in Bethesda for Christmas, the family was already in an uproar. Dylan followed Alex into the condo, where they immediately heard Adelina's voice from a back room. She was shouting. Alex gave Dylan a worried look as they walked in. The first person they saw was Sarah, sitting in her wheelchair near the couch, a book open in front of her. She looked up at them over the top of the book. Her face was shiny with sweat.

"Hey, Alexandra," Sarah had said.

"Sarah!" Alex rushed over to Sarah, who said she was fine, just running a bit of a fever.

The next four days were chaos. Jessica spent the bulk of her time in her room, because every appearance resulted in another outburst of argument between Richard and Adelina.

"You were supposed to be taking care of our daughter!" Adelina would shout.

"I'm fine, Mom!" Jessica replied.

"Have you seen her report card?" Adelina called out.

Richard, as always, retreated. He hadn't regularly occupied the office in the Bethesda condo in more than ten years—it was Carrie's office now—but that didn't stop him from disappearing into the office and locking the door behind him.

The sisters were torn on how to react. Julia was staying with Crank at the Hyatt Regency a block away. She said, "Mom's making a crisis out of nothing, as always."

Carrie was more reserved. "I'm concerned. Dad probably stayed locked in his office the entire fall. God only knows what Jessica's been up to."

Alexandra, who had done more than her share of drinking in college, backed her mother.

Sarah, fighting another infection, mostly stayed in bed or parked in her wheelchair near the couch, glassy eyed from painkillers.

It was an incredibly uncomfortable, tense couple of days. Dylan spent a fair amount of it standing out on the balcony, freezing his ass off, smoking.

This time, he didn't have Crank to keep him company. "Trying to quit, man," Crank said. "I'm not getting any younger."

Dylan gave Crank a wry look. "You're not exactly an old man yet. What are you, thirty?"

"Thirty-three. But that's not the point. Point is, you gotta grow up some time."

"Yeah," Dylan said. "True enough."

The fussing and yelling between Adelina, Richard and Jessica continued right up until the morning after Christmas. It was a little after 11:30 in the morning, and all of the sisters (except Andrea) were seated around the table with their parents, Crank and Dylan. The family only rarely used the formal dining room in the condo, but with this many people, they were seated around the large table. Platters were piled high with bacon and eggs, pancakes and French toast, all of it carefully laid out by caterers from the Hyatt.

"You're staying in Washington," Adelina announced just after breakfast, glowering at Richard. "I will return to San Francisco with Jessica."

He raised his eyebrows, then took his napkin from his lap, carefully wiped his mouth, and tossed the napkin on the table.

"I think that's a good idea," he said. "It appears I need to move back to Washington, anyway, I've been asked by the President to come out of retirement."

With that, he stood and walked out of the room, leaving a stunned silence in his wake.

CHAPTER SIXTEEN
It started in the womb

1. Jessica. April 30

Jessica Thompson leaned against the wall, her eyes drooping, shivering a little.

"Do you need a break?" The question came from Sister Kiara Langley, her therapist. Sister Kiara was a web of contradictions. An African-American from Los Angeles. A Roman Catholic nun with a PhD in psychology. For the last ten days, she'd been in Jessica's room three times a day to probe and ask questions. Questions Jessica wasn't prepared to answer.

For the first several days she'd said as little as possible. A few times she screamed until Kiara left. But by the end of the fifth day, she felt nothing but exhaustion. Her skin and her soul were numb. Everything was numb.

"No," Jessica said. "I'm just…still tired. So tired." She closed her eyes.

"Jessica, I need you to stay awake for a while. I told you, you're going to feel tired for quite a while, and probably depressed. It's a common side effect."

"Yeah, I know," Jessica said. Depressed was an understatement. She couldn't laugh. She just felt dead inside. The night before, a dozen or so of the residents of the retreat had gathered to watch a movie: a romantic comedy. Her mother had laughed, a lot. So had a lot of the others there. But Jessica just sat there, staring. It wasn't funny.

"Why couldn't I laugh?" she asked.

Kiara said, "Well, it's complicated. You know what dopamine is? In your brain? Basically, that's what gives you pleasure. The meth makes it so you can't produce as much of it. And on top of having less of it, the dopamine receptors are…basically burned. There's less of them functioning. And it's going to be a long, long time before those function normally again."

"And in the meantime?"

"In the meantime you stay clean. When you go home, you'll be in therapy. You'll go to a long-term treatment program. But it's mostly up to you. You're eighteen years old. I can't keep you here, and your mother can't keep you here. It's up to you now."

Jessica didn't want it to be up to her. She wanted to just curl up and let someone else take care of her.

"I want to stay clean," Jessica said.

"So what do you need to do, Jessica?"

She nodded, slowly. "Talk."

"Right."

She crossed her arms across her chest. "Can we turn up the heat in here? It's freezing."

"Sure," Sister Kiara said. The nun walked to the door and adjusted the thermostat, then returned to her seat. "Tell me a little about when all this started."

"The meth? Or the other stuff."

"All of it."

Jessica took a deep breath. "It started in the womb, really. My twin got all the personality and smarts and…everything, really."

"What's her name?"

"Sarah. She won't tell you, but Sarah means *Princess*, and that's just what she is. She likes to dress all shocking—combat boots and black clothes and makeup, but even when we were little girls, it was always Sarah who had the attention. Sarah made friends. Sarah smiled, and—she had it all."

Jessica shook her head. "Don't get me wrong. I'm not blaming her for all of this. That was just the way it was. Sarah smiled and everyone came running. Sarah got in trouble, said something funny, and everyone laughed. For me it was just—always a little harder. I stayed quiet and in the background and just…did my thing."

Sister Kiara smiled at her and said, "How did that make you feel?"

Jessica looked away. Then she turned back to Kiara and said, "Sometimes I felt really alone. My oldest sisters were all gone. I used to get along great with Andrea—she's my youngest sister—but she moved away to Spain to live with our grandmother. I did make some friends at school, and…I dated a girl for a while. But she broke up with me."

Jessica looked away again. Up until now, Kiara had mostly just asked questions, but she was certain the admission that she was attracted to girls would prompt condemnation from her. After all, Kiara may have a PhD, she might have been dressed in jeans and a button down shirt, but she was a nun.

Kiara, though, only said, "Talk to me about your relationship with your sisters."

She rolled her eyes. "I have almost no relationship with my sisters. I'm the good one. The quiet one. Besides, can you even *imagine* the pressure I'm under?

Julia went to Harvard and runs a multi-million dollar business she built herself. Carrie went to Columbia and Rice and is a scientist at the NIH for Chrissake. Even Alexandra, she's at Columbia in pre-law and had *perfect* grades and the *perfect* boyfriend and then the *perfect* wedding. Everything's so *perfect* for all of them I could just puke."

Sister Kiara leaned back in her seat and murmured, "Now we're getting somewhere. Do you really feel like their lives are perfect?"

"No," Jessica replied in an empty voice. "Carrie's a widow. She just had a baby."

Kiara looked startled. Somehow her briefings from Jessica's mother hadn't included this bit of information. "Tell me more."

Jessica said, "Car accident last summer. I was in the car too. Sarah was hurt really bad, and Ray—that's Carrie's husband—was killed."

"Drunk driver?"

"No. Murder. Or...murder-suicide, I guess."

"I see," Kiara said, her eyes wide. "Were you hurt?"

"Just some glass fragments. Scratches."

"So what is home life like now? Is Sarah in school? Do you two get in much conflict since the accident?"

Jessica shook her head. "I don't really see her. She stayed with Carrie and my mom in Washington after the accident. I came home with Dad."

Sister Kiara looked troubled. "Are you and your father close?"

Jessica snorted. "Are you kidding me?"

2. Adelina. April 30

The dream always started the same.

It was 1981. She was in what should have been her normal seat, violin at her chin, eyes fixed on Antoni Ros-Marba, principal conductor of the Or-questa Nacional de Espana in Madrid. Eyebrows arched over his rounded glasses, his hair swept back on his head, he held his conductor's baton high in the air. A broad smile on his face as his eyes met her. She knew that he knew she had talent that would one day land her in the first chair. They all did. She held her breath, and the audience stirred in anticipation.

Ros-Marba's arms fell, signaling the music to begin, but she froze. Her stomach twisted in pain. Richard was there, in the audience. Thirty-one years old to her sixteen. Handsome. His dark hair fell down over his forehead, his lips curled up in a cruel grin. He stood, but no one else in the audience noticed as he made his way down the aisle. She couldn't breathe. She couldn't think. Richard reached Ros-Marba and shoved him out of the way effortlessly, and the other members of the orchestra turned away.

Adelina dropped her precious violin. The instrument cracked, fragments of wood flying everywhere. Her right hand uncurled and the bow fell to the floor with a crash.

Richard finally reached her. Almost gently, he reached out a hand and wrapped it around her throat.

"What are you doing up here, Adelina? You know better."

The room was dark and smelled of ammonia and sweat. In the first row of the audience, her mother and brothers slowly turned their backs.

She woke up choking.

A blanket was stuffed in her mouth, balled up in her fist, keeping the pain inside, where it belonged. She lay on her side, curled up, knees drawn up to her chest, the chest pains familiar. She slowly pulled the blanket away from her mouth, once she was sure the accumulated regret and terror wouldn't force its way out in the form of sound.

She was drenched in sweat. It was nearly six o'clock, and the day wasn't going to get started on its own. Out of habit, she rolled over and picked up her phone. No messages. No signal still. Ironic, she thought. For years she'd done everything she could to make sure she was never out of cell phone range. Checking for messages, checking for *that* phone call, was second nature. But when she'd arrived at Saint Mary's ten days ago with Jessica, she'd noticed there was no signal and just shrugged it off. It had been sixteen years. If the call was going to come, it would come. Jessica came first. Richard had the number for the retreat center if there was an emergency.

Not that her children wanted her around anyway.

She slid out of the bed and padded her way to the shower. The rooms here were simple, but more than adequate for her needs. This retreat had been to save her daughter. But she was beginning to wonder if—just maybe—there was hope for her too.

The dreams had been troubling her increasingly in the last few months. Except for a few days at Thanksgiving and Christmas, she'd not slept in the same bed—or even the same city—as Richard. Not since last August. She would have thought the nightmares would get better. She would have thought the anxiety would get better. But it hadn't. In fact, it had been worse, sometimes so bad that she lay paralyzed in bed, unable to function at all.

It didn't make any sense. It was like she was a prisoner, just out of jail, just looking for an opportunity to go back. To go back to safety. To go back behind locked doors.

Ironic, because for thirty years she'd believed that when her children were grown, she was going to leave him at the first opportunity. Instead, her reprieve would soon be over. Jessica would graduate from high school in June (probably) and she would no longer have a legitimate excuse to avoid her husband. She would go back to Washington, the city she hated most of any in the world, and smile and be the diplomatic wife to the new Secretary of Defense and one day she would give up, walk into her bathroom and bleed out because there was no longer any point.

But for now, at least, Jessica needed her. This was their last day at Saint Mary's Retreat. The retreat center was situated on the edge of the Sequoia National Forest, and had provided the most peaceful ten days Adelina had experienced since her childhood. She didn't want to leave.

The days had a structure here. Each morning she awoke and joined one of the three meals served in the common area, sitting next to Jessica, her sullen, resentful daughter. The first three days Jessica didn't eat at all, but since then, she'd begun to astonish everyone in the center, putting away two or three meals at a sitting and sleeping almost all the rest of the time. She'd gained weight, a lot of it, in the last few days. It wasn't enough—even after the weight gain, she was only approaching 90 pounds, and looked dangerously unhealthy.

Their next stop, had this not worked, would have been a psychiatric institution.

After the morning meal, Jessica typically slept most of the morning, then met with Sister Kiara, the no-nonsense nun and therapist who had so impressed Adelina.

Adelina herself walked every morning on the well-marked path through the forest. The sequoias were staggering in their beauty. She found herself stopping for long periods of time. Sometimes to sit. Sometimes to pray. Sometimes to weep. For years she'd held herself aloof, but here, it was impossible to deny the immensity of God. Here, she felt Him just in reach, in the deep shade below the trees, in the glades and the deep foliage, in the flowers that unfolded in the windows of sunlight that shone down to the forest floor.

After her walks, she often returned to the retreat center in a state of tears. Nobody commented on it, except for Jessica. On the third day of her withdrawals, she'd seen her mother crying, and said, "What the fuck is wrong with *you*?"

In the afternoons, she met with Father Ross, one of the spiritual directors.

Ross generally dressed casually in blue jeans and thick flannel shirts, except on the days he performed Mass. All the same, he challenged Adelina.

"Everybody gets forgiveness, Adelina. Even you. That's what grace is."

She just shook her head. They argued. He gave her verses in scripture to read. Some of them helped. Some of them decidedly didn't. But all of them made her think. All of them made her question. She was deeply concerned with both the spiritual and the temporal questions. She couldn't solve the temporal ones...not today, anyway. But her soul, and the souls of her children...that was something else.

But she knew she didn't rate forgiveness.

"Jesus didn't talk about grace," she said.

Ross sighed when she said things like that. "He talked about forgiveness, Adelina."

"He talked about law. He said adultery was forbidden. That even *thinking* about adultery was forbidden. He said that *wanting* to murder was the same as murder. "

"You haven't committed murder, Adelina."

But she wanted to.

Ross took her hands. "Adelina, listen to me. We are all sinners. But you, me, all of us, can be forgiven."

She knew better. But she still prayed.

Her discussions with Father Ross were challenging on a host of levels. Intellectually and spiritually. It was apparent that he genuinely cared about her welfare. It was equally evident that he was hopelessly naive and didn't have the first clue what she was talking about. He lived in a retreat center amidst the sequoias, where God was apparent right outside his front door. She didn't get to live in that world. She lived in a world where charming diplomats turned out to be liars. She lived in a world defined by anxiety and fear. She'd lived in that world for thirty-three years.

Thirty-three years she'd protected her daughters from that bastard. Thirty-three years she'd suffered, alone.

For Adelina Thompson, it was time to leave that world. No matter what it took.

CHAPTER SEVENTEEN
It seems I found one

1. Adelina. February 23, 1981

Adelina Ramos felt her cheeks heat up. The American diplomat, Richard Thompson, had stopped in the shop for the third time in a week. He wore a dark double breasted pinstriped suit with a narrow black tie, and his hair, too long for Spanish tastes, was swept back on his forehead. He had a broad face, blue eyes and a strong chin. She guessed he was somewhere in his late twenties, and by the look of the suit, he was quite rich. Whenever he was there, she stammered and acted like a fool.

Adelina wore an ankle-length white linen dress with embroidered flowers, hand sewn by her grandmother.

The previous week, he'd come into her father's flower shop, three blocks from the *El Palacio del Congreso de los Diputados,* the lower house of the Spanish parliament. He'd come in to place an order of flowers. Dozens of flowers in multiple arrangements to be delivered to the US Embassy, then on from there to the *Cortes.*

Her father, Manuel Ramos, a dour and serious man, took the order. Always polite, but never charming, her father made halting conversation with the diplomat. Richard Thompson, from San Francisco, California. Thompson had a ready smile, startling blue eyes and charming manners.

Three days later Thompson was back to take the initial delivery. This time he wore jeans and a plain black t-shirt, which highlighted a lean but muscular frame. Her father, unfortunately, was out at the time, leaving Adelina to mind the store. She helped him load the flowers into the back of a boxy looking yellow SEAT Bocenegra. The back seat was folded down, so there was just room for the flowers.

"What sort of function are the flowers for, Señor?" she had asked. In Spanish. Most of their rare American customers spoke no Spanish, but Thompson spoke functional, if not perfect Spanish.

"We plan to deliver them to your *Cortes* as a goodwill gesture," he replied.

A week passed after his second visit before he returned again.

"Señorita Ramos," Thompson said when he stepped into the shop.

"Señor Thompson," she replied. "Can I help you with something?"

He smiled, a crooked, wolfish grin. "I came here looking for a flower. It seems I found one."

Her eyes dived for the floor. "You're too kind, Señor."

"Señorita Ramos. In all seriousness, I'm here to see you. I have tickets to the theater for Friday evening. I would be grateful if you would attend with me."

She shifted uncomfortably. "Sir, I'm sixteen."

His eyes widened. "I hadn't realized, Señorita."

Her tone prim, she said, "Even if I wasn't, I have an audition for the National Orchestra on Friday. I'm sure I'll be too busy for you."

"Well, then. Another time."

With that, he whisked out of the shop, and at that moment, she assumed out of her life.

Forty minutes later, the phone rang. She knew who it was. At fifteen minutes before six, it could only be her father, calling to tell her to lock up at six o'clock. That happened once or twice a week, usually when he got caught up having one too many glasses of fino with his friends and cousins.

It was fine. She'd grown used to it. Every day she went directly from school to the shop, where she would do homework at the counter until closing time, often while eating a snack. Her father worked hard. Born the Marquis of Cerverales, he'd lost everything during the Franco dictatorship because of his support of the leftists. He started over in the early 1970s with nothing but a flower cart, but by the time Franco was gone and King Juan Carlos began to implement democratic reforms, he'd built a new life.

He'd lost his title—and nearly his life—but her father still had his bragging rights. He often drank too much at the cafe down the street from the *Cortez*, where he talked of old political battles long since won and lost. During the spring, summer and fall, the cafe spilled out onto the sidewalk. Since November, though, it had been buttoned up tight. It pained Adelina to see her father when he was lost in nostalgia. But she also felt pride for him. Her parents were separated—her mother had returned to live in Calella with two-year-old Luis—but her mother still taught her to take pride in her father.

In the year since her parents had separated, Adelina had stayed with her father. Divorce, though technically legal in Spain for the first time as of that year, was still largely unheard of.

Adelina was in her second year playing violin for the National Youth Orchestra, and her father spent a substantial portion of his meager earnings on her continued lessons. Her hours sitting behind the counter—often with little business—were all she could offer in return.

At five minutes after six she locked the door and rolled the steel shutters down over the front door, then tightened her scarf and tugged on tight leather gloves to ward off the icy wind. It was dark already, and she felt a shiver as she slid the padlock in place to secure the shutters.

She stepped back, startled, as a large truck barreled the wrong way up Calle los Madrazo. The truck spit out black smoke, and she saw soldiers sitting in the truck as it sped away.

Adelina turned in the other direction to head home, just in time to see Richard Thompson approaching. She let out a startled gasp, suddenly very aware of the fact that most of the shops were closed and it was dark and very cold.

"Señorita," he called out. Commanded.

She tucked her head down and began to walk, her shoes clicking on the sidewalk. He followed. "Señorita," he said, his voice louder.

"Please leave me alone." Adelina's voice shook as she said the words. Then she staggered at the sound of a loud explosion.

Thompson stopped in his tracks. Another truck had pulled up to the end of the street, and soldiers poured out of it. They had their weapons at the ready and one of them shouted.

That's when she heard the cracking, high-pitched sound of a machine gun. One, two, a dozen shots, then more. Adelina screamed and backed against the side of the lane as soldiers ran up the street.

Thompson backed up against the wall next to her.

"Señorita, we must get under cover. I'm afraid it's Basque terrorists. Or a coup."

More shots. A lot of them.

Her eyes rolled as she desperately sought an avenue of escape. "Come! Now!" Thompson shouted. He reached out and grabbed her gloved hand. Even though the shots were in the distance, the proximity of the shouting soldiers and the gunshots terrified her. She gripped Thompson's hand harder and ran behind him.

He came to a stop in front of her father's shop. "Unlock it," he ordered. His voice was unnaturally calm, as if he were used to hearing gunfire. "We'll stay in there until the trouble has cleared."

Her hands shook so hard she dropped her keys. He grabbed them and unlocked the padlock, slid the shutters up only halfway, then pulled her inside.

1. Julia. April 30. 1:15 PM Pacific.

Julia Wilson felt disoriented as the driver took the exit off I-105 onto Crenshaw Boulevard. Hawthorne Municipal Airport was a single-runway public airport south of Los Angeles. Julia had called ahead to ensure their charter was ready to fly, including the extra passengers.

Flying a charter aircraft could be expensive. But as often as they traveled during the touring season, it actually worked out cheaper to charter a plane for three or six months out of the year. Operating expenses worked out to about a thousand dollars for every hour they were in the air, but that was *still* cheaper than other forms of travel for a dozen or more people at a time. Several years before Julia had run the numbers on buying a private aircraft and just hiring a full time crew, but the charters worked out to be a lot cheaper.

Her confusion was due to what her sister Carrie had just told her on the phone. "I can't believe that," she said.

"I know," Carrie replied. "He's been lying our entire lives. *They've* been lying our entire lives."

"It doesn't make any sense," Julia said. "It wasn't even Senator Rainsley she had the affair with. It was George Lansing." Her eyes darted to Crank, sitting next to her, and Anthony, who sat in the front passenger seat. Anthony's eyes were wide.

She mouthed, "That is *off* the record. Mouth. Shut."

Anthony mimed turning a key at his mouth.

"I remember you telling me about that...who was George Lansing?"

Julia shrugged. "I didn't really know him exactly—he worked in consular affairs. I just remember Mom spending a lot of time with him in the fall of '96. I stayed as far away as I could. I was busy with school and all that stuff too, I don't really remember that much."

"But Mom told you for sure about him?" Carrie sounded almost desperate.

"Not exactly. No. Now that I think about it, *she* never said she had an affair with him. But she didn't argue when I accused her, either."

"Whatever," Carrie said. "I can't believe she was such a fucking liar."

Julia sighed. "Listen, let me call you back. We're just getting to the airport."

"All right. If she's home...just...I..." Carrie trailed off. Somehow her inarticulateness captured how they both felt.

Julia hung up the phone.

"Everything kosher?" Crank asked.

She nodded. "Yeah, just...you're...wow."

Crank's eyes widened. "Jesus, baby, what's wrong?"

"I'm *fine.*"

"Babe…"

Julia let out a loud groan. "All right, fine. But he has to swear this is all off the record."

Anthony, in the front seat, said, "Of course."

The car came to a stop. Julia huffed and had the door open before the driver could put it in park. Within seconds she was marching across the tarmac, with Anthony and Crank trying to keep up. The jet, operated by a Boston-based charter company, sat on the runway, engines already warming up.

She led the way up the stairs, both of the men following behind her.

Inside the plane, the pilot said, "Ma'am. We're just about ready, once your baggage is stowed."

"Thank you," Julia responded.

The pilot disappeared back into the cockpit. Julia took a seat in one of the luxurious leather chairs. As Crank and Anthony got themselves situated, the flight attendant offered drinks. Julia promptly ordered a vodka tonic.

As the attendant turned away, Julia said, "Make it a double, please."

Crank's mouth dropped open. "All right, Julia. Spill. If he can't hear it, I'll kick him off the plane."

Anthony held his hands up, palms facing her. "With God as my witness. Whatever you tell me is off the record."

Julia rolled her eyes. Then she said, "Fuck it. I don't need to protect him. Turns out, Carrie and Andrea have a different father than the rest of us."

"Wait…what?" Crank said.

Anthony's eyes widened. "You know I suspected as much when I saw the pictures from the wedding last summer. The two of them stand out, a lot."

Julia leaned her head forward. "And *where* did you see the wedding pictures?"

He shrugged. "It's my job to research things. A friend of your sister—"

"Which sister?"

He shook his head. "Alexandra."

"You've been working on this for a while, haven't you? This is all some bullshit smokescreen."

"Yes, and no."

The pilot interrupted, speaking over the cabin speakers. "Flight attendants, please prepare the cabin for takeoff."

"Explain yourself," Julia said.

Anthony sighed. "I followed the court-martial last summer with a great deal of interest. War crimes interest me. Plus, I thought it was an interesting coincidence that it took place in the same province as Wakhan."

"I don't know what that is. Wakhan?"

"Ancient history. Soviet war crimes. Some awful stuff went down in Afghanistan in the early 80s."

Julia shook her head. "That makes no sense…what does it have to do with us?"

"Nothing," Anthony said. "Point is…yeah I'm interested in the foreign policy angle. I'm interested in your history, and your dad's history. Who wouldn't be?"

"Well. I can't give you permission to write about this. You'll have to talk with Carrie about it first, because it affects her first."

"All right," he said.

"Jesus," Crank said. "Whatever. He agreed to keep it under wraps. What the fuck? Who is their dad?"

"Senator Chuck Rainsley."

Anthony pursed his lips. "Senator Rainsley?"

Julia nodded. "That's what Dad reports."

"Jesus Christ," Crank said. "I can't fucking believe it."

"I believe it," Julia said. "You know my mom's fucking crazy."

Crank shrugged. "Well, yeah, but…that's a big deal. And there were three daughters in between. Who does that?"

Julia rolled her eyes. "My mother, obviously."

Anthony said, "Tell me about your mother."

2. Adelina. February 23, 1981

The battery powered radio crackled with confused and conflicting announcements. The new Prime Minister, Leopoldo Sotelo, was dead, murdered by the revolutionaries. No, he wasn't dead, he was held prisoner. The members of the lower house of Parliament were all dead. No, they were held prisoner. The rebels were led by Basque terrorists. Or the Guardia Civil. King Juan Carlos had been killed. Or he was allied with the rebels. The leader of the rebels was Lieutenant Colonel Antonio Tejero, who had already served prison time for involvement in an attempted coup in 1978. None of it made any sense to Adelina. She knew politics from listening to her father—that was unavoidable. But the seizure of Parliament by the Army? It was frightening. What would come of her family? Her father? For that matter, when would she be able to go home?

For two hours, she'd peered out the slats of the metal shutters while listening to the radio. The phone wasn't working. She didn't know where her father was. And the Guardia Civil patrols outside still blocked the street, the soldiers marching up and down, machine guns slung over their shoulder, their breath billowing out in great clouds of frost in the cold air.

Above all, Richard was starting to scare her.

Inside the shop, it was freezing cold, and they had no light except a candle casting weak light through the room. Along with the phone lines, there was no electricity—cut by the rebels, according to Richard. He paced like a caged animal. Angry muscles, sometimes vibrating with tension. Twelve steps, from one end of the shop. Stop. Turn. Twelve steps back.

At one point he spun toward her and grabbed her wrists. "I've got to report in. Stay here."

Then he spun away, pulled the front door open and ducked under the halfway rolled up shutter.

Immediately she heard shouts. "*¡alto! ¡no te muevas!*" Stop! Do not move!

Richard froze, only his feet and legs visible to her. She stopped breathing.

"Who are you? What are you doing here?" The questions were demanding, harsh.

Richard stumbled over his words, answering in halting Spanish, as if he were a tourist who had learned the language from a phrase book. "I—I was the flower shop. Please no shoot."

The soldier, or soldiers—she couldn't really tell how many there were—demanded his papers.

A few moments later, he slipped back in, then closed and locked the door. He closed his eyes. "It appears I'm not going anywhere," he said.

She shivered. His eyes were glassy as he looked at her.

"Don't worry," he said. "I'll take care of you."

"I just want to go home," she said.

"You're a very pretty girl," he replied.

She took a deep breath, her eyes dropping to the floor. Where was her father? Why hadn't he come to her? Soldiers or not, her father would come to her. Wouldn't he?

The radio was going on. Mindlessly. They knew nothing. The radio announcer said that the rebels had tanks on the street in Valencia, and that the army had gone over to the rebels.

Where was her father?

Richard moved by her. He put his hands on her shoulders and ducked his head to meet her eyes. "Do not be afraid, Adelina." His tongue brushed his lips as he said the words. He stood close to her. Close enough she could smell his acrid sweat.

"Please, Mr. Thompson..."

"Call me Richard."

"Richard, stop."

"Adelina," he whispered as if he could taste her name on his lips.

"Stop."

He brought his lips to hers. She didn't respond, but her body shook, frail. In response, he gripped her arms harder, and his lips forced hers open.

"I need you, Adelina." His voice was hungry. He didn't *need* anything. This was desire. It was lust. It was hideous.

She jerked in fear at the sound of a gunshot outside, her heart pounding. That served only to inflame him more. He pressed her against the wall, pawing at her breasts. She could feel his fingertips, gripping as tight as if they were metal, pressing into her skin. Terror flooded through her as she realized that she had no way to stop him. She began to struggle, throwing her arms out and hitting at him.

"*Stop!*" she cried out, tears threatening to spill over.

"Stop fighting me, damn it!" he muttered. Shoving her against a wall. "And what happens if we die tonight? The Army is out there overthrowing your government. If they realize who I am, they'll kill me."

He was crazy. Richard's face was flushed, his breathing rapid, excited. He leaned close and whispered in her ear, "You're going to love it." Then his hands were all over her. Aggressive. Urgent. He began to pull at her dress.

Adelina screamed.

CHAPTER EIGHTEEN
Feliz compleanos

1. Adelina. March 21, 1981

Feliz *compleanos, Adelina. Happy birthday.* Seventeen years old, and her life was already ruined. As she whispered the words to herself, she thought, bitterly, *I'm so sorry, Papa.*

Her father couldn't hear her, of course. She stood, head bowed, in her black dress, the same black dress she'd worn for days. Manuel Ramos had finally returned to his home in Calella, dead at sixty-one years old. And she missed him, terribly.

Her father's death was sudden, but his worry for her had gone on for weeks. She'd wept after the night of the failed coup. She remembered crying as she heard King Juan Carlos give his speech ordering the Army home. She cried for days afterward, and her father asked her over and over again what was wrong.

She never told. Because she believed Richard when he said he would kill her father, kill her little brother, if she ever told. He was a cruel man, who enjoyed lies and pain. He was *evil*. She believed him because of his smell. She believed him because of the ice cold look in his eyes. She believed him because of the way he hurt her.

In the days after, she'd wept. She'd prayed. But she'd kept Richard's secret. Even after he came back and hurt her again and again.

It was agonizing. Agonizing to see the condition her father was in. Agonizing to know she was responsible for his pain. She had begun to waver. Until finally one day, she said, "Papa, I need to talk to you. It's important."

He smiled. Then he said, "As soon as I get back to the shop, Adelina. I promise. I'll only be gone twenty minutes."

Her father never returned. Twenty minutes later he was dead, run over by a truck on Calle Santa Catalina.

"I'm afraid, Papa," she whispered the words. Then she kneeled. The ground was cold and moist, and soaked through her dress to her knees. She whispered, "I'm afraid he'll kill me, or Luis, like he did you. I'm...I'm afraid. I'm so afraid."

She leaned forward, nearly prostrate in front of the grave. "Papa, I'm so sorry. Please tell me what to do. Tell me what to do, Papa."

Her shoulders began to shake in great sobs. Her father was gone, her life was over, and she was going to have a baby.

I should never have let you stay in the city with your father.

The words echoed through her mind. Words that she couldn't erase. Words that crushed her soul.

I didn't raise my daughter to be a slut, Adelina.

The pain was overwhelming. The shame was overwhelming.

Who is he, Adelina?

The questions. The demands. Four days after her father was laid to rest in the tiny churchyard of the parish church of Santa Maria in Calella, her mother dragged her in to the priest, demanding she go to confession. On her knees in the church, in between the Parish priest and her mother, she confessed her sins.

In a sober, cold voice, the priest said the words she'd been afraid of.

"Adelina, I would gladly grant you absolution. But I'm sure you know, I cannot do so if you are not truly in a state of contrition."

She stammered. She begged. She cried. But the priest's words were final. "Adelina. In order to return to a state of grace, you must be truly contrite. You must remove the sin, and regularize your situation."

Fear staggered her. She knew what he meant. She had to marry him. If she didn't—if she told the truth—he would surely hurt Luis just as he'd hurt her father.

She broke down.

"What is his name?" the priest thundered.

"Who was it?" her mother screamed.

Finally, she'd broken down. Out of fear for Luis, she didn't say the worst. She didn't say how it happened. All she said was the name.

Richard Thompson.

2. Julia. April 30.

Julia leaned back in her chair. Furiously, she wiped a tear from her eyes.

"That's it. I know it's ridiculous. I mean, I'm thirty-two years old. But I still—I still resent her. I like to think I could forgive. I don't want to be the kind of person who can't. But when I needed her, she wasn't there."

Anthony flipped back two pages in his notebook. "Okay, let me make sure I've got it straight. You were pregnant. At fourteen."

Julia nodded.

"And your mother?"

"She was—too preoccupied with her affair. Or whatever. I don't know what was going on with her. But I needed her."

"Do you regret the abortion?"

"Asshole." Julia's response left little doubt of her opinion of Anthony's question, but it communicated little in the way of an answer.

"Sorry," he replied.

"Yes, I regret it," she said.

Crank sat up. "You do?"

A tear ran down her face. "Of course I do. If she—or he, I guess—were still alive, she'd be sixteen now, same as Andrea."

Anthony leaned forward and said, "Look, I'm sorry. That was a shitty question to ask. Just...tell me this—"

"Stop."

Anthony stopped. But then he said, "Stop what?"

"Stop probing. You want to write about the album, fine. You want to write a puff profile piece on me and Crank? Go for it. But this is—"

Anthony sat forward. "This is bigger than that. This is bigger than you've ever realized, isn't it? Your father's going to be the Secretary of Defense, and suddenly you're finding out you don't even know who he is."

"Stop." Her tone was stiff, but he kept going.

"Not to mention, one of your sisters was kidnapped. And you don't know who was responsible."

"You can't seriously believe my father—"

"I don't know what I believe, Julia. I think you need to let me pursue this where it leads."

Crank leaned forward. "Anthony. Shut the fuck up."

"Excuse me?"

Julia held a hand up. "Please, Crank. Just—stop a second. I don't know what it is you expect to find."

"I don't either," Anthony replied. "Just bear with me."

She sagged into her seat. "All right," she said.

"Okay…" He shuffled through his notes for a moment, then said, "All right. Your mom was pretty young when they got married, right?"

"Eighteen."

"And she moved to the United States then?"

"Right. I was about three months old when they moved to the U.S."

"Washington, DC?"

"San Francisco…I think. I was a baby."

"Your dad's official bio says he was posted to Pakistan from '82 to '84."

"I guess he was then. At that age I wouldn't have known the difference between Pakistan or Disneyland."

"And your earliest memories?"

"In Washington. I think. I remember when Carrie was born, vaguely."

He checked his notes. "January '85."

"Yes."

"Were your parents close then?"

Julia raised her eyebrows and shrugged. "Not so I could see. I was really young. I don't have a lot of memories from then. Mom used to spend a lot of time in her room alone and Dad was always at work."

"Who took care of you?"

Julia smiled, but it wasn't a warm smile. "Miss Reyes. I remember her. She sang to me a lot. I do remember we'd have breakfast together sometimes on the weekend. Mom would let me sit in her lap. That was before things got really awful."

Crank said, "It's hard to imagine your mother singing."

"She was an accomplished musician, Crank. Why do you think she made all of us learn an instrument? When she was a teenager, she played for the national youth orchestra in Spain."

"What happened?" Crank asked.

Julia smiled and held a hand out to her husband. "She fell in love. It happens, you know."

Crank took her hand. "It does, doesn't it?"

3. Adelina. January 1984.

"**J**ulia, come."

Adelina Thompson took her daughter's hand in hers. In her other hand she held a leather suitcase. She was exhausted, frazzled. Her flight had been delayed, then diverted around a storm cell, finally landing almost three hours late.

The delays were welcome. Except for a few days here and there when he'd gotten leave, Richard hadn't been home since April two years before. Two years she'd had to learn English, to raise her daughter.

Two years to regain her sense of self.

She'd prayed about it. Sometimes she was ashamed, because she knew that despite his lies, Richard's assignment took him to places that were not safe. And more than once, she'd prayed he would meet an accident. That he would leave her with an insurance policy and their house in San Francisco and her daughter, little Julia.

Julia, who was innocent.

Julia, who reminded her every day of how it felt to be used.

He hadn't met an accident, and unexpectedly, he was home a year early. Promoted. His letter and subsequent phone call said nothing of the reasons why. They merely gave instructions, as if she were in the military, to pack their things and fly to Washington on January 28th. It didn't matter that she'd made friends in San Francisco. It didn't matter that she'd found a home in the church there, that she'd tried to reconstruct her life. She didn't belong to herself. Not anymore.

Not as long as he was in a position to hurt her. To hurt her daughter, or her little brother.

The terrifying part was, no one would ever believe her. Richard was charming. He smiled and shook hands and spoke reasonably. He was eloquent, soft-spoken, and generous. He wore beautifully tailored suits and had perfect teeth and in a hundred subtle ways reminded everyone they encountered that she was young, delicate, incompetent.

She was trapped.

As she stepped off the plane and into the jetway, she straightened her dress, then kneeled in front of her daughter.

"Let's get you cleaned up," she said, quickly wiping Julia's face with a napkin.

"Go potty," Julia said.

"In a few moments, Julia. We've got to go see father, first." Her stomach twisted a little in fear at the words. She knew he was only a hundred feet away at the end of the jetway. She straightened Julia's dress.

There was no point in putting it off any longer. She stood up and took Julia's hand and the two of them walked down the jetway.

She spied Richard in the terminal. It had been six months since she'd seen him—he hadn't come home for Christmas, leaving her and Julia to celebrate alone for the second year in a row. His skin was dark from exposure to too much sun, his skin roughened.

She felt a little woozy as she walked toward him. The combination of first-class tickets and a two-year-old daughter meant they didn't check her age on the plane, and she'd had enough drinks to boost her courage and damage her judgment.

"Adelina," he said. He leaned close, pulling her into a not-too-close embrace, and murmured the words under his breath, "It's lovely to see you dear. You've been eating well, I see."

Bastard. "You look well," she replied.

He knelt in front of Julia. "Hello, Julia. Do you remember me?"

"Poppa?" Julia asked.

He put his arms around their daughter. Adelina felt her gorge rise, and she closed her eyes and whispered a prayer to Mary. When she opened them, Richard stood again. He smiled at her in a way that probably appeared endearing to people who walked by them, but which served only to frighten her.

"Come, then," he said. "I'm anxious to show you where we'll be living."

That was simple. He'd purchased the house in San Francisco without consulting her and done the same here. She didn't actually know *where* they were going this morning, which was typical of her whole life. Richard took her suitcase, and she followed, hand clamped around Julia's.

Twenty minutes later they were getting in the car. It was unseasonably warm for Washington, DC in January, which meant the temperature was close to that of San Francisco. The sky was steel grey, threatening rain. Richard had been irritated about Julia needing to use the restroom, as if there was any way Adelina could have controlled that.

"How was your flight?" he asked. "It took long enough."

Adelina shrugged as she buckled Julia into the back seat. "The flight was fine. It took forever. We need to get a car seat," she said.

"A what?"

"My friend Linda has one. It's to protect her."

"She's two years old. I don't think that's—"

"She needs one."

Richard blinked. He wasn't used to her being assertive about anything. "Fine," he said. "Anything else?"

"Yes." She said the word as she got in the front passenger seat of the car.

He raised his eyebrows. And waited, hands on the wheel.

Her heart thumped wildly as she said the words: "I want to go to college."

He shrugged. "And?"

She kept going, so terrified she couldn't stop talking, the words coming out faster and faster. "I know we didn't start off the best—whatever. I'm nineteen. I didn't get to finish high school. I lost everything. I want to go to school. I want to—"

"Fine."

"What?" she asked, her voice raising to a squeal.

"Go. Whatever. But I expect you to host dinners, I've got a lot of important people I need to cultivate for my career."

"Sure. Of course," she said.

He started the car, and as they drove out of the airport, he said, "I don't know why you were so anxious about this discussion. I love you, Adelina. I want the best for you."

Her eyes widened at the words *I love you*.

Despite her fear, Richard kept his word, not interfering when she made arrangements to register at Montgomery County Community College. The home he'd purchased was a surprise. Unlike the old Victorian townhouse in San Francisco, he'd bought an expensive condo in Bethesda. With five bedrooms, it was larger than they could possibly ever need, though she took his injunction to be ready to host *important people* seriously. It was only a few days later that Richard announced in a peremptory fashion, "We're having guests over next Saturday."

"Oh? Who? How many?"

"Let's see—Colonel Chuck Rainsley and his wife. He's retiring in a few weeks and planning to run for the Senate from Texas, and I'm guessing he's going to win. We need to cultivate him. Leslie Collins—he works for some accounting firm in Virginia, but he's a friend of Prince Roshan, who will be here with his wife. George-Phillip, the Duke of Kent, who is playing at diplomacy, he's assigned to the British Embassy."

She swallowed. "Prince Roshan—Saudi Arabia? Will there be any dietary restrictions?"

"That's right. You've been paying attention, I see."

Irritated, she said, "My father was a Marquis, Richard. I've dealt with dinner parties before."

"*Was.* Your father was a near penniless shopkeeper who lost his title and position long before you were born."

She felt her fists clenched involuntarily. She might be stuck with Richard Thompson, but she would *never* let him get under her skin. She *knew* better.

She spat out the words. "Your dinner party will be flawless." Then she turned her back, stomping to the room she'd converted into her own study. It had nothing of Richard in it, and she intended to keep it that way.

CHAPTER NINETEEN
Loved?
Past tense?

1. Jessica. April 30.

The picture on the wall, an Ansel Adams print of a waterfall or a river or a cloud was almost a stereotype. But Jessica let her eyes bore into it, almost as if she would discover real answers buried somewhere in the image. At Sister Kiara's suggestion, she'd tried to run through her catalogue of memories of her father.

They were few. He was always calm. Always collected. Always locked away in his office, or sternly presiding over dinners at which Jessica and Sarah were expected to stay silent. She remembered holidays, around the big dining table. She vaguely and distantly remembered trips to the zoo and Golden Gate Park. Was her father along for those? Her mother? All she could remember for sure was Carrie.

Sister Kiara leaned forward and said, "Do you need a break? I'm reluctant to quit now that you're finally talking." Her smile was easy as she said the words, but Jessica knew she had a point. In her ten days at the retreat center, Jessica had barely spoken a civil word to anyone.

"You're afraid I'll clam up again?"

Kiara raised her eyebrows. Then she nodded, slowly. "Yes. Yes, I am."

"Um…would you mind if I walked down and got some coffee? And we can talk on the way?"

"Yeah," Kiara said. As if reluctant to break the spell, she stood, and the two of them left the office.

Outside, in the cool mountain air, Jessica stopped and looked up at the sky. "Okay, so here's what happened."

With no further transition, she began to tell Sister Kiara her story.

In Jessica's mind, it all went back to the first week of junior year. For ten years, she and her twin had shared everything. Birthdays. Bedrooms. Their crazy-ass mother still bought them matching clothing, and everyone expected them to like the same things.

But they didn't. Sarah liked punk rock, leather and boys. Jessica liked pop, pink and girls.

She still remembered the first time she realized that she wasn't like other girls. Alexandra, Sarah and Jessica were at the beach, five, maybe six years before. It was a beautiful day, unseasonably warm, the sun shining down on them. They were still close then.

At one point, a crowd of high school boys marched along the beach in front of them. Sarah had leaned close and whispered something, blushing.

Jessica didn't feel whatever it was Sarah did. But two months later, she was invited to a party at Liese Hamilton's house. Six girls attended the party, and Jessica stayed over. They sat up talking half the night, and at one point she found herself focusing on Liese's eyes. Pretty eyes. They were sitting close to each other, really close, and Jessica wanted to kiss her very badly.

Jessica didn't think about it again for a long time.

It was funny, really. It's not like being a lesbian was anything that horrible. She lived in *San Francisco*, after all. This was the twenty-first century.

At the same time, in recent years, she'd spent more and more time in church with her mother. She'd hear the words spoken at school, at church, in her life. It wasn't the big things. *Everybody* knew the Catholic church didn't approve of homosexuality. *Everybody* knew that only certain states allowed gay marriage. Those things mattered, but only in an abstract way.

What mattered to Jessica were the small things. Her mother would give friendly advice. *When you find the man you love, don't let anything get in the way,*

Jessica. Because, to her mother, it could be nothing but a man. After all, Adelina Thompson's life had revolved around her husband's for more than thirty years. Jessica's friends would say *Oh, that was gay*. In a thousand small and large ways, they'd express their disdain of all things gay and lesbian.

Freshman and sophomore year in high school, she began to feel more and more isolated. More and more unsure of herself. More and more afraid to tell anyone who she was.

And then it happened. One evening during the summer before junior year of high school, Jessica was standing in line for tea at the Purple Kow when she saw a willowy, blonde girl in a blue dress that matched hers. Her hair was flowing, shoulder length and a deep shade of indigo. And her intense blue eyes tracked Jessica as she got in line.

"I'm Jessica Thompson."

"Chrysanthemum Allen."

Seriously? Jessica thought.

They both ordered German Lite Cheese Cake and iced milk tea, and Jessica laughed at the coincidence. They sat down at the bus stop and began to talk as the cars drove by.

Chrys was seventeen and was starting her senior year. She wore contrast as armor. Indigo hair and conservative dresses. Beautiful lace ruffled tops with pajama bottoms. When she talked about music and math her eyes glowed. Spoken word poetry excited her. The written word not so much—she'd barely passed English her junior year.

A week later, they climbed out Jessica's window and lay on the roof of the back porch, looking up at the stars.

"Sometimes when I look at the stars," Chrys said, "I think everything's actually going to be okay."

"What do you mean?" Jessica had asked.

Chrys clammed up. She always did. She was sexy and alluring. She was maddening. She rarely revealed weakness or concern, and then when she did, it was indirect.

"I know I'm not good at talking about myself," she said, more than once. "But I love you."

And she did. Jessica loved Chrys, Chrys loved Jessica, and that was okay. But sometimes it was so frustrating. Chrys was so *needy* sometimes.

Two days before Thanksgiving, Chrys showed up at her door. Tears were running down her face, and she said, "I was going to text you, but I couldn't do it."

"What?"

Chrys looked pale and sad as she said, "Break up with you."

Jessica backed into the front door of her house, stunned. "What? Why?"

"I love you, Jessica. But I can't."

"I don't understand..."

"You don't have to." Chrys leaned forward and kissed her on the lips, then ran.

Jessica texted her, over and over again. Finally, Sarah shouted, "What is *wrong* with you?" and Jessica screamed, "Leave me alone!"

The next two days were excruciating. Alexandra and Carrie came home for Thanksgiving, then Crank and Julia, and on Thanksgiving night Dylan Paris showed up by surprise and proposed to Alexandra.

It was a giant, chaotic mess. The whole family hugging each other, Alexandra bursting into tears, her mother crying and her father acting as if he cared. The dinner, after the chaos was over, had a slightly frantic air; as if the gossamer threads of joy and love were so fleeting that it would take nothing but a slight wind to blow them away.

After everyone settled down again, Jessica's mom, the insensitive witch, said to her, "You know, one day you'll meet a man who loves you like Dylan loves Alexandra."

For the first time in her life, Jessica cursed at her mother. "Go to hell," she said, bursting into tears, then she ran upstairs and locked her room. She sent the first of what would be dozens of text messages to Chrys then, asking her how she could be so heartless.

A week later, Chrys had shown back up on her doorstep, begging forgiveness.

Telling Sister Kiara about it now was like the wind coming in off the bay blowing the fog away. "The thing is, I really loved her," Jessica said. "I really loved her."

Sister Kiara leaned back in her chair. They were sitting in the small common dining area of the retreat, and Kiara had a steaming cup of coffee in front of her. "Loved? Past tense?"

Jessica's face twisted in pain. Then she whispered, "I'll always love her. But she's dead."

2. Adelina. February 11, 1984

The dining room was set with eight places. Fine china, set off with crystal wine glasses and candlesticks. A sumptuous white tablecloth, and a four course meal centered on roast duck in plum sauce. Adelina Thompson hated her husband. But she would play his game. She had children to protect. She had a little brother to protect.

Julia was down for the night, in the room furthest from the dining room and accompanied by her nanny. Two hired cooks assisted in the kitchen, and two servers helped in the dining room. But this was Adelina's production.

At five minutes before seven, Richard walked into the dining room. His eyes scanned the perfectly set table.

"Where is the wine?"

The server brought him the bottle, a 1976 Cos Pithos Cerasuolo di Vittoria. A very dry wine, detailed, with a brace of acidity, it was perfect for roast duck.

His eyes darted to hers, eyebrows raised. "You chose this?"

Adelina nodded, giving nothing in her expression.

"I approve." No smile accompanied the bare accolade.

She didn't allow herself to feel any pleasure or pride from his approval. She despised him.

A knock on the door. "That will be our first guests," he said.

She felt a brush of contempt for him. Why he felt the need to state the obvious she didn't understand. But something was different about him. In the three weeks since he'd returned from Pakistan, it was clear that he was different. Just an edge of worry. Something had happened there, something that frightened him, and shook his confidence. He'd spent long nights in his study, virtually ignoring her—a relief from his constant physical demands the first months of their *marriage.*

She turned and walked out of the dining room. She had no desire to speak with him. He followed her all the same, and when she opened the door, he put a hand at the small of her back, making her skin crawl. She smiled at him. After all, they were a happy couple.

At the door stood a remarkably tall man with pale blue eyes in the dress blue uniform of the Marine Corps. At his side, a woman perhaps ten years his junior.

"Come in, come in," Richard said, a patently false smile on his face. "Colonel Rainsley, this is my wife, Adelina."

Rainsley took her hand in his. Warm, but not sweaty. No brute force. His eyes met hers directly and she felt a shiver. "Adelina. It's a pleasure to meet you. I'm Chuck Rainsley, and this is my wife Brianna."

"It's lovely to meet you, sir," Adelina said. Her English had improved dramatically, thanks to a year of lessons in San Francisco. "Can I get you a drink?"

Brianna preferred white wine, and Colonel Rainsley asked for a bourbon and Coke. Adelina walked to the kitchen and issued the instructions, then returned to the living room. Colonel Rainsley and his wife were seated already. Adelina said, "Your drinks will be up in just a moment."

Rainsley said, "Adelina, Richard tells me you met when he was posted in Madrid?"

Adelina plastered a smile on her face, hiding the thumping she felt in her chest. "That's right. He stopped in one day at my father's shop—Papa was a florist—and one thing led to another."

"You're quite the catch," Rainsley said.

Adelina felt her face heat up.

"The moment I saw Adelina the first time, I knew I wanted to marry her."

She wanted to scream when she heard Richard's words. Misery competed with rage as she kept a smile clamped on her face. Her chest hurt and she wanted to turn her eyes to the Marine Colonel and say, *rescue me.*

But there would be no rescue. How could there be? Instead, she turned her attention to the Colonel and his wife.

"And where did you two meet?"

Rainsley looked at his wife, adoration clearly on his features. "Ahh, well, the Marine Corps sent me to graduate school at Fletcher in '75."

Adelina raised an eyebrow. Richard had gone to the Fletcher School, though a different year.

"Anyway, we met there. Brianna was majoring in music at Tufts."

Adelina flushed with pleasure. "Music major? What was your focus?"

"Viola," Brianna said. "I've taught elementary school music."

"I played with the National Youth Orchestra in Madrid," Adelina said.

Brianna's eyes widened. "Oh, that must have been amazing."

The two women began to chat about music. For the first time in nearly three years, Adelina found herself discussing something with animation and excitement.

"Tell me more about the Youth Orchestra?"

With pleasure, Adelina began to describe the nearly daily rehearsals in Madrid. The performances at the Auditorio Nacional de Música, and her preparations to audition for the National Orchestra.

Wistfully, she said, "If I'd made it to the audition, I'd have been the youngest violinist in Spanish history to make it into the National Orchestra."

"Really?" Brianna said. "How old were you?"

"Sixteen."

"You must have been *really* good, why didn't you go through the auditions?"

Adelina froze, her heart suddenly pounding. Richard's eyes had darted to her, for just a second, then back to the Colonel. He was listening. And he'd warned her. More than once. She had a carefully reconstructed history, which started with an earlier birthdate.

"Oh," she said, trying to cover with a lie. "My father passed away, and my um, mom, wanted me to come back to Calella…"

She trailed off, and Brianna said, "Oh, I'm so sorry about your father. I—weren't you working at your father's shop when you met Richard?"

A knock on the door startled Adelina. "Excuse me," she said, standing up and walking quickly to the door.

Two men stood there. The first—short, balding, with a ruddy, freckled complexion, wore a rumpled suit. Next to him stood a much taller and younger man with dark hair and green eyes. The tall man wore an impeccably tailored suit.

"Welcome..." Adelina said, trailing off.

Richard came up behind her, gripping her upper arm in his hand. Tightly. Too tightly, it hurt.

"Good evening, gentlemen. Come in." He released the pressure on her arm quickly. It had merely been a reminder. To watch herself.

Thompson presented the two men. "Adelina, Colonel and Mrs. Rainsley, may I present Prince George-Phillip, the Duke of Kent. Prince George-Phillip is with the British Foreign Service. And also this is Leslie Collins. He's a good friend of mine who did some accounting work for the US Embassy in Islamabad when I was there."

Colonel Rainsley and his wife stood.

"Pleasure to meet you, sir," the Colonel said, shaking George-Phillip's hand. Adelina watched as the two of them shook hands, each taking the measure of the other and liking what they saw. George-Phillip was clearly young, in his early twenties, but he had the confidence and bearing of a much older man.

George-Phillip turned to Adelina, his eyes widening a bit. He took her hand and bent over it with a quick kiss. "A pleasure, madam." Colonel Rainsley frowned at the gesture, then frowned even more when George-Phillip turned toward Brianna Rainsley and did the same.

Before they were able to ask for drinks or anyone returned to their seat, the doorbell rang. A moment later, the final guests were admitted. Richard introduced them.

"May I present Prince Roshan al Saud? And his wife Myriam?"

Prince Roshan was in his early thirties. He wore a conservative grey suit with a muted green tie. His wife, Myriam, wore a smart looking red dress.

"If you would like, we can all move to the dining room," Adelina said.

Five minutes later, the assembled company had taken their seats. Richard sat at the head of the table, of course, and Adelina at the foot. To Richard's right, Prince Roshan. Prince George-Phillip was to Adelina's right. Roshan had been seated in the place of honor by Richard primarily by virtue of his proximity to the throne of his country: Roshan was the Saudi Arabian king's son. George-Phillip was a cousin—and a fairly distant one at that—to England's Queen Elizabeth.

To Adelina's left sat Colonel Rainsley, and Leslie Collins was to Richard's left. The two wives, Myriam and Brianna, were in the middle of the table.

Moments after they were seated, a server poured wine around the table.

"Prince Roshan," Adelina said, "would you prefer water or soda in respect to your faith?"

"Wine, please, madam. I am, of course, devout to Mohammed's teachings, but I also live in the modern world." He paused for a moment, and said, "Water for Myriam, though."

"Of course," Adelina replied as smoothly as possible. Roshan was a pig just like her husband. The drinks were poured as Collins, Roshan and Richard began to discuss political developments in Soviet occupied Afghanistan.

"I'm afraid I'm somewhat at a loss with regards to the minutiae of Afghanistan," Prince George-Phillip said in an aside to Adelina.

"You're very young for a Foreign Service officer," she replied. "And a Duke at that."

George-Phillip shrugged, a self-deprecating motion. "I achieved my seat through no skills of my own, of course—my father was killed in a car accident when I was seventeen."

"My condolences," Colonel Rainsley said. "Do you plan to continue his work?"

George-Phillip scoffed. "As head of his private club? Hardly. I have two more years to my Foreign Service commitment, then it's Sandhurst for me." Sandhurst was the Royal Military College.

Rainsley said, "Are you considering the military as a career?"

"I am, Colonel."

"You could do worse."

"I believe you're correct. Plus—let me be frank—my father did nothing to bring honor to our family or country. I feel it's my role to do my part."

At the other end of the table, the three men, Richard, Collins and Prince Roshan, were speaking in low voices. Collins said something that caused the other two men to chuckle.

Adelina turned to Rainsley. "Richard tells me you are considering a run for the Senate, Colonel?"

"Not considering, ma'am. I've made the decision."

"Please, call me Adelina."

"With pleasure. I'm Chuck." He smiled at her. Across the table and in the middle, Brianna Rainsley frowned at her husband.

"What are you plans for the Senate?" George-Phillip asked.

"I'll tell you. I watched my men get butchered in Beirut six months ago, and there was nothing I could do about it, because of bullheaded, incompetent orders engineered directly out of the White House. I plan to make that my first priority."

As he spoke the words, Rainsley's eyes were bright. He was a man on a mission.

Adelina said, "I think that's admirable."

"Not admirable, Adelina, just my duty as an officer to take care of my men."

George-Phillip leaned forward and said, "Would that all officers felt the same, Colonel." Then he did something odd. At the opposite end of the table, Leslie Collins said in a low tone the name of a place—Wakan or Wack Hand or something like that, his voice at a low drone. George-Phillip stiffened just a little at the word, and his eyes narrowed slightly.

Adelina tilted her head. Something was going on there, but she didn't know what. She wondered if it was something she could use against her husband.

3. Jessica. April 30

"The thing was, Chrysanthemum was a basket case. We would date a month, and she'd break it off. No explanation. She'd make crazy demands. I had to show my love by skipping a class. Or kissing her in front of the Cathedral. Or…just…crazy stuff. She needed help."

Sister Kiara said, "Why do you think that was?"

Jessica shrugged. "Drugs. She was abused. Broken home. Who the hell knows?"

Kiara shook her head. "How did she die, Jessica?"

"Last June and July she'd gone off the edge. Really crazy stuff, and in July I broke up with her. I just couldn't take it any more, you know? I loved her, but… love can only go so far. Love can't make someone not crazy." Jessica sighed and leaned forward, resting her head on her hands.

"It was my fault," she said.

"No, Jessica. Chrys's mental health—whatever was going on with her isn't your fault. She made choices. We all do."

Jessica shook her head. "Yeah, but if I'd been there for her. I don't know. I wasn't. And in August, I went to stay with Carrie and Ray in Washington, along with Sarah. And…we got in the accident. Sarah was in the hospital, Ray died. I was out there for a long time."

She sniffed. "Chrys left me a message. Saying she was afraid she was going to hurt herself. She begged me to call her back. And…I didn't get the message. For days. When I got back to San Francisco she was dead."

Kiara closed her eyes. Then she whispered, "What happened to her?"

"Overdose," Jessica said. "It was intentional. She took a whole bottle of pills and drank it down with a bottle of vodka."

Kiara shook her head. "I'm so sorry."

Jessica remembered the blinding pain. She'd come home from Chrys's house that night, her first night back in San Francisco. Her father had left her a note. He'd be out, probably all night, and there was forty dollars to order a pizza or whatever.

She paid a homeless man ten dollars to buy her a bottle of vodka and took it back to her room, where she drank herself to insensibility.

The next weeks were the darkest she could remember in her life. Her father was never home, or when he was, he locked himself in his office. They ate three meals together in as many weeks. She went to school, barely, but racked up an impressive number of detentions, stopping just short of what might result in a phone call to her father.

The house was deadly empty. They'd lived in San Francisco full time since she was six years old, when her father retired from the Foreign Service. The house had always been full of people—her father and mother, Carrie, Alexandra, Sarah, Andrea. But slowly they'd faded away. Carrie went away to college. Andrea went to live in Spain. Then Alexandra left for Columbia. For two years it had been just the twins and their parents, and that seemed awfully quiet.

But it was nothing like the tomb the house had become now. Sarah was in Bethesda, Maryland, staying with Carrie as they both recovered from the mental and physical injuries of the accident that had killed Carrie's husband. Her mother had stayed on the east coast, leaving it to Richard Thompson to watch out for Jessica.

What could happen, after all? Jessica had it together. She was the goody-two-shoes. She had perfect grades. She watched in derision as her sister Sarah got in scrape after scrape. She was better than that.

Jessica came and went to and from that tomb of a house every day. She called her mother twice a week to let her know she was doing fine, even though it was a lie. She went to school when she had to, she ate when she had to, and she sank into a dull but terrifying depression, her only company the sound of echoes as she walked through the house.

The week after Thanksgiving, she went out for the first time since Chrysanthemum's death. A party. Mick Babcock was hosting it, which meant it would be a drunken bash, but she was on the hunt for something more. She wanted to be held. She wanted to be touched. Chrysanthemum's death had left her disastrously lonely. Jessica Thompson wandered into that party a disaster waiting to happen.

Forty minutes after her arrival, she found herself sitting on a couch next to Rob Searle, another senior. Rob had shoulder length hair, long in the front and swept back with gel like a pop star, and a ridiculous peach fuzz mustache. She'd drunk three glasses of vodka-laced punch and smoked a joint, and was feeling almost giddy. That's when he said, "I think we've got something, babe," and grabbed her, bringing his lips down on hers.

Jessica wriggled her arms and legs in shock for just a moment. Then her hand closed on an irregularly shaped object on the table. A *fork*.

In a swift motion, she clenched the fork in her fist and swung it, stabbing Rob in the back.

He screamed, jerking back from her, his eyes wide.

"The fuck! Did you just fucking stab me?"

She stood up, her whole body swaying, and said, "Keep your hands to yourself."

"Jesus Christ, and I thought we had something. Agggh, that hurts!" He bent, reaching over his shoulder, trying to remove the fork from his back. It had penetrated his shirt, driven right through, and opened up a wound in his shoulder that was going to hurt a lot worse when he sobered up.

"Dude, what the fuck happened to you?" It was their host, Mick.

"Bitch stabbed me," Rob said. Then he burst out laughing. Mick let out a loud belly laugh, then reached around and grabbed the fork. A little bit of blood spattered when he pulled it out, and Jessica stood and backed away.

"Fucker," she muttered. Rob just laughed more. She rolled her eyes and walked away. As she headed for the door, Marion Chen blocked her way.

Marion was a pretty girl. Or used to be. She'd have been a senior in high school if she hadn't dropped out in September. Now she worked waiting tables at the Fisherman's Wharf and was saving money to take her GED and start college. Jessica knew her. Or knew *of* her rather—they hadn't moved in the same circles when Marion was still in school, except the last couple of months of junior year.

Marion didn't look so good now. She'd always been pretty, but slightly overweight, at least by unrealistic American magazine standards. Now, the Korean-American girl's face had leaned out, her cheeks slightly concave. Dark circles bordered the bottom of her hollow eyes.

"Jessica." Marion crossed her arms over her chest like a couple of drumsticks.

"Hey, Marion. You doing okay?"

Marion's eyes narrowed. "What the fuck are you asking that for?"

"Just curiosity," Jessica said. "Hadn't seen you in a while." *Not to mention, you look like a fucking concentration camp victim.*

"Yeah, I'm doing fine."

"I'm glad," Jessica said. She started to steer around Marion.

"Hey," Marion said. "I gotta ask you something."

Jessica sighed. This party was a bust. She should just go home. "What?"

"Chrysanthemum told me she kept trying to call you, and you wouldn't answer. She was all fucking broken up about it. That was right before she offed herself. Is it true?"

Jessica closed her eyes. And she couldn't control it, even though she wanted to. A tear ran down her face. "Yeah, it's true. I was in a bad car accident, and my brother-in-law died, and my twin was in the hospital for months, and I didn't return her call for a couple days. Fucking sue me."

Marion winced. "Jesus. That's the fucking breaks. Sorry."

"Shit," Jessica said. "Just…whatever. Anything else?"

Marion shook her head. "You want to blow this place? Let's go get high."

Jessica blinked. Was Marion serious? She looked at Marion's full lips, at her pretty, high cheekbones, and said, "Yeah, let's go."

CHAPTER TWENTY
He's really a fucking spy

1. Adelina. May 8, 1984

"**Something's** different about you."

Adelina froze. She was in the process of putting away groceries, and had unconsciously been humming Tina Turner's new hit, *What's Love Got to Do With It?* For two days, she'd been trying to shut out her news. Not think about it. The implications were terrifying.

She stood up straight. Richard was leaning on the doorframe. His face was openly curious and distrustful.

"What do you mean?" she asked. She set the can of peas down on the counter next to her hand.

He narrowed his eyes. "You've been very cheerful lately. It's nice to see."

Bastard. She was cheerful because for the first time in her life she had some vague idea of what it felt like to be loved. To be valued. Cherished. But now—here—she had to deal with *him.* Her rapist. Her captor. Her husband. She felt a cold chill in her gut, as she always did when he looked at her like this. With lust in his eyes. Richard was rarely gentle, never loving, always contemptuous. Until March, she'd never imagined that making love could be something enjoyable. Something amazing.

He'll kill me if he finds out. Or he'll kill my daughter.

That's crazy, he had responded. *Just leave him.*

You don't know him. He murdered my father.

You don't know that for sure.

I do.

Adelina swallowed. She felt a pit of fear in her stomach, as she often did with Richard. Because she had missed her period. And—it wasn't possible that Richard Thompson was the father. She was trapped. She couldn't leave him because he'd take Julia. Or hurt her. But she couldn't go on like this. Because she was dying inside.

"Seriously," Richard said. "What's going on with you?"

She couldn't meet his eyes. "My class. I'm just really enjoying it. I've made friends." *I'm in love and dying because I can't leave you.* She closed her eyes, trying to force back tears. She had too much pride to let him see her cry.

"Tell me about your friends," he said, his voice cool.

Change the subject. "You tell me about yours. You've been out with Leslie Collins a lot. Is he really an accountant?"

"No," he said, his voice contemptuous. "He's really a fucking spy."

Asshole. "He just doesn't seem your type," she replied, ignoring his caustic response. Ever since the night he'd huddled with Prince Roshan and Leslie Collins, she'd realized something was wrong there. Richard Thompson wasn't the type to ignore genuine British royalty in favor of a jumped up nobody from Saudi Arabia whose only claim to *royalty* was the recent discovery of oil. She knew him well enough to know that if he paid more attention to Roshan than to George-Phillip, something was suspicious.

Unfortunately, she'd had little luck figuring out what it was. Richard was, as always, secretive.

"Leslie isn't the point. The point is your newfound cheerfulness. I want to know what the fuck is going on."

His eyes had narrowed, and she felt the temperature in the room plummet from the ice in his eyes.

Be careful, Adelina. Piss him off, but not too much. She whispered a quick prayer to Mary. Then she shrugged a little. "I turned twenty last month. I guess I realized it's time to make the best of our situation." Swallowing back vomit, she continued with the words she'd rehearsed. "I guess I've been a bit spoiled. I should be more grateful."

"You *should* be more grateful," he said. "I take care of you, don't I? Do you ever have to worry about food? About anything at all?"

Just my freedom, you fucking bastard. "No," she said. "I just never planned to have children."

"What the fuck do you mean?" His tone had a hard edge to it. For a second, she wished the nanny were here, instead of at the park with Julia. He was never violent when other people were there.

She swallowed. "Sorry. I didn't mean to upset you."

"I'm not fucking upset."

She knew the next words would set him off. They *always* did. "Richard, calm down…"

"Don't tell me to fucking calm down. If you hadn't gotten pregnant, I wouldn't have had to deal with an international fucking incident. The agency *made* me marry you."

"Well, my mother made me marry *you*." She knew the next words were going to hurt her. Or rather, *he* was going to hurt her in response to what she was about to say. But right now, she needed him to. Because otherwise, she was going to have no way to explain the pregnancy. So she said the words, quiet, her tone vicious, calculated. "Do you *really* think I'd ever marry my rapist voluntarily?"

Richard's eyes bugged, and he reached out and grabbed her by the throat. Silent, his face controlled, the only sign of his anger those bulging eyes and his hand gripping her.

For just a second, she started to panic. Had she miscalculated? He was always so controlled. She couldn't *breathe*. But then relief swept over when he let go of her throat and muttered in a guttural voice, "You fucking whore."

Then he started to tear at her clothes.

Adelina didn't cry. She didn't weep. A tear slid down her face, a desperate, lonely tear, but she wiped it away before he could see it, and inside she closed her heart, she disassociated, she left her body behind and turned her mind and her heart to a prayer to God to deliver her and protect her daughter. Richard Thompson might have her body, but he could never have her soul.

2. Bear. April 30

Jesus, *Joseph and Mary*, Bear Wyden thought as he got out of the cab on Pennsylvania Avenue. He was frazzled. To say the least.

After his unsatisfactory meeting with Senator Chuck Rainsley that morning, he'd regrouped his team at Diplomatic Security with new instructions. Priority number one was to dig into Richard Thompson's past, but he couldn't tell anyone that.

However, as a matter of *routine investigation*, he'd detailed investigators to pull every detail they possibly could, not only of Richard Thompson's private life, but that of every member of his family. Credit reports, FBI files, even college applications. A search of the National Crime Information System database turned up a hit in San Francisco in February 1990, but the file wasn't actually in the system. Worse, the file, which was on paper with the San Francisco Police Department, was a secured file. He'd had to personally call the chief of police to request a copy, which he'd been told should be faxed to him some time that night.

It was probably some drug addict with the same name. But Bear knew that in February 1990, the Thompsons were in San Francisco on compassionate leave when Richard Thompson's mother was dying.

He felt like he was just getting his teeth sunk into the investigation when Secretary Perry called. It was a short call.

"Meet me at the White House at 3 pm."

It was 2:45, and Bear was being patted down by the Secret Service agents at the Pennsylvania Avenue entrance. He didn't know why he was here. Other than the Secretary of State he didn't know who he was meeting. But he knew the fucking White House was so far above his pay grade that he'd gladly go back to Whogivesafuckistan if it meant he didn't have to deal with this bullshit. Bear was a security agent. A cop. Not a politician. He wanted to retire from the Foreign Service and go look at pretty girls on the beach in Florida—not get retired early because of some stupid-ass political shootout.

But then he thought about that sixteen-year-old girl, Andrea Thompson, taking out two hardened terrorist fuckheads with her bare hands while her father dicked around behind his desk at the Pentagon. That girl deserved some justice, whatever form it was going to take.

Forty minutes later, Bear was still sitting in a waiting room in the West Wing, sending instructions to his investigators via text message and email.

That's when he saw the email from one of his senior investigators.

Mitch Filner was a former CIA operative and had been placed with the US Embassy in Singapore in the late 90s. After a rape charge in Singapore, he was dropped by the agency, but had done some freelance work in Iraq and Afghanistan over the last decade.

Mitch Filner had turned up dead of multiple stab wounds in a dumpster in Northern Virginia. Normally a local crime wouldn't come to anyone's attention, except that a real estate agent had walked into a condo in Bethesda that morning, expecting it to be empty. Instead, the carpet was flooded with blood stains.

The blood was a match for Filner. And the condo had a naked eye view of the Thompson's condo in Bethesda.

What the hell did it mean? Why was a former CIA operative watching the Thompson daughters? At the scene of a shooting from the night before. Something stank to high heaven.

At 3:25, the Secretary of State finally walked into the waiting room. Bear jumped to his feet.

James Perry looked put together and well rested, which was more than Bear could say after digging through Richard Thompson's file all night.

"Bear. Come this way. We don't have time for a briefing."

Bear followed as Perry headed down the hall. A secret service agent walked along with them and opened a door just ahead. For a panicky moment Bear thought they were walking into the Oval Office. But instead, he recognized the figure behind the desk the moment they walked in. Former Senator Ben Olin, now the National Security Advisor to the President.

Olin stood up. Also in the room, unfortunately, was acting-Secretary of Defense Richard Thompson, along with his military aide-de-camp, an Army Colonel. To his left, Max Levin, the Director of the Central Intelligence Agency, flanked by another man with a ruddy, freckled face. In moments, that unfamiliarity was addressed. The freckled guy was Leslie Collins, the Director of Operations at CIA.

Bear stared openly at Thompson and Collins. Thompson was CIA and had been for thirty years or more. There was no doubt about it. There was no way they didn't know each other.

Did Thompson know *Mitch Filner?* How fucking tied up was he with the people who had kidnapped his daughter?

The National Security Advisor leaned forward and said, "Secretary Perry, I've just received the most interesting briefing from the Secretary of Defense and the Director of the CIA. I understand your department is conducting the investigation into Andrea Thompson's kidnapping. Why?"

Perry answered off the cuff and without reference to any notes. "The kidnapping involved foreign nationals who may have been engaged in espionage. One of them we are certain was hired in the past by the Defense Department and CIA for intelligence related activities."

Bear coughed. "Two, sir."

Perry turned towards him.

"Two?"

"I just got the news, sir. A former CIA employee turned up dead this morning. His blood was found all over an apartment which overlooked the Thompson condo in Bethesda."

Richard Thompson visibly started. "What?" Then he turned, purposefully, toward Collins.

Bear thought *that* was fucking interesting.

The National Security Advisor asked, "What do you have to say about that, Max?"

Max Levin was unruffled. Prior to his tenure at CIA, he'd been a Marine Corps General, then head of the National Security Agency. He'd seen his share of crises. "First I've heard of it. What's this guy's name?"

Bear answered, "Mitch Filner."

Leslie Collins shook his head and scoffed. "We fired Filner ten years ago. He raped some girl in Singapore."

Olin, the National Security advisor, closed his eyes and muttered, "Dear God." He appeared to count to twenty. Bear watched as he did it. Finally, Olin said, "All right. For now, State keeps the investigation. The rest of you, turn over whatever they need. We don't need any political liabilities. Is this going to be a liability?"

As he asked the question, he looked at each of the men in the room. His meaning was clear. It was an order. Make this problem go away, before it became a problem for the President.

3. Leslie Collins. April 30

Leslie Collins sat in the back of the Lincoln Town Car. He looked at his watch. He was going to be late for dinner. *Again.*

He shook his head. Then he picked up his secured phone.

"Yeah, Danny? It's Collins. I need a status."

Danny McMillan wasn't just an employee. He was a trusted friend, who had served his time in some nasty places—some of them, side by side with Collins.

"Yeah. Here's what I have. First thing—Carrie and Andrea Thompson called Senator Rainsley's office. They have an appointment tomorrow evening."

"Shit," Collins said. "All right, what else? What are their plans tonight?"

"As I understand it, some of them are going out, but Andrea Thompson is planning to stay in. Our guy on the security team thinks she's burnt out."

"All right. What about the mother?"

"No sign yet. No cell phone signal, no credit cards."

"And the oldest sister?"

"She's on a charter flight to San Francisco right now with her husband and a reporter."

Collins was silent for a moment. "A reporter? Does he have a name?"

"Uh…Anthony Walker. He's an entertainment reporter with the *Post*, apparently."

Collins closed his eyes and set the phone down on the seat beside him. He counted to ten, and then counted to ten again for good measure. Then he picked up his phone. "Are you fucking kidding me?"

"What, sir?"

"Anthony Walker isn't a fucking entertainment reporter, he won a fucking Pulitzer for his international affairs coverage. Walker did a whole feature on Wakhan three years ago when the UN dug up the bodies."

Now it was Danny's turn to be silent at the other end of the line. Finally he came back and said, "What do we do?"

"Take it down. I want everyone who can possibly blow the lid on this thing to be completely discredited. Or dead. How long will it take to execute?"

"Most of it, twenty-four hours or less. GP might take a bit longer, and he's the wildcard."

"All right, pull the trigger. All of them. We don't know who knows what, and I don't see how we're going to contain this thing."

"Done, sir."

Collins hung up the phone. Then he dialed his wife.

"Dear, I'm going to be a few minutes late, traffic coming from the White House."

CHAPTER TWENTY-ONE
I'd never hate you

1. Carrie. April 30. 5:17 pm

"**O kay,**" Leah Simpson said. "We'll have the car brought around at six."

"Thank you," Carrie said. She rocked Rachel in her arms unconsciously as she spoke.

Leah paused as she started to walk away and said, "Listen. I promise we'll take good care of you and Rachel and your sisters, all right? My job is to make sure you're safe."

Carrie gave a half smile. She hadn't felt safe since the day a jeep plowed into her car, killing her husband and upending her life. But saying that sort of thing makes people uncomfortable, so she merely answered, "Thanks."

As if she sensed Carrie's skepticism, Leah touched her arm for just a moment, then stepped away.

Sarah walked into the room, her boots thumping on the floor. She looked strangely subdued in a plain black dress and combat boots. "I'm ready whenever you guys are. I swear to God if I don't get out of this house I'm going to explode."

Carrie touched her sister's shoulder. "Pretty soon you won't be so stir crazy, you'll be off to college."

Sarah snorted. "Yeah, I guess. I just never imagined I'd be home schooling my senior year in high school."

"This year wasn't what any of us expected."

Sarah looked stricken. "Sorry, Carrie, that's not what I meant."

Carrie pulled her sister close. "It's okay. You get to grieve for what you lost too, Sarah. Don't think I don't know how hard it's been for you this year."

"Sorry. I'm gonna listen to some music, just let me know when you guys are ready?"

"Sure," Carrie responded as Sarah broke away. "The car's coming around at six."

Sarah wandered out of the kitchen. Carrie stood and walked Rachel, now fully asleep, back to her crib. Very carefully, so as to not disturb the baby, she laid her on the bed and tucked her in. She stayed momentarily, looking down at her daughter. When Rachel slept, it was with abandon you didn't see in adults. Her arms were splayed out, hands clenched in tiny fists as she breathed in and out.

Sometimes it was breathtaking when Carrie realized how much her daughter looked like Ray. In her smile, and the tiny dimples that formed in the corner of her mouth. She leaned close, closed her eyes and smelled Rachel.

Eyes closed, she felt a rare sense of inner peace. Everything was shifting underneath her. Andrea (and possibly all of them) was in danger, her father wasn't who she thought he was; everything in her life was in question. But she knew that somewhere, Ray was thinking about her. She knew her daughter was right here with her, and that she would do *anything* to protect Rachel. Anything at all.

In the end, that was what mattered. This baby, sleeping right here.

Gently, she kissed Rachel on the forehead and stepped out of the room.

As she walked back down the hallway, she heard Dylan's voice. He sounded tense, aggravated.

"Do we have to discuss this now? Look, I just want to relax, okay? You go out with Carrie."

Alexandra answered him, sounding sad. "Dylan, I don't understand what's wrong."

Carrie paused, not wanting to eavesdrop, but saddened by Dylan's tone of voice when he responded. "I'm just exhausted, Alex. I miss Ray and I'm tired and sick and just...please. Go without me tonight, okay? I'll be fine."

Carrie sighed and kept walking. The tension between Alexandra and Dylan was too much to bear. It reminded her so much of the awful pain and stress she and Ray had been through a year before. She wanted to help, but didn't know how. And, as she walked down the hall and into the living room, she knew there was nothing she could do. Dylan needed to work through this on his own. They—Dylan and Alexandra—needed to work through this together. She could be there for them—to answer questions, to help when they needed it, to listen—but she couldn't make them work it out.

2. Bear. April 30. 5:25 pm

Bear Wyden sat, frustrated, staring at the piles of paper on his desk. Despite the masses of information they'd collected into two days, despite the physical evidence, the background files, he still had far more questions than answers.

Why had Tariq Kouri and his still unidentified confederate kidnapped Andrea Thompson? Motives that made sense were in limited supply. Were they somehow involved in human trafficking? Sex slavery? If so, there were far more likely targets than the daughter of the Secretary of Defense. Bear was ready to rule out coincidence or unrelated motives. Andrea Thompson was kidnapped because of who she was, or who her father was.

Which raised the second question.

Who was her father? Richard Thompson claimed he was. But he looked nothing like two of his daughters, both of whom towered over him. He also didn't act like it. Fathers—even Cabinet level fathers—rushed to the hospital to protect their sixteen-year-old daughters. The fact that Thompson hadn't was the first clue he had an unusual relationship with his daughter. But it went downhill from there. He'd had little contact with her in the three days since she'd arrived in the United States. He'd taken no time away from work. He hadn't spent evenings with her. Something was just wrong there. Everything he saw indicated to Bear that Richard Thompson bore no paternal feelings at all toward Andrea Thompson.

Bear thought through the limited facts he knew:

Richard Thompson had spent his career in the CIA, with the State Department as cover.

Tariq Kouri—the Saudi national who had kidnapped Andrea—had worked as a contractor for the CIA and the Pentagon. Richard Thompson knew him.

Mitch Filner—who had turned up dead—had worked for CIA, until he was fired after a rape accusation in Singapore.

Bear leafed through Thompson's file, returning again to the photograph from thirty years before. His eyes fell on a Leslie Collins in his early thirties. Collins was now the Director of Operations for the Central Intelligence Agency. Why was he at the meeting at the White House yesterday? What did the CIA have to do with investigating the kidnapping of an American girl?

Collins and Thompson had been in the CIA together, but there was little information publicly available about Leslie Collins. He'd maintained an almost invisible public profile until he reached his current position. Bear knew that if he started inquiring about Collins, it would be an immediate dead end.

What about the others who were present that night? Roshan al-Saud was the head of the Saudi Arabian intelligence agency. Wyden had access to his State Department file. He opened the file on his computer.

A grandson of King Abd al-Aziz ibn Saud, Prince Roshan was one of several hundred potential third generation claimants to the throne of Saudi Arabia. He had served his career alternately as a diplomat and a spy, with periods in the embassies to the United States, Indonesia, the United Kingdom and Pakistan, among others.

Bear narrowed his eyes as he scanned through the file.

Roshan was in Pakistan in the early 80s. Bear checked the dates. Roshan was in Pakistan at the same time as Richard Thompson.

A quick Google search established that Leslie Collins was also in Pakistan at the same time, and also established that the other party attendees—Chuck Rainsley and George-Phillip Windsor—were not.

Was there something between the three of them? Had Tariq Kouri also worked for the Saudi intelligence agency? What about Mitch Filner? How did he fit in? Bear checked through the files, but there was little or no information about Filner. They obviously needed to correct that.

What else did he know?

The other kidnapper: they knew nothing about him at all. No identification. His fingerprints and DNA had turned up no matches in any database. A dead John Doe, driving a stolen vehicle. No one of similar appearance had been reported missing in the last forty-eight hours. He was a mystery, and a deep one, and that screamed intelligence agency as well. People left behind footprints. They carried identification, they had fingerprints on file, and they were reported missing when they went missing. Whoever this guy was, he either worked for an intelligence agency or he'd never had any brush with the authorities at all. It didn't add up.

And then there was the British connection, in the form of Charles Frazier, a British tourist who just *happened* to have been shot directly across the street from the Thompson sisters last night. Frazier had been in the United States for less than twenty-four hours on a tourist visa and was now being treated at George Washington University Hospital for his gunshot wound.

Was Frazier actually an intelligence agent? And if so, what was his connection to all of this? Why would the British be interested in the Thompson sisters?

None of it made any sense. Something connected all of this, but he didn't know what it was. And that missing piece of information was the vital piece.

Bear sighed and began to review the file again. The answer was out there somewhere.

The phone on his desk rang.

"Bear Wyden," he said.

"Sir? I'm calling from the classified documents desk. You've received a secure fax from the San Francisco police department."

Bear sat up. That would be the police report. Which contained…who knew what? It was time to find out.

3. Adelina. April 30th. 3 pm Pacific Time

Sister Kiara sat down in the chair facing Adelina. At a right angle to them both, completing the triangle, was Jessica, whose heavy eyelids and posture spoke of her exhaustion. Jessica had slumped deep into the cushions of a couch and looked as if she was having difficulty staying awake.

Tired she may be. But she still looked so much healthier than she had ten days before, when she'd come home in the morning after staying out all night, puking all over the kitchen. Adelina had packed her in the car without hesitation and driven here.

"So," Kiara said. "First, thanks for sitting down with us. The reason I wanted to have all three of us talk—you two are headed home in a few hours. I wanted to talk over plans for the next few weeks, and also see if there are some things we could talk about. Is that okay with both of you?"

Adelina nodded and looked to her daughter. Jessica's eyes went to her mother, then back to Kiara. She nodded, her expression dull.

"Okay, then. First of all, I understand Jessica's going back to school starting next week so she can graduate with her class?"

"That's right," Adelina said. She looked over at Jessica. "It's really up to you. You'll have a lot of catching up to do—but I thought you'd be happiest not being set back a year."

Jessica nodded. "I'd like that, if it's possible."

Adelina swallowed, hard, struggling to contain her emotions. Jessica's voice sounded incredibly sad.

Kiara said, "I think that's a really good idea. But I'd like to talk about a couple of things. First, I've made arrangements for you to meet with a psychiatrist, Jessica. Doctor Ralph Foreman. He's a specialist in addiction and grief counseling. For now, I think twice a week would be a good idea, and he's made the space available. Is that okay?"

"Of course," Adelina said. But in her head, she thought, *Grief counseling?*

"Jessica? You're eighteen years old, so it's your decision."

Jessica nodded.

"I'm going to recommend that the two of you go into therapy together for at least some of those sessions."

Adelina took a deep breath. She'd had so many secrets, for so long. But maybe it was time to let some of them go.

"Yes. I think that's a good idea," Adelina said.

"Finally, Jessica. I think it would be a good idea, now, while we're in a safe space, for you to talk with your mother. About Chrys and Marion."

Jessica's eyes widened, and Adelina felt her heart thump. *Who were Chris and Marion?* She watched carefully as Jessica said, "Do you think…"

Her voice trailed off. Then she looked at her mother and said, "I didn't tell you because I thought you'd hate me."

Adelina's voice was broken as she said, "I'd never hate you."

"Mom, I'm a lesbian. And I fell in love. And she died."

For just a second Adelina felt shock. Her daughter was gay? Reflexively, she fell back for an instant to her upbringing, and she wanted to correct her daughter and tell her that no, she was not a lesbian, and no, she had *not* been in love with a woman.

But then she thought about how alone Jessica must have been. *Alone.*

She pictured her daughter. All alone, her twin injured in the accident. Everyone she could lean on was gone. Her mother gone.

"You…fell in love? And she died?" Adelina's eyes watered, and her breath began to move in and out quickly. "Oh, God, and you had no one to turn to. Baby, I'm so sorry. I'm so sorry I wasn't there."

Jessica was shaking now, her eyes wide, her face twisted in fear. "Mama, you're not mad?"

Adelina reached out and took her daughter's hands. "Come here," she said. Then she sobbed. "I'm so sorry I haven't been the mother you needed. Oh, God, I'm so sorry."

Jessica collapsed into her arms, and Adelina pulled her close. "Baby, I'm so sorry," she whispered. She thought about all the times she'd failed her children. But she wasn't failing this time. She wasn't losing *this* daughter. She pulled Jessica tighter and whispered, "I'm here, baby girl."

In halting steps—a few words at a time, and punctuated by many tears—Jessica began to tell her mother the story of how she fell in love with, and lost, Chrysanthemum Allen. They cried together, and finally Jessica fell asleep in her mother's arms, as Adelina slowly brushed her daughter's hair.

Adelina whispered, "I wish we could stay here longer."

"I know," Kiara said. "But she has you. And you're a good mother."

Adelina closed her eyes, trying to hold back a sob. "I wish that was true. I'd give anything for it to be true."

CHAPTER TWENTY-TWO
On that day
I will punish

Crank. April 30. 2:45 PM Pacific.

The Richmond district of San Francisco was blanketed with fog when Crank pulled the rental car to a stop in front of the house on Cabrillo Street. After the morning flight, it had taken nearly ninety minutes for them to get their car arranged, and then drive into the city.

As he parallel parked the car, the three of them stopped talking. Julia leaned forward, resting her hand on the dashboard and looking up at the house. It looked the same as always. Four stories, light blue brick with white ornamentation, it was one of the most striking houses on the block.

"I don't know why," Julia said, "but I'm actually nervous about this."

Crank looked over at her. It was out of character for Julia to ever admit weakness on any topic. "We'd better head in, then?"

She looked back, meeting his eyes. "Right." Her eyes darted to Anthony, in the back seat. "Tell me again why you're along for this?"

Anthony smiled. "I'm here to help you."

She shook her head then opened the door of the rental car. "Let's go."

Crank opened the driver's side door and stepped out, walking up to the door beside his wife.

After twelve years together, he knew her moods well. But this was unusual. She was pensive and withdrawn in a way he'd rarely seen.

"Hey," he said, his voice quiet. He touched her arm and raised an eyebrow. "I'm okay," she said.

"You sure?"

She nodded, brushing him off, and rang the doorbell to the house. Crank knew she had a key. But Julia had never actually *lived* in this house, so whenever they visited, she was scrupulous about knocking.

Today, however, there was no answer. They waited, and she rang the bell again. And again.

Crank coughed. "You've got your key on you?"

"Yes," Julia said. She sighed. "I don't like using it." She opened her purse and rooted around in it for a minute. Then she fitted a key to the deadbolt and carefully turned it. Crank heard the lock slide, then click, and she opened the door.

"Well, then," she said, her voice low. She paused for a moment more. Then she pushed the door open. It was immediately apparent no one had been home in some days. The mudroom at the foot of the stairs was cluttered with junk mail. Magazines and catalogues, bills and other mail had grown into a small pile behind the door. A rank smell radiated from somewhere inside—spoiled milk or worse.

Julia looked at the pile of mail, then at Crank.

"She's fine," he said. "Just out of town or something. She told your dad she was going to some retreat center."

"For how long?" she said. "I spoke with her on Friday, and this is a lot more mail than that. And that smell..."

She started up the stairs. Crank followed, leaving a bewildered Anthony Walker behind.

The house was quiet, empty. Eerily so. As they looked around the ground floor, with all the lights out and not a soul in the house, Crank realized that he had never once been in this house by himself. It was dark inside, and the quiet was eerie and uncomfortable. It was almost as if the fog outside had seeped into the house, rendering it cold and dark.

Crank thought back. The last time he'd been here was the fall of 2012—Thanksgiving night. Andrea had been in Spain, but the rest of the Thompson clan was on hand, and that night, at least, they were full of drama. Jessica and Sarah were fighting. Alexandra had revealed her sexual assault at school and then Dylan Paris showed up on the doorstep after a cross-country flight. An altogether satisfying night.

The house was very different now.

Cold.

Crank followed Julia into the kitchen. She froze at the door to the kitchen.

"What is it?" he asked, coming up behind her. Then he saw and heard it.

The floor on the far side of the kitchen table was covered in...vomit? Days old. Maybe weeks. Dried out, but crawling with ants and flies. This was the source of the smell. Julia stared for one minute, and then her shoulders shook. Once, twice, then she ran, covering her mouth, for the bathroom.

Anthony came up behind Crank.

"I don't get it," Anthony said.

"I don't either. Adelina would *never* leave her house in this condition unless it were a real emergency."

Crank met Anthony's eyes. Then he said, "I don't know what's going on here. And I don't know why Julia's trusting you. But you better not screw her over."

Anthony said, "That's not how I do business."

"I'm cleaning this shit up," Crank replied.

"Don't. In case—in case the police need to get involved."

Crank sucked in a breath. Anthony was right, of course. You didn't fuck with the scene of a crime, if that's what this was. He'd absorbed that much and more from his father, a retired Boston cop, over the years.

With that in mind, Crank tiptoed around the kitchen. More signs of an abrupt departure. The coffee pot was full, but cold, and it had a spot of mold floating on top of the liquid. Two glasses, dirty, in the sink. On the kitchen floor, near the vomit, a half-gallon of milk in its plastic container, laying on it's side and bloated from expanding glasses. That wasn't going to smell good.

Crank didn't touch anything. "Let's go," he said. "We leave everything as it is. Whatever the fuck happened, Adelina and Jessica left in a hurry."

As they stepped out of the kitchen, they found Julia sitting at the dining table. She had her hands on her laps, her posture straight, staring straight ahead at the wall.

"Julia?" Crank asked.

She looked up at him. "They've been gone a week. At least. How the hell didn't we know? What kind of family are we? My mother and one of my sisters has been missing for *a week* and no one even knew?"

Crank put a hand on her shoulder. "You talked on the phone with her on Friday."

"She sure as hell wasn't here."

"So, maybe she's at that retreat your Dad talked about?"

"Why wouldn't she say anything? Why leave the place such a disaster?"

Crank sighed. "I don't know. I…I don't know. My suggestion…let's take a look around. If we don't see anything, we call the cops."

She swallowed and nodded. "Yeah. Yeah. All right. Check her bedroom and bathroom. Maybe there's some clue there."

She stood and led the way, down the hall, past the closed door to Richard Thompson's office, and up the stairs. The second floor had two bedrooms, Adelina and Richard's.

"Mother's first," Julia said.

"Wait," Crank said. "They have separate rooms?"

"Well—yeah."

"Weird."

Julia nodded. "I guess. It's been that way a long time." She turned the door-knob.

The room was spare. A queen sized bed, a small bookshelf, a bureau and a desk/vanity combo. Adelina had a large walk-in closet, hung with dresses on both sides.

"She didn't pack much stuff," Julia said, looking in the closet. The desk and vanity told the same story. Adelina's laptop was still on the desk, along with a charger cable for an iPhone. Did Adelina have another charger? Impossible to know. Julia walked to the desk and tentatively pressed the power button. The computer, a relatively new MacBook, began to boot up.

"Who leaves for a trip without their laptop?" Anthony asked.

"And without cleaning the kitchen floor?" Julia asked.

They watched the computer boot up, and Crank felt a sick fascination. What would they see when the screen finally appeared? Possibly nothing. Possibly, Adelina's computer would be password protected. Or infected by viruses. Or wired to a bomb which would explode when they finished inspecting it. Who knew?

The computer finally booted to a password prompt.

"Damn," Julia muttered. She slid into the chair, chewing on her lower lip. She reached out and attempted a password. No good. Then she tried another. Nothing. "I could do this all day," Julia said. She tried three more passwords in quick succession. Nothing.

"What have you tried so far?"

"Variations on my Dad's name and birthdate. Her birthday. Her hometown."

Crank's eyes darted across the hall to Richard's bedroom. "Somehow I don't think she's going to use anything of his as a password."

Julia frowned. "Yeah, you're probably right."

"Your parents aren't close?" Anthony asked.

"They're WASP iceboxes," Crank said.

"Not my mother," Julia said. "She's no WASP."

"Fair," Crank replied. She tried another password. Crank wandered across the room. He opened the top drawer of the bureau.

Crank frowned. Half a dozen prescription bottles. Buspirone. Three times a day for anxiety. Amitriptyline for panic disorder. Risperdal for bipolar symptoms.

Crank said. "Your mom is on some serious meds. Take a look at this?"

Julia stood and walked over. Her eyebrows scrunched together. "Panic disorder? Bipolar?" Her eyes darted to Crank's. Then she pulled the drawer out further.

A battered and frayed Bible. Notes were stuffed in the Bible, her mother's dense handwriting on them. She opened the Bible up to one of the well-worn notes.

A verse had been underlined several times and circled in pencil.

Zephaniah 1:9:

> *On that day I will punish*
> > *all who leap over the threshold,*
> *who fill their master's house*
> > *with violence and fraud.*

Julia frowned, confused, and flipped through the Bible again. Another heavily underscored verse.

Psalm 37:

> *For the wicked shall be cut off,*
> > *but those who wait for the Lord shall inherit the land.*

"My Mom was always devout. But this is...I don't know."

Julia lay the Bible down.

"Wait—" she said. She bent down a little, peering in the top drawer. At the very back, another book. She pulled it out.

It was a journal. Her eyes went to Crank's. "I don't know if I..."

"She's missing," he said.

"Right." She took a deep breath then opened it up.

It was in Spanish. Densely written in barely legible handwriting that covered every square inch of the journal's pages. No margins. No paragraph marks. A solid block of text.

On every single page.

"Oh, my God," Julia said. "I feel like I don't even know who she is."

"Can you read it?" Crank asked.

"I hardly know any Spanish," she said. She flipped through. "Some of it I recognize, or...maybe." Her eyebrows furrowed. "This can't be right."

"What is it?" Crank moved closer to her.

"I swear it says, *He raped me again today.* Or violated? I'm not sure, I don't really know Spanish!" Julia swallowed and looked up to Crank. "I'm reading this wrong. It can't be."

"Bring that with you," Crank said.

She began to pace back and forth. Finally, she marched across the hall, shoving open the door to her father's bedroom.

The room was spare. Clothing hung in the closet. Julia began to pull open drawers. Clothing. Another one. Then another. The fourth drawer, she pulled open and dumped out, tossing clothing across the bed. Her face was oddly frozen, confused. She pulled open another drawer.

"Nothing," she said. Then she looked up at Crank. "The office."

He raised his eyebrows. "Your Dad's office?"

Julia nodded. She turned and walked out, then down the stairs.

The office door was closed and locked. Unlike the rest of the doors in the house, this one had a relatively new doorknob, modern, with a metal plate.

Julia let out another curse. Then she said, "Wait...stay here." Then she ran downstairs.

"I don't get it," Anthony said.

"I don't either," Crank replied. "But—she's onto something."

Two minutes later, Julia was back. And she was holding a small axe.

"I'll handle that," Crank said. "If we're doing breaking and entering, let me handle the breaking part."

She snorted. "All right. Have fun."

Anthony said, "Are you sure this is a good idea?"

Julia shook her head. "If you don't think so, go on without us."

Three minutes later, Crank had the door open. Mangled, broken to shreds. But open.

The office was much as Crank remembered it from his one visit in here. Ten years ago? More? A large bookshelf extended from the ceiling to the floor, an entire wall covered in books. The wall with the door was covered mostly in photographs and plaques. Pictures of Richard Thompson with various Presidents: Bill Clinton, Ronald Reagan, George Bush. A photo showed a much younger Thompson in military fatigues, his arm around another man, both of them standing in a desert.

On the desk, a single family portrait with all of the daughters. No pictures anywhere else in the office of Adelina, but each of the daughters had a portrait somewhere on the wall.

Except Andrea.

"That stings," Crank muttered.

Anthony was looking at one of the photos, the one of Thompson in the desert. He said, "That's Vasily Karatygin."

"Who?" Julia asked.

Anthony shook his head. "Highest ranking Soviet defector to the Afghan rebels. He was a Spetsnaz Major—that's the Russian Special Forces, like our Green Berets. He ended up joining Ahmad Massoud's militia."

"I haven't a clue what you're talking about," Crank said.

"I'm sure it doesn't matter," Anthony said. "That was thirty years ago."

"My dad was never posted to Afghanistan," Julia said.

"Well, nobody officially was back then," Anthony said.

Julia wandered around the office, a frown on her face. She began to open desk drawers.

"What are you looking for?"

"I don't know," she said.

Crank slid open another drawer. Files. He pulled one out randomly. It was labelled Wakhan/Badackshan. Idly, he flipped it open, then his eyes widened. He dropped the file. "Jesus Christ," he muttered.

"What is it?" Julia asked.

She reached for the file, but Crank put his hand on it. "You don't want to look at that."

"The fuck I don't," she replied, grabbing the file away from him. She laid it open on the desk and gasped.

The first thing in the file was the photo Crank had seen. A dozen or more bodies, most of them children. Bloated, blackened. Crank winced and looked away.

Anthony moved forward and picked up the file. "Holy fuck, that's Wakhan. Why does your father have this?"

"Wait. What?" Crank said as Anthony flipped through the file.

Anthony said, "Back in December 1983. A group of rebels got their hands on nerve gas and used it on a village they felt was collaborating too closely with the Soviets. As a matter of fact it was Ahmad Massoud's militia, or at least they were implicated."

Julia's eyes darted to the picture on the wall. "Was that guy involved? Kara-tygin?"

"Nobody knows for sure," Anthony replied.

"Whatever it is, it doesn't tell us where Julia's mom is," Crank said. "Let's keep looking."

He pulled another file out of the drawer. Credit card bills. Another file contained what appeared to be a copy of Richard Thompson's personnel file. Crank dumped those on the desk and kept looking.

"Huh," Anthony said, as Crank continued to rummage through the drawer.

"What is it?" Julia asked.

"Look at this," he said. "I think your dad may not have been State Department at all. I'm starting to think CIA."

"What? Dad? No way."

Anthony said, "You never know. Take a look at this." He laid the file on the table in front of her and pointed at something in it.

Crank had frozen, looking at another file. He didn't say anything as he looked at it. His heart was beating heavily.

The file was a police report. February 13, 1990. From the San Francisco Police Department.

The photos made it all too clear what had happened. Someone had beaten Adelina Thompson nearly to death. Swollen face, bloody lip. *Jesus Christ*, he thought, when he saw the sentence, *Victim refuses rape examination.*

Crank looked up at his wife. She was having a lively debate with Anthony about the likelihood of her father being in the Central Intelligence Agency. Laughing a little.

Then she saw Crank's face.

"What is it?"

He shook his head. *Shit.* She reached out and grabbed the file. Then her eyes widened, and she gasped, covering her mouth.

"Oh my God," she whispered.

A lab report fell from the file. Julia picked it up with shaking hands. Her eyes scanned it, then she handed it to Crank.

It was from the DNA Diagnostic Center. The first paragraph read:

Dear Mr. Thompson. Thank you for your recent examination at the DNA Diagnostic Center. At your request, we have examined the samples provided, and can rule within 99.9% probability that the individuals tested are not related.

The lab report was dated February 12, 1990.

"That *son of a bitch*," Julia whispered. Her eyes scanned the file. The photographs of her mother. Beaten and raped. "It says…it says in here that she refused to press charges. The police referred her to the battered women's shelter."

"Fuck," Crank muttered.

"That's not it," she said. "Alexandra was born November 9." Julia began to breathe heavily. Hyperventilating. "She was born exactly nine months after this police report, Crank. Oh, my God. Oh my *God,* and do you know how badly I've treated my mother?" Julia's voice sounded desperate as her eyes swiveled to Crank.

"There's no way you could have known," he whispered.

"She's my *mother*," Julia cried. "Look what he did to her! Is it any wonder she couldn't be there for me? Can you even imagine what she went through?"

She stood up, her fists clenched. Then she cried out. "We have to find my mother, Crank. We *have* to!"

Crank looked up at the sound of brakes out front. His eyes darted to the window. A car had parked out front, and two men got out. Both of them had short, closely cropped hair and muscular builds. Both wore open suit coats.

"Trouble," Crank muttered.

CHAPTER TWENTY-THREE
Those are drugs

1. George-Phillip. 10:35 pm GMT

As was his habit, George-Phillip stopped in to check on Jane when he arrived home a few minutes after 10 pm.

Jane, of course, was fast asleep in her bedroom, her tiny hand curled up, touching her lips, her knees drawn up to her chest under the blanket. She breathed in and out quietly, her raven hair spread out evenly around her head in a fan.

George-Phillip was troubled. He didn't like coming home after Jane's bedtime, regardless of the reasons.

Unfortunately, today at least he had good reasons to be so late. The news from the United States had been increasingly grim as the day went on. George-Phillip spent the day on the phone, his number one focus the shooting of Charlie Frazier. The good news was that Frazier was going to recover—the gunshot wound was serious, but not critical. He would be out of the hospital in a few days.

But not on his way home, most likely.

George-Phillip hadn't received any official enquiries yet about Charlie's status, but he knew it was coming. At some point, the United States government would formally ask the British government if Charlie was an intelligence agent, if only because of the circumstances of the shooting. When that moment came, the British ambassador wouldn't have to lie, because he wouldn't know.

George-Phillip had been called to speak with the Prime Minister, who wanted an explanation of why a British citizen—and employee of the Secret Intelligence Service—had been shot in Washington, DC. That discussion had been unpleasant, but George-Phillip made it absolutely clear. Charlie Frazier's employment was and must remain a secret. He was fairly certain the American government would jerk them around for a few days, asking a lot of questions and delaying Charlie's departure. But in the end they would let it go. As friendly nations, the United States and the United Kingdom maintained a polite fiction that they didn't spy on each other. But everyone in the intelligence community recognized that for what it was—fiction.

In practice, in the years since the September 11 attacks on the United States, intelligence budgets for both the United States and the United Kingdom had ballooned, with each government employing tens of thousands of intelligence employees, military, civilian and private contractors, often in overlapping roles. The United States was clearly worse: George-Phillip had read a report indicating that the US had more than 800,000 individuals with secret clearances, most of them employees of private companies. Undoubtedly some of those were employed spying on the United Kingdom. And, George-Phillip thought, no doubt some of them were using their access to secret funding and information to further their own personal aims rather than their government's.

George-Phillip shook his head. Even here, in the doorway to his daughter's room, he couldn't clear his head of work. He straightened himself, stretched a little, then walked out of the room, gently closing the door behind him. He walked down the hall to his office and mixed himself a whisky and soda.

For a minute or possibly two, he looked out at the square. The trees and shrubbery at the corner were overgrown, obscuring the center of the square with its garden and tennis court.

He sat down at the desk with his drink and began to scan through the evening's accumulated emails.

Five minutes later he sat up, alarm bells ringing in his head. Now *that* was interesting. A report indicated that Vasily Karatygin had turned up in Kabul. The former Spetsnaz major had defected from the Soviet Union in the early 80s and later became a deputy leader in Ahmad Massoud's militia in Afghanistan. It was unclear where his loyalty lay now, if any—but it was clear that he ran a huge opium smuggling operation centered in Badakhshan Province.

Karatygin had been on George-Phillip's radar for thirty years because of his involvement in the massacre at Wakhan. He wasn't one to show up in the Afghan capitol for any reason. It was too dangerous, too many competing interests, not to mention the fact that the Americans had a price on his head.

Was it connected?

George-Phillip had to assume it was. Someone—possibly Leslie Collins, possibly Prince Roshan, possibly even Richard Thompson—was making an aggressive move. But who? And why? Why now?

The phone rang. It was O'Leary.

"George-Phillip here."

"Sir, news."

"Go."

"It looks like our player is Leslie Collins. Surveillance picked him up giving orders. He's going after all of the Thompsons, anyone who can even potentially give information on Wakhan."

George-Phillip muttered a curse. "All right. Even Richard Thompson?"

"As far as we can tell, yes, sir. And—you, sir. I've already mobilized an extra protective detail, they'll be on their way shortly."

"I don't need a protective detail, O'Leary, we've been through this."

"Beggin' your parson, sir, but you do, and they're on the way whether you like it or not."

"Fine. O'Leary, you know what to do? Start making arrangements."

"Yes, sir."

George-Phillip hung up the phone and looked out at the square. Adelina Thompson and her daughters were likely in a great deal of danger. They were the wild card, and in some ways that was his fault. He shook his head, and reached for the phone again.

He didn't hear the gunshot in Belgrade Square before the bullets hit the glass.

2. Dylan. 6:26 pm

Dylan Paris leaned back in his chair and closed his eyes. Carrie, Sarah and Alex had all left the condo about forty minutes before.

It was the first time he'd had any peace in days. He felt as if he might pass out any second, but for the moment he wanted to just rest his mind. Sarah's words the day before had been weighing on him. His best friend weighed on him.

Ray would have said something like, *Man up, Studmaster, and tell her. Ask her for help.* He would have. But asking for help, that was the hardest thing in the world. The thing was, he was stuck. He remembered the moment he'd decided to do it. It wasn't that night in the dorms. It wasn't even at the funeral. It was before Ray had even died. He'd been at the hotel with the rest of the Thompson clan. Alex's dad was there, and he had a gin and tonic, and Dylan couldn't keep his eyes off that drink.

He wanted one so badly right now he could taste it.

You're turning into your dad, Dylan.

Fucking asshole.

But it was true.

"Dylan? Can you come here a second?"

Dylan's eyes popped open. Andrea was standing in the hallway, a confused look on her face. He stood and walked toward her. "What is it?"

"This…" she said, pointing in her room. "I went to check out some of the clothes Carrie loaned me, and…"

Dylan frowned. Inside the closet, underneath the pile of clothes, was a cardboard box. Several plastic baggies were in it, filled with white powder.

"What the fuck?" he asked. He walked closer, and picked up one of the bags. Underneath the plastic bag—money. A lot of it. Twenty-dollar bills, stacked.

"Something's wrong," he said.

"Those are drugs," she said.

"Yeah."

"A lot of them."

"Yeah," he replied.

Her face was pale. "Those weren't in here yesterday, or this morning. I know—I went through the closet before I left to get the blood test this morning. Who was in here?"

Dylan tried to think back. That morning, he and Alex had gotten breakfast at the corner diner while Andrea went with Sarah to get the blood test and Carrie went to the Pentagon. The condo was empty except Rachel and the nanny. And their guards.

"I don't get it," he said. "I think we need to call the cops."

"What? Are you sure?"

"I don't know what's going on, Andrea."

Both of them froze when the phone rang. Neither of them had ever heard it before—it was the house landline.

3. Adelina. 3:30 pm Pacific

**delina** knew exactly when they drove into cell phone range again, because both of their phones started to ring with message after message.

Jessica said. "We're popular, aren't we?"

"It was like this when I drove to town last Friday to talk to Julia," Adelina said. "Sometimes I wish I could just get rid of the damn thing." But of course, she knew she couldn't.

"I got like fifty text messages from Sarah," Jessica said. She frowned as she scrolled through the messages then sat up straight. "Mom!" she said in a squeal.

"What is it?" Adelina said, alarmed by the sudden note of urgency.

"Pull over, Mom. Check your messages!"

"I'm sure there's nothing that urgent—"

"Mom! Do it!"

Adelina didn't argue. She pulled the car to the side of the road and pulled up her messages.

Julia had sent her two dozen text messages. Carrie just as many. One message from Richard. It simply said, "Call me."

"Oh my God," she said, when she saw the message from Carrie: Andrea kidnapped. Call. Now. She looked over at Jessica and said, "Call Carrie now. I'm getting us home. I'll call Julia."

She put the car in gear and began to drive, too fast, out of the mountains. She reached for her phone again to dial Julia's number, when it rang.

She stopped the car again as she recognized the beginning of the incoming number.

She answered it. "Hello?"

"Adelina Ramos, please."

Adelina *Ramos*. Of course he wouldn't use her married name.

"This is she." Her voice shook. She hadn't heard that voice in years except once or twice on television, and it shook her to her core. A yearning she didn't think she was even still capable of washed over her, along with fear, because this phone call could only mean one thing. He'd said he would never call again, unless it was the end. He'd said—to forget about him. To forget about what could have been.

"You need to get them out," the voice said. *Them* meaning her children.

"Are you sure?" she said.

"We intercepted some calls. You need to act right now, you're all likely in danger."

Adelina gasped. "All right. Where do I go?"

"Try to make it across the border. I may be able to get you more help there."

She sobbed. Then she threw caution to the wind and whispered, "I still love you."

There was a long pause. Then the response.

"Always, Adelina. Always."

The phone disconnected. In the seat next to her, Jessica was talking too rapidly. "Yes, of course I'm okay, I've been up in the mountains with Mom. Yeah, at a retreat. It's...complicated. But Andrea...she's okay?"

Adelina dialed Andrea's phone without hesitation. She would be the first and most in danger, followed by Carrie.

Andrea's phone went straight to voicemail. She tried again. No good. Was she back in Spain?

No. The text messages from Carrie were clear. She leaned toward Jessica. "Who are you talking with? Is Andrea with them?"

"No," Jessica said. "Andrea's at the condo. I'm on the phone with Carrie, she's out to dinner with Sarah and Alexandra."

Adelina nodded. "Tell Carrie to make sure she's in a public place with lots of people. Tell her she's in danger."

Jessica's eyes widened in confusion. "What?"

"Just *do it.*"

Jessica started speaking rapidly into the phone again. Adelina dialed the condo.

It rang. Three. Four. Five times. Six.

A moment later a voice answered, a male voice with a voice bordering on a Southern accent.

"Hello?"

"Dylan Paris? This is Adelina Thompson."

"Mrs. Thompson? Everyone's been looking for you!"

"No time for that now. Is Andrea there with you?"

"Yeah..."

"Get her out. You're in danger. Do you understand me? Whatever you do, you need to get her out of that building."

"I don't understand—"

Dylan's voice cut off suddenly. At the other end of the line she heard something terrifying. A loud crack.

A gunshot.

CHAPTER TWENTY-FOUR

Trouble

1. Julia. 3:30 pm Pacific

"**Trouble**," Crank said.

Julia looked up from the file. Crank was standing against the window, his face looking tense and alarmed. "What is it?" she asked.

He shook his head slightly then raised a finger across his lips. *Quiet*. Then he whispered. "Two guys. Suit jackets. They're armed. I don't think they're cops."

Julia stopped breathing. It never occurred to her that they might be in danger. But the last forty-eight hours had changed a lot. Andrea had been kidnapped. Her father worked for the CIA. Her mother had been attacked.

She didn't move. A drop of sweat rolled down her forehead. She whispered, "Crank, I'm worried."

"Out the back door," he said. "Grab the file."

She scrambled to gather up the police report describing her mother's assault. Crank grabbed her hand, pulling her toward the door. A deep anxiety lined his face like nothing she'd ever seen before.

He paused at the door to the office, listening. Anthony also stood stock still, face frozen.

"They're messing with the front door," Anthony whispered.

"Go. Back door," Crank replied, his voice urgent.

They moved quickly, Crank in the lead, pulling Julia by the hand, Anthony following behind. Julia winced at the sound of boards shifting and creaking under Crank's boots.

They heard a loud crack downstairs, and a male voice muttering.

Crank didn't say a word, moving now through the kitchen to the back door. Anthony eased the kitchen door closed behind them.

Eyebrows narrowing, Crank twisted the knob, but the back door didn't budge. The deadbolt, which required a key inside and out, was locked.

"Shit," he whispered. He looked desperately toward Julia.

Footsteps up the front stairs. Hands shaking, she got her keys out of her purse. She only had one key to the house and had never tried the back door. Did it use the same key? She had no idea. She got the key out, and tried to fit it in the lock.

It didn't fit.

The intruders had made it up the stairs. Julia imagined them at the landing, trying to decide whether to move toward the office, the stairs, or the kitchen.

Then she heard a man, cursing, and rapid steps toward the other side of the house. Office it was.

"Block the door," she hissed. She turned toward the kitchen window and unlocked it, then tried to raise it. It didn't budge. Damn it. She had to get it open, and get the bars open, quickly.

While she tried again to raise the window, Crank and Anthony lifted the kitchen table and slid it to the door.

"That's not going to hold them long," Crank whispered.

Footsteps in the dining room. Julia grimaced and let out a groan as she tried again to raise the window.

"Oven," Crank said.

Anthony looked at Crank, then to the oven, and nodded. The two of them raced to that side of the kitchen, then slid the oven out, away from the wall. A loud squeal rose from underneath as the metal scraped against the stone tiles.

Julia heard a shout, then footsteps pounding through the house. At that sound, Crank let out a loud cry as he and Anthony lifted the stove in the air. The gas line stretched to its length, then cracked and broke away from the wall at one of the joints.

"No!" Julia cried.

It was too late. They dropped the stove, blocking the table, just as the intruders tried to open the kitchen door. Julia waited for an explosion, a hissing, but nothing came. Instead, Crank dove for the wall and disconnected the gas.

The kitchen door banged against the table, once, then twice, then again.

"Let's go," Crank said. He lifted a chair, and swung it, wide and fast, at the window. With a crash, the glass shattered, just as a hole was blown through the door. A bullet! Julia let out a scream.

"Fuck me fuck me fuck me," Crank said, fumbling for the lock for the barred windows.

"Got it!" he said a second later. The cage lifted wide, and he lifted Julia off her feet and to the window.

"Go!" Anthony yelled.

The three of them tumbled out the window and onto the stairs, then ran for the gate in the back yard. Beyond was the alley going half a block down a public street. Crank held Julia's hand the whole way, tugging her along behind him.

Less than a minute later, they were out onto the street. Crank led them to the corner and stuck his head out for just a second.

"Gone. They're already gone." He sagged for just a second. Julia collapsed against him.

Five seconds later, with a loud crash, an explosion blasted the house, spewing flame and debris out into the street.

2. Leah Simpson. 6:31 pm

One minute later and three thousand miles away, Leah Simpson stood at the door of the Thompson condominium, a frown on her face. Mick Stanson sat at the desk twenty feet down the hall, cleaning his service weapon.

"What? Who is here?" she asked over the radio again.

John Lochlear, the agent at the front desk, said, "Our relief."

She sighed. What kind of fuck up was this? "They've got valid ID?"

"Yeah."

She frowned in frustration. They weren't supposed to have a relief team here until midnight. "Hold them there," she said into the radio. "Let me call Bear. This is bullshit."

She didn't wait for an answer, instead reaching for her cell phone and speed dialing Bear. The phone rang once, twice, a third time.

"Yeah, Bear speaking."

As Bear answered the phone, she saw the light appear above the elevator. She tensed, even as she said the words, "Bear, is there supposed to be a relief team here?"

His response was instant and vociferous. "No! Keep your guard up, someone just tried to assassinate the head of MI-6."

Leah's first response, before she could even think properly, was to crouch and reach for her weapon. The crouch saved her life—when the elevator door opened, a tall man stepped out and sprayed the hallway with bullets. The burst missed her, but took the top of Mick Stanson's head off, spraying the hallway with his blood.

She ducked back, squeezing her body into the alcove across from the Thompsons.

3. Dylan. 6:31 pm

The sound of the bullets from a light machine pistol, probably a MAC10 or an Uzi, were unmistakable. So was the panic in Adelina's voice over the phone.

Dylan didn't have time to deal with Adelina. He let the phone drop and shouted, "Andrea!"

Without thought, he moved as quickly as he could toward the front door. He didn't have a clue what was going on. But he knew that *someone* had put a great deal of both cash and drugs in Andrea's room. He knew that, for reasons he didn't know about, Adelina had chosen *that moment* to call. And now someone was shooting in the hall?

Coincidences were one thing. This was something else.

"What are you doing?" Andrea shouted as he moved toward the front door.

"Finding out what's going on. Stay down."

She didn't need to be told twice. Instead, she crouched down next to the couch, where she had a line of sight to the front door.

He put the chain on then cracked it open.

Across the hall, Leah Simpson was in the alcove, her weapon out. Twenty-five feet further down, another one of their guards was down, blood splattered all over the wall.

Christ. They were pinned in place. No way to escape. Only one defender with a weapon, and that was a lousy automatic pistol with maybe fifteen shots.

Without looking at him, Leah shouted, "Stay inside."

"I am! How many are there?"

"Three!"

Fuck. There was no hope of holding them off. Dylan left the chain on the door and marched directly to Andrea. His eyes scanned the condo, trying to figure out options.

The balcony. Christ. It was eighteen floors down. But if he could get her to the floor directly below—

"Stay," he called, then ran into Carrie's room, the first bedroom after the living area. He yanked the blanket off the bed and carried it out to the living room.

Five shots in quick succession. Loud. That must be Leah.

"Shit. Andrea—they're after you. You're going over the side. Get into the condo below us, then meet me…in thirty minutes. At the war memorial on Norfolk. If we miss each other there, then the Metro station at midnight. Got it?"

Her eyes were wide as saucers. He shoved the blanket at her. The shooting started again.

"Go! You can do this!"

4. Andrea. 6:33 pm

Andrea crouched on the floor, holding a useless sheet, her heart pounding. Four more shots outside shook the entire floor, the glass sliding doors to the balcony shaking and rattling.

Dylan was in the kitchen, pulling back drawers, an unreadable expression in his face. He strode from the kitchen carrying a butcher knife in one hand and a cleaver in the other. As he passed into the living room, then the front hall, he switched the light out, stationing himself in the darkness, knives at the ready.

"Go, damn it! I'm only going to be able to stop one of them, if that many!"

At Dylan's command, she jumped to her feet and slid the balcony door open. The wind was blowing, warm, from the Potomac River half a mile away. She rushed to the edge of the balcony then sucked in a terrified rush of air.

It was eighteen stories down. The cars at street level looked like toys.

She heard a voice cry out, and Dylan said, "Damn it, Leah's down. You need to go *now*."

Tears began to run down Andrea's face freely. As quickly as she could, she wound the blanket up and knotted it around the balcony railing.

Before she could give it even a moment's thought more, she grabbed the knotted blanket, wrapping it twice around her right wrist. Then she looked back at Dylan as she swung a leg over the edge of the balcony.

He stood, ready, in the darkness. His legs were spread shoulder width apart, knives at the ready. His expression was savage. She met his eyes.

Dylan nodded, his expression an inscrutable mix of love and resignation. His hands tightened around the knife handles. She dropped down over the side, just as the front door of the condo burst open. Dylan crouched, huddled in the darkness behind the door.

Andrea gasped as she swung down and the blanket tightened. Immediately she heard a tearing sound, the fabric not strong enough to hold her weight, and she screamed, unable to see anything but the ground two hundred feet below. Flailing, she reached out and grabbed the rail of the condo below Carrie's, gripping it as tightly as she possible could and pulling herself in.

Tears ran down her face as she got purchase for her feet. Her heart beat in her chest so hard that she thought she was going to die of a heart attack then and there, and as she raised her leg and scrambled over the side, she heard more gunshots upstairs.

Shit!

The balcony door down here was locked.

A man was crouched in the kitchen, clearly in view of her, holding his wife and a small child. He watched her with terrified eyes, but made no move to unlock the balcony, even though he'd seen her come over the side on a fucking sheet.

Andrea didn't hesitate. She picked up one of the cast iron chairs on the porch and swung it.

The glass sliding door shattered inward.

She strode into the condo, her feet crunching on the broken glass. She looked at the man who cowered on the floor with his family and said, "Sorry about that."

Andrea let herself out the front door.

Epilogue

1. Carrie

"**What** the hell?" Alexandra said as half a dozen uniformed police officers, accompanied by their Diplomatic Security detail, burst into the restaurant. They were accompanied by Bear Wyden, the head of the investigation.

Carrie shifted position, her body tensing up. The sudden change alarmed Rachel, asleep in the sling across her chest. Rachel began to stir, then cry.

Sarah stood, alarm on her face.

"What is it?"

"Can the three of you come with us, please?"

Alexandra went pale. "Dylan? Is Dylan okay? What's going on?"

"Ma'am, please," Bear said.

The three women stood. Carrie felt an awful sense of dread. Bear didn't say, *Dylan's fine.* He didn't say, *Don't worry, Dylan will be okay.* Unconsciously, she reached out and took Alexandra's hand.

A moment later, the three of them were in the back of a giant SUV. Bear sat in the front passenger seat as a uniformed DSS agent drove. "Go!" Bear said. "The rest can catch up."

Carrie leaned forward and said, "Where are we going? What's going on, Mr. Wyden?"

Bear rubbed a hand across his forehead.

"Mr. Wyden? Where is Andrea? And Dylan?"

Bear shook his head. "We don't know."

Alexandra gasped. "What do you mean you don't know?"

"Exactly that. At least three men bearing apparently valid IDs attacked the condo. They killed the security guards. It appears, as best we can tell, that Andrea got away. It's...less clear...about Dylan. Two of our agents are dead, and at least three of theirs."

"Who are *they?*" Carrie said.

"We don't know. But whoever it is...your family home in San Francisco has been...destroyed. There was a bomb."

"*Shit!* Julia and Crank?"

"They're being questioned by the San Francisco Police Department now, and we've got agents on the way."

Carrie looked back at Alex, who was sitting, stunned, her face pale. She looked...terrified. She looked like Carrie must have looked in the hospital last August, not knowing if Ray was going to make it or not.

He hadn't. And she...did. And some days, some moments, if it hadn't been for Rachel, she might have wished otherwise.

Alexandra didn't have a baby girl to worry about. Carrie reached out and squeezed her sister's hand. Sarah had Alexandra's other hand. They'd be there for her. She was going to need it, if anything had happened to Dylan.

She slumped back to her seat. She still had no idea what had prompted all of this. She didn't know why Andrea had been kidnapped, or who had attacked them. But whoever it was, whatever it was, it was serious enough they were willing to kill. Whoever *they* were.

"What are you doing to find Andrea and Dylan?" she asked.

"We've mobilized every police department in the region, Miss Thompson."

"Mrs. Sherman, please. Or Carrie. But not...that," she corrected.

"Right. We're on it, Carrie. I promise you, if they're out there to be found, we'll find them."

2. Adelina

The sun had long since set over the Pacific Ocean. Adelina glanced over at her daughter. The one daughter she was in a position to take care of.

Jessica was asleep in the passenger seat, curled up in a near fetal position. She'd been asleep most of the drive, her body still recovering from the drugs which had ravaged her system. When she wasn't sleeping, she was eating. The good news was, she'd gained 15 pounds in the last ten days.

The bad news was, she still hadn't made it back over a hundred pounds.

Just one more score to settle with Richard.

Her phone was off. She'd made one stop, at a bank, where she'd withdrawn ten thousand dollars in cash from her savings account. After that, there would be nothing, because she had no plans to leave an electronic trail until they were across the border, and not even then if possible.

For thirty-two years she'd kept his secrets. To protect Luis, and later to protect her daughters.

But now her daughters were in danger. Her home was gone—she'd seen that much. She didn't wake up Jessica as she drove past the smoking hulk of their house. Nor did she spare a moment's regret for the building that had been a prison for much of her adult life. Instead, she kept on going, turned the car around and got on the highway headed north.

Traffic on 101 North was light. It was going to be a much slower route than the interstate, but she wanted to stay off the main highways. She would take it slow, use pay phones, and keep a low profile until she had Jessica out of the United States. Once her daughters were safe, then she could worry about the rest.

Starting with the unfinished business in that phone call, and the chill those words evoked.

Always, Adelina. Always.

3. Andrea

From the War Memorial on Norfolk Avenue, Andrea Thompson could just make out the mass of police and emergency vehicles crowded around the condominium four blocks to the south. Flashing strobe lights in blue and red illuminated the windows of buildings on both sides of the street, and cars were stuck in heavy traffic on Wisconsin Avenue, angry commuters blocked and unable to get around. Horns honked and angry voices cried out.

As she watched, she could just make out EMTs, not in any particular hurry, wheeling a body out of the building.

Andrea knew she looked like any other teenager in the area, though perhaps not dressed as well. Blue jeans and a pajama top. She had no money, no passport, and no phone. She had people trying to kill her who had the resources to gun down federal agents in a highly secured building. She had a father she'd never met, and a not-father who she wished she'd never met.

She had a mystery for a mother, who—for reasons unknown—knew something was going to happen and called a warning. Too little. Too late.

She fished in her pockets, but found nothing but lint.

Meet me...in thirty minutes. At the war memorial on Norfolk.

Far longer than thirty minutes had passed since Dylan said those words. But she'd hung around, just in case. Hoping Dylan might show up. Hoping he might still be alive, even though she knew she'd left him armed with nothing but kitchen knives, as gunmen came down that hallway.

Gunmen intent on killing *her.*

She sighed. Then turned to walk away. Dylan Paris had sacrificed himself so she could live. She wasn't going to waste that sacrifice.

GIRL
OF
RAGE

Dedication

for Khalil
I am proud of you

Acknowledgements

The book took a lot of help along the way to complete. I'll probably forget some people but I especially want to thank Lori Sabin for your fantastic editing, and Sally Bouley and Jackie Yeadon for your extensive assistance reading through the book.

Thanks to my beta readers: Tanya Hall, Kristen Teaff, Emma Corcoran, Kathy Baker, Wendy Wilken, Dimitra Fleissner, Laura Wilson, Bryan James, Michelle Kannan, Sarah Griffen, Amy Burt, Jennifer Mirabelli, Stacey Grice, Kirsten Papi, Beth Suit, Rita Jenkins Post, Kelly Moorhouse and Kirsty Lander. You guys looked at a lot of first draft material and have my everlasting gratitude.

To the baristas at The Thirsty Mind and Amherst Coffee, where I wrote the bulk of the book: you guys and gals are awesome. Khalil and Amirah: thanks for putting up with your dad being distracted, overworked and sometimes addled. It's been one of the toughest years of your lives, and I'm proud of you both.

To my partner and love of my life, Andrea Randall: thank you for listening to my brainstorms and crazy ideas as I worked through this book. Living with another author means we understand each other, and it also means sometimes we're both in worlds of our own creation. But we always return home to each other. I love you.

Prologue

Do You Trust Me?

Andrea Thompson , May 1, 12:04 am

"Dylan?**"**
As she saw the lean figure limping toward her in the darkness, Andrea Thompson stepped out of her hiding place. Dylan Paris walked unevenly toward her through the dimly lit entrance to the Bethesda Metro Station. He wore a light jacket, even though it was really too warm for it, and a canvas backpack was casually thrown over his shoulder. His face was grim, mouth turned into a deep frown, and his eyes were focused somewhere else, far away from her. At first she thought he was going to walk right by her.

"Dylan?"

He stopped, his hands tightening into fists. His pause gave her a second to look closer at him, but he wasn't reassuring. His face, already unshaven, had dark flecks of dirt or something along his jawline. One of his hands shook, and his shoes were soaked. *Why?*

She'd last seen him as she went over the rail of the balcony. He'd been standing in the darkness, knives in hand, ready to protect her.

Get into the condo below us then meet me … in thirty minutes. At the war memorial on Norfolk. If we miss each other there, then the Metro station at midnight. Got it?

Looking at him now, she wondered what the delay had cost him. Gunmen had been coming down that hallway. She shivered as the realization sank in that this man, who she barely knew, must have killed their attackers with his bare hands. The flecks on his face weren't dirt.

They were *blood*.

"We need to get out of here," he said. His voice was low, and barely contained a hint of savagery.

She nodded. "Where to?"

"I'm gonna make a couple calls, see if I can get us a place to hole up."

"What about the *policia*?" She corrected herself. "The *police*."

Dylan just stared at her, his expression unreadable. Then he said, "Come on." He turned and walked out into the darkness. Andrea followed, down an alley, then onto a crowded street. Bars, people crowded onto the sidewalk. Cars were parallel parked along the street.

Dylan took her upper arm in his hands and said, "We can't go to the police because it was police who came after you in the first place. I don't know who they are. But for now, we're getting you under cover."

She nodded, then said, "I don't know."

Dylan stopped and looked at her. "Your sister's my wife, Andrea. Do you trust me?"

She met his eyes. Dylan—he'd put himself between her and killers. "Yes. I trust you."

"All right, then. No more questions, for now."

He turned and strode away. Three cars down, she saw a Chrysler convertible, the top down, parked illegally next to the fire hydrant, its emergency lights flashing. Dylan paused and glanced around. Then he reached in his pocket and took out a cell phone. He looked at it with cold eyes, his jaw firmly set. He quickly tapped a message into the phone, and with one last glance at the people walking by on the street, he tossed it into the back seat of the convertible.

Then he turned and began quickly walking away, pushing his way through the crowd of young professionals out for drinks. At the next corner, he extended his right arm in the air and flagged down a cab.

The car came to an abrupt stop. Andrea peered inside. The cab itself was light blue, with dark blue and orange lettering on the side. Barwood taxi. Hybrid vehicle. The driver looked East Asian.

Dylan opened the door and said, "Get in."

She didn't hesitate, sliding across to the seat behind the driver. The car was small and clean, and the radio was loud, tuned to a news station. He got in beside her and leaned forward, resting one hand on the back of the seat in front of him.

"Where to?" the cab driver asked.

Dylan shifted in his seat, then he said, "You know any good hotels? Like on the other side of town?"

The driver shook his head. "No good hotels there."

"No, listen … good like … I don't want to get asked too many questions. Pay cash." Dylan reached in his pocket and slid out a hundred dollar bill, then slid it into the driver's hands.

The driver looked at Andrea in the rearview mirror. Creepy eyes.

Then his eyes shifted back to Dylan. "I know place in Maryland. Cash only. No ID."

"Perfect," Dylan said.

As the driver put the car into gear, a raindrop splashed on the windshield. The traffic was slow, but they were moving. Three police cars, lights flashing, rolled by going in the opposite direction. Back toward the condo.

Andrea leaned back in her seat. The last three days had been a nightmare. She'd been kidnapped, escaped, then watched her family fall apart with the realization that she and Carrie had a different father than the rest of their sisters. She'd been faced with assault and attempted murder.

She was exhausted and terrified.

"What's the plan?" she whispered, pitching her voice beneath the prattle on the radio so the driver couldn't hear.

"We hide. Get some rest in a place where we can't be tracked. Then we figure out a plan." His voice was low enough she didn't worry about the driver hearing them over the car radio.

"Why did you throw away your phone?"

He shrugged. "GPS. Someone wants you dead badly enough to either be a federal agent or impersonate one. I don't want to be found. I sent a text to Alex to warn her she wouldn't hear from us."

She sighed. "I thought so."

The raindrops fell steadily now, a rapid drumbeat against the roof of the car. For a few minutes she just listened as the taxi driver navigated traffic and the rain fell against the roof. For just a second, the drumming of the rain took her back to Calella, driving along the beach in the summer rain with her best friends. She wanted to go home.

All of this chaos stemmed from … what? Something about her mother? Her real father, whoever that was? She didn't even believe Richard Thompson's assertion that Senator Rainsley was her father. He'd never said anything true to her before. Why should she believe him now?

She needed answers. She needed to know why she'd been virtually abandoned by her parents. She needed to know why strangers had been trying to kill her.

She needed to know who her father was.

"I need answers, Dylan," she whispered.

He didn't answer right away. Instead he stared out into the rain, his face turned away from her. "I know," he finally said. His tone was desolate.

"I need to know who my father is. And who is trying to hurt me and my sisters."

He nodded.

"Will you help me?"

A handful of raindrops pattered against the roof before he turned and put a hand on her shoulder. "Of course," he said. "I'll help."

PART
ONE

CHAPTER ONE
Them's the rules

Adelina. May 1, 10:15 pm Pacific

The little man grimaced, rubbing his eyes. Adelina Thompson had called three times during the drive north, and he'd promised to stay awake until she arrived. But he hadn't been gracious or polite about it. He was short, with thick glasses that magnified his rheumy eyes, and his pale blue pajamas were threadbare, the vertical blue stripes faded into obscurity. She imagined that winter was tough for him—his knuckles were swollen and arthritic.

He had a business here in the shadow of the northern California redwoods, but it was a business that merely limped along. The prospect of the twenty extra dollars she'd offered for late arrival had been powerful.

The campsite was deep in the woods, and the air was moist and warm. Crickets and frogs and God only knew what else made a continuous buzzing, and the darkness hid the trees and cabins and dangers beyond. It was oppressive. Claustrophobic.

"Here's the key. No noise, everybody's already asleep. You're in the second cabin on the left."

"Thank you," Adelina said. "We won't be making any noise. My daughter's asleep in the car."

"I'll just need to make a copy of your driver's license, please."

She lay her hand on the counter and said, "Oh no ... I'm afraid I forgot it."

The old man narrowed his eyes. "Can't rent a cabin without a driver's license."

She frowned. "We're only here for the night. Can you make an exception? You wouldn't make me and my daughter sleep in the car, would you?"

He grimaced. "Them's the rules," he said, sounding unsure of himself. It was after midnight, after all, and temperatures had been dropping.

"Please?" she asked, leaning slightly forward. "I wouldn't ask if it wasn't urgent. You see..."

"I don't need any trouble," the man said.

"We're no trouble. It's just ... my husband..." As she said the words, she dropped her eyes to the floor.

He grimaced. "Left him, did you?"

"He hurt me," she whispered.

The man exhaled. "All right, then. Fine. I guess the copier's not working. You make sure you're out of here early, mind you. We don't get inspected often, but if the county finds out I'm letting people stay without ID, there'll be hell to pay."

She breathed a sigh of relief. "Thank you."

He frowned. "That'll be forty dollars. Plus the twenty you promised on the phone."

¡Gilipollas! It didn't matter. Right now, the important thing was to get Jessica into a bed and get under cover for the night. She couldn't drive without sleep and Jessica couldn't continue at all. Despite the adrenaline and shock of the news of Andrea's kidnapping and finding their home burning away, Jessica had still slipped into a deep sleep within minutes of getting on the highway. She'd tossed and turned, moaning and resistant when Adelina woke her to eat at a fast-food chain along US 101.

That was the withdrawals.

She won't suffer through the same kind of physical withdrawals you see from alcohol or heroin, Sister Kiara had told her. *But it will be almost as bad in its own way. She's only been doing meth a few weeks, but it might be two years before she laughs again, or feels any joy. That's just what happens to the brain. She's done a tremendous amount of damage to herself. In the meantime, all you can do is love her.*

That, and keep her alive. Jessica had been through a harrowing ordeal on an emotional level, but Adelina knew that the only way she could keep her daughter safe now was to run as far and as fast as she possibly could.

She thought about the voice on the phone ... the voice she hadn't heard in more than a decade.

Always, Adelina. Always.

Hearing his voice again gave her a thick pain like a fist buried in her chest, slowly squeezing the breath out of her. He'd been the love of her life. He'd gone away, at her insistence.

Hearing his voice gave her something she hadn't had in years.

Hope.

So she ran. It's not that she thought Richard would hurt Jessica. He was a monster, but in some ways a predictable one. He wouldn't hesitate to hurt Andrea, most likely, reasoning that she wasn't actually his daughter. But Jessica was his, and he knew it.

But Richard wasn't the only threat. She never knew the details, but something terrible had happened in Afghanistan when Richard was there thirty years ago. Something so terrible it had lain dormant, a secret which had floated some careers and killed others. She thought she knew who some of the players were. Prince Roshan, a charming snake of a man who kept his wives in veils in Saudi

Arabia while sporting around Washington with twenty-year-old call girls on his arm, a man who had smiled at her and been charming and had the same cold, lifeless look in his eyes as her husband.

She thought the other threat was likely to be Leslie Collins, who Richard had insisted for years was nothing more than an accountant. He thought she was stupid, and at times through the years it had served her well to let him think that. It had protected her and her daughters. But Collins was no accountant, and when he finally reached a level where further promotion required Senate approval, the now Director of Operations for the Central Intelligence Agency finally had to go public about his career.

Collins wouldn't hesitate to torture small children to accomplish his goals. She just hoped the rest of her daughters had heeded her instructions to run.

If only she knew what had happened in Washington. She'd called the condo that afternoon and gotten Dylan, her son-in-law. Her instructions were simple. Run, and get Andrea out. She heard a loud crack over the phone, then more, and then Dylan hung up. She knew what the sound was. Gunshots. She'd called again, but it was too late. She kept trying, stopping at rare pay phones along the road—there were few enough of those left—but no one answered at the condo.

It wasn't safe to use cell phones. She'd thrown them into the San Francisco Bay as they left town. Then drove, for hours, north, stopping only for one meal and restroom breaks. In a way, Jessica's deep depression and withdrawal made the trip easier.

But Adelina kept questioning herself. Second guessing. Jessica needed to be in heavy therapy. She needed to be in an environment where she could get treatment. She needed to be examined by a doctor. Instead, she was on the run, and the only thing Adelina could do for her daughter was pray.

Finally they had reached her destination for the first night—a campground in Crescent City, California, surrounded by redwoods and quiet. As she got out of the car, Adelina took a deep breath, the scent of pine and spring flowing into her nose. It was a smell of hope.

She stumbled in the darkness to the cabin and unlocked it, the latch opening with a loud, audible click. The door swung wide. A queen bed and a bunk bed. A small table. No sheets or pillows. They would make do. She had a blanket in the back of the minivan, and bundles of clothing from their bags would have to serve as pillows.

First, she needed to get her daughter inside.

Adelina opened the sliding side door to the van. Jessica was sprawled across the middle seat. Her lifeless brown hair was splayed across her face, eyes closed, and mouth open. Since Adelina had taken her to the retreat to dry out less than ten days ago, Jessica had begun to gain weight. But it still wasn't enough. Her face, red and marked with acne, was gaunt, the hollows in her cheeks heartbreakingly prominent, her ribs clearly visible under her tank top.

"Jessica, wake up. Come inside the cabin and you can sleep in a bed."

Jessica groaned and turned her head into the seat.

"Come on, Jessica. I need you to get up for just a minute."

Jessica didn't stir. Adelina closed her eyes. Her daughter was eighteen years old.

Her daughter was a wreck.

She leaned into the van and tilted Jessica out of the seat, pulling the girl to her shoulder. Jessica groaned and flailed, and Adelina staggered a little under the weight, her knees bending. With a lot of effort, she got her arms around Jessica and dragged her out of the van, Jessica's sneaker-clad feet hitting the ground with a thud.

Jessica groaned and said, "All right, all right. Head hurts." Then she stood, and staggered toward the door of the cabin.

As she stepped inside, Adelina sighed and whispered a prayer. For now—for the next few hours—they were safe.

She leaned against the doorframe for just a second, staring in at her daughter, indirectly lit from the headlights of the car. Jessica had staggered in and fallen into one of the bunk beds. Anyone else who saw this scene would see a strung out kid who might be a drug addict or might be anorexic, a kid who couldn't keep her eyes open, brush her hair or take basic care of herself.

Adelina knew what they saw. She'd seen the looks, in the weeks leading up to their final departure from San Francisco. When Adelina had first returned home, switching places with Richard, she'd given Jessica plenty of leash. But it became clear, quickly, that her daughter was out of control. Conflict and rage. Sadness and grief. It was clear Jessica needed help and wasn't getting it.

In February, she had to drag Jessica out of the house when her daughter refused to even get dressed. They'd gone into the grocery store with Jessica padding behind her, wearing pajamas and flip flops, muttering and cursing at her mother all the way through the store.

She'd seen the looks of curiosity and pity from the young mothers. Disgust from single men. Understanding and empathy from the older mothers and grandmothers.

Nothing was as simple as it seemed. Adelina didn't see an eighteen-year-old drug addict lying on the bare mattress in the cabin. What she saw was a three-year-old daughter twirling in her ballet shoes. She saw the daughter who seemed to take on the pain of her daring, sometimes reckless twin. She saw a young teen, fifteen years old at the time, serious expression on her face, as she played Paganini's 24th Caprice for a packed recital at the Green Music Center. One of the most difficult pieces for violin, and Jessica had mastered it. Of all of her daughters, Jessica was probably the only one who had both the musical talent and discipline to match her mother, and until a few months ago, it had seemed likely she was destined for the San Francisco Conservatory.

When Adelina looked at her daughter, she saw the four-year-old who had once followed Sarah around the house, both of them leaving a trail of chaos everywhere they went.

Adelina walked out to the minivan. She looked around in the darkness. She couldn't see anyone, so she reached far back under the driver's seat and removed the thick envelope full of cash. She wouldn't risk leaving that in the van. She removed the blanket and their bags from the back seat, then carefully locked up the van and went inside.

She closed and locked the door, covered her daughter with the blanket, then curled up beside her in the darkness

Adelina suppressed a tear. She didn't have time to fall apart right now. She'd already done that too many times in her life. For now, she needed to hold it together.

All the same, she missed her little girl.

CHAPTER TWO
Insider

Bear. May 2. 12:10 am.

"**Are** we *finished*? I need to get my daughter to sleep somewhere appropriate."

When Carrie Sherman said the words, her daughter stirred in the sling. The baby had cried most of the last hour, finally drifting off into a fitful sleep. They were inside a sterile office in a building she'd never paid attention to before, a few blocks from the main State Department building. A stream of investigators, uniformed officers, and God only knew who else continued to demand answers. The noise had made for a challenging time, as the team of federal investigators asked questions and then asked them again, over and over.

Where was Dylan? Why hadn't he or Andrea come out with them?

Why were drugs found in Andrea's room?

What did they know about their father's career?

Bear Wyden knew the questions wouldn't get any answers, because he knew that the three sisters knew nothing. But her demanding, arrogant tone infuriated him. People were *dying* out there.

"We're done," he said. "For now, we've got you in a safe house in Alexandria. I'm going to need to get clothes sizes for all of you."

"What?" Carrie asked. "We're not going to a safe house."

"Just for a couple days. Your condo is a crime scene, Mrs. Sherman."

"Fine. I'll need all new baby supplies then too. Diapers. Clothes. Formula. Bottles. Breast pump. Either we get that stuff from my condo or someone buys it. And where are my sisters?"

Bear closed his eyes and heard the phone call with Leah in his mind again.

Bear, is there supposed to be a relief team here?

No, he'd said. There wasn't time to say anything more, because the supposed relief team, led by Ralph Myers—an insider, a fifteen year DSS agent Bear had known for at least a decade—killed Mick Stanton and critically injured Leah.

He'd been frantic. Two hours he'd attended to duty instead of running to the hospital. Two hours. And now he had to listen to this spoiled woman demand diapers and bottles.

"Just in case you missed it, Mrs. Sherman, two of my agents died protecting your family. Leah Simpson is in the hospital. Don't take that demanding tone with me."

Carrie wasn't cowed. "Just in case *you* missed it, Mr. Wyden, my sister and brother-in-law are missing because your team failed to protect them. So don't take that judgmental tone with me."

Bear felt his chest and throat tighten. He closed his eyes and struggled to take a deep breath. His mother had suggested breathing exercises to keep his temper under control through the divorce. Sometimes they actually worked. He turned and walked out of the room and into the hall. He could *not* stay in the same room with that woman another moment.

He paced in the hallway for just a moment then reached for his phone. It rang before he had a chance to start dialing.

Secretary Perry.

Secretary James Perry. Former soldier. Vietnam veteran. US Senator for three decades, then presidential candidate. He'd been Secretary of State for six months, and for reasons that didn't mean one lick of shit to Bear, he'd taken a liking to Bear Wyden.

Bear answered the phone. "Wyden, here."

"It's James Perry, Bear."

"Yes, sir."

"I'm going to ask you about progress in just a moment. But first, how's Leah Simpson?"

Jesus. Bear muttered under his breath, then said, "Critical condition, sir. That's all I know. Hospital wouldn't tell me shit when I called."

Damn it. He couldn't recall the words, but using profanity with the Secretary of State was never a good idea.

"And you're downstairs?"

"Yes, sir."

"Put someone else in charge for the next two hours. You go to the hospital."

Bear choked a little. "Sir, I can—"

"That's not a request. She's your ex-wife. Go find out if she's okay."

"Yeah," Bear replied.

Perry disconnected without any further courtesies. Bear leaned against the wall for a moment.

Bear, is there supposed to be a relief team here?

She was calm. Not panicked. Not even anxious. Concerned. Businesslike. Within two minutes of that call she was lying on the floor, a bullet through her hip and another in her chest. And he was here, babysitting the investigation. Screw that.

He walked down the hall and pushed open the door to the offices assigned to the investigation team. His eyes scanned the room and fell on Scott Kelly.

Kelly was a forty-four-year-old former federal prosecutor from Boston. Precise, competent, exacting. Four years prior, his wife had left him, and he decided he wanted to travel the world. He resigned from his position and joined DSS as a high-level investigator, where his first three-year tour had been in Bangkok. He had slightly prominent jowls and dark circles under his red rimmed eyes, and looked perpetually exhausted. His performance reviews, however, were stellar.

"Kelly," Bear called across the room.

"Yeah?"

"I'm going to the hospital to check on Leah, then out to the crime scene. You're in charge."

Kelly raised his eyebrows. "Yeah? When do I get to sleep?"

"You can sleep when the investigation is over."

"Yeah, yeah, whatever. Go check on Leah."

Bear didn't stick around to figure out what else Kelly might have to say. Everyone on the team knew he and Leah had been married for fifteen years. He didn't need them looking at him, wondering, speculating, whatever. He had a job to do.

He was soaking wet by the time he got to the parking deck, and the drive to the hospital felt like it took days. Even though it was well past midnight, traffic near downtown DC was snarled from the downpour. Bear didn't like to drive at all, not in DC, but under the circumstances he had little choice. It pissed him off that he was stuck in traffic. It pissed him off that someone out there was running circles around his investigation. It especially pissed him off that he still had feelings for his ex-wife. His ex-wife, who left him and remarried a college professor of all things. It pissed him off that from the moment he'd gotten her phone call, he hadn't been able to think about *anything else.*

So he drove through the storm in a fog, the rain drumming against the roof of the car, then he walked through the hospital paying little attention to his surroundings, until he finally reached the trauma center at George-Washington University Hospital—the epicenter of the convulsion which had taken one of his daughters and destroyed his marriage.

He'd been here before. Four years before, to be exact. It was the end, really, of his and Leah's marriage, although neither of them knew it at the time. At the time they thought they were there because their eldest daughter was diagnosed with encephalitis. They thought they were there because loving couples support each other through crises.

But when Leanne died of the brain infection, their marriage died too. Part of Bear's soul died, really. He tried to be there for Leah. He did. But all he could see was their daughter. Dying. He had nightmares—nightmares where he woke up choking, nightmares where Leah was shot on duty, and he'd begun to fight for her to switch to a desk job.

Their mild arguments turned into loud ones, and that was fine, until they went silent. When *she* went silent. One year after Leanne's death, an angry silence reigned over their home. Until she left him. Then Bear was transferred overseas—without her.

The thing was, Bear never said goodbye. Not to Leanne. Not to Leah. Not to his marriage, or his life. So now, being back in Washington—even if only briefly—supervising his ex-wife? Not something Bear wanted. It was old wounds being torn open, problems being stirred up. If it hadn't been for Andrea Thompson's kidnapping, Bear would have spent a quiet week in Washington before being reassigned.

Wouldn't that have been nice?

Shit.

Gary Simpson was pacing in the waiting area. Leah's *husband.*

She hadn't been married long. Only a year ago, Bear had been up to his ears in terrorists and jihadis in Islamabad. But he still called Jimmy and Rebecca, via Skype every Sunday afternoon. The kids were getting older, and it had been a couple of years since the divorce was final, so the fact that Leah was dating shouldn't have been any surprise to him.

Married though? That was a surprise. To Bear, her getting remarried was *final* in a way the divorce hadn't been. So when she broke the news one day via Skype, he congratulated her, and then got off the line as quickly as possible.

He'd never admitted to himself that he'd secretly believed they'd one day get back together.

He'd never admitted to himself that their divorce had broken his heart.

Now he was faced with Gary Simpson, who approached him with a wounded, red-faced expression. Simpson was everything Bear wasn't—an intellectual, a college professor, an academic. Simpson would have set off every alarm Bear had for a limp wristed pretty boy. Except for the fact that he was built like a truck and had earned his first degree, a Bachelors in Economics, with a full scholarship as a fullback at Notre Dame. He'd gone on to earn a Masters and a PhD at Harvard.

In short, Gary Simpson was a man to be reckoned with. And right now his face reflected nothing but rage.

Bear started to back up when Gary got close.

"Gary, chill," he said.

"Motherfucker," Simpson said, preparing to take a swing.

"Gary! This isn't going to help Leah!" Bear got his arms up in a protective stance as he shouted the words.

"You got her shot. Doctors said she might die."

"I didn't *get* her shot, Gary."

Simpson moved to attack again, and Bear stepped back. "Gary. I just came to find out how she is."

"What do you care?"

Bear sighed and dropped his arms to his side. "Fine. Hit me. Whatever. I don't care, Gary. I just want to know how she is." As a final step, Bear closed his eyes and waited, because he knew if Simpson hit him, he was going to *feel* it.

The punch didn't come. After a few seconds, he opened his eyes. Gary Simpson had turned away. "They don't know if she's going to make it, Bear."

Bear muttered under his breath, "Motherfuckers."

"Who *did* this?"

"Don't know yet. It was partly an inside job. And I didn't tell you that. We're working on it, all right? Whoever did this—we'll find them. They won't get away it. I promise."

Simpson leaned close. Bear braced himself, but Gary didn't have any fight left in him. Instead, he whispered in Bear's ear. "Don't just find them, Bear. *Kill* them. Do you hear me?"

"Yeah, buddy, I hear you."

Twenty minutes later, Bear was back on the road. He was grateful, for the ten thousandth time, for Leah's parents. As they had in more than one crisis in the past, they'd stepped in, Leah's mom watching the kids while her dad held a vigil at the hospital. He ached to go to them right now. What kind of father stayed at work at a time like this?

The type of father Bear was. He couldn't go to his kids right now, because he needed to find out who had hurt their mother. So, he drove from the hospital to the Thompson family's condominium in Bethesda.

The crime scene.

Despite the very late hour, traffic was snarled on Wisconsin Avenue. A cluster of police vehicles—both federal and Montgomery County, Maryland—spread out in front of and around the 20-story building, blue lights flashing. One lane of Wisconsin was blocked. Bear pulled his car to a stop, parking half on the sidewalk, and a local police officer in a heavy rain poncho approached rapidly. Bear flashed his badge and said, "I'm Bear Wyden. Diplomatic Security."

The cop backed off immediately. They knew who he was, of course.

Bear sprinted through the rain to the entrance of the building. Two more local cops were there, and they scrutinized his ID while he stood there dripping on the tile floor. One of them made a quick phone call, presumably to ensure Bear was cleared to enter the crime scene.

"Forensics team is upstairs," the officer finally said.

"Thanks," Bear replied. Then he walked toward the elevator.

The ride up to the 20th floor seemed to take hours, and the soft music playing in the elevator didn't help. Finally, the doors opened. A uniformed officer—this one from Diplomatic Security—blocked the elevator.

"Bear," the officer said. Now that he'd verified Bear's identity, he stepped back.

The FBI forensics team had spread out across the entire top floor of the building. From the door of the elevator, the hall went off in two directions, with two doors at each end, a total of four penthouse apartments. As he stepped off the elevator, Bear saw that large sections of the floor were taped off.

Ejected cartridges littered the floor near the elevator, each of them neatly marked. It was clear, from here, what had happened. The shooters—as best they could tell there were three of them—sailed past the ground floor security by flashing their IDs. They rode up the elevator just as Leah was calling Bear to ask why a relief team was coming on duty.

On arrival, they opened fire the moment the elevator opened up. Mick Stanton had been halfway down the hall to the left. Twenty-eight years old. Unmarried. He finished law school at Georgetown and decided a future of poring over the books and writing briefs didn't suit him, so he'd joined the Diplomatic Security Service two years before. A promising young agent, shot in the head.

The shooters shifted their fire to Leah. They'd missed her with their first round of bullets, probably because she'd instinctively ducked. She took out one shooter, midway down the hall, and wounded another before she got hit.

The position of the dead shooter was marked clearly on the floor. That one was Ralph Myers.

Ralph Myers. Bear had known him ten years. He and Leah, back when they were married, had hosted Ralph for dinner at their house. Bear knew a lot about him. He was single. Late thirties. Myers was smart as hell, ambitious. He volunteered for dangerous and sticky assignments, and had spent a lot of years in the Middle East, including Iraq, Pakistan and Afghanistan.

Huh. Suddenly it occurred to Bear to wonder. Was Ralph agency? Did this have something to do with the CIA?

Bear walked on further. On the left side of the hall, in the alcove across from the Thompsons' doorway, was a large bloodstain. Leah's blood. She'd taken two bullets and probably looked dead to the attackers when they busted through the door into the Thompsons.

What happened after that was … less clear.

The first attacker didn't make it through the front door, and the reason was clear enough. His gun-hand had been removed at the wrist with a large meat-cleaver. When they ran the fingerprints they got an immediate hit from the military database. Dylan Paris's fingerprints were on the knife, which was partially embedded in the wall.

The second attacker made it into the condo, but not much further. Another knife—this was a sharp, fourteen-inch kitchen knife—was embedded in the man's back. He lay on the ground, arms splayed out, in the middle of the living area. He had a shoulder holster under his coat, but no weapon.

Presumably, after Dylan killed both attackers, he took their weapons. But there were a lot of unexplained questions here. Who were the attackers? Who were they after? Presumably Andrea Thompson, but what was she up to? After the assorted dead bodies, the second big surprise in this investigation was the discovery of four kilos of cocaine in Andrea's room, along with a lot of cash. The cash and the cocaine were out on the floor, and the cash had been tampered with.

Who did it belong to? Andrea?

Bear didn't buy it. But it looked bad. Especially after she apparently abandoned Dylan and busted through the apartment below in an effort to get away from the gunmen.

If it hadn't been for the insider, it looked very much like Andrea's kidnapping—and the subsequent attacks—had to do with some kind of drug war more than anything else.

Which made absolutely no sense at all, unless she was working for someone else.

If so, that was one cool actress. He'd seen her right after she was rescued from the kidnapping. And not in a million years would he believe she'd been faking the shock and terror of that experience.

But something was clearly wrong here, and the Thompson sisters were right in the middle of it.

CHAPTER THREE
"Damn it, Crank."

Julia. May 1. 11:30 pm Pacific

Julia Wilson ran her fingers through her hair. She was frustrated. It was eleven-thirty, and she and Crank had been at the Hall of Justice, the headquarters of the San Francisco police, for hours. She was more than a little bit tired of being stuck there, answering questions hour after hour.

For the last forty-five minutes, she'd been left alone. That didn't fit well with Julia's normal mode of operating. As the manager of one of the most successful bands in the world and the CEO of her own company, Julia didn't spend time cooling her heels waiting on other people. So less than five minutes after her questioners left the last time, she'd gotten up and walked to the door to demand that the questioning be brought to an end.

That was when she discovered that the door was locked.

Julia didn't panic. She didn't raise hell, or bang on the door, or yell. Instead, cold as ice, she turned and walked from the door and sat back down at the small table. She sat with her back straight, one knee crossed over the other, and she stared at the mirror prominently placed on the wall.

She waited. Minutes went by, then more. She resisted the urge to take out her phone. She'd already received a text message from Carrie with the most essential information. Carrie, Rachel, Sarah and Alexandra were under protective custody somewhere in northern Virginia, under the protection of Diplomatic Security. Dylan and Andrea were missing, but Alexandra had received one last text from Dylan shortly after midnight.

I'm with Andrea. We're safe for now. I'll be in touch. Dylan.

Not enough information to do anything with, but at least they knew he was alive. Which was more than they knew about her mother or sister Jessica. Carrie had filled her in on that, too. Jessica had called, after being missing for days. She was with their mother, and according to their mother, everyone needed to run and hide.

That was oh-so-helpful. Typical of their mother, really. Make a short, cryptic phone call about something urgent and expect everyone to drop everything. It didn't make any sense. But then again, little about Adelina Thompson made sense. Julia had long since made her peace with her mother, and generally wasn't bothered anymore. But moments like this—when the entire family was in danger—she couldn't help but be a little cynical.

But then she remembered the photos. The file.

It was pretty clear-cut. Carrie—Julia's next youngest sister—wasn't related to their father. Therefore, Adelina must have had an affair. That didn't really surprise her—she had known for years that neither of her parents had been entirely faithful.

But the result was a surprise. In her father's files, she'd found the report with the genetic testing. And filed away with it, she found a police report, documenting her mother's brutal beating and rape.

The beating took place one day after the date of the test results.

The conclusion was inescapable. Her father—Richard Thompson—her *father*—had beaten her mother nearly to death. Raped her. *Impregnated her.*

Julia had run it through her mind a thousand times in the last six or so hours and it still made no sense at all. The whole concept was unbelievable. How was any of this possible?

Julia didn't have a chance to completely absorb the news however, because two men had shown up at the house. Normally that wouldn't have fazed her in the least—but Andrea had *just* been kidnapped, everything was confused, and as they tried to figure out what to do, the men broke in. Julia and Crank—along with the reporter from the Washington Post who had been along for the confusing ride—tried to escape out the back door, only to be shot at. They made it out, but it was close.

Then, the unthinkable happened. The men had set off a bomb of some kind in the house. Julia stood there in shock, watching her parents' home burning, until the police and fire department showed up.

And so here she was. Waiting. Because the police had apparently disappeared, leaving her locked in this room. She had to go the bathroom, she didn't know where her husband or sisters were, and every second that went by without answers she got more and more angry. The more she thought about it, the more angry she became. Finally she gave in and began pacing.

And that, of course, was when the police came back in. Julia froze and said in a cool voice, "Unless you're planning on pressing charges for some crime, you need to let me go to the bathroom, then talk to my family, right now. I've done nothing wrong and I don't know why I'm locked in this room."

The detective who had originally talked to her—Detective Sergeant Pam Larson—raised her eyebrows. An attractive woman with dark hair and a slightly red face, she had red cheeks and nose—broken capillaries—the obvious look of someone who drank too much.

Sergeant Larson said, "I think you're going to want to talk to the gentleman."

She didn't say anything else, as a man in an off-the-rack grey suit walked into the room.

He set a briefcase on the table in front of him and said, "Mrs. Wilson, have a seat."

A woman followed him, also in a grey suit. She had prematurely white hair, but unlined skin.

"And you are?"

The man nodded and gave a half smile. "I'm Wolfram Schmidt. Special Agent, Internal Revenue Service, Criminal Investigation Division. This is my partner, Emma Smith."

His voice was smooth as butter, his accent odd, part Texas, part eastern European.

Julia stood there, frozen in place. *Internal Revenue Service?* "I'm sorry ... what? Who did you say you were?"

"IRS, Mrs. Wilson. Criminal Investigation Division. Please ... have a seat."

Julia moved on autopilot, sliding into the seat across from ... what was his name? Wolfram Schmidt. Who inflicts that kind of name on their child? "What can I do for you, Mr. Schmidt?"

He smiled and slid a business card across the table toward her. "Mrs. Wilson. First, I want to make it clear, you are not under criminal investigation at this time."

"I'm sorry?" she said, suddenly alarmed. *At this time?* "Why would I think I would be under investigation?"

What the hell was going on? She thought about the last week. Her mother going missing. Her father preparing to go into confirmation hearings as Secretary of Defense. Andrea kidnapped, then attacked by gunmen. Her heart was beating forcefully in her chest.

What would the IRS want to do with her?

Schmidt seemed unperturbed. He opened his briefcase, took out a manila folder, and flipped through it. His attention appeared to be on the folder, but the game he was playing was familiar. He knew what was in that file. This was all about intimidation.

Julia wasn't easily intimidated.

"Mrs. Wilson. In 2011, there were a series of transactions involving your Barclays International accounts that don't have proper documentation in your tax return. Specifically, there was a sale of stock in Beta Pharmaceuticals. Are you familiar with the transactions in question?"

Julia blinked. She didn't have the first clue what he was talking about.

She did, however, know that she was in over her head. She picked up his card, then said, "I don't think I'm going to answer any questions at this time. My attorney will be in touch."

Schmidt raised his eyebrows. "Are you sure you want to go that route, Mrs. Wilson? We can probably settle this all here and now, plain and simple. I don't see any need to make this an adversarial process."

She shook her head. "First of all, as I'm sure you're aware if you've been researching my company, I deal in hundreds of transactions a year. I have no idea about the specific ones you are talking about. Second of all, I think it would be best if you spoke with my attorney. In fact," she said, standing up, "unless you or the San Francisco Police Department plan on pressing charges or coming up with some other reason to hold me further, I'll be leaving right now."

She backed away from the table.

Schmidt looked up at her. His eyes were blue and clear. Menacing eyes.

"Mrs. Wilson. I wouldn't recommend that."

"Thanks for the advice," she said. "But I'm leaving."

For a second, she thought the police were going to stop her, which wouldn't make any sense, because she hadn't done anything wrong—but who knew what made sense? She was intimately familiar with her business dealings, and there was absolutely nothing of interest to the IRS. If anything, Wilson Enterprises, the holding company for the band and all its assets, overpaid its federal taxes. She was scrupulous about such details, and even if she wasn't, her tax attorneys were.

Something was seriously wrong.

Sergeant Larson, the local cop who had originally questioned her, followed her at the door. "Mrs. Wilson, I'm going to have to ask you not to leave town."

Julia froze in place. Then she turned toward the detective. "Sergeant, are you filing criminal charges against me? Yes, or no?"

The sergeant swallowed, then said, "Not at this time."

"In that case, I'll ignore your request. I don't live in San Francisco; my home is in Boston. If you need to reach me, you can do so via my attorney. Where is my husband?"

"He's being questioned, ma'am," the sergeant said.

"No. Neither of us has committed a crime. We were in my parents' house, which was attacked, and instead of helping us, you've been treating us like criminals. We are *finished*."

As she spoke the words in a sharp tone, she saw a familiar face. Anthony Walker—the reporter from the *Washington Post* who had been with them in the house.

"I'm calling my attorney right now. My husband's attorney. He's going to advise you to release my husband *this instant*. Am I clear?"

"Wait here, ma'am," the Sergeant said. Then she hurried off.

Walker sauntered up. "I was wondering when you would get fed up."

She raised her eyebrows. "What do you mean?"

"I told them to call *The Post's* attorneys hours ago. They've been bluffing. Fishing for information because they don't have a clue what's going on."

"I don't have a clue either," Julia replied. At that moment, she let out a sigh of relief, releasing tension she hadn't even known she was holding in. A door down the hall opened, and her husband came walking out toward her.

Crank Wilson was considerably taller than Julia. Bleached and spiked hair. He wore half a dozen earrings, spread unevenly between his ears.

He gave her a lopsided grin, the same grin she'd fallen in love with when she was a college student and he was struggling as a musician, trading gigs for beer.

They'd had their share of conflict, especially their first three years together. Misunderstandings. Raging arguments. They'd thrown dishes, and on one memorable occasion, Crank had smashed an acoustic guitar against their dinner table, shattering it. Each time they'd apologized, with tears and emotion and love. And over time, they'd mellowed. Her barriers came down as she slowly learned to trust for the first time in her life. He grew up, and over time they discovered that on top of being passionately in love—they also liked each other, a lot. They laughed, and played silly games. They traveled the world together.

As soon as she saw his smile, Julia melted, walking to him and wrapping her arms hard around him.

"You okay, baby?" he asked.

"Let's go," she replied. "We need to go, now."

"Right," he said.

Five minutes later they walked out the front door of the Hall of Justice, both Crank and Anthony trotting to keep up with Julia's pace. At the corner, she raised an arm high, and held it there. It took no more than thirty seconds before a cab pulled up.

"Never fails," Crank said. "Takes me half an hour to get a cab, usually."

"I wonder why?" Anthony said with a smirk.

"No one asked you," Crank replied in a friendly tone.

They all climbed into the cab, and Julia leaned forward. "Hayward Airport, please."

"Yes, ma'am," the cab driver said. "You've got a flight arranged there?"

Hayward was a general aviation airport, of course, and the easiest place to get a private jet in and out of San Francisco. She was happy to be leaving San Francisco. It was her family's home, in theory, but it had never been hers.

Julia, normally scrupulously polite even to people she intensely disliked, didn't reply. It's not that she didn't hear the cab driver. She did, but the words didn't really sink in until Crank said, "Yeah, we've got a flight. We're a little late, so it would be great if you could get us there quick."

As he finished saying the words, he leaned back and whispered in her ear, "You okay, babe?"

She shook her head and crossed her arms over her chest.

I want to make it clear, you are not under criminal investigation at this time.

Which meant nothing. It meant they didn't have anything yet, or they were on a fishing expedition, or they thought she'd done something and might confess. The whole thing reminded her all too vividly of the incredibly painful ordeal her sister Carrie had gone through less than a year before. Investigation at NIH. Husband court-martialed by the Army.

For a second, a flash of shame passed through her. She remembered shying away from Ray when she first heard the news. On trial for war crimes. For killing a little boy. For a few minutes, she'd let herself believe the crappy news she saw in the papers and on CNN.

Oh, Carrie. She wished she'd been better to her sister. She wished *the world* had been better to her sister.

Finally she answered, "I don't want to talk about it here, Crank. Let's get to the plane. I need to know where everyone is."

"All right, babe," he said in a low, deeply concerned voice. "I'll make the calls. You just ... relax."

She could hear the worry in his tone. And she knew it was her own fault in a way. Julia didn't fall apart. Julia didn't freak out. She didn't panic or get hung up on anything and maybe sometimes she just *needed* to. Because right now, all she could think of was her sisters, wondering whether they were okay. Without thought, she found herself dialing her phone.

"Babe, it's almost three in the morning back east," Crank said.

"What about Jessica? Where is she?"

He shook his head. "Carrie texted earlier. Jessica called this afternoon. She's out there somewhere."

"Damn it, Crank."

He put his hands on both sides of her face and leaned close. "Julia. Calm. Okay? It's going to be okay. I promise."

"You don't know that. You can't know that."

"I know you can't fix it all from this cab. We'll fix this, Julia. Okay? But we can't do it, *right now, right here.*"

She swallowed and nodded. Of course he was right. But that didn't make it any easier.

CHAPTER FOUR
Safe House

Alex. May 2. 3:42 am.

I'**m with Andrea. We're safe for now. I'll be in touch. Dylan.**
That was all she had. She didn't know where he was. She didn't know if he was hurt. She didn't know if he was *drinking*. She didn't know if something horrible had happened. All she knew was he was with her sixteen-year-old sister, and that they were safe. *For now.*

Alex had messaged Dylan back at least a hundred times through the night. But no luck. She'd gotten desperate enough that while they were still being questioned at the State Department, she'd shown his text message to her questioners. That had started a flurry of activity, which resulted in absolutely nothing that she could tell.

Sometimes Alex Paris thought she was going to explode from the stress. It seemed like nothing she did made things easier. She'd forgiven Dylan. She'd forgiven herself. She'd done everything she could to protect herself and make herself stronger. She'd stood by him when he struggled with the physical therapy. She'd stood by him when he was drowning in post-traumatic stress. And after a long fight, it had seemed things were getting better. That life was getting better. It had seemed that she was going to get her happily ever after, after all.

But real life didn't work that way, did it?

It didn't. Because shit happened. Best friends showed up with the news that people you loved were criminals. Best friends got killed, leaving behind young widows and unborn children. *Ray* had been killed, leaving a gaping wound in her sister *and* in her husband, and it wasn't fair, because there was nothing Alex could do to heal either one of them. She'd spent the last nine months holding their hands and watching them cry, and watching her husband fall to pieces.

Because that's what Dylan had done. No question. When Ray died, he took part of Dylan with him. In some ways, he'd taken the best part of Dylan. The honorable part, the part who would never lie to his wife. When Ray left, he left behind a shell of Dylan, a Dylan who looked the same and sometimes acted the same, but was actually hollow.

Sometimes Alex felt like it was *her* husband who died, not Carrie's.

That's exactly how she'd felt when they'd gone out. Was it only eight hours ago? It felt like a lifetime. His last words to her had been, *I'm just exhausted, Alex. I miss Ray and I'm tired and sick and just … please. Go without me tonight, okay? I'll be fine.*

So she did. She went out with Carrie and Sarah and the baby. While she was having dinner, armed gunmen had gone after Andrea and Dylan. *Why?* The questioning had been pointed. Did she know about the drugs? Did she know about the money? Both had been found in the condo. Did Dylan have something to do with it? Did she know where he had gone? Where Andrea had gone?

Nothing they said made sense. None of it.

It was nearly two in the morning before the DSS agents had brought them in an armored SUV to a nondescript ranch house in northern Virginia. They could have been anywhere in America. Drab brick. Scuffed hardwood floors. Sliding glass doors to a dark backyard. Well-stocked guest rooms, clean and impersonal. One of the rooms had a crib and was fully stocked with diapers, bottles, powdered formula, zinc oxide, and a hundred other possible needs for Rachel. Someone had been thorough.

The only thing the house didn't have was safety. It was in the middle of nowhere. It was a *safe house.* It merely underscored the fact that someone had tried their best to kill Andrea and Dylan tonight, and that neither of them had surfaced since, except for that one, cryptic text message. Alex already knew every inch of the bare bedroom she'd been impersonally assigned. Roughly 120 square feet. A closet with a sliding panel door. Crappy carpet. Crappy windows, frosted to make her invisible to snipers, she supposed. A queen-sized bed that was far more comfortable than her and Dylan's second-hand bed in New York, but not nearly as welcoming.

It was cold. And she missed her husband.

But missing Dylan was nothing new, was it? She'd had plenty of practice at that.

So Alex lay in bed, watching her phone, waiting to hear from the man she loved. Waiting to hear from the man she knew was fighting to keep his head above water but wouldn't reach out to her for help. Waiting to hear from the man who she'd have done anything for. She didn't cry. Alex Paris was all out of tears. Now she just lay there, waiting. Waiting, and wishing.

In the nearby rooms, she knew her sister Carrie slept, baby Rachel in her crib. At the opposite end of the hall, Sarah. None of the three of them were in good shape, but Sarah, in particular, seemed shaky. She hadn't talked at all in the last couple of hours before they reached the safe house, only answering questions in monotone with as few words as possible.

They'd been in the safe house for two hours almost, but Alex hadn't slept. Instead, she lay there in the bed, staring at the ceiling, wishing she could go back in time and change everything. Her wishing was futile. Frustrating.

She felt like she'd spent most of her relationship with Dylan separated. When they met and fell in love, they'd lived thousands of miles from each other, and that distance had almost killed them. She went to college; Dylan went into the Army. Only through a series of improbable coincidences and near miracles did they have a chance to become a couple again.

Then Ray had to go and die.

She knew it was irrational. It wasn't Ray's fault. It's not like he committed suicide. He was *murdered*. But irrational or not, she was angry with him. She was angry with fate, or God, or whatever it was about the universe that allowed her husband's best friend to die under those circumstances, leaving behind little more than a messy pile of survivor guilt.

Alex sighed. She was wasting her time, rethinking about the same things over and over again. She was exhausted and stressed and worried and there was absolutely nothing she could do about it. She rolled over, staring at the wall. Pale moonlight shone through. She could see the vague shadows of the trees in the frosted glass, swaying and rolling in the wind, the raindrops rattling against the gutters. It must be blowing like crazy, because occasionally the window rapped slightly in its frame.

Dylan and Andrea were out in that.

Somewhere.

CHAPTER FIVE
Something bothering you?

Meredith Collins. May 2. 4:30 am.

Meredith Collins lay in her cold bed alone, staring at the ceiling, listening to the drumming of the rain outside and the echo of her own breath against walls which were too far away in an empty room.

It was half an hour before Leslie usually rose for the day, and he'd already been out of bed for half an hour. It hardly mattered—she knew he hadn't slept. For a week or more, he'd been short with her, he'd been late nearly every night, and he'd spent long hours locked away in his office on the phone.

She sighed. *Poor Leslie.* He'd spent decades working his way up, enduring dangerous tours in places like Afghanistan and Indonesia. He'd devoted his life to his country, to the safety of others, and now he'd finally reached the pinnacle of his career. And instead of being able to relax, instead of being able to slow down and give orders, he'd become more stressed, more overworked, more—*cold*.

It wasn't fair. Logically she knew that high office meant a lot of pressure. More pressure than ever before, because now not only did he have to do a good job, but he had to navigate the political waters of the White House with a fickle, inexperienced President and a Congress which had a vendetta against the federal government itself. It wasn't enough to be good in that environment. You had to be perfect.

But knowing that intellectually wasn't enough to ease her heart. It wasn't enough to stop her from worrying as she watched her husband age before her very eyes.

She slid out of the bed. It was early, but she could at least get some coffee going and prepare to greet the day with some semblance of calm.

The truth was, she rarely knew what to do with her days anymore. Susan, their eldest, had graduated from Princeton and gone on to the FBI—she was now at the academy at Quantico and reportedly doing well. Woodrow and Franklin, the twins, were undergraduates at Columbia.

Since the twins had gone to college, her days were frightfully empty. Quiet. Leslie was gone from 5:30 in the morning until late in the evening sometimes, and their house had been too big even for a family of five, much more so for the two of them. Even when he was home, he wasn't really here anymore. She sometimes filled her days with friends in her bridge club, and served on the board of the McLean Women's Club, but when she was honest with herself, she had to admit that she was unbearably lonely.

She padded down the hall in her bare feet, passing his office on her way to the kitchen. Unusually, the door was cracked. Leslie had soundproofed his office when the children were very young, and out of habit, he always closed the door.

She paused just for a second, her feet faltering, when she overheard Leslie say words that shook her to the core.

"I don't really care, Danny. I want them found, and I want them dead. No more fuckups. Andrea Thompson and Dylan Paris need to turn up in the Potomac. Am I clear?"

She stopped, her feet buried in the thick plush carpet.

Andrea Thompson. Wasn't that—Richard Thompson's daughter? She'd been kidnapped earlier in the week; it had been all over the news. What would Leslie have to do with that? It didn't make any sense. Even though she never got involved in his work, even though she'd never asked questions or wondered or doubted, she found herself paralyzed in the hallway, listening.

"Yeah, I know," he was saying. "But don't worry about that. The Justice Department's going to be holding a press conference this morning. Richard Thompson is going down. We don't have to worry about him anymore."

A trickle of sweat ran down between her breasts, and she felt her chin involuntarily shaking. Richard and Adelina had been friends for twenty years. This—it didn't make sense. Why would Leslie be up in the middle of the night plotting against his friend? Taking about *killing* his friend's daughter?

She stumbled as she moved backward away from the door, and her nightgown caught on a closet doorknob. The thin fabric tore along the seam as she yanked the nightgown. She ignored the damage, instead moving as quickly as she could down the hall to the kitchen. Hands shaking, she poured water into the coffee pot and started it brewing.

She took a breath, trying to calm herself, and looked out the kitchen window into the wet darkness outside. Even though it was very early in the morning, she knew the traffic would already be backed up along Old Dominion Drive, a third of a mile down their driveway. She rarely heard any traffic—the trees fronting the property were too thick to allow much sound through, and the long driveway took a sharp turn halfway there, effectively blocking any lights from the road. Their house was old—a converted farmhouse built in 1842, which was often included in the annual Tour of Homes sponsored by the Women's Club. The house had been a sore point with her and Leslie—he'd wanted to add a substantial addition, but the Women's Club and the Historical Society had fought the addition. So, unfortunately, had Meredith. That was five years ago, but she was afraid he still hadn't forgiven her.

She realized her hands were still shaking as she stood at the window. What had the phone call been about? The coffee pot was almost finished, the machine making the loud bubbling sounds it always made when it was finished brewing. She turned around and let out a startled squeak.

Leslie was in the doorway.

"You scared me!" she admonished.

He walked to the coffee pot casually, then took the carafe out and shook his head. "The machine generally works better if you put coffee grounds in it, dear." He poured out the hot water that had collected in the pot. She'd completely forgotten to put grounds in. She stood there, wringing her hands as he started a new pot, grinding the beans for an unusually long time before scooping the grounds into the filter.

His eyes were lifeless as he restarted the pot. "Something bothering you, Meredith?"

"I... I—"

"Perhaps you overheard something?"

She nodded, still wringing her hands.

"Meredith, what was it your father used to say?"

She knew instantly what he was talking about. Her father—George Mason Cutter—had been a Navy admiral. During World War II he'd flown a F2A Buffalo aircraft off the deck of the USS Hornet before he was shot down and spent nearly 24 hours in the water before being rescued. By the Korean War he was squadron commander and a fleet admiral by the late 1960s, but his career ended under a cloud. An accident and subsequent fire on the aircraft carrier USS Forrestal killed 134 sailors and destroyed millions of dollars worth of equipment. Admiral Cutter wasn't officially held responsible—but he'd been forced to retire, a bitter, aggrieved man. Right up until his death in 2004 at the age of 82, he'd frequently said that no one understood what patriots were forced to do to protect their country.

Civilians never understand, he would say. *Of course it was horrible we lost those sailors. But it was a war. You can't win a war if you don't take risks.*

She sighed. "He used to say civilians didn't understand."

Leslie nodded. In a slow, condescending tone he said, "That's right, Meredith."

"Les ... what don't I understand?"

He turned away from her, a troubled expression in his face. Slowly, he pulled two coffee mugs down from their hooks and walked to the refrigerator, getting out a carton of half-and-half. She stood anxiously; still wringing her hands as he poured the coffee, then poured a splash of half-and-half into each. Neither of them used sugar anymore. He slid her cup toward her.

"How much do you know about what I actually do for a living, Meredith?"

She shook her head and shrugged. The question made no sense. She knew *nothing* of what he did.

"Meredith. My job is to protect the security of the United States. You know that."

She grimaced. "What does that have to do with Richard and Adelina, or their daughter?"

"Well, it seems that there has been more going on there than we realized. In fact, Richard has been involved in some very shady dealings. Treasonous dealings."

"I don't understand."

"I can't explain it all, Meredith. He's involved in some kind of serious drug money laundering, and his daughter, the oldest one, has been assisting him with moving the cash around. Her husband's a rock musician, you know."

Meredith felt her heart slowing down. Of course. There was an explanation, and it was even one that made some sort of sense. Except she couldn't imagine Richard Thompson being involved in anything so sordid. "It all seems so ... greedy."

"That's what happens when people have power, Meredith. They get greedy. I've uncovered some very disturbing history about Richard recently, unfortunately. I had to meet with the Justice Department to turn over a lot of it."

She shuddered. Poor Adelina. She must be heartbroken.

"Why didn't you tell me?"

Leslie raised an eyebrow. "You know the answer to that. It's all classified. You should never have heard what you did hear."

"Explain that, please. Classified or not. I heard you saying ... saying..." She couldn't finish the words. She literally, physically could *not* finish the sentence. That she'd heard her husband ordering the killing of a teenage girl.

Leslie shook his head. "What did you hear, Meredith?"

She swallowed. And whispered, "Andrea Thompson. That ... that..."

"That she was to be killed."

Meredith shuddered.

"Meredith, Andrea Thompson is not what she seems."

"She seems like a sixteen-year-old girl who was kidnapped."

"The news didn't report that the kidnappers were known, vicious killers. Both of them heavily involved in the drug trade and terrorism. The news didn't report that she killed *both* of them with her bare hands. She may be sixteen, but it's likely she's psychotic. Didn't you ever wonder why the Thompson family never brought her around? As best as we can figure, this was some kind of deal gone bad. These are *not* nice people we're dealing with."

"But what about a trial? Bringing her into custody? Why would you—?"

Leslie shook his head. "Sometimes, we can't do things all nice and clean and neat. That's what it means to be in a position of power. You have to make decisions that are the best for all. You know that. Your father knew it too. But the thing is ... I can't sit around and wring my fingers and worry. I have to take action. Richard knows I'm on to him now, and I fully expect he's going to do everything he can to take me down. And—Meredith—he's the acting Secretary of Defense. He has resources at his disposal I can't even dream of."

"Are you in some kind of danger?" She didn't like the way her voice rose at the end of the sentence. It spoke of fear and anxiety and dependency.

He sipped his coffee, and from the set of his lips and eyebrow, she knew he was taking the question seriously. Finally, he nodded and said, "Yes. I'd say I'm in danger. Both professionally and personally. And it's essential I deal with that danger."

"I don't see—"

He held up a hand, cutting her off. "Meredith, Richard Thompson is a dangerous, ruthless man. He's at the top of his career, and he won't put up with any threats. He's right next to the President of the United States. If I don't deal with this, it's not just me in danger, dear. It's the country. It's the President. Now you tell me. What would your father say if he was still alive?"

She swallowed. Of course he was right. She knew Richard. She'd seen, at a few dinner parties over the years, how dominant he was. How occasionally he would say something to Adelina with *just the right tone* and she would go silent. Terrified of her husband. A husband Meredith knew was cold as ice. They'd been acquaintances over the years—friends even. But they'd never gotten *too* close. The Thompsons weren't people you got *that* close to, because it was clear that they only opened up so far.

She sucked in a breath and took a sip of her coffee. Then she said, "Leslie, I'm sorry. I didn't mean to overhear anything, and what I did overhear was none of my business. I trust you. I know you'll do what's right."

Leslie looked at her and said, "You're going to see a lot in the papers in the next few days and weeks about them. Things that will seem crazy—even unbelievable. Do you understand?"

She nodded. "I do."

"Trust me, Meredith."

"Of course."

He took her hand and gave her a smile. But it wasn't warm. Then he turned away, walking back to his office down the hall. Undoubtedly, he would close the soundproof door.

She turned back toward the window. The barest edge of the sunrise was visible above the trees, just a slight lightening of the sky. In another hour it would be completely light. Leslie would be gone to work by then, and she had a meeting this morning to plan the annual Tour of Homes.

Time to put Richard Thompson and his family out of her mind.

CHAPTER SIX
They took everything?

Crank. May 2. 9:25 am.

Crank's eyes jerked open when he felt the wheels of the plane touch down with a loud screech, the tiny jet bouncing and bumping down the runway at Stafford Regional Airport forty miles south of Washington, DC. Instantly awake and craving a cigarette, he slid up the plastic window cover and looked outside.

The sky was ominous, banks of grey and black clouds forming a roof above them. It had been nearly one o'clock in the morning in California before they finally got off the ground, and the second half of the flight had been interrupted by stomach-wrenching turbulence. Five and a half hours later, plus three time zones, and it was already mid-morning here.

Across the aisle from him, Julia stirred, sitting up. Crank looked outside as the plane taxied to the end of the runway and turned to the left. From here he could see Interstate 95, which they would take to get into the DC area.

It was a parking lot. Lines of cars were backed up, unmoving, as far as the eye could see. A moment later the plane turned again to taxi back toward the general aviation terminal, and the view shifted to blissful, peaceful woods, hangers and warehouses. No traffic. Sometimes ignorance *was* bliss. Soon enough, Crank would be stuck in that traffic.

"What time is it?" Julia groaned. This despite the fact that she *already* had her phone out and was checking her email.

Crank didn't answer. He recognized the expression already on her face—a line, slightly off center, creasing her forehead. She was irritated about something.

"What the hell?" she muttered. She started dialing her phone.

"Problems?" Anthony said.

Crank looked back over his shoulder. The *Washington Post* reporter was sitting in the seat behind Crank, covering his mouth as he yawned. His eyes were red and puffy.

"I don't know," Crank replied. "Seems like everything's problems lately."

He stopped talking as Julia finally reached whoever she'd been calling.

"Mary, it's Julia. Talk to me."

Quiet, as Julia listened. Her expression grew more severe, then in a high pitched, strained tone she said, "What do you mean they're taking everything?"

Crank met Anthony's eyes. That didn't sound good at all. It wasn't the sort of thing he'd ever discuss with a reporter, but they had been shot at and nearly blown up together the previous night. If he couldn't trust Anthony Walker at this point, they had even bigger problems than he'd imagined.

The plane came to a stop, lined up with other jets of similar size. Julia immediately unbuckled her seat and stood, walking a few paces behind them. A moment later the co-pilot stepped out of the cockpit. "We'll have you ready to exit in just a moment, Mr. Wilson."

Crank had no idea what the plan was for transportation or luggage. But usually Julia had a car arranged. While she was busy on the phone he asked the copilot, "Um … our luggage? Has our transportation arrived?"

"Yes, sir, I understand there's a car here to take you to Arlington. We'll have your luggage offloaded in just a few minutes."

"Thanks," Crank said. He *did* know they were planning to check into a hotel in Arlington. Which one, he had no idea—he'd never really paid attention to that kind of detail.

"No!" Julia said, too loud, into the phone. "Of course everyone will get paid. Just—tell them to take the rest of the week off. Paid, of course. Yes … I know it's

Monday morning. Yes, I know what that will cost. But everybody gets paid. I'm in Washington, DC right now—or I will be in a couple of hours, depending on traffic. I'll find out what's going on."

Everyone will get paid?

Crank ran those words through his head. What was she talking about? Of course, everyone would get paid.

Julia hung up and looked at Crank, alarm in her eyes.

No. Not just alarm. Her eyes were … almost hollow. She was terrified.

"Jesus, babe, what is it?"

"The IRS. They served a warrant at the Boston office. Everything's been seized."

"What?" Crank said. "What do you mean, everything?"

"I mean *everything*. They took the records, the files, the computers. Mary said they took everything out of the office, told everyone to go home, then hung a *sign* on the front door saying we were closed for business."

As her words slipped into the curse, her tone went higher and higher pitched. "The IRS said we were closed for business, Crank!"

"I'm sure it's just a misunderstanding," he said.

"Doubt it," Anthony muttered.

"What the hell is that supposed to mean?" Julia asked.

Anthony rolled his eyes. "A misunderstanding? The same day your house gets blown up and just a few days after your sister gets herself kidnapped? I'm pretty sure you're a smart lady, Julia. You need to start thinking this stuff through. Because if the IRS is after you, you've got real trouble."

Her eyes flared, and she said, "Thanks for the news, Anthony. Why are you along for this trip?"

He smirked. "Seems to me you could do worse right now than have a journalist on your side."

She took a breath then closed her eyes. Crank could almost hear her counting. He could imagine the words running through her head. *One … two … three … four … fuck it.* Julia wasn't the most patient person on earth. Her eyes snapped open. "My apologies. Let's get to the car. I've got a lot of work to do." She turned and walked toward the front of the plane.

Anthony didn't respond. Julia had the capability to turn on a dime, and Crank had years of experience dealing with her. Anthony Walker was a newcomer.

Ten minutes later, Julia and Crank were sitting on the sleek leather back seat of a Lincoln Town Car, with Anthony in the front passenger seat. The car pulled out of the airport silently. Crank could feel the tension as Julia dialed again.

"Marty? It's Julia Wilson."

Crank nodded, slipping his phone out of his pocket. Martin Barrymore was their attorney.

"We've got problems," Julia said. Then she launched into a narrative about the bombing of her family home, followed by their detention in San Francisco, the questioning by Wolfram Schmidt, that freak from the IRS, and then the news that the IRS had apparently seized their offices in Boston.

Crank was a musician. He was the lead singer and guitarist for one of the most successful bands in the world. He was, technically, a multimillionaire many times over. But when it came to legal or financial matters, he was out of his depth. Quite intentionally, he'd never really taken any interest in the business outside of supporting Julia's efforts. He listened. He knew all about the problems they had with the music being pirated, with declining sales revenue, with counterfeit merchandise. But in the end, it was his job to make music, and Julia's to make money.

So now, in the middle of a crisis?

He felt useless. Worse than useless. Because he couldn't help but wonder if he'd said something to Schmidt that might have gotten them into trouble.

You signed the tax returns, Schmidt had said. *So clearly you're responsible for them, right? Tell me about those stock sales.*

I don't know what you're talking about, Crank had replied. Over and over again.

Anthony twisted around in the front seat and said, "So, you just make the music, right?"

"Yeah," Crank replied. He felt defensive about it. Should he have taken a more active role? Julia loved the business side of things. She always had. But now he wondered if he should have stayed more involved. More engaged. Was he giving her the support she needed? Had his neglect of the business somehow put them in danger?

"You mind if I call in to some of my guys at the national desk? Something stinks here."

Crank met Anthony's eyes. Julia had trusted him this far. And it's not like he had to ask. The guy could go ask whatever questions he wanted.

"Yeah, knock yourself out. Whatever." *Whatevah.* He was tired, and he knew when he was tired his accent was wicked strong. And he didn't really care what Anthony thought anyway.

All the same, he listened as Anthony dialed and started talking.

"Hey, Ron? Anthony Walker. Yeah, listen, got a question for you. I'm sitting in a car right now with Crank and Julia Wilson … yeah, really … anyway, they've run into some issues with the IRS and something stinks … *what?*"

Crank stiffened. Anthony had jerked in his seat, his back stiffening as he said the word *what?* What was that about?

Anthony had taken out his notebook and was scribbling in it as he nodded. "Uh-huh ... yeah ... okay. Isn't that pretty quick?"

The response was loud enough Crank heard it. The guy on the other end of the line said, "Hell, yes."

In the meantime, to his left, Julia was speaking into her phone. "Martin, I get they've got an investigation going. We'll deal with that. But there's due process. They can't just come in and send my employees home and take *everything* from the offices."

Her face blanched a little at the response. "What?" she said. She waited a second, then said, "All right, so they can. But they *shouldn't*. That's where you come in."

She listened, her face looking thoughtful. "Okay ... yeah. Yeah. Right. In the meantime, how do I pay my employees? Our payroll is fifty-thousand dollars every two weeks."

She frowned. "No. That's not acceptable. I can't tell them that."

Jesus Christ, Crank thought. None of this made any sense. And seriously? They paid that much every two weeks? He knew they had a large office full of employees in Boston—twenty-five people, actually—but that was still a lot of money. He tried to figure out the math and got lost. Then he got frustrated. Why the hell didn't he know this stuff?

He turned back to Anthony, who had disconnected his cell phone.

"What the hell was all that about?" Crank asked.

Anthony looked at him, surprise in his eyes, and said: "This is way bigger than I thought."

"What do you mean?"

Anthony grimaced and rubbed the bridge of his nose between his thumb and forefinger. Then he said, "The Attorney General just announced a special prosecutor is being convened to investigate Richard Thompson."

"What?" Crank and Julia said simultaneously. She set her phone down at her side, without any ceremony or word to the attorney on the other end of the line.

"Sorry, Julia. There's supposed to be a press conference at ten. But you know how it is—someone already leaked the story. Apparently there's evidence linking your father to major drug money laundering."

"Bullshit," Julia said.

"Yeah, well, the Attorney General doesn't think it's bullshit. Apparently the IRS doesn't either, because at the press conference they're going to accuse you of managing the whole operation."

CHAPTER SEVEN
Occam's Razor

Carrie. May 2. 9:35 am.

"**M**y computer," Carrie muttered, adding to the list she was compiling on her phone. Her list of things she needed from the condo, if they hadn't been seized as evidence.

"My guitar," Sarah said.

"Sure," Carrie replied. She added it to the list then took a sip of her coffee. Sarah sat across from her, reclined in the thickly padded dining chair, her legs stretched across to another chair. The table was thick glass that colored her legs with a pale blue and slightly obscured and blurred the thick, ropy scars on the outside of her left leg.

Across the economically furnished room from them, Alexandra paced back and forth in front of the sliding glass doors. Every few minutes she checked her phone. A few feet away, Rachel was asleep in the crib someone had managed to procure in the middle of the night.

All three of them jumped when they heard a knock at the front door. From the kitchen, Ben Crosby, one of their several guards, called out, "I got it."

Ben was in his mid-twenties, muscular, short-haired, and bore several weapons. A former soldier, he was jocular, with a ready smile and blue eyes that flashed intelligence and occasional danger. In some ways he reminded her of Ray. Optimistic. Honorable. Probably doomed. Her husband, her poor, demented husband … he'd walked into that trial ready to do battle, optimistic, somehow believing all the way through that doing the right thing would save him. He never expected someone to play outside the rules. He never expected a killer to try to save himself by committing murder.

He never even knew she was having a baby.

She dismissed Ben Crosby from her mind. Bitterness about Ray sometimes filled her thoughts, clouding her mouth with dust. But still, a lot had changed in nine months. Sometimes she went an entire day without falling apart, without her mind turning over again and again what had happened.

But she knew she would never be completely free of it. Free of the grief that continued to overwhelm her if she wasn't careful.

A moment later Crosby returned. Accompanying him was Bear Wyden.

Alexandra froze mid-pace, turning to face Bear, and Sarah looked up from the table, sudden interest in her eyes.

"Anything?" Alexandra asked.

No one had to ask her what she meant. Bear sighed and said, "No sign of Dylan. But we found his cell phone."

"Where?" she asked.

"Young couple from Gaithersburg—they were in Bethesda for drinks last night and left the top down on their convertible. Apparently Dylan threw his phone in the back seat of the convertible. We tracked it by GPS to their home."

Alexandra's face twitched. "No sign of him there? You searched their place?"

"Mrs. Paris—"

"I just want to know if you searched their place? What is the problem—?"

"Stop," Bear said. His tone was firm. "We're doing our best to find him, but this isn't helping."

She shook her head. "Just like you did to protect us, right?"

Carrie interceded, "Alexandra, this isn't helping."

"*You* stop. Just because you lost Ray doesn't mean I'm going to let the same thing happen to me!"

Carrie winced and stood up without thinking. She took a breath, ready to respond to Alexandra's verbal slap with a cutting response, but stopped herself. She took a deep breath and reminded herself how horrible those hours had been after the accident. Ray injured. In surgery. Dying.

She remembered the words he'd said to her over and over again, during their worst times. His words that had calmed, promised, and failed in the end, through no fault of his own. She walked around the table, toward her sister, even as Alexandra's eyes brimmed with tears and she said, "Carrie, I'm so sorry, I didn't mean it—"

"It's okay," Carrie whispered, lying. Sometimes you had to lie to serve a greater truth. She put her arms around her sister and said the words Ray had once said to her. "We'll get through this together. I promise."

At that, Alexandra's slight tears broke down into sobs. "Oh, shit, Carrie, I'm sorry!"

Carrie heard Sarah, behind her, talking to Bear. "Give her a second. She's been a mess all morning. In a few minutes she'll get it together."

Alexandra sniffed and started to try to pull herself together. Carrie took her hand, and said, "Come sit."

Alexandra followed, and Carrie said to Bear, "Can I get you anything? Coffee?"

Bear shook his head violently. "I had a million cups of coffee overnight. Last thing I need right now."

Sarah said, "You haven't slept?"

He gave her a dismissive glance then said, "I came out to brief you ladies on what we know so far, and to ask you a few more questions. Then I'm getting a couple hours of sleep."

"Wait," Carrie said. "I need to apologize for this morning, I was kind of a bitch."

He held up a hand, as if to forestall the apology, and as if she'd been waiting for the queue, Rachel made a tiny coughing sound then began to cry.

Carrie started to stir, but Sarah jumped to her feet. "I've got her, Carrie."

"Just bring her to me," Carrie whispered.

Sarah lifted the baby and gently carried her to her older sister. "I hope the sight of a woman's breasts don't offend you, Mr. Wyden."

He coughed, suddenly uneasy, and said, "Do what you gotta do." All the same, he looked away as Carrie rearranged herself. Awkwardly, his eyes fixed on a spot somewhere far to her left, he said, "No need to apologize. We're all under a lot of stress."

"How is Leah?" she asked. The baby was latched on now. She draped the baby blanket around Rachel and looked in her eyes. They were pale blue, searching, serious. Carrie rarely felt happy or at peace these days. But when she fed her daughter, for the first time in her life she felt the presence of God in the bond between her and that tiny, defenseless baby. Sometimes she looked into Rachel's eyes, and she could feel Ray's arms wrapped around her from behind. His legs clasping her thighs, his eyes as he looked over her shoulder into the eyes of their daughter.

Ray Sherman wasn't alive anymore, but when Carrie gave herself to her baby daughter, she could still feel his breath in her soul. She knew that no matter what happened, she would always feel it.

Now that Carrie had more or less covered herself, Bear looked back toward her and answered the question. His face was surprisingly emotional. "Leah's going to pull through. She took two bullets, and it was touch and go all night. But she's stabilized. Gary—he's her new husband—is staying at the hospital, and I'm going to spend the morning with the kids and hopefully get a couple hours of sleep in."

What? None of that made sense. Unless—wait... "Leah isn't..."

"My ex-wife? Yeah, she is."

"I had no idea," Carrie said, her voice low. She studied him. He was exhausted, his eyes red rimmed, dark bags permanently formed under them. But she could imagine the turmoil he was going through. Leah and Bear might be divorced, but he would have to be inhuman to not be turned upside down by this. "I'm doubly sorry for this morning. I was a raging bitch."

He waved a hand to dismiss it. "All right. So first things first, I want to go over a couple of things with you, and ask you some questions. First—any clue where Dylan and Andrea might be other than the text he sent? Any friends in town? Hideouts? Acquaintances?"

Alexandra shook her head. "I don't think Dylan knows anyone around here."

"No old Army buddies?"

Alexandra shook her head. "None that I know of. Most of..." Alex's voice trailed off.

Carrie leaned forward and spoke in a bitter tone. "Most of Dylan's *Army buddies* are dead, and the ones who aren't are in prison."

Bear grimaced. "Right. The shooting in Iraq."

"Afghanistan," Carrie corrected.

He nodded. "I'm gonna ask you a straight question here. Carrie, it's your condo. Any idea how the drugs or cash got in there?"

Carrie twisted her mouth a little, and Rachel stirred, grabbing at her with a tightly wound fist. "Someone planted it there. I guarantee you Andrea's not mixed up in drugs."

"What about Dylan? I understand they had him on some pretty powerful painkillers after his injury."

Alexandra said, "Dylan doesn't even drink. Much less do drugs." For a quarter second longer than they should have, Carrie's eyes locked on Sarah's. Then she looked away.

Alexandra was fooling herself if she didn't know Dylan was drinking again. Carrie had seen it in the furtive movements of his eyes, in the tension in his body when he was near Alexandra, in the slight shake of his hand. From Sarah's expression, she knew it too. All the same, while Dylan may be drinking again, he certainly wasn't dealing massive quantities of drugs. She didn't know where the drugs in the condo had come from, but it wasn't Dylan Paris.

"All right," Bear said. "So they didn't come from Dylan, and Andrea had literally just arrived in the country. And we *know* she had nothing, because she was kidnapped off the plane and her things were examined and catalogued before they were returned to her. Had anyone else been in and out of the condo?"

Carrie shrugged. "Not in the last week. Family. My father. The nanny. And a bunch of people from Diplomatic Security."

"Does the name Ralph Myers mean anything to you?"

It wasn't familiar, and Sarah also shook her head no. But Alexandra spoke up. "Isn't he one of the guys on your team? He asked me some questions about Columbia. Yesterday? I think so. It's all jumbled together."

"Where was he? Where were you?"

Alexandra closed her eyes and thought. "Carrie was out, gone to see Dad. Andrea and Sarah were at the doctor. Must have been yesterday."

"Where was Dylan?"

"Out on the deck reading a book. We'd … we'd had an argument. Anyway, Ralph said he was on duty and was just curious about how Dylan and I met. He's a nice guy."

Bear frowned. "He was a nice guy. He's dead now."

Carrie flinched, and for just a second she felt a flash of irritation at Bear. She knew it was irrational. But she couldn't stop herself.

"The attackers killed him?"

Bear shook his head. "No, as best we can tell, Dylan Paris did. Myers was one of the attackers."

Alexandra gasped, and Carrie's irritation at Bear shifted to anger. "Mr. Wyden, do you think you can consider—"

"No. I need to know," Alexandra said. "What happened?"

Bear sighed. "We're still trying to reconstruct the events, and some of it I can't talk about. But as best we can figure, when the attack came, Andrea went over the side of the balcony, and Dylan stayed to ambush the attackers."

"Andrea did *what?*" Carrie asked.

"She tied a blanket to the balcony rail and used it to swing down to the floor below, then smashed in their sliding glass doors and let herself out on the 19th floor."

"Badass," Sarah murmured.

"And what happened after that?"

"The shooters killed Mick Stanton, and wounded Leah. Once she was down they busted open the door to the condo. As best we can tell, Dylan was hiding behind the door—he took down one right there, and the other one in the living room."

Carrie said, "He took them down?"

"The evidence seems to indicate he stabbed them with kitchen knives."

Alexandra gasped and covered her mouth.

"At that point," Bear said, "it's not clear what happened next. He had blood in his shoes—it looks like he went into Andrea's room and took some of the cash. We're still reconstructing the scene. But he left the building via the elevator at that point. The car he threw his phone into was near the Metro station, so we think he *may* have gone that way, or he might have taken a cab. We're having some trouble getting the surveillance video from the Metro station analyzed."

"Maybe you should leave him alone," Sarah said.

"Sarah," Alexandra commented. "We need to find him."

"Seriously," Sarah replied. "Think about it. He's taking Andrea underground, because someone is trying to kill her. Will you get that through your head? The last thing he needs is to have the cops breathing down his neck. And frankly," she said, looking now directly at Bear, "you need to spend more time figuring out who is trying to hurt Andrea and less time trying to stop her from getting away from them."

Bear frowned. "I'm going to be straight with you, but you've got to be straight with me. Why didn't any of you tell me the IRS was investigating the family? Don't you think that might have been relevant information?"

Carrie stared at Bear, stunned. "What are you talking about?"

"Don't bullshit me. The IRS seized your sister Julia's offices this morning. They've had an investigation running for some time."

She turned to Alexandra. "Do you know anything about this?" At Alexandra's head shake, she said, "This is the first I've heard of it. I haven't talked with Julia since the middle of the night last night. She's on her way here, last I heard."

Bear shook his head. "No one's questioned you? Asked any questions? Sent even a letter in the mail?"

"From the IRS? Nothing."

"I don't get it." Bear looked genuinely puzzled.

"Neither do I. Just in case you missed it, we've been basically housebound since the day Andrea arrived in the States."

Bear leaned forward and looked closely at Carrie. "Look, Carrie, I know you and I haven't exactly hit it off in the last few days. But I need you to level with me. I don't know exactly what's going on with all of this stuff, but you can bet if what I'm hearing about the IRS is true, you'll have agents coming to see you. FBI, treasury agents, who knows what. You're certain you know nothing of this?"

Carrie looked him in the eye. "I'm certain."

"All right," he said. "I'm going to do everything I can to make sure you're safe. You and your sisters and your daughter. What I need you to do is keep talking to me. You hear me? You *have* to let me know what's going on."

Carrie took a deep breath and sat back. She looked up at the ceiling. Did she really have any good reason to trust Bear Wyden? So far nothing in her experience led her to trust any federal agent. She remembered all too well sitting in a room across from Janice Smalls and Jared Coombs only a year ago as they prepared to destroy Ray's life.

Something about Bear, though ... made her want to believe. He wasn't a soldier—he never had been from what she knew. He looked nothing like Ray. He was a barrel of a man, with few social niceties. But the fact was, she *needed* to trust him.

Before she knew what she was doing, she said, "I think this is all somehow related to whoever my father is."

"Secretary Thompson?"

"No," she replied. "No. Apparently, he ... is not my father."

Bear nodded. "I suspected so. Nor is he Andrea's."

"That's right."

"What makes you think that has anything to do with all of this?"

Carrie shrugged. "Obvious, isn't it? No one's ever tried to kill any of us before. But now, when we're getting blood tests related to a genetic disease? Are you familiar with the term Occam's Razor?"

Bear shook his head. "Afraid not."

"Basically it's a principle used in science—in short, if you have a bunch of competing hypotheses, the one with the fewest assumptions is most often correct. You start out with the simplest explanation and work your way up."

He nodded. "Yeah, they teach the same principle to detectives. Because it's the truth—ninety percent of the time, the obvious perp is the one who did it."

"But not always," Alexandra said.

"No, not always."

Sarah asked the next question. "So what's the simplest explanation here?"

Bear shrugged. "Your father isn't Richard Thompson. Someone else is. And that someone else doesn't want to be found out."

"You would have to be one cold-hearted bastard to kill for that."

"If there's power and money involved, you can assume that. Who are our candidates to be your father?"

"My dad—shit..." Carrie stopped. "I've always called him that. My—whatever he is—says Senator Chuck Rainsley is my birth father. I have an appointment to see him later this morning. Or rather, Andrea and I had one."

"I'll take you," Bear said, sighing. "I'll get with the kids this afternoon."

Carrie sighed. "Thank you."

"There's one more thing you need to consider, Carrie."

"Yes?"

"Whoever is trying to hurt Andrea—if it's because of who her parents are—then we need to be concerned about your safety too. And Rachel's."

CHAPTER EIGHT
Open Up. Police.

Andrea. May 2. 10:15 am.

The rhythmic thumping from the headboard of the room next door did nothing to ease Andrea Thompson's frustration, nor the fact that it had been going in spurts all night. The pattern was clear. Twenty minutes would go by. The door would open, and she'd hear voices. Then the building seemed to shake as the steel door slammed shut, and a few minutes later it would start, usually slow, then faster and faster. Never more than a few minutes. Then the door slammed again. The television Andrea kept on wasn't loud. She didn't bother—it would have to be all the way up to block out the noise from next door.

It was a few minutes after ten and this had been going on all night. An internal debate had been running through her head after she lost count sometime in the early morning, awakened every forty minutes or so. Was the woman next door a prisoner? Was she trafficked? Or a prisoner of her own addictions? Who knew?

What Andrea did know was that she herself was effectively a prisoner, a fugitive. It presented an interesting ethical problem for both her and Dylan. If the woman next door was a prisoner, they should call the police. But of course, the police had clearly demonstrated they couldn't protect her. And Andrea did not want to die.

Right now, however, she was nervous and frustrated and frightened. Dylan had left almost an hour before to get cigarettes and find out what he could of the news. An hour later he still hadn't returned, and she was worried that whoever was after them had somehow found him. Was he laying somewhere injured? Was he dead?

Andrea replayed her doubts and worries over and over again, a never ending loop of anxiety and stress, a film on repeat that kept showing her the same images. Hairy Chest, his dead and swollen face as he collapsed in the car. The sight of

Dylan, psyching himself up to a killing rage, knives in both hands, as she swung down off the balcony. But even further back. The disapproval on her father's face. She remembered the looks he'd given her when she was young, but they'd never made any sense. The looks of slight disgust and solid disinterest. She remembered her mother's tears and protestations that they loved her.

Then why do you keep sending me away? Andrea had asked once. Three years ago? It was right before her thirteenth birthday, in June of 2010. *My birthday is in two weeks. Why are you sending me away?*

Her mother had sighed and said, *It's best, Andrea.*

She *hated* her mother. Her father she could understand—he was a cold bastard and rarely came out of his office to spend even five minutes with any of his children. But her mother? *Why?*

It had never made any sense. Until she discovered that Richard Thompson wasn't even her father. Then the ugly stares, the disinterest, the bitterness of her exile all made sense. Andrea was the evidence of her mother's infidelity. Richard was a bastard, but he was a bastard for a reason. Because of their mother.

Andrea started at a knock on the door. She sat up straight then grabbed for the long serrated kitchen knife Dylan had left with her. She didn't answer the door.

Another knock.

She tensed. Dylan was supposed to identify himself by voice if he came. So who the hell was at the door?

She slipped off the bed where she'd been sitting, and moved in a silent crouch to the door. The blackout curtains were ineffective, weak light slipping around them in all directions, but they were enough to block her view of the outside. She slowly came to her feet and put her eye to the peephole in the door.

She froze. Outside, standing in the oppressively dim light, was the hotel manager or desk clerk, a grizzled Indian or Pakistani with nearly white hair and beard. Next to the manager was a bored looking police officer. The hotel manager said something in words too quick to understand, and the cop said, "No, don't open it. What about the next one? That's where you said the noise was from?"

Shit! Andrea thought quickly. Someone, maybe the hotel manager, had called the cops reporting suspicious activity? Maybe reporting whatever was going on next door?

Did they think she was somehow involved in that?

A moment later she heard the thumping stop next door. A loud voice, the words unclear, then she heard the words clearly. "Open up. Police."

Shit. Shit. Shit. Andrea leaned close to the blackout curtain. Careful to not move it, she put her eye near the gap between the wall and the curtain, trying to get a view of whatever was happening next door.

Movement. Then a loud noise, and the door next door slammed. The cop moved into the room, and the manager stood outside. Loud voices. Shouting. A male voice, the john maybe, begging.

A moment later she saw a man come running out. Grey suit, his shirttail hanging out. He walked past the hotel manager, looked back, and then ran.

The door slammed. Andrea started to back away from the blackout curtain, but then she noticed that the manager hadn't moved. What the hell was going on? He stood, his back to the door, hands clasped behind his back. His right leg bounced a little. He swayed on the balls of his feet, turning slightly toward Andrea's room. She jerked back from the opening.

Then she realized exactly what was going on. Because she heard a female voice cry out. Loud. Someone *had* called the cops, and this was the result. Whoever that poor woman was next door, the cop had decided to exploit her too, instead of helping.

The rage that flooded through Andrea right then was nearly uncontrollable. She sank down, resting on her haunches, shaking with anger. She squeezed the knife in her hands tighter, wanting nothing more than to run next door and use it on the cop who was abusing his position.

Jesus Christ, what could she do about it?

And what would happen if Dylan came back right now? Would he blow his temper? Go next door? Would he get them caught?

Or was Dylan out drinking somewhere? She didn't know much at all about him, except that he was a war veteran. Sarah had said he was a reformed alcoholic who had started drinking again. Andrea knew about addicts and alcoholics, and the one thing she knew was they couldn't be trusted if they weren't in some kind of serious recovery.

The noise started again, the headboard of the flimsy bed banging into the flimsy wall of the crappy room next door, and Andrea realized that she had no choice.

None.

The bathroom had a small window that she could climb out. She stuffed her few things into her plastic shopping bag, then walked to the phone. She closed her eyes, then picked it up and dialed 9 for an outside line. Then 911.

"Prince George's County 911, what's your emergency?"

"I'm calling from the Annapolis Road Motor Inn. A girl was prostituting herself next door, and someone called the police. Now the police came and they're screwing her."

"Ma'am, what is your room number?"

"I'm in 112. They're next door, the door to the right of my room. The police officer is in there right now, screwing her. Do you hear me? Instead of helping her, he's fucking her while the hotel manager keeps watch."

"We're dispatching someone right now, can you tell me your name?"

"No. I have to go."

Andrea set the phone in its cradle and walked to the door. She set the chain on the door and turned the deadbolt. Then she ran for the back window. It was small, but she should be able to fit through. High above the toilet, the glass frosted. She slid the window back.

It stuck.

Damn it. What was she thinking? She should have checked the window first. But the rage, the thumping next door, all of it was just too much. She yanked at the window again, bracing her right leg against the corner of the wall. Slowly, she felt it beginning to separate. Finally, with a sudden crack, the window snapped back and she slipped off the toilet, falling to the floor and hitting her head on the wall. Her vision went white, for just a second.

Jesus. She had to move. Back on her feet, she stretched for the window, lifting herself up and through it with both arms.

Her window was directly above the bed of a white, dirty pick up truck. She let her body fold through the window, hanging on with both arms and flipping over, landing in the truck feet first. The truck was parked in a dirty alley behind the motel. A ten foot high chain link fence, tangled with weeds and brush, was about ten feet from the back wall, the space between worn and potholed concrete. Puddles of filthy looking water filled the potholes.

Andrea jumped to the ground from the back of the truck. Old crushed beer cans and condom wrappers scattered the alley. She ran to the end of the alley then calmly walked out from behind the building. The motel, a grey painted building that looked as if hadn't been maintained since the 1990s sat on a corner of a two lane road and a larger, six lane divided highway. Annapolis Road was lined on both sides by fast food places, mini-malls, check cashing places and pawnshops.

She walked, back erect, across the two-lane road and sat down at the bus stop. Dylan would be back soon—she could keep an eye out for him here.

Three police cars were already in the parking lot of the crappy little motel, lights flashing. She couldn't tell from here what was happening. But she knew she didn't want to be over there.

There was Dylan. He was walking up the street toward her, a new backpack slung over his shoulder and a large shopping bag in his hands. His eyes darted from her, to the hotel, then back to her. No change of expression. The police out front were obvious.

He sat down next to her at the bus stop and lit a cigarette. "What happened?"

With as few words as possible, she explained the situation. When she talked about the police officer exploiting the woman in the room next door, his fists clenched.

"You did the right thing," he finally said.

"We need to find a new place to stay," she replied.

"Yeah. Here, I got you some clothes. I hope they fit. Jacket, pair of jeans. Size six shoes. I thought we'd head to the public library, get on the Internet. I want to touch base with Alex, then we're going to have to disappear again."

Andrea nodded. "Okay, Dylan. It sounds like a good plan. But somewhere along the road, we stop running. I want to know who my father is, and why this stuff is happening."

"Yeah, me too," he said.

They stood up when a bus slowed down. "Let's take this one," he said. "If it goes to a train station, we can go from there."

She nodded, and they waited on the edge of the sidewalk as the bus came to a stop.

Andrea glanced over her shoulder toward the motel. An ambulance had arrived at the hotel, and a young woman was being led to it by two female police officers. She had a black eye.

The no-longer-bored police officer was handcuffed and being led by two of his fellow officers to a car. Andrea gave a grim, satisfied smile and stepped onto the bus.

Adelina. May 2. 6:55 am Pacific

"We have to get going, Jessica. Let's get you together, and then you can sleep again in the car, okay?"

Adelina felt her eyes water with frustration as she finally gave in and physically pulled Jessica up, pulling her legs forward until they dangled off the edge of the bed.

"Mmmmm, I'm okay," Jessica mumbled.

The exhaustion, if anything, was worse now than it had been the first few days after they'd arrived at the retreat. Sister Kiara had been clear about that. Ten to twenty days where Jessica would do very little other than sleep or eat. Six months where she would seem listless. Increased risk of heart trouble, strokes or brain aneurisms because of damage to the blood vessels.

Most meth addicts relapse, Adelina. She'll need a great deal of care and close attention.

Right now Jessica just sagged in place. At least she didn't curl up again. The sun would be up shortly, and she wanted to be out of here within the next few minutes. She couldn't trust that the manager of the campsite would keep his promise. He might realize he had fugitives on the property. He might call the police figuring a reward might be in the offing. He might do *anything*, and she wasn't willing to take a chance.

At the same time, she wasn't taking her daughter out looking like this. Jessica's face was smudged with what looked like dirt. Her t-shirt was rumpled and dirty, which was probably fine—she was a teenager after all—but her hair was also a snake's nest of tangles.

"Hold still," Adelina said. And in the dim light of the cabin in the northern California forest, she began to brush her daughters hair.

"It's okay … stop…" Jessica said, pushing Adelina's hand and the brush away.

"Hush," Adelina responded. She brought the brush back up and began to brush. Jessica's hair had always been lighter than her twin's, brown like Alexandra's—and Richard's. She could see his features clearly on Jessica's face. The squarer than was entirely feminine jaw, the thick, almost luscious eyebrows. Richard had been a handsome bastard, after all.

Of course, that was one of the saddest parts about their marriage. It's not like Richard couldn't have picked up a woman. For thirty years she'd seen a parade of unfortunate women throw themselves at her husband, though it had become less common as they'd grown older. She never cared. If he was busy with someone else, he was far less likely to bother her.

Right now, Richard wasn't her problem. Jessica, her eighteen-year-old daughter, was. Jessica was leaning forward now, her eyelids heavy, and Adelina said, "Come on, Jessica, sit up. We'll be in the car soon."

A few more swipes with the brush brought Jessica's hair into some kind of order. Not beautiful, because large amounts of it broke off every time it was disturbed. Her hair was far thinner than it had been a few months ago. Her whole body was far thinner. Once again, rage at her husband flooded through Adelina. He'd been with Jessica, in California, while Jessica fell apart from grief and addiction.

While Jessica went to parties with guys from school, Richard had been busy in his office doing God-knows-what. Adelina had never trusted him. She'd never loved him. He'd never been her *husband* in any way that mattered. But she'd believed that he'd watch after his own daughter, while she stayed in Washington to deal with the aftermath of Ray's murder and Sarah's injuries.

Instead, he'd just let her do whatever she wanted. She'd signed her own report card and erased messages from the home answering machine documenting her absences from school. While he stayed locked in his office, doing whatever the hell it was he did, Jessica had found their emergency cash fund—ten thousand dollars, sorted in a steel box in the attic—and spent all of it.

While he stayed locked away in his office, Jessica had become a slave. All it took was one night at a party.

Miriam said it was okay, Mom, Jessica had told her, tears running down her face. *She said it wasn't addictive. I didn't know it was meth.*

It was too late. When Adelina returned home from San Francisco, she knew there were problems, but not how serious. She knew Jessica was losing a frightening amount of weight, but briefly, her grades returned to normal. January and February crawled by, with Jessica attending weekly therapy sessions. Adelina began to believe they were home free, until Jessica snuck out on a Friday night in April, two days after her eighteenth birthday. She came home with her clothing torn and dirty and a nasty bruise on her face.

Emergency room. Waiting hours. Long discussions with the doctors and therapists.

Then the ugly news. No available beds for three more weeks.

Finally Adelina decided. She made the arrangements to take Jessica to a private Catholic retreat tucked amidst the redwoods, and hired a doctor and nurse to attend to Jessica during the worst of the withdrawals.

"Almost done," Adelina whispered, as she finished brushing Jessica's hair. She hadn't realized tears were flowing down her face. Almost angry with herself, she swiped at the tears and pulled Jessica to her.

"Can we get some breakfast?" slurred Jessica.

"Yes. Let's go," Adelina said.

She took her daughter's hand and they left the cabin. The sun wasn't quite up yet, but it was close, the sky a vivid rose and orange shimmering through the trees. Adelina led Jessica to the car, then walked around to the driver's side and got in. Once they were both buckled up, she slowly drove out of the campsite.

Adelina shivered when she saw the old man who managed the site. He was standing outside the cabin near the entrance, in a grubby t-shirt, with a suspicious expression on his face. She was grateful he'd let them stay, but it worried her for the future. She thought about his expression as she drove away from the campsite, pondering his suspicious demeanor, then abruptly pulled the car over.

"Whas wrong?" Jessica slurred. She was holding a hand up to her forehead, a pained expression on her face.

"Don't worry," Adelina said. Only she *was* worried. She got out of the car and walked in a circle around it. It was a green Dodge Caravan and looked little different than a million other minivans on the road. Mud splatters on the bottom showed they'd been near the campsite. Adelina walked over beside the road. Thick mud. She leaned over and picked up two fistfuls, then threw a mud clod at the license plate, obscuring three of the letters. It wasn't enough, but any more might look obvious. She shook as much of the mud off her hands as she could and walked back to the car.

Of course, now her hands were covered in mud. She ran her hands along the hood, getting them wet, then reached inside, searching for a napkin or paper towel. Jessica's eyes were wide, but she passed her mother a small stack of napkins.

Adelina wiped her hands as best she could, then got in and started driving. She switched on the radio, switching the satellite radio to the all-news channel. She needed to know what was going on, and if there was any kind of search happening.

Voices. She listened, the voices washing over, something irrelevant. A joint Justice Department and Internal Revenue Service investigation into—

She jerked in her seat just as Jessica muttered, *"What?* Turn it up."

Adelina reached for the dial.

"We're returning to Jim Bowers with WNN News, currently at the Justice Department. Jim, what can you tell us?"

"Hi Bill. Well, what we know so far is that the Justice Department apparently opened an investigation in response to tips received when Acting Secretary Thompson was nominated as the Defense Department head. According to Rory Armitage, this has been—"

"That's the Special Counsel?"

"Yes, Rory Armitage was appointed as an independent counsel by the Attorney General. He's in charge of the investigation."

"Okay. And Armitage felt there was enough information to bring in the IRS?"

"That's right. We don't know the details of their evidence, but the accusations are clear. They're accusing Richard Thompson of outright corruption, documenting bribes and money laundering activities as far back as the 1980s."

"And this somehow involved Crank and Julia Wilson?"

"That's what the IRS believes. And the most bizarre part, Bill, is the involvement of the children. There's speculation that Thompson got into a conflict with a drug cartel, because the family homes in San Francisco and in Bethesda, Maryland were attacked last night. His wife and two of his daughters are missing right now, and the rest are in protective custody."

"Can you tell us something about the search?"

Adelina sucked in a breath. She looked over at Jessica, who sat, eyes wide, confusion on her face.

"I don't have many details, Bill. I know nationwide alerts have been sent out, and an AMBER alert for Andrea Thompson, since she's sixteen years old. I don't think the FBI is holding out much hope of finding them."

Adelina sighed. Nationwide alert. She'd have to be very careful. The police would be looking everywhere for her. She needed to stop. Get hair dye or bleach, do everything she could to change their appearance before the alerts went out far enough that people started to recognize her.

Damn it.

"Mom?" Jessica said, her voice shaking.

"Yes, sweetie?"

"What the hell is going on?"

Adelina sighed. It was a long, painful story. It was a story none of her children knew. It was an ugly story. Everything about their lives had been lies. But wasn't it time to start telling the truth?

CHAPTER NINE
Adelina's daughter

Carrie. May 2. 10:45 am.

Bear squeezed the steering wheel and said, "Have you met Senator Rainsley?" His expression was severe. Before they'd left the safe house, he'd drunk three cups of coffee, explaining that he had been up all night. Earlier he'd said he was going home, but after a brief phone call he'd changed his mind.

Carrie, who wore a simple, but elegant suit, said, "I don't think so. He and my father were political enemies for many years. I remember hearing his name spoken like a curse."

"Interesting," Bear said. "It would tend to back up the idea that he's your birth father. That's an incredibly long running affair, though. You were born, when, 1988?"

"Flattery will get you nowhere. I was born in January '85."

"Okay. So this affair was going on from at least, what, March or April '84 up through … 1996?"

"It had to have been on again and off again. My parents were posted to different cities during those years. Washington, Brussels, Beijing."

Bear nodded. "That makes a little more sense. So, she meets Rainsley in DC sometime in '84. They have an affair. You're born. Then she runs into him again years later. Where were your parents in '96?"

"China."

"Rainsley was in the Senate then. It'll be simple enough to check if he was in China at any point then."

"My dad said so … *shit!*" Tears suddenly welled up in Carrie's eyes. Her *dad.* She sometimes felt like someone had punched her in the face when the knowledge hit that the man she'd always believed was her father wasn't. And not just that he wasn't—but that both of her parents had lied about it.

Why? If her mother didn't love Richard Thompson, why didn't she leave him? Why the pretense? It was clear her mother had never been happy. She'd suffered from depression and anxiety and God only knew what else, and she'd taken that out on her daughters for years.

She sighed. "Julia said she had some news related to all this that she found in San Francisco. But she didn't want to talk about it on the phone and asked to wait until we could meet in person."

"She's on her way to DC?"

"Yes. Last we talked she was stuck in traffic near Fredericksburg."

"Christ," Bear said. "So we'll meet back up with her later."

Carrie sighed. "No news about Andrea? Or my mother?"

Bear shook his head. "No. We've got alerts out for both. Police in both states have pictures, details. But nothing for sure yet."

"And what do you know about Rory Armitage?"

"Armitage? He's the special prosecutor investigating your father—the Secretary of Defense."

"It seems like all of this is happening very quickly. I mean—you know a little about what happened with my husband, Ray, right?"

"A little. I read about it in the papers."

Mention of the newspapers made her stomach twitch. She and Ray had been smeared in the news. "Everything in the papers was wrong," she replied sharply.

"Okay, so tell me what happened."

Carrie swallowed. "Army platoon went off the deep end. They took a lot of casualties, then the platoon sergeant went crazy and shot a civilian kid. Ray reported it several months later, and his sergeant leveled counter charges saying Ray had pulled the trigger. They put him on trial."

"And he was murdered," Bear said.

The word always hurt. It was ugly, and bare, and truthful. It said nothing and it said everything. "That's right," she said. "By one of his fellow soldiers."

"Jesus," Bear said.

"Anyway," she said. "You've got to understand. I've already lost my soul mate. My husband. And … all I have is my family. My sisters. My daughter. You understand? I can tell you this much: Andrea's not mixed up with money laundering or drugs or anything else. Neither is Julia. Whatever's going on with this prosecutor and investigation stinks."

Bear didn't answer. He kept his eyes on the highway as they got closer to the city.

"Why aren't you answering?" she asked. "You think they're guilty?"

Bear shrugged. "I don't have enough evidence to have an opinion. I know your sister took out two experienced killers with her bare hands. I know they found drugs and money in her room. A *lot* of both. I know my ex-wife got shot down trying to protect her, but instead of turning herself in for safety, Andrea disappeared."

"Wouldn't *you*? It's not like she didn't have reason to disappear. Three attacks, Bear. Three. In less than a week. The only conclusion is that *you* can't protect her. Especially when at least one of your own people was involved."

Bear nodded. "Yeah. Yeah, good point. Which is why I'm taking you to see Senator Rainsley. Because everything about this makes exactly no sense at all."

Bear was driving too fast for the wet road conditions as he sped through Arlington on I-66. The speed felt like death to Carrie, and finally she said, "Slow down. My daughter already lost one parent."

He slowed.

Traffic soon began to back up near the Roosevelt Bridge. Soon they were creeping along, cars all around. The Potomac River spread across before them; ahead, the Kennedy Center, the Lincoln Memorial, the US Institute of Peace.

Carrie had avoided this part of town religiously. She remembered the last time—walking with Dylan down 23rd Street to the edge of the National Mall, just a few blocks from George Washington University Hospital, where her husband had been laying. Dying.

It was still close sometimes. The moment the doctors told her she had to make a decision, that he was brain dead, that he would never recover, that there was nothing there but a husk, a body connected to life support.

She looked down at the floor of the car and went silent. It was easier than seeing those places, which for her would always ache with his memory.

Bear frowned and said, "Everything all right?"

She shrugged. "Ray died a few blocks from here. This part of town always reminds me."

Bear sighed. "Sorry, Carrie. For what it's worth, you both got a raw deal."

"You've got no idea."

She turned away from him, resting her chin on a fist and blocking her view of both Bear and the State Department building to their left.

She knew what Ray would have said. Always optimistic, always hopeful. *You just have to pick yourself back up, Carrie. I love you. You can do this.*

He would have encouraged her. To keep going. To do the right thing. To take care of herself and her sisters and especially her daughter. And she would. She'd do what he would have wanted, because that's what you do, right? You just pick up and keep going.

"Almost there," he said.

The Capitol building was in view, the giant cast iron dome with its dozens of columns and ironwork statues stark against the ashen sky. This had once been Carrie's favorite city. She remembered spending her first two years of high school here, before they left for Moscow. She'd come back briefly with Julia, Crank and Sean in 2003. Then finally, in 2013, she'd come here to live. The best and worst year of her life.

She sighed. Right now, she needed to set all of that aside. She needed to remind herself that Ray Sherman wouldn't have sat around sighing. And neither would she. Carrie Sherman was made of stronger stuff than that.

She cleared her throat and muttered, "Sorry about that. I'm good to go now."

"Good," he replied. "We're going to park at Union Station and walk over. That all right?"

"Of course," she said.

They didn't talk as Bear negotiated the traffic near the Capitol building and then parked behind the large marble structure of Union Station. Twenty minutes later they were walking down the sidewalk to the Russell Senate Office Building, where Senator Rainsley had his office. All around them were people who felt at home here: Senate and House aides, lobbyists and lawyers, Senators and Congressmen. People from a thousand different walks of life—from the seven figure lobbyist-lawyers to the minimum wage deliverymen. It was overwhelming. She'd grown up around the Foreign Service; she knew the ins and outs of the government from an early age. There was something comforting about walking down a sidewalk filled with oblivious government functionaries, people who had a sense of purpose, people who believed their lives mattered.

She stared up as they approached the stone and marble Beaux-Arts Russell Building. White columns reached to the upper stories, the windows between them lined up in a row down the block.

It was almost intimidating, she thought, as they went through security and on to the elevators. Inside, past the interior rotunda, was a long marble hallway with twenty-five foot ceilings, imposing marble walls and floors. The entire structure was designed to make visitors feel small, insignificant. And perhaps they were, in the context of history. But she knew that right now, her focus needed to stay very solid.

Bear finally stopped outside Senator Rainsley's office. A large symbol, the state seal of Texas, was mounted next to the doorway.

"You've been here before," she said. "You knew the exact way to this office."

He nodded. "Day before yesterday, as a matter of fact."

She blinked. "In relation to *this* investigation?"

"That's right."

She frowned. "You're not telling me everything."

"Of course not, Carrie. I'm running this investigation. I brought you here as a favor. I'll tell you what I can later, but don't expect me to fill you in on all the details along the way."

She shook her head. "I suppose I should thank you." Instead, she opened the door and slipped into the office.

"Doctor Carrie Sherman," she said to the twenty-something girl behind the counter. "I have an appointment with the Senator."

The girl blinked, startled. "Yes, ma'am." She instantly picked up her phone and spoke into it. "Doctor Sherman is here, Senator."

"I think the Senator warned her to expect you," Bear murmured. "I'm gonna sit out here and send some emails and get caught up on the investigation."

"You don't want to come in?"

"For your reunion with your long-lost birth father? I think I'd rather pluck out my eyebrows. You two have fun."

The girl behind the counter followed the entire exchange; her eyes shifting back and forth like two undersized radar dishes. Carrie ignored her and turned toward the main office as the door opened.

A very tall, trim man stood in the doorway. At six-foot six-inches, he was Ray Sherman's height, and somewhat taller than Carrie. His hair was steel grey, but might have once been dark brown like hers. His eyes were hazel. He looked like he might have a normally ready smile, but right now he wasn't smiling. Instead, his expression was serious.

"Carrie Sherman," he said. "Come in." He stretched an arm out to invite her into his office.

She let out a breath, suddenly realizing that for the space of ten or more heartbeats, she hadn't breathed at all. She stepped forward into the office, her eyes darting around. One wall was covered in memorabilia. Senator Rainsley in a basketball uniform, on the deck of an aircraft carrier, in a Marine Corps Colonel's uniform.

One photograph caught her attention. Rainsley stood in the rain at a podium, the Founders Court at Rice University clearly visible behind him.

"I got my PhD at Rice," she said.

"So you're Adelina's daughter," he said, his voice low.

She turned toward him. His expression was unreadable, but it wasn't what she expected. He didn't show fear, as if he were concerned a fifteen-year affair was about to be revealed, or that she was going to demand blackmail or money. Nor did he look like he was about to welcome a long-lost daughter. She didn't know what his expression meant.

"So you're my father," she said.

His eyebrows scrunched together. "Have you discussed this with your mother?"

"She's missing."

Finally an expression. Rainsley was stunned. "Missing?"

"Yes. She was last seen leaving a Catholic retreat center with one of my sisters sometime yesterday afternoon. Then she and Jessica called, and she told us to run. I have no idea why, and I don't know whether she's alive or dead." Carrie's tone was devoid of emotion as she spoke.

"Christ," he said. "I didn't know."

"You should read the papers," Carrie said.

Rainsley said, "I knew about the attack on your condo. But I've been in meetings all morning. As you may or may not know, yours wasn't the only attack yesterday. The head of British intelligence was attacked in his home at the same time."

She raised her eyebrows then shrugged that off. "I can't even imagine what that has to do with me. But according to … according to *my mother's husband*, you've got some explaining to do."

"I'm not your father, Carrie."

Carrie staggered a little.

He reached out a hand and took her arm. "Come. Sit."

She did, sinking onto a long leather couch. He sat in the chair that cornered the couch.

"I don't believe you," she said. "Look at you."

He sighed. "Believe me. I'm happy to discreetly get a DNA or blood test or whatever to prove it to you, if you like."

"And my sister Andrea."

"Your mother and I were never involved, Carrie."

"Why does my father think you were?"

Rainsley sighed. Then he looked at her and said, "Are you sure you want to open this can of worms?"

Carrie laughed, a little hysterically. "You're kidding, right? Did you just ask me that?"

He chuckled. "I guess you're saying that ship has sailed."

"Just ... if you aren't my father, then why did ... *The Secretary of Defense* ... why did he tell me you were? If you aren't ... then who is?"

Rainsley stood, stretching his long, lanky body. "Okay, first of all, I need to tell you that I don't know all the details."

Carrie crossed her arms over her breasts and raised an eyebrow.

"Fine," he said, defensively. "I'll tell you everything I can. Your mother and I have known each other since ... oh ... 1984 or so. She had just come to Washington, and your father—Richard Thompson, rather—had just come back from his tour in Afghanistan."

"He was never stationed in Afghanistan. We didn't even have an Embassy there in the 1980s."

"Technically I'm breaking the law by telling you this. But Richard Thompson was a CIA covert operative and worked his entire career under diplomatic cover. He was a central figure in arming the Afghan resistance in the early 1980s."

Carrie stiffened. "That's the most ridiculous thing I've ever heard."

"It's true. Do you want to hear the story or do you want to argue with me?"

She snorted. "If you want to fill your office with bullshit, by all means, go right ahead."

He shook his head. "Adelina—your mother—was really quite amazing. I won't lie to you, I was taken with her enough that Brianna had words with me the night we met. She was nineteen, I found out later, but told everyone she was older. Spirited, and clearly afraid of Richard. For a while there, when your father was traveling—which was often—she spent a lot of time with Brianna. They grew to be close friends—or as close as anyone can get to Adelina."

"Wait," Carrie said. "What do you mean ... nineteen ... in '84?" She shook her head. "That's not possible. Julia was born in '81."

"Funny how that works, isn't it? Richard Thompson was on a tour in Spain that year—the year there was a right wing coup attempt. He marries a visibly pregnant sixteen-year-old, then whisks her back to the States and disappears for a tour in a backwater in Central Asia."

"Jesus Christ," Carrie said. "He would have been late twenties then? Early thirties?"

Rainsley shrugged and sank down into his seat. "Yeah. I felt bad for her. She was afraid of him, no question there. I never saw any signs of physical abuse, but who the hell knows? Her fear of him had to be based on *something*. Brianna saw it too, and insisted we have her over as often as possible."

Carrie's stomach turned. She couldn't reconcile that idea with the passionless, cold man who had raised her. But even though he was remote, controlling, she'd never seen him as cruel. She's always seen him as her father.

"I don't understand," she said. "Any of this."

"Yeah. Well ... I'll be honest with you. I was on a crusade then. Planning to run for the Senate. I'd seen my entire command wiped out in Beirut. Largely because of inept pencil necks from Washington like Richard Thompson. So I may have been a little too sympathetic to his wife."

"What happened?"

"She fell in love."

Carrie sat up straight. *"What? With you?"*

He shook his head. "No. Not me ... I don't know who. She never told me. But it was clear. She had a beautiful light in her eyes. And a lot of fear. So when she came to us—I guess it was January 1990—she told us she was in danger. And begged me that if Richard demanded to know—if he accused me of having an affair with her, of being your father—then I was to admit to it."

"Why?"

"I don't know. But I wasn't going to tell her no. I wasn't—look. I don't know how to explain it. She sounded desperate. Brianna and I both worried about her, but she clearly wasn't ready to leave him. She *begged me*. So when Richard called me about it—"

"He called you?"

"Yes. Mid February of 1990."

"Okay. What happened?"

"He called. He demanded that I stay away from his wife. He threatened me, and he threatened to hurt her. It was an ugly conversation. But I kept my promise."

Rainsley turned and stared out the window. His shoulders sagged.

Carrie whispered, "You loved her?"

Rainsley shrugged. "I'm happily married, Carrie. But Brianna and I both cared for her."

"Enough that you risked your career for her."

He kept his back to her and waved a hand in the air dismissively. "I'm a Marine. This Senate stuff is all bullshit. It's like retirement, but more interesting than golf. Brianna wasn't happy, but she agreed it was necessary."

Carrie sighed. Then she whispered, "I'm glad she had someone to love her."

He turned toward her. "She had somebody," he said. "I just don't know who it was."

"Who does?" Carrie asked.

"Her priest maybe? Or God. I wish I knew."

CHAPTER TEN
Shut Her Up

Adelina. May 2. 9:15 am Pacific

Jessica bit into her third burrito as Adelina carefully took another bite of her first. "How come we never drove up here before?" she asked. "It's beautiful."

She was right. They'd just passed over a river in coastal Oregon, and to their right was the exit for Rocky Point County Park. All morning, they'd been driving slowly up U.S. 101 along the coast. There were occasional flashes of ocean as the highway twisted and turned, following the Pacific Coast. Adelina had been following the gas station map she'd picked up somewhere north of Oakland—their cell phones were somewhere in the bottom of San Francisco Bay. That Jessica hadn't really noticed or objected to losing her phone was a sign of how profoundly depressed she was.

The heavy rain that fell overnight had passed, leaving the sky cloudless and blue.

Adelina sighed. "It's complicated."

"You've said that about every question I've asked you this morning."

Adelina sighed. "Can I be honest with you, Jessica?"

Her daughter blinked. "I don't understand."

"You're eighteen years old now. I've been keeping secrets since long before you were born. But this one—I'm afraid if I start to tell you, you'll panic on me. I'm afraid if I tell you too much, you'll go right back to the drugs."

Jessica flinched. She curled up a little in her seat, drawing her legs close to her, and she whispered, "I guess I deserved that."

"The only thing you deserved is love, Jessica. You deserved … parents who weren't crazy." She shook her head, trying to shake off the regret clouding her vision. "I'm sorry I couldn't give you that."

Jessica shrugged and took another huge bite. Adelina had never seen anyone eat so much in her entire life. She hoped she had enough money to keep feeding her daughter. The cash she grabbed from the bank had to last indefinitely, but they were going through it far faster than she'd imagined.

Finally Jessica swallowed and said, "Tell me. Please. I don't care how bad it hurts. It won't hurt as bad as a lie."

Adelina sucked in a breath, trying to hold back a mix of grief and a sad, knee-jerk anger. The accusation was true enough. She had lied. She'd lied to her daughters, and she'd lied to herself.

"I need you to hear me, Jessica. I know you think it won't hurt as bad, but if I tell you the whole story, you're going to feel like someone died."

She looked to her right, meeting her daughter's eyes for just a moment. Jessica nodded, and Adelina looked back to the road.

"Well, then. The first thing you need to understand is that everything you know about your father, and how we met, is a lie, mixed with truth, and mixed with more lies."

"I don't understand."

Adelina sighed with relief when she saw a sign for a scenic overlook. She needed to stop and tell this story when she wasn't driving. She swallowed, took the exit, and two minutes later pulled to a stop in a parking lot overlooking the ocean. Below them, at the bottom of a long steep hill, was the ocean, spreading out before them.

"I was sixteen when I met your father, not eighteen."

"Oh…" Jessica said.

Adelina wished she could think of a way to soften the blow. But she was coming to realize that it was secrets that had poisoned all of her daughters in one way or another. It was lies that had kept them from having a whole mother. So, for the first time, she told the unvarnished truth.

"He raped and impregnated me. He may have killed my father. He certainly made me believe he had. And then my mother forced me to marry him."

Jessica sat, staring at Adelina. She shook her head slightly, dazed. "That's utter bullshit," she said.

"No, unfortunately. It's true."

"Why did you stay with him?"

"I was trapped, Jessica. He threatened to hurt me, and more importantly, he threatened to kill Luis."

"Your brother?"

Adelina nodded. "Luis was two at the time. And my father was dead. I ... I didn't have anywhere I could turn."

Abruptly, Jessica opened the passenger side door, flooding the car with a cool breeze and the scent of the sea, and dropped out of her seat to the ground, nearly staggering. Adelina sat. She'd just told her already fragile daughter that her father was a rapist and a liar. Should she have hidden it? Should she have kept her secrets longer?

Jessica sat down on the low stone wall that edged the parking lot. She pulled her legs up close and wrapped her arms around them, then lowered her face so she was resting it against her knees.

Adelina wanted to weep at the sight. She'd spent so many years trying to protect herself and her daughters, and she'd failed them one by one. Every single one of her daughters.

Slowly, she opened the van door and stood. Jessica's shoulders were shaking. A pit of anxiety in her stomach, Adelina walked to her daughter and sat on the wall next to her.

Without raising her face from her knees, Jessica said, "Either I believe you and lose my father, or I assume you're crazy, and I'm stuck in a car with a crazy person."

Adelina slowly nodded her head and picked at her fingertips, knowing that Jessica's accusations were deserved.

"Father was the only normality we had, you know. Carrie used to sneak us out of the house and take us to the zoo or the park or the pool or the movies or anywhere she could think of, just to get us out of your way. Because you were crazy. You were always screaming or crying or falling apart."

Adelina closed her eyes. Then she whispered, "It's true. Carrie was your mom because I couldn't be."

"Yeah, but who took care of her? Who took care of *Julia?*"

"I think maybe God protected them," Adelina said. "I couldn't. You're right. I was literally out of my mind with fear. All the time. I'm so sorry, Jessica. I'm sorry I failed you."

Jessica choked a sob. "Are you kidding me?" she spit out. "You're *sorry?* Do you know what it's like to not be able to bring your friends home because you think your mother might be having a freak out? Do you know what it's like to grow up in a house where everyone goes from cold to hateful in just a second?"

Adelina took Jessica's hands in hers. She looked her daughter in the eyes and whispered, "If I could take it all back, I would. If I could make it better, I would."

Jessica's eyes welled up, and tears began to run down her face. "Mama," she whispered, reaching out.

Adelina pulled her daughter close. Jessica began to cry. First a thin, reedy cry, but soon she was wailing in great open-throated sobs, her shoulders shaking, her face buried in her mother's shoulder. Adelina knew it wasn't just this revelation she was crying for. She was crying for her lost love. She was crying for her twin, still recovering from an accident thousands of miles away. She was crying for all of the lost moments, the isolation and the quiet cold in their home. She was crying for the father she was losing, the father she'd never had.

Adelina. February 12, 1984

The alarm blared in a grating, angry tone, startling Adelina awake. She rolled over, groggy. She'd been awakened twice the night before by a dream of choking. More specifically, it was a dream that Richard was choking her.

It wasn't the first time, not by any means. But she hadn't had the dream in some time. Partly, she thought, because he'd made no physical demands of her since their first night in Bethesda.

That night, he'd been insistent. He'd arrived home from Pakistan and made arrangements to purchase a brand new condominium in Bethesda, Maryland, right around the corner from the Metro station that was under construction.

"The location will be really valuable once the station is opened," he'd said, droning mindlessly about matters she'd cared little about.

She didn't care how his real estate investments did. She didn't care how his career did. She hated him and how he'd destroyed her life.

Her disinterest had antagonized him, and he'd forced himself on her that first night back, then not allowed her to leave the room, even when Julia's cries from down the hall indicated their daughter had wet her diaper.

Adelina thanked God she'd not had to deal with it since then. And that he hadn't managed to impregnate her that night.

After that night, they'd fallen into an uneasy truce. She promised to handle their social engagements flawlessly. He promised not to hurt her.

It was no way to live, and she needed to find a better answer.

That morning, though, she knew exactly why the dream had come. Normally, the dream was formless, and it always started the same way—Adelina, in the practice hall of the National Youth Orchestra. Richard walked in, always in the black jeans and black t-shirt he'd worn the day he raped her the first time. Smiling. Menacing.

Last night, the dream had been different. Because *he* had been there. The smiling twenty-one-year-old Prince George-Phillip.

You're a charming woman, Adelina, he'd said.

You're too kind, she had whispered.

Every time his eyes grazed over her, she felt herself flush. It wasn't that she hadn't felt desired before. After all, *Richard* had desired her. But it was different. George-Phillip was kind. He'd been interested in what she had to say about the Youth Orchestra and her opinions of international politics, which she'd spent considerable time studying in the last year. His expressive face and animated eyebrows demonstrated how closely he was paying attention to what she said. Adelina might have had to drop out of school, but she was a very intelligent woman. No more than five minutes into their conversation, George-Phillip and Colonel Rainsley both realized that. The conversation had naturally shifted, mostly to the circumstances of Colonel Rainsley's run for the Senate.

"The problem wasn't that the orders were badly thought out," Rainsley had said. "The problem was no one in the White House *cared enough* to think through the implications of putting us there with rules of engagement that wouldn't allow us to defend ourselves. Do you know that was the deadliest day for the Marine Corps since Iwo Jima? And here's the thing—the White House couldn't even decide on a response. Too much political infighting, so we pulled our guys out, used a battleship to bomb the crap out of the wrong people and left it at that. Every single one of those young lives was *wasted.*"

Of course the discussion had circled around politics and international affairs. Richard was a Foreign Service officer, and their guests included people who weren't high government officials yet, but likely would be one day.

Adelina found herself staying careful. Periodically Richard's eyes wandered to her, and it was important to maintain the pretense that she was entertaining their guests solely for his purposes.

In fact, she'd found herself more and more drawn in by George-Phillip. Rainsley, initially, was dismissive of George-Phillip's opinion of anything military. That lasted right up until George-Phillip described the British recapture of the Falkland Islands almost two years before.

"You were part of the landing force?" Rainsley asked, disbelief on his face. "You're too young."

"I was nineteen at the time, sir. After my father passed, I served a two year tour with the 5th Infantry Brigade."

"Under General Moore?"

"Yes, sir, you know him?"

"I do, I was briefly assigned as Liaison to Royal College of Defense Studies in '77. General Moore was assigned there at the time."

Adelina watched George-Phillip, intrigued. At first she'd taken him as a fop. Royal, perhaps, but a fop. But apparently he had enough substance that he'd volunteered to serve in an infantry regiment and fought in the Falklands War, when he could have just as easily sat at home spending his inherited wealth.

Colonel Rainsley had turned his attention from George-Phillip to Adelina. "We should turn the conversation to other topics," he said, "so we don't bore Adelina."

At the opposite end of the table, Leslie Collins and Richard were leaning close to each other, nearly whispering. Prince Roshan seemed equally involved in whatever they were discussing, which left Brianna Rainsley and Myriam Roshan stewing in the two middle seats of the table.

"No need to worry about boring me, Colonel, I'm quite interested in the topic. Unless Brianna or Myriam would prefer we discussed something else?"

George-Phillip gave Adelina a warm look, a slight twinkle in his eye, one side of his mouth slightly upturned. Adelina felt a deep sense of satisfaction at Rainsley's clear look of discomfort.

Myriam Roshan took the opportunity to ask Rainsley a question about his experience in Beirut and to lament the damage caused by the civil war, and the conversation moved on.

That night, Adelina dreamt of George-Phillip. Dreams that slowly turned back to the familiar scene, dreams that ended the same way they always did. With Richard's hands around her throat.

Her eyes had popped open and she sat up instinctively, terror clogging her throat, her heart thumping in her chest. It was four in the morning when she awoke from the dream, and it took her a long time to get back to sleep. She got up and got a glass of water, then went back to her room and lay down alone. With the door locked behind her. When the alarm woke her at six am, she felt strung out. Exhausted.

All the same, she dragged herself out of bed. She didn't expect to see much of Richard, but Sunday mornings she attended Mass at the Saint Jane Frances de Chantal Catholic Church on Old Georgetown Road. Services. Communion. But since her arrival in the United States, she'd not attended confession. Maybe soon, she thought. She'd been telling herself that ever since the day almost exactly three years before when Richard had walked into her father's shop. The day of the coup. The day he raped her.

Adelina left her room cautiously, as always. She didn't know if Richard was home—he often wasn't—but she didn't want to take the chance. Julia would be awake any moment. Adelina wanted at least a few moments before she was. She walked down the hall, passing Richard's closed door on her way to the kitchen. At first he'd balked at the idea of separate rooms, but he'd finally given in, with the admonition that she was to never tell anyone.

People will think we don't love each other. Married couples don't sleep in separate rooms.

We don't love each other, she'd replied. *No amount of lies will change that.*

He'd snarled at her and she'd walked away, knowing that antagonizing him any further was a bad idea.

The coffee pot—a new one, with a built in clock—was already on with a fresh pot.

Thank God. She poured herself a cup, generously adding cream and sugar, and walked toward the sliding glass doors and the balcony. She passed the mantel, with its bizarre decorations, including a gigantic brass head he claimed to have bought in Indonesia. It was heavy. One day she wanted to use it to smash in *his* head.

She slid open the sliding glass door and slipped into one of the cast iron seats at the table overlooking Bethesda, Maryland, and in the distance, Washington, DC. She left the door cracked—Julia would be awake soon. This was the one compensation for living here instead of San Francisco—or, for that matter, Madrid or Calella, or anywhere else on earth without Richard. She loved the view from this balcony, she loved sitting out here and drinking her coffee and relaxing. She rarely had moments of unguarded relaxation. Very rarely. She closed her eyes and leaned her head forward and whispered a prayer.

"Mummy?"

Adelina swallowed and opened her eyes.

Julia had awakened and was standing at the sliding glass door. Her brown hair was tousled, curling around her head, framing green eyes that looked alarmingly similar to Richard's. She wore a blue nightdress with white flowers.

Adelina smiled and stood, then slid the door open slightly.

"Come here, baby," she said. She sat down, and Julia scrambled up into her lap and stretched her arms around her.

Adelina stiffened for a moment, then fought that down and hugged her daughter back, cursing herself. It wasn't Julia's fault Richard had ... it just wasn't her fault. But all the same, every time, she had to fight back the initial reaction. She had to fight against her instinct to shy away, her instinct to not be touched, ever.

"I love you, baby," she whispered in Julia's ears. But she wondered if her daughter would someday wonder why Adelina recoiled against touch. She sat there, holding her arms around that precious baby, and promised herself that no matter what else happened, she'd take care of that little girl.

"I love you, Mummy," Julia said.

The phone inside rang. Adelina felt a flash of irritation as she stood up to go get it, swinging Julia around to rest on her hip. Was it the babysitter again? She was late last Sunday, and Adelina ended up being late for Mass, which was yet another sore point with Richard, because he'd insisted Julia be brought up as Protestant. Not that he would make arrangements for Julia to have any other religious instruction. Nor could he be bothered to take any interest in his daughter in any other way.

You're not even religious! Adelina had shouted. *You're only doing this to spite me!*

She'd lost that battle, and Adelina had learned long since that she simply *couldn't* win all of them. But she would teach her daughter in private, no matter what he said.

Adelina reached the phone and picked it up.

"Hello?" As she answered the phone, Julia began to squirm in her arms. Adelina held on tightly.

"Mrs. Thompson? It's Marcy Whitsun. I'm afraid I'm not going to be able to make it on time this morning."

"That's fine," Adelina snapped. "Don't bother. Don't bother coming back at all."

"Miss Thompson? Wait, it's just that—"

"I don't really care what it is. You've worked for me for three weeks, and this is the second time you've called to say you're late or not coming on Sunday morning." Julia began to kick in her arms, but Adelina held on. She continued speaking into the phone. "I have limited patience. You've reached the end of mine."

She slammed down the phone, hard. Unbidden tears sprang to her eyes. The only thing that tethered her to reality was going to Mass. That was all she had. She *needed* to go. She needed the time.

"Mummy?" Julia said. Her tiny arms were waving wildly. "Mummy? Mummy?"

"*What?*" Adelina shouted.

Julia's eyes seemed to double in size as they filled with tears. Her face began to get red, and Adelina said, "I'm sorry, baby, it's not…"

She didn't get a chance to finish the sentence. Julia's face turned red and she began to scream.

"Oh, for Christ's sake," she muttered. She slid Julia down to the floor, where the girl promptly collapsed and continued screaming. Adelina looked around, her head swiveling round as she searched for her coffee cup, which she'd only had maybe three sips from before Julia awoke.

Julia let out a piercing scream.

And *that* was when Richard's door opened and he shot out of his room.

"Can't you quiet that child?" he shouted. "I'm trying to sleep!"

"Why don't *you* quiet her?" Adelina shouted back. "The only time I *ever* get to myself is Sunday morning, and now I'm losing that too."

His face stiffened, his jaw working, and he reached forward and grabbed the sides of her face and began to squeeze. "I told you to shut. Her. Up. *Do it.*"

His face was red as he said the words, his teeth clenched and his eyes bugged slightly. Adelina began to whimper, the pressure from his hands on the side of her face causing intense pain.

"Stop!" she shouted.

He let go and pushed. Adelina staggered back against the wall.

He sucked in another breath, his shoulders rising, and Julia let out another piercing scream.

He pointed. "That child. If you don't shut her up, *I* will."

Adelina slid down the wall, backing away from him. His words instantly quelled any argument or defiance. All she had to do was remember her father, run down by a truck on a narrow Madrid street, and he instantly gained her obedience. She had a little brother, Luis, to protect. She had a daughter to protect. It didn't matter that Richard was Julia's father. The longer she knew him, the more she realized he simply had no normal human feelings.

She kneeled down and picked up Julia, who screamed even louder. "Stay away from her."

Richard sneered at her. "Gladly. I'm going back to sleep. If you have to, take her outside, but shut her up."

"I'm going to Mass this morning."

He threw his hands up in the air. "Fine! Take her to your Mass! Just shut her up!" Richard turned and stomped off, then slammed the door to his room.

Adelina turned back into the kitchen. Her heart was beating rapidly, and she could feel sweat on her forehead. "Calm down, Julia. You must calm down. Don't disturb your father."

Julia hiccupped and began to whine again. Adelina was desperate. She knew how to take care of babies—after all, Luis had been younger than Julia was now when she married Richard. She'd changed plenty of diapers and fed plenty of babies, and she knew what to do to calm Julia down. But the hardest part was calming herself down, and Julia would not calm down until her mother did. All Adelina could see was Richard, reaching his hands around her throat, ripping her dress, harming the people she loved.

She closed her eyes, desperately trying to breathe as waves of nausea and fear swept through her. "Come on, sweetheart, let's get you something to eat."

Eventually, Julia began to calm, and they sat together on the balcony as Adelina fed her daughter. The sun was coming up now; great bands of red and orange stretching across the sky. Adelina reflected that despite herself, she'd won another victory against Richard this morning. She'd won an essential victory, the fight for her daughter's soul, the fight to bring her daughter up in the Church. The flip side of that was the bleak realization that she'd won that victory not through her own efforts, but through her daughter's.

It was well past one in the afternoon when Adelina returned to the condo. Julia was asleep in her stroller—the long walk back from the church had been peaceful. The sky was a little grey, but by the time she started the walk back home, the temperature had warmed to the low sixties.

Normally Adelina made the walk home regardless of the weather, but that would change if she took Julia with her every week. Adelina didn't mind walking in a raincoat with an umbrella in thirty degree weather, because it gave her time to think. But a two-year-old couldn't do that.

The need to go to confession had been stronger than ever today. The last time she'd gone to confession had been traumatic. She remembered being on her knees in the parish church of Santa Maria in Calella, her mother on one side and the priest on the other, as she sobbed out a half-true story. She was pregnant, and gave the name of the father—Richard Thompson. But she didn't describe the circumstances, because she was too afraid. Too afraid he would hurt her brother, or her mother.

Father Dennis, the priest at Saint Jane Frances de Chantal, seemed like a trustworthy man. She'd watched him over the last few weeks since her arrival in Bethesda. In his early thirties, he had deep brown hair and eyes and moved around the church with deliberate care and courtesy to everyone. He'd made a point of introducing himself at her first Mass, and then sought her out twice since to make sure she was settling in well.

She'd never had cause to doubt a confessor before. The bond between a penitent and confessor was supposed to be inviolate, but she'd learned the hard way that not all men were able or willing to uphold the trust of that sacred bond. After her experience in Calella, she needed to be sure. What would happen if she told Father Tom about her rape, about Richard, about her lies to her family, about all of it? She didn't know. Part of her was deeply afraid he would betray her the same way the parish priest in Calella had done. She couldn't imagine the consequences of Richard in a real rage. For example, if his position were threatened. He'd made it very clear to her that his ambition was both boundless and that she was to do everything she could to support it.

As Adelina rode up the elevator, she felt, rather than saw, Julia begin to stir. Adelina crooned a quiet tune in the elevator, hoping to keep her asleep long enough to take a nap. She decided to take the chance. Next weekend she would go to confession. Her soul was more important than any earthly consequences.

Inside, she stood still and breathed in the calm for a moment when Julia didn't stir. The concierge had let her know that Richard was out. She knew he wouldn't be back until late that evening—whatever Richard did with his free time didn't include her. Sometimes he spent long hours locked in his study, and sometimes he just stayed out. She didn't really care where, as long as she didn't have to deal with him often.

She rolled the stroller back to Julia's room and slowly lifted her out of the seat to the crib, then froze halfway up.

The phone was ringing. *Damn it.* Julia started to stir, but Adelina whispered calming words and slowly got her into her bed. She tucked the blanket around her then stepped back.

The girl didn't stir. Adelina stepped out and gently closed the door.

She reached the phone just in time to hear the answering machine pick up.

"Um … hello," said the voice on the machine. A warm, upper class British accent. She instantly recognized George-Phillip's voice and felt an intense anxiety.

"I'm calling for uh … Mr. Thompson. This is George-Phillip Windsor, you were kind enough to host me for dinner the other night—"

Adelina snatched up the phone.

"Hello? Hello?"

"Um…"

The awkward exchange went silent. Then George-Phillip said, "Is this Adelina Thompson? It's so pleasant to hear your voice."

Adelina felt her cheeks heat up at the same time she felt intense shame. Hate Richard she might, but she was *married* to him. But just hearing the sound of George-Phillip's voice on the phone sent her heart racing.

"This is Adelina," she whispered.

"I—I called to say thank you for hosting the dinner the other evening. It was a distinct pleasure."

Adelina started to answer and found herself stumbling over her words. Flustered, she said, "Thank you. Would you like me to pass a message to Richard?"

George-Phillip coughed. Then he said one word, a word that made Adelina's chest hurt a little.

"No."

She swallowed, waiting for him to speak again.

"Actually," he said, "it's really you I wanted to speak with, if that's all right. You see, I'm still fairly new in Washington, and…"

"Yes?"

"I suppose it would be improper of me to ask you to meet me for lunch."

Extremely improper. But she wanted him to ask her. She wanted it very badly.

"Perhaps," he continued, "you could bring along your lovely daughter. I genuinely do have the highest of motives. You see ... ironically, you're the first person I've really met in Washington my own age."

She wrinkled her forehead. Of course. That made much more sense. Julia would act as a tiny chaperone.

"Of course. I think that's a lovely idea," she said.

"Perhaps Monday?"

"Monday is good. I can meet..." She thought quickly. Nowhere near Embassy Row, of course, though that would be most convenient for George-Phillip. The State Department wasn't far from there, and Richard might well be in that part of town for meetings. "What about ... Matisse on Wisconsin Avenue?"

Matisse was sufficiently distant from the State Department. Richard would be unlikely to be in that part of town. Plus, he hated French food, except when he was trying to impress others.

"That sounds lovely," George-Phillip said.

"Monday then? At one?"

"I will see you then," he replied.

Quickly, before she could acknowledge what she was doing, Adelina hung up the phone. Thirty seconds later, she let out a gasp, and only then did she realize that she hadn't been breathing.

CHAPTER ELEVEN
The Prince of Penguins

Jessica. May 2. 10:14 am Pacific

Jessica Thompson sat on the stone wall overlooking the Pacific Ocean and wondered what it would be like to throw herself off the wall, to roll down the cliff, to die in the cold, heartless waves below. A brisk and cold wind blew a chill right through her soul as she wiped tears and stared out at the ocean, wondering if her mother was a liar or insane. She had a piercing headache; the kind that felt like someone had driven a nail right through her skull. The pain was centered just over her right eye.

Abruptly, she said, "Show me your driver's license."

Adelina didn't balk at the strange request. Instead, she stood and walked to the minivan and opened the door, then took out her purse.

A moment later Jessica was holding the California Driver's License in her hands.

Adelina Ramos Thompson. Birth date: March 21, 1964.

The math wasn't all that hard to work out. Julia was born in December of 1981.

"You were sixteen when you got pregnant."

Her mother nodded.

"But you always said you were two years older."

Adelina sighed. "Your father always wanted it that way. He didn't want to get married in the first place, I think. But leaving a pregnant teenage girl in Spain would have been detrimental to his career." Her face looked wistful as she said the words.

"Why did you marry him?" Jessica asked. "Who marries their rapist?"

Adelina shook her head. "You grew up in a different world, Jessica. A world where girls tweet and post on Facebook and Instagram and marry other girls if they want to. A world where people have heard the terms *date rape* and *sexual harassment* and it actually means something. When my mother realized I was pregnant, she dragged me to the priest to go to confession. They forced me to marry him."

"I don't understand," Jessica said.

"Of course not. To you, some level of freedom has always made sense. When I was growing up, divorce wasn't even legal in Spain."

Jessica shook her head slowly. Her mind was awash with thought, with confusion. Then she said, "Why did you have more children with him?" She felt a stab of pain and something akin to grief. "Why did you have *me?*"

Adelina sighed. "That's a long story. I hadn't planned to have any children after Julia."

"You must have loved him a little, right? To sleep with him again? Otherwise … what about Carrie? If you didn't love him?"

"Dear, Carrie isn't Richard's child."

Jessica winced. "Am I?"

Adelina reached out and took Jessica's hand. "Yes, your father is Richard."

"My father is the man who raped you," Jessica said bitterly.

Adelina closed her eyes. "Yes. I'm sorry."

Jessica gave her mother a scornful look. *"You're* sorry? He's the one who should be sorry." She thought through so many things in the past that hadn't made sense. Her dad, always locked away in his study when he wasn't working. His long trips away from home. His cold demeanor.

Was that why—?

"Mom? Is that why Andrea left home? Is she also not his?"

Her mother nodded. "Yes. I tried. I hated him, but I still tried to—you can't imagine how hard I tried to ... to—"

As her Mom flailed around for the word, Jessica muttered, "You mean, you tried to stay faithful."

Adelina looked down, her face twisted with shame. "Yes. But I couldn't."

Why should she have? Jessica thought. She didn't say anything right away. So much of this made no sense. It was one thing to believe that her father had pushed Adelina. That it had been date rape maybe. That he was drunk or worse. But she couldn't believe the father Adelina described—a cold-hearted sociopath. A man who would murder to protect his secrets.

Who was Richard Thompson? What did she even know about him?

The answer was basically nothing. She knew nothing about her father. Nothing at all.

"Mom ... what happened? *Why?*"

Adelina took a deep breath then began to speak again.

Adelina. February 13, 1984

Adelina Thompson squeezed Julia's hand tightly as the taxi jerked away from the curb, pushing its way into the heavy traffic along Wisconsin Avenue. It was almost one in the afternoon, and grey drizzle chilled everything in the area.

"I'm coll," Julia said.

Adelina walked down the sidewalk and said, "Come along, Julia."

"But I coll!"

"Julia, the word is *cold*. Please enunciate."

"I coll!" She wasn't any clearer, but she was a lot louder.

"We'll be inside in just a moment."

Adelina's heart was racing as she walked to the entrance of Matisse. She didn't think she was likely to run into anyone she knew here, or for that matter, anyone Richard knew. But one couldn't be too careful. Washington, DC might be a large city, but the class of high level government workers her husband belonged to was a small town indeed.

Even if she did encounter someone, she had Julia beside her. She was having lunch with another recent arrival to the city, a *Prince* for God's sake, and no one had any right to question it.

As she entered the restaurant, a mustachioed man, arrogant and commanding, approached her. He wore a tailored Perry Ellis suit, which probably cost far too much for his position. His eyes scanned Adelina and Julia ruthlessly, probably tallying up the apparent value of their clothing and hair accessories, undoubtedly taking note of the diamond bracelet she wore. Richard might be a complete bastard, but he liked her to look the part.

"How may I help you, ladies?"

"I'm meeting a friend … George-Phillip?"

The maître d' raised his eyebrows. "Indeed. Prince George-Phillip will be here shortly. Please, come this way."

She followed, surprised as he led her to a small room in the back. "Please forgive the presumption. A most noxious person has been here stalking the Prince."

"Oh no," Adelina said. "Not a criminal, I hope."

He chuckled. An unpleasant sound. "Not that I'm aware of. A young lady, as a matter of fact."

Adelina gave him a frozen look as he led her to the private dining room. "You are impertinent," she said.

He sniffed and walked away without taking her coat. Not her problem. She took off her raincoat, then Julia's, and threw them on the overstuffed chair in the corner.

"Have a seat, Julia," she commanded, pulling out one of the dining chairs.

The little girl's chin barely came over the top of the table. Her face was set and unhappy.

"It's all right, dear. We'll get something for you to eat in a moment."

"Hunngy," Julia said.

"I am too. What do you say we play a game?"

Julia smiled, a bright, happy smile, and clapped her hands together.

"We're going to guess who's coming in through the door next. You guess first."

Julia's lower lip puffed out. "Don' like this game."

"It's okay, Julia. Just take a guess."

"A penguin?"

Adelina raised her eyebrows. "It could be … it could be indeed. What if it's … a prince?"

Julia smiled. "A penguin prince!"

"Yes!" Adelina cried. "A penguin prince!"

And of course, at that very moment, George-Phillip walked in through the doorway.

"No penguin I'm afraid," he said.

Julia giggled. "You *are* penguin."

George-Phillip looked down. Adelina snickered. He wore a black suit with a white shirt.

"Hmmm," he said, raising his formidable eyebrows. "Perhaps I *am* the Prince of Penguins. But in disguise."

Julia giggled again.

The formerly rude maître d' lifted their coats from the chair, as a hostess pulled out seats for Adelina and George-Phillip.

"It's marvelous to see you, Adelina."

"And you too," she said.

"And Julia. You are, perhaps, the most beautiful little girl in the entire world. I could easily imagine that *you* are a princess. Tell me it's true."

Julia giggled and buried her face in her mother's lap.

"The maître d' told me you were having some trouble with a … uh … stalker?" Adelina said.

George-Phillip grunted. "A little. Do you really want to hear this story? It's dreary."

Adelina smiled. "I'm curious."

"Well, when I first arrived at the Embassy, the charge d'affaires had no idea what to do with me. So he arranged for me to meet with a young society columnist with the *Washington Post*. You might be familiar with her work? Maria Clawson?"

Adelina grimaced. "Horrid woman," she muttered. "I met her at a party two weeks ago. She's a terrible gossip."

George-Phillip grimaced. "Yes, indeed. We dated a few times before I realized how vindictive she was. I broke it off in fairly short order, but I'm afraid she took it hard."

"I'm sure she did," Adelina said.

She was fairly certain Maria had appeared in Washington from the recesses of some empty place in the middle of the country, Kansas or Ohio or Minnesota, and only had pretensions at society. Which would make her doubly offended at being jilted by an actual prince.

"So, Adelina. You know my background. You know my father died, and that I became Duke at too young an age, and served in the Falklands. Yet, I know almost nothing of you."

She smiled and deflected his words by saying, "I'm just a simple woman, George-Phillip. No real story there at all."

"You're from Spain. And I heard you say that you played with the National Symphony? At such a young age?"

"Not the Symphony, the National Youth Orchestra. I played violin."

"Played? Past tense?"

A stab of sadness sliced through her chest. "Played. I've no time for such things in my life these days."

George-Phillip leaned his head slightly to the side. "So sad for one so young."

"I'm not much younger than you," she replied, laughing. "What are you, twenty-one? Two years is hardly *that* big of a difference."

George-Phillip frowned a little. "I thought *you* were twenty-one."

Adelina froze.

"Oh, dear," he said. "How old *are* you?"

"Nineteen," she whispered.

"Hmm," he said. "That rather changes things, doesn't it?"

"Not really. It's just—awkward to explain sometimes."

"There's no need for you to explain anything, my dear. Sometimes we do things when we're young that surprises others."

She didn't know why she said it. She didn't know why. Absolutely nothing forced her. Nothing in her history had given her any reason to trust anyone— much less yet another over-privileged upper class white male. George-Phillip and Richard were probably cousins.

Despite all of that, the words that came out of her mouth were, "And sometimes people do things to young people who have no control over it at all."

He frowned, and she instantly said, "Forgive me. So tell me … what compelled you to ask me to lunch?"

George-Phillip coughed, then stumbled on his words. "I … you see … I needed to…"

Adelina couldn't help it. She felt her face begin to flush, the heat beginning at her cheekbones and working its way down her face to her neck and chest.

"Mamma turnded red," Julia said, helpfully.

"The word is *turned*, Julia," Adelina said.

"Nevertheless, you did turn red," George-Phillip murmured.

"I've no right to turn red," she whispered.

A second later a waitress entered the room, trailed by the maître d'. Within a minute, George had approved the wine and in fluent French, discussed their order.

Adelina's French was slightly rusty, but good enough. She joined in the conversation, and in a few moments they'd finished their order.

"Est ce qu'elle comprend Français?" asked George-Phillip, nodding toward Julia. *Does she understand any French?*

"Du tout," she said. *None at all.*

"Très bien," he replied. *Very good.* He continued in French. "You see, Adelina, I must admit I was intrigued and disturbed by the age difference between you and

Richard, and even more so now that I know you're younger than you said the other evening. You were … seventeen when Julia was conceived?"

"Sixteen," she whispered. "But not willingly. They forced me to marry him."

"They?" he asked.

"My mother. My priest. But you mustn't tell anyone. You mustn't do anything."

"Any man of honor would, and should."

She leaned forward. *"Not* if you would honor my wishes. Richard is dangerous. And I have a four-year-old brother in Spain to protect, along with Julia."

"Surely you don't mean—"

"I mean you must leave it alone."

He sighed and straightened his tie. "Well, then. I'm truly sorry, Adelina. I wish…"

"There's no point in wishing for anything," she said. "Enjoy lunch. That's all there is."

"Oui," he replied, raising a glass of wine to her.

She steered the question away from the very dangerous ground they'd treaded on. "Tell me about your parents," she said.

"I've little to say about them," he said. "My father was a wastrel."

"I'm so sorry," she replied.

He took her hand and said, "It's quite all right. I do have a favorite aunt, the Princess Alexandra. Feisty woman. Her father died while defending his nation, unlike mine."

Adelina smiled. "My father spoke very warmly of her. They met at King Juan Carlos's wedding."

"Really? I believe I'm third cousins or some such with Queen Sophia. What took your father to the wedding?"

"It's a small world," she said. "Richard gets angry when I mention it, but my father was the Marquis of Cerverales, and second cousin to Juan Carlos. He met Princess Alexandra at the wedding, and told the story for years, among many others."

"What happened to your father?" he asked.

She sighed. "He lost everything to Franco. He had to start life over as a street vendor, but he succeeded. Then he was run down in the street. A truck *accident*." Her eyes pricked with tears. "I never had the opportunity to say goodbye to him."

He closed his eyes and reached out, taking her hand. "I'm so sorry, Adelina. Even my father … even four years later … I feel his loss keenly. I can only imagine your pain."

Julia said, "Mommy lost Daddy?" A line had formed between her eyebrows.

"No, sweetie," Adelina said. "I lost *my* daddy."

"Find new daddy?"

Adelina suppressed a sob. George-Phillip said, "Aren't you a sweet and kind little girl."

"Mommy say Jesus loves kindness."

George-Phillip smiled. "And so he does."

The conversation drifted from there to safer topics. The latest gossip from the diplomatic community. Fallout from the invasion of Grenada, the Falklands war, the attack on the Marine barracks in Beirut and the subsequent escalation of the war there, which had resulted in shelling of populated areas of the city in early February. The conviction of an Alabama Klansman who had randomly selected a black victim and hung him from a tree. And the topic which had dominated diplomatic circles for days: the selection of a new Soviet Premier following the death of Yuri Andropov. Politics was a far safer topic.

They moved on to entertainment, television and the media and *Spitting Image*, the satirical and somewhat scandalous puppet show, which had launched on the air the previous week in London. Among other things, the show lampooned the royal family.

"It's really funny," George-Phillip said. "Naturally, someone sent a film of it to the Embassy here. But all the old women running the Embassy were scandalized."

Adelina laughed as George-Phillip described the antics of the show, including the satirical show *The President's Brain is Missing!*

"Oh, how I wish I'd seen it," she said.

He sobered a little and said, "Maybe we can arrange for a showing at the Embassy—"

She reached out and touched his hand. "George-Phillip. No."

"But, it doesn't have to—"

She sighed. "Stop. We really can't see each other after today. This was sweet. And in a different life, things would be different."

His mouth quirked to the side. "Of course. And I'd never ask you to do anything dishonorable, Adelina."

"Gotta go potty," Julia said.

Adelina closed her eyes. She was closer to tears than she'd realized. She didn't need that. "Excuse me," she said, her voice at a near whisper. She lifted Julia out of her seat as Julia said the words, "Why Mommy sad?"

With Julia in her arms, she rushed out of the room. In her haste, she didn't see the young columnist from the Washington Post until she literally bumped her out of the way.

Maria Clawson gasped as Adelina stumbled back.

"I'm so sorry," Adelina said.

She kept moving, trying to bite back the tears. Inside the women's room, she sighed in frustration. She was too late—Julia had already soiled herself. Nearly crying in frustration, Adelina searched her purse for a diaper. She had one, tangled at the bottom with sundry other supplies.

"Mrs. Thompson." The voice was sickly sweet.

Twenty-three-year-old Maria Clawson was slightly taller than Adelina. Pale skin and blonde hair framed a classic Irish face with her upturned nose and apple red cheeks. Adelina wanted to pinch them until she cried.

"Maria. How pleasant to see you." There was no hiding the venom in her voice.

"Having a lunch out with friends?" Maria asked.

"I am. And you?" Adelina wanted to say, *Are you here stalking George-Phillip?* but she knew she couldn't.

"Yes, I'm here with Janna Farrington," Maria said.

Adelina raised an eyebrow, not recognizing the name.

"Oh, you wouldn't recognize her name," Maria said. "She's old Washington society."

Adelina snorted, unintentionally. She did *not* need to make an enemy of a *Washington Post* gossip columnist after all. But she couldn't help herself. "I suppose old Washington society means her money goes back more than ten years? Of course I wouldn't know her. *Society* in Europe goes back a bit further."

Maria froze. She sniffed and turned up her nose, then said, "I'm sure you're familiar with *all sorts* of society in Europe, aren't you Adelina? And really, you should be proud of yourself. Most homeless nobility wouldn't be caught dead marrying rich Americans. But you've done all right for yourself. And I bet Richard Thompson wasn't even as old as your father."

Julia began to cry, and Adelina realized she was holding her daughter's arm far too hard.

"*Excuse me,*" she said, forcefully.

A few minutes later she had Julia sorted and cleaned up. George-Phillip was sitting in the dining room, waiting for her.

"Adelina," he said.

"I really must go," she replied.

"Of course," he said, sadly.

For just a second, she let herself *see* him. He was her age, or close to it. Tall. He was a man, caring and considerate but strong. He was everything Richard wasn't.

He wasn't hers.

She sighed and set Julia on the floor beside her, then began getting her daughter into her coat. Two minutes later, she left the room, walking into the main dining room of the restaurant. Neither she nor George-Phillip had spoken another word.

As she walked out of the dining room, she spotted Maria Clawson, sitting with an older blonde woman near the window. Maria had her claws out as she spoke forcefully to her companion. Then she looked up, her eyes darting from Adelina to the door of the private dining room.

Adelina paused, then saw George-Phillip, standing in that doorway.

She looked at the floor and then walked out without meeting Clawson's eyes.

The entire ride home in the cab, Adelina thought about what Maria would say. If Maria, the gossip columnist, chose to write about seeing Adelina lunching with George-Phillip. It would make for an interesting piece, wouldn't it? Just enough innuendo to smear her and enrage Richard. She thought she might preempt the questions by telling Richard she'd had lunch with George-Phillip. After all, nothing inappropriate had happened. The two of them talked. Two-year-old Julia had been in the room with them the entire time.

But Richard wasn't home that afternoon, or that evening. When seven pm finally rolled around and she had Julia asleep, Adelina found herself staring at her closet.

Staring.

Finally she got up. She paced outside the closet door. Back and forth.

Then she opened it.

On top, on the shelf, in the back, was the dusty case of her violin. She pulled it down and reverently set it on the bed.

She'd loved that violin. It wasn't special. It wasn't an antique. There was nothing to make it stand out from a million other similar instruments. After all, her father might have claimed the title of Marquis, but in practice he was an impoverished shopkeeper, and no mere posturing could bring him into land or titles. He'd saved money for several months in order to buy this instrument.

She opened the case for the first time since her father had died. It was dusty, and she felt the dust against her fingertips with the cloying grip of grief. Slowly, she eased the instrument out. It would be badly out of tune, of course, but she'd forgotten nothing. She quickly tuned the instrument.

Then she began to play. A solitary, lonely note. Then another. And another. And before she knew it, she was playing. One note after another, the rapid-fire introduction to Antonio Vivaldi's *Winter*. Tears ran down her face as she played through the rhythm, a powerful, mournful movement.

The tears came faster and faster, just as the notes did, and she found herself swaying, playing louder and louder, quicker and quicker. The rising notes took over, and for just a second she felt herself close her eyes. She swayed with the music, and she wasn't standing in the prison of her life just outside Washington, DC.

Instead, she was on the floor of the orchestra pit of the National Youth Orchestra, with two thousand people in the audience, her father in the seat of honor as tears ran down his face.

And then she cried out, because for just a second, her father's presence was so real. It was so real it hurt. So real she could smell his awful cologne, she could feel the roughness of his hands as he held hers, she could feel his beard as he kissed her cheek. His presence was so real it ripped her insides out. It turned her love into grief, her joy into hopelessness, her faith into dust.

In a sudden, jerking motion, she lowered the instrument from her shoulder, raised it by the neck, and swung it hard against the wall. The drywall cracked, and she swung it again, harder. This time the instrument itself cracked at the neck, and she cried out in pain.

She swung her violin a third time, as if it really were her past she was destroying. The wood of the instrument shattered, fragments and splinters flying everywhere.

Adelina let the remainder of the wood fall to the floor. Julia was stirring in her room next door, on the verge of crying. The noise. Adelina sank to her knees, gripping her head in her hands. Not meaning to, she found herself holding the sides of her head where Richard had the other day. Like him, she squeezed, as if causing herself pain could shut out the cries of her daughter, as if squeezing her own head could shut out her own cries of pain at the loss of everything.

She lay down on her side and wept.

Jessica. May 2. 11:00 am Pacific

A tear ran down Jessica's face as she listened to her mother's story.

"You smashed your violin?" she whispered.

"Yes," Adelina said. A tear ran down her face.

"Why did you tell George-Phillip you couldn't see him again?"

Adelina stared at the floor, and she whispered, "Because it's a sin, isn't it? I'm married. I was married then. I wanted to see him, so badly. But I knew, if I did, then … well…"

"You were afraid you would love him?"

Adelina closed her eyes. Jessica leaned forward and touched her mother on the shoulder. And then she whispered, "I wish I'd known. Somehow."

"You weren't born yet. Not for a long time."

Jessica turned on the wall, looking out at the ocean. She felt numb inside. Confused. But also relieved. For the first time in her life, her mother made sense.

Her mother made sense. And the sense she made was so heartbreaking and full of grief and sadness and tragedy that Jessica wanted to throw herself off the wall. Instead, she leaned on her mother, and slipped her hand around her waist.

Her mother sighed.

"Did you get to see him again?" she whispered. "Is George-Phillip Carrie's father?"

Adelina took a deep breath and began to speak again.

CHAPTER TWELVE Georgie, Indeed

George-Phillip. May 2.

"**S**ir?" Oswald O'Leary, George-Phillip's special assistant, had opened the door and leaned inside.

"Oh," said George-Phillip. "It's three o'clock, isn't it?"

"Yes, sir. The car is waiting."

George-Phillip stood and straightened his tie, then pulled on his jacket. He felt as if he were moving in slow motion. It was the afternoon of the second day since the assassination attempt, and he'd barely slept since. For one thing, security personnel had been in and out of his house since that night, installing bulletproof glass, armored doors and a safe room between his and Jane's bedrooms.

Moments like that made him question his choice of avocation. George-Phillip would have done just as well financially by following in his father's footsteps— serving on the board of several charities, concerning himself with hunting and drinking, and leaving the public service to men of lesser station. But something of his aunt Alexandra's example had settled in on him at a young age. Princess Alexandra had continued participating in hundreds of royal obligations every year right up until recently, when aging and arthritis had begun to slow her down. So instead of living a quiet life, he'd attended the military academy at Sandhurst.

He'd served his time in the Royal Marines and the remainder of his career in the Special Intelligence Service.

The result? Some lunatic firing a rifle through his office window in the middle of the night from the woods in Belgrave Square.

Except, George-Phillip reflected, he knew full well that it wasn't some random lunatic. Whoever wanted to kill him had also placed a bomb in Adelina Thompson's home in San Francisco and attacked Andrea Thompson and her brother-in-law in the Thompson condominium in Bethesda, Maryland. Whoever it was had a long reach, a lot of resources, and a vendetta that appeared increasingly personal.

O'Leary walked silently beside George-Phillip as they made their way to the elevator. O'Leary was, in some ways, the perfect assistant. The two men had worked together for thirty years, and O'Leary was the *only* person who knew everything he'd worked on—including the Wakhan file, and of course, the links between George-Phillip and Adelina Thompson.

They stepped into the elevator. George-Phillip looked at O'Leary and said, "Any word on the whereabouts of Adelina? Or Andrea Thompson?"

O'Leary shrugged. "We've got people looking for both, but there's a lot of ground to cover. The best bet for Adelina will be when she uses her phone or credit cards, which is bound to happen at some point."

"Unless she threw them away. She must know there are people after her."

"I don't think she's that smart, sir."

George-Phillip grimaced. "She's a lot smarter than you'd think, O'Leary. You never gave her enough credit."

"We have trained agents looking for them, sir. They'll turn up."

"*Safely*," George-Phillip said. "I don't have to tell you that this is important to me on a personal level."

"That you don't, sir."

Two minutes later they were in a car, slogging through traffic to the bridge. It was only a mile and a half to 10 Downing Street, perhaps a twenty-five minute walk. On some days he might have walked it, but that was less of an option with people trying to kill him.

Who was he kidding? This wasn't new. At one time it would have been the Irish he was worried about killing him. Or the Arabs. Now it was … who?

He didn't know. Likely someone inside the CIA. Rogues, perhaps, working for Leslie Collins. Nothing else made sense. Whoever it was, they would have answers soon enough. In the meantime, George-Phillip had other problems.

Once they cleared the guards, the car pulled to a stop in front of Number 10 Downing Street. George-Phillip took a deep breath, then stepped out of the car as the door was opened. A moment later the front door to the house opened.

"Your Grace," said the man who stood in the door, an aide to Prime Minister Duncan Howard. "Come in, please."

George-Phillip felt like a mouse walking into the house of a hungry cat. He smiled and approached the aide, who led him into the entrance hall.

"This way, sir," the aide said.

"Thank you," George-Phillip said. He'd first visited this house when Margaret Thatcher was still new in office. He remembered sitting across from the woman who would become known as the Iron Lady, the first—and still only—female Prime Minister.

I hope you'll be more of a credit to your nation that your father was, Miss Thatcher had said.

I plan to, George-Phillip had replied. *I'm seeking an enlisted position in the Royal Marines, then appointment at Sandhurst.*

Good, she'd said. *I'll speak with General Moore.*

She'd been as good as her word—General Moore had found him a job, and not a desk job. George-Phillip had been trained and went ashore alongside the other Marines.

Duncan Howard, the current occupant of 10 Downing Street, was a mere shadow of Miss Thatcher. An arrogant buffoon who understood nothing of the needs of national security or of the economy, his only overriding goal was his own political preservation.

That said, George-Phillip had to respect the position, though he had none for the man. A moment later, the aide stopped at the door, letting him in.

Duncan Howard stood as they entered the room. He gave George-Phillip a smarmy smile and held out a hand.

George-Phillip took the hand.

"Georgie," Howard said, and then waved vaguely to a scarlet brocade seat. "I'm so pleased to see you alive and well. That must have been quite a fright."

"Indeed," George-Phillip said. He took the proffered seat and waited for Howard to get to the point, doing his best to suppress his irritation at the nickname. *Georgie* indeed.

Howard sat down across from him and said, "Tea?"

"No, thank you."

Howard frowned then said, "Georgie, I called you over here because of a matter which has been brought to my attention. A matter which I'm not really—equipped—to deal with."

"Indeed?"

"How familiar are you with the Wakhan region of Afghanistan? And specifically—what happened during the Soviet occupation of that country?"

George-Phillip grimaced. "I'm intimately familiar with it. You may be aware MI6 conducted an investigation in the late 1980s. It was my first major assignment."

"I am aware. That's why I asked you."

George-Phillip nodded.

"I've received a disturbing report. Disturbing because it was brought to me directly. Disturbing because it involves you. I'd like to ask you to explain yourself?"

"I've no idea what you mean."

"Did you, in fact, find out who was responsible for the massacre at Wakhan?"

"The Afghan Mujahideen was responsible for the massacre, Mr. Howard. Specifically Ahmad Shah Massoud and his confidante Vasily Karatygin."

"The Soviet defector?"

"Yes. He's mainly a smuggler now."

"Where did they get the chemical weapons?"

George-Phillip didn't answer.

"Come now. This is what the report is about. I'm told that you found out who sold them the weapons."

"We did, sir. Richard Thompson, the new American Secretary of Defense, was the leader of the group that got the weapons into the country."

"Dear Lord. Why did we not take action then?"

George-Phillip rolled his eyes. "Ironically, I sat in this very office with your predecessor Mrs. Thatcher discussing this subject, Duncan. We didn't do anything about it for the same reason the American government didn't. Because at the highest levels, *no one cared* about the civilians who were murdered. I was ordered by Miss Thatcher to suppress my findings. We sealed the report in the interest of national security."

Howard looked at him and said, "That decision might still cost you."

"It's already cost me decades of sleep. Why are you raising this now?"

George-Phillip knew the answer. Of course he did. It must be one of the conspirators who had originally covered up the massacre. Perhaps because of Thompson's elevation to Secretary of Defense, perhaps because of the increasing likelihood that Carrie and Andrea Thompson would learn who their birth father was. Something had set this thing in motion and now who knew where it would end up?

Howard leaned forward. "We've been asked by the Guardian to comment on a story they are about to run."

"About Wakhan?"

"About what they are referring to as the cover-up at Wakhan."

"Do you wish me to comment?"

"We're considering pursuing them under section 2 of the Official Secrets Act."

George-Phillip grimaced and shook his head. "I don't recommend it. First, it will make the government look like clowns. We don't need another ABC affair. Second, it isn't even our secret."

Howard frowned at the mention of the ABC trials of 1978, when the government had aggressively prosecuted journalists Crispin Aubrey and Duncan Campbell for receiving official secrets. The trials were a credibility disaster for the government.

"Perhaps, but certainly it's classified information, even if it's not really *ours.*"

"Who is *we* anyway?"

Howard frowned. "The Cabinet, Georgie. The Cabinet."

George-Phillip sat forward in his seat. "Duncan, I'm a member of the Cabinet. We've had no such meetings or discussions."

Howard waved a hand dismissively. "Informal."

"It's hardly a secret anymore, then. If you've discussed this … informally … with the Cabinet, then you might as well take out your own advertisement in the Guardian."

"George, really, that's not—"

"Would you like me to make an official statement?"

"Not yet. Actually I want you to stay quiet until we know which way the wind is going to blow."

George-Phillip sighed and closed his eyes. There were times he wished he'd never heard of Wakhan, Adelina and Richard Thompson, or their daughters. There were times, more and more lately, when he wondered why he hadn't followed in his father's footsteps. The lack of moral courage displayed in Duncan Howard's statement was appalling.

"Duncan, we can't avoid this or base our response on politics—"

Howard cut him off. "Everything is politics."

"Politics got us into this mess in the first place." George-Phillip stood up. *Not just politics*, he thought. *Politics and greed and lust for power.* "I really must go, Prime Minister."

George-Phillip. February 15, 1984.

"George-Phillip, can you come to my office for a moment?"

"Of course, sir."

George-Phillip laid the heavy black receiver in its cradle atop the rotary phone and stood up, stretching his back. He'd been at his desk for several hours, skipping lunch, as he studied the mind-numbing protocol standards required of Embassy personnel. While his goal was to serve in the military and possibly intelligence services, he knew that a brief stint in the diplomatic corps would help. Not to mention the fact that Mrs. Thatcher herself suggested it.

All the same, the minuscule details and gradations of the diplomatic world did not appeal to George-Phillip. Everything from the precise titles to be used when addressing the assistant chiefs of sub-Saharan villagers to the order of seating when meeting with deposed nobles was included. It was all precise, detailed, and utterly bloodless.

The phone call had come from the Ambassador, Sir Francis Galvin. Galvin, who reminded George-Phillip three times per week, without fail, that he was a *self-made* man. A boy who had grown up with a coarse East End accent, Galvin had distinguished himself in the Second World War and was awarded the Victoria Cross by King George VI. Subsequently, he'd traded on that for a career under the Foreign Office and the Diplomatic Service.

Despite his evident valor and the Victoria Cross he still wore daily, he was a monumental todger.

George-Phillip had to respond to his summons. He squeezed out from behind his desk in the tiny office in the basement of the Embassy and ducked his head to miss the large pipe that ran near the door. He stepped out of the door, rearranged his suit coat so that it was a little neater, and made his way down the hallway to the elevator.

George-Phillip was well aware that he was the only person on the Embassy staff who had an office in the basement. Somehow, the Ambassador managed to find homes for 200 diplomats and another 200 support staff, but the Embassy had been too full for George-Phillip.

Not for the first time, as George-Phillip rode up the elevator, he pondered the fact that being 46th from the throne was exalted enough to piss off egalitarians but not exalted enough to actually give him any privileges.

Nevertheless, he made it to Galvin's office in a hurry. George-Phillip was twenty-one years old, and he knew he had to earn his place here.

The Ambassador's secretary waved him in. She had crimped and poufed her newly blonde hair in a way that had become very stylish in the United States but was still a little too aggressive for the British Diplomatic Service. She opened the door for George-Phillip.

Inside the room the Ambassador sat, relaxed in his chair. A glass of bourbon sat untouched on his desk before him.

"George-Phillip. Come in. Have you met Oswald O'Leary?"

O'Leary was an aggressive looking man with the bunched shoulders and flattened nose of a prizefighter. A bulldog of a man.

"Nice to meet you," George-Phillip said.

"O'Leary, this is George-Phillip. Excuse me, *Prince* George-Phillip. Mrs. Thatcher has seen fit to foist him upon us."

O'Leary nodded at George-Phillip then gave him a sideways grin. "Pleased to meet you, sir. Oswald O'Leary. I work here and there."

"He's not allowed to tell you this, Georgie, but O'Leary works for MI6."

George-Phillip coughed politely. "What can I do for you, sir?"

Galvin said, "I presume you've read the gossip column in the *Post* this morning?"

George-Phillip answered very quickly. "Sir, I generally don't bother myself with gossip columnists."

O'Leary leaned forward and said, "How well are you acquainted with Mrs. Thompson?"

"We aren't close," George-Phillip said. "I was invited to a dinner at Richard Thompson's home last Saturday evening—I've written up my report."

Galvin leaned forward and said, "You didn't submit a report about your lunch with his wife on Monday."

"Well, sir, I..." George-Phillip sighed. He had no excuse. The rules were clear—contacts with foreign diplomatic personnel had to be reported. Including spouses. But he knew why he hadn't posted a report. He hadn't planned on telling anyone about lunch with Adelina, but that witch Maria Clawson had made it necessary. "Sir, you are correct. I did not."

"Tell us about your lunch," O'Leary said.

George-Phillip said, "I was quite taken with the young lady. She is ... not happy in her marriage."

"Maybe that's because he's old enough to be her father," O'Leary said.

"He is indeed. She's quite terrified of him—she seems to believe he's capable of harming her."

Galvin blanched. "Surely you can't be serious."

"I'm serious, sir. I felt bad for her. But she was clear we would not see each other again."

"And why was that?" Galvin responded.

George-Phillip sighed. "I believe the attraction was mutual, sir. She—she seemed quite torn and upset by the end of our meal."

O'Leary grunted. "So she doesn't want to see you?"

"I'm afraid not," George-Phillip said.

"We want you to see her."

"Whatever for?"

O'Leary said, "Have you ever heard of the Wakhan Corridor?"

"No—" George-Phillip said. Then he paused and held up a finger. "Wait … I did hear the term mentioned Saturday night. In passing, and I didn't know what it was in reference to."

"You included that mention in your report," Galvin said.

"Yes, sir. But I think it was probably meaningless."

"It's not meaningless," O'Leary said.

"Well, what is it, then?"

Galvin leaned forward and said, "George-Phillip, first I must advise you, this discussion is classified under the Official Secrets Acts. Revealing anything we discuss here would be considered an act of treason to the Crown. You understand?"

George-Phillip stared at Galvin in shock, offended that Galvin felt the need to remind him. He stifled his anger and simply acknowledged the statement.

"I understand, sir."

"All right. Go ahead, O'Leary."

O'Leary leaned forward. "It's like this, sir. On December 12, Ahmad Massoud's militia swung through the Wakhan Corridor. It seemed that one of the local villages had been cooperating too closely with the Soviets. But instead of the typical retribution, they dropped two canisters of sarin into the village by helicopter."

"Good lord," George-Phillip said. "What … what happened?"

"Everyone died. Women, men, children, it didn't matter. Even the sheep and donkeys died."

"So … why are you telling me?"

"Unfortunately, we have reason to believe that the militia obtained the chemical weapons via the Central Intelligence Agency. We don't know if it was a rogue operation or not, but Richard Thompson was involved, along with Leslie Collins and Prince Roshan. I presume you know all three men?"

George-Phillip felt a chill. "Yes. Collins and Roshan were both at the dinner Saturday."

The Ambassador leaned forward and looked at George-Phillip closely. "Georgie, I realize you're still basically nothing more than a kid. But sometimes a nation asks something of its children as well. I trust we have your loyalty and discretion in this matter?"

George-Phillip looked Galvin in the eye. "Ambassador, my great-grandfather was George the Fifth. I know something of loyalty to the crown."

Galvin stared back at him, anger in his eyes. "Aye, well, I'm not interested in your grandfather, I'm interested in you. You're to make friends with Adelina Thompson and find out what you can of what happened in Wakhan. O'Leary will work with you. Am I clear?"

George-Phillip sighed. "Yes, sir. I'll do my best."

George-Phillip. May 2.

"Let me out," George-Phillip said.

"Sir?" said the driver and O'Leary simultaneously. The car was on Millbank, near the Riverside Walk Gardens. The Vauxhall Bridge crossing the Thames was still between them and the headquarters of the Secret Intelligence Service.

"You heard me," George-Phillip said. "Stop the car and let me out. I'll walk from here."

O'Leary leaned close. His voice was low and calm, as if he were speaking to a child. "Sir, someone tried to kill you two days ago."

"So they did. Now stop the car, and I'll walk. Keep nearby and watch over me if you're worried I'll be shot. But I need to be left alone for a few minutes."

"Stop the car," O'Leary called.

The driver brought the car to a stop. George-Phillip was irrationally irritated. The driver didn't stop when he gave the order, only when O'Leary did. But that's how it worked. The higher you went up the chain of command, the less direct influence you had over events. George had felt that frustration often enough before. But now it ached, because Adelina Ramos Thompson was out there somewhere, lost and alone and frightened, with people possibly trying to harm her and her daughters. It ached because *his* daughters were out there, unprotected and unknowing.

She'd never admitted it to him.

She'd never said a word. But he'd known ever since he first saw then twelve-year-old Carrie at a diplomatic function in Beijing, and later, when he saw both of his daughters together on the beach in Calella. It was obvious, because both of them looked so very much like him, and even more so like his cousin Eloise.

George-Phillip had respected Adelina's wishes for thirty years and not revealed himself to his daughters. But she was missing now, and they were all in danger, and now he had to keep his own counsel. No matter what it did to his career or his own personal aspirations.

He got out of the car and began to walk along the narrow plaza fronting the river, then along the Vauxhall Bridge. He was well aware this was the sort of behavior that would see him lambasted in the tabloids. *Giant Eyebrow covers the Thames*, or something equally offensive. But sometimes you simply had to get away. As he walked across the bridge, he studied the headquarters of the Secret Intelligence Service, towering over the bridge and the river. The green glass and stone building was oppressive, a pile of stone and glass straight out of Orwell's

1984. What was truly astonishing was that the plaza between the SIS and the river was open to the public, access to the building and its grounds blocked by a high steel fence.

Inside, it was another story. Inside that building, George-Phillip barely kept control of the pulse of a hundred nations. Some people questioned the need for such an apparatus. Those people wondered why the SIS spied, why they had intelligence operatives operating in every nation on earth, why they worried about nuclear proliferation and terrorists and jihadists. But those people had never looked at the bodies of women and children scattered across a street, destroyed by the bombs of terrorists. People who questioned the need for SIS didn't understand that the purpose of an intelligence agency was nothing more than to protect.

All the same, sometimes the weight of this calling wore down on George-Phillip. The weight of constantly having guards. The weight of his daughter Jane being whisked from primary school to home to other locations with a full complement of guards, because his family was not safe.

The weight of his decisions was what wore him down. His decision to leave behind Adelina, even when he knew that she suffered at the hands of that son of a bitch Richard Thompson.

Adelina, he mused.

Sometimes he liked to play *what if* games. What if he'd gone to Spain instead of the Army the year after his father died? What if he'd been in Madrid the day of the coup? It wasn't *that* unlikely.

It was ridiculously unlikely. He'd been in school, determined to finish his final year before going into the Army. Struggling with his own identify after his father died in a drunken car accident. Adelina had been helpless that day, and ever since. Here it was thirty years later, and he'd never been able to help her.

What if, he sometimes thought. What if they'd said, *the hell with it,* and made a run for Brazil or Thailand or Burma or anywhere else far from the reach of CIA or SIS? What if he hadn't been such a coward?

He paused halfway across the bridge and looked out at the river. It was a grey, cold day.

What would Carrie or Andrea say? If they knew he was their father? If they knew he'd not been courageous enough to fight for them?

Well. It might be too late. It might wreck everything he thought of as a life now. But he was going to fight for his daughters. And … if she'd let him … for his love.

CHAPTER THIRTEEN
Witch, witch, witch, witch

Adelina. February 16, 1984.

"**N**o. I can't see you again."

"Adelina, I must see you."

At his words, she felt the blackness reaching out and grabbing her heart again. Because she *wanted* to see him. She wanted to so badly she could taste it.

She knew that could be nothing but disaster.

"I can't see you," she whispered.

Very slowly, she hung up the phone and closed her eyes, shutting out the darkness.

Jessica. May 2.

Jessica felt her stomach rumble. She hadn't eaten in almost an hour, and for days she'd been constantly ravenous. She hugged her legs tighter to herself and looked out at the water. The talk with her mother had been full of unwelcome revelations, not the least of which was that her father was a rapist.

Or Adelina *claimed* he was. After all, her mother was a lunatic. All of Adelina's daughters knew that. She took enough drugs to tranquilize an elephant. She had fits and breakdowns. She cried randomly and had panic attacks that terrified all of them. She'd more than once freaked out and injured her daughters with both her words and her slaps.

"Jessica?" her mother said.

"Leave me alone," Jessica whispered.

Adelina sighed and stood. Jessica didn't watch her walk away. Instead, she stared out at the ocean and fought to preserve her anger at her mother.

It wasn't that hard. All she had to do was remember too many incidents to count. Especially the worst one, the broken cello, the memory that had preserved for all time her memory of her sister Carrie as a saint and her mother as the devil.

Jessica had been six years old, and it had to have been late October, because she remembered she and Sarah had gone to the Halloween party at the Brewer's old Victorian up the street. Jessica had dressed as an angel, and Sarah as a witch. Black and white. They'd run around holding hands through most of the party and gorged on candy until Sarah threw up on Randy Brewer's Harry Potter and the Chamber of Secrets LEGO set. Randy, five years older than they were, punched Sarah. Sarah threw up again, while Jessica screamed, and their mother took the two of them and Alexandra home in a huff, complaining loudly the whole way that none of her daughters knew how to behave.

The next morning, everything in the house seemed ominous. Their father stayed locked in his office, not an unusual state of affairs, but Mother had been in the dining room the entire morning, sobbing. Jessica didn't remember where Alexandra had been that morning. Maybe she'd had a sleepover.

"Stay out of her way," Carrie whispered that morning. "Don't go downstairs, I'll bring you some breakfast."

"What's wrong?" Sarah asked. As always, Sarah had no sense of self-preservation. She'd constantly antagonized their mother.

"You wouldn't understand, it's something with Julia," Carrie had said.

"Who's Julia?" Jessica had asked.

"Sister, stupid," Sarah said.

"Don't call me stupid!" Jessica shouted. "She's hardly ever here. How would I know?"

"*Are* stupid," Sarah said. Then she reached out and pinched Jessica's arm.

"Stop it, both of you!" Carrie whispered urgently. "Mother's crazy today. *Don't* bother her!"

Sarah looked at the floor and said, "Sorry, Carrie." Her voice was low.

Jessica pinched her back. Sarah swiveled her wide open blue eyes to Jessica and stared. She didn't cry or say anything, but her lips curled up in a caricature of a smile.

"*Stop it!*" Carrie said again. "I'm going to call Julia, and then get you guys some breakfast. Stay up here and out of trouble, okay?"

So the twins stayed in Carrie's room playing with Andrea, who complained because she was hungry. But all three of them knew better than to go downstairs. It had been weeks, maybe even months, since their mother had a breakdown. But they knew.

It was a long twenty minutes later before Carrie came back upstairs. Andrea was crying. "I'm hungry," she cried.

"It's okay, Pooh Bear," Carrie whispered. She began handing out donuts and small cartons of apple juice.

"I wanted grape juice," Sarah said.

"It's all they had at the 7-11, Sarah. Maybe you can have some grape juice later?"

"Okay," Sarah whispered. Her eyes watered.

Now, at eighteen, Jessica understood just how awful it was that their older sister had to sneak out to the convenience store to get them breakfast, out of fear of disturbing their mother who was somewhere near the kitchen. But that was soon overshadowed.

They all froze at the sound of footsteps coming up the hardwood stairs.

"Carrie?" The voice was tremulous, shaky. It sent a chill down Jessica's spine. Their mother had been crying, and that was never good. "Carrie? Where are you? Who were you on the phone with?"

Carrie whispered, "Hide the food."

As the girls scrambled to push their donuts and juice boxes under the bed, Carrie stood up and walked toward the closed door. Stark terror filled Jessica as her big sister opened the door.

"In here, Mother," Carrie said.

Mother staggered into the room. Her face was puffy and red, and her hands were clenched, wringing each other. "Who were you on the phone with?"

"Um, a friend from school," Carrie said.

"*Which* friend?"

"*Witch friend*," Sarah said. Then she giggled.

"What did you say, young lady?" Their mother's eyes narrowed.

Sarah's eyes widened. Ridiculously so. Always defiant, she bared her teeth a little and rolled her eyes and said, "Witch witch witch witch."

"How *dare you?*" Mother shouted, raising her hand to slap Sarah.

That was the moment everything changed. Because seventeen-year-old Carrie grabbed her wrist.

"You're not hitting her," Carrie said. "Not anymore."

The response was instant. Adelina swung her other open hand and slapped Carrie across the face. "*You* don't tell me what to do! *You* don't touch me," she shouted, slapping Carrie a second time.

"Stop!" Carrie cried out as she stumbled back. "Stop, you crazy bitch!"

Mother screamed something unintelligible, and Sarah and Jessica grabbed Andrea and dragged her under the bed. The scuffle got louder, as their mother screamed, and Carrie screamed back, wordless sounds of rage. Then there was a loud crash, and Carrie was on the floor looking stunned next to her cello. Their mother had staggered back to the door, a look of horror and crazed grief on her face.

Mother swept out of the room without another word, and Jessica and Andrea swarmed out from under the bed. Carrie was on her back, her eyes closed in pain. Her cello was on the floor beside her, the neck snapped from where she'd fallen over it.

"I *hate* her," Carrie whispered, balling up into a fetal position. "*Hate.*"

Jessica didn't remember what happened after that, except that Sarah had hidden under the bed all morning, crying and refusing to come out and whispering, "I'm sorry, I'm sorry, I'm sorry, Carrie," over and over again.

The next fall Carrie had left for college, and Jessica never saw her play the cello again.

But she'd won one thing. Their mother never hit any of them again after that.

How was Jessica supposed to reconcile *that* with the image her mother painted of the wronged, raped woman struggling to survive a near psychotic husband? How was she supposed to ever, *ever* think of Adelina Thompson sympathetically?

"I hate you," she whispered, her words barely carrying over the sound of the surf crashing against the shore down below.

"What?" her mother said.

Jessica looked up from her knees and said, "I hate you. You weren't a mother to us. Ever. And now you're taking away my father too? I *hate* you."

Adelina flinched. "I deserve it," she whispered. "I don't expect you to forgive me."

"I don't know how you can even think of forgiveness," Jessica said. "You made our lives hell," she cursed. But as she said the words, tears ran freely down her face.

"I'm sorry," Adelina replied.

"I don't accept your apology. I never will."

Jessica turned away. Remembering Carrie's screams as she shielded her sisters from their crazy mother. Remembering Sarah sobbing under the bed for hours. She remembered Andrea packing to leave for Spain again, never knowing that the reason her parents didn't want her was because her mother had an affair. You couldn't tell a pretty story and apologize and expect everything to be better. You couldn't erase a lifetime of hurt.

Fuck her, Jessica thought.

Adelina. February 17, 1984.

"Come, Julia."

Julia wore a tiny blue dress with patent leather shoes and a matching belt. Lately whenever she moved it was at a dead run, slightly tilted forward with her arms behind her, as if smashing her head into a wall or the floor would be the most natural thing in the world. Completely in character, Julia ran forward at a dead run, straight toward the marble counter behind which sat the stunned concierge.

"Stop!" Adelina called out, reaching out with one hand while she simultaneously tried to balance the stroller, two bags of groceries, her purse and a cup of coffee. Something had to give, and it was the coffee, which fell on the floor and erupted in a brown explosion. Julia's feet slid in the sticky mess even as her arm stayed gripped with Adelina's, and she started to swing around in a great circle as the first bag of groceries fell to the floor.

Inside the bag, a bottle of something smashed open. Peanut butter, maybe, or apple sauce. God forbid it be the wine.

"Julia!" she shouted, even as the little girl's legs started to pump again.

In another moment, she had everything calmed down and her daughter stationary. The grocery bag and her coffee, however, were lost causes.

"We'll bring up the … surviving groceries … Mrs. Thompson."

"Thank you, Harold," she said.

The concierge said, "By the way, a courier delivered a letter for you earlier. From the British Embassy."

Her chest tightened suddenly, almost painfully. "Oh … I'll take that," she said.

He handed over the letter. "I presume it's related to Mr. Thompson's birthday? The courier was very clear to deliver only to you."

Stunned, Adelina said, "Yes … of course." She held a finger to her lips. "Our secret, please. We wouldn't want to spoil the surprise."

The only thing she wanted to give Richard for his birthday was a knife between the ribs. But that wasn't a realistic option. In a sharp voice, she said, "Stay still!" to Julia, then tore open the envelope.

An invitation on heavy cream-colored card stock with gold engraving, handwritten in delicate calligraphy: *You are cordially invited to lunch with His Grace Prince George-Phillip Windsor, the Duke of Kent, Wednesday, February 22, 1984 at Her Majesty's Embassy in Washington, The District of Columbia.*

She rolled her eyes. The invitation was intentionally vague, she supposed, in case Richard had taken delivery of it. *That* would be an ugly situation.

She wasn't having lunch with anyone.

She wasn't.

Especially not at the British Embassy. It was bad enough the Post had mentioned her lunch with George-Phillip at Matisse. Richard hadn't mentioned it yet. Would he? Would he know? Richard was no fool, and the diplomatic community itself was tiny. She couldn't imagine he hadn't heard. Richard was biding his time. Sometime, this afternoon or tonight or next week or next year, he would do something unspeakably cruel. That's how these things worked.

"Come, Julia!" she called, marching away.

The two-year-old ran after her, and grabbed Adelina's hand as they reached the elevator. She took her daughter's hand in hers and rode upstairs in silence. Adelina didn't notice that her other hand was clenched into a fist until she glanced down and saw the invitation was crumpled.

Adelina. May 2.

Adelina sat slouched in the driver's seat of the minivan. The day was beautiful, the sky free of clouds, and the view to the horizon unusually clear. A strong wind blew off the ocean and up into the hills, occasionally shaking the minivan.

Jessica still sat on the wall. Arms wrapped around her legs, face resting on her knees. She wasn't crying. Her shoulders didn't shake, though Adelina had no idea how her daughter sat out there without even shivering.

You weren't a mother to us.

It was true, and she knew it. Her oldest daughter was thirty-two years old, her youngest sixteen. Six daughters, and they all hated her. The worst part was, she knew she deserved it. Jessica sat there on the wall, refusing to talk to her, and she hadn't even been through the worst of it. She knew that it was Julia and Carrie who had borne the brunt of her unmanageable anxiety and fear, her panic attacks, her rage.

She'd have done anything to fix it. *Anything.*

For now, all she could do was help this one daughter. She slid out of the seat again and said, "You don't have to talk to me if you don't want to. But don't you think we should go get something to eat?"

Jessica's shoulders slumped. She nodded her head, and said, "I'm sorry. I don't understand you, but I don't hate you. I really don't."

Adelina sighed. "I wouldn't blame you if you did, you know."

Jessica grunted lightly and gave a tight shake of her head.

"Anyway, let's get moving."

"Where are we going from here?" Jessica asked.

"Well … I'm concerned about being out on the road in the minivan, especially now that we know they're looking for us. It's a matter of time before we get caught. So I thought we'd stop at the next town and get a bus."

Jessica stared at her, her eyes unmoving, unblinking. Then she said, "To where?"

"Canada."

Stunned, Jessica said, "Why?"

Adelina said, "Haven't you been listening to the news? They're searching for us."

"Well, yeah. But … Canada?"

"Yes. We need to get somewhere *safe*," Adelina said,

Jessica sighed. "I don't know how I can possibly trust you."

Adelina reached out and touched her daughter's hand. "I know. But nevertheless, we have to go."

"All right," Jessica whispered.

CHAPTER FOURTEEN
Cat got your tongue, Adelina?

Adelina. February 25, 1984.

In the week after Adelina's lunch with George-Phillip, she avoided Richard and avoided time alone with equal intensity. The daytimes were easy enough to keep busy, as she went about interviewing possible full-time nannies, and took Julia around to meet with several different instructors for piano.

Richard had voiced some choice words about both topics. But Adelina had persuaded him, reminding him that most cultured children played an instrument. Julia was young, but Suzuki method training typically began between the ages of three and five.

I insist on her learning an instrument, she had said.

You should teach her on your violin, he had snarled back.

Of course he was aware of what she'd done to her violin. Richard missed little, but in order to drive it home she'd taken the shattered instrument and left it on his bed.

Richard responded by throwing the violin in the garbage and having a deadbolt installed on his door.

And so things continued. If Richard knew about her lunch with George-Phillip, he didn't say anything. But she was sure he knew. Of course he knew, thanks to that bitch Maria Clawson. There it was, the bottom paragraph in her column. *The Duke of Kent and current junior attaché at the British Embassy, Prince George-Phillip, was seen lunching with Adelina Thompson, the wife of a junior State Department official, at the exclusive eatery Matisse on Monday. Neither of them was available for comment, but this columnist wonders at opportunities for closer U.S. - British relations.*

There was no way Richard didn't know. Maybe he was saving the knowledge for just the right moment. It would be like him, to sit on something for days and make her squirm in fear.

But the days went on with no mention of it, and no further contact from George-Phillip for nearly ten days.

When it came, it was like a bomb. The phone rang at 2:30 in the afternoon. Julia had been difficult that day—extremely difficult. When the new nanny arrived, Adelina made herself a drink and fled to the balcony. She was on her second drink when the phone rang.

She ignored it, choosing to enjoy the unusually warm weather instead.

The glass door slid open. "Mrs. Thompson?"

Jenny Sullivan, the new nanny, held out the phone. "It's Mr. Thompson."

Adelina closed her eyes. She didn't want to talk to Richard.

She had no choice. She reached for the cordless phone.

"Yes, Richard."

"Go get a new dress to wear. Something fancy. We're having dinner with the British Ambassador and guests tonight. It's a black tie affair, very formal."

"The British Ambassador?"

"Yes, and that boy you snuck off and had lunch with. Prince George-Phillip."

Adelina sucked in a breath, but didn't say a word.

"You didn't think I knew about that, did you, Adelina? You should know better by now."

Adelina's words were casual, but she couldn't stop her voice from shaking. "Don't be silly, Richard, it was just lunch. I even had Julia along."

"Of course it was just lunch. Even I know a British royal isn't going to be interested in some peasant slut from Spain. But I don't like being made a fool of in the papers, Adelina. This better be the *last* time Maria Clawson ever mentions my name in her column."

Adelina stiffened in rage. For nearly fifteen seconds she stood there, her teeth clenched, the phone gripped in her hand, unable to say a word.

"What? Cat got your tongue, Adelina?"

"I'll find a dress," she growled.

Then with a swift, smooth motion she slapped the cordless phone against the cast iron table. She hit the phone against the table three, four, then five more times, until the casing finally cracked with a snap and plastic bits went flying everywhere.

Then she burst into tears. She *hated* him. *Hate.*

She closed her eyes and slumped into her chair. Then she whispered a prayer, the words sweeping over her in a torrent. She had to get control of herself and her temper. Sometimes the rage seemed to wash over everything, to black out everything. This was new. As a child or a teen she'd never been prone to fits of anger.

She opened her eyes. Jenny was in the living room with Julia. Both of them stared at her.

Adelina stood and brushed her hands down the front of her shirt. Her temper terrified her sometimes. And embarrassed her. She slid the door open and said to the astonished nanny, "I'm going out."

"Why Mummy break phone?" Julia asked.

Neither Adelina nor Jenny answered the question. Adelina carefully buttoned her coat and walked out of the condo.

Hours later, she rode silently in the car with Richard to the British Embassy. It was dark out, traffic was heavy, and it was stifling hot inside Richard's Mercedes 500SE. She stared out the window, unaffected by the leather seats and polished wood dashboard. Her father had not owned a car for most of her life, and she'd have sooner lived with her daughter in a shack on a rock than in the shifting, often terrifying luxury Richard took for granted.

"You're quiet," he said.

Adelina shrugged. "I'm saving my energy for the dinner."

"Charm them, Adelina."

She rolled her eyes. "Anyone in particular?"

"Eugene Jackson."

"Who?"

Richard huffed in impatience. "I expect you to know these things, Adelina. We've reestablished diplomatic relations with the Vatican. Jackson is Reagan's envoy to the Vatican, and he's been nominated as the first Ambassador."

"Right," she said, holding a hand up. "His confirmation hearings are next week?"

"Exactly."

"Why didn't we have diplomatic relations in the first place?"

"Congress cut funding for the diplomatic mission in 1867, because the Pope banned Protestant services in the city."

"1867? Are you serious? And it took them more than a hundred years to fix it?"

Richard shrugged. "I don't know all the history. The Vatican was invaded and became part of the Kingdom of Italy or some such. Anyway, the British re-established relations last year, and now we have."

"Okay. And why do you want me to charm Ambassador Jackson?"

His eyes narrowed and his fists tightened on the steering wheel as his face flushed red—dangerous signals for Richard. For a moment she thought he was going to say it was none of her business.

After a second, he relaxed, slightly, and said, "Along with being the new Ambassador, Eugene Jackson and his wife are close personal friends of the Reagans. A good word from him to the President could do a lot for my career."

Adelina nodded. "I see. What do we know about him?"

"He's seventy or so. Prominent businessman in California, he helped bank-roll the President's campaign, and he was part of the Kitchen Cabinet." The Kitchen Cabinet was an informal group of conservative advisors to the President—political opponents had accused them of helping to select Reagan's actual Cabinet members.

Richard continued. "He goes *riding* with the President, and he and his wife hosted the Reagans for Nancy's birthday."

Adelina nodded. "Okay. So, charm him. What's his wife's name? Will she be there?"

"Elizabeth. They met at Stanford. And yes, she'll be there."

"Okay. Make nice. Charm him. Consider it done."

In a sharp tone, Richard said, "Don't be fresh with me."

"You're a sociopath and a complete bastard, Richard. Would I be stupid enough to antagonize you?"

Without a pause he reached over and pinched her thigh, hard, through her dress, twisting his fingers. She slid away from him, then grabbed his hand and tried to pull it off as the pain sharpened.

"*I hate you*," she whispered.

"That's fine," he replied. "As long as you do what you're told."

She didn't respond, choosing instead to shut out the pain, staring out the window into the darkness. She reached a hand into her purse and clutched her rosary, tracing the beads with her fingers. She knew well that saying the prayers out loud would evoke an immediate violent response from Richard. So she prayed in her heart, tracing the beads, starting with the Lord's Prayer. Sometimes she got stuck there, praying for protection from evil over and over again.

Twenty minutes later, Richard pulled the car to a stop. Guards at the Embassy gate checked his identification and waved him in. He parked, then came around the front of the car and opened her door. She slid out of her seat, letting the rosary fall back into her purse. He placed his hand on her arm and walked her toward the entrance.

Inside, it was clear this was to be an intimate affair. A dozen men of varying ages were in the room, many of them accompanied by wives or girlfriends. Adelina's eyes sought out George-Phillip.

He was across the room from her, talking with a slightly older woman in a mauve dress. Adelina felt a flash of jealousy, which was ridiculous. She had no claim on George-Phillip. The woman was shockingly tall, at least six feet. Her dark brown hair was cut in a reverse bob, and her green-blue eyes seemed unusually large.

Despite the fact she had no claim on him, he took the woman's arm and approached Richard and Adelina the moment he saw them.

"Mr. Thompson, I'm so pleased you could come," George-Phillip said. "And Mrs. Thompson." He turned to the woman beside him and said, "Eloise, please allow me to introduce Richard and Adelina Thompson. Richard is an American diplomat and graciously hosted me for dinner two weeks ago. Richard and Adelina, this is my cousin, the Lady Eloise Percy."

Cousin, Adelina thought, feeling oddly satisfied. It made sense. Eloise was tall, though not so tall as George-Phillip, and she was afflicted with the same hooked nose and eyebrows that looked powerful on a man but not so much on her.

"Charmed," Richard said. He sounded anything but charmed. The others didn't seem to notice, but Adelina's survival depended on knowing Richard and his moods, including the moments when he was lying or manipulating. His voice was laden with syrup as he continued speaking. "Lady Eloise, it's a pleasure to meet you. I don't believe we've met before. Have you been in Washington long?"

Eloise smiled, revealing two overhanging buck teeth. Adelina knew it was petty, but the teeth pleased her. "This is my first trip to Washington, actually."

"Welcome," Adelina said. "I'm actually new to the city myself."

"Oh really!" Eloise said. "I don't suppose you'd be interested in learning about the city with me, would you?"

Adelina smiled and tried to think of a way to politely beg off the invitation. She had no desire to spend days traipsing around the city escorting some over-privileged British—

"I think that's a delightful idea," Richard said, his voice still sickening. "Adelina was just saying the other day that she doesn't get out of the house often enough. We have a two-year-old daughter, and she's a very devoted mother."

George-Phillip said, "Adelina's father knew Alexandra."

Eloise's eyes lit up. "Oh, really? She's our favorite aunt. Your father is..."

"Juan Ramos, Lady, he was the Marquis of Cerverales."

"Oh, yes!" Eloise said. "I've heard of him. He had some political disagreement with Franco, yes?"

"I'm afraid so," Richard said. His voice no longer held a sickly sweet tone. "Adelina was the daughter of a shopkeeper when I plucked her out of Spain."

Adelina kept a death grip on her smile.

"Don't be so modest," Eloise said. "Our aunt spoke fondly of your father."

"He would have been delighted to know that," Adelina said.

"Oh dear," Eloise said, even as George-Phillip almost imperceptibly froze. "You speak of him in the past tense?"

"He passed away two years ago," Adelina replied. "An accident."

"So sad," Eloise replied.

"Tragic," Richard said in a dry voice. "Oh ... isn't that Eugene Jackson, the new Ambassador to the Vatican?"

He sounded like an idiot, Adelina thought. But he clearly wanted to exit any conversation having to do with Adelina's past.

"I believe so," George-Phillip said. "Oil man, right? Friend of your President?"

"I must go pay my respects," Richard replied. "Adelina?"

"Coming, dear," she said. "Please excuse us," she said at a near whisper to George-Phillip and Eloise.

"Of course," George-Phillip said, his voice low and troubled.

Adelina didn't have time to pay any more attention to George-Phillip, however. Richard had moved very quickly to Jackson, the new Ambassador to the Vatican, and was already speaking by the time Adelina caught up.

"May I present my wife, Adelina?"

"Pleased to meet you, Mrs. Thompson," Jackson said, his eyes dropping immediately to the cleavage at the front of Adelina's bodice. He was a kindly looking man, with salt and pepper hair swept back from his high forehead and deep wrinkles on either side of his mouth. "This is my wife, Elizabeth."

Adelina shook hands and smiled at the older woman. The Jacksons were probably seventy. Elizabeth was a trim woman with white hair just long enough to reach her shoulders.

"Congratulations on your appointment as Ambassador, sir."

"Thank you very much, young lady. Although it's not quite confirmed yet."

"Oh?" Adelina said, blinking her eyes innocently.

"There are a few old bigots still in the Senate," Jackson said. "They don't think we should reopen diplomatic relations at all."

"Oh, dear," Adelina said. "I'm so sorry."

Elizabeth Jackson smiled and said, "It's quite all right, dear. I'm certain Eugene is up to the challenge."

"I'm sure," Adelina said. "I didn't mean to imply otherwise."

"It's all right," Elizabeth said. "I will say, though, that I look forward to returning to Rome."

"How long have you lived there?"

"Two years," she replied. "We rent a townhouse in Celio. I'm trying to persuade Eugene to buy it and just stay there for retirement. It's a lovely neighborhood."

Jackson smiled. "It is. Crowded and dirty and loud, but lovely."

"It's *Rome*," Elizabeth countered.

"True," Jackson said.

Adelina smiled at the older couple then felt a sense of real relief as Richard excused himself. "I always wanted to go to Rome," Adelina said. "I'd planned on going there after I graduated high school, but I got married instead."

"We love it," Elizabeth responded. "It's truly beautiful. Though I do miss California sometimes."

"Not Washington?" Jackson said, raising a bushy eyebrow.

"Pshaw," Elizabeth said, lightly smacking her husband on the shoulder. "Who could miss Washington?"

Adelina felt her lips curl up. "Not me," she said. "I haven't been here long, and I'll freely admit, it's taking a lot of adjustment."

Elizabeth spoke in a kindly tone, like a loving aunt. "Well, you're a very young woman, and I suspect with your husband in the Foreign Service, you'll move a lot in the coming years. I'd suggest getting involved—local charities, or your church, or something. It can be a very lonely life following your husband's career."

"It hasn't been that lonely for you, has it, dear?" Eugene asked.

"You wouldn't know, you silly old man," Elizabeth said.

Adelina's eyes dropped to the floor.

"Thank you for the advice," she said quietly.

The last thing she ever wanted to do was follow her husband's career around the globe. But in her heart, she knew that unless she found a way to break from Richard soon, she might never escape.

Someone moved next to her. She drew in a deep breath and looked up, already knowing it was George-Phillip. She felt her cheeks warm and darted a glance at him, then back at Elizabeth.

"Elizabeth and Ambassador Jackson, may I introduce His Highness, George-Phillip, the Duke of Kent?"

George-Phillip grinned and held out a hand.

Jackson took it in his and said, "It's a pleasure to meet you. You go by George?"

"George-Phillip, generally," replied George-Phillip. "It's nice to meet you. Congratulations on your appointment as Ambassador."

Jackson grinned. "It's mostly ceremonial, to tell you the truth," he said. "As they say, the Pope doesn't have an Army, so as Ambassador I won't have earth shattering matters to attend to."

"Soul shattering, perhaps," George-Phillip said.

"You're a believer?"

"My mother was Catholic," George-Phillip said. "It caused quite a stir when she converted, actually. My father nearly had to abdicate. I'm loyal to the Church of England, as any good third cousin to the throne should be." As he said the words, his face had an endearing grin.

Jackson chuckled. "A diplomat despite your age."

"Forgive the lapse in this company," George-Phillip replied, "but sometimes I think *diplomatic* is a bad word. Perhaps world affairs would be better off and more straightforward if everyone said what they meant."

Jackson's grin actually grew wider. "Young and idealistic."

"You were young and idealistic once," Elizabeth said. "Don't knock him."

"I wouldn't," Jackson said. "Life will do that for him."

"I hope to always be an idealist," George-Phillip said.

His eyes were wide open, bright, and the slight flush on his cheeks seemed to indicate an intense awareness of Adelina. She looked away from him, searching out Richard.

Richard was thirty feet away, in a small knot of diplomats and wives. George-Phillip's cousin Eloise had moved to that group. He seemed unaware of her, but she knew better.

George-Phillip said, "And what about you, Mrs. Thompson? Are you also an idealist?"

For just a second she met George-Phillip's eyes—eyes that stabbed her, gripping her by the throat.

"One can't live on promises and hope," she said.

"I can't imagine what else you would live on," George-Phillip retorted.

"I'm afraid I have to step away," Elizabeth said. "It's been a delight talking with you both."

"I'll get you a drink for when you come back," Jackson said.

Both of them stepped away quickly, leaving Adelina and George-Phillip standing alone. Adelina felt as if a spotlight were on her.

"I must see you," George-Phillip said.

"I can't," she replied.

"I *must*," he said.

Adelina took a step back. She felt tears threatening, suppressed emotion welling up in her throat. She only barely remembered what it felt like to be cared for.

But she remembered all too well what it was like to be at Richard's mercy.

"I cannot," she whispered.

Then she walked away, to the safety of the crowd around Richard.

CHAPTER FIFTEEN
There's my little girl!

Adelina. February 26, 1984.

Julia had been difficult to get to sleep tonight—restless and irritable. Adelina finally gave up and lay down beside her daughter, lightly tapping her on the leg to soothe her. Julia's eyes dipped, opening and closing repeatedly as she fought sleep.

Finally, Julia's breathing evened out, her eyes closed, her cheeks slightly flushed. Adelina sagged against the bed and slowly released her daughter's hand. She desperately needed an hour to relax, uninterrupted. Now that Julia was down, she'd hopefully get it. It would be uncharacteristic of Richard to seek her out—she suspected he was finding some other source of sexual satisfaction than his captive wife, and nothing could make Adelina happier.

The last thing she wanted was Richard *touching* her. Unfortunately, she had to talk with him. She approached him as rarely as possible, but sometimes it was unavoidable.

Her mind kept returning to George-Phillip's words the night before.

"*I must see you.*"

"*I can't,*" she had replied.

"*I must,*" he had said.

George-Phillip didn't understand. He must not believe her when she described the danger Richard represented. Or worse, he didn't care. He didn't care what risk *she* bore, what danger *she* was in.

It seemed likely, until she thought of his kindness, of the concern in his eyes. George-Phillip was not a man looking for an easy sexual liaison, and if he were, he could find much better targets for his lust than Adelina Thompson.

Which left her with one question. What *did* he want?

She was attracted to him. Intensely so. In their few meetings, it had become clear that her desire was mutual. It was also equally clear that it was impossible. Even if her husband weren't dangerous, the fact was, she was *married*. She didn't love Richard—in fact, she hated him. But she still had to live with herself, and no matter how much she hated Richard Thompson, she'd married him in the church. She was married in the eyes of God. Those were the only eyes that really mattered.

She stood, slowly, taking care to not disturb Julia. As she came to her feet beside the small bed, Julia's breath paused for just a moment. Adelina waited to see if her daughter would open her eyes—if she would clench her fists or turn red in the face or scream loud enough to draw Richard's anger. After a moment, Julia settled back into the bed a little deeper, her tiny chest expanding as she breathed in.

Adelina stepped into the quiet hallway. From Julia's room, she could see down the hallway: two more bedrooms on the right side of the hallway, three on the left. The master bedroom, Richard's, at the end of the hallway. Thank God this place was huge. Adelina had taken the furthest possible room from her husband.

His bedroom door was cracked several inches. She walked toward the door, feeling a sense of dread. His open door might mean he was careless, which occasionally he was. Or it might mean he was preparing to assault her. He'd only done that a couple of times since he'd returned to the United States, though.

As she got closer to the door, though, she realized that it was carelessness. And something else. He was on the phone with someone, his words falling out in an uncharacteristic rush.

"Christ," he said. "How was I supposed to know Karatygin was going to use it on civilians? I thought we were all done with this."

Silence. What was he talking about? What was used on civilians?

"Bullshit, Leslie," he said, his tone harsh.

Was he talking to his accountant friend? Leslie Collins?

Accountant, hell, she thought. She didn't know what Leslie Collins was, but he was most definitely not an accountant.

"Fine. I'll go and calm down Prince Roshan and then we'll move on, all right? I don't ever want to talk about this subject again."

He slammed the phone down, and Adelina's heart suddenly lurched. What if he realized she'd been standing here? What if—

It was too late. He stood in the doorway, still wearing his suit and tie. One eye narrowed slightly more than the other one and he demanded, "How long have you been standing there listening?"

"I didn't really hear anything—"

"Sure you did. I *know* you heard something. Tell me what." His eyes were cold as he said the words, his expression calm. Calculated.

She swallowed then tried to speak. But she found herself stammering, the words colliding at her lips and unable to come out except in a jumble.

"Let me help," he said, his open hand swinging at her.

She couldn't move away fast enough. His slap hit her on the ear, staggering her.

"*Stop,*" she cried out.

"I'll stop when you answer my god damn question."

"All I heard was you say something about civilians, and that you need to calm down Prince Roshan. I don't have a clue what it's about."

Another slap knocked her back against the wall.

Against her will, tears ran down her face. He placed his palms against the wall on either side of her head and pressed his face in close to hers.

She cringed, turning her face away from him.

"Let me be clear about one thing, Miss Adelina. Make no mistake that my daughter would be far better off with a white woman as her mother."

She froze.

"You just remember that. You *never* talk to anyone about anything I say, do you hear me?"

She nodded, trying to suppress the tears.

He shouted. "Do you understand me? Answer me!"

"Yes," she whispered.

Down the hallway, she heard the sound of Julia sputtering in her bed. *Damn it.*

"Please don't wake the baby," Adelina whispered.

"I'll do whatever the hell I want," he whispered back.

"Mama?" The word rang out from down the hall. Julia stood in her doorway, a hand stretched out to steady her. "Mmmm wet."

"Right here, Julia," Adelina said, her voice shaking.

Richard grimaced, and then in a display of frightening calculation, he winked at Adelina. He broke into a broad smile and turned toward their daughter.

"There's my little girl!" he nearly shouted in a cheerful, warm voice.

Julia broke into a smile, her cheeks puffing out.

Richard lifted Julia high in the air and she giggled.

"Da!" she said, a smile on her face.

Adelina. February 27, 1984.

When Adelina awoke the next morning, Richard was gone.

He'd scrawled a note on a small sheet of paper, torn off of a pad with the heading, "From the Desk of Richard Thompson."

The note read:

Dearest Adelina, I must travel to Saudi Arabia and possibly Pakistan in the next few days. I'll be in touch.

She sagged in relief when she read the note.

Dearest Adelina. As if. He must have thought the nanny would see the note. Or he was truly a sociopath. She didn't know which, and right now she didn't care. What she knew was that his absence meant an unexpected reprieve from the daily grinding fear that she didn't realize had overwhelmed her for the last month.

Month, she thought. It had only been a month since he'd returned to the United States. Only a month since she'd left San Francisco to occupy this condominium on the edge of the nation's capital.

As she stood there, tears running down her face, she tried to picture how she was possibly going to survive her marriage to Richard. During his assignment in Pakistan, it had seemed bearable. She'd been alone with her daughter in San Francisco. She'd made friends, gotten involved in the church. She'd begun to have a life again.

His return had swept all that away. Again. And he might be gone today, but she knew he'd return, tomorrow or next week or next month, and his return would spell the return of instability, of fear, of the lies and twisted behavior. As she thought about it, her breath sped up, and she could feel the tightening in her chest, the constricting threads of fear tugging at her neck.

She forced herself to breathe, but even her breathing became ragged.

As the wave of panic swept over her, she began to pray, head bowed, until she fell to her knees. She didn't realize she had tears pouring down her cheeks. She didn't realize her shoulders were shaking.

She didn't realize that she was coming apart at the seams.

She sank down into her prayers, her fingers unconsciously running along the beads of her rosary, her lips moving silently, trying to calm the terror.

"Mama?"

Julia's voice didn't initially break into her consciousness.

"Mama? I'm hunngy."

This time she heard Julia, the high-pitched whining voice breaking over her prayers.

"Hunngy. I'm hunngy."

God damn it, couldn't she see—

Adelina froze. Of course she couldn't see the condition Adelina was in. Julia wasn't even three yet.

She took a deep breath and opened her eyes and said in a shaking voice, "Okay, Julia. Want to come pray with me first?"

"I hunngy," Julia said. Her eyes were huge.

Adelina let out a staggered, broken breath and stood up. The fear wasn't gone. It felt like a huge welt on her chest. She furiously wiped at the tears that had fallen down her face and lifted Julia to the sit on the counter.

"I'll make you some breakfast," Adelina said.

"Some cereal?" she asked, words coming out automatically. Heart still thumping rapidly in her chest, she turned to get the cereal, but Julia said, "Wan' ice cream."

"No ice cream, Julia. You can have cereal or yogurt."

"Ice cream!" Julia demanded. "Wan' chocolate!"

Adelina closed her eyes. "I don't have chocolate ice cream."

She took down the cereal and poured it in a plastic bowl, then added milk. In three weeks she'd be twenty years old. The thought made tears run down her face again. She was twenty, and her father was dead, and her life was hopeless.

She set the bowl on the highchair tray then lifted Julia into the chair. Julia began to scream. "Ice cream! Ice cream!"

Adelina wanted to scream too. She readjusted the tray after bucking Julia in. Julia was full out crying now, and Adelina was desperate just to get her to *shut up*. The pain in her chest was getting worse, and all she could think of was the fact that she wasn't even twenty years old yet and she wanted out. She wanted her mother. She wanted her father. She wanted her life back, and she couldn't have it.

She sank back against the counter, the screaming from Julia unabated. Julia hit her bowl with a fist and it went flying, spattering milk and cereal on the wall.

For just a second Adelina felt rage flood her again. She turned away, walking into the living room and clenched her fists at the side of her head. She fought down the urge to scream, to yell at Julia, to throw something, to *break* something. She fought it down, but as she did so, she felt the tightening in her chest worsen.

The knock on the door startled her.

Oh, thank God! That would be Jenny, the nanny. Adelina rushed to the door and opened it in a rush.

Jenny was twenty-two—three years older than her employer—and a student at University of the District of Columbia. She was smart and pretty.

Adelina was envious. Jenny might be dirt poor, taking on this job to help buy her books for her night courses, but she was making choices for her own life. Choices that had been taken from Adelina.

"Bless you," Adelina whispered urgently. "She's a terror this morning. Come in."

Jenny's eyes widened at the sight of the screaming Julia in her highchair and the mess of cereal and milk splattered on the wall.

At the sight of Jenny, Julia screamed even louder. "Mommy! Don' go! Don' go! Mommmmyyyyy!"

Adelina swallowed the pain in her chest. "It's all right, Julia. I'll be back soon." She gave her daughter a kiss on the cheek and rushed back to her room to change. With luck, she'd have time to stop for a cup of coffee in relative peace, outside the house, before she went to the church.

Adelina. February 27, 1984.

"Bless me, Father, for I have sinned," Adelina whispered as she made the sign of the cross. Father Dennis waved his hand and muttered a blessing, and she felt a shudder as she said the next words. "Lord, you know all things. You know that I love you. It has been three years since my last confession."

Father Dennis shifted his position. Though the church had confessionals, Adelina had requested they meet in his office. She knelt across from him, and occasionally her eyes darted to the purple stole he wore. On one level, it was calming, reminding her of the presence of God and of Father Dennis's authority.

On another level, it terrified her. After all, it was the Parish priest in Calella, acting under the authority of God, who had ordered her to marry Richard. If only she hadn't had to move to her mother's home in Calella. If only her father hadn't died.

If only she'd never met Richard Thompson.

She took a deep breath, not knowing where to start.

"You may begin," Father Dennis said.

Her voice tiny, her body full of shame, Adelina said, "I don't know how to."

He reached out and rested a hand on her shoulder. "The Lord knows the story already, Adelina. If you're penitent, then just tell it however you can."

She nodded, and, horrified, choked back a sob. Sniffing, she said, "These are my sins."

She squeezed her eyes closed, tightly, and whispered, "For three years I've lied to everyone around me to protect my brother."

"What have you lied about?"

"My age. My husband."

"Tell me the truth now."

She choked on the words. Then she spit them out. "I was sixteen, and he raped me. I hate him. Father, I know he's my husband, but I *hate* him. Sometimes I imagine him rotting in jail. Or in hell. I think of the most dreadful things."

Father Dennis paled. "Your husband raped you? Before you were married?"

She nodded. The tears were streaming rapidly down her face now, and she shook, terrified.

"I'm so sorry, Adelina, I had no idea. Did you report it to the police? Wait, now you … how did you end up married?"

She struggled to get her mouth around the words. But then she told the story, of how her mother had dragged her to the parish priest in Calella.

He muttered to himself, then said, "I'm so sorry, Adelina."

"That's not the worst of it," she said. She looked up, looking in his eyes, and she said, "Father, I've fantasized—about killing him. About … about running away. Sometimes I get so angry I'm afraid I'll hurt my daughter."

"You must learn to control your anger, Adelina."

"I pray for that every day," she whispered.

"Continue to do so. You mustn't hurt your daughter. Or your husband. I believe—Adelina, I believe you should report this to the police. Or allow me to do so."

Terror flooded Adelina. She jerked back, and said, "You wouldn't!"

He smiled reassuringly. "I wouldn't, unless you gave me permission. You remember the story of Saint John of Nepomuk?"

She shook her head. "I … no."

"Saint John was the confessor to the Queen of Bohemia. It seemed that Wenceslaus, the King, thought the Queen was committing adultery, and ordered John to divulge the secrets of the confessional. When he refused, the King had him tortured and murdered, then thrown in the river."

Adelina shivered, imagining with horror what it must have been like for the priest. "And he didn't tell?"

"No, Adelina. He went to his death to protect the Seal of the Confessional."

"My priest didn't. He told my mother when I learned I was pregnant."

Father Dennis closed his eyes. "He committed a grave crime in doing so. I assure you, God will deal with him. But I can promise you, no such thing will happen now."

She looked at Father Dennis and said, "Is it a sin to hate my husband?"

He sighed. "Perhaps not so uncommon a sin, and given your circumstance—the fact is, if you are truly contrite, you shall be forgiven. I would urge you to consider what I've suggested to you. Your husband committed a crime, and against a child."

"I can't," she whispered. "He'll hurt my brother. He's threatened to before, and I believe him."

Dennis sighed. "Then I suggest you pray. Perhaps you can be a moderating influence on Richard. And you can still raise your daughter. Do you intend to have any further children?"

Adelina shivered. Then she whispered, "I'd rather die."

"I must advise you against artificial contraception."

Adelina nodded. Birth control was the least of her worries.

"Finally—though I know this is hard given the circumstances of your marriage—you must remember that Richard is your husband. Cleave to him, and perhaps you can somehow bring him back into the path of God. Is he Catholic?"

She shook her head. "Anglican," she said. "But not devout. The only thing he believes in is himself."

"Teach him as best you can. Perhaps through your daughter."

Adelina knew the advice was sound, but all the same, it made her want to vomit. She felt more desperate than ever.

"I will," she whispered. "What is my penance?"

"I'd like you to read First Peter, chapter three, and think on the instructions given within. Not just of wives, but also of husbands. You're subject to him, but you can also set an example, and bring him to the Lord."

She nearly recoiled from him. She would read the verses. But they frightened her.

"Yes, Father."

He brought her the book and they read it together. As they read the words, she felt fresh tears begin to stream down her face.

Wives, in the same way, accept the authority of your husbands, so that, even if some of them do not obey the word, they may be won over without a word by their wives' conduct when they see the purity and reverence in their lives.

The words made her angry. She felt her fists clench, and her first thoughts were rebellious. She didn't want to be an example to Richard. She wanted to *hurt* him. She wanted to walk away. She wanted him to go to hell.

She closed her eyes. Mary hadn't taken the easy way out. When she realized the fullness of God's plans for her child, she didn't run away. She didn't hide her child. She let him be raised up, exalted, hammered to the Cross in shame and disgrace and terror and pain.

Adelina didn't have that sort of courage. She could admire it. She could wish for it. But how was she to live it?

Father Dennis began to pray. "God, the Father of mercies, through the death and resurrection of His Son has reconciled the world to Himself and sent the Holy Spirit among us for the forgiveness of sins. Through the ministry of the Church, may God give you pardon and peace, and I absolve you from your sins in the name of the Father, and the Son, and of the Holy Spirit."

Adelina bowed her head and choked out the word, "Amen."

As she left the church, she kept thinking to herself that she felt no relief. She felt no guidance. God and the Church expected her to simply be submissive, to let Richard continue to do whatever he wanted.

It was wrong. It was *so* wrong. She found herself running as she exited the front door and rushed down the front steps. It was cold again, winter returning with fierceness, a chill biting right through her inadequate clothes. The sky was nearly black with dark, roiling clouds. Her heels clicked on the front steps as she ran down them, barely paying attention to what she was doing. Tears ran down her face, and she began to sob as she started to sprint.

But then she came to a sudden stop. Because a car stood next to the curb, and standing next to it, blocking her way with an open and hopeful expression on his face, was George-Phillip Windsor.

PART TWO

CHAPTER SIXTEEN
Calling in a favor.

Andrea. May 2. 1:45 pm.

"**I'm** getting kind of hungry," Andrea said.

"Yeah, me too," Dylan said. "We'll get something after this."

As he spoke, his eyes scanned the desks where the library patrons sat at the computers. Just to be on the safe side, they'd taken the Washington Metro out to the Virginia suburbs. The library was busy, and the dozen computers lined up on three long tables were all in use. The library was well lit by long lines of overhead fluorescent lights, and the place was crowded. At the opposite end of the building, a large crowd of children sat in a circle around the librarian, who was reading a story. Young mothers stood nearby, some of them chatting, others reading, all of them looking relieved to have a few minutes' break from their children during story-time.

"There," Dylan muttered.

A woman at one of the computer tables stood and shouldered her bag, then walked away.

Andrea breathed a sigh of relief when she saw the woman hadn't logged out. They'd been surprised to learn that access to the computers in the library required a current library card—which neither of them had.

She followed Dylan as he slumped into the seat and opened up a web browser. He started with *The Washington Post*.

"Jesus," he muttered.

Andrea felt her eyes widen. The entire front page of the website was devoted to the attack on the Thompsons, underneath a huge headline.

Secretary of Defense Elect's Family Homes Attacked
Adelina Thompson, Two Children
Missing: Sources Speculate Drug Connection

Underneath the headline were smaller stories and photographs, including individual photos of her mother, Jessica, Dylan, and Andrea. Andrea felt her breath accelerate as she squeezed in beside Dylan and looked at the story. The newspaper also had photos of the entrance to the Bethesda condo and the burned out house in San Francisco.

"Jesus," Dylan muttered again. His voice was low. "I talked to your mother last night. Just for a second—that's when the shooting started."

"Do you think she's hurt?" Andrea whispered.

"Probably on the run," he said. "She called to warn us to get you out. It was just too late."

"What the hell is going on?"

He shook his head. "Beats me. All I know is, we're staying under the radar until we know more. Check this out." He pointed.

One of the several articles described a press conference that morning. It didn't make any sense. Richard Thompson was accused of corruption and money laundering. The feds had put out a warrant for her *arrest* as a conspirator.

"That's what the drugs were about," he said, "and the money." He looked at her. "I bet the bills we have are marked somehow."

She nodded. "Maybe we can go … I don't know … buy a bunch of prepaid credit cards?"

"Not too many in any one place. If the money gets tracked—say through a bank—it might link back to the card. We'll buy a few at a time in several different places, I think. And … new clothes. Haircuts."

"You could use a shave," Andrea said.

Dylan grinned, his teeth showing up white in the midst of a darkening beard. "That's what Alex always says. But that photo shows me clean shaven, so I'm gonna let it grow."

"We can't go back to the hotel."

"Nope," he said. "Pretty soon they'll match up the fingerprints, if not today, then tomorrow. And then the surveillance cameras will show up on the Metro."

She grimaced. "What do we do?"

"Hold on. I'm not out of options yet. But once we're finished here, we've got to book."

He turned back to the computer and opened up Facebook, then logged in. Then he typed in a name: Christopher Mendoza.

The page that came up showed a grinning man with short-cropped black hair and a five o'clock shadow, wearing a grey sweatshirt with the word ARMY on it. The *About* section on the page said, "US Army, Arlington, Virginia."

"Who is that?" Andrea asked.

"Old friend," Dylan replied. He opened up a message box and typed in the message: What's up, Border Bunny?

The response was nearly immediate: Redneck motherfucker. What do you want?

Andrea sucked in a breath. What did *Border Bunny* mean? *Motherfucker* she could figure out.

Dylan: Calling in a favor. Priority 1. Need help now.

Mendoza: Wut u need?

Dylan: Place to sleep. And a ride. I'll explain later, but if you help me you could go to jail.

Mendoza: Sick. Where?

Dylan: Clarendon Metro. 3 pm.

Mendoza: See you, Bacon Bits.

Dylan laughed silently, then typed in the search bar. Alex Paris. Andrea's sister's profile showed up immediately. Dylan pulled up the message box and typed in: Andrea and I are alive and well. In hiding. I'll be back in touch as soon as possible. Stay low. Keep your status updated so I know you're okay. Love u.

Then he logged out without waiting for an answer. He looked over his shoulder, then pulled up the drop down menu. Delete cookies. Delete history. Then he logged out of the computer.

"All right. Let's go." He stood, and Andrea followed. Both of them walked as casually as possible toward the door of the library. Andrea could see Dylan was nervous. Like he thought someone was watching them, or they were in danger. His back was tense, muscles in his arms bunched up, his neck tightly wound.

She touched his arm and he froze. "Is something wrong?" she whispered.

He shook his head. "Come on," he said. His voice was curt, almost rude.

She didn't understand why he was always such a prick. What did Alexandra see in him?

She followed him anyway. What choice did she have? Once they were outside, he turned quickly to the right and walked down the sidewalk. A cool wind was beginning to blow, and since they'd been in the library, the sky had become much more cloudy.

Lips compressed tightly, he walked. His right leg was a little stiff—the leg that had been nearly destroyed during the war.

"One of the librarians was watching us as she talked on the phone. She was sweating."

"You think she recognized us?"

"Yeah. We gotta get to the Metro right now. Cops might be on their way already."

She nodded. They were less than half a block from the station entrance.

That's when she heard the sirens.

"Shit," he muttered. He didn't falter, his legs moving, one step in front of the other. "Mess up your hair," he said conversationally. "In your face a little."

He turned and walked backward, casually lighting a cigarette. A police car rounded the corner, drove past the Metro station, and then passed them. Another sped past. Both police cars had their blue lights flashing, but no siren.

He took a deep drag from the cigarette and turned around again. "Come on." He ducked into the entrance to the Metro station, tossed his cigarette to the ground, and swiped the Metro card he'd purchased from a machine earlier that day. She followed.

The inside of the station was crowded. It wasn't quite time for rush hour, but there were far more people in the station than they'd seen when they arrived an hour before. Dylan led her down the escalator to the platform, then stood leaning against a pillar. She leaned against it too, facing him.

"I'm worried, Dylan," she whispered.

He grimaced. "It's going to be okay."

He said the words, but she could see his eyes, and Dylan was a terrible liar.

"You don't look like you mean it."

He shrugged. "Maybe I don't. Ray used to say that shit to me. It's gonna be okay. Don't worry, he'd say. It's all good. But sometimes it's not." He looked away.

Andrea sighed. First rule of being on the run with Dylan: don't tell him when you're feeling anxious. Because he can't help.

"What happened to you?" she asked.

He rolled his eyes. "I'm fine."

Yeah, right. She turned away from him. She could feel wind blowing from the tunnel, and a moment later saw headlights. With a loud roar of brakes and a rush of wind, the train entered the station.

She turned to him as the train was coming to a stop. "I know you lost your friend, Dylan. But you need to get yourself together. You've got a lot more you *could* lose."

His mouth opened, but he didn't say any words. She walked away and stepped on board the train. He followed a moment later. A loud ringing peal burst from the overhead speakers, and the doors closed with a thumb. She scanned the car. No seats, so she wrapped her left hand around one of the stainless steel poles. Dylan took the pole opposite the car from her and glared.

As the train pulled out, he said, "What exactly does that mean?"

She sighed. "I'm worried. I'm worried because you sound like a pessimist and you look like a drunk and my life depends on you. That's what it means."

"I'm the guy who took those killers on with a knife to protect you," he muttered.

"I know that, Dylan. Don't think I'm ungrateful. I'm telling you, I'm worried about you. You know my sisters said it too. Carrie said you haven't been the same since Ray died."

He looked as if she'd punched him between the eyes. "He was my best friend."

She leaned close as the train car swayed, a loud screeching sound from the tracks below. "You should honor his memory, then."

Dylan's eyes widened. He shifted his position and turned away from her, looking out the windows of the car into the blackness of the tunnel.

He sighed, then said, "You're right. I know it. It's been almost nine months since he died. I'm stuck. All I can remember is seeing him in that hospital bed, with his body all screwed up, then the funeral. He had a lot of life left in him."

She reached out with her right hand, the one that wasn't wrapped around the steel pole, and took his arm. "It's going to be okay, Dylan."

He gave a small laugh. "You *do* look like you mean it."

She shrugged. "I do. Some things we can do something about. We can run and protect ourselves. We can do our best for the people we love, for the people around us. We can push for—for truth. For doing the right thing. But some things we *can't* control. And that stuff—it's out of our hands. All I know is I've got family I love. Uncle Luis and Abuelita, and my sisters. You, even."

He nodded. He didn't say any words. Just nodded.

"All right, then. What's next?"

He gave her a soft grin. "We go see Mendoza."

"Who is this Mendoza? He's Spanish?"

"Guatemalan, I think. Or Texan. I don't know. Anyway, he's wired, and he owes me some favors."

"*Wired?*" she asked.

"Wired in. I think he can get us fake IDs. Give us a place to stay. And he feels like he owes me a favor."

"What sort of favor?"

"I knew him in Afghanistan. He broke an ankle two months into our deployment, so he basically missed all the fun."

What sort of fun? she wondered. Her impression had been that Dylan was very bitter about his experience in Afghanistan. Sometimes the things he said made no sense. Or maybe she just didn't grasp his bizarre language.

"Can you trust him?"

He shrugged. "Yeah, I can trust him. I told you, we served in Afghanistan together."

Andrea said, "I thought Ray was falsely accused. By his Sergeant."

Dylan froze, stricken. He stared at her, his mouth open for a minute, then he nodded. "Yeah," he whispered. "That's true."

"Dylan…"

"Just leave me alone. We trust Mendoza because right now we don't have any other choice."

She stared at him. "All right."

Ten minutes later the train came to a stop at Clarendon Station. Dylan bent his knees as the train pulled into the station, peering out the window, looking for police. When the doors opened, he said, "Come on."

The platform was uncomfortably hot, air blowing from the tunnel. The train on the opposite track pulled in and disgorged its passengers. Andrea was suddenly crowded in, people on all sides, elbows and briefcases and backpacks. Dylan grabbed her arm and pulled her along with the crowd.

Conversationally, he said, "Look over there, near the station manager."

Andrea's eyes darted to the small office encased in glass near the turnstiles. Two police officers stood there, scanning the crowd.

Her heart began to pound, and she shook her head, letting her hair fall partly over her face. Dylan scanned the crowd, then made a snap decision. He walked over to a teenager, a boy with spiked hair. He whispered something, urgently, as the crowd rushed past them. Another inbound train pulled in. Dylan stuffed something in the teenager's pockets, then turned and took her arm again. "Head low," he said.

They walked toward the turnstiles. The cops were still scanning the crowd carefully. There was no way they were going to make it by.

Until the teenage boy suddenly shouted at the opposite end of the platform, letting out a loud *whoop, whoop, whoop!* and waving his arms in the air. One cop, then the other, looked toward the teenager.

"I WANT TO FUCK SOMEBODY!" shouted the teenager.

Someone in the crowd tittered, and the cops shook their heads simultaneously, then began to push their way through the crowd.

Andrea and Dylan had reached the turnstiles. They swiped their cards and went through just as the cops reached the other end of the platform. Andrea took one last look—the teenager stood between the two police officers, a grin on his face.

They rode up the escalators and reached the top right in the middle of the crowd.

"Over there across the street. That's Mendoza in the green car."

The car was an Oldsmobile, probably thirty or more years old. It was twice the length of most of the other cars on the block, and it wasn't just green, it was a loud, fluorescent green that probably stood out in satellite photos. A twenty-something man—Christopher Mendoza—sat behind the wheel.

Mendoza saw them in the crowd, but Dylan didn't acknowledge him, instead turning down the sidewalk away from the station.

At the end of the block, Dylan said, "Here he comes."

She could tell, because the rumbling of the engine underneath the hood of the Oldsmobile was shaking the newspaper stands half a block away. The car pulled to a stop at the corner. Dylan opened the back door for her, then ran around to the passenger side and got in the front passenger seat.

The back seat had been leather once, but now consisted largely of grey duct tape. The seat was large enough she could have laid down lengthwise and almost slept comfortably. As it was, she slid to the center of the seat.

"Chris Mendoza," said the driver, holding a hand back to shake. "I used to hang out with this jerk."

She smiled and shook. "Andrea Thompson."

Mendoza put the car in drive and sped away when the light turned green. He turned to Dylan and said, "I saw cops going in the station—how'd you get past 'em?"

Dylan smirked. "Paid a teenager to make an ass of himself."

Mendoza chuckled. "Well, let's get out of here. I went online and checked out the news after we talked. You got some big guns after you. What the hell for?"

Dylan looked over his shoulder at Andrea. Then he shrugged. "Don't know. But whoever it is, they're serious."

"Yeah, you aren't kidding," Mendoza responded. "Anyway, we'll get you under cover. You need anything?"

"New clothes. Haircuts. I've got a ton of cash—I want to buy some prepaid credit card and disposable phones."

Mendoza nodded. "Can do all that. What about ID?"

Andrea said, "The police have my passport. Everything, really."

Mendoza looked in the mirror and met her eyes. Then he looked back to the road. "We can cover that. I know a guy. He's good."

"How long?"

"Rush job? I don't know. Usually he takes a week or two. Sometimes I help arrange some IDs for the local high school kids."

Dylan snorted. He turned in his seat and said to Andrea, "Mendoza had a whole operation going. Buying and selling shit we couldn't get through the PX. I swear to God guys all over the FOB were crying when he broke his ankle."

Mendoza chuckled as he slowed the car at a red light. Andrea half listened. She didn't know what a lot of the words Dylan said meant. Was the PX some kind of supply shop? Store? What was a fob? She didn't know, and somehow she didn't think the details mattered. What mattered was Dylan's manner. As he talked, he seemed animated, his eyes wide, a light and easy tone of voice.

Andrea had only met Dylan twice before: at his wedding with her sister Alexandra, and a few months later after the accident, when Ray was still hanging onto life, then the days they'd spent around each other over the last week. Dylan seemed to be unstable. Humorless. But in Mendoza's presence, a different Dylan emerged. He laughed and seemed less grim.

Was it merely the presence of an old Army buddy? And if so, why didn't Alexandra affect him that way? After all, as Alexandra had said no less than 99 *thousand* times, she and Dylan were soul mates.

Whatever that meant. Instead of speculating any further, she sat back in her seat and tried to relax as Dylan told their story to Mendoza. He went into a lot of detail, taking his time.

When he'd finished, Mendoza looked in the rearview mirror and caught her eyes again. "You seriously went up against those guys in the car and took them out? *Then* jumped off a twenty-story building?"

She swallowed, but didn't answer.

Mendoza had pulled up to a driveway, in front of an old townhouse. It was brick, surrounded by yellowing grass, and toys were scattered around the front porch. He twisted around in his seat, and raised a hand to her, fist closed.

"Respect," he said.

She touched his closed fist with her own. And didn't say a word as they got out of the car.

CHAPTER SEVENTEEN
What's your plan, Paris?

Dylan. May 2. 4:00 pm.

"**M**ama! This is my friend, Dylan Paris, and his sister, Andrea." Dylan breathed a sigh of relief as Mendoza said the word. From then on, if anyone asked, Andrea was his sister.

Mendoza's mother was not what Dylan expected. She wore a black dress with a cowl-neck collar and a strand of unusually large pearls. When they walked in, she was sitting at a table with three other women, all of them elegantly dressed and with cards in their hands. Dylan looked at the cards—they were unlike any he'd seen before. Colorful, with swords and cups and coins instead of the suits he was used to.

"Dylan and Andrea? I'm Sofia. It's nice to meet you." She set her cards face down on the table and stood, then muttered, "And don't you card sharks touch mine."

She walked over and took Dylan's and Andrea's hands.

"Nice to meet you," Dylan said. "I don't see how such a beautiful woman ended up with *him* as a son, though."

Mendoza punched Dylan in the shoulder even as his mother blushed.

"Thank you, dear. Are you just visiting? Do you live around here?"

She was a nice lady. But Dylan wasn't planning to tell anyone the truth about anything right now. "We're from Raleigh, ma'am. North Carolina." His accent wasn't exactly North Carolina, but only a Raleigh native would be able to tell the difference.

"Oh, isn't that nice. I got a speeding ticket in North Carolina once," she said.

Dylan chuckled. "Most people can't get away fast enough," he said.

"Ma, we're gonna grab some lunch, all right? Then we've got some errands to run."

"You go ahead, I've got to get back to my game," Sophia said.

Mendoza led Dylan and Andrea into the kitchen.

Andrea said, "It was pleasant to meet you," as they left the room, and Dylan thought he might have to come up with a better cover story. *He* could pass off North Carolina. Andrea couldn't, not with that Spanish accent.

"So what's the plan?" Mendoza asked.

Dylan looked at Andrea. She looked back at him, her expression not giving him a clue. He spoke. "Can we hole up here for a couple days? And then we'll make ourselves scarce. I don't want to put you in any danger."

"Danger is my middle name," Mendoza said, pushing his chest out.

"Yeah, well, maybe it's yours, but I don't think it's your mom's."

Mendoza nodded. "Truth. All right. I'm thinking we go for a completely new look, right?"

"Yeah," Dylan said.

"Let me get that rolling, then. I gotta ask you one question though—you got enough cash for all this? The IDs are gonna cost. I can spot you some … I still got a little in the bank from Afghanistan."

"Nah," Dylan said. Mendoza didn't have to offer, but in some ways it relieved Dylan that he did. "We're good."

For the next several minutes Mendoza puttered around the kitchen like an old woman. Dylan and Andrea stood there in uncomfortable silence—Andrea sipping a glass of water and Dylan just watching. Mendoza seemed different.

They'd been friends at Fort Drum, then deployed to Afghanistan together. Just a few weeks into their deployment, Mendoza had broken his ankle, a nasty compound fracture, during a firefight.

He used to joke and laugh a lot more, Dylan thought. Now, Mendoza had a haunted look. He didn't talk as much, and he certainly didn't laugh as much.

It worried Dylan. He didn't say anything right away, letting Mendoza finish putting together a salad.

"All right," Mendoza said. "Hope you guys don't mind some greens. They're good for you, make you live longer."

"That looks wonderful," Andrea said.

"Rabbit food," Dylan muttered. "Ah, well."

Mendoza grinned. "We'll take it out on the porch, and if you don't like it you can throw it to the rabbits, all right? Some live in the neighborhood."

Outside, Dylan sat on a cast iron seat and soaked in the sunshine. The backyard was simple, with neatly cut grass and a wooden fence surrounding it. Toys were scattered here and there.

"You got a little sister, right?" Dylan asked.

"Two. Twelve and seven. They'll be home from school soonish."

"And you doing okay?"

Mendoza met his eyes. "Why do you ask?"

Dylan shrugged. "You don't seem yourself is all. You don't laugh."

Mendoza chuckled a little. "You should look at yourself, *amigo.* You look like someone died."

Dylan shrugged. "Someone did."

Mendoza's lips tightened in a straight line. "That's right. A lot of someones."

Andrea looked confused. Mendoza leaned forward and said to her, "Bunch of our guys got killed in Afghanistan. Or after, with Sherman and Hicks."

"Hicks is the man who killed Ray?" she asked.

Dylan nodded. "Yeah. He was—just really messed up."

"Everyone was, except me," Mendoza said. "I broke my ankle and went home and missed out."

"Good thing," Dylan said.

Half an hour later they were back out in the car. Mendoza drove them first to a stylist on Columbia Pike.

It wasn't anything like the barbershops Dylan usually frequented. For one thing, the pictures on the walls showed a wide variety of hairstyles, not a single one of which looked normal. Spikes and mohawks in a thousand variations. He watched as Andrea walked around. Her eyes narrowed in, finally pointing.

By the time they left, Andrea didn't look like herself. Her hair, mostly dark brown, was now completely black, except a wide alternating turquoise and violet streak across the front and down the left side of her face. Her hair had been cut into a reverse bob, and both eyebrows had been plucked and shaped, giving a significantly different look to her face. Older, narrower, with her cheekbones far more prominent than before. Dylan thought there was no mistaking that she was sister to Sarah Thompson, but she looked nothing like before.

Dylan's hair and eyebrows were three shades lighter, a blondish brown, and his unshaven beard was neatened up and trimmed. He looked at himself in the mirror for a long time—the change in appearance had an odd effect on his mood. Even as a teen he'd never paid much attention to his personal appearance other than trying to stay generally neat. But this was an intentional look, and that felt strange.

"Ladies man," Mendoza muttered, half sarcastically, when Dylan finished.

"You should get yours done," Dylan replied.

"Nah," Mendoza said, running his fingers through his thick black hair. "Nobody touches the locks."

Andrea giggled, and Dylan smiled. It was the first time he'd seen her really laugh.

"All right," Mendoza said. "Time to complete the look."

Dylan muttered curses to himself, but followed.

An hour later, they had discarded their clothes. Dylan had shifted from his typical khakis and flannel shirts to more businesslike pants and a button down shirt. Andrea wore a red and black flannel dress.

"You look like the 1990s," Mendoza said to Dylan.

"Shut up." Dylan chuckled. Then he adjusted the plastic-rimmed rectangular sunglasses he'd bought. "These are hideous," he said.

"No," Andrea said. "They look good. And the point isn't for you to be fancy. It's for you to be hidden."

Dylan nodded. "Yeah, yeah, that's easy for you to say. You don't suddenly look thirty."

She smiled. "What's next?"

Dylan thought a moment. Before leaving the condo the night before, he'd reached into the bag and randomly stuffed stacks of bills into his own bag. Once he'd finally counted the stacks of money, he'd been stunned. He'd barely scratched the surface of the bag full of money they'd found in Andrea's room. But that scratch had contained 32 stacks of bills totaling 80,000 dollars.

He didn't know where the money had come from. Or why they'd been attacked. But he knew that right now they needed to stay hidden, and the money was going to help.

"Mendoza, how much time do you have?"

"I'm all yours, man."

"I want to buy some pre-paid Visa cards. Bunch of them. But you can't just walk into one place and buy a lot … so I'm thinking half a dozen stops. And then I want to pick up some burner phones. Four phones, a dozen SIM cards."

"All right."

"Okay … I got one last thing for you."

"Yeah?"

"How much is that piece of shit car worth?"

"I don't know … two thousand?"

"I'll give you six for it. We're gonna need wheels."

"Done. And I got a text back from my guy—he's gonna meet us to do the IDs."

Andrea. May 2. 6:00 pm.

Andrea sank into the booth, exhausted and with aching feet. Dylan, looking equally exhausted, shrank into the faux-leather upholstery across from her. He had a bleak expression on his face as he looked around the diner.

"What's up, man? You look like someone pissed in your Cheerios." Mendoza was sitting next to Andrea, and was far more alert than he had any right to be. Of course, he hadn't spent the night being attacked by assassins, then holed up in a shitty hotel in the worst neighborhood in suburban Maryland.

"Nothing," Dylan said, shaking his head absently. "Missing Alex a little—we usually eat at this diner down the street from campus. Looks kind of like this place."

Mendoza shrugged. "She'll be all right, man. Don't fret. It's you two I'm worried about."

Dylan just looked away from Mendoza, his eyes tracking the approaching waitress. Mendoza shifted position, unhappily. Dylan knew he didn't like not being the center of attention, and he didn't at all like Dylan ignoring him.

"What's your plan, Paris?"

Dylan looked back at Mendoza. "We crash at your place tonight. I think we're all set to fly under the radar now, so in the morning we start searching for Andrea's father."

Andrea sat up. "Where are you going to start?"

"We start with our burner phones. I want to ask some questions of your oldest sisters. Find out what they remember. Carrie was in Spain with you when you were a baby, right?"

Andrea nodded. She thought about that album, and the damnably out of focus photographs. She opened her mouth to speak, but the waitress arrived, and they hurriedly placed their orders.

Who *was* the man in those photos? She wished she'd had more of an opportunity to look at them. It seemed like it was an eternity ago that she'd sat down with her sister Carrie, looking at the album from Spain. That was only on Tuesday. She closed her eyes, picturing the man in those two photos again. His face had been slightly blurred, but it was clear enough to see his eye color matched hers, as did his slightly aquiline nose. The man in the photo was easily six-five.

But she had no idea who he was, and Carrie didn't remember either. Maybe Luis or Abuelita would know. She needed to call them both anyway. They'd have heard about the attack by now and would be terrified. She felt awful she hadn't gotten in touch already, but there had hardly been an opportunity.

She could tell her voice sounded tired when she said, "I think we should ask Luis."

Dylan looked confused. Andrea said, "My uncle—Mother's younger brother. He's *much* younger. I think she was sixteen when he was born. He might know who the man at the beach was. Or other details I don't know about."

Dylan started nodding as she spoke. "Okay. We got something there. Do you know if Carrie has those photos on her Facebook page?"

Andrea shook her head. "I don't think so. I'd never seen them before."

"Okay," he said. "We need to get her to post them. I want to do image searches on all the people in the photos. Everyone you don't know. Who knows what might turn up there?"

"Julia might know more," Andrea said. "She's the oldest. I mean—I was born in China. She was already a teenager. She must have seen something, right?"

"She's never really talked about it with me much, but I get the impression she saw way too much in China," Dylan said.

Their waitress was already on the way out, carrying a heavy tray of food. "Food's coming," Andrea said.

"About time," Mendoza said. "I got a question. What if this isn't about the blood tests at all?"

"What do you mean?" Andrea said.

"Well, look—I get it. Your dad isn't your dad. And you got attacked. But no one attacked—what's your other sister's name? Carrie? Right?"

Dylan raised an eyebrow. "It was her condo we were in," he said.

"Yeah, yeah, I know. I'm just saying—don't close off possibilities. If your dad is into bad shit," he said, nodding at Andrea, "there could be all kinds of possibilities. Plus, it's not like this is the first time. I mean, Ray was murdered."

Dylan frowned. "That's not happening to anyone else."

"Good luck controlling that, Dylan. No wonder you look like crap if you think you could have done anything to save Ray. You were in New York when it happened, right?"

Dylan grunted. "Yeah, I know. I tend to blame myself for stuff that's—"

"Stuff you couldn't do nothin' about. I get it, Dylan."

"Yeah, yeah. I can at least protect *this one*," he said, pointing at Andrea.

The statement, and the fierce look on his face, sent shivers down her spine. She couldn't get her mind around the fact that less than twenty-four hours before, he had fought gunmen *with a knife*. To protect her.

"Good. There you go. Something you can do," Mendoza said.

"Leave him alone," Andrea said.

"Do *what?*" Mendoza replied.

"Dylan's had a rough time. Let him alone."

"You don't need to protect me," Dylan said. His tone was harsh.

"You don't need to protect *me*," Andrea replied.

Dylan rolled his eyes. "People are trying to kill you."

"Yeah, I know that, Dylan."

He closed his eyes. And then he said, "I'm so tired I could collapse right here. I can't eat a bite."

"Go get some rest," Mendoza said.

"Yeah," Dylan replied. "But do me a favor. Is there some place busy, like a mall, not close to where you live?"

"We could go up to Tysons, maybe. It's a big mall. Crowded. But we gotta be back at my place by 9, so you can get your IDs."

"Yeah … let's do that. We'll call Alex and Carrie, then toss the first SIM card in the garbage and head to your place. And get some sleep. I don't know about you, but I'm desperate."

"Let's go," Andrea replied, heart suddenly beating faster at the thought of talking with her sisters.

CHAPTER EIGHTEEN
One of the little people

Anthony. May 2. 1:00 pm.

Anthony Walker felt a wave of exhaustion slip over him as he slid into the chair in front of his desk at the offices of the *Washington Post*. Spread in every direction across the floor around him was the staff of the entertainment section—a dozen reporters, editors and photographers, two research assistants, and his boss, Linda Halloran.

Linda wasn't exactly a friend. In fact, the day he'd shown up at her desk, she'd looked up at him with scorn. "I know you think you're better than the rest of us, Walker. But foreign correspondents put their pants on the same way as everyone else. While you're working for me, you're one of the little people. Understand?"

Her attitude was unjust. Anthony might have been a foreign correspondent, but he had professional respect for everyone at the paper.

Personal respect—now that was something different. In the few short months he'd been in exile at the entertainment desk, Linda had gone out of her way to assign him to the crappiest possible stories. He'd covered the free weekly plays for toddlers at the National Theater. He'd interviewed Efua Lawal, the Nigerian pop singer who'd been arrested in New York with two prostitutes and fourteen grams of cocaine. He'd spent *two entire weeks* in January covering Justin Bieber's arrest in Miami.

Prior to January 24th, he'd never even heard of Justin Bieber.

Only a few weeks left and he'd be out of this hell. But then the call came early last week. *Morbid Obesity* was recording a new album. Would he do a profile of the headliner, Crank Wilson, and his wife, Julia? As an added incentive, Julia Wilson was the eldest daughter of the newly nominated Secretary of Defense.

Anthony jumped at the chance. It would be far more interesting than any other stories he was likely to get.

Julia and Crank had presented far more of a story than he'd bargained for. First, Julia's youngest sister had been kidnapped the day she arrived in the States, setting off a media firestorm. Now someone had blown up their house, the IRS had shut down their business, and Julia's father was under investigation.

Not your typical entertainment desk story.

Anthony logged into his computer, then picked up the handset for his phone and dialed into his voicemail. He opened up a notebook and began writing down the messages. Two from Linda Halloran, sometime yesterday evening. A call from his mother. Bill Lieby, his best friend and a foreign correspondent for the *Post*. The final message was from Jackson Barlow, the executive editor. *That* message had been left at 12:30, only half an hour ago.

Anthony pulled the phone to him and dialed.

"Jackson Barlow's office." A pleasant voice, but an unfamiliar one. Did Barlow have a new assistant? He was notoriously grumpy and went through executive assistants at a pace of two or three per year. It was a miracle the paper had never been sued—or at least, as far as Anthony knew it hadn't. That didn't rule out the possibility that something had been hushed up. Anthony had wondered more than once if Barlow was a womanizer in addition to being so grumpy. It would explain the continuous parade of new pretty young girls working for him. Over the phone, at least, this one sounded young.

"Is Jackson in? This is Anthony Walker, I just got back in the office."

"Oh! Mr. Walker! Mr. Barlow's in conference room A. He told me if you called to send you right there. The meeting just started."

"On my way," Anthony said, already rising to his feet and grabbing his laptop.

As he did, his eyes fell on one of the several monitors mounted not far from his desk. The screen showed a CNN news feed. Prince George-Phillip, the head of the SIS, was standing in front of a podium speaking into a microphone as reporters waved their arms. The headline flashing across the bottom of the screen read: *Terrorists attempt to assassinate British Intelligence head.*

Anthony shook his head as he turned away, heading toward the elevator. He'd interviewed the tall, gangly George-Phillip four years before, when the Prince became the first head of the Secret Intelligence Service to ever give a public address. The London newspapers liked to make fun of George-Phillip's admittedly ridiculous eyebrows, which were constantly in motion whenever he talked. But it was clear enough to Anthony that the newspapers missed his most important features—the intelligence behind those cool blue-green eyes was fierce. George-Phillip Windsor was a worthy head of the Intelligence Service.

As he walked from the elevator to the conference room, Anthony thought he'd have much preferred to be covering the story of George-Phillip's assassination attempt instead of whatever was going on with the Thompson family.

Then he froze, his hand on the door to the conference room.

Wasn't it an odd coincidence that someone had attempted to assassinate the head of British intelligence at the same time the children of the US Secretary of Defense were attacked?

Anthony's mind raced as he opened the door, and he didn't really pay attention to the dozen or so people in the room as he entered. He thought about the photographs he'd seen of Carrie Sherman and her sister, Andrea. Two remarkably tall women with very dark hair and blue-green eyes. *Was it possible?* What an incredible scandal that would have been: the wife of an American diplomat, pregnant not once, but *twice*, with children of a member of the British royal family.

Jackson Barlow stood at the head of the table. "Welcome back to Washington, Anthony. Nice of you to join us."

"Uh … thanks, Jackson."

Anthony forced his attention back to the present. He glanced around the room, taking note of the occupants.

Jackson Barlow, the executive editor of the paper. David Samuel, the National Desk editor, plus four reporters from his team. Jim Hsu, Anthony's old boss on the World Desk. Bill Leiby, and several other foreign correspondents. Two legal reporters and a politics reporter.

From the people in the room, it was easy enough to deduce which story *this* meeting was about.

"Have a seat," Barlow said. "I understand you spent yesterday and this morning with Julia Wilson?"

"And her husband, Crank," Anthony said, giving Barlow an insincere smile. "He's got a new album coming out soon."

Barlow met Anthony's eyes. "Understood. You still have access to them?"

Anthony nodded. "Yes. They want their side of the story out there."

"Okay. I want to hear your take."

Anthony looked around the room. He didn't know what anyone else in here had. Some of them would undoubtedly be buying the special prosecutor's story—that somehow Richard Thompson was involved in money laundering and more, and had enlisted his daughter's aid. Anthony didn't buy it.

He looked Barlow in the eyes and said, "We don't have enough information. But the idea that Richard Thompson somehow enlisted his children in a giant money laundering scheme is doubtful. Honestly, I don't think Julia Wilson is that stupid."

Barlow nodded, then said, "Okay—if that's the case, what's the real story?"

Anthony looked around the room. Why the hell was Barlow putting him on the spot like this?

"I don't know, Jackson. I've been stuck in moving vehicles since early this morning. But I think that's what we need to find out. What's the real story?"

Barlow shook his head and smiled. "All right. Here's what we're going to do. Legal team—I want you guys to concentrate on the actual investigation. What does the independent prosecutor know, or what does he think he knows? What's the IRS doing? Why did they seize Julia and Crank Wilson's assets? National desk—you guys follow up on the political side. What's going on with the Pentagon? Is Richard Thompson going to step down? Is Congress getting involved? What else?"

Anthony said, "I want to know if there's a link to the assassination attempt on the head of SIS."

Barlow's eyes nearly bugged out. "*What?* There's no link there, Anthony."

"Probably not. But the timing is curious."

"There was probably an earthquake in Mumbai last night too. That doesn't mean it's linked to Richard Thompson."

"No ... but this is different. How often are there attacks on multiple people at high levels of intelligence agencies of different countries on the same day?"

"Richard Thompson isn't—"

"He's CIA. Not State Department."

"Bullshit. Where do you get that?"

"From his own files. When Julia and Crank Wilson busted into his office last night they had me along for the ride. There's more here than meets the eye, Barlow."

Barlow gave Anthony a cool look. Then he took a deep breath and closed his eyes.

"Fine, Anthony. You're off the entertainment desk. I want you in charge of the team for this story."

Anthony tried to fight back a grin. And failed. He was going to be back in his element. As he stood up, Linda Halloran stirred in her seat.

"Jackson," said Linda. "Anthony's got live assignments on the entertainment desk. He needs to finish those."

Barlow dismissed her with a casual hand wave. "This is priority, Linda. Anthony—your show. What do you have?"

Anthony felt remarkably little tension in his stomach. This was a chance to get his life back. He was going for it. He walked around the conference table, picked up a dry erase marker, and wrote in large bold letters:

Same-day assassination attempt
Wakhan massacre?
R. Thompson - sexual assault of his wife 1991?

The others in the room stirred as he wrote the second and third line. To Anthony's right, Jackson Barlow frowned.

Links between GP and R. Thompson?
R. Thompson - CIA career
Missing: Adelina Thompson, Dylan Paris, Andrea Thompson, Jessica Thompson

He stood back and looked at the white board.

"What am I missing?" he asked.

"What the hell is that about Wakhan? And sexual assault?" Barlow's voice was harsh as he asked the question.

Anthony said, "What we found in Thompson's office was ... serious. First, Adelina Thompson was only sixteen when she conceived her first daughter. Richard Thompson married her when she was seventeen and already pregnant."

"Holy shit," someone muttered.

"Second—we found a report of a paternity test, determining that Carrie Sherman was not Thompson's daughter. The very next day, after the report was written, we have a police report. Adelina Thompson was assaulted and raped in February 1990. She refused to press charges, but according to the San Francisco Police, her husband was the prime suspect."

Silence had fallen across the room. "Finally—and this is the most confusing part for me—Thompson had a file with information about the Wakhan massacre in his office. Nothing classified there, everyone knows the massacre took place. What I want to know is this: did he know about it when it took place? Richard Thompson was assigned to the US Embassy in Pakistan in 1983."

"Motherfucker," Jackson said.

"I'll look into the Pakistan stuff," said Bill Leiby. "And the links with Prince George-Phillip. That's really interesting. Did you know he was involved with the SIS investigation into Wakhan?"

Anthony's eyes widened. "Are you serious?"

Leiby nodded. "My timing may be off—it was, I don't know—'84 maybe? The results never made the light of day, but I remember George-Phillip asking questions one day—"

Leiby's eyes widened and met Anthony's.

"What?" Anthony said.

"Understand, he was a kid then. Twenty-one maybe? I was on the diplomatic beat at the time. And there was some fuss—the British Embassy made a formal complaint to the paper."

"About?"

"Our society page columnist wrote something about George-Phillip and Adelina Thompson being seen having a private lunch together."

Barlow nodded. "Yeah, that happened. Maria Clawson wrote the story, I think."

Anthony frowned in distaste. Maria Clawson was a gossip blogger, specializing in destroying people's lives. "Clawson worked for the *Post*?"

"Until the late 90s," Barlow said.

Anthony shook his head. "Jesus. Before my time. So—George-Phillip and Adelina Thompson had lunch in the 1980s. Anything more?"

Barlow shrugged. "No idea."

"We'll find out," Leiby said.

"All right. We need to find out what the British concluded in their investigation of Wakhan. And I think we need to do our own investigation again."

Linda Halloran said, "What about the political implications? Does anyone know if the President will keep backing Thompson's nomination?"

Barlow shook his head. "I'll be stunned if he does. And that's going to get ugly."

Anthony responded, "Everyone else will be covering the political angle. Does it hurt the President? How will this affect polling numbers? They'll all miss the real story."

Barlow pointed a finger at Anthony. "You better get the real story for us."

Anthony nodded. "I'm on it."

Julia. May 2. 2 pm.

The phone rang four times. Five. Six. Then it cut over to voicemail.

"You've reached the personal line of Richard Thompson. I can't take your call right now. Please leave a clear message and a phone number."

Julia clicked disconnect. She'd left messages already. Several of them, in fact. Her father wasn't answering his phone.

Of course, he was the Secretary of Defense. *Plus,* he'd gotten news that morning that the Justice Department was investigating him under charges that were clearly ridiculous.

But he still needed to answer his damn phone.

She put her cell down and looked around the suite they'd checked into in Arlington. She needed to *do* something. She needed something to fix, something concrete to put her hands on. Carrie was back at the safe house, but neither she nor Julia knew the address. Her lawyer was meeting with the Internal Revenue Service, and there was absolutely nothing Julia could do to help that situation. She'd spent an hour on the phone with employees, both reassuring them and making sure their immediate needs were taken care of. But she felt a pit in her stomach. Payroll was in a few days, and the corporate accounts had been frozen, along with her and Crank's savings and investment accounts. Their cash account had a lot of money in it, but not enough to cover payroll for any length of time.

Julia stood and paced. In the next room, behind a closed door, she could hear Crank practicing. He had the volume low, which was good. He'd been working on several new songs, and she'd been pushing. Pushing, because in some ways, the most recent songs he'd written seemed like rote. Morbid Obesity had been together more than a dozen years, and had released 8 albums. They'd done so many tours that the hotel rooms and suites across the globe had long since merged together into a hazy mess. But the music had always been cutting edge, emotional, deeply connected to who they were as people. Lately, though, it felt like they were following a formula.

She stood for just a second, tilting her head and listening to the tones of the guitar through the closed door. Hard to hear, but whatever Crank was working on, it had an odd, catchy, syncopated beat.

She reached for her phone again. Maybe Carrie had gotten clearance to meet.

It rang before she could touch it. She froze. The word "Dad" appeared across the front of her phone.

Answer. Decline. The two choices felt like the choice between good and evil, and she didn't know which was which.

She stared at it. Her tongue felt like copper. She picked the phone up, tapped on the "answer" button and spoke without a pause for thought or breath, her words as much of a surprise to her as they would be to her father.

"Where's my mother?"

Stunned silence at the other end. Then he said, in a perfectly calm, placating voice, "I don't know, Julia. I don't know where she is."

A cold rage wrapped around her heart. "Why did the IRS close my offices this morning? What the hell is happening to our family, *Father?*"

"Julia, I am returning your call. I did not expect to be spoken to this way."

"I didn't expect to find out that—that…" She couldn't say the words.

"Find out what?"

"I read the police report."

"What police report? I have no idea what you are talking about." His voice sounded damnably reasonable.

"Let me refresh your memory, Father." Her voice was cutting and sarcastic and bore thirty years of lies and hurt. "The day after you found out Carrie wasn't your daughter, Mom was beaten half to death and raped. Does that ring a bell?"

"Julia, where did you—"

"In your office, Father. You don't even deny it?"

His response was unexpected, both harsh and insistent. *"In my office? When?"*

"Yesterday. Right before two thugs broke into the house, tried to kill us, then set off a bomb."

Silence. After a few seconds, he said, "There's a great deal more to this than you realize, Julia. You mustn't jump to conclusions."

The bedroom door opened, and Crank appeared in the doorway. "Hey," he said. "You won't believe this song—" He froze and stopped talking when he saw her expression.

"What else can I do, Father? Apparently neither of my parents can be bothered to tell me the truth about anything. What else am I supposed to do other than come to my own conclusions?"

"I've never lied to you, Julia."

"What?" she shouted. "You've never lied to me? What about the affairs in China? What about my sister not being my sister? What about you raping my mother? What about the fact that she was a *child* when she got pregnant with me? You've never lied to me?"

As she cried out the words, she saw it. Julia had been—eight years old? She had run downstairs that day, holding hands with Carrie. They had been giggling, free. It must have been a Saturday, and they both had Valentine's candy from school. They'd been playing and laughing, but she remembered wondering why Mary, the nanny, looked so distressed.

That morning, she and Carrie had run into the family room and jumped on the couch together, then Carrie said, "Why Mommy cry? Mommy? Why Mommy sad?"

Her face had been bruised, and she'd lay curled on the couch, eyes red with tears, reading a book. Her arm was in a sling.

"I'm not sad," their mother had said. Then she tried to smile. "I'm just a little sick."

"Sick make you purple?" Carrie said. Then she giggled and ran to their mother and wrapped her arms around her, and Adelina winced. Carrie said, "Kiss make Mommy better," and leaned up and kissed her.

Valentine's, Julia thought. She hadn't thought about that day in years. But she'd seen the police report last night. Her mother hadn't been sick. She'd been beaten and raped.

I'm not sad. I'm just a little sick.

Just a little sick. That was a couple days after Valentine's, a couple days after the police report indicated she'd had cracked ribs.

A surge of rage swept over Julia. In a low voice she whispered into the phone, "You've never done anything *but* lie to me."

Then she put the phone down. Bright sunlight poured into the hotel room, but she felt dead inside.

"Babe?" Crank said in a low voice.

Julia turned to her husband. She opened her mouth, but couldn't speak. There were no words. Nothing. She thought of all the times she'd been at war with her mother. The cruel things her mother had said. The constant warfare.

Why? Why had her mother been so hateful? Was it all fear of her father? Why had she had the affair? Her mother had been sixteen when she became pregnant with Julia.

And fifteen years later, Julia got pregnant, and aborted the child. A child who would have been Andrea's age now.

A child she'd never be able to hold or kiss or love.

She knew it wasn't logical. She knew it didn't make any sense at all. But suddenly tears were running down her face, and Julia let out a low growl. Crank instantly moved to her, putting his arms around her.

"It's okay, babe," he whispered.

"No," she said. "It's not. It'll never be okay." Then a wave of agony hit. Not physical pain, but spiritual agony, remorse and grief and loss for the thing she'd always wanted but never had. "I have to call Carrie," she whispered.

He broke away from her and she dialed Carrie's number.

"Where are you?" she asked as soon as Carrie answered. "Did you get the address?"

Carrie gave her an address. "Call me when you're less than five minutes away. I'm not supposed to tell anyone where we are, so we won't tell our security until the moment you drive up."

"Perfect," Julia said. "I'll call. We need to talk."

Julia turned to her husband. He had a concerned expression on his face, his eyes wide, eyebrows raised. "Let's go?" she asked.

Five minutes later they were in a rental car. Crank drove while Julia fidgeted with her phone.

"Talk to me," he said.

"I keep thinking about Belgium. I remember being so alone. I don't ... I mean, I get it that she must have been afraid of him. She must have been crazy sometimes. But why didn't she just leave him?"

She closed her eyes, not expecting an answer from Crank. Julia didn't remember the flight to Belgium, but she did remember being angry they had to leave San Francisco and her friends.

The last day in San Francisco.

Her mother had been in rare form that day, trying to herd three children, get the house packed and arrange everything by herself. For several weeks Mother's patience had been short, as she became alternately inconsolable and angry.

Where had her father been? Julia had a vague memory that he'd met them in Brussels—for most of the three years before leaving for Belgium, he'd only been home for brief visits.

Julia clearly remembered the meltdown right before they left for the airport. The cab had been waiting at the front steps for several minutes as Adelina corralled three children and half a dozen bags. Julia had already seen the signs, the stress lines appearing around her mother's eyes, the thinning lips stretching across her mouth.

They had been standing on the front steps as her mother panicked, searching around.

"Julia, watch your sisters, I left one of my bags." She ducked in the front door.

Julia took six-year-old Carrie's hand in her left, and Alexandra's in her right. Alexandra immediately began to pull away, and Carrie shouted, "Stop, you're holding my hand too tight!"

Carrie had reached over and pinched Julia's arm. Julia spun toward her sister, and Alexandra's hand got loose, sending the toddler spilling down the steps.

Carrie screamed and Julia felt her heart in her throat. Alexandra had been— maybe fourteen months? She hadn't been walking long, and when she fell it was like watching a limp doll just fall end over end.

Her tiny face instantly turned bright red and she began to scream. The cab driver got out of the car and shouted, "Is she okay?" just as their mother came back outside.

Adelina had let out a cry and rushed to Alexandra, yanking her out of Julia's arms. "I can't trust you alone for *five seconds*!"

Julia remembered feeling—injured? Hurt? Her mother's words dug deep.

"Is okay, Mommy," Carrie said. "She not broken."

Adelina had sniffed. "No, she's not broken."

"I want to go see *Daddy*," Julia had said.

Her mother had looked at her with weary, incredibly sad eyes, and said, "Well, you're going to get your wish, Julia. Go get in the car."

The bitterness made her choke. Thinking back now, Julia found herself questioning everything she'd ever believed about her mother and father.

She said to Crank in a broken, strained voice, "Everything I've ever believed is upside down."

Crank nodded, but didn't say anything. He reached over with his right hand and intertwined his fingers with hers.

"Things were good in San Francisco. I remember that. Mostly. Not always—I remember my mom being sick and hurt after Valentine's the year Alexandra was born. When he beat her up and … and…"

Her voice trailed off. She couldn't say the words.

"It's okay," Crank said.

Julia forced the words out. "When he raped her. I remember it, but I didn't know what it meant. I just knew she was sick, and I was mad because she couldn't do anything for a few days and we were stuck with the nanny. And then she got so sad when we went to Belgium." Julia moaned a little. "Oh, God, she was so sad. And I was mad at her. Because we were going to see Daddy, and I didn't know why she was sad."

Crank turned the car onto the highway. "No way you could have known what was going on with her."

"True," she said, "but still. I keep thinking about those three years in Belgium. Barry looked after Carrie and me sometimes. Alexandra had a governess. I barely remember seeing Dad. They were already sleeping in separate rooms. I guess they always did and I just didn't think anything of it."

"You were so lonely," Crank murmured.

"I was," Julia said. "But I never realized—what must it have been like for her? Did they hate each other? Dad—I don't get … I don't get any of it. I mean—do you know how many years of therapy I've gone through, thanks to her?"

It was a rhetorical question of course—he'd been right there with her through it all. He knew all about her therapists.

She closed her eyes. She remembered the day she'd confronted her mother right before leaving for Germany. Julia had spit out bitter words. *Why wouldn't you help me? Why weren't you there when I needed you?*

Even then, during that confrontation, her mother had hidden her father's secrets. And during the drive to the airport the next day, her father had calmly and smoothly lied to Julia. He'd lied to her about when and how he'd met her mother. He'd lied to her about his posting after that. He'd lied to her about being in therapy. He'd lied about *everything*.

But so had her mother.

Julia shook her head. She didn't understand any of it. She looked at the cars ahead of them on the highway, an empty feeling settling over her. Her company had been shut down by the IRS. Two of her sisters and her mother were missing. Nothing made sense any more.

She sat straight and slowly closed her eyes. She was not going to cry. Not now. She had too much to do, too many problems to deal with, too many people depending on her, not the least of which was Carrie and the tiny little baby who was going to need help to live.

CHAPTER NINETEEN

Suspended.

Bear. May 2. 8 pm.

"**Yeah,**" Bear muttered into his phone, fighting to force his eyes open. He groaned and shifted position, sitting up, disoriented. Light flooded his eyes and he squinted them, realizing where he was.

The hospital. He'd spent the afternoon with the kids after dropping Carrie Sherman back at the safe house, then slept for two hours, then he'd come here. Leah was in intensive care, and Gary, her giant pug of a husband, was pacing at the other end of the waiting area.

Bear sat up, when he heard the voice on the phone. It was the Secretary.

"Bear, I need you to come in."

"Yes, sir," Bear said, desperately suppressing a burp, his entire chest rumbling. "What … sorry, sir … I'm a bit groggy."

"Be in my office in an hour."

"Yes, sir."

Shit. Bear took the phone away from his ear as Secretary Perry hung up. He looked at his phone, uncomprehendingly. It was 8 pm. He'd been asleep for two hours. Not enough to feel rested, but plenty to make him feel desperate.

He stood up, staggering a little, wishing he hadn't quit smoking. Jesus, he needed to get some coffee. And a shower. Did he have time for a shower? Maybe, if he booked it right now. He walked to the other end of the waiting room.

"Gary," he said.

"Motherfucker," Gary said.

"How is she?"

"Not awake yet. But she's in recovery."

Bear sagged. "The kids?"

"Your mom's with them."

"Okay," Bear said. He looked at his phone and said, "The Secretary just called me. I gotta go in."

"Yeah, whatever."

Bear shrugged. He and Gary were never gonna be pals.

"Call me if anything changes."

"Yeah, all right."

Bear put a hand out and briefly rested it on Gary's shoulder. Gary froze.

"Gary. She's gonna be okay."

Initially Gary didn't respond. He just stood there, his entire body a jumbled mass of tensed muscles. Bear felt him shaking, all 220 pounds of packed muscle vibrating like a well-tuned instrument. For just a second, he thought Gary was going to slug him. Instead, he sagged.

"Yeah."

Bear stepped back and let his hand drop. He didn't want to push his luck, nor did he feel much appreciation for the irony of comforting the husband of his ex-wife. Miss Manners didn't give out any scripts for *that*.

He left the hospital as quickly as he could. At 8 pm he could count on a long wait at the subway station, or an equally long wait for a cab. Or he could just walk or run it. It was twelve long city blocks back to his apartment, probably a fifteen-minute run. Far quicker than waiting for a cab.

He opted to run. Maybe that would help wake him up some.

Bear hadn't counted on the heat. Washington, DC—the entire East Coast really—had just been through an unusually long and cold winter. Bear hadn't fully adjusted to the sudden change from winter to summer with barely any transition at all. The air was soupy, thick with humidity and street smells. And, instead of sneakers, he was running in business shoes.

Asshat. Sometimes Bear's internal monologue was less than diplomatic.

He was soaked with sweat by the time he reached his tiny apartment. For just a second, when he walked in, he was disoriented. Twenty-six hours had passed since he'd gotten the phone call from Leah.

Bear, is there supposed to be a relief team here?

No. No relief team.

It was an ambush, an ambush by at least one person who was supposed to be on their team. A betrayal by a long time DSS agent, and Bear still had exactly nothing to go on.

Bear left a trail of dirty clothing from the door to the shower, and washed his hair and body in record time, the water turned all the way up, pounding his sore and exhausted body with the hottest water possible. He was red faced and relaxed when he stepped out and began to dry himself off, only to discover that he'd failed to wash his armpits, which still smelled pretty dodgy. Whatever. He sprayed himself with deodorant and got dressed quickly, wearing the thickest socks he had because he'd developed a blister on the back of his ankle on the run over.

He picked up his shoes and started to put them on. They were scuffed all to hell. 8:32, and he had twenty-eight minutes left before he had to report to the secretary's office. He took thirty seconds to apply polish to his shoes, ninety seconds to chug a Red Bull and fifteen seconds to reach in the drawer for his laptop so he could check his email.

Then Bear froze. The laptop wasn't in the drawer.

His kitchen table was completely clear.

Oh, shit. When he'd left the apartment twenty-six and a half hours ago, he'd left at a dead run. Shots had been fired at the Thompson condominium, his ex-wife was in the line of fire, and he didn't take a minute to lock up the classified documents that had been sitting on his kitchen table. Classified documents, which included the personnel file of the former spy turned diplomat turned Secretary of Defense-elect Richard Thompson.

He could see it in his mind's eye. The file, carefully opened on the table, where he'd been reading it.

He traced his movements the night before. He'd left the office a few minutes after 5:30. The classified documents desk had called him after receiving the fax from the San Francisco police. The police report.

It still made no sense. Adelina Thompson sexually assaulted, and her husband the suspect, more than twenty years ago. She'd refused to testify and the case had been closed with what looked to Bear to be unusual dispatch. Bear put the file, along with Thompson's personnel file and background documents on Wakhan and Pakistan in the 1980s, into a bag and walked out of the building.

He'd walked out of the building with a bag full of improperly secured classified documents. Then, when he found out his ex-wife had been shot at, he'd left them out on the table.

Shit. Shit. Shit.

He was shaking. He looked at the clock. 8:38. Twenty-two minutes. It was a twenty-minute walk from here to Main State, and typically four minutes from the entrance to the elevator and then up to the 7th floor.

He needed to leave right now. Instead, he walked over to his closet and kneeled at the floor safe. Maybe he'd forgotten. Bear had slept a total of three hours out of the last forty-eight. He was functioning on empty. Maybe he'd just forgotten.

He dialed the combination, but got it wrong and cursed in frustration. Then he tried again, and opened the safe.

It was empty.

No classified documents.

No nothing. His passport, birth certificate, a thousand dollars in cash, and other documents were gone, including the three surviving photos of his and Leah's wedding, which he'd locked in the safe to ensure he didn't burn them while drunk. Everything was gone.

Shaking, Bear shook his head, then stood up. He had to get to the Secretary now. He had nineteen minutes. He ran out the door, letting it slam shut behind him, and hit the down elevator button.

Then he stood there. The left elevator was on 18, the right on L. Neither moved.

Christ.

He shifted his weight back and forth from one foot to the other, limbering up. He was going to have to run. It wasn't far, straight down New Hampshire Avenue to 23rd Street, then left, through the George Washington University campus and there it was. He walked it every day.

He didn't run it twice a day. He wished he'd worn sneakers. Finally. The elevator was moving.

"Oh, there you are. Mister Bear!"

Christ. It was Millie McPherson, the widow who lived two doors down from him. Millie was a blue-haired old woman who had, from her patterns of speech, probably grown up on an antebellum plantation in central Georgia. She had on a sixty-year-old yellow sundress, patent leather shoes and a bow in her hair, for Christ's sake, and her smile revealed a full set of unnaturally straight teeth.

"Oh, hey there, Miss Millie."

"Do you have time to chat for just a moment, Bear?"

The elevator was moving now, coming up, floor 7, 8, now 9.

"I don't, really, I'm kind of on an emergency call, if the freaking elevator ever gets here."

"It won't take but a moment, sugah, I promise."

"Maybe you could ride the elevator down with me, Miss Millie." He wanted to be polite. He really did. But the elevator dinged and the doors opened and he stepped inside. He stabbed the L with his index finger as she tottered over toward the door.

"Wait..." she called.

He pretended to reach for the door to stop it and said, insincerely, "Oh no," as the door closed.

The elevator started moving and he prepared to run.

Two minutes later he was out the front door of the building and on his way. It was 8:47, and he had thirteen minutes to make a twenty-minute walk. He ran as quickly as he could.

It was a warm Friday night in Washington, DC near DuPont Circle. The crowds were out in force, people spilling onto the sidewalk and traffic jammed up, nobody moving in their cars except the cabs who drove recklessly in between other lanes and sometimes narrowly missing bumping onto the sidewalk. Bear ran through a crowd of twenty-something college students who crowded the sidewalk, all skinny jeans and halter tops and skin everywhere, an appalling display of youth and beauty and crushing envy which Bear might have normally enjoyed. Tonight he had no time and no inclination, pushing past the kids aggressively, his passage evoking cries and curses.

Finally he was free, headed down New Hampshire Avenue. He dodged traffic at the intersections, only having to stop when he finally hit K Street with its wall-to-wall traffic. He checked his phone. 8:55. *Damn it.* There was no way he'd make it in time.

No matter. The moment the light changed he launched himself across the street, hearing the screech of tires as an overly aggressive cabbie had to suddenly stop. Down 23rd Street, past George Washington University Hospital where Leah was recovering from the gunshot wounds, and on toward Main State.

It was five minutes after nine when he arrived, breathless and sweaty, at the Secretary's door.

He knocked, sucking back breaths. He had to compose himself before that door opened. He took a last shuddering breath, then tried to hold himself calm as the door opened.

It was the Secretary himself at the door. A tall and gaunt man, James Perry had once been a naval riverboat captain in Vietnam, and later a United States Senator. His runs for the Presidency had ended in failure—Republicans labeled him as too wonky, too intellectual, too weak-kneed, to be President. Bear admired him, though in general his attitude about Democrats was to be appalled at their lack of fortitude or patriotism. But in Bear's eyes, no one could question Perry's courage or his patriotism.

"Bear, come in. I was starting to worry."

"Sorry about that, sir," Bear gasped out.

"Bear … you all right?"

Bear followed Perry into the dimmed office. "Yes, sir," he said.

The Secretary's office was large, with a sizable sitting area marked with ornate couches and tables. His working space, a large mahogany desk, was at the opposite end. Wide planked hardwood floors stained a deep reddish brown stretched across the broad space, contrasting with the white walls, elegant wainscoting and elaborate molding.

"Have a seat, then," Perry said, walking over to the desk and indicating a chair that sat at an angle to the desk. Bear took a seat, sucking in another shuddering gasp of air as he did so, trying to be discreet.

"Are you *sure* you're all right?" Perry asked. "Breathe, man."

"I'm fine. I was running late so I actually ran over here from DuPont Circle. I live over that way."

Perry raised his eyebrows. Bear noticed for the first time that the eyebrows were shot through with white. Perry must dye his hair.

"I see," Perry said. "First, how's Leah Simpson?"

"She's out of surgery, sir, and in recovery. The last news we got was that her prognosis was good."

"Good, good," Perry said, nodding. "And the Thompson daughters. They're still at our safe house?"

"Yeah," Bear said. "Though Carrie Sherman blew the location earlier, with one of the other sisters."

Perry frowned. "How did she do that? You didn't take their phones?"

"They aren't prisoners, sir."

"True. All right, that's what it is. Tell me what else you have?"

Bear sighed. Then he said the first thing that came out of his mouth. "Nothing, sir. Or—very little."

Perry bit his lip. Jesus. He was *personally* interested in this, not just professionally.

Bear said, "We know that Adelina Thompson lied about her age. Not on official documents, but socially. She was actually sixteen when Richard Thompson knocked her up."

"Okay. What else?"

"She had an affair. Who with we don't know, but two of the daughters aren't his. And we know that when he found out, he beat her up and raped her."

Perry blanched. "What? Are you serious?"

"Yeah, unfortunately. It happened in 1990."

"I didn't know about that. What's your conclusion about Richard Thompson's original employment?"

"Thompson was CIA."

"Right. You saw that Henry Kissinger signed his recommendation. He was National Security Advisor then. Richard Thompson was CIA."

"But CIA puts people in diplomatic cover all the time."

"Of course they do, Wyden. Tell me how that works."

Bear nodded. Of course. When CIA needed to place someone, they created a cover *with the cooperation* of State.

"He was some kind of a long term plant," Bear said. "But for what purpose?"

"Think about the crew running CIA then. George Bush and William Colby and Kissinger. Those guys thought they could do anything. The CIA was running assassination programs and drugs and all kinds of stuff. I think Thompson was a recruit, and they placed him at State. Then Kissinger came over here too, as Secretary."

"What does all this have to do with *now?*"

"I don't know yet. But I can tell you this—Thompson's got some enemies. They're trying to take him down, and they don't care who goes down with him. Things are changing very rapidly right now."

Bear's mind turned to the missing files.

"Right. I get that," Bear said. "Sir, we may have one problem. I suppose I'm reporting myself. I had Thompson's personnel file along with some other classified documents about Wakhan and Pakistan at my apartment. I didn't properly secure the documents last night when the shooting was reported. And when I finally got back tonight—they were gone."

Perry sat back and rubbed his eyes. Then he said, "We *do* have a problem, then."

Bear waited. It was a problem all right. DSS sacked people for far less. People *went to jail* for less.

Perry looked up and said, "You should know, the reason I called you in—I got a call from the White House about an hour before I called you."

"Yes, sir?"

"Thompson's nomination is being withdrawn by the President. He's going to hang him out to dry, which I think is well deserved."

Bear nodded. That was good news. But not if they took down his daughters with him. Bear didn't know the oldest daughter Julia, but he knew Carrie had been through too much already.

"I was ordered to hand over the investigation to the independent prosecutor and the FBI. They're doing a joint investigation with the IRS and Secret Service. We're out of it."

"Yes, sir," Bear muttered. He didn't want to be out of it. He wanted to know who had shot Leah.

"The thing is," Perry said, his voice quiet. "There's something that isn't right here. Something just doesn't make sense. Richard Thompson is a snake. But drug money laundering? I don't buy it. Not at all."

Bear was confused. He looked at Perry and said, "So … what happens now?"

"Well, obviously I have to take you off the case," Perry said. "We'll have your team here turn over whatever they have, which isn't much from what you've led me to believe. And—given what you've reported to me, I may have to temporarily suspend you, with pay, while I investigate."

Suspended. That was a blow. Bear sat back, nodding. Then he realized Perry was staring closely at him.

"Now, Bear, I can't tell you what to do with your free time, if you're suspended. But I'd expect you'd be careful."

Huh. What was he saying? Go investigate on your own? Was he saying he'd cover for him? Or was this one of those situations that happened sometimes, where people just got hung out to dry? He'd be out there with no professional backing, no actual business being on the case. He wouldn't have a budget, or a right to carry a weapon except for self-defense, with no jurisdiction to do anything at all.

Did it even matter? He thought for just a second about his ex-wife, fighting for her life in the hospital. About Andrea Thompson, on the run and not even knowing who her father was. He thought about Carrie Sherman, fighting for the life of her daughter.

He nodded slowly. "Sir, I apologize. I suppose I'll have to accept the suspension. How long will I be suspended, sir?"

"I'd say indefinitely. Until I can complete an investigation. Right now I'm a little busy, though."

"Yes, sir. I understand." Bear stood. Then he let an uncharacteristic grin appear on his face. "You know, sir, for a Democrat, you're all right."

Perry winked. "You are too, Wyden. You know what to do now."

CHAPTER TWENTY
I haven't been honest

Sarah. May 2. 5 pm.

The text message came in first, and Carrie looked at her phone. Her eyes narrowed, and she looked at Sarah.

"Sarah, do me a favor," Carrie whispered.

Sarah's eyes narrowed. In the months since the accident, she'd gotten to know her much older sister a lot better. And right now Carrie's posture radiated tension. Her back was unusually straight, and Rachel, normally a fairly docile baby, was starting to squirm.

"What's up?"

"Go over to the front door. I want you to watch. In a couple of minutes a car's going to pull up. Julia and Crank. Make sure they let them through."

"I thought Bear said we couldn't give anyone the address," Sarah whispered.

"It's Julia," Carrie replied, even as Sarah stood.

On door duty was Lucas Steelman, a twenty-four-year-old uniformed agent of the Diplomatic Security Service. Sarah was sure he'd changed his name, or just made it up, or found it in a puddle of pure testosterone. No one was actually named anything so stupid.

On the other hand, he *was* easy on the eyes. The name might be stupid, but it fit. An obvious weightlifter, his biceps bulged underneath his sleeves, which looked tailored for someone just slightly smaller. Extremely muscular. In fact, Sarah thought, he looked like a lunk. A delicious lunk, but a lunk nonetheless.

She was pretty sure Eddie could take him in a fight. Eddie was a pretty big guy too, but more importantly, he was smart as hell.

Right now Steelman—she couldn't think of his name without wanting to chuckle—leaned against the wall near the front door, whistling in a low tone.

She leaned against the opposite wall. "Hey."

He looked at her with impassive eyes. "You aren't supposed to be at the door." But his eyes grazed slightly down to her chest, as she knew they would. She leaned back against the wall a little more, her back arching slightly, probably setting off every serotonin receptor in the poor guard's brain. His eyes widened slightly, but she thought it was unconscious.

"This job must get boring for you," she said in a low tone. Her voice laid out a lure at the end of a not very long line. He wouldn't take long before he started nibbling.

"Sometimes. You do a lot of waiting, but then when the chips are down, you gotta man up." Now his eyes were fully on her. Predictable. He was hooked. Already.

"Have you done that sort of thing often? Where you had to um … man up?" She let one side of her mouth curl up a little, and parted her lips just slightly. This was ridiculous.

He shrugged, failing to appear modest. "I'm a federal agent. You do what you gotta do. Say, how old are you, anyway?"

"I turned eighteen three weeks ago," she said, intentionally making her voice a little husky. She crossed her legs at the ankles.

Agent Steelman blushed, his ears turning bright red. Sarah almost burst into laughter, but she needed to keep him occupied for at least another minute or so. Instead, she licked her lips.

That was when the grey rental car turned into the driveway. Steelman instantly tensed, reaching for his sidearm.

"Stop," Sarah said. "That's my sister Julia and her husband."

"What the hell?" he shouted. Four agents ran up to the car, weapons out, shouting.

"Stop them! That's my sister."

"Son of a bitch!" he muttered. He opened the door and snarled, "Stay here!" She watched him as he charged out the front door, shouting to the other agents, who quickly lowered their weapons.

A pale faced Crank and Julia Wilson emerged from the car. Immediately, the four agents hustled them into the safe house, where a tense Ben Crosby confronted Carrie.

"Someone want to explain what the hell just happened here?" he demanded.

"I think the answer to that is obvious," Julia replied.

Crosby ignored Julia, facing Carrie. "We explicitly told you not to tell *anyone* where you were."

Carrie shifted Rachel in her lap. The baby, whose arms were flailing around, began to burble as Crosby spoke.

"I'll thank you to not shout at me," Carrie said. "You'll scare my daughter."

"What the hell were you thinking, Carrie?" Crosby's face was red as he spoke.

The baby chuckled, a deep gurgling sound, and began waving her arms at Crosby.

Sarah leaned against the wall and snickered. Crosby's angry face looked funny anyway, almost like a caricature, but the laughing baby just topped off her sense of the ridiculous. His face worked in indescribable antics, his jaw twisting a little, and finally Carrie spoke, since he'd apparently lost his capacity to do so.

"We're not prisoners, Crosby. This is my sister, and she's as much a part of this as the rest of us. And since you weren't telling us anything, I took it in my own hands. End of discussion."

Crosby shook his head. "I'll be reporting this to Bear."

Scorn filled Carrie's face. "Report it to the *President,* for all I care. I understand you're trying to protect us, and I'm grateful. But I'm not keeping my sister away."

He sighed and walked away. Lucas walked by Sarah, diverting his eyes from her. He knew he'd been had.

As the agents walked away, Carrie stood, holding Rachel in the crook of one arm, and reached for Julia. "Thank God you're here," she whispered and they embraced.

The two eldest sisters held each other for a long time. Crank walked over to Sarah and said, "Hey, kiddo," then pulled her into a hug. "You hanging in there?"

"Yeah," Sarah said. "You?"

"Julia's carrying the brunt of all this. I don't even know what's going on, really."

Sarah shrugged. Of course Julia would. Her oldest sister had left home when Sarah was little more than a toddler. She was confident, assertive, and competent. She managed the band and ran her own company and never seemed entirely human to Sarah. She remembered times when she was younger, when Julia would visit, or they would meet her. The house would fill with tension, their mother sometimes angry and inconsistent. But those visits were few and far between, and became less and less frequent over the years as Julia's career became more and more successful.

It wasn't exactly that Sarah didn't love her eldest sister. She did. It was more that she just didn't know her that well. A long gap of years and experience left them distant, and she didn't know how to bridge that gap.

At the opposite side of the room from Sarah, Alexandra stood in the doorway, looking just as unsure as Sarah felt. Of course, she'd been a gigantic bitch to Carrie earlier, and Carrie would undoubtedly tell Julia about it. The two of them were very close. Sarah looked at Alexandra. She loved her sister, but didn't always like her. Alexandra was the middle sister, and never seemed quite sure of who she was. It was as if her older sisters had taken all the talent, leaving Alexandra nothing but sheer determination to push through.

She at least had that in spades. Sarah met Alexandra's eyes for just a second. As if they'd shared an invisible signal, both of them moved to the center of the room and hugged Julia.

When they parted, Julia said, "Listen—we need to catch up. On a lot of stuff. But in particular—Crank and I found some stuff in Dad's office you need to know about."

"In Dad's office?" Carrie asked, a frown pulling down the corners of her mouth.

Julia nodded. Her eyes darted to Crank, and she described the scene they'd found at the house in San Francisco last night. Sarah's eyes widened at the details. Jessica and their mom were gone. Vomit on the floor in the dining room, and a spoiled gallon of milk in the middle of the kitchen floor. The *diary*.

Julia handed the diary to Carrie as she spoke. She spoke words that Sarah barely comprehended. Their mother was sixteen when she got pregnant with Julia.

Sixteen. Julia looked at Alexandra with what Sarah would have sworn was a pitying look, then showed them the police report.

Sarah blanched at the pictures, but froze, keeping her reaction to herself. Alexandra was pale, a hand covering her open mouth. She began to shake violently, and Carrie said, "Alex, it's—"

"Leave me alone," Alexandra said. "That's not possible. You're *lying.*"

"Alexandra," Julia whispered. "I know this is hard…" Her voice trailed off.

Sarah looked at Alexandra, her mind calculating the months back from Alexandra's birth to the assault.

There was no question. If their father had raped their mother, and the police report and documentation of the assault was accurate, then Alexandra had been conceived in that rape.

Horrified, Alexandra stood. "Leave me *alone*," she demanded. Then she stumbled off to her room, slamming the door shut behind her.

Alexandra. May 2. 8 pm.

When Alexandra's cell phone rang three hours later, she almost declined the call. It was from an unfamiliar number with a 571 area code, and she didn't even know where that was. She was groggy from crying until she fell asleep. She'd ignored Carrie's entreaties to open the door earlier—she just couldn't face it. After the third ring, she picked it up, suddenly in a panic.

"Hello?" Her voice was urgent and cracked a little.

"Hey, babe, it's me."

Panic and elation ran simultaneously through Alex and she urgently whispered, *"Oh my God, are you okay?"* As she did it, she found herself looking around. Was Ben Crosby around? Or one of the other guards from State Department? They'd report Dylan in an instant.

She looked out in the hallway, then hurried down the hall to the bathroom and closed the door behind her. As Dylan spoke, she turned on the shower, letting the water run.

"I'm okay," he said. "Andrea's okay. We're hiding out for now."

She closed her eyes, pressing a hand to her chest. She knew she couldn't ask where he was. But she ached to know.

"Are you safe?" she whispered. Tears formed up in her eyes, involuntary tears that she couldn't do anything to stop, and they began to run down her cheeks.

"We're okay for now. You'll probably get some questions at some point. But there was a bunch of cash in the apartment."

"Bear told us," Alexandra said. "He said they found drugs too."

"Yeah. And I don't know where they came from. Andrea doesn't either. Alex, someone set us up."

Alexandra whispered, "Bear said you killed the intruders to protect Andrea."

Silence. Breathing on the other end. Then he said, "I don't want to talk about that. Not now. I've got too much to focus on."

Oh, Dylan. She couldn't even imagine what he was going through. "You know I love you," she whispered. "No matter what."

"I know," he said. "And I love you. Now talk to me. What's going on? I've tried to check the news but it's all bullshit."

She sighed. "We're at a safe house. State Department security picked us up during dinner last night. Right after ... right after ... you were attacked."

"You're safe there?" he asked.

"We've got guards. A bunch. Julia and Crank are here now, at least for tonight."

"They've got trouble," he said.

"Yeah. You read about it?"

"It's all over the place. It's bullshit."

"That's not the worst of it. Carrie went to see Senator Rainsley. He's not her father. But ... Dylan..." Her voice began to shake. The bathroom was beginning to steam up, and she sat on the closed toilet seat and wrapped one arm across her stomach.

"What is it, babe?"

"See, my dad found out Carrie wasn't his. Julia had ... she had a report from some testing place. It was from February 1990. And ... the next day my Mom got beat up. Like ... badly. Assaulted and raped, and the police thought it was my dad. Everyone thinks it was my dad. My sisters do."

"Yeah? It wouldn't surprise me."

She flinched. She knew Dylan and her dad had never gotten along. Her over controlling father had run a background check on Dylan when they were still in high school. She still didn't know exactly what had occurred when Dylan and her father had talked back then, and she didn't really want to know. Dad was overprotective. But he couldn't be—evil.

"Dylan, it's ... you don't understand. It was ... it was almost exactly nine months before ... before ... I was born."

She closed her eyes. She couldn't say the words, even to herself. That her mother had been *raped*. That she was the product of a rape. Unwanted. Just a ... a thing.

"Jesus, babe," Dylan muttered. "Are you serious?"

She closed her eyes. "It can't have been my dad. He would never do that."

Dylan was silent for a few seconds. Then he took a deep breath and said, "I love you, babe."

"I love you," she whispered back. "Dylan..."

"Yes?"

"When can you come home? When will it be safe?"

"I don't know," he said. "But I promise I'll be careful, and I'll take care of your sister."

"Will you stay in touch?"

"Yeah. I'll be calling from different numbers, and at random times, okay? So keep an eye out. I don't know who is after us, so we're keeping a really low profile. And I want you to be careful too. Stay in the safe house, or wherever you can that's safe."

"I will," she whispered.

"And Alex ... I need you to hear me for a second."

"I'm listening."

He exhaled slowly. Then he said, "I haven't been much good since Ray died. I know that."

Her voice cracked as she spoke. "Dylan, you don't have to—"

"Yes, I do." His interruption was forceful. But then he paused a moment and said, "I've been a disaster. I've been a lousy husband. And I haven't been honest with you."

"Dylan..." She felt her heart twist at his words.

"Stop interrupting and listen to me. The thing is ... I ... shit. I can't say it."

"You can," she said.

He groaned. Then said, almost whispering, "I've been drinking again."

"I know," she replied.

"I'll get help. I promise."

She leaned her head back against the wall, letting the steam envelop her. Then she whispered, "You know I'm proud of you. And I love you. I'm here, Dylan."

"I know. I won't screw it up anymore."

"Maybe you should consider AA like your mom?"

He sighed. "I—I can't do all that God stuff. You know that."

"Will you just think about it? You've been trying to do everything on your own, Dylan."

He didn't answer right away, but after a few seconds of silence, he said, "Yeah. Yeah, I'll think about it."

She sighed, then said, "Thank you for telling me, Dylan. You know I love you."

"And I love you," he responded. "Listen—keep watching your Facebook. I'll call or message when I can. And I want you to keep your status updated and message me so I know where you are. Okay?"

"I will. And Dylan?"

"Yeah," he said.

"I love you. No matter what. Just come home."

"I will," he said. And then he hung up the phone.

CHAPTER TWENTY-ONE
Why is he still alive?

George-Phillip. May 2. Midnight.

"**Really,** sir, I don't see how I'm going to be able to continue in this work if you cannot keep regular hours. It's past midnight. Poor Jane nearly cried herself to sleep when you didn't come home. I should tender my resignation right now."

George-Phillip sighed. Jane's nanny, Adriana Poole, stood erect in the doorway of his office, color on her cheeks, as he sagged into his chair. She was right, of course, and normally George-Phillip fought to ensure that he was home at a reasonable hour, even if it meant working late into the night after Jane was in bed.

"Miss Poole, I'm going to ask you to bear with me for a little while on this. Unfortunately we have a crisis developing."

"What crisis?" Her voice was high pitched and loud enough to be heard at Whitehall.

"Please, Miss Poole, lower your voice." His tone was urgent as he spoke. Jane's room was right down the hall, and she'd already been disturbed enough.

"The only crisis I see is a daughter missing her father."

"It seems likely I'll have a great deal more time soon enough," he said. The words escaped from his mouth before he could do anything about them.

"Whatever are you talking about, sir?"

"I just told you we have a crisis brewing. There's a possibility I'll be forced to resign. In the meantime, I've just found out I must travel to Washington in the morning, and I need you to look after Jane. You simply cannot quit now."

"You're leaving! Now? After some lunatic shot at the house just last night? I think you've lost your senses, sir."

George-Phillip groaned. He might be a Prince and a Duke and a member of the Prime Minister's Cabinet, but this twenty-four-year-old girl routinely dressed him down, and he couldn't do anything about it *because she was right.* He couldn't leave his daughter now, when she was terrified after the attack on the house.

He thought it through for five seconds, then said, "Well, you'll both have to come with me, then."

"To America?" Adriana screeched.

"Yes, to Washington, DC. I don't know how long we'll be gone—perhaps a week."

"I couldn't. I don't have anything to wear."

George-Phillip closed his eyes and took a deep breath. Then he counted slowly to ten. And then ten more, just for good measure.

When he opened his eyes, she still stood there. "Miss Poole, I'm asking you to please accompany my daughter to Washington, DC. It's urgent, and at least for the next few days, I will not be able to spare the time to find someone else. I'm begging you. It's a matter of national security. I must go."

She was silent for just a moment. Then said, "All right, then, sir. If it's a matter of national security, you should just say so. I'll get my things packed."

"We'll leave for the airport at six in the morning."

"Yes, sir."

Adriana bustled away, thank God. George-Phillip turned to his desk and sighed. He was exhausted. Not long after he had returned to his office after the meeting with the Prime Minister, the call had come in. Richard Thompson was facing indictment in the United States. The political wheels in Washington were spinning, and no one knew where they were going to end up.

George-Phillip's eyes fell to his desk. Inside, the file. He knew that if the contents of that file were to be made public, Richard Thompson's career would be over, and his wouldn't be the only one. Over the years, he'd often revisited the decision to bury what had happened, to bury it right alongside the bodies of the civilians who had died there. A generation had passed, governments had risen and fallen, the Cold War had come to an end and yet the secrets of three decades ago still lingered, poisoning the well of the present.

George-Phillip reached in his desk and took out the file. The original report of his own investigation. Interviews and documents. Records meticulously kept for three decades. He carefully slipped the file into his steel walled briefcase and secured the briefcase itself to his desk. He checked the time, then dialed O'Leary.

The phone rang only once before a curt voice said, "O'Leary, sir."

"It's C," George-Phillip said. The nickname, just the letter C, had been the traditional name for the Chief since Sir Mansfield Cumming, the first Chief of MI6, had signed his papers that way. "Any updates?"

"None, sir, but our investigators seem to think she went south. We're watching the border crossings in San Diego, among others. But if she's using cash, we might not be able to track her."

"All right, then. And Andrea Thompson?"

"Last known location was a motel in suburban Maryland, sir, just outside Washington, DC. Seems she heard something suspicious in the room next door and called the police. They found her fingerprints all over the place. Sir—the hotel was a nasty one. Prostitutes and drug dealers."

George-Phillip winced. "Keep looking," he said.

"We will, sir. I've got my best people on it."

"Good, good. I know I can trust you with this. Any leads on who attacked the Thompsons?"

"None, sir. They were professionals. I'm guessing Middle East."

"All right. I'll be on a seven am flight. Just keep me informed."

He disconnected the phone. Four more hours and he'd have to be back up and getting ready for the flight. Time to get some sleep. He stood and let his eyes fall on the window, now covered with a steel plate until the window was replaced with bullet-resistant glass. The shots had narrowly missed him last night—it was pure dumb luck he hadn't been killed. But he still didn't understand *why*. Was it the Wakhan file? Or something else entirely?

Leslie Collins. May 2.

Leslie Collins tried to remind himself to pause every day when he entered the lobby of the original headquarters building at Langley. There, against the north wall of the lobby, was the Memorial Wall. 102 stars carved in the wall, each of them representing an agent who had died in the line of duty. More than a third of those agents were unnamed—represented *only* by a star. Their names, their operations and their deaths were still a matter of national security.

Collins reminded himself once again, as he exited the building, that he had a responsibility to those 102 men and women. A responsibility to protect the integrity of the agency, to protect its secrets, to protect the nation the agency protected. Sometimes, however, meeting that responsibility required sacrifices—sacrifices that he found personally distasteful, and in some cases immoral. But one didn't just decide to do what one wanted, after all. The purpose of having government agencies, the purpose of having checks and balances, all of it was built to ensure safety and security. As a part of that system, Collins felt that sometimes you had to set aside your personal desires and beliefs.

His feet echoed off the floors of the lobby as he walked toward the front door. Even in an agency that ran 24 hours a day, 365 days a year, it was quiet in the late evening. Watch officers and other essential personnel worked late into the night, but the bulk of the agency's personnel commuted to the office just like any other government employee in Washington. He stopped at the door, looking out across the vast parking lot. He could hear crickets and frogs and God only knew what else from the woods around the two hundred fifty acres of land occupied by the agency.

He jumped a little, startled, when his cell phone rang. Only a dozen or so people had his personal phone number. The dozen included his wife, his pastor, and the President, among others.

He sighed when he saw the name on the phone.

Richard Thompson.

His car let out two loud beeps as he pressed the unlock button on his keyfob and disarmed the alarm. He answered the phone.

"This is Leslie Collins."

"Leslie. *What the hell?*"

"Richard, this is not a secure line, as I'm sure you're aware."

Richard's reply was ragged, angry. "I don't really care, Leslie. Can I make that more clear? I do not care."

Leslie sighed and opened the door of his 2014 Volvo S60. Initially Leslie had objected on political grounds to buying a European vehicle. But Meredith had driven one owned by one of her silly friends, and had convinced him to take a test drive. The handling and leather seats convinced him. He passed his old 2010 Cadillac to her and took the new car.

He always felt calm when he sat in the leather seat.

"Richard, you may not care, but I do."

"What do you know about this investigation?"

The voice automatically spilled over to the car speakers as he cranked the car. Hearing Richard Thompson's disembodied voice surrounding him was more than a little bit disturbing.

"I don't know anything about it, Richard. But I would take it seriously, if I were you."

"Bullshit you don't know anything, Leslie. You went to school with that son of a bitch, Armitage."

Rory Armitage was the special counsel investigating Thompson. He had also been Collins' college roommate. Not that it mattered.

"Armitage is just doing his job. I can't imagine where he came up with such a wild theory. *Drug money laundering?* Really? I can't imagine there's any truth to it, Richard. Unless..." Leslie's voice trailed off with a suggestive silence.

"You son of a bitch. You planted this, didn't you?"

Collins sighed. "Richard, I'm finding your wild accusations a little disconcerting. I know you are under some stress right now. Maybe you should consider taking a step back—or even seeing a therapist. I'm concerned about you."

Thompson didn't respond. The silence at the other end of the line troubled Collins. Thompson, when calm and organized, was a formidable enemy.

After a moment, Collins said, "Richard, are you there?"

"I'm here," Thompson replied. "Leslie, I want you to be careful. You don't want to mess with my life."

Collins raised an eyebrow. He put the car in reverse and backed out of his reserved parking space, then turned, heading into the darkness toward the checkpoint at the entrance to the headquarters. For just a second, his headlights illuminated three pairs of glowing eyes—deer on the edge of the parking lot, just on the other side of the fence. Sometimes they played hell with the motion sensors on the edge of the property.

He thought it was curious Thompson didn't talk about his wife or daughters. Or was he so self-absorbed and narcissistic that he didn't worry about them at all when his own position was at risk? That was kind of sad, wasn't it?

"Richard, listen, I'm driving now, I've really got to go. Let's talk next week, all right? We'll do lunch."

"I'm not *doing lunch* with someone who screwed—"

The words cut off when Leslie's hand brushed the disconnect button on his steering wheel. He waved to the guards at the gate, then pulled out onto Colonial Farm Road, headed south toward Georgetown Pike. This late, traffic should be finished and he could be home in ten minutes.

Unfortunately, the phone rang almost immediately. *Unknown number?*

There were only a few people it could be. He answered.

"Collins here."

"Leslie. How pleasant to hear your voice."

Collins involuntarily stepped on the brakes, causing the car behind him to swerve dangerously. He got himself under control and driving again almost instantly. The cultured voice on the other end was familiar. Roshan al Saud—a member of the royal house of Saudi Arabia, and director general of *al Mukhabarat*

Al A'amah—the Saudi Arabian Intelligence Agency. Educated at the best British boarding schools, Roshan gave off a polished, highly educated air which fooled everyone except those, like Collins, who had seen him torture captured Russian prisoners with a refined and frightening cruelty.

"Roshan! It is very good to hear your voice. You are well? I understand you're in the United States."

"I am, briefly. And I'd very much like to speak with you privately."

Leslie checked the time. "You're at your home?" he asked.

Roshan owned an exclusive thirty-room house less than a mile away from Leslie's.

"I am."

"I'm on my way. You caught me at the perfect time."

Collins disconnected the phone and drove. Traffic on Georgetown Pike wasn't heavy, but it wasn't especially light either. Sometimes, especially if there was rain or snow, you could get tied up here for hours. But it was warm now, a little humid, and after a long nasty winter, most Washingtonians were out relaxing instead of working.

It was fifteen minutes later when he pulled up to the gate of Prince Roshan's property. He slid down the window as the guard approached. The guard—a man in his early thirties with cold looking eyes and a thick five-o'clock shadow, stared at Collins for fifteen long seconds.

Then he said, "Mr. Collins, please pull up the driveway. You'll be met at the house."

Collins was familiar with the Saudi's routine. He'd been here as a guest many times before. As he parked the car and got out, he was startled to see that it wasn't a guard who opened the front door—it was Prince Roshan himself.

Roshan, like Collins, was no longer a young man. Roshan had once been the unofficial leader of the small group of western intelligence agents working together in Afghanistan. Collins remembered riding together in a truck to Badakhshan province, at one point hiding under the floorboards with Thompson while Prince Roshan negotiated with the Russians.

That was a long time ago. Now, Roshan was portly, with prominent, almost puffy cheeks and a salt-and-pepper beard.

For official functions, Roshan wore robes and red and white checked *keffiyeh*. But at home, he typically wore blue jeans and a t-shirt. Roshan was a traditional Saudi man only when it came to how he treated his wife and his public appearance. In private, he indulged in all the luxuries Western culture could provide.

"Leslie!" Roshan said, a genuine appearing smile gracing his face. "Come in, come in! It's been too long. How is Meredith?"

Leslie grimaced. "She's fine, Your Highness. Just fine."

"Come in. You know better than those niceties, Leslie. I won't stand for titles." As he spoke the words, Roshan rested a hand on Collins' arm, as if to emphasize the words and his affability.

"Roshan. You've always been a good friend. How is Myriam?"

Roshan led him into the house mumbling meaningless platitudes about his wife. Myriam al-Saud effectively didn't matter. Disenfranchised by the culture and law of her own country, she had less role in her husband's life than the models who shamelessly accompanied him to expensive dinners and shows at the Kennedy Center whenever he was in Washington.

Roshan poured Collins a glass of Eagle Rare Single Barrel Bourbon. Collins sniffed it, the smell of charred vanilla and old oak and leather filling his nostrils.

He took the smallest of sips, then murmured, "This is very good."

"Be my guest," Roshan said. He poured himself a drink and tossed it back, then sat in the deep leather chair across from Leslie.

"My friend, we have a problem."

"We?" Leslie replied.

"Yes. *We.* The problem has several heads, and any one of them could harm both of us, and our countries."

"Thompson," Collins said.

"Indeed. He's sinking."

"We need to make sure we don't go down with him," Collins said. "There are a lot of loose ends. I'm particularly concerned because it looks like the oldest daughter may have information about Wakhan now. They broke into his office in San Francisco. God only knows what he had in there."

Roshan frowned. "Your people are responsible for the destruction of the home?"

Collins nodded. "Not agency. Independents."

Roshan frowned and his eyes narrowed. He looked away from Collins for a moment, then looked back. "Leslie, I'm concerned you've lost your nerve. Not just attacking Thompson's family, but by doing it so—ineptly. Letting a sixteen-year-old girl get away? What were you thinking?"

"You're aware of who the girl's father is?"

"Of course. He presents no risk to us."

Collins rolled his eyes. "He's the only person outside of our circle who knows what really happened at Wakhan."

"If he knew, none of us would be in our positions."

"He *knows.*"

"What makes you think that?"

Collins closed his eyes. "He confronted me about it."

Roshan sat up straight. "*When?* And why didn't you say anything?"

"I had it contained. That was in '84."

"Why is he still alive, then?"

"Are you serious? His cousin is the Queen of England. Besides, as I said, I had it contained. He was having his tawdry little affair with Thompson's wife. We didn't have to threaten him—we threatened her. That shut him up."

Roshan shook his head. "Not good enough. What are you doing now?"

"I had a team try to get him, but they missed. We'll try again. In the meantime, Thompson is thoroughly discredited, and Prince George-Phillip will be soon. Nothing they say will matter within the week. I'd expect the President to withdraw Thompson's nomination any moment."

"Good. And the rest of them? All this violence has done nothing but attract attention."

"We're backing off. Surveillance, but that's it. We planted drugs and money in the Thompson condo, and we've registered several accounts at friendly banks in the Caymans to Thompson. The IRS will likely find those within a couple more days."

Roshan nodded. "And Windsor? Do you really believe he is contained?"

Collins thought about it. The threat of killing Adelina Thompson was no longer going to be enough to keep George-Phillip quiet. That had probably passed years ago. Which meant they were going to have to find some new way of dealing with him. Or dispensing with him.

"I don't think so," Collins said.

"Leave him to me, then," Roshan said. "I have assets which make more sense for this. You focus your efforts on discrediting Thompson."

"Agreed," Collins said.

Then he took another sip of his bourbon. It really was quite good.

California. May 2.

The campsite was bathed in red and orange light, slanting through the redwoods, as Nick Larsden drove his 2008 Hummer into the camp. He scanned the area. It was an out of the way campsite, the facilities neglected and worn. The camp office, next to the entrance, was old and the white paint was peeling. Except for the beat up rusted truck next to the office, there wasn't a single vehicle.

Nick had been working his way up the coast all day, stopping at drive-thrus, campsites and any other likely place. An adult woman and her teenage daughter in a minivan shouldn't be that hard to find, but so far, he'd not had any luck. And he was pretty sure he wasn't the only person looking. The price dangled in front of him for finding the women was high.

Nick was a former soldier turned private investigator and later bounty hunter. Mostly he worked for ridiculously low fees, chasing men who were on the run after not paying alimony, so when the call came in, he didn't question it. Especially when the caller, a stuck prig with an Irish accent, indicated he was willing to pay a significant deposit.

"Where do you want me to bring them?" he had asked.

"When you find them, contact me for instructions."

That was more than a bit unusual. Nick suspected the caller wanted the women dead or missing. That was fine, Nick supposed, though he wasn't a big fan of making war on women. But sometimes you had to do what you had to do. When it happened, though, he was going to insist on the money up front. The original price had been enough for him to retire from this business for good. Nick wanted a nice place in the mountains, paid for, where he could hunt and have his dogs and not have to worry about the stress of day-to-day bullshit.

He slid out of the cab of the Hummer. An old man approached. He was short and scrawny, almost diseased, and his clothes didn't fit. Thick glasses revealed eyes that were oddly magnified.

"You looking for a campsite or a cabin? How long you staying?" the old man asked.

"I'm looking for two women," Nick said.

He held out a sheet of paper he'd printed that morning. Two separate photos: the one of the older woman looked like it came from a newspaper, and the one of the teenager was a selfie from her Facebook page.

The old man's eyes narrowed when his eyes hit the paper. *Bingo.* He'd seen them.

"I've never seen them," the old man said.

Oh, ho. He was going to make things difficult.

"You sure, old man? They're running from the law."

The man's eyes widened a little, and he sucked in a breath nervously. No wonder he looked so poor. Nick would have bet this guy played poker—and lost his shirt every time.

"I don't know what you're talking about," the old man said.

Nick sighed. He glanced around the campsite again, just to make sure. Not a soul around.

With violence so sudden the old man never saw it coming, Nick reached out and grabbed the old man's hand and twisted it. The first bone in his wrist snapped almost instantly and the old man screamed.

"Now tell me the truth, you old fuck. Did they come through here?"

"Yes! Yes! They slept in Cabin 3 last night. Left early this morning, before sunup. The girl was drugged or something. They paid me an extra twenty dollars! Now let go!"

Nick looked at the old guy for a second and frowned. "What else can you tell me? Were they still driving a minivan?"

The old man nodded urgently. "Plates was covered in mud. I don't know where they went. Headed north, I think, they turned right out of the camp."

Nick looked around the camp one more time, still absentmindedly twisting the old man's wrist, provoking moans from the man. He didn't suppose he'd find anything in the cabin, but he should check.

"Did she show you her license or anything? You got any record?"

The old man shook his head. "No. I'm supposed to. State inspectors. But ... Gawd, *please stop! That hurts!*"

Nick sighed. "You just failed your inspection," he said.

Then he reached out with both hands, grabbing the old man by the neck, and lifted him into the air, one forearm across the man's Adam's apple. He squeezed hard, and the old man twitched several times, then sagged, already passed out. Nick kept holding him, blocking his windpipe.

"Sorry about this, man," he said.

He held the man until he was sure. No pulse. Then he dropped him to the ground and walked to Cabin 3.

The door was unlocked. The old man hadn't cleaned the cabin, of course, but he didn't see anything of use. A woman's elastic hair band. And that was it. He shrugged. At least he knew they'd been here. Headed north.

Canada? He guessed so. But the odds of catching up with them were slim indeed with the information he had.

He shook his head, eyes falling on the old man again. What a waste.

CHAPTER TWENTY-TWO
Señora? Are you all right?

Adelina. May 3.

The pothole must have been large enough to swallow up a smaller car. As it was, the back end of the bus bounced in the air with a loud thump, and Adelina felt herself bounce right out of her seat for just a second. Jessica moaned and began to slide out of her seat. Adelina reached over and tugged her eighteen-year-old daughter back into her seat like she was a toddler.

The bus was crowded, and would have been reasonably well appointed, except that the air conditioning had failed sometime not long after Jessica's birth. The heat was a physical thing, alive with motion, like an unseen reptile under the surface of a Louisiana swamp, green and obscure, thick and dangerous. The upholstery in the seats was torn, and the baby two rows up from Adelina and Jessica had cried for the entire three and a half hour ride from Tacoma.

The passengers were a mix. At least two dozen men and women Adelina judged to be migrant workers. Hispanic, poor and tired. Two rows in front of her and across the aisle, a man slept with his head thrown back in the seat, mouth open, completely ignoring the squalling baby directly across the row.

The man fascinated Adelina. He wore blue jeans, threadbare but not torn at the knees and leather work shoes which had been resoled more than once, apparently by hand. He'd likely done it himself—nowadays it was cheaper to buy a throwaway pair of shoes from Walmart, produced by near-slave labor in a third world country, than it was to have a pair of custom shoes resoled by a cobbler. The stitching along the edge of the leather sole was slightly uneven.

His sweatshirt was clean but old, the elastic near the wrists worn and loose, threads spreading apart, with deep stains in the elbows, which Adelina knew wouldn't come out no matter what he did. But it wasn't his clothes or his shoes that caught her attention. It was his craggy face, weathered, worn, his skin indistinguishable from the leather on his boots. Deep laugh lines radiated from his eyes and creases around his mouth. His mouth was open, asleep with the kind of abandon usually only seen in small children, despite the fact that the man was missing most of his teeth.

He looked not much different from her father, Juan Ramos, in the years before his death. Exhausted, yes. Tired from the weight of years of too much work and too much worry. But her father had also been content in the last years of his life. After he and her mother had separated, he'd been happy in a way she admired to this day. He laughed, he cried, and he loved life with an abandon she only wished she understood.

The man on the bus looked like that. He looked exhausted, and despite her poverty, her fear, her danger, she wanted to help him.

That was laughable. How could she help anyone now?

Closer to the front of the bus, four hikers rode together. They were in their early twenties—the two men with flannel shirts and brand new sandals, the women in color tank tops and too tight jeans. Two girls out with their boyfriends. Their backpacks took up too much space in the overhead racks, forcing everyone further back in the bus to jam their bags together, while the Birkenstock-clad college kids were largely unaware of the bus full of humanity behind them. Adelina thanked God that despite the problems her daughters had, despite the fact that they largely hated her, she'd sent them out into the world with a deep sense of caring and charity and love for the world around them.

The thought filled Adelina with a staggering sense of loss. She'd failed them in so many ways, and now she didn't even know where all of her daughters were. She'd seen the headlines. Andrea was missing along with Alexandra's husband. She'd never approved of Dylan, not until he'd made his cross-country trip to San Francisco to propose to Alexandra. But that had shown both courage and commitment, and he'd shown it even more in the way he'd supported Carrie after Ray died.

She bit back her tears and looked out the window. The bus was nearing Bellingham now, their last stop. She wasn't sure what to do from there. She had their passports, thankfully not the official diplomatic ones. In her experience, diplomatic passports did nothing to speed up travel, and often slowed them down. Because they were unusual, immigration officials everywhere tended to stop, look closer, and ask more questions.

Questions Adelina did not want to answer. When she crossed the border out of the United States, hopefully within the next twenty-four hours, she wanted it to be quick, routine, and no-nonsense. She wanted to attract no attention at all. She wanted no questions asked, until she got to the Canadian border officials.

The question was, could she make it? Despite the fact that she'd traveled to a dozen or more countries in the last thirty years, and lived across Europe, Asia and the United States, she'd never actually crossed the US borders into Canada or Mexico. Would they check her identification as she left the country? Would a routine check turn up the fact that she was missing and cause them to detain her?

She was afraid that's exactly what would happen. And if they did that, she didn't know what was likely to happen to her.

Well, she'd cross that bridge when she came to it. She craned her neck, looking off into the distance. Both sides of the highway were crowded with greenery, trees and lush bushes. Cars were passing them on both sides, the bus slowing down a little.

Her breath caught a little when the bus changed lanes to the far right, then slowed even further, the loud diesel engine decelerating with a whining sound. The bus slowed even further, then came to a stop. She craned her neck around, but couldn't see through the back—no windows, and the angle didn't allow for a decent view.

The heat inside the bus was oppressive, the smell of sweaty men filling the space.

Adelina forced herself not to panic when two men in dark green uniforms walked up along the side of the bus. They wore green Smokey the Bear hats and short sleeve uniforms with a bright yellow patch on one side. Customs and Border Control.

She swallowed. How could they have been found? She'd paid cash for their tickets and hadn't used her debit cards since leaving San Francisco. She hadn't shown identification to anyone since leaving San Francisco either.

The two men stepped aboard the bus, just as two more agents appeared, one of them female. The two who boarded the bus were a study in contrasts. The first, a tall man who obviously struggled with his own addictions. Balding, red faced, with a belly that cruised over the top of his belt much the way the bulbous prow of an oil tanker extended over the water, he looked uncomfortable and hot, with a sheen of sweat reflecting the outside sunlight.

His darker haired partner was shorter, more compact and far more muscular, with sculpted magazine quality biceps underneath a perfectly tailored uniform. Hispanic, he looked Puerto Rican or possibly Dominican, with dark skin and a thick carpet of hair. He reminded her of an older version of Eddie Vasquez, the college student and EMT who had been pursuing Sarah ever since the accident last year.

The shiny faced one called out in a voice intended to be authoritative but in fact just sounded hoarse. "All right, everyone please have your identification ready to examine. This is a routine stop, we're from Customs and Border Protection."

A series of curses ran through Adelina's mind even as Jessica stirred beside her. What would she do? What would they do? She was sure they were looking for her. Why else would the Border Patrol pull over the bus?

Why had she thrown away her phone? If she could have called someone—Carrie, or Julia, then at least they'd know her fate. Then she'd be far less likely to simply *disappear.* But it was gone, and there was nothing she could do about that.

The shorter Border Patrol officer repeated his partner's words in badly accented and translated Spanish. He might look at home in San Juan, but English was clearly his first language. Interesting he was the one doing the translating. It must be like being typecast as an actor.

The two agents had already stopped, dealing with the four Patagonia and Birkenstock-clad hikers with their manicured nails and three hundred dollar backpacks. One of the women, a petite blonde twenty-year-old in a Whitman College sweatshirt, was exclaiming out loud to everyone who could hear that *she was white.*

The shorter Border Patrol agent looked irritated and the woman's friends looked appalled. Adelina just shrank into her seat. She wanted this to be over as quickly as possible.

That didn't seem likely. The short agent had lost his patience. "Lady, either give me your ID right now, or you can do it at the station."

"I don't have to give you *anything.* I'm an American citizen, and I know my rights. I don't understand why you don't check out *him!*" As she said the words, she pointed directly at the old man two rows in front of Adelina, now awake and serenely watching the Border Patrol. Adelina could see a U.S. passport neatly resting in his hands.

"Crazy bitch," the taller agent muttered. He wiped a handkerchief across his forehead, then said, "I'm asking you a simple question. Are you an American citizen? Show me your ID. "

"My head," Jessica murmured. She squinted, looking up to the front of the car, and muttered, "Can't they be quieter?"

Chaos erupted. One of the two boys jerked to his feet for all of one half second. He immediately found the front of his shirt bunched up in the fist of the smaller Border Patrol agent.

"*Sit down!*" snarled the agent.

The bus driver leaned his head against the steering wheel, apparently giving up on going anywhere any time soon. The blonde girl shrank into her seat, suddenly realizing how serious this was. She was shaking and began to fumble in her purse.

"It's right here," she said in an unsteady voice.

"Yeah, lady, it's too late for that," one of the agents said. "Stand up, and step off the bus."

Slowly, the woman stood, her face serious. She stepped off the bus, and the two agents on the outside escorted her out of sight.

"Jesus," Jessica muttered. "What a stupid bitch."

"*Jessica*," Adelina said, "I don't care how—misguided—that girl was. You don't need to use that kind of language."

Jessica started to tense and give her a scornful look—then looked down at her lap. "Sorry," she said. As if she'd suddenly remembered something.

The two agents were now systematically—and uneventfully—walking down the aisle. Examining passports and driver's licenses. Adelina watched as the agents made their way down the aisle. The legality of what they were doing was actually questionable. But that was beside the point. They were doing it, and she didn't have any choice but to comply.

The agents had reached the seats two rows in front of her and Jessica. On the left side, the old man. He smiled pleasantly and handed over his passport to the taller, sweaty agent. It looked worn, well used. The agent looked through it, eyes examining the photo, then looked back up at the old man.

"You're a U.S. citizen?"

"I am," the old man said.

"Where are you traveling to?"

Adelina knew well that the man didn't have to answer that. But he did. "My granddaughter lives in Bellingham. She's going to give birth to my first great-grandchild soon enough."

The sweaty agent wiped his forehead again, then said in a sour voice, "Congratulations." He thrust the passport back at the old man, and moved to the next row.

The shorter agent had moved past the couple with their crying baby, and was now only a foot and a half from Adelina.

In the row directly in front of her were two men, African-American, and both showed their driver's licenses.

"You're a U.S. citizen?" asked the agent.

"Yes, sir," both answered.

Adelina's tongue and cheeks were stiff, her neck aching. She had a hard time focusing as the agent asked more questions of the two men in front of her. Her heart was beating too fast, and a numb, tingly feeling began to expand from the tip of her tongue.

The sweaty agent was now at her row, talking to the two women directly across the aisle from Adelina.

"Mom," Jessica said.

Adelina was frozen, her mind turned inward to that cold February night a couple of months before her seventeenth birthday, when Richard Thompson had raped her. To the emotional torture he'd subjected her to. The psychological games. The one time he'd really beaten her, after he learned Carrie wasn't his.

She'd tried to love her daughters. But it was hard. Four of them, *his*. Four of them the product of rape and lust.

She looked at her wrists, and thought of Julia, who had once attempted suicide. Adelina would die before she went back. The pain in her chest was tighter and tighter. Cutting.

"*Mom,*" Jessica hissed.

"Señora? Are you all right?"

Startled, she looked up. The shorter agent—the Hispanic one—stood in front of her. She didn't know how long the fear had paralyzed her. She didn't know how long the panic attack had gripped her.

"Sorry," she muttered. She reached in her purse and handed over her passport. Then immediately froze in terror. *She'd handed over the wrong passport.*

As the wife of a senior U.S. diplomat (and now Cabinet member) she carried two passports: one, her personal one, the other, her official diplomatic passport.

Her eyes, wide now, jerked to Jessica, who also sat frozen, arm extended, holding out her personal passport for the agent.

"You're a U.S. citizen?"

"Yes," Adelina croaked.

He looked at her passport. "Birthplace is Calella in Spain? Where exactly is that?"

"It's on the Mediterranean," she said. She coughed.

"You all right, ma'am?"

"The bus is hot, I just need a drink of water."

Jessica chimed in, "We're on a day trip and decided to take the bus instead of drive. Boy, was that a mistake."

The man gave Jessica an odd look, then his eyes went back to Adelina. He casually held up the passport. "Hey Perkins, you ever see one of these? Diplomatic passport."

The taller agent, an irritated expression on his face, shook his head. "We don't have time for that, Alvarez. If she's a citizen, move on. *Christ*, this bus is hot."

The shorter agent—Alvarez—chuckled, then handed the passport back to her. He looked at Jessica. "You two be careful. And get your Mom some water, she doesn't look good."

Both agents moved on to the next row, and Adelina sagged into her seat.

CHAPTER TWENTY-THREE
You Don't Understand

Carrie. May 3.

"I don't understand," Carrie said. "You're saying we're losing the safe house? The protective detail?"

Bear's jaw worked as he looked away from her. Teeth nearly clenched, he said, "It's out of my hands, Carrie. The entire investigation is being turned over to the special prosecutor and the IRS. I was ordered to stand down—in fact, I've been placed on administrative leave."

Carrie frowned. She didn't pretend to know the intricacies of government investigations and jurisdiction. But given that the IRS was investigating the family—and not the people who had attacked them—none of this seemed good.

"So when do we have to be out?" she asked.

"This morning," he said, his voice low.

Carrie sighed. Then she turned away from Bear and sank into her chair.

Julia, still sitting on the couch next to Crank, said, "We'll need to rent a suite, I think. The most secure hotel we can find, and we'll hire bodyguards."

Carrie shook her head. "Your accounts have been frozen, Julia."

"Only the business ones. My personal account's still accessible. It's enough to last a little while."

"Why are you placed on leave?" Sarah's voice, from the doorway, was aggressive, pitched a little loud and monotone.

Bear looked across the room at her. Then he said, "I was up late last night reviewing files related to your case, when the call came about the attack. Unfortunately I left the file out on my kitchen table—and someone broke into my apartment while I was out. The files are gone."

Carrie frowned and met Julia's eyes. Then she looked back at Bear.

"What was in the file?"

"Your father's State Department personnel file."

Sarah muttered something under her breath. Carrie couldn't hear it exactly, but it sounded suspiciously like *motherfucker.*

"So what do we do now?" Carrie asked.

"I want you to meet Anthony Walker," Julia said to Carrie. "I think he can help."

"The reporter?" Bear said. "That's a bad idea."

"I disagree," Julia said. "It's not like the government is helping us. Somebody is trying to destroy our family. We don't have time to screw around."

Carrie stared at Julia aghast. She'd spent more than a year avoiding reporters, ever since the calls started coming in when charges were filed against Ray. They'd been hounded by the media, caricatured, and it hadn't stopped after Ray's murder.

"I don't know," Carrie murmured.

Julia leaned forward and took her hands. "Listen—I know you don't want to, and I know why. I've been dealing with the press for years, I get it. But I'm telling you—this guy's straight up. And if anyone can get to the bottom of it, he can."

"This is a bad idea," Bear said.

"I don't know if I can trust a reporter," Carrie said.

"Look. Let's meet with him. If you decide you don't trust him, we don't have to talk with him anymore."

Carrie sighed. Her mind kept going back to Ronald Lafferty, the reporter from the *New York Post*. He'd harassed Ray for weeks, then shown up at the hospital during their three-day vigil after the accident.

Lafferty had penned a front page poison article attacking her and Ray less than a week after Ray's death. All so he could get his damn story. The story was filled with lies and innuendo with lots of descriptive detail, but little or no truth. Julia had offered to sue, and briefly tangled with the lawyers at the *Post*, but it didn't go to court.

Carrie sighed. "I'll talk with him. But I'm skeptical."

Bear frowned. Then he said, "It's your call, I can't stop you. But I think you're making a mistake. You can't trust some reporter."

"Can we trust you?" Carrie asked.

Bear flushed. "That's your call, too, now, isn't it? I'll tell you this much: I want to know who shot the mother of my children. You can cooperate or not, but I'm on this case until they shoot me."

Carrie turned to Julia, then to Alexandra, sitting quietly by herself. Alexandra gave a minute nod. Carrie nodded.

"All right. I'll meet with him. Bear—will you sit in on that too? We need all the help we can get."

George-Phillip. May 3.

Wouldn't it be wonderful, just once, to do something without fourteen layers of scrutiny?

The thought ran through George-Phillip's mind as he looked over the statement the flight attendant handed him, detailing the extensive charges either he, or the agency, or possibly the royal travel budget, would have to pick up for this flight. Ninety-two thousand pounds sterling for the roundtrip to Washington and back.

It seemed odd to him that Cabinet members—and, for that matter, members of the royal family, other than Her Majesty—often flew scheduled commercial flights. But increasingly the split personality of the British public meant restricted public resources. While the Queen always flew charter jets, or the shorter range jets of the 32nd Squadron of the Royal Air Force, all such flights came from the travel budget, which was limited.

The rest of the family typically flew commercial, except for special circumstances. Prince Charles had seen that such circumstances were increasingly rare, after his *six-hundred thousand pound* roundtrip to South America had caused significant public scandal. And that trip for an environmental jaunt—irony indeed. Now, as a result, George-Phillip had to figure out how in hell he was going to possibly *personally* pay for a charter flight across the Atlantic, which was required for official business.

Whatever. Let the newspapers bray. He wasn't flying his daughter commercial—not two days after an assassination attempt—and he wasn't leaving her alone in London.

Right now, Jane was asleep, stretched across the row of seats across from George-Phillip. Her nanny, Adriana, was in the row across from her, reading a paperback novel with two cupcakes on the cover. She'd been wide eyed, watching out the windows as the flight took off four hours before, and silent since then. Jane, on the other hand, had taken to her first flight as if it were her twentieth. She'd barely paid attention as the flight took to the air, instead keeping her nose buried in *Discovery Box*, her favorite periodical. That was actually fairly typical for Jane—she would appear to not pay any attention at all to new experiences, until the next day. Tomorrow, she'd be able to talk about nothing else.

That tendency worried him. Because on the way to the airport this morning, she'd talked and talked and talked about waking up to the sound of gunshots two night earlier.

For the first time in the thirty years of his career, George-Phillip was considering retiring. Jane had already lost her mother.

For just a second, George-Phillip felt a lump of unhappiness. He'd lost the love of his life years ago. Then he'd married a good woman, a kind woman, a woman who he'd imagined spending the rest of his life with. But their marriage had lasted just three years.

He closed his eyes and gritted his teeth. He didn't have time for such nonsense.

Opening his eyes, George-Phillip flagged down the flight attendant. "Bring me a Pimm's iced tea, please, and a telephone."

"Yes, sir."

The phone came quicker than the drink, which was unfortunate. But he would have to settle for what he could. He leaned toward the window, looking out at the glare. Far below were the clouds, and below that, ocean in all directions. He looked back toward his daughter and his decision was made. When this crisis with the Thompson family was over, he was resigning from the government. He'd given thirty years of his life to the Queen. The remainder would belong to Jane.

Lifting the phone to his ear, he dialed.

"Aye," said the gruff voice of Oswald O'Leary.

"It's C," said George-Phillip. "Any updates?"

"Yes, sir, I do. One of our agents in California has a lead on Mrs. Thompson, sir. I'm told she's running south toward Mexico, and fast."

Damn it, George-Phillip thought. He'd have some influence if she were able to get to the Canadian border. Trying to cross into Mexico, however, would be hazardous. Security on the American border with Mexico was far more aggressive than the Canadian border—not to mention the dangers of drug wars and corruption, which had rocked the northern cities of Mexico in recent years. What was she thinking?

He sighed. He hadn't actually seen or spoken with her, other than a few short words, in sixteen years, and even then she'd changed a lot, twisted by anxiety and fear.

For the hundred-millionth time, George-Phillip found himself wishing Richard Thompson were dead.

"All right. Keep tracking her. I don't even know who all is after her at this point, but I want Adelina Thompson and her daughters protected."

"Aye, sir. I'll do the best I can."

They disconnected, and George-Phillip looked out the window at the clouds below. O'Leary would be on a flight to Washington the next day, but his role had become so important that George-Phillip insisted they take separate flights so one of them was on the ground at all times.

His affair with Adelina had been doomed from the beginning. He remembered those intense months in 1984 so clearly. She'd been terrified of Richard—terrified he would hurt her, even more terrified that she would lose Julia if they separated. They'd had the conversation too many times to count.

You should leave him.

I can't. You don't understand.

But he did. He understood she was terrified. But sometimes he wondered if her fear was warranted, or if it was all in her head.

He had stopped wondering after his investigation of Wakhan began to make real progress.

George-Phillip shook his head as he looked out at the clouds and the ocean far below. That had been the one and only time he'd ever broken the classification rules. In fact he'd violated the Official Secrets Act and every principle of his profession.

It had been an early-March day and the sun was dazzling over Washington, DC. Adelina had gotten away with an excuse of a nonexistent bridge game with equally nonexistent church friends. Instead, they met at an overlook high over the Potomac River on the George Washington Parkway. There, surrounded by forest overlooking Washington, DC, they could talk in private even as cars raced by on the parkway behind them.

"Before we go any further, there's something you must know," he had said.

"Are we going further?" she asked, raising one achingly beautiful eyebrow.

He said, "Regardless. You need to know that while my interest in you is purely personal, I do have a *professional* interest in your husband."

"Don't call him that. Not in private. Publicly he may be my husband, but privately, he is my jailor. My rapist. Don't you *ever* call him a husband."

George-Phillip had sighed. "Nevertheless, he is my target."

Her eyes widened. "Are you saying that you started seeing me in order to get to him?"

George-Phillip shook his head. "No. The two things happened independently of each other. But the bottom line is, something terrible happened in Afghanistan last year, and I believe Richard was involved in it."

"Nothing he did would surprise me."

"Did you expect him back from his tour so soon?"

She shook her head. "No, in fact, he originally said he would be in Pakistan for three years, and that I could expect to see him only occasionally for vacations." Her mouth curled into a bitter smile. "I'd looked forward to having him gone. But it turned out to be less than two years."

"When did you learn he would be coming back to the United States?"

"He called in mid-December to let me know he wouldn't be taking leave for Christmas. And that I needed to have the house packed and ready to move to Washington by the end of January."

George-Phillip had felt his heart sink then. The massacre in Badakhshan province had taken place on December 12. There was no question—someone at the U.S. State Department, or more likely the CIA, had ordered Thompson out of there following the massacre.

"Does that change anything?" Adelina asked him.

"Nothing could change what is between us," he had said. And he meant it. But it turned out to not be true. The next few weeks had been the most intense in his life. Was the affair sweetened by the fact that it was forbidden? He didn't know for sure. But he did know that in the nearly thirty years since then, he'd experienced nothing so emotionally intense as those weeks in the Spring of 1984 when he fell in love with Adelina.

Thirty years may have passed, but the intensity of the emotion never faded—it merely became a dull ache, one that was occasionally improved and even appeared to be in complete remission, but always returned. That was partly because he'd never known why it ended. The end came suddenly, without warning, and without explanation. On an afternoon in late May 1984, he'd called her and she didn't call back. Not that day, or the next.

Up until that point they hadn't gone more than a day without talking. George-Phillip worried, but didn't panic. Until the next day, when she didn't return his call for the third day in a row.

On the fourth day, George-Phillip was recalled to London for several days of meetings as a result of his report on the Wakhan massacre, and it was two weeks before he returned to Washington.

Two weeks during which she'd neither answered the phone nor returned his calls.

Frantic upon his return to the United States, George-Phillip rented a car and drove directly from National Airport to the Thompson condominium in Bethesda.

It was hellishly risky. But after three weeks without a response, he'd thought nothing but the worst. Was she dead? Had Richard finally done away with her? On his arrival at the building, he walked past the concierge as if he belonged there and stepped into the elevator and pressed the button for the penthouse.

Sixty seconds later he was knocking on the door of the condo in unison with the beating of his heart. He felt his pulse in his neck as he waited. The pulse in his neck pounded harder with each second.

An unfamiliar woman opened the door—not Jenny Sullivan, Julia's nanny. This woman was young—probably eighteen or nineteen, with long blonde hair.

"Can I help you?"

George-Phillip had coughed and said, "Is Mrs. Thompson in?"

The woman at the door said, "Wait right here." Then closed the door in his face.

He cooled his heels in the hallway. Ten seconds. Twenty. Thirty.

Finally Adelina opened the door. A ridge of tension ran down the center of her forehead like a furrow through the plowed field, the strain evident in her posture and in the flash of her eyes.

"What are you doing here?" she hissed.

"I just returned from London, and since you aren't returning my calls, I felt it necessary to come in person."

"I'm not returning your calls because I don't want to talk with you."

"Why?"

She rolled her eyes. She *rolled her eyes.* He'd spent weeks feeling shut out, frustrated. Concerned about her safety. Wondering if she was even alive. He'd felt … angry. Afraid. Worried. And she rolled her eyes?

His face must have shown some of what he was thinking, because she stepped away from him, her face suddenly closed and wary.

"*Why?*" he asked. "Did I offend you somehow? Did I hurt you? Did *your husband* suddenly become the man of your dreams?"

Adelina's response was instantaneous; a loud ringing slap that stung his face. "How dare you?" she asked. "You know what he did to me."

George-Phillip staggered back. "And I know what you've done to me, Adelina. You've broken my heart."

"I never want to see you again," she said.

He closed his eyes, forcing himself to contain the overwhelming pain her statement brought on. "I don't understand you, Adelina."

She sobbed. "Please, George. Just go. Leave me."

She stepped back inside and closed the door. Twelve years would pass before he saw Adelina Thompson again.

CHAPTER TWENTY-FOUR
The Most Important Weapon

Alexandra. May 3.

"**Excuse** me a moment," Alexandra said, stepping away from her sisters. They had just arrived at the Crowne Plaza in Arlington, where Julia had rented a suite.

"Hey," Carrie said, catching her eyes. "You okay?"

"Yeah," Alexandra replied. "I'm good."

She stepped into the bedroom at the end of the hall and dropped her bag on the bed, then took out her phone, urgently checking to see if he'd contacted her. Nothing from Dylan, but she had a friend request on Facebook from a Sherman Roberts. The name tore at her heart. Roberts and Sherman were Dylan's two best friends from the Army—both of them dead now.

She accepted the request then checked her messages.

His was obscure.

SHERMAN ROBERTS: Hey you. I was browsing profiles and saw yours and thought we should get to know each other. If you get my message, let me know.

She wondered if he was online right then. Maybe? She tapped in her response:

ALEXANDRA PARIS: Hi there. I don't usually talk to strangers.

His response was immediate. Her phone rang, but there was no caller ID. She scrambled to answer it.

"Dylan?"

"Hey, babe. Where are you?"

"We've moved to the Crowne Plaza in Arlington, Virginia. The DSS isn't giving us protection anymore."

"Son of a bitch, are you serious? Why not?"

"They're not in charge of the investigation anymore. It sounds like that's the Justice Department and IRS. They're after my father. But Julia's working on hiring private security."

Silence at the other end of the line. Breathing. Finally, Dylan said, "I want you to make sure you've got a retreat. Fire escape. Anything. Make sure you've got a way out. And you need to buy a gun."

"Dylan, I've never fired a gun—"

"Alex. These people are serious."

She closed her eyes. Less than forty-eight hours before he'd killed two armed attackers while protecting her sister.

"Okay. Okay. I hear you, Dylan."

"Me and Sherman taught you how to protect yourself in a fight. What's the most important weapon you have?"

Jesus Christ, she thought. His voice was intense. "My brain," she whispered.

"That's right. You have to stay one step ahead. What's the plan from here?"

"We're meeting with Bear in a little while, and some guy from the Washington Post who Julia knows. She says she thinks he might be able to help us. Right now we need information."

"Right. We especially need to know who Carrie and Andrea's father is."

Alexandra sniffed. "Yes. You're right."

"I'm tossing this SIM card when we're finished talking. But I'll keep watching the Facebook account. Drop me a message and I'll call within a couple of hours. All right?"

"Dylan..." she said.

"Yeah?"

"Be careful."

"I will," he replied. His voice was sober. "I love you."

Julia. May 3.

The hotel telephone was loud and jarring, unsettling in a world where 99 percent of phone calls had a pleasing ring tone. Julia stood and walked to the phone and lifted it to her ear.

"Hello?"

"Mrs. Wilson?"

"Speaking," Julia said.

"There's a Mr. Anthony Walker here to see you."

"Send him up, please."

She hung up the phone and glanced over at Crank, who stood at the bar mixing a drink. "Fix me one, please?" she asked.

"Strong?"

"Yes. Better make it a double. What about you?" she asked Bear, who was standing in the corner sending an email on his phone.

"No, thanks," Bear said absently.

Carrie was lying on the couch nearby, her face exhausted, and Rachel stretched out across her chest asleep. The baby's eyes were closed, her tiny hands curled into fists.

Crank held out the glass to her, a vodka tonic. She sipped it, sighing in relief. Sarah was on the balcony, headset in her ears, her head moving as she listened to music. Alexandra had disappeared to her room the moment they'd arrived in the suite.

A knock on the door. Julia set her drink down as Crank opened it. He put a finger to his lips and whispered, "Quiet. Baby's sleeping."

Anthony practically tiptoed in, his eyes falling on Carrie and Rachel. Carrie didn't open her eyes, but said in an even voice, "It's fine as long as you don't shout. Forgive me for not getting up and introducing myself. I'm a mattress right now. An exhausted mattress. My name's Carrie Sherman."

"Anthony Walker," he replied in a bemused voice. His lips were curled up in a slight smile, and his eyes scanned Carrie longer than Julia was comfortable.

Intensely protective of her younger sister, Julia's eyes narrowed. "Anthony's a *journalist,*" she said, in a none-too-friendly tone of voice.

Anthony raised his eyebrows. "I am. By the way, I've got a question for you. I know you guys ruled out Senator Rainsley. But—odd question, but the dates line up. And so do some other things. Do you remember George-Phillip Windsor?"

"Who?" Carrie said.

Anthony passed his phone to Julia, who stood to take it. A sudden squeeze in her chest hit when she looked at the photo.

Anthony said, "You recognize him."

In a higher pitched voice than she expected, Julia said, "That's George Lansing. He worked for the British embassy when we were in China. My mother—she had an affair with him."

"Let me see," Carrie said. "I never knew what he looked like."

Julia handed the phone to Carrie, realizing that the resemblance was too clear. "It's obvious now, but I never saw it before. That was a long time ago, and I had a lot going on."

Carrie's eyes widened when she saw the picture. Her hands started to shake, and she said, "I know him. He spoke at my graduation. And ... and ... he's the guy from the pictures. From Spain. I think."

"I don't know who George Lansing is," Anthony said. "Unless that was just the name your mother told you."

"Wait," Julia said. "You said—"

"I said George-Phillip Windsor. As in, Prince George-Phillip. He's like a second or third cousin or something to the Queen of England. *And* the head of the Special Intelligence Service."

Carrie let out a loud cough. "I'm sorry, but *what?*" The baby stirred, but Carrie shifted anyway, sitting up and trying to settle Rachel in her lap. "Are you saying *he's* my father? That my father is some … somehow connected to the British royals? I *know* him—he gave the commencement address at Columbia when I graduated. I shook his hand."

Anthony said, "I don't think there's proof."

"Well," Julia said. "Tell us what you have."

Alexandra, standing in the door of the suite, said, "Yes. Tell us." Her face looked stunned, and she walked forward, facing Anthony.

Anthony looked back and forth between the sisters and Crank. "Okay. Here's what I know. The timing is right. I think they met sometime in the spring of 1984. George-Phillip was a junior diplomat at the British Embassy. I don't know where they met, but we can place them in a restaurant together in late February, 1984. In fact, you were there too, Julia."

Julia felt as if she'd been punched. "I was *there?* How do you know?"

"A gossip columnist spotted your mother and George-Phillip and wrote about it."

Julia felt her stomach churn. "A gossip columnist? Anyone I know?"

"Yeah," Anthony said, his voice apologetic. "It was Maria Clawson. From what I hear—and this is all hearsay—she dated George-Phillip briefly. Before he met your mother. And—well—she didn't take his rejection well at all."

"Jesus," Crank muttered. "That gossipy bitch smeared Julia all to hell twenty years later. What the hell?"

Julia took Crank's hand and squeezed it. "She's out of business now."

Maria Clawson was out of business only because Julia had personally funded a lawsuit against her. A nineteen-year-old college student had been raped by a popular football player on campus at the University of Alabama, and when she went public, the media came out swinging, Maria Clawson in the lead, smearing the girl. The girl won her lawsuit and a settlement big enough to permanently shut down Clawson.

"So I ate at a restaurant with this guy. Where did they meet?"

Anthony shrugged. "No idea."

"I can probably answer that," Bear said. He'd been quiet up until that moment, but Julia looked at him now. "In your father's State Department personnel file, we've got a photo of your parents along with George-Phillip. It was taken in the condo you live in now, in February 1984."

Carrie shook her head as she rocked Rachel back and forth. "The timing's right. I was born the next January."

"Right," Anthony said. "And then George-Phillip was in China for a year, from May '96 to May '97."

Julia closed her eyes. "That's the year I was—falling apart."

"The twins were born in April '96," Carrie said.

"And Andrea in June '97, which means she could easily be his daughter. Both of you could be."

Julia met Carrie's eyes. Carrie shrugged, her expression empty of emotion.

"I don't know what to think," she said.

"So Mom had an affair with some British prince who blew in and charmed her," Alexandra said sarcastically.

"I think it's crazy she stayed married, considering what happened," Carrie said.

"What exactly happened?" Alexandra asked. "He wasn't convicted of anything. He was *suspected*. They didn't arrest him. They dropped the charge."

"Yes, Alex," Carrie said. "Because he was a rich diplomat. You think he would have stayed out of jail if it hadn't been for that?"

"I am *not* the child of a rape," Alexandra shouted.

The baby started to stir, a rough cry slipping out. Alexandra covered her mouth.

"If I read her diary correctly," Julia said, "you are. And so am I."

"What about the twins?" Alexandra said. "You think they are too? Or is there some other affair waiting in the wings?"

Julia leaned forward, resting her head in her hands for just a second. Then she got up and walked over to Alexandra and faced her. Alexandra looked scared, her eyes an open window into confusion and shock.

"Alexandra, this is a shock to all of us. And we don't know the answers to a lot of this. But—just—right now, try to keep an open mind, okay? We're here for you. Whatever happened with our parents, we know who *we* are. We know what we've been through together. Okay?"

Alexandra took a deep breath. She nodded, silently. "All right," she whispered. "Sorry."

"It's okay," Julia soothed. "It's okay."

No one else spoke for a minute. Then Julia took Alexandra's hand and led her to the couch and sat down.

"Okay," Julia said. "So we have this Prince George-Phillip and my mother meeting in early '84. And we think he's likely to be Carrie and Andrea's father. We know they were together at least twice in '84, and I remember seeing him in Beijing."

"And he looks just like the mystery guy in my photo album. *And* he showed up at my graduation."

Anthony looked confused, and Julia said, "What mystery guy?"

Carrie sighed. "When I went to Spain with Andrea in 2002, there was a guy in two different photos—one on the beach and one in the town square. He's standing off to the side watching us, and neither picture was focused very well. But he looks a lot like your George-Phillip. I guess the deciding thing is height—is George-Phillip tall?"

"Really tall," Carrie said.

Anthony nodded. "Six-six maybe. Gangly. Hair and eyes like yours, but he's got these huge bushy eyebrows. Be grateful you didn't inherit those." The last words were said with a subdued grin.

Carrie laughed, a short, bark-like laugh. "I suppose. Now the question is, how do we get in to meet George-Phillip?"

"You don't," Anthony said. "He's the head of the British Intelligence Agency. It would be like asking for an appointment with the director of the CIA."

"Or the Secretary of Defense?" Carrie challenged.

"Hmm—good point. Except you don't have those kinds of connections in the British government. Do you?"

Oh, shit, Julia thought. For the first time in this discussion, she wanted to run. She wanted to just get up and walk out. Because *she* did have those kinds of connections in the British government. Or at least one.

Harry Easton.

Harry had been her first love, if you could call it that. Nineteen years old, a fourth year at the International School of Beijing when she started there at fourteen. He'd swept her off her feet. He'd treated her like dirt, pressured her into sex way too early, got her pregnant then dumped her. He'd ruined her life, at least for her high school and early college years.

He was currently the Deputy Head of Mission at the UK Embassy in Washington.

Julia only knew about that because of an article in the *Post* three weeks before, detailing the implementation of the latest trade agreement between Britain and the United States. Harry had been quoted in the article.

She sighed out loud, then said, "I know someone at the Embassy."

For the first time since he handed Julia her drink, Crank spoke up. "Fuck, no."

"Crank, it's necessary—"

"No. We'll find another way. He screwed you up way too much. I won't have you going to him asking for a favor."

Bear interceded. "What are we talking about here?"

Carrie sat up, clutching Rachel to her. "Julia, no. I can find another way."

Alexandra looked baffled, and Anthony's eyebrows drew together as he put together the story. "You aren't talking about—"

Julia spoke in a loud, sharp tone. Not a shout, but loud enough to cut through the sudden chaos. "Everybody be quiet! *I'll* be the one to decide who I talk with."

Silence from the others.

She took a steadying breath and said, "All of that happened almost twenty years ago. I'm going to go make the call." She stood, and Crank rose with her.

"Crank—I need to be alone, all right? *Please?*" She looked in Crank's eyes, trying to communicate through that gaze how much confusion and discomfort she felt. She needed to do this alone. She needed to process this call by herself, and not have to talk about it in front of other people.

He gave a minute nod. He understood.

She was ashamed of the sudden relief that flooded through her. So she leaned forward and kissed him on the corner of his mouth, then walked away from the group and into the bedroom, closing the door behind her.

She sat down on the bed and closed her eyes, puzzling through the feelings that flooded through her.

She was a grown woman in her early thirties. She ran a multi-million dollar corporation, moving hundreds of people all over the globe. She was competent, skilled, and in command of her own life.

But inside, part of her was still that desperately lonely fourteen-year-old girl who was abandoned emotionally by her parents, who'd gotten involved with a much older boy who took advantage of her loneliness and insecurity. Some days, even though she'd met the love of her life, she still woke up with a gaping pit of need that could never be filled. Even after twelve years with Crank, she still sometimes looked at him like he was a stranger. Not because of him, but because deep inside, she couldn't trust, couldn't open up, couldn't reveal the terrified little girl inside.

She didn't want to make this phone call.

So she unlocked her phone and dialed 411. An automated voice asked her for the listing she wanted. "Washington, DC. The Embassy of the United Kingdom."

A toneless voice, a computer, which had no understanding of the emotional weight of its words, said, "Stay on the line to be connected."

Two clicks, and then a ring. Another ring. She felt queasy and wrapped her left arm across her stomach. A third ring, then a pleasant female voice answered.

"Embassy of Great Britain. How may I help you?"

Julia cleared her throat. Then said in a voice far too tentative for her liking, "Harry Easton, please."

"May I ask who is calling?"

"Please tell him it's Julia Wil—Julia Thompson. He'll remember me from the International School of Beijing."

"Yes, ma'am, please hold."

Julia cleared her voice again. She would *not* let her voice shake when she was speaking with Harry.

Then his voice. The same melodious voice which had once whispered in her ear, *That wasn't so bad, was it?* Only now he sounded tentative and uncomfortable. "Julia."

She cleared her throat, suddenly choked with anxiety. She couldn't force any words out.

"Hello? Julia?"

Get. A. Grip. She clenched a fist and said, "Harry. Hello."

"I was ... surprised ... to hear it was you." His voice sounded oddly tentative. "I've seen the news about your family—I'm sorry to hear you've had such tragedies."

Julia reminded herself that Harry Easton had no power over her now, unless it was power *she* gave him. And she wasn't going to do that anymore. Not after all these years.

"Honestly," she replied, "I didn't expect to be calling you. But I'm finding myself in need of a favor. And you're the person in a position to assist."

She heard him take a deep breath. He waited a moment, as if he couldn't find the right words to say. Then he responded in a low, sober tone, "If there is anything in my power, I will. I owe you that much, certainly."

Prepared for—arrogance, or anger, or contempt—Julia hadn't expected that tone of voice or those words. She flinched.

"I—" she started to speak, but cut herself off.

"Listen, Julia..."

"No," she responded. "You don't need—"

"I do," he said. "I ... I've carried regret for many years for the way I treated you. I was so terribly wrong."

Julia wanted to scream with rage. She wanted to throw her phone across the room. She wanted to shout at him, or scream, or do anything she could to throw the words back at him, to not have to hear the remorse and sorrow in his voice. *He didn't get to be sad about what he'd done. He didn't get to ask for forgiveness.*

She shook. But she didn't say anything. Finally Harry spoke again.

"Julia, I'd never dare or presume to ask for your forgiveness. But all the same, I hope one day you'll offer it. I'm deeply sorry. I'd do anything to change it."

All of it flooded back. All of it. The shame and fear and sadness. The horror of walking through the halls of high school her senior year, with the words *slut, whore* whispered around her. The awful photo. The crushing shame, and the sharp pain in her wrist when she sliced it open.

She'd thought that she had left it behind. She'd thought that it didn't affect her anymore—that her career and her life with Crank had robbed those experiences of their power to make her hurt. But she hadn't. She hadn't healed, she hadn't walked away from it, and some of it still had the power to drag her right back.

But now she had a choice. Now she had a choice to move on and grow up and live her own life. It was the choice she'd made every day for the last twelve years, and the choice she was going to keep making.

There was no choice really. Not if she wanted to live the life she wanted. Because the only way to release the power Harry Easton had over her was to give up any power she might have over him. She heard the sadness in his tone. The shaking in his words. Somewhere along the way, he'd gained some—what? Wisdom?

She exhaled, letting out the tension. She hadn't even realized she'd been holding her breath. With that rush of air out of her lungs, she felt herself let it go.

"What happened?" she asked. "What changed?"

"Everything," he said. "But—the big thing was—I'm a father now. A little girl, she's three. And some day she's going to be in school and will be around boys and all I can do is pray she'll be treated better than you were. I'm truly sorry, Julia."

Julia closed her eyes. Something so simple, yet profound. A baby. Harry had no way of knowing that Julia couldn't have children. He had no way of knowing the utter rage she carried. A tear rolled down her cheek. Harry Easton walked away with some remorse, but he got to have a daughter. But thanks to him, thanks to the back-room abortion in that awful clinic in China, *she* would never bear a daughter of her own.

She didn't want to forgive him. She didn't want to let him off the hook. She wanted to reach through the phone and tear his guts out.

Julia closed her eyes. She thought of the affirmations her therapist had given her, and the prayers she'd learned to say. She sought the inner peace that was sometimes so elusive.

Finally, she whispered, "I forgive you."

Then she clenched her fist against her stomach, because she didn't know if she meant it. But even if she didn't, she had to act like it.

Harry gasped. Then, incredibly, she heard him sniff, as if he was tearing up. "I don't deserve that," he said, his voice broken.

She sighed. "Let it go, Harry. Move on. Raise your daughter, and protect her."

"I will," he replied.

"Now for the favor I need."

"Anything."

"My sister Carrie and I need to meet with Prince George-Phillip."

There was a stunned silence at the other end of the line. Finally he said, "Surely you're kidding."

"No, Harry. It's important."

"I don't—Julia, he's the head of the Special Intelligence Service. And a member of the royal family. I've got no power to arrange such a meeting."

"I need you to try," she replied.

"I would have to go well outside normal channels to arrange such a thing. Which means I'll need to give explanations."

She sighed, and said, "It's intensely personal."

"What personal business could you possibly have with him?"

She coughed. Then said, "This is related to the attack on my sisters. If you can get the message to him that Adelina Thompson's daughters want to meet with him, he'll know what it is about."

"Not *Richard* Thompson's daughters?"

Julia snorted a bitter laugh. "He'll understand either way."

"Then I'll do the best I can. Can I reach you back at this number?"

"This is my cell."

"I'll be in touch, Julia."

CHAPTER TWENTY-FIVE
Mister Oz

Dylan. May 3.

It was late afternoon, almost evening, as Dylan looked out the window of the kitchen. Mendoza sat at the table smoking a cigarette in front of an untouched deck of cards. Dylan imagined Mendoza's mother would give him hell later for smoking in the house. Andrea sat across from him, scanning through the Washington Post on the tablet they'd bought the night before. Along with the tablet and half a dozen disposable phones, they'd bought pre-paid SIM cards from several locations, dragging Mendoza along for a three-hour odyssey from store to store.

Dylan still worried that it would be dangerous to get online, but they had little choice. They needed information.

"Look at this," Andrea said. "It says your President is caught in an internal dispute about whether or not to rescind the nomination."

"Yeah?" Dylan said.

She slid the tablet across to him and he scanned the article. Dylan didn't follow politics at all, so most of the names mentioned in the article were unfamiliar. But one thing was clear—the President was caught in a bind, whether or not to support his nominee for Secretary of Defense. The confirmation hearings were set to begin in just a few days.

"I bet the President's hoping your father will withdraw."

"Richard Thompson is not my father," she said. Her tone was final.

"You know what I mean."

"I do. But I'd prefer you spoke with some precision. At this point we don't know who my father is, but we do know that man is not him."

"Okay," he replied. Slowly.

A large black SUV with flashy chrome rims was coming down the street. Dylan leaned a little closer to the window to see it. It came to a stop directly in front of the house and the door opened. A man got out—short black hair, black stubble darkening an angular face.

Dylan tensed, and Andrea followed his lead, rising half out of her seat. "Heads up, Mendoza. You know this guy?"

"Yeah. Relax. He's our delivery guy. Just stay here."

Mendoza stood and walked out of the kitchen. Andrea pointed to the other exit from the kitchen, a side door that led to a narrow space between homes. Dylan leaned back and unlocked the door, then carefully turned the knob to crack the door. He wanted to be able to move quickly if they needed to.

A minute went by, then another. Dylan could hear voices in the front entrance, Mendoza and the other guy, but he couldn't tell what they were saying.

A year ago, Dylan would never have doubted Mendoza. They'd served together. But things were different now. For one thing, Mendoza got hurt and left their unit early on. For another, the members of Dylan's platoon had turned on each other like frenzied sharks when it came time to save their own asses. Dylan trusted nobody but family now. Slowly and casually, he slid his hand under his shirt and rested his hand on the pistol grip of the weapon he'd taken from one of the dead killers. It was a .45 Glock patterned after the M1911 Colt automatic, and felt comfortable in his hand.

Andrea raised an eyebrow.

"Just being careful," he whispered.

The front door closed with a thump, and Dylan heard footsteps coming back toward the kitchen. His grip tightened on the pistol.

Outside, the guy with the SUV was walking back to it.

Mendoza froze in the doorway when he saw Dylan. "Paris—everything okay?"

"Yeah, man, it's all good."

The guy out front got in his SUV and drove away.

"I got your IDs. They're pretty good."

Mendoza dropped a card in front of Dylan and another in front of Andrea.

Dylan raised his eyebrows. It was a Tennessee driver's license in the name of Sherman Roberts. He flipped it back and forth. It looked real enough, including a bar code on the back.

"The bar code doesn't actually work. You don't want to get pulled over with that, all right? But it'll pass for hotels or whatever."

Dylan said, "This looks good. How's yours?"

Andrea passed hers over. It was indistinguishable from a real driver's license. Mendoza's *friend* had given her a couple of years, but the date on the license made her 18 rather than 21. That was good—she looked too young for that. They needed to stay as discreet as possible. He handed the card back to her without comment.

"We'll need to get going soon," Dylan said. "I don't want to put you in any more danger than I already have."

"Don't worry about me, man."

Andrea was already up.

Dylan said, "Let me check in with Alex real quick." He reached for the tablet and logged into Facebook and his new account.

He had a message from Alex.

Tell Andrea to Google Prince George-Phillip.

Weird. He showed the message to Andrea, whose eyebrows drew together.

"Do it," she said.

Dylan typed in the words on the screen. A moment later Google returned the Wikipedia results along with a photograph. Andrea, standing over his shoulder, cursed under her breath. Then she said, "That's the man who was in the photos from Spain."

Dylan looked through the Wikipedia entry. It was detailed.

"He was stationed with the Embassy in Washington, DC in the early 80s," he said.

"What about the 90s?"

Dylan looked up at her then pointed at the screen.

Her face stiffened. "He was in China."

"The resemblance is pretty strong," he said. "You and Carrie both look like him."

He scrolled down further.

She sucked in a breath and said, "Stop."

She hunched down next to the table, her face close to the tablet. The screen had stopped on a photo. George-Phillip, in a military uniform, complete with sash and medals. At his side was a little girl in a dress with red polka dots. The little girl had raven hair and green eyes. She could easily be mistaken as Carrie or Andrea's sister.

"I don't get it," Dylan said. "Your mom had an affair with this guy?"

"I guess so," Andrea said. "And not a short one. Carrie's twelve years older than I am." Her face settled into a thoughtful expression. She took the tablet and typed into it.

"I don't understand," Mendoza said.

Dylan nodded toward Andrea, then started to explain. But he stopped when Andrea let out a string of curses in Spanish.

"What is it?" he asked.

"He's coming to Washington," she said. "He has a meeting with the President tomorrow."

Dylan looked at her. "Okay, and...?" His voice trailed off.

She looked at him with calm eyes, and Dylan knew what she wanted to do.

"That's crazy talk, Andrea."

"I haven't said anything yet."

"It's still crazy."

"Crazy or not, if he's my father, don't you think it's time?"

Blaine, Washington. May 4.

Nick Larsden was frustrated.

Since early Friday morning he'd been on the road, working his way up the West Coast of California, then Oregon and Washington. A frustrating and probably futile search, he'd thought, until he stumbled on their campsite in California yesterday. Two hours after leaving the old man dead at his campsite, Nick had found the minivan. It was parked in the grocery store parking lot next to the Greyhound station in Medford, Oregon.

The license plates were a match, and more importantly, he'd found evidence in the van itself: the daughter had left piles of food wrappings, fast food bags and other garbage on the floor behind her seat. When Nick opened the glove box he found what he expected to find: the van was registered in the name of Richard

Thompson. That must be the woman's husband. She'd abandoned her van and taken a bus, sometime that morning.

Nick followed the trail. From there it wasn't difficult to figure out. She'd probably arrived there at nine or ten am. The next buses north were to Seattle and Bellingham at ten and ten-thirty. And the Bellingham bus continued on to Blaine, on the Canadian border. He would bet anything the woman and her daughter were on that bus.

He had looked around the bus station. Medford had a tiny station and probably didn't have more than two dozen passengers a day. He'd flashed a fake badge at the woman behind the counter, identifying himself as a State investigator, then shown her the pictures of Adelina and Jessica Thompson.

Verification. He had been eight hours behind them, but the bus would be stopping along the way. Maybe he could catch up before they tried to cross the border.

Unfortunately, it wasn't to be. The bus started with an eight-hour lead, and got to Blaine ahead of him by three hours. There was no sign of the woman or her daughter.

So now he watched and waited, an unread newspaper in front of him at the cheap table in the corner of the McDonald's. The Sumas border crossing was only two hundred yards away, several lines of cars backed up waiting to cross the border. It seemed like a lot of traffic for a Sunday morning. The day was clear and bright, but a lot cooler than the San Fernando Valley where he lived.

His phone started to vibrate. UNKNOWN CALLER. Interesting. He picked it up and answered the call.

"Hello?"

The caller had a thick, gravelly Irish accent. "Mister Larsden, this is Oz."

"What can I do for you?" Larsden responded, his tone respectful but quick. It was a thin line—Mister Oz, who was obviously using an assumed name, had offered a million dollars for this job. *A million dollars.* Larsden wanted that place in the mountains very badly.

"Your friends assured me you'd be able to accomplish this job. But it seems you are not making any progress."

Larsden gritted his teeth, then answered in as calm a voice as he could muster, "I'm in Blaine, Washington, I've traced them to the border. It looks like they're going to make an attempt to cross into Canada."

"Mister Larsden, they must not make it to Canada. Do you understand?"

"I may not be able to prevent that."

"You will if you want to continue in your line of work. Or any line of work. Do I make myself clear, Larsden? Adelina Thompson and her daughter must not make it to the border alive. I don't care what you have to do."

"Roger that." He dropped his voice to a whisper. "And what am I supposed to do after I start killing people in sight of the border guards?"

"I suggest that you make sure you are unseen."

Christ.

"Make it three million."

"Excuse me?"

"You heard me. When this job started you just wanted them caught. Now you've changed it to murder. If it's that important, then you pay."

Hesitation at the other end of the line. Then the response: "Fine."

"I'll be in touch," Larsden said, his voice back at a normal tone. Then he hung up the phone and stood up. No one in the dining room appeared to notice anything unusual. Now the only question was when would Adelina and Jessica Thompson show up? Or had they already crossed the border? He didn't have any way of knowing.

For now, he needed to find a good vantage point where he could take a concealed position with his rifle. It wasn't ideal, but he had few other options. He walked out into the parking lot, the breeze raising goose bumps on his skin. He checked his watch. It was 11 am.

The cars were backing up Cherry Street, away from the border crossing. Across the street was the pedestrian lane. A scattering of people walked toward the metal turnstiles, which marked the border. Once they crossed through, there was no immediate re-entry to the United States. Instead, the next stop was Canada's Customs station.

Nick paced the parking lot for a moment in frustration. They might have walked right out of the bus station and directly to the border. They might already be in Canada.

He didn't know why *Oz*, his unnamed benefactor, wanted to ensure they didn't make it across the border. But the job had come to him through Marky Lovecchio, an old Army buddy. When Nick got out of the army, Marky had gone on to a career in Special Forces. In 2006 he'd left the military for a private military contractor—the pay was a hell of a lot better, he said, and you got to pick your own weapons. Marky had a lot of contacts, and vouched for *Oz* and his ability to pay astronomical sums.

"I worked for him befoah," Marky had said. Even after fifteen years away from East Boston, Marky still couldn't pronounce his Rs. "He goes by *Oz*—I don't know his real name—but the cash is real enough. I did a couple jobs for him last year."

"Any idea who he is?" Nick had asked.

"Nah. I think he's some mucky muck in England. Or the IRA. I don't care who he is, his money's green."

That was all nice, but now Nick was stuck with a job that would pay well if he could complete it, and threats if he didn't. And there was no guarantee the two women had even come this way—

Wait.

His eyes followed Cherry Street back up the block. A turn next to the gas station led off to a couple of commercial buildings. Beyond that, some houses and woods. He took out his phone and pulled up the maps application. Harrison Avenue on this side of the border dead-ended into a farm, less than a hundred yards from Boundary Road on the Canadian side of the border.

There was nothing but a field there. *Was there even a fence?* No way to know from what he could see. But he imagined himself in the shoes of Adelina Thompson, running, fast. Trying to hide from the cops and from whoever was after her. To her, wouldn't it make a lot more sense to cross *anywhere* other than an official border crossing where she might be stopped and questioned?

As quickly as he could, Nick got into the vehicle and started it up. He drove to the exit of the McDonald's. Traffic—way too much traffic. Cars backed up from the border station right into the intersection. He nosed his Hummer into the intersection, provoking a series of wild honks from cars. He pushed forward, slightly bumping a rusted antique Oldsmobile.

In the distance, way down at the end of Harrison, he saw what he was afraid of.

Two women, one of them anorexic, walking in the shade of the trees as if they were just out for a stroll.

He laid on the horn.

CHAPTER TWENTY-SIX

One Shot

Dylan. May 4.

Dylan turned toward Andrea, easing his hands on the wheel a little. His knuckles were white.

"Once you get out, I want you to walk leisurely. Wait until you hear the horn honking before you do anything. Once you hear that, you'll have sixty seconds, tops, to make it over the fence. Then it's up to you."

She nodded, her face grim. She was wearing a tough pair of jeans and a heavy hooded sweatshirt labeled "George Mason University."

"Once you get in there, you look for the residence."

"Right. It's the two-story brick building. We looked at the satellite photos, Dylan. I'm not an idiot."

"You're anything but. But we're attempting something stupidly reckless, Andrea. You only get one shot."

She nodded. "All right."

"What do you do if the guards catch you?"

"Throw up my arms and yell that I'm seeking political asylum. Then tell everyone, loudly, that I'm Prince George-Phillip's daughter."

Dylan nodded. Traffic began to move and he hit the gas. Mendoza's old green Oldsmobile shuddered, spitting out a cloud of black smoke as it lurched forward. He glanced over at Andrea. She looked terrified.

"I'll be praying for you," he said. The words felt odd in his mouth.

She shook her head. "Bullshit you will. But I'll take it anyway."

"I can always try," he replied. "I don't *think* I'll get struck by lightning."

She chuckled. "I'm sure you won't." She craned her neck.

He followed the direction of her gaze.

On the other side of the street, headed Southeast on Massachusetts Avenue, traffic had slowed to a crawl, snaking slowly around a grouping of three police cars with lights flashing. Dylan kept his face impassive as he scanned the police cars. Two of them were District of Columbia police, and the third had a smaller logo on the door. As they got closer, he saw it clearly: Diplomatic Security Services. They were parked in front of the Embassy of Japan, and several uniformed police stood in front of the fence, blocking a group of twenty or so protesters from the front of the building. Ranging from their teens to an old lady in a wheelchair, they waved signs reading, "Stop the slaughter," and "Honk if you love dolphins."

A huge banner waved in the air, held up by two young men. The banner was full color, displaying a bloody beach strewn with the carcasses of dozens of dolphins.

Dylan flinched at the blood. He hated the sight of killing.

"You okay?" Andrea asked.

"Yeah. Fuckers." He honked the horn and waved at the protesters. "Almost there," he said. They were crossing a bridge now, heavy trees on both sides of the road. Dylan turned on his right hand turn signal then pulled to a stop just after 30th Street.

"Here's where you get out. You've got three minutes."

Andrea looked him in the eyes. "Dylan—be careful."

"Same to you."

She nodded, then reached over and squeezed his arm. She stepped out of the car, just as a cab behind Dylan started honking his horn. Dylan stayed there while she looked both ways, crossed to the yellow lines, then cut between cars and started walking down Whitehaven Street, a small street bordered by the Brazilian Embassy and several very large houses.

Once she was on her way, Dylan hit his left turn signal and pulled back into traffic. He drove intentionally slow, swerving the Oldsmobile slightly left and right, enraging the cabbie behind him. A moment later, he approached the British Embassy on the right side of the road.

Dylan had studied the satellite photos and images on Google as closely as possible. While those images told him nothing about the security setup at the Embassy, he knew that the first two driveways in front of the residence buildings were blocked with steel bollards before the fence and gates. He'd never get the Oldsmobile past those. The grass in between driveways was blocked with solid looking brick planters bordered by a well manicured lawn. It was attractive, but also functional.

The third entrance, however, didn't have the steel bollards. A solid looking gate stood between two stone pillars, with a small guard booth just inside the gate on the left. The stone pillars were capped by carved gryphons.

Just to add to the chaos when he arrived, Dylan turned on the radio at full volume. The sound of Jason Derulo singing *Talk Dirty to Me* blasted out of the car, the subwoofers in the trunk vibrating the windows of nearby buildings. Dylan came to a stop in the road, his left turn signal on. The guard stepped out of the booth, staring curiously at Dylan from the other side of the fence.

That lasted until Dylan turned and stepped on the gas, accelerating rapidly toward the fence.

George-Phillip. May 4.

The newspaper headline was troubling, but not nearly as troubling as some of the quotes inside the lead article. Heads would roll, and quite possibly some at the newspapers would be tried for violations of the Official Secrets Act, but that didn't erase the damage. In some ways it would make it worse. The Special Report had been online for less than ten minutes before the first phone call came in. George-Phillip had just finished breakfast. Now he sat staring at the screen on his tablet, wishing he'd waited to eat.

Special Report. MI6 Insiders Accuse
Government of Covering Up Afghanistan Massacre

This is a Guardian Special Report.

Related Special Reports:
   * Who Was Involved in the Massacre?
   * Interviews with Survivors
   * How the Tragedy Unfolded

On an ice-cold night in Afghanistan in December, 1983, the villagers of Bozai Gumbaz were huddled in their mud huts and yurts, large round portable structures used by the nomads of the steppes of Central Asia. For four years, war had raged in Afghanistan, following the 1979 Soviet invasion. But for the poor villagers of the Wakhan Corridor, a finger-shaped protrusion from Afghanistan squeezed between Pakistan, China and the then-Soviet Union (now Uzbekistan), the war was remote. The villagers and herders of this region, once part of the Silk Road, had largely been bypassed by the war. With no roads, no structures, and few mineral resources, there was little here to interest outsiders.

Unbeknownst to the villagers that night, the war was about to reach out to them. Two unmarked helicopters left the mountains of Pakistan and crossed the Hindu Kush Mountains into the Wakhan Corridor. At approximately midnight on December 13, 1983, they came to a hover over the village. Survivors described a punishing whiteout as fresh snow was blown into the air by the rotors of the helicopters. No one on the outskirts of the village (those who survived) could have imagined what happened next. Villagers, standing in their doors and windows gawking at the helicopters, began dropping in their tracks. Men, women and children died within seconds, their village washed with a cloud of sarin, a deadly chemical warfare agent that can cause nearly instantaneous death to those exposed.

More than six weeks passed before word of the massacre reached the outside world, and three more months before the first outsiders reached the village. Two investigators from Helsinki Watch (now Human Rights Watch) trekked on snowmobiles from Pakistan into the country. What they found became an international crisis, with U.S. President Ronald Reagan denouncing the Soviets for using chemical weapons in Afghanistan.

Our investigation, however, has shown that the chemical weapons were provided not by the Soviets, as the entire world assumed in 1983, but by a group of American and Saudi intelligence officials led by the current Secretary of Defense nominee Richard H. Thompson (shown in a 1985 photograph, right). Further, according to confidential sources within the Special Intelligence Service, it was learned by The Guardian that current SIS Chief George-Phillip Windsor (second cousin to Her Majesty) was responsible for the investigation and later cover-up of the massacre.

George-Phillip closed his eyes as he read the last paragraph. His ability to influence events in Adelina's favor was about to come to a difficult end if he didn't get ahead of this.

Where did his responsibility lie? Was it to continue to protect a past Prime Minister, and by extension, the entire government? Was it to Adelina? Or to those poor villagers who had never had an advocate? Or, for that matter, was it to Jane, who had already lost her mother?

George-Phillip sighed. His daughter. She'd been the most cheerful of babies, always smiling and burbling and drooling. But after Anne died, she'd cried for months, inconsolably. He'd done everything he could, including taking a lengthy absence from SIS, but it wasn't until he'd hired Adriana Poole that Jane began to recover.

Adriana was flighty. Sometimes George-Phillip thought she was genuinely stupid. But she was also kind, and cared very much for Jane—no matter how indifferent she was to Jane's father. Like any man and woman in their position—a wealthy widower and a young woman of good stock, they'd both tossed around the idea, but quickly ruled it out. Two less compatible individuals had probably never existed.

He stood up and walked to the window, then looked at his watch. It was 2:00 pm. O'Leary should be in shortly. Not a day went by when George-Phillip didn't thank God he had the pugnacious little man working for him. He turned back to the article and read further.

According to the Guardian's sources inside the MI6, Prince George-Phillip led the investigation into the Wakhan massacre in the spring of 1984 while he was assigned as a medium-level attaché at the British Embassy in Washington, DC. His final report identified Secretary Thompson—then a low-level state department functionary—as the ringleader of a small group of intelligence officials responsible for delivering the chemical weapons to Ahmad Shah Massoud, the leader of an anti-Soviet militia operating in Badakhshan Province.

According to a senior MI6 official, Prince George-Phillip's report fingered those responsible, and then recommended burying the report.

George-Phillip muttered a curse. The last paragraph was patently untrue. He'd recommended confronting the United States publicly over the issue. But the Iron Lady had not only given the order to suppress the report, she'd also made a very persuasive argument. People today forgot that in the early 80s, the United States and Russia were poised to destroy the earth with their nuclear weapons. The Cold War was at its peak and George-Phillip's report would have created a tremendous propaganda victory for the Soviet Union and undermined everything the Queen's government had worked for.

The argument felt hollow with the retrospect of time, and the years of staring at the photos of the twisted and bloated bodies of children. He wondered how he would explain the decision to his child. Jane would know nothing of the Cold War and Ronald Reagan and Mutually Assured Destruction. She would understand only that children and their mothers had been murdered and a generation had passed and no one had done anything about it. No one had done anything for those children.

George-Phillip wondered how he would explain his actions to God, were he called to account today. He sighed. He had so many regrets. So many. He remembered one of his last conversations with Adelina, when he'd begged her to leave Richard and run away with him.

You don't mean it, she had said. *Your sense of duty is too strong to run away.*

He'd last seen Adelina in China a lifetime ago, in the fall of 1996. The American Embassy had hosted a dinner for the officers of the British and Australian Embassies along with their wives—even in the 90s, the diplomatic services of all three countries were still dominated by men. By that time George-Phillip was a senior intelligence officer, but publicly he was a junior attaché for the Diplomatic Service. With his cover as a junior diplomat, he was required to attend such functions.

The meal had been tense, unusually quiet for a diplomatic function. All of George-Phillip's instincts had screamed that it was time to force the issue, insist that Adelina leave Richard. How was it even possible that the other Embassy personnel were not aware of the painfully obvious dysfunction of that family? Adelina mumbled through the meal, never taking her eyes off her plate, responding to queries about her health with only the barest of courtesies.

George-Phillip had frozen when he saw eleven-year-old Carrie for the first time. She stayed through the dinner then was escorted away by a governess. Unusually tall for an eleven-year-old, she had raven hair and blue-green eyes, and a slightly upturned nose that looked nothing like her mother or her father. She looked a great deal like his first cousin, Eloise Percy, right down to the glint of mischief in her eyes. Moments after the introduction, George-Phillip's eyes darted involuntarily to Adelina, whose face revealed nothing.

She'd never told him that Carrie was his daughter. But it was obvious, now that he'd met the girl. He didn't understand why. Nor could he erase the sudden surge of anger at the thought that he had a daughter who had been kept from him.

Adelina's eldest daughter Julia, fourteen years old, had a haunted, pale look about her face. George-Phillip had been alarmed to see that miscreant Harry Easton, the Ambassador's son, corner her after the meal, speaking urgently, his hands waving all over the place while she shrank back. Her curly brown hair was a disorganized mess, hanging in her eyes, and she kept her face pointed to the floor. Midway through the meal, she disappeared entirely, and so did Harry.

Neither Richard nor Adelina noticed. Adelina kept her head low, obviously terrified of Richard, who occasionally whispered urgent words in her ear. Every time he touched her she flinched.

George-Phillip had wanted to scream, because everyone else ignored all of it. He found himself questioning his own perceptions. Was everything normal and it just seemed wrong in his eyes? How could they just stand around and drink and laugh and enjoy themselves when everything was so obviously wrong?

He finally ran out of patience. Ronald Easton, the British Ambassador, was deep in a conversation with Richard Thompson, and Adelina had just broken away from a talk with the Australian Consul-General when George-Phillip approached her, his heart thumping.

"Hello, Adelina, how are you?"

She froze, her eyes darting to him, then away. She didn't say anything.

"You haven't called," he said.

"I'm pregnant," she whispered.

He swallowed. "You didn't tell me about Carrie."

"That's because I want to live," she whispered. "He put me in the hospital when he found out she wasn't his. I don't know what he'll do when he finds out I'm pregnant again."

"Is the baby—is the baby mine?" he asked, his voice low and urgent.

"Yes. Of course. I never *voluntarily* touch him."

Of course he knew that. He looked her in the eyes and said, "Adelina, you must leave him. He's destroying you *and* your children."

"You don't understand what you're asking. If you did, you wouldn't say that. I'd lose my children. I'd lose everything." Her face shifted to a smile and she said in a much louder voice, "Yes, I enjoyed the show very much! I'm hoping we can take Julia to see it, I think she'd love it. She's very musically inclined."

George-Phillip restrained himself from jumping back in disgust when Richard Thompson casually clapped him on the shoulder. "Prince George-Phillip, it's a delight to see you again."

"And you, Ambassador."

"Please excuse me," Adelina said. "I must find Julia, she seems to have snuck off."

George-Phillip grimaced. "I'm afraid she was speaking with Harry Easton a little while ago, and he's gone as well."

Adelina's lips pursed and she nodded. She stepped away, walking toward one of the side doors of the room.

George-Phillip found himself drawn into a policy discussion with Richard Thompson. It was bizarre and irritating, and as a diplomat he had to just bear it. Walking away from the American Ambassador just wasn't done. But where did she go? His eyes scanned the room over and over again, but she never reappeared.

She never reappeared. Not that day, not that month.

The diplomatic community was small, and word began to spread. Something had happened to Adelina. Or possibly one of her daughters. Harry Easton vanished from Beijing in June, sent back to London even though his father still had another year as Ambassador. Adelina Thompson wasn't seen at all, and when Richard Thompson attended functions without her, he would simply say that she felt ill.

Finally, in May of 1997, George-Phillip had reached the end of his assignment in China. He gave up any pretense of discretion and showed up at the Thompson's apartment the day before his departure. He knocked and knocked, and finally a young American woman answered.

"Miss Adelina ain't here," the woman said. "She can't see you."

"Tell her it's George Lansing."

"She can't see you," the woman said again. Then she leaned forward and whispered, "She told me to give you this, if you came. But she doesn't want to see you no more. Go back where you came from and leave her in peace. That woman deserve some peace."

She held out a thick, cream-colored envelope the size of a greeting card.

George-Phillip staggered away, walking down the block toward the entrance to the compound. It was late afternoon, and a black Ford pulled up to the gate—one of the many cars hired by members of the diplomatic community. Three girls stepped out of the car and quickly walked inside the gate.

The oldest, fourteen-year-old Julia, walked with her head down, her curly brown hair hanging almost in her face, books clasped to her chest. She kept her head down and rushed past George-Phillip without a word.

Behind her, twelve-year-old Carrie walked, holding the hand of her sister. The one Adelina had named for George-Phillip's aunt, Princess Alexandra. Carrie towered over the young and fair-haired Alexandra. For a moment she met George-Phillip's eyes.

"Good afternoon," he said to her.

"Hello," she said. She gave him a brief, impersonal smile, then tugged her sister along. "Come on, Alexandra. Let's get inside. I bet Grace made cookies again."

George-Phillip had walked away quickly, struggling to hide the tears that came to his eyes as he walked away from his daughter. His daughter that didn't know—would never know—that he even existed.

At the gate, the guard waved him out and he tore open the envelope.

It contained a note.

For my safety, you must never contact me again.

The envelope also contained an ultrasound. The baby was a girl.

Over the years since, George-Phillip had kept tabs on Adelina, of course, as well as all of her daughters. Through O'Leary, he'd kept a discreet eye on the girls, and when he learned that Carrie and Andrea were in Spain in 2002, he'd taken the very risky step of going there by himself to get an in person look at his daughters. He'd stayed in the background, but he'd longed to reveal himself to them. Four years later he'd made arrangements to give the commencement address at Columbia University the year Carrie graduated with her Bachelor's degree, and so was able to shake her hand and smile at her and say congratulations when she accepted her degree. She didn't know, of course. How would she? He doubted she even remembered his existence. He was just an old man who had spoken at her college.

He'd never had any indication Adelina wanted him to contact her. He'd never heard from her again. And finally he'd given up and moved on. He'd married Lady Anne, and they'd had a child, and then in due course his wife died. And now—more than anything—he wanted to know where his daughter Andrea was, where the love of his life Adelina was.

The knock on the door startled him. He turned away from the view of trees and large brick houses just on the other side of the fence.

"Come in," he said.

The door opened. It was Oswald O'Leary. He looked unusually flustered.

"What do you have?" George-Phillip asked without preamble.

"Nothing solid, sir, but one of our agents reports tracking her near the Mexican border. It seems she's trying to get across the border."

"And do we have anyone on the Mexican side of the border? In case she makes it across?"

"We've got a small team in Tijuana sir, watching the border crossing. If she goes across there, we'll get to her right away."

George-Phillip nodded. "All right. That's good news, I suppose. And how much is this all costing us?"

"We're up to four million, sir, I'm afraid. All the subcontractors. They charge a pretty penny in the States."

"Bastards," George-Phillip muttered. "All right. Keep going."

"Yes, sir." O'Leary started to turn away, then put a hand to the earpiece he always wore. His face tensed, a look of concern flashing across it.

"O'Leary?"

"A disturbance at the gate, sir. Nothing to worry about."

Jessica. May 4

"Here," Jessica's mother said.

Here was a muddy field, knee-high grass mostly trampled by cattle or illegal aliens or who knew what. What Jessica did see was obvious. A small concrete pillar about three feet high on the other side of the field marked the border. A road and some houses were just beyond.

A loud honk down the street caught Jessica's attention. She looked that way. Three blocks away, back at the intersection near the border station a gleaming black sports utility vehicle—a Hummer, she guessed—was nosing its way into traffic and snarling traffic. Her mom stopped and looked too.

"What the hell?" Jessica gasped as the Hummer bumped into another car, shoving it out of the way.

Her mother stood for just a moment, both of them tense.

The Hummer slowly pushed another car out of the way. The honking was coming from multiple vehicles now.

Jessica looked across the field, then back at the Hummer.

"Mom," she said, her voice quavering. "Run. Let's run. *Now.*"

Adelina, suddenly breathing rapidly, nodded.

Jessica grabbed her mother's hand and pulled, plunging off the street into the muddy field. Instantly her canvas shoes soaked through, the cold mud gripping at her feet like the undead trying to pull her under. Her heart sank. If the entire field was this muddy, it would take them all day to make it across.

More honks from the intersection.

Jessica felt panic descend. In the last few days someone had kidnapped her sister, attacked her other sisters, and bombed their house. Something had gone terribly wrong.

"Run!" she screamed as Adelina stumbled. She leaned down, putting her arms underneath her mom's and tugging her back to her feet. Hand in hand, they began to run across the field.

Thirty feet into the field, Jessica's left shoe was yanked off her foot by the mud. She didn't stop to do anything about it, because the Hummer was free of the traffic now, and speeding up the three blocks toward them, engine roaring. Instead, she kept moving as quickly as possible. Somewhere behind the Hummer and toward the border station, she heard a police siren.

They had at least seventy-five yards to go across the field. Jessica felt pain in her forehead as she ran, staggering, pulling her mother. Adelina was only fifty, but she wasn't athletic and had suffered a lifetime of stress. She struggled to make it across the field, her face turning red.

The sirens were getting louder behind them. Jessica hazarded a look behind her when they'd made it halfway across the field. The Hummer had bounced to a stop just off the road. The driver's side window rolled down.

Another police car appeared on the Canadian side of the border, screeching to a stop in the road. Two police officers got out of the vehicle.

Jessica screamed, "Help us!"

A loud crack sounded behind them, and a splat just to her right as a bullet struck the ground.

The two Canadian police jumped behind their car as the rifle shot rang out. The pain in her forehead sharpened, blooming down her neck and into her right arm. Jessica staggered.

CHAPTER TWENTY-SEVEN
The Darkest Valley

Adelina. May 4.

A **delina** cried out when Jessica suddenly faltered beside her, sinking to her knees in the mud. Panic flooded her. Had her daughter been shot? Where? Behind her, she heard another shot, and a bullet grazed her arm. She pulled Jessica to the ground, then lay down on top of her, putting her body between the shooter and her daughter, praying the grass would be enough to stop the bullets.

"Help us!" she screamed.

More shots rang out, this time from the Canadian side of the border. These gunshots were higher pitched, not the deep bass of the rifle.

Jessica's face was grey, and her eyes were wide open. Her left eye was dilated, rolling around independently of her right eye, which was focused on Adelina. She was breathing heavily, her mouth moving, but no sound was coming out other than a high-pitched breathy wail. Her right eye was wide, terrified. Adelina couldn't see any injuries, no blood. *What was wrong with her?*

"It's going to be okay," Adelina whispered. "I'll protect you." She began to recite a prayer as she held her daughter's hand and looked in her eyes. "The Lord is my shepherd, I shall not want. He makes me lie down in green pastures ... he leads me beside still waters; he restores my soul. He leads me in right paths for his name's sake."

Adelina flinched at the sound of another rifle shot. The bullet slammed into the mud six feet away from her. Another hit three feet away.

"Even though I walk through the darkest valley, I fear no evil ... for you are with me ... your rod and your staff—they comfort me..."

Sirens went off somewhere behind her, and she heard the rumble of the Hummer turn into a roar. Suddenly it was receding, and the sirens were following. She lifted her head and looked around, then directly at the Canadian police.

"Help me! My daughter's hurt!"

Across the field, two U.S. Border Patrol vehicles were parked, even as two police cars raced after the speeding Hummer.

Three Border Control officers were getting out of the vehicles and stepped into the field.

Adelina began to panic. She couldn't let the Border Patrol take her or Jessica. She leaned down, putting her arms underneath Jessica's armpits, and lifted her to her chest, backing toward the Canadian border.

She continued the prayer, silently, even as she pulled her daughter away from the Border Patrol, who began to run.

> *You prepare a table before me*
> *In the presence of my enemies;*
> *You anoint my head with oil;*
> *My cup overflows,*
> *Surely goodness and mercy will follow me*
> *All the days of my life,*
> *And I shall dwell in the house of the Lord*
> *My whole life long.*

Adelina staggered as she bumped into the concrete post marking the border. She fell to her back, dragging Jessica with her.

"I'm Adelina Thompson," she gasped. "My husband is the Secretary of Defense of the United States."

She saw the Canadian officers look stunned, even as the Border Patrol officers stopped just on the American side of the border.

"I claim political asylum. I need urgent medical care for my daughter. Please help me."

She looked the officer in the eyes.

He nodded then said to his partner, "Call for an ambulance," as he kneeled beside Jessica.

George-Phillip. May 4.

"What sort of disturbance?" George-Phillip asked. He glanced out the window. He could just barely hear the sound of a horn and the awful bass sound of a car stereo. The music sounded obnoxious, low and grating.

"Some drunk American crashed into the gate, sir. Nobody hurt. The security guards are dealing with it."

"Well, then. Keep me updated. It's Sunday, and I need to be with my daughter."

"Very well, sir."

George-Phillip left the small office. The official residence, which was reserved for visiting dignitaries, had four bedrooms on the first floor, plus several other assorted rooms—sitting rooms, offices and kitchens, along with a small locally hired permanent staff.

He walked down the hall by himself as O'Leary turned toward the exit. He reached his left hand out and opened the polished hardwood door to the playroom.

Jane was on the floor, humming to herself as she played with a doll set. Adriana was across the room from her, knitting a scarf or something.

As the door opened, Jane's face brightened.

"Daddy!" she cried, jumping to her feet.

She ran to him and he lifted her into the air. She threw her arms around him. He was always surprised by how solid she was, and tall for a girl her age. He held her in his left hand and tickled her, causing her to convulse with giggles.

"Miss Poole, I thought I would take Jane to the zoo this afternoon. You may come along if you'd like, or if you wish to have the day off to explore the city, that's fine as well."

Adriana stood and said, "If it's all the same to you, sir, I'll come along."

"The zoo? Take me to the zoo? Zoo!" Jane crooned.

"Yes. We'll go see the pandas, I think."

"And the lions!" Jane threw her head back and roared.

"She should have a bit of a snack first, sir, begging your pardon. She usually has a snack about 2:30."

"By all means," he said, sharply bothered by the fact that he didn't know that. He spent far too little time with Jane. It was time to rectify that.

He opened the door. At that moment one of the security guards appeared, running down the hall.

"Your Highness, please stay in the room for the moment."

"Excuse me?"

"There's an intruder on the grounds, sir."

At that moment he heard a shriek, then a loud thump just down the hall. A high-pitched voice, female, shouted, "Don't shoot! I'm looking for asylum!"

A male shout, then another thump, then he heard a scream. Then words he was stunned to hear, shouted down the hallway.

"I'm Prince George-Phillip's daughter!"

Silence. It sounded as if they had the female intruder subdued.

I'm Prince George-Phillip's daughter! It couldn't be. Could it?

"Step out of my way, please," George-Phillip said to the guard.

"Your Highness, wait until the area is cleared—"

"You heard me," George-Phillips said. He set Jane down, and said, "Stay back." Then he pushed his way past the guard.

At the end of the hall, two security guards had wrestled a young woman to the floor. One kneeled on her back, preparing to tie her hands with plastic zip-ties.

She looked up at him with big blue-green eyes.

"Let her go," George-Phillip said.

One of the security guards looked up at him, stunned.

"Let her go, right now," he commanded.

Both guards stepped back. Slowly, Andrea Thompson came to her feet, her wary eyes on George-Phillip and Jane. She was mussed, a little bit of dirt on her face, her black and turquoise hair tangled from wrestling with the security guard. He thought about what he'd read about her. How she fought her way free when she was kidnapped, and somehow climbed down from a twentieth floor balcony when killers were after her. This young woman, his daughter, had far more internal resources than he could have ever imagined.

Thirty years of painful regret welled up in George-Phillip at that moment. Thirty years of regret that he'd not been able to protect Adelina, that he'd never known Carrie or Andrea, and that he'd never been a part of their lives. Worse, he saw all the pain and fear in her face. Fear that he would reject her, that she'd be alone, fear that he wouldn't admit the truth. He felt his cheek suddenly twitching, his uncontrollable damned eyebrows working their own dance on his face, and then a tear ran down his cheek.

"Jane," he said, his voice low, shaking. He motioned for her to come out into the hallway. "I'd like you to meet your sister. Her name is Andrea."

Andrea's eyes widened and began to water.

Jane clapped her hands together. "Sister!" she shouted. She stepped fully into the hallway and ran to Andrea, wrapping her arms around the sister she'd never met.

Epilogue

Dylan. May 4.

I thought *the British didn't carry guns.* Dylan's brain was foggy. He hadn't been driving that fast when he hit the gate, maybe 15 mph, but the sudden impact had still jolted him hard. The music was still blaring out of the speakers, THUMP THUMP THUMP, obscene lyrics, booty calls, talk dirty.

He shook his head and looked back up into the barrel of the pistol.

"Step OUT of the CAR!" shouted the man with the gun.

"WHAT?" Dylan shouted. "I can't hear you!"

"Step out of the car *now!*"

Dylan heard sirens in the distance. Lots of them. The music changed. Pitbull and Kesha. Timber. Yelling. Going down. Twerking. *What is all that noise?* Dylan reached out and turned the stereo off.

"No need to be so freaked out," he said. "Sorry, I didn't mean to fuck up your gate—"

"Get out!" shouted the guard.

"Okay, okay, okay…" he said. He opened the car door and stepped out.

Immediately one of the guards slammed him up against the car. Dylan felt his ribs bruise. He didn't resist as they pulled his arms behind him.

He felt his mouth curl up in a slight smile, remembering Alex muttering, *What is it with you and cops?*

He needed to stall them and keep their attention for a few minutes, and give her some time to get into the residence. He didn't know if she'd made it yet— probably not, it was too quick.

Slurring his words, he said, "Where's Harry?"

"There's no one named Harry here, you wretch—"

"What do you mean?" he asked, still slurring his words. "Captain Harry. Er … Captain Wales, I think they called him. I was in Afghanistan with him."

Take that, motherfuckers. Actually, he'd never been anywhere near Prince Harry, though he'd been in Afghanistan at the same time, at least from what he'd read in the papers at the time. But this was a good time to stretch the truth.

"I didn't mean to break your gate. He tol' me to stop by. He said any time."

The guards went into a huddle. Traffic on Massachusetts Avenue was at a complete stop now. Gawking drivers who were already slowed by the protest at the Japanese Embassy were now presented with even more of a spectacle with the fluorescent green Oldsmobile in the driveway of the British Embassy.

Good. Dylan was hoping this would all be sorted before the DC police arrived.

That's when he heard one of their radios. Shouts.

"Intruder spotted entering the residence. Full alert. Full alert."

The bad news was, that prompted the guards to knock Dylan straight to the ground. One of them kneeled on his back, his knee grinding into Dylan's spine.

"Take it easy, bud, I'm not resisting," he murmured.

Two extremely long minutes later, a radio call came. He heard an argument, but couldn't see anything with his face pressed to the grass. It was getting itchy down here. He hoped he wasn't going to jail again.

Then he heard a voice. "Let him up. We've got orders to let him in."

"What?" one of the other guards said. "Bullshit."

Mutters. More argument. Then he was hauled to his feet, and the guards were opening the gate.

"I'll drive your … your … car … inside," one of the guards said.

Their leader said, "Follow me, sir. You're to be taken to see the Prince, God knows why."

Dylan coughed, then composed himself. Unable to help himself, he winked at the security guard, and then followed him into the Embassy compound.

Adelina. May 4.

Adelina clutched the coat the police officer had lent her. It was cold, especially with the water and mud soaked through her clothes. The ambulance was so loud she couldn't hear what the emergency medical technicians were saying. But it didn't sound good. They'd run an IV and were checking Jessica's vitals as the ambulance raced down the highway.

One of the EMTs leaned close to her and said, "We're going to Abbotsford Regional Hospital."

"What's wrong with her? She wasn't shot."

"Ma'am, it looks like a stroke. How old is she?"

"Eighteen! She can't have had a stroke."

"There are good doctors at Abbotsford, they'll do their best to help her. But I need to ask some questions, all right?"

Adelina nodded, clutching the coat.

"Is she doing any drugs? Or alcohol?"

"None right now. She just got out of a drug detox."

The EMTs looked at each other, then back at her. "What was she using?"

"Alcohol. And … crystal meth."

The EMT nodded. "That might explain the stroke. Is she taking any medication?"

"Ibuprofen. She's had terrible headaches. And she's eating enough for three people. I thought she was getting better!"

"She probably was. But your run across the border may have just been too much exertion. Meth can damage the blood vessels in the brain, unfortunately. How long have you two been on the run?"

Adelina sighed and thought back. Three days? Four? She couldn't even remember. "A few days."

The EMT nodded. "All right. An immigration officer will meet us at the hospital to discuss your asylum application. In the meantime, she'll be getting the best care possible. I promise we'll do our best."

Adelina nodded, looking at her daughter. Jessica's skin was grey, her eyes staring up at the ceiling. She was still awake and obviously frightened out of her wits.

Adelina didn't know what was going to happen from here. But she knew no matter what, she was never going back to Richard. She'd do everything she could to protect her daughters. She'd find Andrea. And for Jessica, right now, all she could do was comfort her. She reached out and took Jessica's hand.

GIRL OF VENGEANCE

VENGEANCE

A Novel
by
Charles Sheehan-Miles

RACHEL'S
PERIL

Dedication

for Amirah
My Girl of Courage

Acknowledgements

This book took a lot of help along the way to complete. I'll probably forget some people but I especially want to thank Lori Sabin for your editing, and Sally Bouley for your extensive assistance reading through the book. Thanks to my beta readers: Emma Corcoran, Kathy Baker, Dimitra Fleissner, Laura Wilson, Bryan James, Michelle Kannan, Sarah Griffin, Amy Burt, Jennifer Mirabelli, Stacey Grice, Kirsten Papi, Beth Suit, Rita Jenkins Post and Kelly Moorhouse. You guys looked at a lot of first draft material and have my everlasting gratitude.

As always, to Andrea Randall: thank you for everything along the way. You listen to my fears and frustrations and deal with my crazy insecurities even as we wind our personal and professional lives together. I thank God every day for having you in my life.

Prologue

In the silence of the room, the knock on the door startled Carrie and Sarah. Carrie jerked in her seat and looked up, just as a youngish looking doctor with slightly too long hair stuck his head in the room. Doctor Willis was older than he looked, and Carrie had as much confidence in him as she had in any doctor, which wasn't much. Willis wore a white lab coat with a pocket protector, pens in several different colors poking out of the pocket.

"Mrs. Sherman? May I come in?"

The question was rhetorical, of course. She wasn't going to stop him. A nurse or physician's assistant accompanied him—Carrie didn't know which. The nurse was in her thirties with severely cut blonde hair.

Carrie gave him a weak smile and shifted in her seat. Her left hand rested beside Rachel in her baby carrier. Her right instinctively reached out and took Sarah's hand. Sarah gave her an almost imperceptible squeeze.

"We're ready to begin prepping baby Rachel for the transfusion. But before we start, we need to take a moment to go over the procedure again."

Carrie nodded. She'd been over the procedure a thousand times in her dreams. She'd talked about it with the nurses and doctors, and gotten a second opinion, and when that one confirmed the bad news, she got a third opinion. The results were unequivocal—her daughter suffered from Thalassemia Major and would need regular blood transfusions for the rest of her life, which would be cut short unless she could find a bone marrow donor. Now, at six weeks old, they couldn't delay her first transfusion any longer. Rachel was listless and pale; her eyes and skin had a slight yellow tinge.

"Okay, in a few minutes the nurse-team will prepare her. You'll be able to stay with her the whole time, of course."

"What about Sarah?" Carrie asked.

"Of course she can stay. Now, we need to go over the risks again."

"I'm familiar with the risks," Carrie said.

"I know, but it's the rules."

Carrie sighed and nodded. She'd spent far too much time in hospitals. She knew the drill. "Go ahead."

"Okay … so generally transfusions are one of the safest possible procedures. But there are some risks. First, of course, is the risk of infection. That's substantially reduced by the fact that Sarah donated the blood."

Carrie squeezed her sister's hand again. Sarah's hands were soft, except the tips of her fingers. Those had heavy callouses from her many hours of guitar playing.

"Our second risk is a hemolytic reaction, or allergic reaction. Transfusion reactions are rare in newborns, and Sarah's blood is a good match, so it's unlikely. But it is possible. We'll introduce the blood slowly, so we can monitor her for side effects."

Carrie swallowed. "Okay."

"Those are the main short-term risks. And, as you know, we've gone over the long-term risks. Monthly transfusions will cause an iron buildup in her system. She'll have to begin regular chelation therapy at a year to eighteen months old or risk organ failure."

"Right. Unless we can find a bone marrow donor."

The doctor nodded. "Which we'll keep searching for." He rested a hand on her shoulder. "Listen, Carrie, you've had a hell of a time. I promise you we'll do everything we can for Rachel. Okay?"

Against her will, Carrie's eyes watered. She *hated* not having control of her emotions, but ever since Ray's death she'd been on the verge of tears half the time. Her stomach wrenched at the thought. Sometimes the ache of loss was just too much. She needed Ray here with her. She *needed* him. She rolled her eyes up to the ceiling and nodded, trying to keep control of her face and the watering of her eyes, but that didn't work so she squeezed them shut.

"It's going to be okay." A whisper. And for just a second she felt a hand on the side of her face, brushing along her jawbone. Her eyes jerked open, but the doctor was halfway across the room, and Sarah was answering a text message.

She shook her head, confused and brushing off the disturbing feeling. Dr. Willis held out a clipboard.

"Okay, Carrie, if you can sign here. This just acknowledges that I've walked you through the risks of the procedure. Nurse Reynolds?"

The nurse said, "I'm to sign as a witness. Do you understand what the doctor just told you about the risks?"

Carrie was irrationally irritated. She knew she had to sign. She knew the medical procedures. After all, she'd had to sign the papers allowing them to let her husband die. Shuddering, she took the papers and pen that Doctor Willis held out. She scrawled her signature on the document and said, "Yes. I understand."

"All right," he said. "The nursing team will be in, in just a moment." He took the clipboard back from her and walked out of the room.

Fifteen very long seconds passed by, then Sarah said, "You all right? You looked like you saw a ghost."

Carrie sniffed, then reached over and unbuckled the straps holding her baby in the carrier. She lifted Rachel to her and snuggled her daughter. It was comforting. She didn't have Ray, but she had a piece of him, the little girl he'd left behind. The little girl who Carrie would do anything for. She took a long shuddering breath then changed the subject. For right now, talking about Ray or Rachel was just too raw.

"What's going on?" she asked, nodding toward Sarah's phone.

"Alex just texted me and said turn on the news."

Carrie arched an eyebrow. They didn't have a television in the exam room in the hospital. Sarah's face was a little pale.

"What is it?"

Sarah handed her the phone. She was shaking.

Carrie had to reread the headline three times before it made any sense.

WIFE OF U.S. SECRETARY OF DEFENSE REQUESTS POLITICAL ASYLUM IN CANADA
Cross-border shootout ends in hospitalization of 18-year-old daughter

"Oh, my God," Carrie said. "Political asylum? What?"

"I have to go there," Sarah said.

"To Canada?" Carrie demanded.

Sarah nodded. "If Jessica's hurt, I've got to go to her."

Carrie sighed. "Of course." She paused a second, scanning through the article. It described how their mother had dragged Sarah's unconscious twin across the international border even as a shooter was trying to kill them both. The shooter—the paper read 'the *alleged* shooter'—had been captured by the Border Patrol two miles south of the incident following a high-speed chase. Jessica's injuries weren't described in the article.

Unconsciously, she pulled her daughter a little closer to her.

A single knock was followed by the door opening. Two people stepped into the room—nurses or physicians' assistants. The first, a copper-haired woman, said, "Hello, and how is baby Rachel doing today?"

She walked toward Carrie and reached to take the baby. Carrie pulled Rachel closer.

The woman stopped and said, "Sorry—I'm Melissa, the NICU charge nurse. I'll be supervising the procedure today. May I take the baby?"

Carrie was uncomfortable and tense, but she nodded and held Rachel up an inch.

Melissa, the nurse, took Rachel expertly from her hands and laid her in the plastic bassinet. Rachel's arms and legs contracted and she let out a cry.

"Oh, you're such a sweetie," the nurse said in a sing-song voice, scrunching up her nose. Rachel cooed. "I bet your mom and dad are so proud of you! I bet they are!"

Rachel smiled up at the nurse, even as Carrie flinched.

A second nurse entered the room. Expertly, the two of them began moving around Rachel, laying out towels and other equipment. The second nurse positioned a catheter next to a tiny needle, still in a sealed plastic wrap.

Melissa said, "Get a 25 gauge, please." She began to swaddle the baby, leaving her right arm out.

The second nurse nodded. Melissa said, "This is Jodi. She's one of our NICU nurses."

Jodi smiled and took out a needle, slightly smaller than the one she'd previously placed on the table. A set of tubes stretched across the room, and various kinds of equipment were lined up. Both women wore gloves.

"Mom, we're connecting monitors to watch her pulse and respiration and other vitals right now. Then we'll start the lines. She's going to cry a little bit at first, I don't want you to panic."

Carrie nodded and squeezed Sarah's hand again. She was breathing too quickly and closed her eyes for a second, trying to force calm.

It wasn't working. The second nurse, Jodi, held a pacifier with some liquid, and Rachel happily sucked on it as Melissa taped a board to Rachel's arm and attached the various monitors and sensors. Then she wiped a brown fluid on Rachel's upper arm.

In a low voice, concentrating, Melissa said, "Start the line."

Jodi ripped open the plastic packaging on the smaller needle. Carefully, her face pinched in concentration, she pushed the needle into Rachel's arm.

Rachel let out a choked cry, then a full-throated scream. Carrie flinched as the baby began to struggle inside the swaddling as her face turned bright red. The screaming got louder and Jodi shook her head, just once, negatively.

"Try again," Melissa said, her voice quiet.

Jodi nodded and pulled the needle back. *Oh, God. She missed.* Rachel's mouth was wide open, screaming as loud as Carrie had ever heard her. She sniffed and squeezed Sarah's hand tighter. But she refused to close her eyes or look away from her daughter. She was stronger than that. She'd watched helplessly as her husband drifted away into death. She could be there for her daughter.

After preparing a new needle, Jodi pushed it in again as Melissa held Rachel down with one hand and dripped fluid from the pacifier with the other.

"Got it," she whispered. She expertly inserted the plastic catheter. Rachel screamed louder, and Carrie's vision blurred as tears rolled down her face.

Carrie struggled to hold back a sob.

Jodi attached a tube to the catheter.

"Ativan," Melissa said. She looked up at Carrie. "Mom, that's the pain killer. It will help pretty quickly."

Jodi inserted a hypodermic into the line. Rachel continued to cry, her tiny mouth and eyes wide open. Tears rolled down Carrie's face, mirroring the one on her daughter's.

Damn it, why couldn't you be here, Ray? For the millionth time, she cried out inside, *Why?*

PART ONE

CHAPTER ONE
His Highness The Prince

Dylan. May 4.

Dylan Paris still felt a little woozy, a sharp pain stabbing his forehead as he walked between two Royal Marines. They wore sharp uniforms—form fitting navy blue suits with white belts, rank insignia on the shoulder just like U.S. Marines (though upside down to Dylan's eyes), and white leather-brimmed officer's caps with a red band. Unfamiliar insignia graced the collars and belts, and they wore medals on their chest rather than ribbons. Despite the finery, they wore serviceable sidearms, mean-looking Glock 17 pistols with a dull black finish. These guys were for real. And they were pissed.

At Dylan.

It was all right. He was alive, and by the fact that he was now being escorted into the Embassy for an interview with Prince George-Phillip, he guessed he'd successfully distracted the Marines long enough for Andrea to make it over the wall. His hands were zip-tied behind his back, and his head hurt, but he was pretty sure she'd made it.

Mission accomplished.

The Marines didn't take him toward the main Embassy building, a modern three-story glass and brick structure which dominated the grounds. Instead, he followed them (or rather, was frogmarched in between them) toward the three-story brick building he recognized from the satellite photos as the VIP residence. His heart was pounding. What if Andrea was hurt?

At the sound of a roaring engine, Dylan glanced over his shoulder. The fluorescent green Oldsmobile he'd bought from Mendoza now had a Royal Marine behind the wheel. It was moving into the Embassy compound. He turned back to their destination.

The temperature dropped rapidly when they stepped into a large, dimly lit foyer inside the building. Dylan's eyes scanned the room, noting the three other exits and the broad staircase, which circled around the left side of the room. The floors were highly polished and sported a twenty-foot wide Persian carpet, which probably cost more than Dylan's lifetime income.

The first Marine said, "Stay here," and the second grabbed Dylan's arm. The first then walked away, his heels clicking on the marble floor.

That was the first chink in their armor. Real soldiers didn't click their heels; they wore combat boots. Dylan continued to scan the room, noting escape routes along with more prosaic details like the crown molding. A moment later Clicking Heels came back down the hall and announced in stentorian tones, "His Highness The Prince will see you now." The guards then took him by both arms and guided him down the hall to a scene that looked nothing like he expected.

Prince George-Phillip he recognized instantly. For the one thing, the family resemblance was startling. He was at least six feet six inches—Ray Sherman's height. Tall and lanky, with thick eyebrows and a hawk nose, but otherwise with facial features similar to both Carrie and Andrea. His eyes, deep blue-green, were watering slightly.

"This is your accomplice, then?"

Andrea, who stood several feet away, nodded. Beside her, a girl—maybe six or seven years old—stood holding Andrea's hand. The girl looked just like Andrea. Then she spoke in a wary voice. "Yes."

"Remove the restraints, please," the Prince said to the guards. "Please have Gertrude set up coffee and drinks and lunch. In the sunroom. Jane will be joining us—"

One of the Marines spoke rapidly. "Your Highness, I must insist—"

"You'll insist on nothing. I realize their entry was unconventional, but here they are." Without another word, Prince George-Phillip dismissed the Royal Marines and approached Dylan. "I'm George-Phillip. And you are?"

"Dylan Paris, um ... sir. I'm Andrea's brother-in-law."

The heel clicker produced a pair of scissors and cut the zip tie. Dylan immediately brought his hands in front of him and rubbed his wrists. Then he shook the hand Prince George-Phillip extended.

Andrea spoke immediately. "You acknowledge you're my father, and you expect us to be able to just sit down for a cozy lunch?" Her voice was a high tension wire, ready to break at any moment.

"No, Andrea. But I'd like a chance to get to know you and for you to get to know me."

Her expression remained blank, guarded. She nodded once. Dylan breathed a sigh of relief. He guessed he understood her hesitation. After sixteen years of being rejected by the person she *thought* was her father, it was no wonder she was gun shy about opening up to this remote man she'd never heard of until yesterday.

"Dylan," Andrea said. Her eyes were wide and her jaw was clenched as she spoke the words, and her vocal inflection strange. She was on the verge of hysteria. "Did you know I have another sister? Who I've never met? Jane, meet my friend Dylan."

Her eyes watered, and mouth closed, she released a low rumbling growl in the back of her throat in an effort to suppress her tears. George-Phillip looked at her aghast, as if he'd never seen a woman cry before and had no idea what to do.

Maybe he didn't. Dylan looked at him, met George-Phillip's eyes, and then jerked his head toward Andrea, trying to mentally send the command, *Hug her, damn it.*

Dylan didn't know if George-Phillip got the message from his bad miming, or if his human instincts had suddenly clicked in, but regardless of the cause, the Prince moved toward Andrea with his arms out and a sympathetic expression on his face.

"There, there," George-Phillip said. He rested his hands on Andrea's shoulders. "There's no need to cry. This is one of the happiest moments of my life. I want it to be the same for you."

Andrea began to shake, violently, and she sobbed, unable to contain the tears. George-Phillip pulled her to him and put his arms around her. Andrea stayed still, arms at her sides, but she couldn't contain her crying. She sobbed, loudly, the pent up terrible grief of a lifetime of hurt. George-Phillip murmured some meaningless sounds, and Jane put her arms around Andrea's right leg.

"Why are you sad?" Jane asked.

That just caused Andrea to sob more. Finally, she managed to compose a meaningful sound, a single word that rang out in the room with far more weight than he would have guessed possible.

"Why?"

After she said the word, she pushed back against the Prince's chest, forcing him to release her. Fiercely, she wiped her face with the sleeve of the George Mason University sweatshirt they had bought—what ... two days ago? Dylan couldn't keep track any more.

"Andrea ... my daughter." As he said the word *daughter*, Prince George-Phillips eyebrows seemed to do a solo dance, rising high up on his forehead. Hard to imagine, Dylan thought, that a man with no poker face at all could survive as the Chief of Intelligence of a large country.

George-Phillip continued. "Are you asking why I'm your father? Or why you never knew about it?"

"All of it," Andrea demanded. "I want to know everything. I want to know why I was dumped off in another country and never knew either of my parents. I want to know why ... why..."

She paused, trying to compose her face, then said, "I want to know why I was left to believe I wasn't worth loving."

George-Phillip looked somber. Dylan was usually a pretty good judge of people. There was no question in his mind that the Prince was sincere. Men didn't get that close to crying unless they were devastated.

"I'm so very sorry, Andrea. It breaks my heart that you didn't grow up feeling loved."

"You already broke mine," she responded.

George-Phillip sagged. "Indeed. And Carrie's, I suppose."

"My mother would never have been..." She whispered, "...beaten and raped if she hadn't gotten pregnant with Carrie. It was *your* fault."

"That happened first nine months before Julia was born," he replied in a sad voice.

Andrea closed her eyes. "They met in Spain. When she was eighteen. You're telling me he forced her then?"

George-Phillip sighed and said, "I'm deeply sorry to be telling you this, Andrea. It happened when she was sixteen. And her father died a few weeks later."

"I don't ... why did she marry him?"

"She was forced, Andrea. By her priest and her mother. Those days, things were different, especially in Spain."

Andrea shook her head forcefully. "No. *Abuelita?* Not possible. She would never force her daughter to marry a rapist." She hissed the next word. *"Never."*

Dylan hoped Andrea wouldn't piss off Prince George-Phillip to the point where they were forced to leave. He didn't know what kind of legal limbo they were in—would they be arrested the moment they left the Embassy? For that matter, the police probably didn't know where they were.

He didn't think George-Phillip would do that. But neither of them really knew him, did they? And he *was* the head of the British intelligence agency. You didn't get to that kind of high-level position without the ability to make some cold-hearted decisions.

Prince George-Phillip remained patient. He said, "I know there is much you don't know, Andrea, and much that you have every right to be angry about. I'd like to tell you as much as possible, if you'll let me."

With a quick, firm nod, she said, "Yes. Fine. And I am hungry. Wrestling with your guards is a lot of work."

"Come, then. Both of you. Jane, go wash your hands, and you may join us in the sunroom."

Prince George-Phillip showed them where they could clean up—the *water-closet,* he called it—and a few minutes later Andrea, George-Phillip, Dylan and Jane were sitting at a cozy table in a room dominated by large windows on three sides. Surrounding the sunroom was grass, leading off to the trees and the row of houses on the other side of the fence.

With a wry smile, George-Phillip said, "We'll have to do an audit of security here," he said. "If you'd been an assassin I would have been done for."

Dylan thought the Prince was right, of course. Even though Dylan had distracted the Marines, a sixteen-year-old should never have made it into the building.

A woman wearing a knee-length double-breasted tunic poured tea for all of them. There was no sugar in sight, unfortunately.

"Summer sausage rolls, Your Highness, with mini sandwiches and custard kisses."

Jane's face lit up at the last and she reached for the pastry.

George-Phillip blocked her hand with his. "Have a sandwich or two first, Jane."

The little girl pouted, but obeyed. Andrea watched with misty eyes, and Dylan—whose childhood had been a mess of alcoholics and abuse—understood exactly why. It's what he had always wanted too—a simple, domestic existence, with parents who cared.

Andrea said nothing—simply watching, her eyes moving back and forth between the father and daughter.

"You should know," George-Phillip said conversationally, "I've come to the conclusion that my career is interfering with me spending time with Jane, here. Regardless of what happens with the current scandal, I intend to resign my position as Chief. I've no right to ask this, Andrea—but I'd like you to consider coming to London with me. When you have the opportunity. I'd like for us to get to know each other."

Andrea didn't reply. An awkward silence fell over the table, and Dylan leaned forward. He cleared his throat, covering it with his closed fist—*should he have used his napkin?* Then he spoke. "Do I call you … Highness? Or sir? Or…"

"In public, Highness or Your Grace is generally my title, but here, please call me George-Phillip. Do I have it correct that I have you to thank for my daughter still being alive?"

Dylan gave a wry smile. Not in a million years was he going to call a royal prince by his first name. "Sir, Andrea did that all on her own. She's just about the most courageous person I've ever met."

Prince George-Phillip gave his daughter a warm look. "Would that you hadn't had to deal with those situations. But I'm proud and amazed at how you handled them."

"I was just trying to survive," Andrea said, shifting in her seat. Dylan tried to parse out George-Phillip's sentence, but it still didn't make sense. Would that … what?

Without preamble, George-Phillip said, "I think you should both stay here for the time being. You've been on the run and in hiding, and this is the safest place for you. Not to mention that until things are sorted out with the American investigation, both of you are wanted by the police here."

Dylan met Andrea's eyes. She was impassive. He nodded to her, as imperceptible of a motion that he could make.

She nodded back, then her eyes cut back to George-Phillip. She pursed her lips for a moment then spoke. "Yes, we'll stay. I have a thousand questions for you."

"I'll tell you everything I know," George-Phillip said in a soothing tone. "You can ask anything. Within the bounds of the confidentiality required by my position, I'm an open book to you, daughter."

"You say that my—the person I *thought* was my father—" she whispered the next words, her eyes darting to Jane, "raped my mother. And that she was forced to marry him?"

George-Phillip nodded. "She was seventeen when they actually married. Your eldest sister Julia was born a few months later."

"When did you meet my mother?"

"In the winter of 1984. We met in February, at a dinner party here in Washington. I was new in the city, and so was she. Richard Thompson was traveling much of that spring, back and forth to Central Asia. Your mother and I fell in love."

In the back of Dylan's mind, the worst ran through his head. *Why the hell didn't you protect her, then?* He didn't say the words out loud. It wasn't his place. But he hoped Andrea would ask.

"And so Carrie was conceived," Andrea said.

"Yes."

"And what happened after that?"

"I didn't know about Carrie for many years after that. I … in May of that year … I'd just returned from a trip to London. She broke it off with me … with no explanation. I didn't see her again for twelve years."

Andrea gave him a pained look. "Did she tell you later?"

"Yes, when we encountered each other in China. We were both a little older and wiser then. But Adelina … it was tragic. He'd destroyed her spirit. The bright, courageous woman I'd known had become a mouse in public, never contradicting anything her husband said. She told me that the reason … the reason…"

George-Phillip's face twisted in pain.

"Da?" Jane said. "What hurts?"

George-Phillip placed his left hand on Jane's shoulder. And his right hand on his chest. "My heart hurts, Jane. My heart."

Jesus, Dylan thought.

George-Phillip said, "Jane, I think it's time for you to go see Adriana."

Jane's eyes watered. "I want to be with my new sister."

"I promise you can later. Right now, we need to have some adult talk."

She climbed down from her seat, as always looking precarious—as if she might any instant go flying in one direction while the chair went in the other—then walked around to his chair the long way around the table, passing Andrea and Dylan along the way. She stood on her tiptoes and gave the sitting George-Phillip a kiss.

"Play with me later?" she asked.

He nodded and said, "Yes, of course."

"Will you play with me too, sister?" she asked Andrea.

Andrea might be distrustful of George-Phillip, but it was clear she held no reservations about her six-year-old half sister. Her eyes went glassy, and she nodded and said, "Yes, I'd love that."

A few minutes later, after the little girl had left the room, George-Phillip continued. "While I was out of town, out of the country, Adelina had realized she was pregnant. And she believed that Richard would kill her, or Julia, or possibly her brother Luis, if he found out she was pregnant. She believed he was a complete sociopath. I don't know if that's the case or not, but she provoked him into attacking her. So that she could convincingly make him believe that Carrie was his."

Andrea winced. Seemingly without volition, she reached out and grabbed Dylan's hand.

"I tried to persuade her to leave him. I did. I'd have gladly given up my career and taken her hand in marriage. I wanted that more than anything else in the world."

"But you didn't," Andrea said.

George-Phillip gave her a sad smile. "I didn't. When we met again in Beijing … many years had passed. Your mother and I … resumed our affair. But with very strict rules that *she* set. You see, a great deal had happened in the years we didn't see each other. Richard began to suspect that Carrie wasn't his child, because she was so incredibly tall. He took her to a lab and had them both tested. And when he found the results, he beat Adelina almost to death."

Andrea winced. She didn't say anything, just listened. She hadn't touched the food.

"Later, she told me what those years were like. Your family moved a lot—based in San Francisco, then Belgium for three years, then China. Your father had the perfect deep cover—he was Central Intelligence Agency, but as far as the world was concerned, he was a diplomat. That gave him license to operate anywhere. As the years went by, he kept her off balance. Randomly he would terrorize her—keeping her anxious and confused. That just got worse as the years went by."

Andrea gritted her teeth. "She was crazy," she said.

"What do you mean?" George-Phillip asked.

"You describe a victim who was terrorized by Richard Thompson, but what I remember is that she was crazy. She'd break down at the slightest provocation. She was completely unpredictable—the same behavior that one day resulted in a mild scolding would, the next day, provoke screaming rage. She cut us to pieces with her words."

Dylan sighed. He knew what that was like—his father had been a complete bastard and a drunk. For the first time, he felt real sympathy for his mother-in-law. Adelina Thompson had been the terror of all of her daughters. He'd never imagined she'd undergone that sort of trauma.

George-Phillip's eyes watered at Andrea's words.

George-Phillip. May 4.

She cut us to pieces with her words.

Oh, Adelina, why didn't you leave him when I asked? When I begged?

He tried to imagine the Adelina he'd known being abusive. He couldn't. She had been kind and honest and terrified. She'd been anxious often. She'd told him how she'd struggled to separate her daughters from the emotional devastation of their father.

He remembered sitting with Adelina in the Maryland suburbs of Washington at an anonymous restaurant, sometime in April 1984.

It's not Julia's fault that he's her father, Adelina had said. *She deserves all of me, but sometimes I flinch back.*

George-Phillip had sighed, slightly squeezing his hands at his temples. *Please leave him, Adelina. I'm begging you. You deserve so much better.*

Adelina had smiled, a wide, false smile that didn't hide her glassy eyes. *Do you know what he sent me the other day, George-Phillip? He's in Pakistan or some place, but he stopped in Spain long enough to take a picture of my brother. It was a threat.*

George-Phillip had shuddered. A few weeks later she broke it off with him.

He shook his head, coming back to the present. Right now, Adelina wasn't his problem. Convincing his daughter—*his daughter!*—that she could trust him—

that was the task at hand. He looked Andrea in the eyes and said, "I'm so sorry. I didn't know that it had gotten so bad."

Andrea shook her head, her mouth turning up on one side, her expression of skepticism breaking his heart. "Of course you didn't know," she said. "You weren't there."

He was shaken, and covered it by taking a drink of his tea, giving him a few seconds to compose himself. Finally, he said, "Of course, you are correct. I *wasn't* there. And regardless of the reasons—which there were many—there's no real excuse."

Andrea looked at the floor. Then she said, "But you came to Spain. The first time I went there with Carrie."

George-Phillip smiled. "I did. And other times. I was at your concert two years ago. You have a beautiful singing voice."

Andrea blushed. "You were there?"

"Of course. I couldn't make it often, you see, without revealing something. But when there were opportunities to not be observed—I tried to take them."

Every summer in Calella, on Friday nights in the old town, there was a series of live performances. When he'd learned that she would be performing in one, he had discreetly traveled to Spain. He remembered standing in the back of the crowd that milled around the square, and Andrea's nervousness when she walked out on the stage. She'd hesitated at first and looked at a woman he now realized must be her *Abuelita*, or grandmother. Then she smiled, a beautiful smile, and began singing *a cappella*.

He didn't understand the words—George-Phillip spoke fluent French, but no Spanish—but her expression, her vocal intonation made it clear she'd inherited her mother's gift for music. His eyes began to mist again.

"Forgive me," he said. "I'm afraid I haven't a firm grip on my emotions today. I'm wondering—have you heard from her? Do you have any idea where she might be? Your mother?"

Dylan and Andrea looked at each other before speaking, a look that was heavy with meaning.

Dylan leaned forward and said, "Sir ... I spoke with her very briefly. On April 30th. It was right before the shooting started."

George-Phillip sighed. "That was the last time I spoke with her as well."

Dylan tilted his head to the right, raising an eyebrow. "I thought you guys weren't talking."

"We weren't," George-Phillip said. "But I was tracking the family as closely as possible when I got word Andrea was going back to the United States. There are some people with powerful secrets who want them kept. I think they thought that if it came out in public that Richard had raped his wife, his whole career might come under fire. Which would risk exposing Wakhan."

Dylan flinched. "Wakhan? In Badakhshan Province?"

"You're familiar with it?"

Dylan grimaced. "I served in Badakhshan Province during my time in Afghanistan. We didn't get out to the Wakhan Corridor though. Too remote—not even the Taliban is interested in that place. What is it they're trying to keep secret? And what does Richard Thompson have to do with it?"

George-Phillip sighed. Then he said, "What I'm about to tell you is highly classified. But *The Guardian* actually broke the story today, so that secrecy is of dubious value. In 1983, a group of Afghan militia dropped nerve gas on a village in Wakhan, killing everyone in the village. Two CIA officers and a Saudi intelligence officer procured the nerve gas from Russian stocks. Richard Thompson was one of them."

"Holy shit," Dylan said. Then he flushed, an uncomfortable red running down his cheeks and neck. "Excuse me, uh, Highness ... uh ... sir."

George-Phillip chuckled. "Really, man, I served in the Royal Marines. I've heard salty language once or twice. In any event, I was already on high alert after Andrea's kidnapping." He turned and looked at his daughter, musing for just a moment on how incredibly courageous she'd been. "You really are something," he said. "Any man would be proud to call you his daughter, you know."

She just looked down at the table. She didn't trust him yet, of course. That would take time. He just hoped he would get the time.

"In any event," he said, "we were monitoring the communications of certain people who were known to associate with Tariq Koury."

"Hairy Chest," Andrea said.

George-Phillip raised his eyebrows.

She responded, "That's what I mentally called him. The entire flight over he sat next to me, with his shirt unbuttoned halfway down. It was disgusting."

"I see," George-Phillip said. "You understand Koury was an intelligence operative with nearly twenty years of experience. He started out with the Saudi *mukhabarat,* but went on to freelance. He was very dangerous. You're a very resourceful young lady to escape him."

"I didn't kill him," she said. Her eyes were watering as she said the words.

George-Phillip tilted his head.

She went on. "The police killed him and his partner. I just—struggled to survive. The newspapers keep saying I somehow killed those two men with my bare hands. It's not true."

"Unfortunately, the newspapers often write things which are untrue," George-Phillip said.

Dylan frowned and muttered, "Ain't that the sad truth."

The guesthouse butler appeared at the door. "Your Highness, the Ambassador wishes to see you."

On a Sunday? It had to be about the disturbance. He stood, wiping his mouth with the linen napkin, and said, "Excuse me a moment, Andrea. Dylan."

He walked to the door, glancing back once. Andrea and Dylan were huddled together, talking already. He walked out the door.

Stephen Easton was a younger version of the doddering old fool who had been Ambassador to China when George-Phillip was stationed there in the mid-nineties. Much like his older brother Ronald, Easton had traded on his good family name and wealth to get ahead in the diplomatic service. Neither of the brothers had ever really accomplished anything, though Ronald's son Harry—currently an attaché on the staff here at the Embassy—did go from scandal to scandal throughout his formative years.

Easton leaned on his cane as George-Phillip approached. He was approaching seventy years old and looked every second of it, thanks to a lifetime of heavy foods, sitting behind desks, and drinking plenty of port.

"Your Highness," Easton said.

"Ambassador."

"Your Highness, I must protest. I'm given to understand that a pair of intruders invaded the grounds of the Embassy, and instead of turning them over to the proper authorities, you have taken them in and given them lunch? What has gotten into you, sir?"

Easton's face was already turning red. George-Phillip promised himself that he wouldn't antagonize Easton too much—the old blowhard was likely to pop off with a heart attack at any moment.

"Ambassador, one of the two intruders is my long-lost daughter."

Easton's eyes widened. "Dear God, it's true?"

"It is, Ambassador. She's had a dreadful week. People are trying to kill her, and it is my intention to keep her here, safe and protected. This is not negotiable."

Easton shook his head, waving a hand vaguely in the air. "Surely, a hotel nearby with proper security…"

George-Phillip raised his eyebrows. "That is not an option."

"Is it true that both of them are fugitives from American law enforcement? Do you realize the sort of international incident you might be precipitating?"

"There will be no international incident if the Americans don't know they're here. Will there?" George-Phillip raised his eyebrows and leaned close, restraining his urge to verbally flatten the old man. *She's my daughter.*

"Your Highness, they mustn't be here more than a few days. I won't allow it."

George-Phillip sighed. A lot could happen in a few days, and there was little he could do to prevent it. He still didn't know where Adelina was, nor had he spoken with Carrie. Not to mention that terrible article in *The Guardian*.

"Fine, then, Ambassador. I should be able to make other arrangements in a few days."

Stephen Easton started to turn away, but then turned his head back toward George-Phillip, his myopic eyes huge in the thick lenses he wore. "Your Highness … how much of this has to do with the article in the Guardian?"

George-Phillip sighed and said, "It's tied closer than I'd like. But I assure you that the accusations against me are false, and I shall prove it in due course."

Easton raised his eyebrows and minutely shook his head. The old man was skeptical. "Well, then," he said and turned away.

George-Phillip turned to go back into the sunroom, but saw his assistant for thirty years, Oswald O'Leary. O'Leary was Irish, short, with the face of a pug. Foul-mouthed, unconventional, and brilliant, he'd served George-Phillip tirelessly for decades, and he was the only person who had George-Phillip's full confidence. Now he stood at the door looking grim.

"What is it, O'Leary?"

"He's right, you know, Highness. No good can come from you harboring them here."

"Someone is trying to harm my daughter," George-Phillip said.

"She should be turned over to the American authorities. She'll be safer there anyway."

George-Phillip muttered an internal curse then said, "I thank you for your advice. But she's staying here. What do you have for me, O'Leary?"

"Highness, Adelina Thompson turned up."

"Dear God, where? Mexico?"

"No, sir. Canada, actually. She and her daughter crossed the border on foot. It seems there's not even a fence on the Canadian border. They ran across as someone was shooting at them."

"She's still with her daughter?"

"Yes, sir. Jessica Thompson is in the hospital, sir."

Alarmed, George-Phillip said, "Was she shot? Is Adelina all right?"

O'Leary shook his head. "Not shot, sir. I don't know all the details yet—only what's been reported in the news. We don't have anyone on the ground yet. But the Canadian media is reporting that Adelina Thompson is demanding political asylum."

George-Phillip gave O'Leary a grim smile. "It's about time," he said. "I must get back—thank you for the update, O'Leary."

George-Phillip stepped past O'Leary, reaching for the door, when O'Leary touched his arm.

"Highness? Remember that Adelina Thompson is not the nineteen-year-old girl you once fell in love with. She's..."

"She's what, O'Leary? Old? As are we both."

"No, Highness, that's not what I meant. She's ... not healthy. Mentally."

Anger flooded through George-Phillip. "Well, maybe it's time she was given the opportunity to heal." He pushed past O'Leary.

CHAPTER TWO
He won't stop until I'm dead.

Adelina. May 4.

"**Mrs.** Thompson? I'm Liam Tremblay, with Citizenship and Immigration. I've been assigned to your asylum case."

Adelina came to her feet. Tremblay was an unprepossessing man, roughly thirty years old. He had a crooked and mashed nose, which looked as if it might have been broken in a fistfight, but he wore a respectable looking suit.

"I understand your daughter is undergoing some serious medical issues, so I won't bother you today if you don't have time to talk."

Adelina shrugged helplessly. "My daughter is in treatment right now, I've got nothing but time."

"I hope her prognosis is good..." He raised the pitch of his voice slightly at the end of the sentence, as if he were asking a question.

Adelina looked at the floor. How was she supposed to answer that? Her daughter had become addicted to crystal meth. She'd done irreparable harm to her body and her brain. She might survive the stroke, but it was equally likely there would be more.

"All we can do is pray," Adelina said. Which was bitter. She'd prayed for a lifetime, to no avail.

Tremblay sighed. "I see," he said in a soft voice. "I'm sorry."

"Please, Mr. Tremblay. What can I do for you?"

"Well, Mrs. Thompson, I'm the preliminary immigration officer. What I'm empowered to do is to reject your request for asylum out of hand, if I determine there's no merit to it, or I can forward it on to the tribunal which will make a ruling after a hearing."

She nodded. "My claim is valid," she said, her voice confident.

"Be that as may, the process must be followed."

"How long does it take?" She needed *time*. If Canada wouldn't take them in, maybe the United Kingdom would. *Somewhere*. She needed time to find out why Richard was sending assassins after her and Jessica.

"Well, ma'am, if we go forward with your case, then your hearing will be within sixty days."

"And how long does it take to make your decision?"

He smiled at her. "That I can do with a simple interview, here and now."

She breathed a sigh of relief.

"Please. Please, go ahead."

"All right, then. I'm going to ask you a few questions. I want to make it clear right up front, as a matter of normal rulings, we don't accept asylum cases for people who crossed the border from the United States."

Anxiety shot through her. "Why not?"

He gave her a gentle smile and held a hand palm up. "Normally," he said. "The fact that someone was shooting at you when you came across the border changes things. Typically, the reason is because the U.S. and Canada have an agreement that if a refugee reaches our borders, then they must apply in the first country reached."

She nodded. "Okay. I understand. That makes sense. But I'm a refugee *from* the United States."

"That may be a first, ma'am. So I'd like to take you through some questions to determine the validity of your case. I'm going to ask you some basic questions. Please answer them briefly and truthfully."

He took out a notebook and a pen, then perched a pair of reading glasses on the end of his mashed up nose. The reading glasses hung a little crookedly.

"Mrs. Thompson, first of all, where were you born?"

"Spain."

"Do you hold Spanish citizenship?"

She shook her head. Another pang of loss. "No. I renounced my Spanish citizenship at the time I obtained United States citizenship. That was in 1987."

"I see. Why did you not keep dual citizenship?"

"My husband was an American diplomat."

"When and where did you marry?"

"In Calella, Spain. April, 1981."

"Why did it take so long to get your U.S. Citizenship?"

Adelina stared at the man. Wondering if she was making a mistake. She'd kept Richard's secrets for thirty years, to protect her children, to protect her brother. But then she remembered. Richard had hired killers to kidnap their daughter Andrea. He'd sent killers after her and Jessica. He'd finally gone insane. There was no more keeping secrets.

In a flat, toneless voice, she replied, "Because Richard didn't want anyone to know he'd raped a child. So we waited until I was significantly older than eighteen."

Tremblay coughed, his eyes slightly bugging. "Please clarify."

"I was sixteen when Richard Thompson raped me. He was a serving diplomat in Spain at the time. He then murdered my father a few weeks later, when my father became suspicious. My mother and priest forced me to marry him when they realized I was pregnant."

"Dear Lord," Tremblay said. "Yet, you've stayed with him more than thirty years."

"It's not that simple that I could just walk away. I had to stay to protect my children and my brother," she said. "They're worth a lifetime of torture."

"Why did you flee now?"

"My youngest daughter, Andrea, is not his. When he learned she was coming back to the United States, he sent assassins after her. And me."

"Andrea Thompson," he mused. "I saw a great deal in the news about her. And you believe that if you go back to the United States, you'll face risk of further attacks?"

Bitterly, she said, "He won't stop until I'm dead."

Tremblay closed his notebook then took a sheaf of paper out of his briefcase. "Wait just a moment, please. I'm going to approve your case to go forward, which is going to raise a stink since you're from the United States. You'll likely be facing some media attention. Sorry about that."

Adelina gasped. He dialed his phone, and a moment later was speaking with someone. "Yes. Yes. I need a date. Okay..."

Tremblay hung up the phone and scribbled a date into a blank at the top of the stack of forms.

"Your hearing date will be June 26th. In the meantime, you'll need to fill these forms out completely. You have fifteen days to complete them and return them to me. I'm issuing you and your daughter two-month visas. Welcome to Canada."

Adelina burst into tears. Tremblay looked helpless, so he continued to awkwardly fill out paperwork and look away while she tried to collect herself.

"I'll need to see your passports, ma'am. Do you have your daughter's?"

"I do," she said. She fumbled in her purse and passed over their personal passports. Tremblay scanned them with his phone then took pictures of the photo pages. A moment later he stamped both.

"Thank you," she whispered.

"My pleasure, ma'am. Do you have a place to stay while you are here?"

"Not yet, but I have money to rent a couple of rooms. For now I'll stay at the hospital until Jessica is recovered."

He smiled and passed her a business card. "Here is my number in case you need to reach me. I'm based out of the border station in Abbotsford—the one you sneaked by when you crossed that field. I hope you'll allow me to help if you need anything at all."

She gave him a smile, and he left. Her heart was pounding, hard, a feeling that was all too familiar. A full-blown panic attack was on the way. She closed her eyes and began to pray. Once they started she couldn't stop them. Every time. Her heart rate would increase, then chest pain, and unbearable fear in her body.

She didn't have to have a reason. She'd begun having them in Belgium more than twenty years ago, when Richard cruelly tormented her with words and threats, leaving her unbalanced and terrified.

You know, he said once, *it's only a twelve-hour drive to Calella. And I've never met young Luis. What is he, thirteen now?*

You leave him alone!

Then you behave, he had snarled back.

The random cruelty he'd begun to visit on her had begun after he'd learned Carrie wasn't his daughter. He didn't need to make threats. He'd thoroughly cowed her with the hideous assault in February '90, which had impregnated her with Alex and left her with lifelong scars.

She stared at the door, beyond which the doctors were treating Jessica. She hated herself for not leaving him thirty years before. He'd threatened all along that he would hurt their children, that he would hurt her, that he would kill Luis. If she "misbehaved." But now he'd done it anyway, and Jessica was in the hospital, and she had no one but herself and Richard to blame for it.

The pain in her chest was worsening. It always did. The first time it happened, in 1991, she'd been rushed to the hospital, thinking she was having a heart attack. *No,* the doctors informed her. Nothing physically wrong with her at all. They suggested Paxil, a powerful antidepressant.

She tried it, but it made her feel like bugs were moving under her skin. For the next twenty years she went through a series of different anti-anxiety and anti-depressant medications. Her doctors were baffled.

But she did remember, one day not long after Julia went off to college, Doctor Thornton spoke with her. *No amount of medication will stop anxiety that's well-founded in something in your life, Adelina. Is there something I need to know about?*

She behaved. She denied it, changed doctors and stayed terrified.

She clutched her fist against her chest and whimpered. The pain was severe.

"Mrs. Thompson—are you all right?"

She looked up, tears in her eyes. It was a nurse. "Panic attack," she whispered. "I've had them before. I normally take Ativan when I have one, but I don't have any."

"Let's take you down to an exam room," the nurse said.

"No! I need to stay near Jessica."

The nurse smiled. "Jessica's going to be just fine. The doctor is actually on her way to see you now."

Hope suddenly flooded through her. "What? Really?" She shook so hard her teeth rattled against each other, and it seemed like an hour before the doctor appeared.

"Mrs. Thompson? I'm Linda Gates, the chief of neurosurgery."

Neurosurgery. That's what Carrie's husband Ray had ... before he died. She looked up. A tall woman with long blonde hair tied in a bun stood in front of her. She wore a white coat with blood stains on it. Adelina continued to shake.

The surgeon continued. "So ... first of all, your daughter is in recovery. She had a hemorrhagic stroke, not an obstructive one. That means blood was pouring into her brain when you arrived at the hospital. Once we clearly identified that, she went immediately into surgery. I was right down the hall at the time she was brought in. We cleared out most of the blood and repaired the damaged vessel."

"She'll fully recover?" Adelina asked.

"It's too soon to tell, Mrs. Thompson. Your daughter had a life-threatening stroke. I understand she was a regular crystal meth user?"

Adelina nodded. Ashamed. "Yes."

"I'm so sorry," Doctor Gates said. "That's heartbreaking." She reached out and touched Adelina's shoulder. "Panic attack?" she asked.

Adelina nodded, quickly. Tears rolled down her face.

"She said she's had them before," the nurse said. "And she takes Ativan."

"Well. You don't have any here with you? Is there anyone at home who can bring it to you?"

Adelina shook her head. "We're … refugees, I guess. She had the stroke when we were attacked just before crossing the border from the United States. I've asked for asylum."

"Oh, dear. Well … I'll write you a prescription for Ativan then. Good luck with your application."

Adelina sank back into her chair. Three people in a row had been incredibly kind to her. She thought about how isolated she always was. It had been since the 1980s when she last had friends. Richard had put a stop to that, insisting that she never go alone anywhere except church or school events.

I don't want you hanging out with the Rainsleys any more. Charles always has his eyes all over you, and Brianna does too.

They're friends, she'd replied.

You don't get friends, Adelina. You raise your daughters and go to church and you behave. Understand?

As the years went by, she'd hated Richard Thompson more and more.

Bear. May 5.

"Scott Kelly speaking," said the rough voice on the line.

"It's Bear."

"Bear! When are you coming back?"

"Heh, that's a funny joke. I'm suspended, asshole."

"Yeah?"

"You got time to meet? I got some questions for you. It's about your sisters." Kelly didn't have any sisters, and Bear knew it.

"Sisters? Yeah, sure. Where?"

Bear thought for a moment. Huh. He knew a good place with a loud fountain. The International Monetary Fund had a large building at 19th and Pennsylvania, which wasn't a bad walk from State or from Bear's apartment.

"Meet me at 19th and L. Coffee shop in the lobby of the IMF building."

"I'll be there in twenty minutes," Kelly said. "You're buying."

"I'm unemployed, motherfucker."

Kelly laughed and hung up the phone.

Eighteen minutes later, John "Bear" Wyden walked into the ground floor of the tan stone and glass headquarters of the International Monetary Fund. Outside, like all government and quasi-governmental buildings in Washington, the building was surrounded by concrete bollards and plants, which looked decorative but were designed to protect against car bombers coming into contact with the building.

Inside, only a small area was open to the public, a coffee shop on the ground floor and a cafeteria on the second floor, accessible via escalator. Otherwise the building had fairly tight security, with armed guards checking credentials and running people through metal detectors.

Bear walked toward the coffee shop and muttered a curse. Kelly had beaten him there. Which meant Bear was buying.

Kelly joined him in line. In a conversational tone, he said, "You won't believe who I talked with for the first time ever this morning."

"Yeah? Who's that?"

"A certain Vietnam vet turned Senator turned Cabinet Secretary. He called me up to tell me that I'm officially in charge of the State Department side of the investigation—that you've been suspended indefinitely. He also told me that *informally*, I'm to cooperate with you. Which I would have done anyway."

Bear chuckled. "I bet that caught your attention."

"What is going on, Bear? The IRS and Justice Department just crawled up my ass. They're all over this investigation, Diplomatic Security is just peons now. I'm making copies of documents for the independent counsel."

They had reached the front of the line. Bear ordered a thick mocha with whipped cream and a chocolate croissant, one of his several vices. Kelly snorted when Bear placed the order, and said, "Give me coffee and a donut."

Two minutes later they were sitting next to the loud, glistening marble fountain in the ten-story atrium. "All right, so who is actually running the show now?"

"Guy named Rory Armitage. Independent counsel, he was contracted out by the Justice Department and handed a whole bunch of investigators and a near unlimited budget."

"You'd have to have that to go after the Secretary of Defense."

"Yeah, well, he doesn't have a chance in hell of being confirmed as Secretary now. His hearings start tomorrow, and I'm guessing the President will pull the plug before then."

"All right. So who else?"

"The other biggie is some guy from the IRS ... Smith ... no ... crazy name ... Schmidt. Wolfram Schmidt. From *Texas* if you can believe that. The Justice Department guys are working with DEA to try to track down drug connections because of the stuff they found in the sisters' condo. IRS is following the money. They've found a bunch of accounts in the Caymans registered to Thompson. Lot of money there, a lot of recent large transfers."

"That's crazy," Bear said. "What else?"

"You heard Adelina Thompson and her daughter Jessica turned up? They ran across the border of Canada on foot while some asshole was shooting at them with a rifle. The daughter's in the hospital now. And get this: Adelina Thompson—the wife of the Secretary of Defense—asked *Canada* for political asylum from the United States, because she claims her husband hired assassins to kill her."

"Whoa," Bear said. "What happened to the shooter?"

"He tried to get away, but the Bellingham Police got him. And now they've got a big jurisdictional dispute going on, because the shooter was arrested in Bellingham, but the Justice Department and Customs and Border Protection want him."

"Huh," Bear said. "What's his name?"

"Nick Larsden. He's a … a grifter. Small time bounty hunter from LA, he makes his living tracking down bail jumpers. He makes a big deal about having been a veteran, but he was a personnel clerk in Germany when he was in the Army. Failed as a private investigator, then migrated into bounty work."

"That's a big help, Kelly. It's huge. Larsden's the guy I want to talk to."

"Good luck. Everybody wants a piece of him. What's your angle? Why are you working this on your own?"

"Let's just say something about the official story stinks. Richard Thompson may be a scumbag, but I don't buy that his daughters were his couriers and enforcers and shit. That's crazy."

Kelly shrugged. "I've seen crazier."

"Yeah, well, I'm operating on the assumption that there's a different angle. For one thing, from what I understand, Thompson's daughters found files related to the Wakhan Massacre in his office, right before the house was destroyed. Then a few days later, the Sunday *Guardian* runs a special report implicating Thompson in the massacre. I want to know what the links are, and who else was involved."

Bear's mind ran back to the photograph in Thompson's personnel file. The photo which was stolen from his apartment, along with the rest of the documents. He remembered who was in the photo. "Here's who I'm interested in … Prince Roshan of Saudi Arabia. Leslie Collins. Richard Thompson. Prince George-Phillip of England."

Kelly's eyes widened. "You don't think small."

"That's why they call me Bear."

"Bullshit. They call you that because you're so hairy."

"Seriously. I need to know everything I can about those four."

"You want everything. Files on the chiefs of intelligence of three countries, including ours. Access to a criminal who the feds are fighting over."

"Yeah. Can you make it happen?"

Kelly stared at him. Then he said, "I'll do what I can."

"I'll be headed west then, on the cheapest flight."

"Yeah? You going on vacation?"

"I was thinking Washington State."

"Nice. Catch you later, Bear."

Bear stood up and stretched. He walked out of the building, thinking hard. How the hell could he get at Larsden? And who hired him? Richard Thompson? That didn't make sense, unless he had a massive vendetta against his wife. Which was possible. He'd never seen two people less suited for each other.

He needed more information, and he didn't have any resources. As he walked up 19th Street, headed back to DuPont Circle, his mind circled around and around. Then he landed on a neat solution. He knew somebody with access to high-level officials, lots of staff and information, and who had no trouble flying all over the place chasing information. It went against every instinct he had, which meant it might be an awful idea—or a brilliant one.

His brow furrowed. Then he took the phone out and dialed 411.

"*The Washington Post*, please. Editorial offices, not subscriptions."

He was connected sixty seconds later. It took a couple of minutes to get through receptionists, but then he landed directly in Anthony Walker's voicemail.

"Yeah—Walker. This is Bear Wyden. Call me." He gave the number and hung up.

He sighed as he walked. He felt better rested today than he had since Andrea Thompson had arrived in the United States on April 28th, one week before. Leah was stabilizing, and she was awake and crabby as ever. The kids had to be told they couldn't climb all over her due to holes in her body. Teenagers—just like toddlers.

Leah, he thought. *Time to move on, Bear. She's remarried.*

Yeah, he knew.

His cell phone rang. It was a 202 area code—Washington, DC. He answered.

"Mister Wyden? It's Anthony Walker."

"Call me Bear, please."

"All right. Call me Anthony. What can I do for you?"

"I think you and I have some things in common right now. Want to get together?"

"Sure. I'm at the Thompson condo right now. The FBI forensics team turned the condo back over to Carrie."

"I'll head up the red line then, and meet you there. I need to talk to them, too."

"See you shortly, then."

CHAPTER THREE
The road to hell

Andrea. May 5.

Andrea leaned back in her seat, luxuriating in the rare feeling of relaxation. The morning sunlight shone through the glass of the sunroom, and for the first time since her departure from Spain a week before, she'd slept the night through.

She still didn't trust Prince George-Phillip. She might never. But at least, for once, she felt safe.

Just outside the glass door of the sunroom, Dylan sat on a bench. He had a cigarette in his right hand, and a pen in the other, writing furiously in a small notebook Andrea hadn't seen before. She didn't know what he was writing about, but his expression was pained, sometimes furious. Dylan had barely been civilized when he first woke up, and immediately poured the coffee and went outside, leaving Andrea to Prince George-Phillip—*her father.*

"Your friend has a real storm on his brow," George-Phillip observed.

Andrea shrugged. "He served in Afghanistan. And Ray Sherman was his best friend."

George-Phillip's face softened. "Carrie's husband."

"Yes," Andrea replied.

"I want to reach out to her." As he said the words, his eyebrows moved furiously. Andrea tried to interpret their dance, but she couldn't.

"Why?" she asked.

George-Phillip blinked. "What do you mean, why? She's my daughter, just as you are."

Andrea sat up, studying him. Then she said, "Don't do us any favors."

"I truly wish I hadn't hurt you so terribly." He sighed as he said the words.

"El camino al infierno esta empedrado de buenas intenciones," Andrea muttered. *The road to hell is paved with good intentions.*

George-Phillip raised an eyebrow.

"Don't worry about it," she said. "Just … this is all a shock. I just wish I could trust it."

George-Phillip sighed. "I do too. It will take some time, but I promise you, I will prove it to you, and to your sister Carrie."

"So what's next?" she asked.

"I have a meeting with your President this morning, and several other meetings in the afternoon with the Ambassador and others. This evening I would like to have you and Dylan for dinner. And—I'd also like to invite your sisters. Carrie, at least, and the others if they wish to come."

"I think Alexandra will come," Andrea said. "Dylan's wife."

"Yes. I'll have an invitation sent. Is she likely to be at the condo?"

"I have no idea. Last time I was there, someone was trying to kill us."

"Indeed. I'll find out where they are. Is there anything you need in the meantime?"

"I need to call my uncle and grandmother in Spain."

"Of course. Feel free to use the phone in the parlor, just through that door."

He stood, and so did she. She felt awkward. She didn't even know what to call him. "Um … um … Your Highness?"

George-Phillip's eyebrows twitched uncontrollably. It was almost funny. His words were sobering, however. "I'd be grateful if one day you would consider calling me *Father*. But in the meantime, George-Phillip will do. Please, no titles. Not between us."

Andrea swallowed. Then she said, "George-Phillip, then … I … I know I must seem ungrateful or … I don't know." She wanted to stomp her foot in frustration. Andrea didn't get tongue-tied. She rolled her eyes up to the ceiling, because she felt a sudden welling in them. Then she said, "I've always wanted a father who loved me. Who cared about me. And I never understood why *he* didn't. I never understood why they sent me away. So forgive me if you seem to be too good to be true." Then she held her breath and blinked her eyes, willing herself *not* to cry.

He looked at her with a loving expression and said, "Take as long as you need, Andrea. I understand that I'll have to earn your trust."

Then he was gone. She considered storming outside where Dylan was. Yelling. Throwing something. She didn't know what to think, how to react, how to behave. She didn't know what to believe. There was no doubt what he said was true. He *was* her father.

But the rest of it. Could she possibly believe him that her mother had told him to stay away? That she'd *begged* him to stay away. That he'd wanted to reach out to her, that he'd wanted to meet her all along, that somehow he'd watched her and paid attention and showed up at the festival when she sang.

Why had Abuelita never told her?

Adelina. July 5, 1994.

"All right," Bear Wyden said. "You're cleared to go, but I want you to check in with me when you cross into France and again into Spain. You understand? I know Washington says the threat to you guys is over, but I just want to be sure."

"Thank you, Bear," Adelina said. "You can't know how much this means to me."

"I got a pretty good idea," he muttered, tugging at the straps on top of the Fiat Tempra station wagon, a vehicle that Adelina hated. The suitcases were just as secure as they'd been for the last fifteen tries.

"Girls, get in the car, please," she said. "Julia!" she called. Julia was clear across the garage, sitting on the hood of a highly polished classic Fiat. Normally she would have been horrified to see one of her daughters behaving that way, but Adelina had a special place in her heart for Corporal Barry Lewis, the strapping young Marine who had been assigned as Julia's guard. Twelve-year-old Julia had a massive crush on her bodyguard—whenever he was around, her face would flush red and she would stammer and stutter. Lewis took it all in good humor and spent a lot of time with her even when he was off duty. In some ways he'd become a surrogate father for Julia. A father she needed, given the emotional absence of her real father.

"Julia! Come!"

"Go on, princess," Lewis said. "I'll see you in a few days."

Julia blushed bright red at the word *Princess*. Then she jumped off the hood of the car and ran across the garage. Carrie was already buckling in. Adelina winced a little as she lifted almost-four-year-old Alexandra into her car seat and began buckling the straps. She'd infuriated Richard again, this time by not remembering the correct military rank of the Danish military attaché. He only rarely used physical violence with her anymore, preferring to keep her in continuous low-grade terror.

Whatever his current state, he'd agreed to her driving to Spain with their daughters for a week-long visit with her family. It would be the first time she'd been home since her wedding.

Adelina got into the driver's seat. Julia was buckling in next to her, and her lower lip was pouting out. As Adelina started the car and put it into gear, she said, "What's wrong, Julia?"

A moment later she was driving out of the Embassy compound and onto the streets of Brussels, Belgium. Of the cities she'd lived in so far, Brussels was probably her least favorite after Washington. In San Francisco, she'd mostly felt a sense of freedom—at least until the night Richard almost killed her (*the night*

Alexandra was conceived, whispered her unconscious—she shoved the thought down). Washington had mostly been terror. Belgium was unstable. One day he was incredibly kind, the next cruel and erratic. She lived in a constant state of tension and fear, and the panic attacks continued to grow worse all the time.

As she drove into the traffic, she considered turning around. What if she had a panic attack on the road?

She looked over at Julia again. Tears were running down the girl's face, smearing her mascara. *Her mascara?* When did she start wearing makeup? She thanked God Lewis was an honorable man and looked at Julia as a daughter, because the girl had no sense at all when it came to him.

"Why the tears, Julia?"

"I don't want to go to stupid Spain. I want to stay with Daddy."

Bitterness swept over Adelina again, but she swallowed it. "We'll be back in a week, dear. Your father has important meetings this week"—*with prostitutes and his secretary, undoubtedly*—"he won't be around to look after you."

Julia shook her head and looked out the window. She muttered something under her breath.

"What did you say?" Adelina asked.

"I said, that's nothing new. No one looks after me except Corporal Lewis." Her tone was sullen.

Adelina looked in the rearview mirror. Carrie was already wrapped up in a book. *Steel Beach* by John Varley. She didn't understand Carrie or the strange things she read. Science fiction mostly, but also a fair amount of romance. The girl was smart beyond her age and had abandoned young-adult books by the time she was nine.

She looked so much like George-Phillip sometimes it broke Adelina's heart. It broke her heart that she would never see him again, and it broke her heart that he didn't know his daughter. She often wished she'd acceded to his demands—that she'd run away, that she'd given in.

But when she thought that way, her mind always returned to Richard's threats. The most recent had been crude. She'd walked into her bedroom and found a photograph on her pillow. Black and white, it depicted a young man—fifteen or sixteen years old, with a crude crosshair drawn over his face in black Sharpie.

It was her younger brother, Luis.

She was stunned, really, that Richard had allowed her to make this drive. But he'd been distracted, preparing for the upcoming NATO summit, and for a moment the leash loosened. She took immediate advantage.

On the dashboard, she had taped the map, which Corporal Lewis had painstakingly highlighted in red. Beside it, directions were handwritten and also taped to the dashboard. Lewis and Bear had been fanatically protective of Adelina and her daughters, as if they sensed something was seriously wrong in her family but didn't quite know what it was.

Julia had slipped on a headset and put a cassette in her Sony Walkman. It had been one of her Christmas gifts, and she listened to it constantly. She never wanted to do her piano practice, but there was no question she loved music. Although Adelina had doubts about some of the "music" Julia listened to. Right now it sounded like the croaking of frogs was leaking out of her headphones.

"Julia," she said. "Turn that down."

Instead of turning it down, she turned it up. It *did* sound like frogs croaking, with a haunting violin in the background.

"Julia," she said again.

No answer.

"Julia!" she said sharply.

Julia glared at her, then said, "Leave me alone," and whipped her face away from Adelina, her brown hair flying everywhere. She curled up, leaning against the window and staring out.

Andrea. May 5.

Why had Abuelita never told her?

The phone George-Phillip had indicated was visible through the doorway. It was an oddity, an antique, a rotary phone with an ivory handle and gold inlay. It was highly polished, and she was almost afraid to touch it. The phone sat on a fine looking table with a marble top and mahogany legs. Two luxurious high-backed chairs upholstered in sapphire brocade flanked the table.

She'd never used a rotary phone before, but she understood the principal of the thing. She sank into one of the chairs, much more comfortable than it looked, and awkwardly picked the handset up out of the cradle. She reached out and began dialing.

011 ... The first number took forever, the dial cranked around all the way, then circling back, odd clicking sounds coming from the headset as the dial turned. It was difficult to imagine how people could have used these things regularly without wanting to smash their head into the phone. As she watched it turn, she felt her anxiety increase, her stomach tensing.

34 ... The country code for Spain. She'd known how to make a direct dial international call since she was ten years old. She wasn't sure that was knowledge any ten-year-old needed.

937... She continued dialing the nine digits of her grandmother's phone number. And as she did so her jaw hardened, her hand squeezing the grip of the phone hard enough her knuckles were white.

As she finished dialing, she heard silence for a moment, then a series of clicks and hisses. She didn't use landlines generally, and certainly not antique phones. But a moment later the phone at the other end began ringing, a shrill burst of two tones, pause, two tones, pause.

"*Diga*." *Speak.* It was Abuelita's voice.

Andrea couldn't breathe for a moment. She sniffed, horrified at herself, then said, "*Abuelita*, it's Andrea."

"*¡Gracias a Dios!* Thank God you called, I've been so worried about you!" Her grandmother paused for a moment—as Andrea knew she would—then launched into a tirade. "Why have you not called me? It's been a week, and all I see is headlines that you've been attacked and kidnapped and running for your life. Have you lost your mind? Andrea, I want you on a plane home today! Today, do you hear me?"

Andrea heard the phone thump, and then her grandmother shouted, "Luis! Luis! Come here now! Andrea is on the phone, tell her she must come home *now*."

Luis was there? It was Monday morning; he should be working in Barcelona.

"Luis!" her grandmother screamed.

"*¡Abuelita!*" Andrea shouted into the phone. Unconsciously she stood up and began pacing, forgetting that the phone was *wired to the wall*. The pretty gold telephone base fell off the table, stretched out the cord and tugged Andrea toward the floor. Awkwardly, she fell to her knees and grabbed at the base with her free hand, trying to keep it from landing on the cradle and hanging up the phone. Her grandmother was still shouting in the background, so Andrea had an opportunity to right the phone and get it back on the table, then sit on the edge of the chair again.

A moment later, a harried sounding Luis came on the line. "*¡Muñequita!* I'm so glad you're okay, we were terrified."

"Thank you, tío," she replied. "I need to speak with *Abuelita*."

"What? You don't even ask how your poor uncle is doing?"

"I'll ask in a minute," Andrea said, her voice cold. "I have *other* questions to ask right now."

"I don't like the sound of your voice, *Muñequita*. Tell me what is going on. *Madre* has a weak heart."

"I *must* speak with her, Luis."

"Fine. Fine! And if your poor old grandmother has a heart attack, you will feel guilty the rest of your life. Yes? Is that what you want?"

"Luis, I'm *begging* you." Her voice was ragged as she said the last words.

He didn't say anything else. A moment later, her grandmother came back on the line.

"Andrea, it's time for this nonsense to end. I didn't raise you to be disobedient, I expect you to—"

Andrea interrupted. "Why did you never tell me my mother was raped? And that my father is *not* Richard Thompson?"

Her grandmother said, "Is your mother telling those lies again? I am so disappointed in her. She was not *raped*. Her father, *he* let that man touch her—"

"*Stop!*" Andrea whispered. Hot tears ran down her face, a sudden pang of disappointment gouging a hole in her heart. "Did you force her to marry him? Did you?"

"Of course not. I would never do such a thing. She threw herself after that man."

"You *lie*," Andrea cried out. The tears were running freely now. "He raped her, Abuelita. He did."

"It's not true! Your mother lies to you! You *know* you cannot trust her."

"*She* didn't tell me," Andrea whispered. "*She* didn't. My father did. My real father. And the police report. He did it again. After they were married. More than once."

Her grandmother gasped. "Where do you get these crazy ideas? Your *real* father? I don't know what—"

"Did you know he was coming? When he showed up at Miguel's wedding? And on the beach? At my concert?"

Abuelita didn't answer. On the other end of the line, her breathing was hoarse. "Andrea..." she finally whispered.

"*Why?*" Andrea said.

"She was *lying*." Her grandmother repeated the words again, and again, as if saying the words repeatedly just might make them true. As if saying those words was a talisman that would protect her from what she'd done to her own daughter. "She was *lying*."

"No, Grandmother," Andrea said. "She wasn't. And that changed everything. It ruined her life, and it twisted all of her daughters' lives."

"No," her grandmother whispered. Andrea heard the phone thump against the table a continent away. She waited, thinking Luis would pick it up. She waited, but no one ever picked up the line. After five minutes, the knife-edge tone of the off-hook signal sliced through the silence into her chest, cutting her loose from the only family she'd ever trusted.

Adelina. July 5, 1994.

It was nearing midnight when Adelina drove the last few blocks to her mother's flat in Calella. Even though she hadn't been here for more than a decade, the blocks surrounding the flat were familiar. She had few good memories here.

Adelina had come to live with her mother after her father, Juan Ramos, had been murdered, most likely by her now husband. She'd spent those weeks in terrible pain and grief, occasionally walking or sitting for hours along the beach. She could still taste the bitterness of her tears in those months. It took her years to reach any internal peace about her mother's role in her marriage. If she had any at all. Whatever peace she once had was shredded by driving down these streets.

All three girls were asleep. Julia was still curled up against the window, her tape long since ended. Carrie was halfway sprawled across the back seat, and Alexandra was asleep in her car seat, pacifier in her mouth. Adelina brought the car to a stop half a block from her mother's flat, and with tired eyes she stared up at the windows, which were undoubtedly open this time of year to let a breeze through. The windows were dark—everyone had gone to sleep, she supposed, even though they knew when Adelina would be arriving.

That was a bitter thought. She hadn't seen her mother or brother in a dozen years. The least they could do was stay up past dinner time. But then she saw a shadow pass in front of the window, and a flickering light. They were home and awake after all, but the lights on this side of the flat weren't on.

She still didn't want to go up. What would she say? She was regretting having made this trip. The conversation with her mother two days ago was difficult, to say the least. They had little in common, little to say to each other. Adelina asked about Miguel and Luis, and her mother asked about Richard, which merely put a sour taste in Adelina's mouth. But she couldn't pass up the opportunity to get out from under Richard for an entire week, and the girls did deserve to know their grandmother.

She didn't know if their grandmother deserved to know them.

She sighed and pulled the car to a stop in the tiny parking lot behind the apartment building. She didn't know which spot was her mother's. She would find out soon enough—she pulled into the only empty spot then turned off the car. Despite the late hour, loud music poured into the streets from a bar nearby, and she could hear people talking and laughing. It was July in a resort town on the Mediterranean—the night sounds would continue until two or three in the morning. Even so, she could hear the crash of the surf against the beach, and the sound instantly took her back to Ocean Beach, where she often walked in the mornings during her too brief time in San Francisco.

Julia stirred in her seat. Adelina leaned in and touched her on the shoulder. "Julia, wake up, we're here. Carrie, you too."

Both girls grumbled, but she got them moving. Alexandra began to whine as Adelina woke her to get her out of her seat, but settled in Adelina's arms as she walked out of the parking lot and around to the sidewalk and the front of the building. A man stumbled toward them, partially shadowed from the streetlamp, and Adelina instinctively gathered her daughters around her. And that's when it hit her.

Adelina had been sixteen when Richard raped her. Now her *daughter* was almost that age.

Without volition, her heart suddenly began racing, her pulse pumping loudly in her ears, a sharp pain in her chest, terror closing her throat and mind. She staggered, clutching at her chest, and Julia cried out, "Momma?"

Unbidden tears began to run down Adelina's face as her chest tightened in even more pain. "*Madre de dios,*" she whispered, not realizing she'd fallen to her knees with Alexandra still calmed in her arms. "*Help me.*"

"Momma!" the girls screeched, terrified. *Momma!*

***

Dreams.

Adelina was floating, and it was peaceful. She was sitting on the edge of North Beach, the sun shining down on her like the love of God.

But she knew Richard was coming home soon. The sky was getting darker, heavy with dark clouds. She felt a raindrop, thick like oil, one, then another, the fat drops crashing against the ocean, drumming, pounding, crashing, aching, like hammers against a metal roof, and she was in the flower shop again, but not with her father. *Richard* was there and she was just a girl bound for the National Youth Orchestra and he took it all away.

She screamed.

***

"She's waking up."

Her eyes slid open, vision blurred. She looked up. Her mother was sitting there next to Luis. Luis was a big strapping sixteen-year-old with a huge grin.

"Hey, big sister," he said. Adelina's eyes were getting heavy again.

Adelina's eyes bored into her mother's. "Why did you make me marry my rapist?" she demanded, her voice heavy.

"I didn't *make* you marry anyone, Adelina. What are you talking about? How dare you?"

"Get out. You've made my life a *living hell!*" Adelina screamed. "Get *out!*"

She screamed long after they were gone, until her throat was raw, and the cool medication ran through her veins and took her back into a deep sleep.

***

"Mr. Ambassador, we recommend against taking her now. Your wife has been through a terrible shock and needs medication and treatment."

"She'll get treated in a hospital with American doctors. She wouldn't have had these problems in the first place if she hadn't come to Spain. None of them are coming back to this place. *Ever.*"

CHAPTER FOUR
What hearing?

Leslie Collins. May 5.

Monday morning was never pleasant for Leslie Collins, but after the longest week of his career, *this* Monday was the worst he could imagine. As always, he'd gotten out of bed at 4 am, beginning his day drinking coffee as he reviewed the intelligence summaries of the day. It was more of the same. Violence spreading in the Ukraine as nationalist and pro-Russian forces came into conflict. The German newspaper *Bild am Sonntag* had somehow gotten wind of the fact that the US had sent specialists from FBI and CIA to advise the Ukrainian government on how to stop the rebellion in Kiev. Leslie made a note to have someone follow up and find out the source of the leak. Iraq had just finished its bloodiest month in a year, with more than 750 Iraqis killed in April, most of them civilians. As always, Leslie bristled at the implication that the Agency should be doing more there. If Congress and the President would give him the resources, he could do something. As it was, the President had crippled the Agency.

At least he wasn't heading up the NSA. Edward Snowden's revelations of NSA spying had diverted a lot of attention from CIA in recent months, and while technically they were all on the same side, Leslie wasn't above a little interagency competition. Collins had come to believe that his career was going to mirror that of his predecessor George H. W. Bush, who had moved from the Director of Central Intelligence to Vice President and finally to President. He had the ability. He had the ambition. One day he would be at the helm, and he would destroy al-Qaeda and ensure his country's safety.

Review of his official files completed, he turned to his less official reports. And he froze.

Adelina Thompson had been shot at crossing the border into Canada? And she had asked for political asylum? Asylum was the craziest thing he'd ever heard, first of all, but he'd been very clear with Danny McMillan that there was to be no more violence directed at the Thompsons. He had more than enough paper trails established to ensure that Thompson was destroyed, and more violence would only serve to raise suspicions. What he needed right now was for the independent prosecutor and the grand jury to indict Richard Thompson. Smear his name until nothing he said was believable, before he went public about Wakhan and somehow tried to blame Collins for it.

Christ, he thought. If his role in Wakhan—or Andrea Thompson's kidnapping, for that matter—ever came to light, he could forget about his ambitions. Was Danny trying to sabotage him? Danny had to know he was replaceable—after all, he'd taken care of Mitch Filner, who had *once* served as Collins' chief confidential aide.

He picked up the phone and started dialing, never mind that it was 4:30 in the morning.

The phone rang—once, twice, three times. Then a groggy voice answered. "Hello."

"McMillan. It's Collins."

At the other end of the line, was a muttered curse and fumbling. Then the sluggish voice said, "Do you know what time it is?"

"I don't care what time it is. What the hell happened on the border yesterday?"

"The border with where?"

"With Canada, you idiot. Why did you send someone to attack Adelina Thompson? I thought I made it clear I didn't want any more violence."

Silence for just a second, then McMillan said, "Collins, I don't know what the hell you're talking about. I didn't send anybody after her. We've been watching, and that's it. I didn't even have a bead on her. She turned up?"

"She turned up at the border crossing with a former soldier in pursuit, then demanded political asylum. Which she's not likely to get; it's Canada, after all. But I guarantee you it's going to make a lot of news."

"I don't know what that's about, Collins."

Leslie thought furiously. If McMillan's people hadn't shot at Thompson's wife, then who did? And why? It didn't make any sense.

Richard Thompson. May 5.

I understand, Richard. I really do. But the political liability at this point is massive. And we can't have the Secretary of Defense wrapped up in a scandal on the eve of his confirmation hearing.

Richard Thompson gritted his teeth in rage as he sat in the back of the car and rode back toward the base at Fort Myers. As always, traffic in and out of Washington was snarled. At least he didn't have far to go, Fort Myers was right across the river. He presumed that he would have some days to clear his personal property out of the house there. The bigger sting was the President just dropping him. As if he had no confidence that Richard would survive this storm.

Survive he would. But first he had to make it through the next few days. And those would be difficult enough.

The last week had consisted of nothing but wave after wave of shocks. First, the news that Adelina's daughter, Andrea, was coming to the United States, after he'd expressly ordered Adelina to keep her away. It was bad enough that Carrie's height continually reminded him that Senator Chuck Rainsley had been with Adelina—*Senator Chuck Rainsley, of all people*—but to have a second daughter by him. It made Richard queasy to think of it.

In truth, he'd tried to be a good father to both of them. But he just couldn't stomach it when it came to the youngest girl. He supposed it was because he knew from the first that she wasn't his. Carrie he'd had as a baby, and it stayed that way until she'd had her blood typed at six years old. With Andrea, he knew from the beginning—he knew in the surest way possible that he was not her father, because he hadn't touched that hag since the night he'd, in a drunken stupor, forced himself on Adelina and conceived the twins.

Richard Thompson no longer drank to excess.

His phone rang. Richard almost pressed the ignore button, because he recognized the number. It was Joseph Bergmann, the senior staffer of the Senate Armed Services Committee. Bergmann had been a thorn in his side for weeks as he'd prepared for his confirmation hearings—hearings that had been scheduled to proceed in the morning, but were now pointless. But the fact was, this scandal wouldn't last. He'd be cleared soon enough, and then hopefully he'd be able to move on with minimal damage to his career.

"Richard Thompson speaking," he said, answering the phone.

"Ambassador Thompson, this is Joseph Bergmann."

Ambassador Thompson, not *Secretary* Thompson. Clearly Bergmann had gotten the word already.

"I suppose you've heard the President is rescinding the nomination?" Richard asked.

"I have, I'm sorry to hear that, Ambassador. Please allow me to offer my condolences. I'm sure when all this is sorted out you'll be back on top again."

"Thank you, Joseph," Richard replied in a dismissive tone. He didn't need sympathy from a mere Senate staffer. "If there's nothing more, I'll—"

"Actually, Ambassador, I was just calling to verify that you'd gotten word the hearing is being moved to the Central Hearing Facility in the Hart building because of the increased interest from the public and media."

"Excuse me?" Richard said. "*What* hearing? Why would you hold confirmation hearings when my nomination has been withdrawn? Get it together, man."

Bergmann's tone went cold. "There's no need to be rude, Ambassador. In fact, Senator Rainsley insisted on going forward with hearings into your conduct at the Central Intelligence Agency, and specifically events in Badakhshan, Afghanistan in 1983."

For the first time in years, Richard was rendered speechless. He sat in the seat, phone at his ear, unable to speak, unable to think of what to say. *Your conduct at the Central Intelligence Agency?* He'd never been officially associated with the Agency except in the very early 1970s. Some people in the government were aware of his role at the Agency and the State Department, but they were few indeed.

Chuck Rainsley, the bastard who had seduced his wife, was one of those people.

Bile flooded through Richard Thompson. He wanted to hurt someone very badly. *No one* took what belonged to him. And Chuck Rainsley had been undermining Richard's marriage and his career for more than thirty years.

"Ambassador? Are you still there?"

Richard shook his head, suddenly aware that Bergmann was still on the line. "Of course I'm here. And I have no intention of showing up for your fishing expedition. As it stands, I'm no longer a part of this government."

"Ambassador, I wouldn't recommend that. When you get back to Fort Myers, you'll find a subpoena waiting. Senator Rainsley is in a rare mood, and I suspect if you fail to appear you'll be cited with contempt of Congress."

Richard closed his eyes. He responded in as calm a demeanor as possible. "Fine, then, I'll see you in the morning."

Bergmann hung up without further comment. Richard thought through the appalling events of the last few days. Andrea kidnapped—most likely by thugs working for Leslie Collins. That inept son of a bitch was doing everything he could to undermine Richard and prevent him from becoming Secretary of Defense. But he wasn't the worst of it. His wife—his *stupid bitch of a wife*—had made an international laughing stock of him. *No one* asked for political asylum *from* the United States. People came here to be free. They didn't run away. Yet that whore had dragged their daughter across the border and asked for *political asylum.*

It was all over the networks. The Secretary of Defense's wife flees, claiming he's trying to murder her. The Monday morning *Washington Post* had his and Adelina's photo on the front page. The headline read, "Embattled Secretary of Defense nominee's wife flees country claiming abuse."

He wanted to put his hands around her neck and watch her slowly turn blue. He wanted to watch her eyes bulge. He wanted to feel her terror. He *hadn't* been trying to kill her, but that said absolutely nothing for her future. And her stupid brother Luis should start counting his days. He'd *warned her.* For thirty years he'd warned her.

And not just her. Chuck Rainsley. He remembered how he'd shown up at their condo back in 1984, self-absorbed and fancy in his Marine Corps uniform, all smiles and loud exhortations of his own heroism. As if getting all your men killed made you a hero.

He knew what to do. He took his phone back out and dialed. Moments later, the phone was answered.

"Richard!" The cultured, rich voice of Prince Roshan al Saud was friendly.

"Roshan, how are you? I understand you are in the United States?"

"Only for a few more days. I intended to ask you to dinner, but I know you've had a great number of challenges in the last few days."

Richard waved a hand. "It's quite all right. However, I'd like to meet for a bit if you have time."

"Are you free this morning? I'm just leaving a meeting at the Embassy, I'll be back home in twenty minutes."

"That's perfect."

He leaned forward and said, "Driver, change of plans. We're going to Langley, Virginia."

Twenty minutes later, the car pulled into Prince Roshan's palatial Virginia home. He waited for the driver to come around and open the door, then got out of the car, carrying his briefcase.

Roshan met him at the door. He wore a conservative looking grey suit and red tie, with a pin representing the Saudi flag pinned to his lapel. It bizarrely reflected the de rigueur Washington uniform since September 11th, 2001, which required men in any government role to wear an American flag, as if that somehow proved their loyalty. Roshan's greying hair and beard served to highlight his dark skin. His fat, puffy body, with rounded cheeks and a prodigious belly, was a caricature of his former self.

Richard weighed no more than he had when the two men met in 1983, and he took Roshan's weight gain as a lack of self-discipline.

Of course, that wasn't the only sign of a lack of discipline. The endless parade of call girls was another, as was Roshan's DUI two years ago. Roshan had been behind the wheel, careening through downtown drunk when he drove his Maserati through the front windows of an old townhouse on 16th Street. The State Department had to go to considerable effort and expense to cover the incident up, and to bribe both the appropriate officials and the elderly widow who owned the house.

However, right now, Roshan looked fine, besides the bloodshot eyes. "How are you, Richard?"

"Good, good!" The two shook hands, then Roshan took his shoulders and grinned. "Come in, please."

Moments later, Roshan served Richard a gin and tonic without asking what he preferred, pouring the gin from a bottle of Hendricks. Richard sipped. Roshan had made the drink stiff.

"I hear things are rough for you, my friend," Roshan said in a sober voice.

Richard nodded. "A little, but not as bad as it appears. May I be frank?"

Roshan nodded.

"Leslie Collins is behind much of it. The financial stuff, the accounts in the Caymans? That's all his work. No one else it could possibly be."

Roshan leaned forward and said, "We have several mutual problems. Collins is one, I agree. He's a loose cannon. But that's not all. You saw the report in *The Guardian?* It's everywhere now. And you've been named in it, along with Prince George-Phillip. You understand how wrong this could go. I'd expect your Congress to announce an investigation within a week."

Richard grimaced. "Already happened. And I bet you can guess who is behind it."

Roshan rested an index finger against his cheek. "Rainsley?"

Richard nodded. "He wasn't satisfied with fucking my wife. Now he wants to destroy me. But I'm not going to let that happen."

"What will you do to prevent it?"

Richard took a sip of his drink. He loved Hendricks gin. In a dry voice, he alluded to his thoughts. "Roshan, you and I both know that we did everything we could to keep Collins under control in Afghanistan. I was as appalled as anybody that he would commit the crimes he did there."

"Yes, Richard," Roshan said in as unnatural a tone as Richard had ever heard. "We both felt that way. But how can we prove it?"

"Believe it or not, Collins received an official reprimand. It was classified, of course. But it's not beyond belief that it would be leaked now, given the circumstances. Possibly to the special prosecutor, which might divert them from me."

Roshan chuckled. "I'm not surprised you kept some insurance around Collins, Richard. It makes me wonder what you have on me."

Richard smiled. "I *trust* you, Roshan."

Roshan nodded. Richard knew Roshan didn't believe his polite lie.

"All right, Richard. I will help take care of our mutual friend. You concern yourself with Rainsley and make sure that document gets leaked to the right people."

Marky Lovecchio. May 5.

The death metal blasting out of the speakers of Marky Lovecchio's 2014 Dodge Challenger was loud enough that the rearview mirror vibrated with every thump of the bass drum. He liked the music. It drove out the ugly thoughts, and Marky had plenty of ugly thoughts, whether it was memories of his first enlistment (Somalia) or his last (the Sunni triangle), whether it was his failed marriage or the accountant who had seduced his wife while he was in Iraq. Sometimes his ugly thoughts were of prison, where he'd ended up after he beat said accountant within an inch of his life, then threatened to shoot his wife in the face. It had been ugly there for a few minutes, the standoff with the police, but he finally dropped his weapon. Suicide by cop wasn't his style.

Three years later he'd gotten out. He couldn't go back in the military, not with a felony conviction, but that didn't stop a career with a private military contractor, which paid better anyway. Lately he'd been taking on jobs for the mysterious Oz, an Irish gentleman (possibly) who had been keeping Marky busy for more than a year with jobs big and small, some interesting and some not so much.

The latest job was a problem. He'd been ordered to track down a woman and her daughter. It should have been simple. The woman's house in San Francisco was bombed (he didn't know by who) and it turned out she was pretty smart, disappearing off the face of the earth. Lovecchio had drifted south out of San Francisco, showing pictures everywhere he could, until this morning, when he saw the woman's picture on the front page of the paper. She'd gotten away, making it across the border into Canada.

That was a problem, but not as big as the next problem. When they ran across the border, Nick Larsden had been in pursuit, and fired shots across the border after them, which was a big no-no as far as cops on both sides of the international border were concerned. Then Nick had the bad grace to get caught.

He and Nick had gone through basic training together, way back in 1994, and when Nick had told Marky he was looking for work, Marky hooked him up with Oz.

Big mistake. Now Marky was waiting for a phone call, and he had a pretty good idea what that call was going to involve.

For now, he sat in his car along an overlook, watching the ocean far below. He loved the Pacific Ocean. But not as much as he loved getting into the shit. Somewhere along the way in Iraq, he'd gotten the taste for it. He felt invincible—he'd been through five combat tours in three theaters of war. Lesser men all around him had fallen to bombs and bullets, disease and suicide. Marky just kept going.

Sometimes he thought he was immune. He had to be. In October 1993 he and his squad had been separated from the main body of Bravo Company, 75th Rangers in Mogadishu and fought their way through half a dozen city blocks surrounded by literally *thousands* of pissed off Somalis. 18 Americans dead, 80 wounded, somewhere upward of 3,000 Somali casualties, and Marky had walked through it without a scratch. Twelve years later, as a senior sergeant in Special Operations, he'd been briefly captured in Fallujah in the Sunni triangle, only to have a squad of Marines come in fast and dumb into the building he was being tortured in. The result, fortuitously, was four dead Hajjis and one free Marky.

Lately though, he'd been starting to wonder. Like, maybe there was something more to life than all this bullshit. He didn't like running around shooting at people, and that's what the jobs for Oz had consisted of, at least in the last couple of weeks. That was bullshit.

But he also knew that once you were on the hook, Oz didn't take no for an answer. Which was why he was sitting here in the car, waiting for the phone to ring.

Waiting. Waiting.

The volume on the music was so loud that he jumped when the music suddenly cut off, replaced by the ringing of his phone through the car speakers. He quickly turned the volume down then answered.

"Lovecchio."

"Mister Lovecchio, this is Oz." Oz—or whatever his name was—did not sound happy. As always, his voice was gravelly, the Irish accent a quarry full of age and aggravation.

"Hello, sir."

"We have a problem, Lovecchio."

"Yes, sir. Nick Larsden?"

"That's right. First, he had the woman in his sights and let her cross the border. Second, he let himself get captured. If he's in custody, then he can talk."

"Yes, sir."

"You're going to correct that situation. Do I make myself clear?"

Marky nodded slowly, even though he knew Oz couldn't see him. He'd had the feeling it would come to this. Marky owed some level of loyalty to Larsden—after all, they'd both served in the Army at the same time, though Larsden was nothing but a paper pusher. But he didn't owe him *that* much. Larsden had screwed up and he couldn't be allowed to keep screwing things up.

Worst of all, Larsden knew Marky's name.

"I'll take care of him, sir."

"Good. Let me know when it's done. It needs to be quick, before he tells the American police anything. Am I clear?"

"Yeah. He's in the Bellingham jail. I know how to take care of that."

"Then the woman and her daughter."

"Yeah?" Marky asked.

"Yes. They're in a hospital in Abbotsford. Once you've taken care of Larsden, then I'll get you more details."

"I'm on it, sir."

Oz hung up without another word. Seconds later, the Bluetooth switched back over and the death metal came back on the radio, once again causing the rearview mirror to pulse. Marky started the car and backed out of his parking space. It was a four-hour drive to Bellingham.

CHAPTER FIVE
He's not my father.

Bear. May 5.

When Bear stepped off the elevator on the 20th floor, he immediately saw two armed and uniformed security guards standing in the hall. A third was at the opposite end. All three wore tactical vests and carried both pistols and rifles.

The occupants of the other three penthouses must be overjoyed.

Bear walked down the hallway toward Carrie Sherman's condo and one of the guards immediately approached him. The other stood back, hand on his hip, while the first said, "You're here to see Mrs. Sherman? Identification, please?"

He took out his Diplomatic Security Services identification and badge and showed it to the guard. He approved of their thoroughness. The guards wore the logo of Pinkerton Security Services, a firm that had been doing security and private investigation since before the Civil War. Julia Wilson, who was undoubtedly paying for this, didn't kid around.

A moment later they cleared him to head into the condo.

Bear's first impression was utter chaos. He'd last been here on Friday night, a few hours after the attack. The forensic team had been through over the weekend, searching the entire condominium, and they'd left behind a tremendous mess. They hadn't made any attempt to clean up the fan of blood stains on the wall near the front door, where Dylan Paris had cut off the hand of one attacker with a meat cleaver, then stabbed the other in the back during a short and extremely violent melee.

He continued inside.

Carrie Sherman was standing in the middle of the chaos. Papers everywhere. The coffee table turned over. Bookshelves emptied, the books scattered in a pile on the floor. Knick-knacks taken from the mantle and left—somewhere? Carrie's face was strained, angry.

Across the room from her, Anthony Walker was gathering up a pile of papers and stacking items. He could hear the others—Sarah and Alexandra, he supposed—talking in another room.

When Carrie spied him, she said, "Was it your people who did this?"

Bear shook his head. "FBI forensics. Normally they straighten up after themselves. This was—excessive."

"Well, you can help straighten up."

Bear grunted. "Sure. I need to ask you guys some questions, and have a talk with Walker here. What brought you out here anyway?"

Anthony shrugged. "I had questions too, but when I walked in the door, Carrie put me to work."

Bear chuckled.

Carrie was staring at the mantle. She muttered, "The goddamned head is missing."

"The *what*?"

"My father brought back this stupid head from Indonesia or someplace. It's been on this mantle for thirty years or more. It's gone."

"The forensics team should give you a list of anything they removed from the apartment," Bear said.

Carrie muttered something under her breath and walked out of the room.

"She's cranky," Bear said.

"Wouldn't you be?" Anthony replied.

Bear surveyed the ruin of the room again and frowned. "Yeah."

Anthony stood and faced Bear. "So what's this about?"

Bear said, "First, what I'm about to tell you isn't official."

"All right," Anthony said.

"I've been temporarily suspended by the Secretary." He made air quotes as he said the word *suspended*. "DSS is officially off the investigation."

"Gotcha. But you're doing some looking on your own?"

"Exactly. Something stinks in this investigation. I'm trying to find out what."

"So what do you want from me?"

Bear shrugged. "I'll help you, you help me."

Anthony nodded. "Information."

"That's right," Bear said.

"Agreed."

"What do you say we sit down? I want to go over what we know. What you know, what I know. Who did what, and when."

"Let's move into the dining room," Anthony said. "I want to lay this out."

The formal dining room was twenty-five feet long and had a table capable of seating sixteen. Highly polished wide plank flooring and extensive crown molding gave an impression of luxury and wealth.

Bear said, "I've seen a picture of this room. The Thompsons used to host dinners here. There's one in particular I keep getting stuck on."

Anthony raised an eyebrow.

Bear said, "The guests were Prince George Phillip. Prince Roshan al Saud. Leslie Collins. Chuck Rainsley."

"Are you serious? When was this?"

"February of '84."

Carrie, walking by in the hallway, stopped and stood in the door. Beside her, Julia touched her arm. Both of them were listening.

Anthony said, "February '84 was not quite three months after the Wakhan massacre."

"What does that have to do with us, though?" Julia said, interrupting. "Why did Dad have pictures and files about that?"

Bear stared at her, stunned. "He had pictures? Of Wakhan?"

"Yeah," Anthony said, his voice grim. "It was unmistakable."

Bear said, "Before Thompson's personnel file was stolen, I read through it. It looks pretty clear that Thompson was stationed in Afghanistan in '83. So was Leslie Collins. And—Prince Roshan was also in Afghanistan at the time."

Anthony said, "I want to suggest an idea here."

"Go," Bear said.

"Okay, so … Richard Thompson goes to Afghanistan. Let's say, just for speculation—that it wasn't the Russians who gassed that village. We'll speculate that *The Guardian* is correct, and it was Afghan militia, backed by Thompson. And not just him, but that Collins and Roshan were involved."

"Okay? But what does that have to do with now?"

"I'm getting there," Anthony said. "First—again, according to *The Guardian*, and also some of my co-workers at the *Post*, Prince George-Phillip was responsible for the British investigation. Second—he is Andrea and Carrie's father."

Bear shook his head and said, "That's confirmed now?"

Carrie nodded. "Andrea and Dylan turned up last night after Andrea jumped the wall into the British Embassy."

Bear chuckled. "That girl has more balls than a basketball team."

"I've received an invitation from the Prince to come to dinner this evening."

"All right. So—he's your father. Which means he and your mother had an affair—what—when?"

"Spring of 1984."

Bear nodded. "Then at some point later on, they got back together. When? Where?"

Julia said, "In China. 1996."

Bear said. "What I don't get is this: who tried to kidnap Andrea? Why?"

Anthony said, "To … keep the affair secret? Who would want to do that? I assume George-Phillip."

"Maybe. The Guardian says he suppressed the findings of the investigation. Why? Something to do with her? With Richard Thompson? Was someone else involved?"

"Maybe he was threatened somehow?" Julia said.

"Or *she* was," Carrie replied.

"We know that he had *some* reason to suppress the findings," Bear said. "We know your mother had a long-standing affair with Prince George-Phillip. And, based on the police report, your mother and father didn't have much love lost between them."

Carrie said, "He's *not* my father."

Julia closed her eyes and sighed. "He is mine. But the more I learn about him, the more disturbed I am. I've seen the police report you're talking about. It raises a lot of questions. So does her diary."

Bear said, "Her diary?"

Julia nodded. "Yes. It's—in Spanish—difficult to read handwriting. But she makes it clear that she felt like she was a prisoner."

Bear sat down in one of the embroidered dining chairs. "I don't get it," he said. "There's something we're missing. All right … who are our suspects?"

Anthony's eyes darted to Carrie and Julia. Then he said, "I don't think we can rule out Richard Thompson."

Bear felt his stomach tense. "Yeah. Yeah, I don't think we can either. Especially if he knew Carrie and Andrea weren't his kids."

Carrie sighed and sat down at the table. Julia walked up behind her, resting her hands on Carrie's shoulders.

Carrie said, "He knew. He told me Chuck Rainsley was my father. But Rainsley said no, and now … well, you know."

"Okay, so Thompson is one possibility. What's his motive?"

"Revenge?" Anthony said. "He's still pissed his wife had an affair. He was fine until Andrea came into the country."

"Okay. Who else?" Bear asked.

"Leslie Collins," Anthony said.

"Okay," Carrie interjected. "Who is this Collins guy?"

"He's Director of Operations at the CIA," said Julia. "He's basically the second-in-command. I remember him, sort of. He used to come over and meet with Dad. Mom always got weird when he was around."

Carrie raised her eyebrows. "How long ago?"

Julia shrugged. "When I was in high school. Sometimes he'd come over and he and Dad would lock themselves in the office for hours. Mom and Dad had Collins and his wife over for dinner a few times. Can't remember her name. Mary? Meredith? I think I may have met him before that, when I was really little. I'm not sure."

Bear grunted. "Okay. So Richard Thompson and Leslie Collins are both suspects. Who else? Who would need to keep your parentage a secret?"

"Mom?" Julia asked.

Carrie shook her head. "No ... but what about my father? My *real* father?"

Anthony nodded. "It would make for a ferocious scandal. George-Phillip isn't that close to the throne, but he is a royal Prince. Plus, the head of the SIS. He's got good reason to keep your parentage under wraps, Carrie. I'd be careful. Especially if you're going to the Embassy for dinner."

Carrie looked at Anthony thoughtfully. Then she nodded, once, slowly. "I will. My daughter needs me. I'll be careful."

Bear looked back and forth between Carrie and Anthony. She was still grieving, of course, though it had been close to a year since Ray Sherman died. But one day she would heal. And Anthony Walker could do a lot worse than Carrie Sherman. He kept looking at her kind of like a sad puppy dog. She was indifferent, or at least still too bludgeoned by pain to respond to any stimulus other than protecting her daughter. But something in Bear wanted to protect both of them.

Right now, though, he had more important things to think about. Like finding the son of a bitch who had shot his ex-wife.

"All right, all right. So we have three suspects. Anyone else? What about the attack on Friday night? Not to mention whoever shot at your mother on the border yesterday."

Anthony said, "I think Richard Thompson could be a suspect in all three. If he wanted Andrea out of the way. But Carrie has the same father ... and apparently he knows it."

"Plus," Bear said, "the drugs and money were planted by somebody. And they've been used by the special prosecutor as ammunition in his campaign against Thompson. Don't forget the grand jury will be meeting soon."

Anthony nodded. "So the drugs and money were planted by someone else. To smear Thompson?"

Carrie looked back and forth. "What if it was this Leslie Collins? He and Dad ... I mean ... whatever we call him ... he and *Richard Thompson* were involved in the incident in Afghanistan. Now he wants to shut my dad up, smear him, whatever. So he sets up a scheme to discredit him."

Julia nodded, rapidly. "That would explain the mysterious accounts in the Caymans I keep hearing about. Maybe."

"So how do we figure out who it is?" Anthony asked.

Bear answered. "Well, we've got two prisoners. Joe Paretsky is in Federal lockup—he was one of the shooters in Bethesda last Tuesday, when you guys were going over to dinner. The one Dylan Paris took down. We've identified him, but not who he's working for, and he's not talking."

"And the other prisoner?" Anthony asked.

"Nick Larsden. He's in the Bellingham City Jail, and the feds are fighting for jurisdiction. They've got him for at least one murder in California, the owner of a campsite just out of Redwood City. He's the guy who was shooting at Mrs. Thompson and Jessica when they tried to cross the border yesterday."

Anthony's eyebrows ran together. "I think that's our guy. Plus, I know a guy in the Bellingham PD."

"Yeah?" Bear said.

Anthony nodded. "Yeah—you know I went embedded as a reporter in Iraq. One of the guys in the platoon I went in with, he works for the corrections department there. Or he did."

"Call him. I think I see a trip to the West Coast in my future."

CHAPTER SIX
It's your mother

Carrie. May 5.

As it often was, traffic along Embassy Row headed toward downtown Washington, DC was snarled. Carrie normally needed to feel in control—and preferred to drive herself for that reason—but today she was grateful that one of the Pinkerton security guards was behind the wheel of the black Suburban. She sat in the back seat with Alexandra, fidgeting and nervous.

Another black SUV—the guard had referred to it as a *chase car*—drove closely behind them. Carrie kept looking down at the invitation. Cream paper with gold and black lettering.

You and your guest are invited to dine with
His Highness, Prince George-Phillip
at the Embassy of the United Kingdom,
4 pm on the Fifth of May, 2014.

His Highness, Prince George-Phillip, was apparently her father. And this invitation felt all too formal to her. Too distant. On the other hand, what else could he have done? Called her up and said, "Hey, this is your birth father. Want to get together?"

Obviously that made no sense. And even though part of her wanted to meet George-Phillip and learn just what had happened between him and her mother—another part just wanted to turn her back. She had nothing to lose by walking away—right now she didn't have a father at all. Not meeting George-Phillip wouldn't change that.

On the other hand, meeting him—that held another kind of risk. A risk of getting hurt again. She'd lost her husband and her father. She didn't want to lose anything else.

But then her eyes fell on her sister. Alexandra. The middle child. She'd never been sure of herself, never had the confidence that Carrie and Julia had, never had that spark of brilliance that Sarah and Jessica had. But one thing she had was strength and loyalty. She wouldn't shy away from any risk. She'd *chosen* that risk, she'd chosen to love a man who was broken by war and trauma. And despite the pain that came with that, she was richer for it.

Carrie closed her eyes. She'd also chosen. Ray had been dead now longer than she'd even known him. Nine short months from the day they met to the day he died. They were the hardest, most difficult and yet the best months of her life. She wouldn't go back and change them. She wouldn't give back *one ounce* of grief and loss if it meant losing even the slightest memory of Ray.

Ray—ever courageous, ever honorable, would have chuckled and pushed her to go on.

So, instead of panicking, or withdrawing into herself, Carrie did the only thing she could, the thing she was fated to do, the thing that defined who she was. She reached out and took Alexandra's hand and squeezed it gently, reassuringly. "Dylan's going to be fine," Carrie said.

"Thanks," Alexandra whispered. "I know. I know he will."

Carrie sat back in her seat and stared into space. Everything was upside down and confused. She thought of the phone call earlier, as she'd been trying to make some order out of the chaos of the condominium. It was the house phone that rang, and she'd rushed to it, not recognizing the 604 area code.

"Hello?" she'd said.

"Carrie, it's your mother."

"Mom?" she had nearly screeched. "What's happening? I saw the news— you're in Canada? Is Jessica okay? What happened to her?"

"Slow down, Carrie," her mother had said, even as the other sisters crowded around Carrie. Then Mother began to speak, but Carrie missed the first few words, because something was *different* about her mother. She sounded—not strained, or panicked. She didn't know what she sounded like.

"... so for now we're just outside of Vancouver, and I think we'll be here for some time. Jessica's in intensive care."

"What happened? Did she get shot? I heard there was some kind of shootout?"

Her mother had sighed. "No. Your sister is very sick, Carrie. She—she got into using meth somehow. She's addicted."

Carrie winced and almost doubled over, involuntarily clutching her stomach with one hand. Julia, alarmed, put her hand on Carrie's shoulder. Carrie waved Julia off, then said, "Mother, how—when— I don't understand."

"It happened this winter, when your father was locked up in his office."

Carrie had gone cold. "He's not my father."

Silence for a moment. Carrie's sisters, Julia, Alexandra, and Sarah, blanched. They all expected the same thing Carrie did—a hysterical rage response.

Instead, her mother had simply said, "No, he's not. Your father is Prince George-Phillip."

Carrie had put her hand to her mouth and sobbed. Then she had whispered, "Why did you lie to us?"

Her mother gave the strangest answer, an answer that made no sense, an answer that she couldn't understand. Her mother had answered, "To save your lives."

Now, hours later, she still didn't understand. And she didn't know if she ever would.

Carrie unconsciously slid down into her seat a little when she saw the two news vans parked in front of the British Embassy, and the crowd of reporters and cameras arrayed along the sidewalk. She knew they couldn't see into the SUV—the tinted windows were so dark you had to press your nose into the glass in order to make out anything. But all the same, the sight of cameras, of reporters—it took her right back.

The driver swung the car into the driveway of the Embassy, making no concessions to the reporters who had to scramble out of the way.

"Jesus Christ," Alexandra muttered, unconsciously echoing Dylan.

The clamor outside the car was crazy. The guard cracked the window, rolling it down just a few inches. He spoke with the Royal Marine who guarded the gate, then a moment later, the gate opened. The SUV and chase car entered the Embassy compound, pulling to a stop in front of a three-story red brick building. Half a dozen Royal Marines in uniform were at the front of the building. Two of them approached the car, one opening the door almost immediately as it came to a stop.

"Doctor Sherman? Mrs. Paris? Come this way, please. Quickly, we're still in sight of the reporters."

Alexandra got out on her side, and Carrie slid across and followed her out. Quickly, they followed the Marine up the steps. Almost one hundred feet behind them, at the fence, she could hear shouting. The reporters called her name.

She hustled inside, entering a well-appointed, air-conditioned room. The anteroom had highly polished marble floors, the center covered with a beautiful Persian carpet. Across the room from her stood Prince George-Phillip, holding the hand of a precociously tall six or eight-year-old with raven hair and blue green eyes. An older version of that girl—Carrie's sister Andrea—stood a few feet away.

Alexandra didn't wait for introductions. She launched herself at Dylan, who gasped as he touched her, his face the expression of a drowning man who'd just gripped a life preserver.

"I missed you," Alexandra sobbed. "God, I missed you."

At the same time, Andrea ran to Carrie and the two women embraced. Carrie gripped Andrea tightly, as if she could somehow know by touch whether or not Andrea was well.

George-Phillip gave Alexandra and Dylan a brief, kind smile. Immediately Carrie liked him better. Then he looked back at Carrie.

"Carrie," he said, tentatively. "I'm George-Phillip."

Carrie's eyes darted to the little girl, then to Andrea.

"You're my father," Carrie said.

He nodded slowly. "I am. I'm so sorry I couldn't tell you before."

She walked closer, as if to study him. "We shook hands the day of my graduation from Columbia."

"We did," he said. "It was one of the proudest days of my life."

Carrie felt as if she were swimming in uncontrollable currents. She'd once thought she was closer to her father than her mother. But so many things made no sense. His remote behavior. His long absences, both traveling and locked up in his office.

She remembered discussing Ray's trial with her mother, and her father saying, *Perhaps we can find a more suitable topic for discussion. I find this entire subject distressful on the day my daughter got married.* She remembered when she found out her father had hired detectives to run background checks on Dylan and his mother. So much never made sense.

Abruptly she said, "I don't know if I'm prepared for any more terrible revelations. It's been a tough week."

He held out a hand. "I understand, Carrie, and I'd like to—I don't even know where to begin."

Carrie took his hand. His hand was warm, and dotted with age spots. His eyes were tired, but they were her eyes. She smiled at him, trying to reassure, and said, "Why don't we start with a drink, then, and we can talk."

Gratitude flashed openly in his eyes. She glanced over her shoulder at Alexandra and Dylan. They'd sunk into a couch, whispering to each other, oblivious to everyone else in the room. Carrie turned back to Andrea and pulled her sister into another embrace.

"I'm so glad you're safe," she whispered. "We were so afraid for you."

Andrea shook in her arms.

After a moment, they broke apart, and she said, "And who is this?"

She knelt down in front of the little girl.

"I'm Jane," the little girl said. She wore a blue dress and patent leather shoes, too formal for a child this young.

Jane, Carrie repeated in her mind.

"I like your dress, Jane. I'm Carrie."

"Daddy says we're sisters. You and me and Andea." She stumbled over Andrea's name. "I never had a sister before."

"Well," Carrie said, suddenly stifling a sob. She couldn't force her eyes to stop watering though. She tried. Every time she cried, she thought she'd run out of tears. But there were always more. "Now you've got a lot of sisters. Now and forever, if—if our father says it's okay."

"I want nothing more in this world," George-Phillip said, his voice low.

"Can I pick you up?" Carrie asked Jane.

Jane nodded, and Carrie stood. She reached out and lifted Jane up and slid her onto her hip. She said, "I've got a little girl too. Though she's a *lot* smaller than you are."

"Smaller? I like that. I'm always the smallest," she said, her voice sounding sad. "What's her name?"

"Rachel," Carrie answered.

George-Phillip smiled and led them into a sunroom. As they walked in, he said to Dylan, "We'll be in here, whenever you two want to join us."

Dylan looked up and said, "Thank you, sir." His voice was rough.

Jane asked, "Is Rachel a sister?"

Carrie smiled and sat down on a wicker couch, keeping the little girl in her lap. "No, she doesn't have any sisters yet. I'm her mommy."

Jane said, "My mommy's in heaven now."

George-Phillip looked stricken, his eyes bleak. He whispered, "Pancreatic cancer."

"I'm so sorry," Carrie said. She looked back at Jane and whispered, "Sometimes sisters can be like mommies too."

Andrea slid in next to her and said to Jane, "It's true. Sometimes they can take you to the zoo. Or give you Band-Aids when you're hurt. Or get you ice cream, and give you hugs, and take care of you when you cry. Sometimes big sisters do things like that."

Andrea gave her a meaningful look, as if to say, *I remember.* Then she said, "Carrie was like that for me when I was little, just like you."

Goddamn it, Carrie thought, stifling more tears.

"You know, I never thought I would see you—the three of you—in the same room. If only your mother were here," he said.

Carrie looked up at George-Phillip. "Can you tell me about her?"

George-Phillip tilted his head. "What do you mean?"

Carrie took Andrea's hand in hers without even thinking. "What I mean is … what we know is a mother who was … erratic. Mentally ill. Sometimes the rage got so bad she would completely lose it. She'd scream at us, and … rarely …

would hit us. I want to know why. Why did you fall in love with her? Who was she before … before all that happened?"

George-Phillip's face took on the bleakest expression she'd ever seen on a man's face. Jane stirred in Carrie's lap and said, "Da, may I go play?"

"Of course, Jane. Let's go find Miss Adriana." He stood, and said, "Excuse me just a moment."

As he walked out of the room, Andrea said, "I'm not sure I care what she was like."

Carrie sighed. "I'm not sure what I want anymore. Except the truth. I want to know the truth. All of it."

"Do you think he'll tell us?"

Carrie shrugged. "As much as anyone else in the world will." Her eyes shifted to the glass and the grounds outside. "So … please tell me … how you ended up here anyway."

Andrea shrugged. "Alexandra told Dylan to Google George-Phillip. We did—and so we drove over here. Dylan crashed his car into the gate to distract the guards and I climbed over the back wall."

"It's a good thing you weren't an assassin," Carrie said.

Andrea said, "They caught me before I got to him. But I screamed loud enough he came looking for me."

The door opened, and George-Phillip walked back in. He smiled and said, "Young Dylan and his wife are still sitting on the couch. They love each other very much, don't they?"

Carrie smiled. "They do."

He sat and said, "She reminds me a little bit of her mother too. Though Alexandra does have a look of her father about her."

Carrie glanced at Andrea, then back at George-Phillip. "He raped her, you know. When he found out I wasn't his daughter. He beat her nearly to death, and raped her."

George-Phillip flinched. "I'd have done anything to prevent it," he said. "I didn't know until much later. She named her Alexandra as kind of a poke in the eye. Your mother's a courageous woman, but she's also been trapped in a prison for many years. I tried to persuade her to leave, but she was always convinced Richard would harm one of you, or her brother."

"Luis?" Andrea said.

George-Phillip nodded. "I don't know if it was a real fear or not. But it was enough to keep her entrapped."

"You understand," Carrie said, "how difficult this is? Everything we've ever believed is upside down."

He nodded. "I'll try to give you everything I possibly can. I can't even imagine the difficulty you face."

"When did you meet her?"

He smiled. "We met in February of 1984, just a few weeks after your mother arrived in Washington, DC. I was on assignment here at the Embassy then. Though I didn't live in such luxurious quarters." He said the last with a wry smile. "My office was next to the boiler in the basement back then."

He smiled. "Your mother hosted a dinner party—that's when we met. For a nineteen-year-old, she was incredibly poised. Everyone believed she was older, of course. I remember she captured the attention of everyone there. I thought Colonel Rainsley was going to embarrass himself, to be honest."

"Rainsley was there? Senator Rainsley?"

He nodded. "That's right. Your mother ended up being good friends with Brianna, though I don't think she ever confided the nature of her marriage. But they had music in common."

"And why did you end up involved with a married woman?" Carrie asked.

He sighed. "Of course, that was my downfall. I could see even at that party that something was broken between the two of them. He was so much older than she was, and she was terrified of him. But I had no idea how serious it was. Remember that back then, she was not much older than Andrea."

Fascinated at this view of a mother she'd never really understood, Carrie leaned forward and said, "What ... what was she like?"

George-Phillip smiled, his eyes twinkling. "She was fierce. Passionate. Your mother loved music ... did you know she'd played for the National Youth Orchestra? She smiled, even when she was falling apart inside. She was fiercely protective of you girls. When we first met it was just Julia, of course. What a little rascal. Two years old and full of fire. I think your mother would have gone to hell and back to protect her. Adelina was the strongest woman I've ever known."

Carrie shook her head. "I find that difficult to believe. All of it."

"Can you imagine any other reason she stayed with him all those years? Other than to protect you?"

"Tell me more." Carrie's words were a demand. She felt an urgency to ferret out this woman who she'd never known.

George-Phillip shrugged. "We weren't together very long then. A few short months. Richard spent much of the spring going back and forth from Afghanistan and Pakistan, trying to bury any backlash from the Wakhan massacre before it destroyed him. We took advantage of that. Whenever we were in public—not often—Julia acted as chaperone. I finally rented a studio apartment in Chevy Chase, not far from your condominium. We could meet discreetly there. She was terrified Richard would find out and harm her brother, or harm Julia."

He closed his eyes. His voice shook unevenly as he said the next words, "I married, many years later, but I've never loved anyone the way I loved her. I've regretted it my entire life that I did not just—take her. That I didn't fight hard enough, or strong enough to pull her away from him. When I think about how much he hurt her, how changed she was when I met her again in China, so many years later..."

He shook his head, bringing his hand to his mouth. "I would do anything. *Anything*. To take it back. To protect her."

"Why did you leave? Was it because you found out she was pregnant?" Carrie didn't voice the words, *with me*. But they fell in the room anyway.

George-Phillip shook his head. "No ... Carrie. Adelina broke it off with me without explanation in late April '84. I swear to you, I didn't know you existed until 1996."

"Tell me. When did you see her again?" Carrie's demand was sharp.

George Phillip. May 1996.

By the time Prince George-Phillip got off the airplane in China—commercial, of course—and cleared customs, he'd been en route for more than seventeen hours, thanks to an unnecessary layover in Paris. He was hot and tired and desperately needed a good night's sleep.

That, unfortunately, was not to be. A young woman, perhaps twenty-five, waited for him at the end of the terminal with a cardboard sign discreetly labeled "GP." He'd been told to expect her. Wendy Li was a British citizen, born in Cambridge, but her parents were native Chinese. She spoke fluent Mandarin. Purportedly a protocol officer for the Embassy—she was, in fact, the deputy chief of station for MI6. She was exceptionally young for that role, but the combination of an internal shakeup and her own expertise had catapulted her career forward.

"Hello, Your Highness," she said. "Is this all your baggage?" She directed an assistant to collect the bags. "Come this way."

"Thank you. Miss Li, is it?"

"Yes, sir."

George-Phillip was thirty-three years old, and his actual job in China was to be the chief of station for the MI6 in China—the most senior position he'd held to date. His "official" position was Senior Attaché with diplomatic service, a job with so few specifics that he could do virtually anything he needed. Like Wendy—and anyone else who works for the secretive intelligence organization—he required an official, diplomatic cover for his job, which was, of course, to spy on the Chinese.

It wasn't the glamorous job people would expect. Spying typically involved finding people in sensitive positions, determining their weaknesses, and exploiting them. Sometimes the weaknesses were simple—greed, sexual peccadilloes and other means of turning people against their country. Sometimes they were more complex: people who sold out their country believing they were patriots. The most useful asset MI6 had in the Chinese government was secretly a Christian convert who worked in the Chinese Foreign Ministry. The Chinese government, of course, suppressed Christianity along with all other religions. That oppression gave spies a wedge.

As they got into the chauffeured car, she said, "Forgive me, Highness, we do have one issue. Are you fully up to date on the tensions between China and the US?"

"Yes, unless something happened while I was in the air." She was referring, of course, to the spying scandal erupting in the United States, which was severely straining relations in Beijing. Chinese intelligence operatives had stolen significant nuclear secrets from the United States, and as of yet no one knew the extent of the damage.

"Nothing new, sir. Except the American Ambassador had an extremely ... tense ... meeting with the Chinese premier today. There's some concern that the Chinese may retaliate in some way, so most of the NATO allies and Australia will be attending a large reception this evening at the US Embassy. As a show of solidarity, sir. I'm aware how long you've been in the air—but the Ambassador would like you to attend."

He frowned then said, "All right. I'll need to shower and shave, and someone to press one of my suits. They're certain to be rumpled. And perhaps some coffee." George-Phillip didn't typically drink coffee. But he'd been awake so long now it was necessary.

"Of course, sir."

"Who is the US Ambassador anyway? Isn't there a new one?"

"Richard Thompson, sir. Previously he was the US Ambassador to NATO."

George-Phillip felt a chill. He didn't answer, just murmured, "Hmmmmm."

"Sir? You know him?"

Damn. His expression had betrayed him. "I do. But it's been many years. What's your impression?" George-Phillip asked the question just to get her talking so he didn't have to.

"Honestly, sir, something about him ... bothers me. I'm usually a pretty good judge of people. But I can't make him out. He's stone cold."

"Is he married?" George-Phillip didn't breathe after he asked the question.

"Yes, Your Highness. Younger woman, her name is Adelina. They have five children."

"Five? That's quite a lot, isn't it?" *Five? She'd had four more children with him? What the hell?*

"I believe the last two were twins, they were born this April. Confidentially, sir … I think she's afraid of him."

"His wife?" he asked. He arched an eyebrow, trying to look surprised.

Wendy didn't look fooled. She raised a skeptical eyebrow right back. "Yes. His wife. I think she's afraid of him. You know her too, don't you, sir?"

George-Phillip frowned. "You don't miss very much, do you, Miss Li?"

She shook her head. "Very little. Is there something there we should be worried about?"

George-Phillip grunted. On the one hand, it wasn't an appropriate question for a subordinate to be asking. On the other—she had a point. "No. There might have been, many years ago. But that's long since over."

The look of concern didn't leave Wendy's face. But she wisely chose to steer the conversation away from Adelina. "Thompson has been the Ambassador since last October. It's been a difficult time—with the spying revelations, relations with China and the US are souring rapidly."

"Indeed," George-Phillip said. "Spying is one thing. Nuclear secrets are another. It's difficult to blame the Americans for their response."

"Yes, sir."

Ninety minutes later, George-Phillip and Wendy Li arrived at the US Embassy compound and were cleared through the gate. He felt somewhat refreshed after the shower, but nothing would completely do it other than a lot of sleep. Which he was unlikely to get in the next couple of days. So be it. He had a job to do, and sleep wasn't in the job description.

George-Phillip and Wendy were late, but not too much so. It never hurt to be close to the last to arrive anyway. As he walked into the ballroom in the Embassy, his eyes scanned the room and the sixty or more guests who were crowded in various circles and groupings.

He immediately recognized some faces. Rick Smith, the Australian Ambassador to China, and of course Ambassador Ronald Easton, who stood next to his American counterpart—Richard Thompson. Thompson stood in profile to George-Phillip. His expression was grave as he and Easton spoke. Richard had aged, his hair gone grey in the dozen years since they'd encountered each other. He must be in his mid-forties.

Adelina wasn't standing with Thompson, which was a good thing. After a moment, George-Phillip found her. She was standing near the back wall of the ballroom, talking with a young girl. Adelina's back was to George-Phillip. She looked much the same, her back still well toned, exposed in a backless dress. After five children, her body had changed, of course—broader hips and larger breasts. She was lovely. He froze, unable to focus clearly as he looked at the young woman.

Fourteen, he guessed. Curly brown hair, large pretty eyes. Julia. She wouldn't remember him, of course—she'd been a mere toddler when he last saw her. She'd turned into a beautiful young woman.

For a moment he gave into a fantasy that she was *his* daughter, that he and Adelina could have had children. But of course, that was impossible. *Five* children. He wondered if she'd finally been emotionally seduced by her husband.

For the last decade and more his mother had constantly harped at him. Get married. Have a child. But he'd kept a false hope, all along, that one day she would leave him, that a miracle would happen and he would be with the woman he loved. But at the moment he saw her again for the first time, he didn't feel that longing, he didn't feel that love. What he felt was *anger* and *hurt* and *grief* he hadn't imagined he was capable of.

"Your Highness! Welcome to Beijing."

Startled, George-Phillip averted his eyes from Adelina and Julia, only to come face to face with Ronald Easton, the US Ambassador, and Richard Thompson.

Automatically, a smile lit across George-Phillip's face, though it was no more sincere than the friendly face Thompson showed.

"Ambassador Easton! Ambassador Thompson! A pleasure to see both of you again!"

Easton smiled. "Prince George-Phillip, I'm pleased to have you here. So you know Richard?"

Forcing his thoughts away from Adelina, he replied. "Indeed. Ambassador Thompson once hosted me for a *very* interesting dinner at his condominium in Washington, DC."

Julia was walking away from Adelina now. Likely leaving, she was young to attend a diplomatic ball of this nature. Adelina turned around and her eyes locked on his. The shock was obvious. Her eyes widened and watered, and a hand involuntarily covered her mouth. Almost instantly, however, a mask descended on her face, her hand dropped to her side, and she looked away.

"Perhaps, then, you can settle a friendly wager for us," Easton said. He stank of whiskey. "Richard here maintains that it was the advances of John Hawkins on ship building that allowed for English settlement of the Americas. But I have the correct answer—that it was the defeat of the Spanish Armada in 1588. What do you say?"

Easton was a boor. But he was the Ambassador. "Both answers are equally true, Ambassador—the defeat of the Armada would not have taken place had it not been for the improvement in ship building."

"Spoken like a true diplomat, Your Highness," Thompson said. His eyes were cold and his voice low. "You used a lot of words and avoided the question entirely. Bravo."

Thompson was decidedly unfriendly. Did he suspect George-Phillip's affair with his wife? Or was it something else entirely? Had he somehow guessed George-Phillip's involvement in the investigation of the massacre at Wakhan? Whatever it was, even Easton noticed, his face sobering as he heard Thompson's tone.

The three men engaged in small talk, maddening small talk, as George-Phillip kept his eyes everywhere *except* on Richard Thompson's wife, who moved from group to group like a good hostess: entertaining, friendly but not too friendly, a smile always on her face.

Finally, George-Phillip managed to offer his excuses and step away from the two Ambassadors. Unable to face any more meaningless conversations, he stepped into the hallway, needing to have a few moments of solitude. His eyes scanned the hallway looking for the water closet.

He was almost at the end of the hallway when he heard her voice behind him. "George-Phillip."

He froze, his spine rigid. He couldn't show his face. He *couldn't*. He closed his eyes and took a deep breath. "Adelina."

He heard her footsteps, heels clicking on the marble floor, as she approached. He slowly turned around.

"I ... I..." her voice trailed off.

"You miss me?" he asked. "You're sorry for breaking it off with no explanation? You're sorry you broke my heart? What is it?"

Her eyes filled with tears. "I'm sorry," she whispered.

His shoulders sagged. "What am I to say?"

"Just ... tell me you're well."

George-Phillip felt his eyebrows twitch, and he narrowed one eye, trying to hold in the wave of emotion that flooded him. He looked up at the ceiling, unable to control his grief. "I must go, Adelina. Please ... just..."

"I didn't have any choice." The pain in her voice was palpable.

George-Phillip gritted his teeth with an anger he didn't know he contained. "You didn't have a choice? I would have protected you, Adelina. I would have protected your daughter."

He turned and nearly staggered down the hall. She ran after him, calling his name. *There.* A door labeled *Men.* He pushed it open, stepped inside, and leaned against the wall.

CHAPTER SEVEN
Don't patronize me.

Carrie. May 5.

L **ooking** back, Carrie vaguely remembered the night George-Phillip referred to. She'd only attended two or three diplomatic functions in her eleventh year. But she had been a poised eleven-year-old, and her mother had given her permission to accompany Julia for the first hour of the reception. She must have missed him by minutes.

Did she remember seeing George-Phillip? She couldn't recall. The room had mostly been filled with adults, almost all of them shorter than she'd been, and she had stayed close to the wall at the side of the room, Julia at her side, until their mother sent her away. They'd been in Beijing for months by that time, but that was the first time she'd been accompanied by armed guards.

"I remember the reception you're talking about," she said. "The twins were born a month or two before that, and Mom had been—especially difficult. It's not that she doesn't love the twins—but I don't think she'd planned on them. I don't think she'd planned on *any* children really."

George-Phillip nodded. "No. But she still looked on all of you as gifts from God."

"She didn't act like it," Andrea said. Her tone was bitter.

"No. But I don't think you realize how much it cost her."

"How could I?" she riposted. "I don't know her. She never talked to me. She sent me away."

George-Phillip closed his eyes. "Of course you don't. I'm sorry."

"*Tell me,*" Andrea said. "She couldn't. So you have to."

He nodded and began speaking again. "I didn't see her again for several weeks. The diplomatic community is small, of course, but not so small that you see people routinely unless they are friends. And Richard Thompson and I were never friends."

"I can imagine," Carrie said.

His lips turned up in a wry smile. "Anyway. It was … four or so weeks later, at the end of May, and the United States Embassy was holding a service for Memorial Day." He paused a moment. "That's not a holiday we have in the United Kingdom, but our Remembrance Day in November is similar. In any event, it's fairly common for allied Embassies to attend such functions, especially in a country like China where the diplomatic community is so isolated. So I made arrangements to represent the United Kingdom."

He leaned back, his face thoughtful, and said, "I knew, of course, that your mother would likely be at the ceremony. And I knew I needed to stay away. But I couldn't. As soon as I arrived, I ran into Richard and Adelina. It was a bad day for her. I'd never seen her so lost, her eyes searching everywhere, her hands twitching."

Carrie spoke in a soft, urgent voice. "It was awful. I remember that day. Julia had somehow gotten spots of bleach on her dress, and Mother screamed at her. It was garbled and confusing and … frightening, really. Then when our father came into the apartment, she went suddenly silent. Whispering at Julia in an urgent tone to change her dress, to get into something more appropriate, to *hurry.*"

George-Phillip shook his head. "She was terrified," he murmured.

"I think so," Carrie said. "But *we* experienced it as crazy."

Carrie could almost feel the pain and regret radiating from George-Phillip as he closed his eyes, not responding to her words. After all, pain and regret were the emotions she was most familiar with. It was easy to recognize a kindred spirit in pain. She continued. "Anyway, she calmed down a little once Julia was dressed and we were on our way. But … you know what I remember?"

Oh *Christ*, she thought. She started to shake a little.

"What is it?" George-Phillip asked.

"He kept leaning over in the car. As he was driving. And he'd whisper. I thought it was romantic whispers, you know? She kept … shivering, and jerking away from him. She had goose bumps on the back of her neck. All I could think of was how angry I was because she'd treated Julia like dirt and here she was…" Carrie closed her eyes. She remembered what she'd thought. The words had come unbidden to her mind, *I hate her. I hate her. I hate her.*

"You couldn't have known," George-Phillip said. "You were a child."

She sighed. "I know. But I still wish I'd understood. I wish I could take back how much we all hated her. She didn't deserve it. Tell me what else happened."

George-Phillip nodded. His eyes were a thousand miles away. "I ended up seated next to your family—Adelina in between me and Richard. You were on the other side of him."

Carrie thought back, trying to remember if she'd known George-Phillip then. She vaguely remembered a man sitting next to her mother, but it was maddening really, to know her father had been *right there* and she hadn't realized. Of course the adults hadn't deigned to actually introduce the children to anyone. The ceremony had gone on forever—she remembered feeling tired and frustrated, and whispering to Julia, "Will this *never end?*" Of course she would never have said those words to her mother or father—*damn it!* She kept doing that. Richard Thompson *wasn't* her father and she didn't have a clue what to call him. She missed George-Phillip's next few words, but brought herself back to the present as quickly as she could.

"...I could tell something was very seriously wrong. But I couldn't *do* anything. So we sat there for the first forty-five minutes of what seemed like an excruciatingly long ceremony. Finally, Richard was called up to speak."

Carrie nodded. She remembered that. It had been blisteringly hot. By the time Richard went up to speak, her dress was sticking to her back, and even with the broad floppy hat she wore, her skin was starting to feel distinctly hot.

"While he was up there—it was no more than twenty minutes—I was able to talk with her very briefly. Even though I'd only just found out about you, Carrie, I still loved her. And I was worried. Deeply worried."

"Why?"

"She didn't sound like herself. The woman I fell in love with was—vivacious. Energetic. Even in the midst of her awful marriage, she was still inherently an optimistic, cheerful and spiritual person. But when I talked with her at the Embassy, and again that Memorial Day, it was clear she was profoundly damaged. Her voice and inflection were slower. Tired. Sad." His voice dropped to a whisper. "I hated seeing her like that. She was such a kind and caring soul, to see her abused in such a way as to break her spirit ... I wanted to kill Richard Thompson."

Carrie closed her eyes. It was too much. Too much to imagine the kind of life her mother had. Carrie had undergone the most excruciating pain she could imagine in the last nine months with the loss of her husband. But at least Carrie still had her sisters. She still had Ray's memory. She had his best friend.

But Adelina Thompson had lost *everything*. And not for nine months. Not for nine years. She'd been forced to marry Richard Thompson *thirty-three years* ago.

Carrie felt a tear run down her cheek. She whispered, "I've hated her all my life. I've always believed my father was the sane one. I've always believed she was *hateful*, but it wasn't that at all. She was *tortured*."

Andrea stood up and began pacing.

Memories kept washing over Carrie. Julia shouting, "I want *Daddy!*" Her mother collapsing on the sidewalk in Calella, and their terror until the ambulance came. Her mother breaking down after Maria Clawson had begun writing about the family, week after week, posting vicious blogs about Julia and both of her parents, derailing her father's posting to Russia. She remembered her mother lying on the couch, her face red and puffy, on Valentine's of 1990. Carrie stifled a sob. She'd thrown a *tantrum* because her mother wouldn't take her to the church Valentine's party.

She knew about the harm her mother had done. The freak outs and the pain and the screaming and the horrible things she'd said. But she also remembered her mother rushing to her defense when Ray's mom had gone off into crazy town after the accident. She remembered finding herself back at the condo after Ray's death, unable to understand how she'd even gotten there, and her mother lying down beside her and holding her as she cried for what seemed like days.

"If I never do anything else in my life," she said, "I'll make it up to her. I will." She looked up at Andrea. Andrea nodded in agreement.

Andrea. May 5.

"What happens with us?" Andrea asked. As she asked the question, she waved her hand in the general direction of George-Phillip.

"What do you mean?" Carrie responded.

George-Phillip leaned forward in his seat and said, "Perhaps I could…"

Carrie nodded in response. Andrea waited to hear what he would say.

"Obviously I've been … no father to you at all. Either one of you. And I know there's nothing I can do to go back and change that. All the same though … I would like to get to know you both. I would like to … try … somehow … to make amends to you both. It is my intention to retire from my position once the current unpleasantness is over. Perhaps you'll consider coming to London?"

Carrie slowly nodded. "It's possible. I have work commitments, of course, so timing might be challenging."

Andrea shrugged, not knowing how to answer. "I don't know. I'd have to speak with my grandmother about it." Her response was automatic, but a stab of concern and worry hit her. She didn't know where her relationship with *Abuelita* stood. Her grandmother had lied to her. And not about something small. "I don't know what to think anymore," she continued. "No one—not my mother, my grandmother, not you—no one has ever told me the truth. About who I was, or why I wasn't wanted. Why should I believe you now? And what does all this have to do with why someone tried to kill me?"

George-Phillip nodded. "That's a very good question."

Irritated, Andrea said, "Don't patronize me."

He shook his head in response. "I don't mean to. It doesn't all make sense."

"Tell us what you know. Or what you guess."

"All right. First, I believe your kidnapping was originally planned by Leslie Collins, the Director of Operations of the Central Intelligence Agency. Not an official operation, you understand. But on his own."

"Why?" Andrea asked.

"I think he believed that your presence in the country, and specifically the blood tests, would lead to questions which would ultimately reveal what happened in Wakhan."

"That makes no sense it all."

"It does if you know—as he does—that I was responsible for the original investigation conducted by the British government. You see, Collins and Richard Thompson, along with the current Saudi intelligence minister, were the three prime movers in delivering chemical weapons to the Afghan militia. The three of them have been trading favors and boosting each other's careers ever since. But their cooperation depended on secrecy."

Carrie sat forward. "And you've known about it? All this time? Wait … since when?"

"1984."

Carrie slumped back in her seat. "Why did … if you knew he was responsible for it, why didn't you report it then?"

"I did. My official report directly addressed that, and recommended that the issue be brought up with the United Nations Security Council. I was overruled."

"I don't understand why."

"Carrie, it was the Cold War. The Soviets had invaded Afghanistan, and their occupation was brutal. At the time, the United States and the United Kingdom used Wakhan as a tremendous propaganda tool against the Soviets."

Andrea didn't get it. "Okay … so after I escaped the kidnapping … that brought media attention to the family. It seems like it would make it more likely all of it would come out."

"Exactly," George-Phillip said. "Once you escaped, it threw a huge wrench in the works. We intercepted some phone calls last Friday. As far as I can tell, Collins decided the only move left to make was to completely discredit Thompson. He had an agent planted in your Diplomatic Security Service, who placed the drugs and money in the condo and launched the attack against you. As you may know, someone fired shots at my home at nearly the exact same time. At me, rather."

Andrea sat back, shocked. "I didn't know that."

"Right. Now the question is, what is their next move? Thompson's role in Wakhan is public now, thanks to *The Guardian*. But whoever planted the story adjusted just enough of the truth to also tarnish me. The way *The Guardian* reports it, I was part of the cover-up. I believe Collins was likely responsible for that as well. Again, because it attacks the credibility of anyone who can go after him."

Carrie said, "I don't see how he could possibly have done all this in just a few days."

George-Phillip responded, "It isn't possible. I suspect he began planning it and putting it together the moment your father was raised as a replacement for Secretary of Defense."

"But that was only three weeks ago."

"No, Carrie, it was many months ago. The President knew the former Secretary was very ill. Your father was approached about the job in December of 2013."

"Six months ago." Carrie's face was grim as she said the words.

Andrea said, "Then who tried to kill our mother? Someone chased her to the border and shot at her there. Collins? Why?"

George-Phillip leaned his head in his hands. "I'm not sure. The news media is speculating there's some kind of drug war connection. Perhaps Collins thought he could reinforce that narrative? The shooter was captured, by the way."

Carrie said, "Right. Nick Larsden. Bear and Anthony were discussing that earlier, they want to go out to Washington to see if they can question him."

"Bear and Anthony?"

"Bear Wyden—he's with Diplomatic Security. And Anthony Walker is a reporter with *The Washington Post*." As Carrie said the words, her face flushed a little. Just a tiny bit. But enough it caught Andrea's attention. George-Phillip did not appear to notice, and Andrea thought it best to not say anything.

"I know Walker," George-Phillip said. "He interviewed me a couple of years ago. I rather liked him."

Andrea said, "Okay, so this Collins guy tried to have me and my mother killed. And you. He wants to burn the house down before anyone gets wind he was involved in this massacre. So how do we get ahead of him?"

George-Phillip's brow furrowed. "I think we need to prove, publicly, that he was involved."

"Won't that look like it's just defensive?" Andrea asked. "That you or ... Richard Thompson ... are trying to muddy the waters?"

"It might," George-Phillip said. "But the report I wrote was unequivocal, and the evidence implicating Collins was fairly clear."

"That report needs to be publicized."

"I'm afraid it's highly classified. I would need to consult with the Prime Minister before releasing it."

"Can you do that?" Carrie asked.

"Yes," George-Phillip responded. "But first, I believe dinner should be ready. Why don't we gather your sister and brother-in-law, and we'll dine."

Andrea nodded. She was famished and needed to rest a little. She still didn't understand all of what was happening. But tendrils of trust were beginning to grow. George-Phillip seemed sincere. And the truth was, she *wanted* to believe him. She was tired of being hurt. She was tired of carrying around the knowledge that her supposed *father* never wanted her.

A few minutes later, Alexandra and Dylan joined them in the large dining room around a large table. As they took their seats, Dylan's eyes darted back and forth between George-Phillip and his daughters.

"Wait a minute, I just thought of something. If he's your dad," Dylan said, waving a hand in George-Phillip's direction. He grinned. "Wouldn't that make the two of you ... Princesses?"

"Dylan," Carrie said. "That's ... ridiculous."

"It's not really," George-Phillip said. "I'm styled Prince because my grandfather was George VI. But I'm extremely far outside of the line of succession. Jane is not considered a *Princess,* but she will inherit the title of Duchess. I'm truly not certain where the two of you will fall. To some extent that will be up to Her Majesty to decide when we make your parentage public. You'll certainly want to come to London."

Andrea slowly shook her head. "Neither of us are citizens of the United Kingdom."

George-Phillip smiled. "I promise you, we will sort that out. I'm not sure the time is right to make it public, however."

"Why not?" Dylan asked.

"I want to ensure that you are all safe first. Andrea and Dylan, I believe you should both remain here for the time being, at least until we can sort out whether or not you'll be charged in relation to the attack on the condominium."

Andrea nodded. That made sense.

"Carrie—my understanding is that you've lost your Diplomatic Security protection?"

She nodded.

"Quietly then, for now, I intend to inform the President that the two of you are my children. And I'm going to request that you be provided official protection until all of this is resolved. I may be able to obtain assistance from the Special Escort Group as well, but they'll need clearance."

"Thank you," Carrie responded.

The remainder of the evening seemed to Andrea to be almost … normal. Whatever that was. For the first time since leaving Spain, Andrea found herself laughing and enjoying herself. After dinner, they moved to the parlor, where Jane snuggled in Carrie's lap as they all talked. George-Phillip told them about his late wife Anne, and Carrie told him about Ray. For a little while, Andrea found herself feeling the warmth of a real family, no matter how odd it was.

George-Phillip sent Jane off to bed at eight. A few minutes later, Carrie said, "I'll need to get going too. It's not really fair leaving Rachel with Julia this long. But I wonder … George-Phillip … perhaps Alexandra can stay here with Dylan?"

Alexandra flashed a grateful smile at her, and George-Phillip assented. Soon after, the party broke up, and Andrea returned to her room on the second floor, overlooking the grass she'd run across to break into this building just a day ago.

She rummaged in her bag, pulling out one of the throwaway cell phones she and Dylan had purchased a few days before. She turned out the light and got into bed, then sent text messages to Luis and then Sarah.

A response from Sarah came almost immediately.

Hey, what r u up to? Are you at the Embassy?

Andrea responded, **Tired. Still here. Safe. Carrie is on her way back to the condo.**

Sarah: I'm not there. Snuck by the guards, I'm at Eddie's.

Andrea smiled. Eddie was Sarah's boyfriend, a muscular emergency medical technician who was working his way through med school at George Washington University.

Andrea: Good! Have you heard from Mother? Or Jessica?

Sarah: Jessica's awake and recovering. Mom's weird.

Andrea: How?

Sarah: She's nice. I don't get it. I don't get her.

Andrea: We've learned a lot from GP. I think he still loves her.

Sarah: Details?

Andrea filled in some of the details George-Phillip had related. As she was typing out the story on the tiny cell phone keys, she was concentrating so hard she didn't notice the lock turning behind her.

Andrea: So, GP thinks it's Collins who sent the attackers. And that we might still

Andrea barely had a second to move when she sensed, rather than saw, the door open behind her. She jumped up, tangled in the blankets, but she was too late. Her vision went black, spotted with stars, when a heavy fist hit the back of her neck. She fell forward on the mattress then suddenly felt her own pillow shoved against the back of her head. A knee pressed into the small of her back, the weight of a heavy man on top of her. She struggled to throw him off, pushing to the left, then the right.

Then, a voice. Near her left ear, muffled by the pillow, the voice said in a contorted tone, "This is a gift from your *father*."

A crushing pain in her back as the man kneed her in the spine. She tried to scream, but the mattress was pressed against her mouth, the pillow crushing her head. She struggled, her hands grasping for something, anything.

Her hand closed on something. It was metal, cylindrical. A *pen?*

She closed her fist around it and swung downward, as forcefully as she could.

The man howled as the pen connected, gouging into his skin. She pulled back and hit him again, then saw stars when he pummeled her.

"Run away," he said. "Run fast, or you'll die."

Then he was gone, the door shutting behind him. She heard footsteps receding down the hall, and she curled up, gasping for air, her heartbeat racing, the pulse whooshing in her ears.

Whoever it was had a key. Had George-Phillip sent them? Was it all a lie, and he just wanted to lull her into trusting him? Was there something else?

She became aware of a repeated buzzing. Vibrating.

The *phone*. It was silenced, but vibrating. She grabbed for it, pulling up the messages.

Sarah: You still there? Details?

Sarah: Andrea? Are you okay?

Sarah: Andrea! Call me!

The phone showed two missed calls from Sarah's number. She dialed without thinking.

"Hello? Andrea? Are you okay?"

"No," she gasped. "Someone attacked me. In the room."

"Holy shit," Sarah said.

Her mind racing, Andrea knew she had to leave. Right now. "I've got to wake up Dylan—wait…"

She stopped. Dylan was still wanted by the feds because of the attack on the condo. One of the attackers had been a federal agent after all. He was safe here, with Alexandra.

"No … he'll be safe here. Can you … can you get a car? Can you come get me? I need to find a place to hide."

"Where? I'm on my way."

"There's a park across the street from the Embassy. Let me know when you're close. I'm going to have to sneak out somehow."

"Be there soon, sis. I love you. Stay safe."

"I will," Andrea said.

Just to be on the safe side, she pushed and pulled, blocking the doorway with the heavy bed. Then she began to gather her bag, with the cash, spare phones, fake ID and Visa gift cards. She began to get dressed. It was time to go back into hiding.

Then she waited. One minute turned into five, and five into twenty. Thirty-three minutes after she'd called Sarah, her phone vibrated again.

Text message.

Sarah: Five minutes away.

That was it. Andrea came to her feet and threw on the backpack. She un-latched the window and opened it up. A few feet from the window, a long metal gutter ran to the ground. Leaning out the window, she grasped the gutter, then let her body swing onto it. Slowly she slid to the ground.

There would still be guards out here. It was about seventy feet to the fence, which stood in the shadow of a line of trees. But the darkness wouldn't do her any good—she was certain the Royal Marines guarding the place had night vision equipment. She'd just have to run.

She took a deep breath then sprinted for the line of trees. The good news was they weren't expecting anyone to try to *escape*.

She was halfway there when she heard a dog barking, then another. Fifteen more feet and she was under the trees, then fifteen more before she reached the tree closest to the fence. She took a running leap and grabbed a branch and pulled herself up. She slid up the trunk, reaching for another branch.

Shouting, and footfalls. A dog, and a man, running toward the fence. A shout. "Who goes there!"

She pulled herself up another branch, then another. She was above the top of the fence now. As quickly as she could, she stood on a branch that leaned toward the fence, and grabbed another one above her head. She worked her way out the branch.

"Stop!" A shout from below. A guard. Two of them, and more coming.

She didn't have time. She leapt, grabbing the top of the fence and flipping over, then slid down the fence, coming to rest on the outside, facing the two Marines.

"Tell the Prince I'm sorry," she said. "But it's not safe." Then she ran.

She ran through the brush, headed toward Massachusetts Avenue as quickly as she could. She could see heavy traffic moving up and down the street. It was close to midnight, she thought. Finally she reached the street. A gap in traffic—she ran through it, stopping on the double yellow line. Horns blasted at her as drivers crossed by her in both directions, then another gap, and she was across. She heard shouts across the street, and a siren in the distance.

Then she heard Sarah's voice. "Andrea! Over here!"

She turned that way. Twenty yards away, the park was dominated by a memorial, a stone wall with an oddly disembodied head attached to it. She saw the name *Khalil Gibran* as she ran toward Sarah, who was comically straddling a huge Harley Davidson motorcycle. Her tiny legs barely reached the gearshift, and the helmet she wore seemed badly oversized.

"Are you kidding me?" Andrea shrieked. "How did you even drive that thing?"

"Can you drive one?"

"Yeah. Slide back!"

Sarah handed her another helmet off the back. "It's Eddie's," she said. "He kinda doesn't know I took his bike. I left him a note. Let's go! I hear sirens!"

Andrea got the helmet fastened and straddled the bike. She cranked it, the machine roaring to life underneath her.

"Ready?" Andrea asked. At Sarah's nod, Andrea eased the bike into the traffic, headed north away from the Embassy.

"Where are we going?" Sarah shouted.

Andrea paused for just a second. Then she said, "Want to come with me to see Mom and Jessica? I've got questions I need answered."

Sarah thought for just a second. Then she shouted. "Hell, yes!"

Andrea nodded. "Let's go!"

CHAPTER EIGHT

Rogue

Anthony. May 6.

"**I think** you should let me do the talking," Bear said, his voice low. "I'm a cop. I know these guys, even if I don't know them personally."

Anthony shook his head as he eased the rental car into the parking station of the Whatcom County Sheriff's Department. "Listen—you may know cops, but I know Sergeant Coyle."

"How?" Bear asked.

"81st Brigade Combat Team. Coyle was National Guard, gunner on a Bradley Fighting Vehicle. I was embedded with his unit. It was my first overseas assignment."

"Yeah? What year?"

"2004. They lost a lot of guys during their tour there. I spent three months humping around Iraq with Coyle's company."

"Gotcha. Okay, you do the talking."

Anthony nodded, reaching to turn the key to the off position. He pulled the key out and stuck it in his pocket. "I've kept in touch with those guys over the years. Coyle went back again in 2009."

Anthony got out of the car. It was chilly out, and the sun wasn't up yet. Their flight had arrived at Bellingham International Airport at 6 am after a flight featuring vomit-worthy turbulence, and then Bear had insisted on a search for a newspaper stand. He still didn't feel completely steady as he locked the car and crossed the street, Bear beside him.

At the front, Anthony opened the door for Bear, who walked in and immediately flashed a badge at the cop at the entrance. "Bear Wyden. US Diplomatic

Security Service. This is my partner, Anthony Walker. We're here to see Sergeant Coyle."

The cop at the desk, who looked not a day older than 18, appeared rattled when Bear mentioned DSS. *Good move*, Anthony thought. The young cop picked up the phone on his desk and dialed.

Five minutes later a door opened to the rear of the lobby, and a large man, completely bald, walked out. He wore the brown uniform of a sheriff's deputy.

"Walker!" he shouted. He walked over and grabbed Anthony in a bear hug. Anthony returned the hug, slapping Coyle on the back. "Get in here!" Coyle said. The kid at the desk looked bewildered.

Two minutes later, Coyle had ushered the two men to his desk and put two cups of coffee in front of them without asking. He leaned close enough to Anthony that he could smell the pungent tang of Coyle's chewing tobacco.

"First things first," Anthony said. "How's Rogue?"

Coyle shook his head. "Shit. He's not good. He was in the VA hospital for a couple months earlier this year. He got in a fistfight with a cop."

Anthony shook his head. During the tour in 2004, Rogue—his actual name was Manfred, of all things—had been the youngest member of the unit, at seventeen years old. His mother had to give him written permission to join the National Guard. Six months into the deployment, he'd been riding in the back of a hummer when it hit an IED—an *improvised explosive device*. The incident had earned Anthony the trust of the soldiers in the platoon. While they fanned out in a protective circle around the Humvee to fend off attacking insurgents, Anthony dropped his camera in the dirt, bandaged Rogue, then held his hand keeping him calm while the insurgents were shooting at them. He'd never forget the moment Sergeant Mumsford walked up to him, balled a fist and tapped him on the chest. "You may be a reporter but … that was okay, man."

Unfortunately, Rogue's extensive injuries required immediate massive painkillers. Morphine, and later valium in the hospital, Oxycontin on his return to the states, and when the Army cut that off, he moved on to illegally purchased drugs. When he got caught, the Army threw him out with a bad conduct discharge, which made him ineligible for veterans' benefits.

Mumsford—by then retired—and Coyle contacted Anthony, which resulted in a front page profile of Rogue and how he'd been screwed by the Army. His veterans' benefits were restored, but his psychological health was still a disaster.

"Oh, man," Anthony responded. "How'd he stay out of jail?"

Coyle shook his head and jerked a thumb toward his face. "I know the guy. We talked it out, no charges pressed, but we drove him down to the VA and checked him in. He'd said several times he wanted to kill himself."

"Jesus," Anthony said. He wished there was something he could do for the poor kid.

"All right. So what's the scoop about this guy Larsden? Why do you need to see him? Why does everybody else on earth want him?"

Anthony and Bear looked at each other. Bear shrugged. Anthony said, "All right, this has got to stay close, Coyle, okay? People's lives are on the line."

"Go for it."

"Did you hear the news last week? When the Secretary of Defense's daughter was kidnapped? Then his house got blown up, and his daughter's condo attacked, and now this guy here is your suspect for shooting at his wife?"

Coyle nodded.

"We're trying to track down who he's working for."

"News said it was rival drug lords or some crap like that."

Anthony shook his head. "You of all people know how the news gets things wrong."

Coyle nodded, thoughtfully. It had taken months before anyone in the unit had trusted Anthony, primarily because previous reporters they'd worked with got so many facts wrong.

"If it isn't drug lords, who is it?"

Bear leaned forward and said, "You know who I am?"

"Diplomatic Security. State Department, right?"

Bear nodded. "We're pretty sure the person behind all this works for a three letter agency."

Coyle's eyes widened. "Are you serious? It's a fed?" He looked at Anthony for confirmation.

Anthony nodded. "CIA."

"All right. So the FBI's going to be here at ten am to question him. So you've got until eight, then I need you out of here. All right? I kinda want to keep my job."

Anthony sighed in relief. Finally they might get some answers. Coyle stood and led them down the hall. Halfway down, he opened a door.

"You two can wait in here. We'll have him here in 5 minutes."

So they waited. Bear laid the newspaper on the table with the banner face down then sat down in one of the four small wood chairs arrayed around a table. He leaned the chair back against the wall, crossed his arms over his chest, and closed his eyes. Anthony felt unreasonable irritation. How could he possibly go to sleep that easily? Instead, he stood, bouncing on the balls of his feet and pacing. The room didn't look like he would have expected—a large one-way glass mirror. Instead, high in the ceiling, a black bubble was mounted in the ceiling—a camera.

After two minutes, Bear said, "Anthony, chill. You don't wanna be all nervous when Larsden gets in here. You're in command of the situation. Not the perp."

Anthony intellectually recognized the good sense of Bear's statement, but emotionally he was still tense. He wanted answers. He wanted to know who was gunning for Carrie and her family. Larsden had those answers.

His brow furrowed. Interesting that his mind had focused in on *Carrie* and her family.

Not that he disliked Carrie. He didn't. And she *was* the caretaker of what seemed to be an infinite number of sisters. But she was also a fairly recent widow, which made her off limits, and the subject of an ongoing investigation, which made her doubly off limits, and seriously what was he doing thinking about her when he was supposed to be thinking about—

The door opened. Coyle stepped back in the room, his arm cuffed around the bulging upper arm of a large man with a severe crew cut. The man—Nick Larsden, he presumed—had a network of tattoos scrawled up and down his arms. *Interesting*, Anthony thought. He recognized the US Army Special Forces motto—*De oppresso liber*—tattooed on Larsden's upper arm. But Larsden hadn't been Special Forces. In fact, he'd been a personnel clerk. Maybe that would be a wedge. A two-tour combat veteran like Coyle wouldn't think much of that either.

"Sit down," Coyle said. To emphasize his point, he pushed Larsden down into one of the chairs. Once Larsden was sitting, Coyle unlocked one handcuff then locked it to the steel table. Only after that ritual was complete did he say, "*Mister* Larsden." His emphasis on the word Mister was a little ominous. "Allow me to introduce my colleagues from Washington, DC, Misters Wyden and Walker."

"Are you fuckin' serious?" Larsden said. "Is that like Laurel and Hardy?"

Bear leaned forward and slammed a fist on the table with a crash that hurt Anthony's ears. "You don't want to mess with me. I'm with the Diplomatic Security Services, and my normal interrogations are with al-Qaeda trained killers, not two-bit washed up personnel clerks like you."

Larsden immediately tensed up, his face turning red. "I ain't no personnel clerk—"

"Shut up!" Bear roared.

Anthony kept absolutely still. He'd never seen a police interrogation before, other than on television. He didn't have any gauge of whether or not Bear's methods were conventional or not. But the room went absolutely silent.

Bear leaned forward and said, "I want to make things absolutely clear to you, shitbag. The woman you were taking potshots at was the wife of the Secretary of Defense of the United States. Do you understand what I'm saying?"

Bear flipped the newspaper over. Right on the front page was a full-color photo of Richard and Adelina Thompson, underneath the headline, "ASSASSIN SHOOTS AT SECRETARY OF DEFENSE'S WIFE." Underneath that, in smaller but still bold letters, "Adelina Thompson demands political asylum in Canada."

"Motherfucker," Larsden muttered. "No one said she was ... what the hell?"

"You're mixed up in some bad shit, Larsden. This is way over your head. What were they offering you? Fifty thousand? A million? Whatever it was, it's not worth the electric chair."

Larsden jerked in his chair. "Electric chair! Hell no, I didn't hit her, she got away, right?"

Bear shouted, "Her teenage daughter's in the hospital, shitbag!"

Anthony didn't say a word. Technically what Bear said was true. Jessica Thompson was in the hospital, though not of a gunshot wound. Larsden didn't need to know that.

"What do you want from me?" Larsden demanded.

"I want to know who you're working for. I know you didn't think this stupid operation up yourself."

"I don't know!" he cried.

Bear leaned over the table, shouting in his face, "You better know, asshole!"

"Bear," Anthony said.

"WHAT?" Bear shouted at Anthony.

"Maybe I can ask him some questions?"

Bear shouted, "We're not asking him *shit* until he gives me a name!" But even as he shouted, apparently out of control, his right eye winked at Anthony, just out of Larsden's sight.

Christ, Bear was a hell of an actor.

"Seriously, let me try," Anthony said.

"If he doesn't talk he's *dead*," Bear shouted. "Do you know what they do to people in prison who kill little girls?"

"I'll talk!" Larsden said. "I'll tell you whatever you want to know. But I never met Oz! I don't know his name!"

Bear whirled toward Larsden. "Oz? Who the hell is Oz?"

"I don't know," Larsden said. "English, or maybe Irish. Real bastard. This job was supposed to be a simple bounty, going after a couple of fugitives. Then when I caught up with them, it turned into murder. And the bastard said if I didn't follow through, he'd make sure *I* ended up dead."

Anthony said in a calm voice, "So you decided to murder a woman and her child to save your own skin?"

"Wouldn't you?" Larsden said. "No bullshit. I took the job, but I didn't know it was going to turn into all this."

"What was the payoff?" Anthony asked.

"One million," Larsden replied. "When he announced I had to kill them to keep them from crossing the border, I told him he had to make it three. He didn't even blink."

Bear said, "Did you meet this *Oz* in person?"

"No," Larsden replied. "Phone call only. An old Army buddy put me in touch with him."

"*What* old Army buddy?" Bear asked.

"Marky Lovecchio. I knew him in Germany."

Anthony leaned in. "How many jobs have you done for this guy?"

"Oz? This was the first one. And let me tell you, I'm regretting it."

"Little late for that," Bear said. "You should have thought of that before you took out a rifle and started shooting at people."

"Yeah…"

"Where's Marky Lovecchio from?" Bear asked.

"Boston."

Anthony said, "Did you see a phone number? When Oz called?"

Larsden shook his head. "Nah. It always said unknown caller."

"English accent?" Anthony said.

"I don't know. English. Scottish maybe. Irish. I don't know. He sounded like that actor … the old one … Liam Neeson?"

That's not very useful, Anthony thought. "What else did he tell you? Anything?"

"He was pissed she got so close to the border. He said I had to do *whatever it took* to make sure she didn't get into Canada."

"Well you blew that, motherfucker," Bear said.

"So what's next? Do I get immunity if you catch him?"

Bear snorted. "Are you serious? You haven't given us anything yet. Immunity is something you *trade* for."

"I've told you everything I know."

"Yeah? I don't believe it."

For the first time in the interview, Coyle interrupted. "Anthony. Time's up."

"All right, asshole," Bear said. "You're about to go through the ringer. IRS and FBI and Border Patrol and I don't know who all else wants a piece of you. They'll mess you up so bad you won't even know your name. So you better think it through. We're the only ones who can protect you. You better come up with some answers. We'll be back in the morning."

Adelina. May 6.

Adelina Ramos Thompson slowly opened her eyes. She was in a reclining chair, her feet up in the air, and she felt groggy and more than a little exhausted.

As always, her eyes immediately darted to her daughter.

Jessica had awoken from the previous evening, for about three hours. She was lucid, aware of her surroundings, and bitterly spiteful. Adelina withstood the onslaught of verbal abuse for almost an hour before she finally slipped out to the waiting room. Under the influence of medication, Jessica had fallen back asleep. Only then did Adelina return to her daughter's room.

She felt like a coward. She should have stayed, no matter what Jessica had said. But … she was human.

I hate you, Jessica had said. *You were a whore. You cheated on our father. I don't believe your lies.*

It had gone on and on, until Jessica finally turned away from her. Time passed and the verbal attacks began again. Adelina sat there, not hiding the tears that ran down her face, but also not replying in kind. Jessica's words hurt. They wounded, like bloody stab wounds left open, but Adelina reminded herself that Jessica didn't know what she was saying. She didn't have the facts, and she was going through hideous and painful addiction withdrawals. Worse, her speech was slurred, the left side of her mouth drooping almost imperceptibly.

While Jessica was asleep, Adelina got on her knees in the corner of the room and prayed for Jessica's recovery. She prayed that one day her daughters might forgive her—or, if they couldn't do that, that they would at least find peace.

She'd finally fallen into a fitful sleep, still on her knees. A nurse found her there and helped her stand on unsteady legs, pain radiating up through her knees. She had stumbled to the chair and collapsed.

Now, Jessica looked better. Her skin wasn't so sallow, and her breathing was steadier than it had been the night before. And that was a blessing. For the first time in days, she knew where all of her daughters were. Julia, Carrie and Sarah had all moved back to the condo the night before, and hired armed guards for protection. Alexandra and Andrea were at the British Embassy in Washington, DC, along with Dylan. She didn't dare hope to see George-Phillip again—she'd hurt him too much to ever expect that—but she knew that unless he'd changed profoundly in the last sixteen years, he would do everything he could to protect her daughters.

Adelina would never forget those months. Never. She had lost hope in Belgium, lost all pretenses that she could ever have a life. Her hospitalization in Spain, initially just a few days, extended to weeks in Belgium after she'd woken up in a panic attack and the doctors had to restrain her to keep from clawing her own skin off. Weeks she'd spent in a drugged haze, while they tried antipsychotic medications on her. *Clozapine,* which gave her dizziness the first three days, then caused seizures on the fourth day. *Risperidone,* which took away the terror but caused uncontrollable trembling and insomnia and the worst migraine she'd ever had. It was four weeks before she'd stabilized on *imipramine* and low doses of *risperidone,* which reduced the anxiety but also made her listless and vacant, with frequent trembling. Better that than another panic attack.

Almost ten weeks after her hospitalization, she returned to the Embassy in Brussels in mid-September. Julia had been cold on her return, turning her nose up and walking away. Carrie, always the sweetest of children, had come to her and hugged her, whispering, "I missed you, Mommy." Alexandra, almost four, had been full of nonsensical questions.

The months following her hospitalization were hazy to Adelina. She vaguely remembered packing as the tour in Brussels was coming to an end, but the memories were confused and unfocused. She'd tried to reach out to Julia, but the poor girl had been so hurt and confused that she'd refused any contact, spending all of her time in the garage with Corporal Lewis, who Adelina thanked God for every day. At least *someone* was watching out for her, because it was clear that during her hospitalization, Richard had barely seen the children.

The drugged haze continued as they spent several months in Washington, DC in 1995—months Adelina could barely remember now, except that it was one of the very rare times in their marriage where Richard had insisted she sleep with him. Those occasions, no more often than every few weeks, had filled Adelina with rage and self-loathing as she lay there, unmoving, disassociated. One night in May, in the room in the condo, he'd cursed at her when she winced at their painful intercourse.

You're a dried up old whore, he'd said in response to her body's inability to lubricate.

Maybe if I didn't hate you with every fiber of my being, my body would respond differently.

His response had been immediate and violent. But his attempts to have sex with her began to become less and less often, and the very last time had been in September 1995, just before he left for China.

By that time, she knew she was pregnant with twins.

The children had to switch schools in the fall when Richard was assigned as Ambassador to the People's Republic of China. The panic attacks and anxiety had returned in full when she'd stopped her medication due to the pregnancy.

The flight over had been miserable. Richard had flown separately, as he often did, leaving Adelina to handle the travel arrangements for the children. Twenty-four hours travel time, seventeen of them in the air, with a teenager, a pre-teen and a toddler, made the stuff of nightmares. She'd been in the bathrooms on the planes half a dozen times vomiting. Julia was sullen, almost never taking her headphones off long enough to help. Carrie had been a godsend, holding hands with then four-year-old Alexandra as Adelina juggled the luggage while they made their way through the connecting stop in Los Angeles. Then, in Narita International Airport in Tokyo, everything went to hell in an instant. They'd stepped off a moving sidewalk into the crowded terminal, hundreds of people moving in every direction. Adelina had been awake more than twenty-four hours, and she stumbled, setting the bags down and searching for information about their connecting flight.

Then a chill had gone down her spine when Carrie screamed, "Alexandra! Momma, I can't find her!"

Adelina shouted, "What?"

Carrie was standing there, eyes wide, panicking. They were surrounded by people and Alexandra was nowhere in sight. Julia had taken up a position against a wall, headphones on.

"Alexandra!" Adelina screamed out the name in a voice loud enough to be heard across that part of the terminal. "Alexandra!"

She'd turned to Julia and pulled the headset off. "Help me find your sister!"

Julia, not fully aware of the situation, shouted, "Leave me *alone!*"

A mix of panic and rage swept over Adelina. She reached out and slapped Julia full across the face. Julia's face jerked back at the slap, and Adelina shouted, "*Don't* you talk to me that way. Help me find your sister!"

Julia looked stunned. It was the first time Adelina ever struck one of her children, and remorse and horror instantly swept over her.

"Alexandra!" Carrie cried, not seeing what had happened behind her. A red mark had bloomed up on Julia's face. Adelina turned away, calling Alexandra's name again.

It took forty-five minutes before airport security found her. She'd wandered into one of the smoking lounges, where she'd panicked, crying in the corner.

They'd missed their connecting flight.

The next few months were a nightmare for Adelina. This pregnancy was *different* than her first three. She was older, of course, thirty-one years old, but that wasn't old to have a baby. But it was her fourth, and twins, *and* she'd just been taken off powerful antipsychotic and antidepressant medications. Almost instantly after coming off the meds, the fear and anxiety returned, her mind constantly wrapped around itself, twisting in fear. She took to writing in the margins of her Bible, and in a tight scrawl in her journal, filling every page right out to the margin, desperately trying to contain the uncontrollable emotions which were tearing her apart.

She remembered meeting with Charlotte Kelly, the only western obstetrician working in Beijing.

This pregnancy will be different than your others, Adelina. The hormones are twice as much or more. And as you get further along, you're going to be much larger. I want you to get as much rest as you can. Are you staying off your feet?

Adelina had laughed. *As much as any parent of three children can. My youngest is four.*

Get some help. You're going to need it. I want you back every two weeks. We're going to consider this a high-risk pregnancy.

High-risk pregnancy. Everything about her life was high-risk. She wasn't ready to have another child, much less two more. She knew she was a terrible mother—every time she saw the sullen rage in Julia's face she knew it. Julia became so involved with school activities that fall that Adelina rarely saw her. It felt as if Julia was more and more withdrawn, but she wouldn't talk with her mother, and Adelina had no idea how to help. She was overwhelmed and terrified.

Shouldn't the morning sickness be over? She'd asked Doctor Kelly late in the fifth month of her pregnancy, just before Christmas.

It's not always predictable, especially with multiples.

Predictable. It felt as if she spent half of each day vomiting.

One night in late January, Julia didn't come home from school. At first Adelina didn't worry. Julia had been late often this year, and usually got rides from her friends—Lana, the daughter of the Australian Consul-General, and Harry Easton, the son of the British Ambassador. But that night, she didn't appear *at all.*

She had called Lana's parents: the girl had been home for hours. Ronald Easton had answered and verified that Harry was home and hadn't seen Julia since he'd left school that day.

Where was she? For that matter, where was Richard? As he often did, he hadn't come home that evening. Usually she was glad when he gave his attention to whores and massage parlor girls instead of her, it meant that she would be left alone. But with their oldest daughter missing, things were different. Adelina lay on the couch, clutching her chest, unable to breathe, her chest tight with tension. What if she lost the babies? What if Julia didn't come home? What if Richard had finally lost it and done something to their daughter? *WHERE WAS SHE?*

At ten o'clock that night, Julia stumbled in, half covered in snow, her eyes wet with tears. She was pale, strung out as if on drugs, her eyes dilated. Adelina pulled herself up, barely able to move with the weight of the twins, and half stood, half rolled off the couch.

"Where were you?" she had screamed. "Julia! Where were you?"

Julia's eyes had widened, and she'd instantly screamed back. "Why don't you ask me *how* I am, Mother? Don't you care? Don't you care about *me?*"

Adelina back, "You can't just run off anywhere you want, Julia! You can't just do whatever you want! It's dangerous! *Don't* you turn your back on me!"

In the other room, Alexandra began to cry—a little at first, then a loud scream.

"See what you've done, you bitch!" Julia shouted. "Leave me alone!"

Without thought, rage swept over Adelina. For the second time as a parent, she hit one of her children—a loud, stinging slap that knocked Julia to the floor.

Stunned, Julia stared up at her, her face horrified and grief-stricken. Then she screamed, "I hate you! I hate you!" She stumbled to her feet and ran out of the room, slamming her bedroom door shut so hard the frame rattled. The next morning she was running a fever, and stayed home from school for a week.

Seven years passed before she learned what had really happened to Julia that night. Julia confronted her in their dining room in San Francisco demanding to know why Adelina hadn't been there for her daughter's darkest moment, when the fourteen-year-old Julia had come home from a back-room abortion.

The winter of 1995-96 had been the culmination of years of suffering. Finally, on the first of April, the twins were delivered. She took her first dose of risperidone in nine months less than twenty minutes after their delivery. Almost immediately she began to come out of her emotional tailspin.

Then, at the beginning of May, George-Phillip appeared in her life for the second time, and once again changed everything. His arrival was no less transformative than the sunrise after a long night, and despite herself Adelina quickly fell for him again. He was everything she'd ever wanted or cared about—loving, caring, respectful. He asked her what he thought and genuinely listened to the answers.

She hadn't planned to see him again. She hadn't planned to fall in love with him again. When she saw him at the Embassy reception, her first intention had been to avoid him entirely. Adelina was in the back of the ballroom, talking with Julia and Carrie. Both girls wore well-tailored dresses, with their hair and makeup professionally applied. It was Carrie's first official function.

"You've both done a very nice job tonight," Adelina was saying, knowing that the words would be ignored by Julia, who had barely spoken with her in the last six months. Carrie, however, brightened at the words.

"Does this mean I can do it again?" Carrie asked.

Adelina didn't answer. She'd stiffened, her heart suddenly racing, despite the heavy medications she'd been taking again since the birth of the twins. She froze, staring in the mirror at the front entrance to the hall. George-Phillip was there, unmistakably him despite the dozen years since they'd seen each other. He was accompanied by a slightly younger Chinese woman. A girlfriend? It didn't seem likely—her posture looked like that of a colleague, not a lover.

"Mother?" Carrie asked.

Adelina didn't answer. Her eyes were on the man she'd loved—and sent away. The memories were still fresh. Finding out she was pregnant. She'd provoked Richard into raping her, so that he wouldn't suspect adultery. Then she sent George-Phillip away, unable to cope with the hideous shame of the repeated rapes, the adultery, the ugliness of her own life.

The subterfuge had worked for several years, but Carrie looked so different from Richard, and was so tall even by the age of eight, that he'd secretly gotten DNA testing for both of them. He'd stayed away for a couple of days right before Valentine's that year then showed up unexpectedly. With flowers. She'd taken them, suspicious, but didn't understand the danger that was coming. When she sniffed the flowers, his fist came out of nowhere, knocking her down. By the time it was over, she had two broken ribs and was pregnant again.

She'd told herself that she was over George-Phillip. That she didn't love him anymore. Maybe even that she'd never loved him at all.

But one sight of him in the mirror swept those lies away.

"Mother?" Carrie had asked again.

"What?" she had responded.

"Oh, never mind!" Carrie said, her eyes watering. Julia shook her head slowly. Adelina didn't need to translate the look of contempt that her oldest daughter gave her.

"Go," Adelina said. "Just go."

The two girls walked away, and Adelina promised herself she'd stay away from him, she wouldn't put herself into harm's way, that she wouldn't put her *heart* at risk again. Her resolve lasted less than twenty-minutes when she saw him walk to the back hallway.

A month later she saw him again, and this time, she did something she knew was wrong.

"I miss you," she had said.

He had closed his eyes. Then whispered, "You broke my heart, Adelina."

"I broke my own," she had replied, her voice toneless.

Two weeks later, she told the nanny that she was going out, found a pay phone and called the British Embassy.

"I need to see you," she had said.

"I don't think that would be a good idea," he had responded, his voice redolent with pain.

"I'm begging you," she whispered. "There are things you do not know."

And so it had started again. Now—seventeen years later—she sometimes had to ask herself—did she regret it? Any of it? What if she'd never met Richard Thompson? What if she'd never been raped, and gone on to audition for the National Symphony, what if her father had lived?

The problem was, all of those dreams meant that her daughters would never have lived. And as she looked at Jessica—sick, weak, in danger—she knew she'd never make that trade. They were worth *anything*.

Her thoughts were interrupted by a knocking on the doorframe of the hospital room. Her eyes shifted to the door.

A tall man in a well fitted but off-the-rack suit stood in the doorway. "Mrs. Thompson?"

"Yes?"

"My name is Wolfram Schmidt. I'm a Special Agent with the Internal Revenue Service, and I'd like to ask you some questions."

CHAPTER NINE
Isn't it obvious?

Adelina. May 6.

"**I**'m sorry, you're who? From where?" Adelina's response wasn't particularly useful, but it stalled for a moment while she collected herself.

"My name is Wolfram Schmidt. I'm a Special Agent with the Internal Revenue Service."

Adelina's heart was thumping. She stared at Schmidt. She was stunned he was even here. After all, she was outside the borders of the United States. He had no jurisdiction.

"What can I do for you, Mr. Schmidt?"

Schmidt took the question as an invitation. He stepped into the room, and she stood, unsteadily, before he could say anything.

"Let's step outside," she said. "I don't want to wake my daughter."

He assented, and she stepped outside the room directly behind him. Once outside, he stepped across the hall. Adelina followed, staying a little more than arm's length from him.

"Mrs. Thompson ... first of all, I'm aware from the headlines that you've applied for asylum in Canada. I want to be clear that I've got no power here. I can't arrest you, or force you to come back. I can't make you do anything. You could call the police if I'm bothering you."

She studied him. His little speech was obviously a ploy to mollify her, to gain her trust. The problem was it worked, at least a little.

"I'm not quite ready to call the police. What exactly *is* it you're here for?"

"Well, I'm hoping you'll cooperate voluntarily. As you may know, the Justice Department has appointed a special prosecutor to investigate your husband's activities. Among others, the FBI and Internal Revenue Service are part of that investigation—I'm the lead for the IRS side of the investigation."

"You're also investigating my daughters."

Schmidt nodded, slowly. "One of them. Specifically Julia Wilson and her husband."

"Tell me why?"

Schmidt said, "First, you're aware that the President first raised the possibility of your husband—"

Adelina interrupted. "Please don't call him that."

Schmidt's eyes widened and his nostrils flared slightly. He was surprised, Adelina thought. "All right," he continued. "The President first contacted Ambassador Thompson in December to discuss the possibility of him becoming Secretary of Defense. It was already clear that his predecessor's health was failing."

Adelina nodded, encouraging him to continue.

He said, "The initial background checks cleared, of course, though there were some curious gaps in his resume. Those fairly quickly came to light, however, when we learned that Ambassador Thompson had been affiliated with the Central Intelligence Agency for many years. Effectively, he was on loan to the State Department."

What? The CIA? Adelina was stunned. She shook her head, slowly. "I—how is that possible?"

"You didn't know?"

"I know virtually nothing of him beyond the little he chose to reveal over the years. We are not close."

"You managed to have six children with him."

"Not with my consent," she said in a flat tone.

Schmidt was taken aback—his eyes widening, his nostrils flaring slightly. "I see. You understand that's immaterial to this investigation."

She shrugged. "The investigation is your problem, not mine."

"It might become yours, of course." He frowned. "After all, your name is on the tax returns."

"My name, but you certainly won't find my signature. I've never signed a tax return in my life. Mister Schmidt—tell me what I can do to help. I promise you, Richard is no friend of mine, nor is he a husband. Now that I'm finally safe from him, I'll be filing for divorce as soon as humanly possible. I'll gladly testify against him if that's what you need. But I can tell you, without question, that Julia had nothing to do with his schemes."

"Mrs. Thompson—your husband has half a dozen accounts in the Caymans, and there may be more elsewhere that we haven't uncovered yet. He has unreported assets in those accounts in excess of ten million dollars."

"I'm not surprised," she responded. "He's a snake and a liar."

"Were you aware of the accounts?"

"No," she replied.

Schmidt leaned forward and looked her closely in the eye. "Mrs. Thompson—please answer this carefully. Last Friday night, just before armed gunmen attacked your daughter's condominium in Bethesda, you placed a call to the condominium. That call lasted for less than 30 seconds and it was moments before the first shots were fired. Tell me why you placed that call."

Adelina felt her heart thump. Of course they would have pulled the phone records by now. Did her phone show an incoming call? Perhaps it might, perhaps it might not. She'd been stunned to learn, four years before, that George-Phillip had moved from Britain's Ambassador to the United Nations post and taken over the Secret Intelligence Service. Had he been an intelligence agent all along?

Like Richard?

She swallowed and said, "I can't answer that just yet."

Schmidt raised his eyebrows. "Why not?"

"I cannot."

"Mrs. Thompson, it appears from the sequence of phone calls that you had some advance warning of the attack, and you were trying to warn your daughter. Is that the case?"

She shook her head. She hadn't planned on contacting George-Phillip. But now there was no choice.

"Mrs. Thompson. You understand how this looks?"

"Ask me again tomorrow."

"I don't understand."

"Not all secrets are mine to reveal, Mr. Schmidt."

"Do you plead the Fifth Amendment, Mrs. Thompson?"

"We're outside the borders of the United States, Mr. Schmidt. You have no jurisdiction here. I promise I'll tell you when I can."

"Why did you apply for asylum?" he asked.

She smiled bitterly. "Because my *husband* sent armed assassins to kill me. As you may know, he is a high government official. I have nothing I can do to protect myself other than run."

Schmidt sighed. He reached in his pocket and took out a business card. "I have business this afternoon in Bellingham. The man who shot at you is in jail there, and I'll be questioning him this afternoon. In the meantime, if there is anything you can think of—please call me."

"I will. Thank you, Mister Schmidt."

He turned and walked away. Adelina's shoulders sagged. She needed to call George-Phillip now. She had no choice. Time to talk to the nurses and find out where she could make that call. But, as she turned away, she heard the words, "Momma?"

Adelina ran back to Jessica's room. George-Phillip and the IRS could wait.

Sarah. May 6.

Sarah grinned. The sky was slowly turning from black to rose, highlighting the trees in silhouette as they continued down Interstate 76. She was exhausted and ready to stop. She could feel the vibration of the bike in her bones.

There. The first exit in Ohio. They'd driven for five hours, stopping only for gas and coffee, their goal to place as much distance between them and Washington, DC as possible. As they approached the exit, she nudged the bike over into the next lane, slowing down to fifty miles per hour. They'd carefully stayed between five and ten miles over the speed limit and avoided high traffic areas, not wanting to be flattened by a long haul trucker. But for the last two hours, they'd mostly had the highway to themselves.

Sarah did not relish the idea of dying in a motorcycle accident. But even as she drove up the exit ramp, slowing to a stop, she exulted a little. Eddie wouldn't be happy she'd stolen his bike, but he'd understand. And she was finally *free*. For more than ten months she'd been confined to the hospital and then the condo. A cripple. She'd nearly lost her leg to her injuries and the later infection, which kept her in a wheelchair for months, then on crutches for more months. But she'd been completely on her feet since early March, and worked out every day, performing the exercises her physical therapist had assigned, then doubling up on that.

Carrie would have a conniption, of course. She drove a gigantic armored SUV, the biggest and heaviest vehicle she could find, ever since the accident. Sarah understood it, of course. Fear could make you act out in strange ways. For Sarah, that had meant pursuing an obnoxious, in your face recovery. For Carrie, it meant ordering her life into such a tight structure that nothing could impede the walls of the little prison she was constructing for herself.

Sarah wouldn't accept any walls, not Carrie's, not her mother's, not even her own.

Andrea, hunched over behind her on the bike, pointed to their right. A sign that had clearly been erected sometime in the 1970s read *Pamela's Diner*. The light in the letter E had burned out. Behind the diner, a Motel 6. They would accept cash for sure. She goosed the bike forward, trailing her toes on the concrete until their speed picked up enough to balance them. She was almost too short to manage the bike, but Eddie had taught her how to drive it a week before Andrea came to the United States.

Bet he regrets that now, she thought, her internal voice a little smug.

When she cut the engine, silence instantly fell over them. It was jarring, the silence seeming louder than the 1340cc engine that powered the bike, a 2003 Sportster with metallic blue and chrome trim. Andrea climbed off behind her, stretching her impossibly long frame as Sarah slipped off the motorcycle. Both of them took off their helmets.

"We made good progress," Andrea said.

"Yeah. Long way to go, though." Sarah's response felt stiff. "Let's get some breakfast."

Andrea nodded and turned toward the diner. Sarah followed, her thoughts suddenly circling around the fact that she didn't know what she had to say to Andrea. They'd talked a little bit about boyfriends a few days before—before killers had attacked the condominium and Andrea went on the run. Before they knew that an English prince was Andrea's father (something Sarah thought was a gigantic laugh). But really she didn't know her sister. Andrea had effectively stopped living with them when Sarah was in the second grade, and her visits home had become infrequent. She knew Jessica and Andrea had once been close. But now? She didn't think anyone was close to Andrea.

Could she blame Andrea for having strong armor? Sarah couldn't even imagine what it must have felt like to believe that your parents didn't want you. She knew Julia and Carrie had uncovered a lot of things about their mother recently ... that she'd lied about her age, and that she'd been effectively raped and kidnapped from her home. But even so, *both* of their parents had a lot to answer for when it came to Andrea.

Sarah paused to stretch again before they entered the restaurant. Her muscles felt compressed, and her legs still hadn't stopped vibrating. Worse, her left leg—the one that had been badly injured and broken in the accident—*ached* like it hadn't in a very long time. Of course, she had more hardware in her leg than a Home Depot, with all those pins and screws rattling around on the bike it was no wonder she hurt.

Andrea opened the door for her, and Sarah limped into the restaurant. Then the two of them waited at the front door.

Immediately she saw herself in the large mirror near the hostess station at the front of the restaurant. Both of them with dark hair, almost black, with streaks, Sarah's white and Andrea's turquoise. Both of them wore mostly black, though Sarah's skirt was plaid over black leggings. In the mirror, they looked a little comical—Andrea was a full foot taller than Sarah.

Andrea grinned at Sarah in the mirror as the hostess led them to a table. For the next several minutes, they both studied the menu, ordered their food and drinks, then sat back and looked at each other.

Sarah said, "I feel kind of awkward. I mean, we're sisters, but we don't know each other very well, do we?"

Andrea nodded, her expression a little sad.

Sarah said, "Thanks for calling every week after I got hurt. It meant a lot to me."

Andrea shrugged. "You needed it. I could tell."

"I felt so alone. Especially at first, when I thought I was going to lose my leg. And I thought I was going crazy sometimes, with just me and Carrie and Mother. Your calls helped ground me."

Andrea said, "I wish we could have spent more time together. You know—growing up."

Sarah said, "Me too."

"Do you remember going to the zoo? When we were little?"

"Yeah. Carrie used to take us all the time. And to Golden Gate Park." Sarah studied her sister for a moment. They both shared facial features from their mother—the same small, slightly upturned nose, the green eyes and nearly black hair. But Andrea and Carrie had gotten some serious mutant tall genes from their father.

It felt weird to say that word in reference to someone else. "What was it like? Meeting your ... your dad?"

Andrea sighed. "I don't know really. He seemed really nice. But you can't trust that, can you?"

Sarah said, "I don't know. Maybe sometimes you have to trust something."

Andrea stared at her sister, letting her big green eyes stare. Then she nodded, once. "Maybe you're right. But how do you know when?"

Sarah shrugged. "I've got a lot of questions for Mother."

"Me too."

"There are a lot of things I feel like I should know about you. What's your favorite color?"

"Blue," Andrea replied. "You?"

"Isn't it obvious?" Sarah asked, gesturing to her all black clothes.

Andrea chuckled. "How come you and Jessica are so different now?"

Sarah's mouth turned up in a half-smile. "We always were. I think she felt like she had to somehow compensate for … something. I don't know what. It seemed like I constantly got in more trouble while she constantly became more prim."

Andrea said, "I don't see how she got mixed up with drugs."

Sarah shook her head. "I don't either. I feel like I missed something crucial, and it pisses me off. We haven't gotten along the last couple years, but she's still my twin. I should have known."

The waitress arrived with their breakfast. They stayed silent as their food was arranged, then Andrea said, "I don't want to stop long. Let's sleep a couple hours then get on the road again, okay?"

Sarah nodded. "Yeah. It's a long way before we'll get there."

"You could have picked a more practical mode of transportation," Andrea said.

"More practical than a Harley?" Sarah asked. She grinned. "What country have you been living in?"

Two hours later, they were driving west again.

George-Phillip. May 6.

It was a little after four in the morning when George-Phillip awoke, fully awake though it was still very dark. He was already an early riser, and the addition of jet lag guaranteed insufficient sleep for the next several days. He stumbled out of bed and took care of his morning routine, then glanced into Jane's room. His daughter—*youngest daughter*—thankfully could sleep anywhere, any time. She would still be out for at least a couple more hours.

He closed the door, then stepped out of the suite, intending to head downstairs for a cup of coffee, a habit he'd picked up during his first time in Washington, DC thirty years before.

A Captain of the Royal Marines was waiting for him along with O'Leary when he got downstairs.

"Your Highness," the Captain said, coming to attention.

"Good morning, Captain," George-Phillip said, his eyes moving to O'Leary in question.

"George-Phillip, I'm afraid we have bad news," O'Leary said.

"Sir, the young lady ran last night. She climbed over the fence and ran."

Stunned, George-Phillip asked, *"Which* young lady?"

"Andrea Thompson, sir," O'Leary said.

George-Phillip shook his head. "When did this happen?"

"Just after midnight, sir."

"And you're just telling me now?" George-Phillip shouted.

The Captain looked at O'Leary, confused. O'Leary looked uncomfortable. "Sir, that was my order—we couldn't get her, someone met her with a motorcycle and she was gone before our men even made it to the gate. Nor could we pursue her—after all, she wasn't a prisoner."

"She is my daughter!" George-Phillip shouted

The Captain's eyes widened and he took a step back. O'Leary, however, stepped forward, placing a hand on George-Phillip's arm. "Your Highness, I'm well aware of that. But you are also the Chief of the Secret Intelligence Service. You can't allow your personal considerations to interfere with that, sir."

Rage gripped George-Phillip. His response was delivered in an icy tone. "You take too much liberty, Oswald. I can't even imagine what you were thinking. Do we have *any* idea where she went? Who she went with? Why she left?"

The Royal Marine Captain shook his head. "No, Your Highness. Her room was locked from the inside, and while the bedclothes were a mess, there's no sign of a struggle. She took her bag and went out the window, sir, then ran for the fence."

George-Phillip said to the Marine Captain, "Go wake up Dylan Paris. And I want to see the video from the security cameras. Has anyone told the Ambassador?"

O'Leary said, "Is that wise, sir?"

George-Phillip said, "Twice now, a sixteen-year-old girl has evaded our security. Think about it, Oswald. I want to know why she ran. We just had dinner last evening and agreed that it would be safest for her to remain on the Embassy grounds."

He half turned away from O'Leary, but O'Leary grasped his arm. "Sir—have you considered that maybe some of what they are saying in the media about her is true?"

George-Phillip said, "I'm well aware that you always opposed my involvement with Adelina Ramos—"

"*Thompson,* Your Highness. Her last name is *Thompson.*"

George-Phillip turned back to O'Leary, jamming his index finger into O'Leary's chest. "O'Leary, we've been friends and colleagues for thirty years. But I'm telling you now that you are pushing this too far."

"Yes, Your Highness. Of course."

"You may go. I want an update as soon as possible. O'Leary—don't fail me. I want my daughter found and protected."

O'Leary said, "Yes, Your Highness." Then he turned away. He stumbled once as he stepped away.

"Oswald? Are you all right?"

O'Leary looked back. "Of course, sir. I turned my ankle when I was inspecting where she went over the fence."

CHAPTER TEN
Evil empire.

Richard. May 6.

The Central Hearing Facility in the Hart Senate Office building was the largest hearing room on Capitol Hill, with seating for up to several hundred spectators. The seal of the United States Senate, which displayed a flag with thirteen stars over a ribbon labeled *E Pluribus Unum,* dominated the marble wall at the head of the room behind the dais where thirteen Senators were seated. On either side, wood paneled walls were punctuated with openings behind which reporters with cameras were preparing to film the hearing.

The room was full, every single seat taken. Unlike the typical Congressional hearing where one or two members of Congress showed up to make a few comments for the cameras, for this hearing every single Senator was already seated and ready to begin their questioning.

"The hearing is about to come to order, sir," said the nameless intern who had accompanied Richard Thompson to the anteroom. "You can go in now."

Richard didn't bother answering. Instead, back straight, head high, he walked down the aisle at the center of the hearing room. A hush fell on the room as the hundreds of spectators realized he was approaching the witness desk that faced the Senators on the dais. Much as had been the case fourteen years before, when Senator Chuck Rainsley sat at the head of the Senate Foreign Relations Committee blocking Richard's appointment to Moscow, Rainsley was back, now as head of the Senate Armed Services committee. The turncoat had even politically survived the switch from Republican to Democrat in 2003, just after the invasion of Iraq, and despite his obvious leftist leanings, had managed to claw his way to the head of the most important and most powerful committee in Congress. Richard remembered all too well the political circus of his confirmation hearings as Ambassador to Russia more than a decade ago. Rainsley had put every possible obstacle in his way, dug deep into his personal life and then blindsided him with closed, classified hearings where his CIA career was examined.

Richard *hated* this oppressive, noxious room and the chairman who sat at the head of the table. For thirty years Chuck Rainsley had been his nemesis. Richard didn't allow himself to blink as he walked up the aisle, meeting Rainsley's eyes defiantly. Despite the flashes of dozens—possibly hundreds of cameras—Richard made his way up the center of the aisle without pausing or even noticing the barrage. None of the people out there really mattered. Now it was between him and Rainsley.

"All right," Rainsley said, his appalling Texas drawl elongated for the cameras. He looked at the other Senators and said, "Y'all all right?"

When there was no response, Rainsley banged a gavel on the table. "Good morning, everybody. This committee was originally scheduled to consider the nomination of Ambassador Richard Thompson to be Secretary of Defense. As I'm sure y'all are aware, yesterday the President withdrew the nomination. However, this committee still has business to address with Ambassador Thompson. Now, for the moment, we're going to skip right over the reports of drug money laundering and corruption, as well as the reports of millions of dollars of assets secreted away in the Caymans."

Richard seethed at Rainsley's response. In one sentence, Rainsley had dismissed any possible discussion of the lies he'd been accused of, even as he gave credence in a public hearing to those accusations. Rainsley, once a straight shooting Marine (or so he claimed) had become familiar with the wily, slippery ways of Washington. It made Richard sick enough that he wanted to walk out and go wash his hands.

"Today," Rainsley said, "we will begin by addressing a report which appeared in *The Guardian* newspaper in London the day before yesterday."

Rainsley paused for a full twenty seconds to allow the reporters to get a better angle with their cameras. Then he said, as dramatically as possible, "Thirty years ago, in one of the bloodiest incidents of the Soviet invasion of Afghanistan, a tiny village in an out of the way corner of the furthest province from the Afghan capitol was gassed with sarin, the deadliest nerve gas ever invented."

Richard felt his lip turning up in contempt of Rainsley. He forced it down. It was essential to maintain his diplomatic facade.

"For those of you not familiar with the military," Rainsley said, emphasizing (for the three people left in remote rural Alaska who didn't know) that he'd once been a Marine, "just a single drop of sarin is deadly enough to kill a person instantly. In this incident in Afghanistan, two helicopters delivered the chemical weapon in the dead of night and dropped it on unsuspecting villagers. According to Human Rights Watch, more than two hundred and thirty men, women and children were killed. Even the *dogs* died, as did a Human Rights Watch investigator who came into contact with the poison three months later."

The room was silent. Rainsley had absolute mastery over his audience, his words articulate and persuasive. Those words were being broadcast across the nation and the world. If Richard couldn't counter them effectively, it didn't matter what he did. His career would be over irrevocably.

Rainsley spoke again, this time his voice loud, outraged. "Ladies and Gentlemen, colleagues of the Senate—for thirty years we have believed that the Soviet Union was responsible for this massacre of innocents. Who here doesn't remember President Reagan citing the massacre when he described the Soviet Union as an *evil empire*? And yet ... how shocked we would all be to learn that it wasn't the Soviet Union at all who was responsible for the massacre. Instead—a rogue CIA operative, operating with little or no oversight."

Richard normally had complete control over his facial expressions and responses. But at the phrase "rogue CIA operative," he shook his head with contempt.

Rainsley pointed a finger. "According to a report leaked this week to a British newspaper, *this* man, former Ambassador, most recently acting Secretary of Defense, was responsible for procuring the weapons. He was responsible for delivering them to the Afghan militia, which then dropped them on unsuspecting civilians. Instead of protecting the civilians of Afghanistan, we did just the opposite. We laid waste to them."

Rainsley shook his head, sadly. Then, just in case no one knew, he said, "When I served in the Marine Corps, we knew a different kind of war. We learned to face our enemies. We learned to protect innocent civilians. The deadliest mission I ever served on, our job was to *keep the peace*, not to make things worse."

Rainsley was working himself up into one of his trademark tantrums, his face turning bright red. One of these days, he'd have a stroke. When that day came, Richard hoped he'd be there, to help Rainsley along to the other side. For the time being, he tried not to roll his eyes.

"I must not go on," Rainsley said. "My outrage knows no boundaries."

Your morals know no boundaries, Richard thought, staring at the man who had violated his wife, *impregnated her* not once but *twice*. He should have insisted Andrea be aborted. Adelina would have refused, but enough sedatives could approximate consent.

Rainsley yielded to the ranking member, a nonentity from the minority party. The tea party might hold sway in the House of Representatives, but here in the Senate, liberal democrats had a grip on all of the gears of government, especially the most powerful committees. Richard listened to Lewis's opening statement with complete indifference. This committee might think it was important, but in fact all it did was rubber stamp the President's nominations. Instead of listening, Richard looked up at the ceiling. The room had acoustical tiles in the ceiling to ensure those in the back could hear. Unlike the ancient hearing rooms in the other office buildings on Capitol Hill, this one was modern, sleek, as was the building that housed it. Richard preferred the original buildings. Whoever had commissioned this glass and concrete monstrosity ought to have been shot.

An interminable period of time later, Richard glanced at his watch. It was almost 11 am, and the members of the committee still hadn't finished their opening statements. He reminded himself that the entire purpose of this hearing was to show the constituents back home that the Senators were doing something. That's why they were taking all the time. He looked behind him for a moment, at the large crowd.

Richard blinked. In the front row, in the rows reserved for journalists ... it was that bitch Maria Clawson. No longer a too-thin social climbing gossip columnist, she was now old, angry and bitter. When she saw Richard looking at her she raised her notebook in the air, just slightly, then smiled at him, as if to say, *I'm going to screw you all over again.* Yeah, he remembered her. He remembered her poison pen, her sourceless blogs that implicated him in supposedly forcing Julia to get an abortion. As if he'd had any clue the girl had gotten herself pregnant. He'd made it clear to Adelina thirty years ago that his name should never again appear in one of Clawson's columns, and she failed to prevent it. He'd made sure Adelina regretted that failure. But the satisfaction of seeing her cringe, the pleasure of her capitulation, had done nothing to relieve the seething anger and blackness that stirred inside of him.

He turned back to the front, taking his eyes from the noxious woman.

Finally. Richard snapped back to reality as Rainsley was saying, "Richard Isaiah Thompson, raise your right hand and repeat after me. Do you swear to tell the truth…"

Richard repeated the words mechanically. He didn't care for the use of his middle name. The name Isaiah was marble and ice, it was murder, it was *private.* Never in his life had he used his middle name. He didn't even know how Rainsley knew his middle name, unless Adelina had told him during one of their trysts.

"Do you have an opening statement, Mister Thompson?" Rainsley said. Dispensing with the honorifics.

"I do, Senator." Richard's voice was cold as he spoke.

"Please proceed."

Richard stared up at the dais. Rainsley was in the center. To his left and right were six Senators on each side. This committee (like all of them) tended to be white, male and wealthy. Richard's natural constituency. But he couldn't discount the fact that 7 out of 13 members of the committee were Democrats, who would gladly throw him to the wolves if it meant they could extort one more dollar out of the government. The Republicans on the committee weren't allies either—they were weak, ineffectual, divided and terrified of losing their seats to Tea Party insurgents.

"Mister Chairman, distinguished members of the committee, please allow me to state, first of all, that the charge I was in any way involved in the Wakhan massacre is not only unfounded, but a grave injustice. In my detailed comments I will make it clear to you that not only am I completely innocent of these charges, but, in fact, I tried to prevent the massacre *and* reported it through official channels after the fact. *Second.* I will demonstrate that the ludicrous charges currently being examined by the grand jury and the special prosecutor are manufactured by the very man who committed the massacre and is now attempting to destroy me in order to save face."

"That will be quite the feat, Mister Thompson," Rainsley said. "However, your money laundering activities, or lack thereof, are not of interest to this committee. I'm certain the grand jury will take care of *that.* This committee *is* interested in those matters that affect the national security of the United States. Clearly, the provision of weapons banned under the Geneva conventions to terrorist organizations is one of those matters. You'll restrict your answers to that."

Terrorists? Rainsley managed to escalate with every word he spoke. The mujahideen of the early 1980s were American allies, regardless of the atrocities they committed in 2001. Richard leaned forward and said, "Senator, official US policy in the 1980s was to assist the mujahideen. While I gave no one chemical weapons, you can hardly retroactively label them terrorists."

Rainsley smiled, as if to say, *Checkmate.* "Mister Thompson, the same allies you speak of killed thousands of Americans on September 11. Call them whatever you like, but the fact is those Americans are dead."

"Mister Chairman," called out the ranking member, Senator Lewis. "In the interest of time, can we skip the bandying of words back and forth and deal with facts?"

Rainsley nodded. "Of course, Senator. I will concede to you—please ask the first question."

Lewis nodded, then leaned forward. Based on the opening statements, it appeared that the Republicans on the committee were tentatively supporting him—most likely because doing so allowed them to oppose the administration, which had dumped him like a piece of garbage. Lewis's glasses hung at the end of his nose, his bald head glaring under the bright lights. His blue eyes looked at Richard over the top of his glasses.

"Ambassador Thompson ... I'd like to begin by recognizing that all of us on this committee are aware of your long and distinguished history in service to this country. And even if some other members of this committee have forgotten, I remember that the United States armed the mujahideen specifically to defend against the invading Soviet Union. That said, chemical weapons are a serious matter. Please answer for the committee the following question. Did you take part, in any way, in the provision of chemical weapons to the Afghan militia?"

Soft ball, Richard thought. Perfect. "I did not, Senator."

Lewis nodded, his eyes scanning over a sheet of paper. Then he looked back up at Richard. "Do you know who did?"

"Yes, Senator. I reported the crime in 1983. The perpetrator was Leslie Collins, the current Director of Operations of the Central Intelligence Agency."

Julia. May 6.

Martin Barrymore was the quintessential Long Island WASP lawyer. Five foot eight, grey haired, balding, and deep inside his very small heart, he had a little bit of murder in him. As general counsel of Morbid Enterprises, Inc., Julia and Crank's holding company, he'd tackled a lot of issues. Copyright and trademark violation, contract negotiation, mergers and acquisitions. Taxes were never an issue, because the company was scrupulous about paying them. But now, he was heading up the team of tax attorneys who were preparing to deal with the Internal Revenue Service, and Julia was grateful for him.

The two of them, along with two tax attorneys who reported to Barrymore, rode up the elevator to the ninth floor of the IRS headquarters in Washington, DC. Julia was relieved Crank hadn't come—he'd have been far too likely to make flippant comments about how they might not escape from the building alive.

All the same, he'd insisted on something useful to do.

Look, Julia—I don't feel like I'm pulling my weight. All I do is write songs and sing. You're doing everything for us.

But Crank, she'd said, *that's what we've always done. I'm okay with that, I want you to be able to write your music and not worry.*

He'd grinned and said, *This is a crisis, babe. You take amazing care of me. But you gotta let me help.*

So they'd discussed it, and Crank had flown up to Boston first thing that morning. He would be meeting with the staff of the Boston office, and dispensing three weeks pay—in cash. It's all they had in their personal bank accounts, and the possibility of checks bouncing had resulted in a large cash withdrawal. That might be all the staff would get unless Barrymore could get the IRS to agree to free up some money.

Crank would be good at that. He didn't realize it, but over the years, he'd become a natural leader. Confident, bold, but warm and approachable. Everyone felt comfortable approaching him—whether it was network anchors, overenthusiastic fans or roadies who'd been working for the tour for a week. Sometimes she had to step in the way just so he could get some songs written. He didn't like to say no, didn't like to disappoint people.

For now, he'd be fine. A small pit of anxiety turned in her stomach. If she couldn't get the money freed up, then their fifty employees and their families would be out of luck. No severance pay, no nothing. It was grossly unfair, and according to Barrymore, it was also likely illegal. She was counting on his ability to fix that situation quickly. He'd already drawn up papers to file suit in Federal District Court if this meeting didn't go well.

"This way, please," said their escort, a youngish looking woman who had introduced herself as Jayna McCloud. An intern probably; Julia would have put her at twenty-one at the most.

She led Julia, Barrymore and the tax attorneys to a conference room at the end of the hall. The conference room was cheaply appointed. Painted walls, a pressboard conference table (attractive and functional, but cheaply made), chairs that looked half decent but were not ergonomically sound. She guessed if the IRS used these chairs throughout the headquarters, there were a lot of people out with bad backs.

At the table sat three people. The first, at the head of the table, Julia recognized. Emma Smith had been one of the agents who had questioned her in San Francisco what seemed like a lifetime ago, but was in fact just a few days.

"Mrs. Wilson, thank you for coming today. Allow me to introduce Cliff Shriver from the FBI."

To her right, Shriver was a man in a decently tailored grey suit. His jacket was open, and his sidearm, a gleaming black pistol in a shoulder holster, was clearly visible. A badge hung from his jacket lapel.

"And this is Scott Kelly from Diplomatic Security Services. Scott isn't here on an official basis, but he's asked to be in on this meeting because he said he has information that may be helpful to us all. It's up to you whether or not he stays."

"Pleasure to meet ya," Kelly said, his voice a clear Boston accent. He had dark circles under his eyes, the kind you got from years of sleep shortages. He reminded her a lot of her father-in-law Jack, a retired Boston cop.

"I think that will be fine," Julia murmured.

"Julia?" Barrymore asked quietly.

"It's fine," she said. "I want to clear this up as quickly as we can."

Emma Smith nodded in approval. "Please have a seat then."

Julia sat at the end of the table opposite Smith and studied her adversary. Her two in the morning impression of the woman hadn't changed—her skin was smooth, unblemished and free of makeup. She looked to be in her late twenties, or would, but her hair was white. Not bleached, not blonde, but prematurely gray and white. *Interesting*, Julia thought.

Smith said, "Mrs. Wilson, this is an informal meeting. It's not a hearing, and you're free to go at any time. Your attorney is here to advise you on your rights, of course, but I want to make it clear that while you have the right to not say anything at all, if you *do* say anything, we might use it in our investigation."

Julia leaned toward Barrymore, who said, "It's standard. I'll watch out for you here." She nodded.

"Thanks," Julia said. Barrymore responded to Smith. "We're looking forward to clearing this up."

"All right. I want to start with the accounts in the Caymans."

Julia nodded, not saying anything. She'd heard the reports in the media, but that's all she knew. "I'm not actually aware of any such accounts."

Smith opened a folder and slid half a dozen sheets of paper down the table. Barrymore retrieved them and showed them to Julia.

"These are powers of attorney, registered with HSBC, Butterfield Bank, Cayman National Bank, First Caribbean and the Royal Bank of Canada, all operating on Grand Cayman. They authorize you to establish accounts on behalf of your father. Do you recognize them?"

Julia shook her head. They were, in fact, powers of attorney. More disturbing, they all bore her signature. They were all dated December 19 and 20, 2013. Which was alarming. She and Crank had stayed overnight on Grand Cayman en route from Europe to Washington, DC.

"I've never seen these," she said. "That looks like my signature, but I didn't sign these documents."

"Where were you on December 19th and 20th, Mrs. Wilson?"

"I suspect you know the answer to that question," she replied.

"Were you on Grand Cayman Island with your husband?"

"Yes. We were on our way to the States to spend Christmas with my sisters."

"How do you explain your signature on these notarized documents?"

"I can't explain them. This is the first I've ever heard of them."

Smith nodded.

Kelly leaned forward and said, "Can you think of any reason why someone would go to this much trouble and expense? After these accounts were established, more than twenty million dollars was deposited into them. We haven't been able to trace the source."

Julia frowned. Then she said, "Do you know when my father was first approached about taking the Secretary of Defense job?"

The three federal agents looked at each other, mystified.

Julia nodded once. "From what I've been told, it was in December 2013. Right around the same time these documents were signed."

Bear. May 6.

Neither Anthony Walker, not Bear Wyden were accustomed to staying in luxurious accommodations. So after they left the county jail, Bear suggested they check into the local Days Inn there in Bellingham and make that their base of operations for the next couple of days.

"Sure," Anthony had said. An hour later, they had checked in. Anthony went to work on his laptop, making phone calls and generally making a nuisance of himself.

At one point, he looked up from his laptop, his eyebrows scrunched together and a line running down his forehead. "Didn't you say you ran the security detail for the Thompsons in the nineties?"

"Yeah," Bear had replied.

"What were the girls like? Julia and Carrie?"

Bear shrugged. "Kids. Julia was the oldest; she was typical eighth grader. Pissed at the world and especially her mother. Carrie was a sweetheart. Why do you ask?"

Anthony shrugged. "Just wondering."

"Yeah, well wonder quietly." Bear, who had an incurable sleep deficit, lay down to take a nap. He closed his eyes, lulled by the clickety-click sound of Anthony's keys on the laptop.

It was tranquil for a change, and Bear found himself drifting off shortly after noon. That made it all the more alarming when the door to the hotel suddenly burst inward and someone shouted, "Freeze, FBI!"

Bear froze. So did Anthony, his fingers still poised on his laptop, cell phone at his ear.

Five seconds later the room was full of fully armed and pissed off federal agents. Bear was thrown rudely to the floor, where his hands were cuffed with zip ties behind his back and his sidearm was taken away. Anthony was also face down in the carpet, his cell phone beside him face down. Bear instantly found himself wondering—was it still connected to whoever Anthony had been talking to? Hopefully they were connecting a recorder.

Footsteps. He craned his neck as far as he could, but he could only make out a pair of not very well polished wingtips and grey suit pants.

"Let him up," a voice said.

He was hauled upward by his arms and came to rest face to face with a tall man with swept back salt-and-pepper hair and a hawk nose.

"Agent Wyden," the man boomed. "I'm Wolfram Schmidt. Internal Revenue Service—and I'm in charge of the Thompson investigation."

Crap. That was quick.

"Hey," Bear said, giving Schmidt a disarming grin. "Great to finally meet you!"

Schmidt narrowed his eyes. "It's not that nice to meet you, Wyden. You're suspended. And no longer associated with this investigation. What brings you to Washington?" His eyes flitted toward Anthony. "And in the company of a journalist, I see."

"Well, you know, you can't always pick your friends..."

"Shut up. What the hell are you doing here, Wyden?"

"Officially?" Bear asked.

Schmidt rolled his eyes. "Yeah."

"Nothing. Nothing at all, officially. I'm suspended. But, the thing is—"

"Shut up."

"It's hard to answer your questions if I shut up."

"Jesus," Schmidt said. "Untie them. Wyden, sit down."

An agent cut the zip ties holding his wrists. Bear didn't argue—he just sat down on the end of one of the beds. Anthony was maneuvered to sit next to him, and Wolfram Schmidt with his swept back hair sat down opposite them.

"Seriously, Wyden. Quit screwing around and answer my question or you'll find yourself arrested for obstructing justice. You showed up before anybody else to question Larsden, and now he's dead."

CHAPTER ELEVEN
That poor boy

Anthony. May 6.

You *showed up before anybody else to question Larsden, and now he's dead.* What the hell? "What happened to him?" he blurted out.

Anthony's mind crowded with questions. If Larsden was dead, then their only link to Oz was Marky Lovecchio, and they still hadn't identified him. Was that actually the guy's name? If so, they should be able to find him on Google or some public records. Facebook, some other social networking, credit checks. No one was completely invisible.

Schmidt gave Anthony a withering look. "I don't even know why you're part of this discussion. This is an ongoing investigation and—"

Bear interrupted Schmidt. "Yeah, I get it, ongoing investigation, can't comment, yada yada yada. What the hell happened to Larsden? He was the picture of health four hours ago."

Schmidt said, "Off the record, someone shanked him, and naturally no one saw anything. He bled out in the county jail before anyone even knew what happened."

"Son of a bitch," Bear said. He looked at Anthony and both said the same word at the same time: "Oz."

Schmidt blinked. His response was sarcastic. "Oz? Are we going on a trip?"

Bear looked at Schmidt. "I'll tell you everything I've got. I mean everything. But I need you to know, I know for a fact the sisters weren't involved in whatever is happening here. Their father is a complete slime bag, but they weren't involved."

"Yeah? What about Julia Wilson? She's got an enormous stake in whatever the hell is going on."

Anthony shook his head. He was certain Carrie and her sisters weren't involved. "I'd stake my reputation on it. They've been set up. The question in my mind is when did you start your investigation? When did this whole thing kick off?"

Schmidt looked back and forth between Bear and Anthony. Then his posture changed, very subtly—his shoulders lowered just a fraction of an inch, as if he'd relaxed just slightly. His eyes darted back and forth between Bear and Anthony. "For the record, our investigation began officially in January."

"What kicked it off?"

Schmidt said, "Banks are required to report suspicious activity. We received a notice in January of what looked like a strange pattern of activity in a set of corporate accounts in Atlanta. We followed up and what we found was money churning. Small deposits and withdrawals, all of them less than a few hundred dollars to a few thousand, but many of them a day. Someone was funneling a busload of money through these accounts. The company we were looking at didn't even really exist. Shell company, owned by another shell company, and none of the officers and directors were real people.

Bear asked, "When were these accounts opened?"

"All of them in December and January."

"And how did it lead back to Thompson?"

"Stock transactions. There were half a dozen equity sales in one of Julia Wilson's accounts, which had already been flagged by the IRS, but only for verification. But then we saw a large cash transfer from one of Wilson's corporate accounts to the Caymans. That led us to pull records there, and they matched up. The accounts in the Caymans were the destination of the cash transfers out of Atlanta. But the only link we had was to Julia Wilson. And there wasn't enough there."

Anthony asked, "How do you get from there to seizing their assets?"

"No more," Schmidt said. "I've got questions for you. What is Oz? Or who?"

Bear said, "Oz is British or Irish. We don't know anything else about him, except that he hired Larsden." Bear summarized the questioning for Schmidt, including the news that Oz had been introduced to Larsden by an Army buddy named Marky Lovecchio.

"That ought to be easy enough to follow up," Schmidt said. "We know when and where Larsden was in the Army—process of elimination from there. He can't have served around many people with a name like Lovecchio."

Bear said, "So, now that we're working together—"

Schmidt shook his head. "Nobody is *working* together. I'm conducting an investigation. You're obstructing justice."

"Bullshit," Bear said. "You haven't even looked at *why*. Why would someone with a forty million dollar successful company get involved with cheap money laundering? Or for that matter, why would Richard Thompson?"

"Greed. Simple as that. Who the hell knows why any people do this stuff?"

Anthony shook his head. "Not Thompson. He's greedy for power—not money. I think you need to ask what happened here. Because it looks to me like someone duped you in an effort to discredit Thompson."

Schmidt shook his head. "I don't buy it. I'm willing to explore it, but I don't buy it. What I do know, Wyden, is that *you* aren't on this case anymore. And I don't want to get wind that you're going around questioning my witnesses, or butting your fat head into this investigation. Larsden was an *essential* witness and now he's dead. I've got half a mind to arrest you right now."

Bear growled, "You'd be better off putting your resources into finding out who the hell had him killed."

"I intend to do that. But you stay a thousand miles away from this investigation. Do you understand me?"

"Yeah, Schmidt. I get it. Just tell me one thing first."

"What?"

"What was your mother thinking when she named you?"

Schmidt stood up, irritation on his face. "My father and grandfather were named Wolfram, thank you. Once again, Wyden, I'll thank you to mind your own business." He looked at his compatriots and said, "Let's go."

Schmidt and his bevy of IRS and FBI agents left the room. One overenthusiastic FBI agent gave Bear the finger on his way out. Bear shook his head.

So much for interagency cooperation, Anthony thought. "Was that smart?"

Bear shrugged. "It's the IRS. What else can you do?"

Anthony chuckled then shook his head. "What now? Larsden was our best lead. Who the hell is Oz?"

Bear sighed. Then he said, "I think we go see Adelina Thompson now. Otherwise, I'm out of options."

Anthony thought about how Carrie and her sisters reacted every time their mother was mentioned—an almost palpable tension. He hadn't been able to work out why they were so sensitive about their mother. But now it looked like he was going to get the chance.

"Sounds good," he said.

Anthony thought back to his last sight of Carrie, calmly going through the disaster of her ransacked home, baby strapped in a sling at her side. She'd been calm, collected and organized, even in the midst of disaster. She had lines of strain and stress around her eyes, but she was a beautiful woman.

He shook his head. He didn't have time to be thinking about Carrie, nor would she be interested in the midst of her grief and worry about her daughter.

But still.

Alexandra. May 6.

Dylan spun around after pacing the length of the room for the five hundredth time. His back was a line of strain and anger, his hair still tousled from sleep.

"What I don't understand is why she didn't say anything. Or leave a note. Are you sure something didn't happen?"

Alexandra sank into a chair as Prince George-Phillip answered Dylan's question. George Phillip was sitting in a chair across from Alexandra. "Of course I'm not sure. How could I be? All I know is that she went out the back window shortly before one am and ran across the grounds, climbed a tree and went over the wall before anyone could get to her."

"Something must have happened," Dylan said. "Don't you have security cameras?"

"Outside. Not in the residence. But nothing unusual showed up. No one came or went."

"Then it must have been someone in the residence, sir. That's the only option. She wouldn't run on her own." Dylan's voice was sharp, unpleasant. "I need to go find her."

"I wouldn't advise that," George-Phillip said. "You're still a fugitive. The moment you leave the Embassy you'll find yourself in jail until they finish the investigation. You did kill a federal agent."

Dylan shook his head. "I can't just stay here and do nothing."

"Dylan," Alexandra said. Why did he have to be so stubborn? There was nothing he could do. She was just as worried about Andrea as he was, but *someone* needed to keep a cool head.

"Stop," he said. "I *have* to do something. Can you imagine Ray just standing around waiting?"

"Dylan," Alexandra whispered, her heart sinking. "Stop. If Ray were here, there'd be nothing he could do either. We don't have enough information. She could be anywhere."

Dylan stopped and stared at the ceiling and sighed. "This is so frustrating," he groaned.

"I agree," George-Phillip said. "But I'll tell you that I've got all possible assets looking for her, and the search is being run directly by my assistant, who is the most competent man I know. If anyone can find her, O'Leary can. And there's absolutely nothing you can do to help Andrea or Alexandra or their sisters if you are in jail."

Dylan nodded. "I know," he said in a tense voice. Then he exhaled, and in a slower, lower tone he said, "I know. In the meantime, what *can* I do?"

"I want you talk with O'Leary. Let him know what you can about what she knows, where she might go. You two were on the run for a short period—did you use cash? How did you communicate?"

"Cash, gift cards, burner phones. She can stay hidden if she wants, she knows how. But it's dangerous out there."

Alexandra sighed. "You're forgetting Sarah's with her."

Dylan said, "Sarah's a kid. They both are."

"I wouldn't underestimate either one of them, Dylan."

"It's not a question of underestimating them. You didn't see the people who came after her, Alex. They were killers." His voice was fierce, the tension behind his words as sharp as a straight-razor.

She closed her eyes. How was she ever going to get her husband back? It was as if the war had reached out and swallowed him back up, just like it did Ray. He was here, and completely alert and aware. But he wasn't. As she watched him, she thought about the long months of recovery from his injuries. Walking, and later running beside him around Central Park as he healed his body. But healing his mind was another thing entirely. That wouldn't be finished in a week or a month or a year. She could almost see he was on the edge of a meltdown.

Alexandra stood up and put her hands on his shoulders, effectively stopping him midstride.

"Dylan," she said.

"Look, I just *can't* not do—"

"Dylan!" she said. "*Stop.* She's going to be okay. You can't fix this. Please let it go." Then she wrapped her arms around him as tight as she could.

For a second, he didn't move. Then his shoulder sagged, and his arms wrapped around her, and he said, "I'm sorry. Shit. I'm sorry."

They stood and swayed together for a few moments, slowly calming down. Then she stirred when she heard a throat clearing behind her.

Shit! Prince George-Phillip was still standing there.

"Forgive me," George-Phillip said.

"No ... forgive me," Dylan said. "I'm just not used to sitting around."

George-Phillip gave him a disarming smile. "I understand completely. You've got a very smart woman here, Dylan. Listen to her."

Dylan hung his head. "Yes, sir."

"I really must step away," George-Phillip said. "I promise I'll let you know the moment I hear anything."

"Thank you, Your Highness," Alexandra said. She knew for Dylan words like that must be incredibly awkward, but she'd grown up around diplomats. Titles were routine. She waited for George-Phillip to leave, then turned back to Dylan.

"I love you, Dylan."

"I love you," he whispered back.

Carrie. May 6.

Carrie looked at the phone sitting on the table in front of her. Forty minutes before, she'd taken Rachel, who seemed to be running a slight fever, and put her down for her nap. Rachel was listless, and didn't want to drink, which left Carrie with swollen and painful breasts. She'd pump in a few minutes, but right now she was trying to decide what to do about her cell phone. In the background, the television was turned to CSPAN, where Richard Thompson was live on television, testifying before the Senate Armed Services Committee.

She'd missed two phone calls while putting Rachel down. One from Sarah, who hadn't come home the night before. She'd also sent a text message: **I'm with Andrea, headed west. Don't worry about us.**

The other call was from an unknown number, but the voicemail was from her mother.

She sighed and closed her eyes. Deal with Sarah first. She sat on the couch, tucking her feet under her and facing the silent television. The cameras were focused on Senator Chuck Rainsley, his grey hair looking white under the bright lights. When had she met with him? Two days ago? Three?

She wondered if Richard had been lying to her about Rainsley, or did her mother lie to him? Was he sitting there in front of that committee now, thinking that the man who had cuckolded him was the same man questioning him?

Carrie shrugged. The web of lies was so complicated that she had no idea what to think.

You were five before I knew. We'd already ... bonded.

The subtext, of course, was that had he known she wasn't his daughter, he would have shoved her aside, disregarded her, maybe sent her away *just like he did with Andrea.*

Richard Thompson didn't deserve this much of her attention. She picked up the remote and turned the television off, then dialed Sarah's number.

The call went straight to voicemail. Of course. Carrie's stomach twisted a little, realizing there was no putting this phone call off. She thought about the last time she'd seen her mother, five months ago. She'd never gone so long without seeing her, but they'd still spoken regularly. She'd never been close to her mother—a lifetime of hurt prevented that. But she'd never, ever forget how her mother had stood up for her at the hospital, how she'd hugged Ray and burst into tears when she learned of their secret marriage. She'd never forget those black days after he died, days when she couldn't even get out of bed. Days when she wanted to die. Despite their painful past, their conflicts and sometimes their hate, her mother had been there for her and Sarah.

Her hand shook as she reached out and picked up the cell phone again. She dialed the unfamiliar number slowly, each digit heavier than the last, until it felt like she couldn't possibly dial the last number. But then she did.

She put the phone to her ear, trying to ignore the twisted feeling in her stomach. She didn't know the woman she was calling. Except that she'd suffered unspeakably, and Carrie—along with *all five* of her sisters—hadn't known, hadn't guessed, and for a lifetime they'd blamed her for it.

One ring. Then a second. Click. Then the voice she knew so well, high pitched, the very faint Spanish accent. "Hello? Carrie?"

Carrie's throat closed and she leaned forward, left hand across her stomach. She tried to say something. Anything. But no words came out.

"Carrie? Are you all right?"

"Mother," she whispered.

"Carrie, what's wrong?"

"I'm so sorry," Carrie whispered. Tears began running uncontrollably down her face. *Goddamn it!* She hadn't meant to fall apart. "I'm so, so sorry, Mother."

"What? Whatever for? Carrie, you must tell me what's wrong."

Carrie sniffed and blinked her eyes, rolling them up toward the ceiling to try to control the tears. But she couldn't, they just kept coming. She felt desolate. She whispered, "Julia found the police report, Mother. And the pictures. From Valentine's day."

Her mother sucked in a breath, and Carrie spoke again. "She found the diary. We would never have looked at it, not in a million years, but you were *missing.*"

"*Madre de Dios,*" Adelina whispered.

Carrie said, "I didn't know. *We* didn't know. We thought … we thought you were … crazy. That you hated us. We thought … we thought *he* was the sane one."

Adelina whispered, "All I ever wanted was to protect you."

Carrie sobbed. "You did. You did the best you could. Mom … I met my father. My real father. He seems like a good man. He told me … about you two. About … what happened to you in Spain. It wasn't perfect, Mom, but you *did* protect us. We just didn't know. I'm so sorry. I'm sorry I hated you."

"Carrie, you don't have to—"

"Please forgive me?" Carrie whispered.

"Of course. Carrie, you're my daughter. I'm the one who … I'm the one who needs forgiveness. From all of you."

"No," Carrie said. "It's…" She closed her eyes. Her mother sounded—she sounded as if the weight of her remorse would crush her. "I forgive you. You did the best you could, Mom. And … you don't know how much it meant to me. After Ray died. You saved my life. I wanted to die. And you gave me the courage to go on."

At the other end of the line, she heard her mother's voice catch, then sniffing. More tears. She waited, taking a deep breath.

Carrie felt … empty. Drained. The tears still ran down her face, but they weren't tears of grief. They weren't the desolate, awful tears and emptiness and death she'd felt after Ray died. They were tears of … relief. Of redemption. Of … joy? She'd lost a lot … but she'd gained something too. A father she'd never known. And a mother she'd never known either.

Both of them took some time to pull themselves together. Adelina was the first to speak.

"So you met Prince George-Phillip? Where?"

"He's in Washington, Mother. I don't know exactly why, but I understand he had a meeting with the President."

Silence at the other end of the line, except for her mother breathing.

"Mother, what is it?"

Her mother sniffed. Then she said, "I never stopped loving him, you know. I'd have given anything to have had a life with him. Except for you girls. That was the one price I couldn't pay."

Carrie closed her eyes. The tears threatened to overflow again. She thought about the unspeakable suffering her mother had been through. To protect her daughters. To protect *Carrie*. She whispered, "It's not too late."

In a sad voice, Adelina said, "I broke his heart, Carrie. Twice."

Carrie closed her eyes. Then in as forceful a voice as she could muster, she said, "Mother. It's *not too late*."

Adelina sighed. Then she changed the subject. "Tell me—where are your sisters? I've been out of touch too long."

"You first," Carrie said. "How is Jessica?"

Adelina sighed. "She's stable and in recovery. It was … you can't imagine, Carrie. You're a mother now … but to see your daughter go through that … she was addicted to meth, Carrie."

Carrie sucked in a breath. "How?"

"Grief and neglect and the wrong crowd all at once. After she and Richard came back to San Francisco last fall he retreated to his study and more or less ignored her. What he didn't know … what none of us knew … was that her girlfriend had killed herself."

"Oh no," Carrie gasped. "Which friend? Who?"

"Her girlfriend, Carrie. Jessica was in love with the poor girl."

"Oh…" Carrie said.

Adelina sobbed, then said, "She was afraid to tell me. She thought I'd hate her because she was a lesbian. My own daughter. That's how badly I've failed."

"*You didn't fail,*" Carrie said. "Mother … you didn't. You're human, and there's only so much any of us could do. And … none of us were there for her. None of us."

Abruptly Carrie remembered the Christmas before last. When she'd fallen in love with Ray (a stab of pain that they'd never celebrated Christmas together) and the morning when she'd gone downstairs and found her mother in tears.

Was I that terrible a mother to you girls?

Carrie remembered that she hadn't been able to say anything reassuring. She'd merely said, *You've mellowed out a lot over the years.* As if that did anything but dig the wounds in deeper. A few minutes later, Adelina had said, *I know you've always watched out for your sisters, you've always tried to fix things for them. And I'm grateful for that … especially … during those times when I couldn't be a good mother. You were a mother to them.*

Carrie sighed. Now it all made sense, it made a kind of terrible and heartbreaking sense.

"So … Jessica fell in love. And the girl committed suicide. And she was all alone and got mixed up in drugs." The prompt steered her mother back onto the subject.

Adelina began speaking again. "When I got out here I got her into therapy. But I didn't realize how serious it was, until a few weeks ago. She came home late after going out without permission. She had blood on her forehead from a fall, and then she started vomiting. Carrie … I was … in a rage at first. Screaming at her. But then she had a seizure."

With the last word, Adelina's voice dropped to a tortured whisper and she continued. "She fell to the floor and her arms and legs were moving uncontrollably, and ... it was the most terrifying thing I'd ever seen. I called 911 and an ambulance came and got her to the emergency room."

Carrie closed her eyes. That explained the scene Julia had described at the house. There simply hadn't been time to clean up.

"Where are the rest of my daughters, Carrie?"

Carrie sighed. "Julia and Crank are staying at the condo with me for the time being, but Crank had to fly up to Boston this morning. The IRS has ... well, they've frozen their assets. He went up there to pay their employees in cash, and Julia is here dealing with the IRS. She'll be back this afternoon, I think."

Adelina sighed then said, "I met the lead investigator from the IRS. He seemed reasonable."

Carrie raised an eyebrow. "Really? When?"

"He left here a couple of hours ago."

Carrie let out a breath and said, "I'll let Julia know."

"And the others?" Adelina asked.

"Well, Dylan is trapped at the British Embassy for the time being. So Alexandra is there with him. I don't know how long that will last, though. The media picked up on it this morning. He ... well, there's no making it softer. When the condo was attacked on Friday, he killed two of the gunmen. One of them was a federal agent."

As Carrie said the words, her eyes involuntarily darted to the hallway floor. The carpet had been ripped out there by the FBI forensics lab. She presumed because it had blood on it.

Adelina sighed. "That poor boy. He already had a heavy enough burden on his soul."

Carrie whispered, "Yeah. He does. So that leaves Andrea and Sarah. Andrea *was* at the British embassy as well, but apparently last night she ran—jumped over the fence. George-Phillip called me this morning."

"Why?" Adelina cried.

"I don't know," Carrie said. "But Sarah stole Eddie's motorcycle and apparently picked up Andrea. Sarah sent me a text saying to not worry. But she didn't answer when I called. I'll try again as soon as I can."

Carrie looked around and said, "It's weird, really. Rachel's asleep. It's the first time I've been alone since last August. Since ... well, since Ray died."

Adelina spoke quickly. "You're alone? Do you have any protection there?"

Carrie nodded. "Julia hired bodyguards. I think we're as well protected as we can possibly be."

Adelina sniffed again. Then she said, "Will you send this number to the rest of the girls? It's a prepaid cell phone."

"Yes, of course," Carrie said.

"And kiss your lovely daughter for me," Adelina said. "I'm sorry I haven't been able to meet her yet."

Carrie nodded, more tears beginning to slide down her face. "I will. And Mother, you stay safe. Please? Can Julia send *you* bodyguards?"

"We'll see. I think I'm okay for now. It's unlikely even Richard could find someone willing to murder publicly in a hospital."

Even Richard? Did her mother think it was he who had attacked them?

They said goodbye and Carrie walked in the other room to check on Rachel. Her daughter looked a little flushed, hair damp. She touched Rachel's forehead. She was hot to the touch. Troubled, Carrie went in search of a thermometer.

CHAPTER TWELVE

Perfect love casts out fear

Sarah. May 6.

As they rode northwest, the sun setting in a blaze of reds and yellows, Sarah's eyes burned and she felt a heavy blanket of fatigue drape her body. Sixteen hard hours of driving on just two hours of sleep, and she was ready to collapse.

All around them, nothing but trees, grass, green and more green. The air was noticeably cooler and less soupy than late spring in Washington, DC, and the air was cleaner too. But even the cool air, the new scenery and the constant vibration of the motorcycle weren't enough to keep her awake.

She tapped Andrea on the shoulder. Her younger sister had been driving for most of the day, and seemed to have unlimited energy. But, even though it had been nine months, Sarah was still recovering from a horrific injury.

And then there was the Jeep.

It happened not long after they'd switched driving at two in the afternoon. Andrea had been driving most of the morning, with just two stops for the bathroom and then a quick fast food lunch.

"I'll drive," Sarah had said.

"You sure?" Andrea asked. "You look tired."

"I'm fine," she responded. She *was* tired, but she wasn't going to let her younger sister shoulder the entire burden of this drive, injury or not. It had been many months since the car accident. She should be able to manage this now. So she got on the bike, determined to do her share.

The first twenty minutes were completely uneventful. Not too much traffic, and it was a beautiful day. Sarah felt confident and happy.

And then there was the Jeep.

It was large, forest green with a chrome grill, and appeared in her rearview mirror. The license plate was blue and red, almost like the Virginia plates she'd once seen emblazoned with the letters GR8 DAD. Sarah felt her throat close up, the muscles in her arms and chest tense. She began to breathe rapidly and felt a pain in the center of her chest.

She accelerated and switched lanes to try to move away from the Jeep as unspeakable terror rose in her throat. She knew it wasn't *that* Jeep, the one that had ended Ray's life and nearly her own. She knew it couldn't be. After all, Sergeant James Hicks, the man who had gotten behind the wheel of that Jeep with murder in his heart—he was dead.

That didn't make it any easier. Because she felt tears in her eyes and her vision went slightly blurry.

The Jeep appeared again. One lane over, no more than ten feet away from her. Sarah panicked, jerking the bike over slightly, running them almost into the truck in the left lane. That only increased the panic, her heart suddenly beating wildly, and she twisted the accelerator in her right hand.

The bike responded instantly, and they leapt forward. Sarah leaned forward, even as Andrea tightened her arms around Sarah's waist. She sped the bike forward, switched lanes, then switched again, weaving around the cars ahead of them.

Andrea tapped on her shoulder, hard, then screamed almost in her ear, "What are you doing?"

Sarah's panic hadn't subsided. The Jeep was no longer in the mirror, but it was still in her chest, and she pulled to the side of the road, letting the bike coast the last few feet, then she shut it off.

"What's wrong?" Andrea had asked.

Sarah hadn't answered, just pushed herself off the bike as quickly as she could, walking to the grass on the shoulder. She threw her helmet on the ground and fell to her knees, then puked, acid and bile splattering the grass.

Then the thought struck Sarah. Is this what her mother had felt like all those years? If so, no wonder Adelina Thompson had seemed crazy, because Sarah couldn't breathe.

Andrea had knelt beside her and put a hand on her shoulder. "What happened?" she had whispered.

"Nothing," Sarah said, tears springing unbidden to her eyes. "Nothing at all. Everything."

"It's okay," Andrea responded.

After that, Andrea drove.

At the next stop, just outside Minneapolis, they sat down to discuss the route. "It's still another 26 hours driving time," Sarah said, her face glum. She looked up at Andrea, then said, "I can't make it. Not without a lot of rest. I'm sorry, Andrea. I'm just not—"

"It's okay," Andrea responded. "You're still recovering. What are our options?"

"I think Amtrak has a northern route. I don't know if they go through here. Or we could fly?"

Andrea shook her head. "My identification is fake. I don't even have a passport, the police took it when I was kidnapped."

Sarah sighed. Her eyebrows furrowed, then she said, "What about a charter flight? How much of that money do you have left?"

"I can't imagine what that costs," Andrea said.

"A lot," Sarah responded. "I think. Julia and Crank have to hire one on contract, they said individual charters were way too much."

Andrea winced. "Train then."

They got lucky. At ten pm, they boarded the westbound Amtrak Empire Builder bound for Seattle, Washington. They'd be there at ten in the morning on Thursday, a lot sooner—and more refreshed—than if they'd ridden the Harley the entire distance.

Sarah sent a text to Eddie: **Please forgive me. I left the hog in Minneapolis. I promise I'll get it back to you.**

She waited nervously. Thirty seconds later, he texted back. **You're really going to make me choose between you and my bike?**

Sarah let out a nervous laugh. If he could joke, then it wasn't *too* bad. She texted back: Is there any doubt of the outcome?

This time the reply took a lot longer. Long enough to start making her nervous. But then it came: **No. I'd choose you.**

Well, *shit,* she thought. Unfamiliar emotion washed over her. Affection. Maybe even love. When she thought about Eddie, it gave her chills sometimes.

He'd once said to her, *I think I fell in love with you the moment I saw you.* That was a neat trick, considering that when he first saw her she was unconscious with her left leg crushed between the driver's seat and door panel of Carrie's Mercedes.

Eddie had seen her at her worst, cursing in rage and pain when the morphine wore off, filthy and covered in vomit and in so much pain she hated the world. She didn't understand why he'd stayed through all that. And when she asked, he just shrugged and said, *It's all good, I got nothin' else to do.*

Which was bullshit. He was pre-med at George Washington University, and worked part time as an EMT, and was heavily involved on campus as well.

Well, she wasn't going to complain.

As exhausted as they both were, Andrea and Sarah began to drift to sleep almost immediately after the car pulled out of the station, the car rocking a little as the wheels clicked on the tracks. Sarah felt her eyes getting heavier and heavier, and she fell straight into a dream.

She was still in the train car, and Andrea was curled up asleep next to her, her long legs curled up almost to her chest. But no one else was in the long car. Sarah stood and looked around. It was dark outside, the sky the color of India ink, no lights or passing houses or streets. Nothing. The car rocked under her feet, unsteady, and she carefully stepped down the aisle toward the next car. Instead of the black rubber mat she thought the train had as its floor, it was cold, hard stone or marble, polished to a high shine. The reflection of the floor reminded her somehow of a promise she'd made, but she couldn't remember what it was.

She knelt down, tracing the hard floor with her fingertips. What had she promised?

She didn't know. It felt like it was a million years ago. She stood, and walked down the hallway toward the sliding doors ahead. It was silent in the hospital corridor, the walls the same tan fabric she remembered from the previous summer, artwork engineered to be offensive to no one spaced evenly along the walls.

Beyond the door it would be plainer, the walls simple off-white, the waiting room opening into the intensive care unit. She didn't want to go in there—too many bad memories. Too much terror. But even so, she felt herself drawn toward the sliding double doors. She felt herself shiver. It was cold—the kind of cold that claws its way into your bones and won't let go no matter how hard you fight. She wanted to go anywhere else but this antiseptic place where the smells assaulted her nostrils and burned into her brain.

But she kept going. As she walked closer, the doors slid open, and a little boy ran by with a Spider-Man T-shirt and a blue and orange baseball cap. She turned to say something, but he was already gone before she could take a breath.

She shivered. Something about that boy was important. But what? She didn't know. She shook her head and turned back toward the doors and walked through.

Her brow furrowed. It wasn't at all what she expected. Instead of a cold and antiseptic intensive care unit, the room beyond was … well … not a room. It was almost a jungle. Lush tropical plants were everywhere, growing under the bright sunshine. Sparrows were scattered about on the ground, pecking at it, and high up in one of the trees, a sloth hung from a branch, basking in the sunshine.

Then she saw him. In a clearing surrounded by half a dozen trees was an Adirondack chair covered in peeling white paint. Ray Sherman sat in the chair, inexplicably wearing khaki shorts and a grey Army T-shirt. His feet, resting on a tree stump, were bare. Another taller tree stump acted as a table, and a green drink in a martini glass rested on it. Ray wore a floppy canvas hat and was reading a book.

Confused emotions flooded through Sarah as she realized this must be a dream. Ray was dead, after all, and it really wasn't fair that Sarah should see him in a dream. That should be Carrie.

Not that she was making any sense at all. It's not like she had any control over her dreams. But she stood there and studied him anyway. He looked different than the last time she'd seen him. For one thing, he was relaxed and was wearing civilian clothes instead of his camouflage uniform.

That made no sense. Sarah had never seen him in his duty uniform, just the dress uniform he'd worn to the wedding. Or had she? Why would she expect him to be wearing that? She shook her head, because she didn't understand. But he was clearly there, his stubble making it clear he hadn't shaved that morning. He reached out and took a sip from the martini glass.

She shook her head then cleared her throat.

Ray glanced up from his book and smiled.

"Hey," he said. "I was wondering if you were ever going to come by."

"Come by? What is this place?"

He shrugged. "I don't know exactly. It's a good place, though. Have a seat?"

She started to say, "There aren't any seats," but before the words came out of her mouth, she saw that there was one, another Adirondack chair complete with a footstool and a drink.

Bemused, she sat down. The chair was solid enough.

She sighed, and said, "Carrie misses you terribly. It's been hard for her."

He nodded. "I know. I miss her, too. Heaven is nice and all … but seriously, it won't be complete until I know she's safe. Until then I just hang out here. I've been catching up on my reading. You … you can't imagine how beautiful it is here."

"Oh, yeah?" she asked, feeling like an idiot.

"Yeah. You know how it is, there's never enough time to read everything you want when you're alive. But now I've got all the time in the world."

Ray might be dead, but he was still weird.

"You know things have been pretty crazy. Rachel's sick. And they don't know if she's going to get better."

At that, he looked troubled. "I know," he said. "Sometimes I wish I could … you know … do something. But I can't … well … it's complicated. In the end, she'll be okay. We all will."

Sarah closed her eyes. He didn't understand. They were all in tremendous danger. "Ray … things are bad."

He nodded. "I know. But you know what to do. You always have."

She shook her head. "I don't. Can you show yourself to Carrie? Even in a dream?"

He sighed. "I … I can't. It makes it harder for her. I tried to stick around last fall, you know. I did for a long time. You were a terror for your mom." His face sobered. "Carrie was so sad, it broke my heart. But then one day I knew it was time. I said goodbye when you guys were at the zoo."

He didn't make sense at all. Sarah wanted to shake him. "Ray … what do I do?"

He took his feet off the stump, leaning forward and planting his bare feet on the ground. He looked her closely in the eyes, studying her for a moment. It was unnerving, his eyes boring into hers. This didn't feel like a dream at all, and her heart began to beat rapidly, almost as if another panic attack were coming. Even the thought made her muscles tense.

"It's okay," he whispered. He rested a hand on her shoulder. "What you do is love." He looked around then waved his hands vaguely toward the trees and jungle that surrounded them. "All of this … all of us … everything. You love. You … forgive."

She took in a deep, shuddering breath. She thought again about her mother and the panic attacks and how much they hurt and terrified her.

"I'm afraid, Ray. I'm afraid."

He smiled, and said, "Well, perfect love casts out fear, Sarah." He reached out and with a bare fingertip, touched her cheek. "You can do it. Everything you need is right here. In your heart."

She closed her eyes. For just a second, a tendril of memory took her back to the hospital, to a moment of crisis, when Ray had saved her life.

She didn't understand. That never happened. She drifted, and opened her eyes, and Ray was gone, and she was in her seat on the train, rocking back and forth as the tracks rattled beneath her, and she heard his words, *Perfect love casts out fear.*

She let her eyes close again and drifted into a deep sleep.

CHAPTER THIRTEEN
CALL ME, URGENT

Julia. May 6.

"**Mrs.** Wilson, I want to tell you I appreciate your cooperation. I'm going to instruct the bank to free up your operating accounts so that you can make payroll."

Julia sagged in her seat in relief. The operating account wouldn't last long—maybe three months—but at least she'd be able to pay her employees. She closed her eyes for a moment, rubbing the bridge of her nose with two fingers and a thumb, then looked back up. "Thank you, Miss Smith."

Barrymore—Julia's lawyer—leaned back and said, "We've provided you with full financial records of the company—with all the information you could possibly need. What else can we do to help here? As I stated this morning, my client is innocent of any wrongdoing and we want to help this investigation succeed just as much as you do."

The IRS investigator, Emma Smith, said, "I'll have my team look over the documents and we'll get back with you. I do appreciate your cooperation."

Smith stood, followed by Kelly and Shriver from Diplomatic Security and the FBI. Julia and Barrymore, with their assistant attorneys, also stood. In an awkward exchange, Smith, Kelly and Shriver all passed business cards to both Julia and Barrymore, then they all shook hands. It felt like the end of a standard business meeting or negotiation. Not a near apocalypse. Her mind was unfocused for a moment as Emma Smith made small talk.

Julia had never been much for idle chatter. But she couldn't vent her frustration until she was out of the IRS headquarters and on her way. In the elevator, she said, "Marty, do you need a ride back to your office?"

"Nah," he said. "I walked over, it's only a few blocks."

As he spoke, he was turning his phone back on. He gave her a sideways look, and opened his mouth as if he were going to ask what had happened during the brief period she'd met alone with the investigators. Julia started to turn her phone on, pointedly ignoring his unstated question then realized she was still holding the business cards. She glanced at them. Standard government business cards—the seal of the agency they worked for, name, phone number. But Scott Kelly's had a short handwritten note on the back. It said, "Call me for anything." A 703 area code number was handwritten below it. 703 was Northern Virginia—Kelly probably commuted to DC from Virginia. That would be his cell phone then. She put the card in her purse. Allies were necessary, wherever they could be found.

The elevator opened just as her phone finished booting up, and as they walked out the door of the building, the chime of several text messages rang out. She ignored them, dialing the Pinkerton driver instead. Moments later, a sleek black Escalade pulled up to the curb. A bodyguard jumped out of the passenger seat and opened the door. Julia slid into the car and turned toward Marty, standing outside.

"At least you're well protected," he said.

"It's costing enough. I'll catch up with you later. Let me know if you hear anything." He waved and walked away, and the driver closed the door. She glanced at the text messages on her phone. Four of them were routine business related messages. One from Crank said: **All okay in Boston! The team is confident. On my way back, see you about nine. Love you, babe.**

She smiled wryly as she texted him back: **IRS went well. Update later, but we'll be able to stay open for now.**

Then she looked at the last message. It was from Mike DeMint, the band's publicist. **CALL ME, URGENT.**

Mike didn't use hyperbole, and an all caps message with the word urgent in it meant just that. She dialed the number.

"Julia?" he answered immediately. "Problems."

"Mike, what's up?"

"Okay, so you're gonna be pissed. Are you sitting down?"

"Yes, Mike, I'm sitting down. What is going on?"

"It looks like Maria Clawson is making a comeback. She was all over Fox News this afternoon as an official commentator on your father's hearings, which aren't going very well."

Julia burst out into language that would have made Crank blush if he'd heard it. When she calmed down, she asked, "What else?"

"That's not the worst of it. She's trying to tie it all up with the IRS investigation into your company. You're going to have to respond."

She found herself shaking her head as the car pulled out into traffic.

"I'm not responding to anything, Mike. Not without a lot more information. What exactly did she say?"

"She's got a long blog post today. It digs back into your father's hearings as Ambassador to Russia back around 2000. And mentions you and ... your past. When you were in high school."

Another string of curses from Julia.

"Anyway ... looks like she's trying to make a comeback—at your expense. The blog post was ... sensationalist. Stupid. And it stops short of libelous; you're going to have a very difficult time doing anything about it. And it was big enough that she's out there now in public."

Julia closed her eyes and took a breath, then said, "Let me look at her blog, I need to get caught up."

She disconnected the phone. Moments later she was on Maria Clawson's website, which had been inactive for three years.

Now it had a sensational headline at the top.

UH OH: RICHARD THOMPSON AND JULIA WILSON
BACK IN THE NEWS WITH NEW AND IMPROVED SCANDAL: WILSON MUM ABOUT ACCUSATIONS OF DRUG MONEY LAUNDERING

Julia felt bile in her throat. Side by side photos at the top of the page, which was designed like a late 1990s Geocities website with flashing icons and multicolored text, showed her father at the witness table, right hand raised in the air, and an incredibly unflattering photo of Julia and Crank which had graced the cover of *National Enquirer* two months ago. In the photo of her and Crank, she was leaning over to pick her cell phone off the ground where she'd dropped it on the sidewalk. The asshole photographer had manned to get a shot right up her shirt at a particularly graceless moment.

Crank had stopped making a habit of punching photographers ten years ago, but there were times when she wished he'd start again.

The first three paragraphs of the blog post held no surprises—a recap of the hearing. She scanned through it, interested in how it had gone, but still incredibly resentful of her father's lies. From the tone of the article, the Armed Services committee had raked her father over the coals.

But the third paragraph started to get interesting.

Not surprisingly, unnamed sources within the Special Prosecutor's office have named Julia Wilson (wife and manager of obnoxious rocker Crank Wilson) as her father's primary accomplice, by funneling millions of dollars through a network of shell companies and hidden accounts in the Caymans.

Loyal readers will recall that this is not the first time the two have been linked in scandal. Suspicions that Thompson had arranged a secret abortion for his then fourteen-year-old party-girl daughter delayed Thompson's nomination as Ambassador to Russia.

Party-girl. The accusation didn't have the frightening sting it once held. During the first period of Clawson's campaign against her father, Julia had been under eighteen, and Clawson never identified her by name. But a photograph that should never have been taken surfaced on the Internet—a photograph of Julia, fourteen, lying across the laps of two boys.

She'd been fourteen, scared, abused and desperately lonely and afraid. Harry Easton, now an attaché at the British Embassy in Washington, DC, had been her much older boyfriend back then.

She closed her eyes and shoved the old fears and resentments back. She didn't have time for this. She could not fall apart. Carrie and her other sisters needed her. Her employees needed her.

She moved on from the blog post to *The Washington Post*.

Front and center on the paper was the same photo of her father at the witness table. She scanned through the article and winced. Twelve paragraphs in—far down in the article, but still present—Maria Clawson surfaced:

Media critic Maria Clawson linked the current outrage to a series of past scandals involving the Thompson family, including an accusation that Ambassador Thompson arranged a secret abortion for his then fourteen-year-old daughter Julia. In an interview on Fox News, Clawson said, "Before she started managing her drug-promoting counter-culture punk band, Julia had a history of drunken and drugged outbursts which scandalized the diplomatic community. It's common really—the overprivileged kids of the rich and famous going crazy is almost a stereotype. It's a shame, really, because with her platform, Julia Wilson could do some real good in the world."

Julia wanted to kill someone. Starting with that bitch Clawson.

She dialed Mike DeMint back. He answered on the first ring.

"Mike, I want a strategy. We need to hit back and hard. What do I do?"

He didn't hesitate. "You go on the air. Take her on directly. Tell your side of the story, especially the impact her blog had on your life. I'd suggest something like Barbara Walters. She's retiring in a couple weeks, I bet she'll do it. You're a huge catch."

Julia shook her head, feeling nauseous. Then she said, "All right. You make the arrangements and let me know. We'll take it all public. Let me just get permission from my sisters. Some of the story is theirs."

"Yeah, whatever. Just let me know quick. Your window to strike back is short."

"How short?"

"With media cycles the way they are? I think you need to move tonight and probably interview tomorrow. I'll do a brief statement tonight and get it on the website and social media."

Julia closed her eyes and counted to five thousand. Or maybe five. She *hated* dealing with the media. "All right," she said. "Do your worst."

She disconnected the phone. Traffic was unusually light for DC. Of course, their interview with the IRS had run very late, a marathon session. The clock on the dashboard reported 8:30 pm, which was past time for rush hour. As the driver sped up Wisconsin Avenue toward Bethesda, she texted each of her sisters, telling them her plans. If they were going to survive this, all of this, they had to be there for each other like they'd never managed before.

Fifteen minutes later, the SUV came to a stop in front of the condo.

"Wait a moment," the driver said. The bodyguard got out of the car and joined two more who were working the lobby.

What felt like thirty minutes later, but was actually only thirty seconds, one of the guards opened the door. "Mrs. Wilson, I'll escort you inside."

As she got out of the car, her phone started to ring. She took it out and answered without looking at the caller ID as she followed the guard to the front door.

"Julia." She felt a chill. It was her father. Her gut reaction was to hang up the phone.

You've never done anything but lie to me.

Those were the last words she'd said to her father. When was it ... four days ago? He'd tried to make excuses, to avoid taking responsibility for what he'd done to her mother. *Her mother.* Adelina Thompson had been the most hideous figure in her life. Frantic. Often crazy. Screaming attacks and rage and bitter, hurtful comments.

I woke up to find you on Maria Clawson's website nearly having sex with a drug addict.

Julia had responded, *No, Mother, we were just kissing. Believe me, I know the difference.*

I'm sure you do. Her mother's barbed response had wounded.

I didn't raise my daughter to be a slut.

The words still bled, no matter how many years had passed.

Alexandra lost in the airport. *Can't you do anything right?*

Alexandra hurt when she fell down the steps. *I can't turn my back on you for thirty seconds!*

Yes, the words still hurt, but she saw new scenes now, heard new words. Carrie, six years old, throwing a fit because their mother couldn't play with them. Adelina had been black and blue. She hadn't gotten off the couch in days.

The police report.

The words had been stark. Incredibly damaging.

Contusions around neck.

Third, fourth and fifth ribs on the right side cracked.

Blunt force trauma.

Her father had been the suspect. The attack had happened *one day* after the report came back showing Carrie wasn't related to him.

She walked forward into the lobby of the condo, her heels clicking on the floor, and it felt as if she were running a gauntlet.

His voice sounded ragged. Exhausted.

"Hello, Father," she said. Cautious.

"Julia. Darling."

She blinked then said, "What do you want?"

"I wanted to talk to my daughters. And Carrie won't even answer my calls."

She sighed. "Yet you think I will?"

"You're my oldest daughter, Julia. We've always understood each other."

She took a breath. "I think you presume a lot more than you ought to. I think you've left a lot to be explained."

"Of course," he said. "And I'll answer whatever questions you have. Julia … you and the other girls … you're all I have."

She let out a breath. "Not Mother?"

"Your mother is unstable. You *know* that."

"I don't know what to believe from you."

His response was firm. "Believe this. I've had the worst day of my life today. I've faced the most brutal Senate hearing you can imagine. And I'm devastated that you girls would believe *her* over *me*. After all she's … done. Julia … please. All I ask is that you listen. Meet me for a drink and we'll talk. You'll see. You're the only one who will listen to me."

Her mind went to the photos in the police report. Her mother black and blue. The DNA results. The lies about her mother's age. But then she knew he was right about some things. Her mother *was* unstable. Her mother *had* lied to them all, over and over again. And he was her father. He'd always been the stable one. What if there was a real explanation?

"I don't know what good it will do."

"Julia, you're my daughter. You and I … we've always been the closest. I'm begging you. Hear me out."

She sighed. Then slowly, she said, "All right. Let me tell Crank, and we'll meet. Where?"

CHAPTER FOURTEEN
A six-foot-deep hole

Julia. May 6.

The lounge in the Bethesda Hyatt Regency was small and elegant, sitting just to the side of the open atrium that towered above them. On the other side of the bar, a young man, possibly twenty-five, gently played a highly polished grand piano. It was Tuesday evening, so the lounge wasn't very crowded, but it was relatively dark. Julia and her father sat at a table in the back corner, far away from the other patrons.

"All right," she said as the waitress walked away with their drink orders—double whiskey sour for her father and club soda for Julia. She craved a drink right then. But this wasn't the time. "You wanted to talk. I'm listening."

He frowned and loosened his tie. Julia blinked then glanced at her purse, resting on the seat of the chair to her left. Her father was one of the most stilted and anal-retentive men she'd ever met. For him to do anything so human as to loosen his tie in public showed a level of discomfort that stunned her. But she kept that reaction to herself. Julia had learned a great deal from both of her parents, and one thing she knew how to do expertly was out-WASP her father. She betrayed no reaction to his discomfort.

"First of all—Julia … I need you to know I'm disappointed. Disappointed that after all I've done for you … as close as we've been … that you would assume the worst without even giving me an opportunity to explain or defend myself."

Julia didn't respond. How could he possibly think his actions were defensible? What could he possibly say?

"Well?" he asked.

She shrugged minutely. "What do you want me to say? I saw the police report. You both lied about Mother's age. You both lied about Carrie and Andrea's birth. Dad ... the police report ... she had broken ribs. She was beaten and raped."

Richard closed his eyes and exhaled. He didn't answer right away, but the skin between his eyes formed a furrow just above his nose. He rubbed the bridge of his nose between his thumb and fingers. Julia looked away. She was well aware she had the exact same mannerism when confronted with extreme stress.

"First of all—yes, your mother and I lied about her age. We were ... young, and in love. And in Spain it didn't matter at all that she was seventeen when we married. But I knew full well that would be frowned upon when we went back to the United States. So we publicly fudged the numbers. It never occurred to me it would become a big deal. Who could have predicted how wrong everything has gone in our lives, Julia?"

"And Carrie and Andrea? Dad ... that's not exactly a small lie. She had an affair with a British Prince? For fifteen years or more? Dad, I don't know about the rest of my sisters, but I feel betrayed. Why did we never know? And the police report? What happened? Why?" She shook her head, speechless. At the word *Prince* his eyes had widened slightly.

"What's this about a Prince?"

She raised her eyebrows. "Surely..."

Richard shook his head in disgust. "You see? This is just one more example of her lies. She swore to me that Senator Rainsley was the father. It almost destroyed our marriage, you know. I mean ... I wasn't perfect. And as I told you before, when we were in China, I ... was briefly involved with another woman. I made my amends. But this ... I assume you're referring to Prince George-Phillip?"

Julia nodded slowly.

His response was fierce. "She never told me *that*. She lied to me about who she'd had the affair with. Or perhaps she slept with both of them. I wouldn't put anything past her. Julia, I don't know how you can sit there and make accusations against me when you *know* how unstable she is."

Julia flinched. Of course she knew her mother was unstable. Not just unstable, but downright crazy sometimes. She closed her eyes, mind drifting back to that awful night in Spain when her mother had collapsed, gibbering in fear. Carrie and Alexandra had been too young to do anything, both of them panicking. They'd arrived in Calella late, it was dark and the streets had been crowded with men and women out partying and drinking. Julia hadn't known what to do. She didn't know their grandmother's address, she didn't speak Spanish, she didn't know *anything*. Her mother hadn't been able to do anything at all to protect her daughters, then or ever.

Why would I want to know? Why would I ask when my oldest daughter had become a drunken slut?

It didn't matter how much time had passed, or how many times they had nice Friday afternoon chats on the phone. It didn't matter how much Adelina Thompson had done for Carrie and Sarah after the accident. Those words couldn't be taken back, ever. She didn't believe her father, but she didn't believe her mother either. She didn't believe anything at all.

Julia slowly nodded. "Yes. I know she's unstable. But how else am I to interpret that police report? And it happened the day after you found out about Carrie."

"Julia, yes, I had a paternity test. I'd suspected for a long time that your mother had an affair with Chuck Rainsley. The first time he ever came to our house for dinner, she spent the entire time blushing and chatting with him. I spent a lot of time that spring overseas, mostly in Pakistan and Afghanistan—"

"Anthony Walker said you were probably CIA and not State Department. Is that true?"

Her father blinked and his mouth tightened. "The Post reporter?"

She nodded.

"He's astute. I was an employee of the CIA for many years, Julia, under deep cover as a diplomat. It's not all that uncommon. And don't talk to me about hiding things from you. No intelligence agent tells their children what they do for a living. That would have put you all in significant danger."

"So why tell me now?"

He shrugged. "I retired twelve years ago. I can't discuss specific operations with you or anyone, but my employment with the CIA will be widely public by morning. It was disclosed at the hearing today."

"So back to ... the affair. And the police report."

"Right," he said, taking a deep breath. "So, I suspected the affair. It was little things. Unexpected moodiness. Did you know that one time she smashed her violin? And left it in pieces on my pillow?"

A sudden flash of memory, one of Julia's earliest. Carrie was a baby, sitting in her highchair screaming, her little face bright red. She might have been a year old? Julia had been ... four? She'd been sitting in the corner, tearing the pages out of a book she'd found. Julia didn't know if they'd had a nanny then, but she must not have been there that day, because Adelina had seen her and screamed.

Julia, what are you doing? The scream had startled her, and then Adelina snatched the book out of her hands. Julia remembered blood suddenly on her hands, pouring out of two of her fingers. Paper cuts, she realized now. She'd started to shriek, and Carrie was shrieking, and her mother had grabbed her by the wrist and dragged her toward the kitchen doorway where Carrie's highchair was. The screaming got louder and somehow they shuffled and Julia could still remember the slow motion when Carrie's highchair tipped over backward, the terrifying smack as it hit the hardwood floor.

Julia shuddered. Yes. She could easily imagine her mother leaving a broken and smashed violin on her husband's pillow. Adelina Thompson had been dangerously unstable their entire life. In retrospect, she realized that it was a lucky thing Carrie hadn't fractured her skull that day.

She redirected her attention to her father, who was still speaking.

"...when the report came in, I confronted your mother. She'd *lied* to me, Julia. *For years.* So, of course, I confronted her. Adelina was hysterical ... she went berserk. She screamed at me and threw things. Julia, I swear to you, I would never lay a hand on your mother. I loved her. I always loved her. And you know that. I stayed with her despite her *years* of infidelity. The fact is, Adelina is mentally ill. She always has been. What kind of husband would I be to leave her when she was sick?"

Julia grimaced, shifting uncomfortably. What her father said was true. Her mother *was* clearly mentally ill. Julia had witnessed too many years of panic attacks and anxiety driven freak-outs to come to any other conclusion.

"So what happened?" she whispered.

"She ran. Out the door, and out into the street. I confess, I thought she was just angry, and going for a walk to cool down. Sometimes she did that ... Adelina is a passionate woman, but not one who deals with personal confrontation very well."

No kidding.

"When she didn't come back after an hour, I called Melissa Brewer and sent you girls over there, and I drove, looking for her. We didn't have cell phones then, of course, so all I could do was search, then check back at home every once in a while to see if she'd come home. I was frantic."

As he told the story, Julia found herself nodding. Unfortunately, so far it was completely believable.

"So ... by ten that night, I was panicking. I called the police, but they told me they couldn't do anything until she was gone for twenty-four hours."

"So what happened?" Julia asked.

"At one am the phone rang. It was Adelina. She was calling from ... from a pay phone in the Tenderloin."

Julia sucked in a breath. Her father looked ashen as he continued his story.

"I immediately went to her. I don't know if you know what it was like back then—San Francisco now isn't what it was twenty-five years ago. Back then the whole district was ... massage parlors and cabarets. Whores and pimps and drug dealers. Homeless men sleeping in doorways. Junkies and transvestites and derelicts. I found your mother at a bus stop on this filthy street corner. Her clothes were torn and she was glassy eyed—drunk or drugged or I don't know what. She was battered and bruised and..."

He stopped speaking and stared off into space. Julia didn't react.

He swallowed and looked back at her. "I don't tell you this to bullshit you, Julia. It's what it was. She was in bad shape. I took her to the hospital, and we were hours waiting in the emergency room. Finally they saw her, and that took hours more. It was about three in the morning when the police questioned me. It was routine—they *always* question the husband when a woman is assaulted."

He sighed and shrugged. "It was awful. Just ... awful. Julia ... I love your mother. And I second-guessed myself for years. Should I have just let it go and not confronted her? I felt responsible. It's not as if I didn't know that she was unstable. And it just got worse. We went to Belgium and ... well ... you remember her hospitalization."

Julia stared at the table. Of course she remembered. She remembered every slap, every bitter word.

"Julia, I swear to you, I never laid a hand on your mother. And I'd do anything for her to be healthy again. We once loved each other ... surely you know that. She was ... so beautiful when we met. Young and happy and full of life. I know things were awful when you were a teenager, but don't you remember when you were little? She used to take you to church, and sometimes we'd have lunch afterward?"

"I remember," Julia said. Her eyes watered.

Richard. May 6.

When Julia's eyes watered, he knew he had her. Julia had always been his closest daughter, the most loyal. From the time she was a toddler, he'd done everything he could to ensure her loyalty and love. And done just as much to ensure that she felt nothing but fear of her mother.

"Of course I remember." She stared at the table, as if she were reviewing memories in her mind. And he knew that many of those memories were of hugs from him. Throwing her up in the air as they laughed. Embracing her as she came off the stage at her first piano recital.

"Do you think that's why she went so crazy and distant when we were in Belgium and China? Because of the assault?"

He shrugged, but inside, he was filled with glee. He needed Julia as his ally, and it was clear he'd won her over, or at least begun to. "I don't know. Her psychiatrists suggested that it might be some post-traumatic stress. But some of the instability was there even before."

Julia sighed. "What about Andrea?"

"What about her?"

Julia winced. "Why was she ... why did she spend so much time in Spain growing up?"

Careful. Julia and her sisters had almost fanatical loyalty to each other. If she detected any hint of hostility toward Andrea, he would lose her. So, he drove another nail into Adelina's coffin. "I should never have given in to her on that. Adelina wanted it. She said that at least one of her daughters should grow up Spanish. It was irrational."

"But you told Carrie that it was ... you hadn't ... bonded with Andrea."

He leaned forward and looked at her with a serious expression. "It's true, I guess, though I'm ashamed to admit it. Would I have allowed Adelina to send her away if she were mine? I guess ... I wouldn't have. But it's what your mother wanted. And, I guess the truth is, sometimes I found it was easier to give in to her rather than have to deal with months of hysteria."

He ran a hand through his hair, knowing the gesture of insecurity would help persuade her, and that his self-deprecation would come across as honesty. Disarm her suspicion.

She shook her head, then said, "Is that why you never protected us from her? Because it was ... easier?"

He closed his eyes. Better to take the hit on this one and win her over. He spoke in a low tone. "I suppose it was. And I'll regret that to the end of my days."

"I know you did the best you could," she said. *Excellent.* She continued. "But I've still got questions. Why the kidnapping? The IRS investigation? What the hell is happening? And why did you have that file in your office? The one with the pictures of the ... dead bodies from Afghanistan?"

He cursed at himself for the instinct that had led him to keep those photos, to keep that file. Nothing in it had been classified. Nothing in it that hadn't made the papers. But those photos—they showed a power that had awed him. A single bottle, tightly secured inside a steel container. That was all it had taken to kill the entire village. And that power had been in *his* hands. But that, he could never admit to. He might feel his own thrill—much as he'd felt when the truck he'd driven had smacked into the body of Manuel Ramos, smashing the pompous old man's body and cracking his skull open like a rotted watermelon.

"You should never have seen that. It wasn't classified anymore, but it ought to be. Back in 1983 Afghan militia attacked a village with chemical weapons and killed everyone."

"I know about the incident, I've read a fair amount about it."

Of course she had. She was his daughter far more than Adelina's, and he knew she wouldn't walk into a meeting like this without being prepared. But he was ten laps ahead of her—no matter how fast she was, she wouldn't be able to gain control of the situation.

He said, "Then you probably know that at the time, the United States blamed the Soviet Union for it. But what no one knew was that Leslie Collins was responsible for it."

"Leslie Collins? As in the Leslie Collins you used to have over for dinner all the time?"

"Yes. I didn't find that out until much later, of course, and reported it as soon as I knew. But the higher ups in the Agency at the time decided to cover it up instead. Because it was in the interest of national security."

"And you went along with that?"

"I had no choice, Julia."

"So why all the stuff that's happening now?"

He looked at his daughter. Time to plant a seed that would drive a wedge between his daughters and George-Phillip. The thought of that man made him seethe. How the hell had Adelina managed to keep a secret like that all those years? He remembered how many times over three decades he'd had meetings with George-Phillip. Talked over drinks at Embassy functions in different countries. How many times he'd *touched his hands*. Richard wanted to vomit at the thought of it. He wanted to kill. Instead, he spoke in a calm and rational manner.

"Actually I think there are two things happening here. And you gave me the last puzzle piece."

"What piece?" she asked, arching both eyebrows.

"Well, first, I think Collins knew that if I took over as Secretary of Defense, I'd move to have the cover up of Wakhan declassified finally. That would end his career and likely see him in prison. I believe he engineered the secret accounts to discredit me. And you, unfortunately, are an innocent bystander. I assumed he was behind the kidnapping as well. It certainly made the drug money angle more convincing. But now I wonder if something else entirely happened with Andrea."

"What?" She tilted her head. She was hooked.

"Prince George-Phillip, of course. Can you imagine what a scandal it would be if it became public that he'd had a long-standing affair with Adelina? With two children? The easiest way to handle that would be to ensure that those children no longer existed, wouldn't it?"

Julia winced, a slight furrow appearing between her eyebrows. She reached into her purse and took out a tattered, tightly bound book.

"One more thing. What about this, Dad? It's Mother's journal. And it says you raped her."

Christ, that crazy bitch kept a journal? He cursed at himself. How had he missed that? He knew for sure she hadn't kept one in the eighties—he'd thoroughly searched her room, more than once, when she was at church. Carefully, he tilted his head. Then he said, "It's not true, obviously. Let me see it."

She stared at him, her face obviously reluctant.

"Come on, Julia. It's me. You *know* me," he said.

She closed her eyes and sighed. "I don't think you should read it," she said. "It's private."

"Julia, you know I have her best interests in mind. I'm deeply concerned about her."

Her hands shook as she passed the book to him. He studied it. Black leather cover. It was *old*, the paper slightly browning, the entire book slightly curved, as if it had been bound up inside a vase and bent permanently. *Where had she kept it?*

He looked at Julia and raised an eyebrow. Her expression was skeptical. But it was also hungry. Julia *needed* an answer that made sense. Her desperation for order in her life, her desperation for approval—it was plainly obvious. Just as plainly obvious that he was the only one who could provide her with that. Her nothing of a husband couldn't. She'd married him because she could control him. Crank wasn't her equal in determination or in intelligence, and his education was worse than third-rate. Only his freak talent with the guitar, and the business management she'd learned from her father, gave Crank the massive success he so richly did not deserve.

Richard flipped open the journal. He grimaced. The journal was a densely packed block of letters starting on the first page, the handwriting deeply slanted and barely legible. Good God.

"It's worse than I thought," he muttered.

"What?" Julia asked.

"Isn't it obvious? There's no paragraph marks here. No margins. This is the journal of a crazy person." He flipped through the first few pages. Richard was fluent in Spanish—after all, he'd been stationed there and helped assist the organizers of the February 23rd coup.

He stopped on the sixth or seventh page, and the words leapt out at him. *Richard murdered my father.* He kept flipping through. Pages and pages of rambling about God and the devil. He turned the journal to Julia, who he knew full well couldn't read Spanish fluently.

"Look here," he said. "She rambles on for pages and pages about the devil. It makes me wonder if she was hallucinating."

Julia shook her head sadly. Richard took the book back and continued flipping through. An account of her hospitalization. On another page, she wrote, *I hate myself for breaking George-Phillip's heart. But what else could I do?* He grunted in disgust and passed the journal back to Julia.

She should have done what she was told. Richard wanted nothing more than to punish her. Instead, he looked up at Julia and said, "Julia. I know you've—you've had a difficult relationship with your mother in the past. But I need your help."

He leaned close and looked at her with the most sincere eyes he could. "Julia, I don't know if you can forgive her. But you have to recognize that she was sick. We need to help your mother, Julia. We need to get her back to the United States. I … I hesitate to say this … but I'm starting to think that it's time we considered some inpatient options for her."

Julia flinched. "Like … a mental hospital?"

Like a six foot deep hole in the ground. "Yes. She needs competent medical care, and I've never believed that quack she goes to knows what he's doing." He looked down at the table and ran his hands through his hair again. He didn't want to overplay his cards. But he also knew that this conversation was *essential.* He looked back up at Julia and said, "Julia. Can you forgive your mother? Will you help me?"

She met his eyes. He could see the vulnerability in her eyes. The desperate need for approval which had driven her career and her life. She would do as he asked. She *would.*

Then she nodded. "Of course I'll help."

CHAPTER FIFTEEN
No, ma'am. He's dead.

Bear. May 6.

The nurse at the desk looked irritated when Bear asked for Adelina Thompson. She waved down the hallway and said, "You'll find her at the end of the hall with the security guards. Room 201."

Bear smiled and said, "Thank you, ma'am." He walked on, Anthony at his left side. Immediately, the correct room became apparent. Two men in black quasi-military uniforms flanked the door in an uneasy triangle with an officer of the Royal Canadian Mounted Police.

One of the men saw them coming and approached. His sidearm was visible in a shoulder holster. *That* was unusual for Canada.

"Can I help you?" the man asked.

Anthony said, "We're here to see Adelina Thompson."

"And you are?"

"You can tell her it's an old friend," Bear interjected. "Bear Wyden. She'll remember me from Belgium. And let her know we come with news from Carrie and Julia."

The guard looked at him suspiciously and consulted a sheet of paper. Then he said, "Your name isn't on the list of permitted visitors. Wait here." Then he waved at the other guard, who took a blocking position in the hall as the first one went back to the door.

The badges on the uniform looked almost official, unless you looked closely. The center showed an eye, like the CBS logo, with a triangular shape spreading out from the center. Like an all-seeing eye. Creepy. The words on the badge said Pinkerton Security Services.

Bear waited impatiently. It had been one long as hell day, starting with a crack of dawn flight west. Once they'd finished here, they were headed back east on a red-eye from Vancouver to Washington, DC. Thank God *The Washington Post* was paying for the flight. Finally, the guard came back.

"All right, you're cleared. You carrying?"

Bear shook his head. He wasn't officially on duty. The last thing he needed to be doing was carrying his service weapon across international borders.

The guard patted them both down—not a perfunctory search, but really looking. Finally he waved them in.

Inside the room, an emaciated teenager lay on the hospital bed, the back of the bed configured to allow her to sit up comfortably. Her eyes were hollow, but Bear could see that she had the potential for real beauty if she gained a little weight. As it was, she clearly wasn't healthy. He recognized her from the portrait in Richard Thompson's office at the Pentagon, as well as many photos displayed in Carrie's condominium. Jessica, who had been born after Bear last saw Adelina Thompson.

His eyes shifted from the daughter to the mother. Adelina was still an attractive woman. He'd guess she was fifty years old now. Over the years she'd put on some weight, and giving birth to six children had changed her body significantly. But her eyes were still wide, her hair black and twisted carelessly into a knot over her shoulder. She stood as Bear and Anthony entered the room.

"Bear," she said, walking forward with a half smile.

He smiled at her. "You remember me," he said. "It's been a long time."

"A long time, but how could I forget the man who protected my family and my daughters?"

"You're still as lovely as always," he responded.

Adelina said, "Jessica, this is Bear Wyden. He headed our security detail in Belgium in the nineties. It must have been nearly twenty years ago."

"Almost exactly," he responded. "This is Anthony Walker. He's a friend of Julia's, and a reporter for *The Washington Post*."

Adelina's eyes widened. "A reporter? Friends with Julia? I find that … surprising."

"Friends may be an overstatement," Anthony said. "But we've been working together. Julia's come around to the idea that it's time to shed some public light on what's been happening to your family."

Adelina's eyes darted back and forth between the two men. Then she said, "You have my undivided attention. I never expected you to pop up out of the woodwork. What brings you to Canada, exactly?"

Bear said, "I know you were away, so you may not know the extent of the details. But when your daughter Andrea arrived in the United States last Monday, I was assigned to investigate her kidnapping. I'm still with Diplomatic Security, of course. I assigned a protective detail to guard your daughters, but they were attacked again on Friday night. I've been doing everything I can to track down those responsible for the attacks. Our best lead was Nick Larsden, the man who shot at you and your daughter as you were trying to cross the border."

"Was?" she asked nervously. "He's not free, is he?"

"No, ma'am. He's dead."

Adelina blanched.

He went on, "Someone in the jail knifed him. We don't know who, or whether it was for hire or just a bizarre coincidence. Anthony and I interviewed him early this morning, but we didn't get a chance to finish."

"Why not?"

Bear looked at Anthony, as if to ask Anthony's opinion. Should he tell her the truth? Anthony raised an eyebrow. That was the opposite of helpful. He turned back to Adelina and laid his cards on the table.

"We're not here in any official capacity, Adelina. Secretary Perry *officially* relieved me of duty a couple days ago."

She raised an eyebrow. "And unofficially?"

"Unofficially, he's very suspicious of … the entire situation. So when the IRS and the special counsel took over the investigation, he cut me loose to find out what I could find out."

She nodded slowly then said, "That sounds like him. I appreciate your candor."

"You know the Secretary?"

"Of course," she said. "He and Chuck Rainsley are very close friends. And I was once friends with Brianna Rainsley. So we came into contact with each other a great deal in the 1980s."

Bear and Anthony looked at each other. Well, that verified one question. But they still had plenty more. "All right," Bear said. "Will you talk with us?"

"I'll be happy to. On the record or off. If Anthony here wants to print my story in *The Washington Post* I couldn't be more pleased."

Anthony grinned. "I'd *love* to get your story."

"In the meantime," Bear said, "I've got a number of very specific questions I'm hoping you could help us with."

She nodded. "Please, go ahead."

"Would you rather talk in private somewhere?" He nodded meaningfully toward Jessica.

Adelina looked at her daughter. Something unspoken passed between them, then Adelina looked back at Bear. "It's fine. We can talk in front of Jessica."

Bear raised his eyebrows. "All right. I'd like to start with Nick Larsden. Have you heard of him before? Had any encounter with him?"

"No." Her tone was flat as she answered the question.

Anthony said, "Mrs. Thompson ... I was with Julia when she broke into your husband's office. I saw the police report. And ... I saw the diary."

Adelina winced. Then she said, "Then you know what he did to me."

Anthony nodded. "It's true?" he asked.

"Yes. I was sixteen when he raped me the first time."

"Have you ever heard of anyone who went by the name of Oz?" Anthony asked.

Adelina froze at the name. Her eyes widened and her skin went pale. "Oz?" she asked.

Adelina. May 6.

Oz.

Of course. Why hadn't she realized it before? The name sent chills down her spine.

Jessica looked at her, as did the two men, and it was obvious they could see her reaction.

She sighed and said, "Yes, I've heard the name. How did it come up?"

Anthony and Bear looked at each other, then Bear said, "Nick Larsden said he was hired by someone named Oz."

Adelina swayed on her feet, then said, "I need to sit." She stumbled across the room to one of the chairs and fell into her seat. Anthony and Bear followed her in, taking the two wooden visitor chairs.

"Mrs. Thompson? What can you tell us?"

The first time she'd heard the voice, she hadn't known he went by that name. It was just a voice. A guttural, mean sounding voice. It sounded as if the owner of that voice just wanted to reach out and *shake* someone. It was a voice you didn't want to cross. And back then, Adelina had already been terrified every minute of every day. She didn't need any more fears. But she got them anyway.

It happened in 1984. A few days before, she'd manipulated Richard into losing his temper. Into *raping* her. Her purpose, of course, was to have a plausible date when she could have become pregnant, because the two of them hadn't touched each other since the move to Washington.

She'd never felt so dirty. Not even the first time he'd done it. Because this time it was to conceal a lie. A lie she was responsible for. And no matter the reason, no matter how horrible he was, she felt in her heart that she was the one who was wrong. She was the one who was defiled. She was the one who God would judge.

She'd already decided that she wouldn't see George-Phillip again. She *couldn't*. She loved him like she'd never loved anybody. Every time she thought of him, her heart ached—her whole body ached. But if she continued to see him, it would still be in secret. It would still be dirty. And eventually, she knew, Richard would find out the truth. And then he would kill her, or the baby she had inside of her.

She'd already decided, but then came Oz.

It was almost two in the morning when it happened. Richard had flown to London for a meeting, and she and Julia were blessedly alone in the condominium. When the phone rang, the bell was harsh in the darkness.

She stumbled out of bed to the kitchen grasping for the phone, her heart suddenly racing. No one called at two in the morning. Certainly not Richard. It had to be something awful. Had something happened to Luis? Had that bastard finally followed through on his threats and done something to her baby brother?

"Hello? Thompson residence," she gasped into the phone.

"Mrs. Thompson," a voice said. A voice that sounded like the gravel at the end of a long dirt road. Irish accent.

"Who is this?"

"A friend," came the reply. "We have a mutual friend. The Prince is returning to Washington, Adelina. Stay away from him. Do you understand me? You stay away from him, or you'll suffer for it."

Rage flooded through her. It didn't matter that she'd made the decision to say goodbye. Suddenly awake and alert, she spit into the phone, "Who is this?"

"You heard my warning, Adelina. Stay away from him. Don't answer his calls. Don't see him. Or you and I will have a personal problem."

Angry beyond words, Adelina said, "And what exactly does a personal problem entail?"

"Why don't you check young Julia's bedroom to find out?"

Adelina threw the phone at the floor and ran for Julia's room, her feet slipping on the kitchen floor. She screamed silently as she went down on the floor. She scrambled back to her feet, down the hall, opened Julia's door, and snatched her daughter out of the Snuffleupagus toddler bed Richard had bought for her a few weeks before. Immediately Julia began wailing, startled out of a deep sleep in the middle of the night.

Adelina switched on the light and checked Julia for injuries and marks of any kind, even as the girl screamed, her hair tangled in her face.

"It's okay," she whispered, holding Julia to her.

Then her eyes fell on the wall.

A large sheet of white poster board was pinned to the wall ... directly above the toddler bed. A crude, hand drawn representation of Snuffleupagus, Julia's favorite Sesame Street character, had been drawn on the poster board.

A red letter X was scrawled across the creature's chest. In red letters beneath the children's show character were words, printed in large block letters. The message said:

HEED MY WARNING. OZ.

Now, as Adelina told the story to Anthony and Bear, the full weight of the fear swept over her again and she began to shake. "Whoever Oz is ... he, or someone who worked for him, was *inside the condo* and put that poster board up, then left, before calling me. They could have killed us. Or taken Julia. Anything. I wouldn't have been able to do anything to stop them."

"What did you do?" Bear asked.

"The only thing I could do. I broke it off with George-Phillip. I gave him no explanation—I didn't even give him the opportunity to talk about it. I broke his heart."

To her left, sitting in the bed, Jessica listened with wide eyes. Adelina hadn't told her about Oz yet, or why she'd broken it off with George-Phillip. Now her daughter sat there with tears freely running down her face.

Bear asked, "Did you ever hear from him again?"

"Once," Adelina said. "In November 1996. I was pregnant with Andrea at the time."

"What happened?" Bear asked.

"The last time I saw George-Phillip was at an Embassy dinner. For several months we'd been secretly seeing each other. He would ... he would sneak into the compound with false identification in the middle of the day and we'd go off together. I kept fooling myself that it would be all right, that somehow we wouldn't be found out, that somehow I could protect my daughters and still have him. But then two things happened."

The first, of course, was when she missed her period. They had been careful to use contraception despite Adelina's religious qualms, but due to the heavy medication she was taking already, her doctor had flat out refused to prescribe birth control.

She knew. Her last pregnancy with the twins had been extremely difficult and she knew exactly what morning sickness felt like. For three weeks she'd been nauseous, but she'd pushed that to the side, wanting to ignore it, wanting it to be anything but what it was. But when she missed her period, there was no way to ignore it. She bought a home pregnancy test and the result was positive.

Adelina was pregnant and it was impossible that the baby was Richard's. She would sooner die than kill her own baby, and she had no desire to touch Richard ever again. He had no desire for her.

For a week after she discovered the pregnancy, she was paralyzed. She didn't return George-Phillip's phone calls. She thought, she wrote in her journal, and she prayed. Useless prayers, she'd believed at the time. But she couldn't hide forever, and a few days later the US Embassy hosted a dinner for the officers of the Australian and British Embassies. Such affairs were common, and as wife of the Ambassador, she had no excuse for not attending.

Protocol placed her at her husband's left hand, directly across from George-Phillip, who sat to Richard's right. Through the meal she barely spoke, keeping her eyes on her plate.

At one point Richard said in a tone only she would identify as deeply sarcastic, "Not feeling well, darling?"

She simply shook her head. He leaned over and gripped her arm and she flinched.

"Your job is to entertain our guests, Adelina," he whispered.

She attempted a smile, then stood up and said, "Excuse me."

She hid in the restrooms, but of course that didn't last lone. Before long, she was circulating in the room, attempting unsuccessfully to make conversation. After escaping from a conversation with the Australian Consul-General, she heard George-Phillip's voice behind her.

"Hello, Adelina, how are you?"

His voice made her heart sink. For days she'd been debating what and how much to tell him. She looked at him and felt her eyes water. She wanted so badly to collapse into his arms, to sink into his love. She wanted so badly to run away with him.

"You haven't called," he said. His eyebrows were sunken close to his eyes in consternation.

She wanted to make an excuse. She wanted to tell him … she'd been busy, she'd been taking care of the kids, she'd been washing her hair. Instead, she blurted out in a whisper, "I'm pregnant."

His Adam's apple bounced in his throat as he swallowed. "Is the baby mine?"

"Of course. I'd never touch him unless he forced me."

He looked so sad her heart broke. "Adelina, you *must* leave him. He's destroying you and your children."

She thought about the photos she'd received every year on Luis's birthday. Photos taken surreptitiously. Luis at school. Luis eating ice cream. Luis at his first job waiting tables. His eighteenth birthday party. Every single year. Richard wanted to remind her. And then, of course, there was the man he sent from London all those years before. *Oz.* If Richard's goal had been to cow and terrify her, he had succeeded.

"You don't know what you're asking. If you did, you wouldn't say that. I'd lose my children. I'd lose everything." Anxiety twisted through her as Richard approached from behind George-Phillip.

"Of course, I enjoyed the show very much! I'm hoping we can take Julia to it, you know she loves music."

Richard casually clapped a hand on George-Phillip's shoulder. His voice was jovial, suspecting nothing. "I didn't get to tell you at dinner, Your Highness, how much a pleasure it is to see you again."

"And you, Ambassador," George-Phillip said.

He smiled, an insincere diplomatic smile. Adelina knew what his *real* smiles looked like. And she was terrified she'd never see that smile again.

"Please excuse me," she said. "I must find Julia."

That night, she had confronted Richard in his office. All five of their daughters were home, which meant this was the safest time. He was unlikely to assault her with Julia and Carrie in earshot. He looked up at her puzzled when she walked in. She never entered his office.

"What is it, *darling?*" he asked, his tone nasty.

Her chest tightened up, pain curling like smoke across her sternum, and she found herself short of breath.

Richard's chin set. "What is it, Adelina? You've interrupted me. Explain yourself."

She closed her eyes. And then she said the words that she thought might end with her death. "I'm pregnant."

He stood, his face suddenly red, eyes wide, mouth twisted in a rictus of rage. "Pregnant," he said, his voice a curse. "I would think that would be biologically impossible."

He stood and walked around his desk. Her eyes followed him, never wavering, because he held a brass letter opener in his hand. She began to shake as he reached her side of the table. Then she saw it. *He* was also shaking. But not with fear or rage. Almost with excitement.

Her eyes followed the letter opener. He held it toward her stomach then pressed it against her. Not hard. Just enough to slightly hurt.

"Is this an immaculate conception, Adelina? Did your God plant a baby in you to save us all?" His tongue lightly licked against his lower lip as he spoke. Anticipation. He was going to hurt her badly.

Then he leaned close, his lips right next to her ear. "Or did Senator Rainsley plant this baby in you too? Is that where you were running off to during the day lately instead of paying attention to our daughters? I wouldn't have thought he was in China long enough to make you pregnant."

He brought his forehead to hers, leaning against her. "What would you do with your poor Catholic morals if I order you to abort your fucking baby? If I tell you to have it *cut out of you?* What would you do if I told you that if you didn't, I'd take Carrie and sell her to the highest bidder? I'm sure some of those perverts in the Yakuza would love a twelve-year-old white girl, huh? Would you kill this baby to save that one?"

Adelina shuddered. Involuntarily, tears began to run down her face. She closed her eyes. She couldn't show weakness. He fed on fear. He fed on weakness. He was *evil*.

"Answer me, you cheating whore," he demanded. "Shall I cut the baby out of you right here?" He pressed the letter opener against her again, harder this time, hard enough to really hurt.

"No," she gasped.

Abruptly he turned away. He strode away from her and stood behind the desk. "Have your baby," he said. "Maybe I'll smother it in its sleep. Maybe it's time I paid a visit to Luis. Or maybe I'll just torture you until you finally end your own worthless life. Get out of my office."

She had done as he ordered. But that wasn't the end of it. Because two days later, she woke up in her bedroom with a hand over her mouth. She struggled, but realized she was pinned down somehow. She couldn't move her limbs at all.

Hot stinking breath blew on her face, smelling of rot and mud and tobacco. Then the intruder spoke. She recognized the voice, even all those years later. It was Oz.

He spoke in a guttural Irish accent. "I told you to stay away from the Prince. And you disobeyed."

"Please don't hurt me," she whispered.

"This is your last chance. I'm not going to kill you this time. But if you ever see him again, you *and* your daughters will die."

The weight had lifted off of her. "Last chance, Adelina. Make the right decision."

Then he had run out of the room. Moments later, she had stumbled out of bed, running to check on her daughters.

They were in their beds, and safe.

As she finished telling the story, Bear shook his head. "Did you ever find out who Oz was?"

"No," she replied.

"Did you ever talk with George-Phillip about it?"

She closed her eyes. Then whispered, "I never spoke with him again. I had to protect my daughters."

She heard the sympathy in Anthony's voice as he asked her the next question. "Did Richard get his revenge, Adelina?"

She slowly nodded and tears ran down her face. "He did. I don't want to talk about what he did. He made my life miserable for a long time. And the older Andrea got, the clearer it became that she wasn't his daughter. I finally sent her away for her safety. I was afraid he'd lose his temper some day and kill her."

She opened her eyes. Then she said, "It was at its worst when we lived in Bethesda after we got back from China. On a few occasions he physically hurt me. Especially when Maria Clawson began to write about him regularly. Write about *us*. Poor Julia had gotten mixed up with some very bad stuff in China, and a photo circulated amongst the students. She got her hands on it."

She looked down at the floor. Unable to say it. Unable to forgive herself. She whispered, "He … tortured me. Every time she wrote a new column, it was more … more vitriol from him. More pain. More threats. I thought more than once about just throwing myself off the balcony."

Anthony said, "Adelina. I don't know if you'll ever be able to get a legal judgment against him. But I want to bury Richard. I want him to be thrown down so low that he never gets back up again. I want to tell your story."

Adelina shuddered. She didn't speak, but an unexpected voice did. To her left, in a vicious tone, Jessica said, "Do it. Bury him. Don't ever let him hurt her again."

Anthony looked at his watch. "We've got about four hours before we have to leave. Bear, are you up for this?"

Bear shrugged. "Do what you gotta do. We aren't getting an earlier flight."

Anthony said, "First, you need to understand—I need people who can corroborate your story, or parts of it. Will George-Phillip admit the affair?"

"I don't know. You'll have to ask him."

Anthony nodded. "Your daughters will remember some things. What about Chuck Rainsley?"

Adelina swallowed. "Maybe Brianna Rainsley. She didn't know the extent of it, though. But there is one person who did, if he's still alive and you can find him."

"Who?"

"Father Dennis from the Saint Jane Frances de Chantal church in Bethesda. I'm sure he's moved on somewhere else by now."

"Will he talk?"

"I'll give you a letter from me, with written permission."

"Okay. One other thing. Can you think of anyone who knows about what happened in Afghanistan?"

She shook her head. "Leslie Collins, I'm sure. And Prince Roshan. If I had to guess, it was the three of them. They were thick in the eighties. They thought I was too stupid to understand they were up to something."

"Anyone else?" Anthony asked.

"There was another name ... Karat ... Karak..."

"Karatygin? Vasily Karatygin?"

"Yes! I'm sure that's it. You've heard of him?"

"I have," he said. "He was a Russian special forces major, he converted to Islam and defected in the 1980s, then was the second-in-command of one of the Afghan militias for a long time. He's still there ... keeps a low profile, mostly involved in opium smuggling, I think now."

She nodded. "I know I heard his name more than once. But I can't guarantee it's him. Nor do I know if he'd talk to you."

"Well, we might have to find out. Do me one favor though."

"Yes?"

"Prince George-Phillip I have to see. I've interviewed him before, but if I go through official channels, it will take weeks. Can you get me in to see him?"

She looked distressed. "We haven't seen each other in seventeen years. I'm certain he hates me. I broke his heart and never explained why."

Anthony shook his head. "All right. Maybe through your daughters. I believe Carrie met him yesterday."

Adelina whispered, "Yes. She told me."

"All right. I'll start there. Can we get started with some questions?"

"Yes. But one thing first."

Anthony raised an eyebrow. "Yes?"

She whispered, "When you talk to him ... tell him ... tell him I'm sorry."

Marky Lovecchio. May 7.

The phone ringing was harsh in Marky Lovecchio's ear. Who the *fuck* was calling him at six o'clock in the morning?

He took his hand off the tits of the stripper he'd brought back from the bar the night before. He'd flashed several hundred-dollar bills at the club, enough to get the attention of several of the girls. Then he'd made his pick and brought her back to the cheap and nasty motel room.

She was hot, but a lousy lay. Fucking tease. He decided he was going to wake her up with a good fucking whether she liked it or not.

He untangled himself from her then picked up his phone.

"What?"

It was Oz. "Lovecchio. I trust you're having a good time spending my money?"

"It's my money now. I took care of him, didn't I?"

"You did. And that was good work. But I have another job for you."

Lovecchio muttered a curse. The girl was stirring; bleach blonde hair stringy along her back.

"I'm not in the market right now, Oz. I need a little time to relax."

"You can relax after you're finished, Lovecchio. The woman who Larsden let get away? She's with her daughter at the hospital in Abbotsford."

"Canada?" Lovecchio blurted.

The girl was definitely stirring now. She slid out of the bed and walked toward the bathroom.

"Yes, Lovecchio. Canada. The woman is in room 201. I don't care what happens to the daughter, but kill the woman."

Christ. He said, "How much?"

"We'll call it half a million. That's what I was going to pay your friend before he fucked it up."

"Whatever. Fine. I'll do it. How soon?"

"By tonight."

He started to respond, but Oz hung up.

"Hey," he called to the girl in the bathroom. "Come here!"

She muttered something incoherent. He looked around. Her skimpy dress was on the floor.

A second later she came out of the bathroom. He looked at her, his eyes grazing over her obvious implants, the curve of her hip. He didn't care if she couldn't fuck. He'd do the work. "Come here," he said.

She shook her head, a cigarette dangling out of her mouth. She reached for her dress. Bitch. He stood and walked toward her. "You're not finished yet."

PART TWO

CHAPTER SIXTEEN
Here's my theory

Anthony. May 7.

"**You** look exhausted." Given that Carrie was pouring a fresh cup of coffee as she said the words, Anthony decided he could forgive her.

"We flew back on the red-eye," he said. "I came straight here from the airport."

She nodded. "Cream and sugar are over here. Meet you on the balcony, it's beautiful today."

"Okay," he said.

He put too much sugar in his coffee then noticed the mug. It bore the logo of the United States Army, which reminded Anthony once again that Carrie was a widow, and a fairly recent one at that. The shelves and walls displayed a number of photos, including two from Carrie and Ray's wedding. From the look on both of their faces, you could tell they were deeply in love. And he'd died only a few months later.

Anthony leaned a little to see out of the kitchen toward the balcony doors. Carrie and Julia were sitting together at a cast iron table. He walked down the hall to the restroom and slipped inside. Out of curiosity and little more he opened the medicine cabinet.

The top shelf had several prescription bottles, including a Xanax prescription for Carrie filled only a few days before. He closed the door to the cabinet. He needed to mind his own business. He was a reporter, but he was also human, and needed to treat people decently.

Two minutes later, he joined Julia, Carrie and Rachel outside. The women sat across from each other as they sipped their coffee. As he seated himself he couldn't help but notice the contrast between them.

Their appearance, of course, was quite different. Julia was average height for a woman, about five feet four inches. He was used to seeing her brown curly hair tied in a businesslike bun, but here, in her family home, she had her hair down, draping both shoulders. She wore faded jeans and a *Trampled by Turtles* T-shirt. A rock band of some kind? He didn't know. Her hair was relaxed, but she didn't seem to be. Her back was straight, feet flat on the ground, and occasionally she drummed her fingers on the side of her mug.

Carrie, on the other hand, was slouched in her chair. The baby lay in a seat next to her chair, and Carrie's knees were drawn up in front of her. Her dark hair, almost black, draped over her shoulders.

"So tell me about your trip. Did you learn anything?" Carrie lifted her coffee cup to her lips after she finished speaking. She closed her eyes and inhaled, taking in the rich smell of the coffee, then sipping it slowly, her slightly pink lips touching the mug.

Anthony tore his eyes away from her. "Well … we've got a name. But it's almost certainly a pseudonym. Oz. Your mother's encountered him twice before, once in the eighties, then again when you all were living in China. We've got good reason to believe the same man is responsible for hiring Nick Larsden to kill your mother. Unfortunately, we couldn't question Larsden any more … he's dead."

Julia said, "I thought he was captured. I didn't hear anything about him being wounded in the news."

"He wasn't wounded by the police, he was knifed in the jail. I doubt it's a coincidence. He'd already told us about Oz though. We'll track down who he is."

Carrie sucked in a breath. "So … I don't get it."

"Well, here's my theory," Anthony said.

"Your theory?" Julia asked.

He nodded. "You've got two sets of killers, operating with different but similar motives. One *was* trying to keep a lid on who is behind the massacre at Wakhan in the eighties. Whoever that was—and my working theory is that it's Leslie Collins at the CIA, or possibly the head of the Saudi intelligence service—they moved to discredit your father and anything he might say as soon as his name was floated as Secretary of Defense."

"Okay," Carrie said. "And the second?"

"Oz. I'm guessing unrelated to the first set of killers. Whoever Oz is, he *twice* did everything short of killing your mother to keep her away from Prince George-Phillip. I'm guessing those attacks, and Andrea's kidnapping, have something to do with hiding your parentage, Carrie, and Andrea's."

Carrie sat up straight, color appearing on her cheeks. "It's not George-Phillip."

He shook his head. "No. I'm certain it isn't. For one thing, why would he have to threaten her to keep her away?"

"Richard, then," she said. Apparently she'd settled on calling him that instead of *Father.*

"That's what your mother thinks," Anthony said.

Julia started to speak, then stopped and seemed to reconsider whatever it was she was going to say. Finally, she said, "How does Jessica seem?"

Anthony raised his eyebrows. "Honestly?"

Julia bit her lip. Then nodded. "Yes."

"She's really sick. She's way too thin, and looks … washed out. I think she's going to be a long time recovering."

"And Mother?" Carrie asked.

"My impression?" Anthony asked. "That's a woman on a mission, and I wouldn't want to be Richard Thompson right now."

At his response, Julia pursed her lips a little. Her reaction seemed off, and Anthony didn't understand it. He kept his mouth shut.

"So what's next?" Carrie asked. He met her eyes. Blue-green. Large, framed by long eyelashes. No wonder her soldier had fallen for her.

"Well, part of it depends on you. I need to get in to see Prince George-Phillip. There are a bunch of points in Adelina's story he can corroborate. I need at least two sources to run this stuff when it's this sensitive. I'm going to try to track down your mother's confessor from the 1980s. She gave me a letter for him with written permission to discuss her. And then I'm off to Kabul to see Vasily Karatygin, who may or may not be able to give me the information I need about what happened in Wakhan."

"You're going to Afghanistan?" Carrie asked, her tone a little shrill.

"Yeah. I need sources, I can't run this story on speculation."

She looked away, her lips tightly closed. When she turned back to him, her eyes had lost their warmth. Anthony frowned, suddenly feeling off balance. He said, "You've got a lot of bad associations with Afghanistan."

She shook her head in disgust. "Afghanistan reached out and destroyed my life. It took my husband and broke his best friend. It's still coming back. With all the news that's been coming out, Ray's back in the news cycle. Did he do it or didn't he? CNN called me at *midnight* to ask if I'd comment on the special report they're doing on war crimes in Afghanistan. They're tying Ray in with Robert Bales, who killed all those civilians in 2012, and including a story about Wakhan. As if Ray could have been responsible for something that happened before he was even born. *I hate them!*"

She said the last few words with such ferocious intensity that Rachel's eyes popped wide open beside her. The baby immediately began protesting with loud gurgling noises.

"I have to go." Carrie's voice cracked, as if she were on the verge of tears. She snatched up the baby and slipped inside the condo.

Anthony exhaled. He hadn't realized that he'd stopped breathing during her brief monologue. He was shaken by the force of her emotion—and his own reaction to it.

Then Julia said in a low, threatening voice. "I don't know what kind of game you're playing, Anthony. But if you mess with my sister, I'll destroy you." Then she stood too, leaving Anthony sitting alone on the balcony.

Carrie. May 7.

In the room she'd once shared with Ray Sherman, Carrie sat on the edge of her bed looking down at her daughter. Carrie had tears in her eyes, unbidden tears that did nothing but infuriate her.

Rachel lay on her back on the bed. She was still hot this morning and seemed listless. Carrie sighed. She'd take Rachel's temperature in a few minutes. She leaned forward and cooed at her baby, then kissed her on the cheek.

Rachel gave her a big toothless smile. Carrie smiled back, ignoring the tears that were threatening to spill over, and kissed Rachel's other cheek. Rachel gave a small laugh. That escalated to a shower of kisses and loud, happy laughing and gurgling.

Carrie sighed. She was frustrated and confused and more than a little bit angry. Angry because she shouldn't have reacted that way to Anthony's announcement he was going to Afghanistan. He was a journalist, and she barely knew him, and it wasn't really any of her business anyway. But her instant reaction to his news was—fear. Anxiety that he would be hurt.

She sighed a little as she lifted her daughter's arms, evoking more baby laughs. Anthony Walker.

She shook her head. He was a foreign correspondent for Christ's sake, which was just about as dangerous—or even more—as being a soldier. She'd *read* Anthony's dispatches from Iraq when he was embedded with a US Army platoon. His life was dangerous, no life for someone with a family, and on top of that, he wasn't even that good looking. Ray hadn't even been dead a year and she felt *incredibly* disloyal to even be thinking of Anthony that way.

Ray hadn't even been dead for a year! What was wrong with her?

She lifted Rachel to her chest and let the tears spill over. She knew exactly what was wrong with her. She was hideously lonely. She'd met her soulmate and married him and lost him all in the course of nine months. And nothing would ever be the same.

CHAPTER SEVENTEEN
Small
breakthrough

Bear. May 7.

Bear grumbled to himself as he crept forward twenty feet then stopped again. I-66 out of Washington was a parking lot. As far as he could see there was no accident—these were just normal traffic conditions for this early in the morning, just another day in Washington.

Bear *hated* Washington. But he also knew he was never leaving, because this was where his kids lived. He was going to be here for the indefinite future anyway. His appointment to the Joint Terrorism Task Force hadn't been endangered yet by his supposed suspension, or the loss of classified documents—but that didn't mean it wasn't coming soon.

Ten more feet. Stop. At this rate he wouldn't get to Leah's place until ten or ten-thirty. He was exhausted and wore rumpled clothes, eyelids heavy after taking the red-eye back to Washington. But what else could he do? After their arrival at Washington Reagan National Airport at six am, he and Anthony went their separate ways—Bear had gone back to his apartment just long enough to shower and change then get back out on the road.

His phone rang. He fumbled for it.

Scott Kelly.

He answered. "Kelly, what's up?"

Kelly's Boston Irish accented voice sounded out of the car speakers. "I hear you had a run-in with the IRS yesterday."

Bear chuckled. "Yeah, you could say that. Schmidt is not happy that I'm on the case. Not happy at all. What's up at your end?"

"Small breakthrough actually. Or a big one, maybe."

"Tell me."

In the right lane just ahead of him, a rusted red pickup pulled ahead. The driver to Bear's right—driving a Prius no less—was staring at his phone, probably watching porn or reading a Russian novel. Either way he didn't move fast enough. Bear launched his car into the opening, achieving nearly forty feet in one stretch.

Kelly continued yammering on, unaware of the deadly combat Bear was engaged in.

"All right. First, you remember kidnapper two? The one Andrea Thompson said was American?"

"Yeah. She said he called himself Dan."

"Right. We couldn't get a match on his prints, nothing. Nothing in the FBI database, nothing anywhere. Anyway, on Thursday the Pocatello, Idaho police put out a missing persons report. Thirty-one year old Army veteran missing. His mother called it in, but the local police took forty-eight hours to put out an alert. They must have figured he went hunting or something."

"Yeah?" Bear asked. His reply was laced with sarcasm. "That's our guy? Some guy who used to be in the Army just randomly hooks up with one of the most dangerous mercenaries in the world to kidnap Andrea Thompson? I need more, Kelly."

Kelly lashed back. "Let me finish the story, Bear."

The guy in the Prius was honking his horn. Bear didn't flip him off, even though he wanted to. But he did goose the car forward. Morning commutes were only won with guts of steel and the instincts of a hunter. Bear laughed at his own idiocy.

"All right," Kelly said. "So we went to the Army. It was a match. Picture matched. But the Army's pissed, because kidnapper Dan's fingerprints don't show up in their database. And his DNA didn't match up either."

"He wasn't actually in the Army?"

"No, he was. That's where it gets interesting. His name's Tyler Coleman. I went and talked to his company commander. Someone deleted the records, Bear. They deleted the computer records, but there are still paper records of his enlistment. This was our guy for sure. He was Special Forces for one enlistment, 2001 to 2005. Then he disappeared, apparently taking his permanent military record with him."

Bear squeezed the steering wheel. "Fucking CIA."

"That's it. Emma Smith—she's the IRS second-in-command—pulled his social security and tax records. From 2006 until 2011, he supposedly worked as a technical specialist for an outfit called Brennan Holdings in Northern Virginia."

"Bullshit," Bear said.

"Yeah, exactly. Brennan Holdings is a CIA front company. We're trying to find out what he did for them, but during that five-year period Customs and Immigration shows two *dozen* times he left and entered the United States. And then nothing. In 2001 he paid cash for a big house in Idaho, bought some vicious dogs and basically retired."

Bear grunted. He was driving at least four miles an hour now—maybe even five. "At twenty-something years old? I must be in the wrong line of work."

He thought through the implications. Tyler Coleman "retired" from the CIA in 2011. Something stank. "What did the IRS say about his income since 2011?"

Kelly replied, "He reported less than thirty thousand in income in 2012 and 2013. The IRS might have never noticed—we're talking about rural Idaho, the median income out there is pretty low. But here's the kicker, Bear. I talked with the Sheriff out there. Coleman's been arrested for disorderly conduct, public drunkenness and assault in the last three years. He beat up some guy in a bar and did three months in the county jail. His fingerprints should have come up in the National Crime Information Center, Bear. But his record was wiped from there too. And that was *after* he left the Agency."

Bear gripped the steering wheel with both hands. He was moving at a good clip now, almost as fast as a bicyclist. Uphill. With a flat tire.

Maybe not. Brake lights came on in front of him again. Bear sighed as he came to a stop. He was a tenth of a mile from the exit. He could walk faster than this.

"Okay. So the CIA was somehow involved in kidnapping Andrea. Or maybe a rogue element inside CIA. What else?"

Kelly said, "You won't like the next part."

"I didn't like the last part. What is it?"

"The guy Leah tagged the other day, before—" Kelly didn't finish the sentence. *Before she got shot.*

"Yeah," Bear said. "Go on." Kelly was talking about the bizarre melee that had happened in the street in Bethesda the day before the condominium was attacked. A British tourist had been shot, and one of the shooters killed. The other one was tackled by Dylan Paris and then arrested by Diplomatic Security.

Kelly said. "Two things. First, the British tourist? He wasn't a tourist."

"Who was he?"

"Name is Charlie Frazier. We're certain he's MI6."

Bear let out a curse. "What the hell?"

"Yeah, exactly. And here's where it gets really strange, Bear."

"It's not strange yet?"

"The shooter was Saudi Mukhabarat."

Bear didn't answer. He just sat breathing. In his mind, he thought back to the photograph. 1983. Leslie Collins, Prince Roshan, Richard Thompson. All three were in Afghanistan together.

"Kelly. Listen to me. I got it. I know what's happening now."

"Well don't keep it to yourself."

"It's not one group of bad guys here, Kelly. It's two. Or more. One side is Collins and Roshan and Thompson. They were involved in the Wakhan massacre, Kelly. I bet they engineered it. And now, their mutual paranoia is taking them down. Collins thought if Andrea Thompson's parentage came out, it would be enough of a scandal to bust the whole story open. But his actions precipitated that instead of preventing it."

"What would her parentage have anything to do with it? She's a bastard child of a prince. It's not unique."

"Her father conducted the formal investigation into Wakhan for the British government, Kelly."

Bear was missing something. Who the hell was Oz? Did he work for Thompson like Adelina thought? Or worse, did he work for George-Phillip? Maybe Adelina was all wrong about her former lover. Maybe he'd kill his own children to keep a scandal from happening.

"Kelly, you ever hear of an intelligence operative who goes by the name Oz?"

"Oz? Like the Wizard?"

"Yeah."

"Nah."

Yes! Bear had a clear path to the exit. Or close enough. Less than two hundred yards down the emergency lane. He slipped the car into the emergency lane and sped up, ten miles an hour, then twenty, then thirty, the cars to his left flashing by.

Bear spoke again. "Kelly, look into it. This guy's nasty, and he's been trying to keep Adelina Thompson away from Prince George-Phillip for thirty years. I don't know what else he's done, but he's the guy who hired the gunman who went after her on the border."

"All right. I'm on it."

Blue flashes. *Shit!* Bear saw the lights in his rearview mirror as he pulled off onto the exit. The police car rode up right on his bumper. Damn it. Looks like a State trooper.

"Kelly, I'm being pulled over."

On the other end of the line, Kelly let out a guffaw. He silenced himself for just a moment then burst into heavy belly laughter.

"Shut up, Kelly." Bear pulled to a stop, then reached for his wallet and folded it to show his diplomatic security ID and badge.

Then he waited. The cop was still sitting there behind the wheel, probably watching the end of his movie on the computer in the car.

Bear waited another very long minute, then opened the car door and started to step out.

"Sir! Get back in the car!"

"I'm with Diplomatic Security—" He raised his hands in the air, one of them holding the badge and ID.

"I don't care who you're with, get back—is that a gun?"

Instantly the situation became much more serious. The State trooper pulled his sidearm and pointed it at Bear. Bear didn't move a muscle.

"I want you to place your hands on the roof of the vehicle sir. Do *not* make any sudden movements."

Bear rolled his eyes, then slowly turned to the car and put his hands on it. "I'm not dangerous, officer. I'm an agent of the Diplomatic Security Service. My ID and badge are in my—"

"Shut up."

"Well, that's not polite," Bear muttered.

The officer took Bear's pistol from his shoulder holster then took the badge and ID from his right hand.

Then he left Bear standing there and walked back to his cruiser. Bear started to grumble, but then another cruiser pulled up, lights flashing. What the hell?

From the inside of the car, Kelly's disembodied voice sounded out.

"Bear, you still alive?"

Bear didn't dare move. But he shouted into the car. "I think I'm under arrest!"

Kelly didn't answer, instead bursting into laughter. Again.

Bear sighed. Then he called into the car, "Look into Oz, will you? I'm on my way to Leah's if the cops ever let me go."

"I'm on it!" Kelly replied, chuckling.

With friends like that, who needed enemies?

George-Phillip. May 7.

Wednesday morning's *Guardian* carried a giant headline.

AFGHAN GOVERNMENT FILES COMPLAINT WITH WORLD COURT

Prime Minister tells Guardian, **"Being a Royal won't protect Prince George-Phillip from prosecution."**

The article was filled with dozens of manifest falsehoods. Some were simply from ignorance—such as mistaking the International Criminal Court with the World Court—two very different bodies with very different jurisdictions. But some of the mistakes in the article were clearly otherwise motivated. Whoever had leaked information to *The Guardian* had a copy of the report George-Phillip had filed in 1984, but it was clearly filled with distortions.

George-Phillip was considering leaking the actual report. He wasn't sure what else would accomplish the job of clearing the air. And he couldn't very well protect his daughters if he was facing a trial.

He set the paper down on the expansive desk. The office in the family quarters at the Embassy was quite nice, bigger than George-Phillip's office in London and certainly far more traditional. He'd never cared for the steel and glass headquarters of MI6. Outside the window, he could see the crowd of protesters outside the fence. Dozens of them, and the crowd was growing every minute.

Justice for Afghan Civilians, one sign read. *Civilian Blood is on Your Hands!* said another.

He studied the protestors for a moment. They were young and old. Big and small. A broad range of people who were genuinely outraged that the facts of the murder of hundreds of civilians had been covered up for so many years. He felt sympathy for them. He'd felt the same outrage. He remembered that day in Miss Thatcher's office. Shaking.

It's a miscarriage of justice. Prime Minister, if we sit on this it will tell the world we approve.

Prime Minister Thatcher had merely shook her head. *No, Your Highness. As it is, the world believes the Soviets are responsible. If they learn the truth, it will be a massive victory for Chernenko.*

Chernenko is an old man! George Phillip had replied. *He'll likely be dead within the year.*

But the Soviet Union will still be there, Your Highness. For now, the truth must stay hidden.

George-Phillip had collapsed into a chair. In a quiet voice, he'd said, *And what of Richard Thompson and Leslie Collins? Prince Roshan and Vasily Karatygin? They'll just go free after such a massive crime?*

She'd shrugged then said, *God will deal with them.*

Perhaps God would, George-Phillip thought. But he also thought that God mostly worked through human agencies.

A knock on the door. George-Phillip turned away from the protestors and said in a loud voice, "Come in."

The door opened. It was Oswald O'Leary.

"Come in, old friend," George-Phillip said. "I suppose you've heard the news I'm recalled to London."

"I have, Your Highness. No doubt you'll put an end to all of this when you arrive."

"Do you see them out there?" he asked, pointing to the street.

O'Leary's nose wrinkled, as if he smelled something bad. "It means nothing. There's a protest every day in Washington."

"It means something," George-Phillip said. "Those people in that village. Their blood cries out from the ground."

"Very poetic, sir. But not practical."

George-Phillip shook his head. "Always practical, my friend. I've known you thirty years and little changes."

"Always the idealist, sir. I've protected you from yourself for more years than you know. What will you do now?"

"I will tell the truth. My daughter called me not long ago. She's asked me to speak with a reporter from *The Washington Post*."

O'Leary's eyes widened. "Your daughter, sir?"

"Carrie, of course."

"I wouldn't advise it, sir. I truly wouldn't. I know Carrie and Andrea are your daughters, but clearly Andrea doesn't want to be. She ran away when you provided her shelter. And the other one … she was married to a war criminal."

"Oswald," George-Phillip said, an edge forming in his voice.

"Sir, you know I've never approved of your affair with Adelina Thompson. If she knew, the Queen would—"

"You go too far, Oswald."

O'Leary faced him without flinching. "I look out for your best interests, Your Highness. I always have. You realize that *none* of this would be an issue if you hadn't had that affair in the first place. Sir, I'm begging you. *Do not* talk to this reporter."

George-Phillip shook his head. "I admire your conviction, but this is the course I must take. In the meantime, I have a task for you, O'Leary. And there could be none more important."

O'Leary sighed heavily. Then he said, "Yes, sir. What is it?"

"Oswald, I'd like you to go to British Columbia, to carry my best wishes to Adelina. I want you to ask her and her daughter—all of them, if she wishes—to join me in London. And if she agrees, I want you to escort her and keep her safe."

O'Leary looked stunned. "Sir? You can't be serious—"

"I've never been so serious, Oswald. I know you don't approve of her. I know you disagree with me. But you're also my most trusted aide. You're my most trusted *friend*, Oswald."

O'Leary closed his eyes. Then he nodded, once. "Of course, Your Highness. Whatever you wish."

CHAPTER EIGHTEEN
Leave them alone!

Adelina. May 7.

Adelina Thompson stared at her temporary cell phone as if it were a snake about to betray her. It lay on the plastic tray table, amidst the debris of Jessica's breakfast. Adelina had bought coffee and a croissant at the coffee shop in the lobby of the hospital. After days here, she was ready for a hotel room, a bed and a shower. But she wouldn't leave Jessica alone here. Not after all that had happened.

Jessica didn't appreciate it, of course. She was eighteen, and what eighteen-year-old appreciates their mother? Certainly none of Adelina's daughters had.

Except Sarah. Sarah, who had surprised her. Sarah, who had pulled through such incredible and excruciating pain and become a stronger woman for it.

Sarah … who had whispered in her mother's ear, just before Adelina left for California after Christmas, "I'll miss you, Mom. Thanks for everything."

One day, though, Jessica would understand. Jessica wanted nothing more than to be left alone. But the fact was, she'd been left alone too much, too long.

So, for the time being, they were staying here. They had the security guards Julia had hired, and Jessica was recovering in a safe place now. Safe physically, anyway. Every few minutes she looked back at the phone.

Carrie had sent her a text that morning. It was brief and to the point.

Mom. Prince George Phillip would like to speak with you.

Following that sentence was a telephone number. 202 area code. Washington, DC. George-Phillip was staying at the Embassy. Her daughters had visited him.

She wanted to call. She didn't dare.

Except for the phone call before she fled the Bay Area, they'd exchanged no words since before Andrea was born. What reason did he have to call her now? And what would she have to say to him? She still loved him, but what did that really mean, when she'd rejected him in order to protect her children so many years before?

He'd married. Adelina had watched from afar, but even minor royalty had media coverage of their weddings—especially when they were prominent diplomats. His wedding to Anne Davies had been covered in the celebrity magazines and gossip blogs, and Adelina had read every word, studied every picture.

Lady Anne was much younger than George-Phillip. She had blonde hair and blue eyes and was nothing like Adelina. She looked … wholesome. Beautiful, well-bred, almost certainly well educated. Adelina felt a painful mix of emotions when she looked at the photographs. Pain. A vague warm happiness for George-Phillip that he had finally found someone to love. But also a stabbing pain. All those years he'd stayed single … more than twenty years after they'd met. But marriage. Marriage meant he'd given up. That he'd moved on. That he'd finally let go of their shared dream together. The night of the wedding, after spending hours locked in her room looking at the photos online, she'd collapsed into her bed and wept, because that was it. She'd lost all hope.

Two and a half years later, the poor woman succumbed to pancreatic cancer. A hideous and aggressive disease.

He must have been heartbroken. The news media had reported they had a single daughter, Jane. But she'd been unable to find a single photograph of the girl. George-Phillip must keep her tightly under wraps.

Adelina picked up the phone. She turned it over in her hands, trying to decide. She should call. She wanted to call. But she was terrified. Would he only talk to her out of some sense of duty to the past? She couldn't imagine it would be anything else. But she couldn't let her life be driven by fear anymore. She dialed 1-2-0-2-

Then one of the security guards knocked. A moment later he ducked his head into the room.

"Mrs. Thompson? Two young ladies here, they said they're your daughters."

Adelina gasped and stood up. "Let them in, please."

A few seconds later Andrea and Sarah walked into the room. Andrea wore tough blue jeans and a T-shirt. Her hair had been dyed, black and turquoise. Sarah wore her customary black, with fishnet stockings and combat boots.

The three of them stood, frozen, the two girls facing their mother. To the side, not forgotten, Jessica slept peacefully.

"Hello, Mother," Andrea said.

Adelina sniffled, trying to hold back tears. She approached Sarah and Andrea and said, "I'm so glad you're here. I've missed you terribly."

Sarah approached and put her arms around Adelina. "I've missed you too, Mom."

Adelina squeezed her arms around Sarah tightly. Then she looked up at Andrea. Her youngest daughter. The daughter who had born the price, more than any of the others, of Richard's sickness and violence and Adelina's terror. She whispered, "Andrea."

Andrea walked toward her and put her arms around both Sarah and her mother. They stayed that way for a long time, swaying slightly, until Andrea broke off the hug and stepped back. Sarah followed suit.

"Have a seat," Adelina said. "How did you get here?"

The two girls looked at each other and exchanged a secret look. Then Sarah said, "The first half by Harley, but we took Amtrak for the second half."

Adelina looked at Andrea. "I understood you were safe at the British Embassy. Why did you leave?"

"Someone attacked me ... and ... I had a lot of questions."

Adelina sat up. "In the Embassy?"

Andrea nodded. "Yeah. I was getting ready for bed and texting with Sarah. A man came in and tried to—I don't know if he was trying to hurt me or kill me or what. But I pushed him off, and Sarah picked me up."

Adelina closed her eyes. "I'm so sorry, Andrea. For everything. But especially for you being in that kind of danger. Everything I ever did was to protect you girls. But I've not exactly succeeded there, have I? Tell me what you remember about the attack."

Andrea began to describe what happened. What the room was like. The man's smell. Then she said, "He had a thick Irish accent. Deep voice."

"Oz," Adelina whispered.

"What?" Sarah asked.

Adelina explained. As she finished telling the story, she said, "I always thought he worked for Richard. But now I'm beginning to doubt."

Andrea said, "Do you think it's possible it was the Prince? That's what the man said."

George-Phillip? No. Adelina shook her head. "No, I don't think it's possible he's changed that much."

"Well, he came from *somewhere*," Andrea interjected. "And there can't be that many people who have access to the royal residence at the Embassy."

Adelina sighed. "The man who shot at us at the border worked for Oz. I'm afraid he won't rest until I'm dead."

"I don't understand," Andrea said. Her eyes were watering, and she spoke at a whisper. For just a moment, the standoffish, armored young woman looked like the little girl she'd once been, and it felt like a stab through Adelina's heart. "I don't understand any of this. I wish none of it had ever happened."

Marky Lovecchio. May 7.

Making it over the border had been a breeze. Marky had shown his driver's license to the Canadian border guards and they'd passed him into the country. Simple as that. They hadn't even searched his Challenger, almost a disappointment since he'd stashed his guns. There was no point in taking unnecessary chances, and he knew a guy in Vancouver who got him a pistol. It wasn't ideal—a .32 calibre popgun. But it ought to be enough to do the job.

He was disappointed he hadn't been able to stick around in Seattle. That stripper had been a live one, and he'd wanted to stick around with her in the hotel room for another day or two. But no such luck. He wasn't fucking with Oz.

The hospital didn't look much like private hospitals in the United States, or at least not like the ones Marky had been to. This was more like a VA or Army hospital—everything worked, everything necessary was there, but it wasn't lushly appointed with expensive carpets and artwork. Marky was grateful the morning had been chilly. It was May, and wearing a jacket would have raised questions if it were hot. As it was, he was easily able to conceal his weapon underneath his jacket.

He wandered down the second floor wing, his sneakers occasionally squeaking against the institutional floor. He'd passed the cancer ward and pediatrics. Ahead, a crowded nurses' station. His target was in room 201, which would be down the hallway to the left if he was right.

There. The nurses' station was at the intersection of two hallways. To the left and right, patients' rooms. Ahead, more hallway, and probably more rooms.

Marky had been through this before. All you had to do was look like you knew where you were going, look like you knew what you were doing. Nobody questioned you if you were confident and bold. He turned left. At the end of the hall were two security guards. One was sitting in a chair, his telephone out, sending a text message. The other was across the hall from him, leaning against a door frame. A nurse was walking toward him, and behind her a teenage girl with black and turquoise hair. She was hot, and he leered at her as she passed him going in the opposite direction. But he didn't have time to screw around. He looked back toward the guards. Neither of them had stirred, the one at the door lazily looking in his direction.

That was going to be a fatal mistake. Marky wasn't lazy, and he was prepared for these two. He should be able to take down the first before the guy sitting down texting even knew what was happening. He passed another room, the smell of ammonia and an underlying earthy smell wafting out of the room. Some old person dying maybe?

Marky casually slid a hand into the back of his waistband as he got to within twenty feet of the inert guards. The standing one started to move, but he was too late. Marky squeezed the pistol, firing a .32 calibre bullet straight into the guard's eye.

Sarah. May 7.

As Andrea left the room, almost in tears, her mother started to stand.

"Let her go," Sarah said. "I think it's going to take some time. Everything she thought she knew has changed."

Her mother sighed, then sank back into her seat. Jessica was beginning to stir.

"You know I would have done anything to keep her. Except risk her life. Richard would have killed her. He told me that, and I believed him."

Sarah shrugged. The words made her feel—bleak. Empty inside. "I've spent the last two weeks taking in a lot of things, Mother. I learned about how you and Dad met ... what he did to you. I learned two of my sisters had a different father. I learned a *lot*. But ... that just makes things harder, you know? What used to make sense doesn't."

Her mother nodded, her face lined. Adelina looked sad. *Old*.

Sarah reached over and took her mother's hand. Then she said, "I know this, Mother. All of us are your daughters. It might not be easy … but that will never change."

Her mother's eyes misted over. Sarah didn't know what might have happened next, because she froze at the sudden loud *pop* just outside their room, loud enough her ears instantly started ringing. A second one, then a third. *Gunshots.* It couldn't be anything else. Sarah fought her suddenly rising panic.

Jessica jerked up in the bed. Sarah grabbed her around the waist and lifted her off the bed as if she were a rag doll, even as her mother came to her aid. They dumped the now screaming Jessica on the floor.

The doorknob turned. Sarah didn't stop to think. She dove over the bed, grabbing for the door, and leaned against it.

"Sarah!" her mother screamed.

The door pushed inward, pushing Sarah back. She let out a howl, her boots scrambling for purchase as she tried to close the door. She tried to force it closed, but couldn't. Then suddenly the pressure let off the door and she flew forward, losing her footing. Her vision went black when her head connected with the heavy wood panel, then she was thrown back, the door bursting inward.

Sarah landed half on her left leg, the one she'd injured the year before, and immediately collapsed, the muscles in that leg not strong enough for sustained work.

A man wearing jeans and a Black Sabbath T-shirt and a black jacket filled the doorway and raised his pistol, aiming at her mother.

Adelina. May 7.

"What…" Jessica asked in a half scream as she tried to get to her feet.

Adelina pushed her daughter down. "Stay down!" she screamed.

The room had filled with smoke and noise, Sarah howling with what sounded like rage, and Adelina turned back toward the door just as it burst open, throwing Sarah back against the bed with a loud thump.

Terror filled Adelina at that moment, terror that she wouldn't be able to protect her daughters, that she wouldn't be able to see them grow up and get married and have the lives they all deserved. Terror that she wouldn't be able to make amends to her daughters, that she wouldn't live long enough to beg for their forgiveness.

The man in the doorway was large and muscular. A black leather jacket over a T-shirt and blue jeans. Smoke clouded the room from the gunshots he'd already fired, but that was nothing to the gaping black hole of the pistol he lifted up and aimed directly at Adelina.

Everything seemed to slow down to a sickening slowness. Jessica started to move again and Adelina held her left hand out as if to signal *stay*.

Then two arms and two legs were suddenly wrapped around the killer from behind, one hand grabbing at his gun. A flash of black and turquoise and arms and legs moving everywhere and Adelina realized that Andrea had jumped on the killer's back. Her daughter let out a feral shriek and screamed, "Leave them *alone!*"

Andrea had one hand on the guy's gun arm and another wrapped around his face. The pistol was aimed slightly toward the ceiling, and it went off, once, twice, then Sarah ran headfirst at the man, hitting him in the gut with her head. He let out a scream as one of Andrea's fingers sank into his left eye, blood bursting out and down his face. Then Sarah stood in front of him and grabbing at his gun hand with her two hands, she kicked him hard, in the knee.

He collapsed with a scream as Adelina's daughters swarmed over him. Andrea took his gun away then tied his wrists behind his back.

Only then did Andrea, still on her hands and knees, look up and call out. "Mother! Are you okay? Is Jessica?"

Adelina collapsed into her seat.

CHAPTER NINETEEN
Realpolitik

Richard. May 7.

The first thing Richard Thompson saw when he entered the Senate Central Hearing Facility for the second day in a row was that even more people packed the room today than had the day before. Industrious Senate aids had added more rows of chairs, all the way to the back doors. Along each wall on the left and right side of the room were television crews, and additional cameras were crowded on the floor area between the dais and the witness table.

It was officially a media circus. The morning papers had been clear enough. *The New York Times*—always reliably liberal—had called for a public trial of both Thompson and Leslie Collins. The conservative *Washington Times*, on the other hand, had landed squarely behind both Thompson and Collins, labeling them as heroes for taking the war to the Soviet Union. CNN and Fox News talked of nothing else, with pundits on both sides of the aisle calling each other traitors, liberals and a host of other names. The news coverage was ubiquitous, with reporters digging into everything they could find about his history, his family's history.

The networks were digging up archive footage of his Senate hearings in 2000, his diplomatic mission to Iraq just before the invasion in 2003, and even footage of the February 23rd Coup. Left wing commentators openly speculated that Thompson and the CIA had been behind the right-wing paramilitary units that had taken over the Spanish capital. His entire career was being sifted with a fine-toothed comb, right alongside Julia's. He'd also seen coverage of her career—Morbid Obesity's first appearance on television, their first album going platinum, Julia speaking to reporters from Hollywood to Moscow. The reporters took the accusations in the IRS investigation as fact, and clearly someone on the grand jury was leaking information to the press.

None of the reporters had any real facts to speak of.

But they didn't need any, did they? Richard knew that well enough from the debacle of his nomination as Ambassador to Russia.

Consequently, it was with considerable trepidation that Richard now entered the hearing room and walked, head high, between the massive crowd. Toward the front of the hearing room were the officials, journalists and lobbyists who could afford to hire line-sitters to wait in the hours before the hearing. In the middle and back of the room were the members of the public who'd been lucky enough to get close to the front of the line. They were probably a mix of activists and others who were affiliated with left-wing organizations. But sprinkled in the crowd were at least a dozen men and women in military uniforms. Perhaps people who had served in Afghanistan? Who knew why these people were all here.

He was halfway up the aisle when two men stood up. Both of them were dressed in ridiculous looking baggy sweatshirts and pants and had unkempt hair. They held up a banner between them. It read "Justice for Afghan Blood."

Next to them a young woman stood up. If she'd bothered showering she might have been attractive, but as it was her hair looked a little greasy, her face pockmarked with pimples and scars from old pimples. She shouted, "Justice!" then reached into her purse and swung her left hand back, as if she were a baseball pitcher, and *threw* something across the room directly at Richard.

He jerked back and away from the projectile even as someone in the audience screamed, and his eyes tracked on the object. A balloon. A *water balloon*. It splashed down into the crowd to Richard's right, and dark red liquid exploded across half a dozen people, who began shouting and yelling.

Capitol police rushed into the now roiling crowd and hustled the activists away, even as others assisted those who had been splashed.

With blood. Real blood. Richard could smell it. Half a dozen drops had hit him, a few in the face and his hands and probably a few more on his suit. He took out a handkerchief and wiped his face and hands then turned back toward the front of the hearing room, where the witness table faced the gathered Senators.

The smell was awful. He had almost reached the front of the room when his eyes locked on Maria Clawson's.

That whore.

Richard was certain that somewhere along the way she had probably been involved with Chuck Rainsley. Nothing else could explain her long standing hostility to him. He'd felt glee when Julia had funded the lawsuit that wiped out Clawson's career. But now, the witch was back. She was making a comeback of her career on the back of Richard's disgrace.

Disgrace.

That was the word his father, Cyrus Thompson, had once used. Richard shuddered and continued his walk down the gauntlet toward his waiting execution.

He grunted as he reached the front row. Three seats from the aisle on the left side, studiously ignoring Richard, was Leslie Collins. Deputy Director of Operations of the Central Intelligence Agency. His former *friend.* Richard thought it was laughable that Collins would show up here in person to watch Richard crash and burn. Two seats down from Collins was a thirty-year-old Saudi in a dark suit and wearing the traditional white *keffiyeh.* He recognized the man, Prince Roshan's eldest son Ahmed.

Ahmed had the courage to nod at Richard. More courage than that snake Collins showed. Richard turned toward the front of the room. The Senators were all seated, waiting for him, fangs drawn and dripping with his blood.

Richard might be losing, but he would take some of them down with him.

That was something else Cyrus Thompson had taught him. Even as the old bastard was dying, he'd held on to his grudges, his hatreds, his contempt, including his hate and contempt for his own son.

Richard took a seat at the table and looked at his watch. If they started on time, the hearing would begin in three minutes. In the meantime, he sat up, his back straight, pride in every line of his body.

Disgrace.

Yes, that's what his father had said. *Disgrace.*

The word had been his response to the death of Cyrus Thompson IV—Richard's elder brother.

It was the summer after Richard's freshman year at Harvard. Cyrus, two years ahead of him, was entering his final year. Something had always been different about Cyrus. He was thinner than Richard, smaller. Where Richard played rugby and lacrosse and joined the rowing team when they were at Exeter, his older brother had been bookish and introspective.

One night just a few weeks before Cyrus's death, they'd sat on the roof of Kirkland House, four blocks south of Harvard Yard.

"You know Father hates me," Cyrus had said.

Richard had remained silent, just looking up at the stars.

"It's true," Cyrus had said. "I'm a joke. He wanted someone to take over his businesses and his life. Instead he got me. I'm scrawny and read books and what I really want is to be a professor. Right here. But even this ... Father selected Kirkland House. The *jock* house, as if I would ever fit in here. It was his, so it had to be ours."

Richard sighed and took a drink from his hip flask. He had a warm glow growing in his stomach.

"I just give him what he wants," Richard said. "It's easier."

"That's easy for you to say. You want the same things he does."

Richard shook his head. "No. I'm going away. Far away. Screw him. I'll be on the other side of the world, and Father can find someone else to take over his metal shavings or whatever the hell it is he makes."

Cyrus sat up, startled. "Where are you going?"

Richard said, "Can I tell you a secret? A real secret—you can't say anything to anybody."

"Of course."

Richard looked over his shoulder, even though he knew no one else was up on the roof. He whispered, "Last month I met a recruiter for the CIA."

"*What?*"

Richard nodded. "They won't do anything until I graduate, of course. But he said they're looking for people with language talents and who can move around with rich people. Diplomats. Whatever."

Cyrus was dumbfounded. "But ... but ... what if you end up in some place like Vietnam?"

Richard shrugged. "Better with the CIA than as a draftee. Speaking of which ... how are your grades?"

Cyrus had been placed on academic probation during the first semester. One more failed class and he'd be booted out of Harvard—and would lose his draft deferment. There were always ways around such things, of course, but Richard and Cyrus both knew that their bastard of a father wouldn't use them. He'd sooner send his older son off to be killed in some jungle than he would recognize that he wasn't a clone of his father.

Cyrus sighed at the question. Then he whispered, "I'm failing."

"*Why?*" Richard said. "You're just as smart as I am. Smarter."

Cyrus shrugged and looked away. "I don't know. Sometimes it's just hard to care."

Three weeks later final grades had been published and it became official. Cyrus was kicked out. His draft lottery number had already been called, and only the student deferment kept him out of the Army.

They'd returned home to San Francisco, and both brothers had been called into their father's office—the same room that once became Richard's office after the old bastard died. Father had hugged Richard and smiled at him, complimenting his grades and his lacrosse trophy.

Then he turned to his elder son. "I'm ashamed of you, Cyrus. You're ... a disgrace to your family."

"Father ... what should I do?"

Cyrus Thompson III just stuck his nose in the air and looked away from his son. "I suppose you'll have to go to war. Maybe it will finally turn you into a man. Get out of my sight. You disgust me."

Cyrus fled. Richard stood there without responding. His father turned toward him and said, "Your brother isn't capable of leading a squad of mice out of a paper bag. You'll take over the business when I retire."

Richard shrugged. "Don't count on it, Father. I may have other plans."

His father's face had turned red, and he shouted, "You'll make plans I approve of and none other!" he'd thundered.

The next morning, Richard had found his brother, swinging from the rafter in the attic.

Days later, at the funeral, his father had repeated himself, but in a new and more hideous way. "His death was just as much a disgrace as his life."

Richard retained that word. *Disgrace.* He remembered it, kept it, used it, felt it. For the next decade he ignored his father's entreaties to return to San Francisco, instead embarking on his career with the Foreign Service and his much more secretive career with the Central Intelligence Agency.

They spoke, regularly, on Christmas and Easter. But Richard didn't return to San Francisco. He didn't witness the slow deterioration of his family's four-story Victorian in San Francisco. He didn't witness the slow deterioration of his father. It wasn't until 1983, more than ten years after the death of his brother, that he returned to the city he'd once called *home*.

It was during a short leave from Spain. He'd been under intense pressure from his superiors—both because of the failed coup, which *would* have put in place a sympathetic government, as well as his involvement with the underage daughter of a deposed Marquis. The Agency's position was clear—don't make waves. Don't do anything that could call attention to the Agency. Marry the girl and shut her family up.

He did. And when he arrived in San Francisco, it was in preparation for sending his new wife home. He found his father bedridden. His health wrecked by syphilis, which had gone untreated and undetected until it was too late. Partially paralyzed and blind, the old man's internal organs were failing and he likely only had a few weeks to live.

Married, are you? His father had raged. *To some Spanish slut?*

Richard had responded with disdain. *She's the daughter of Spanish nobility, if you care, Father. I don't. What I do care about is that she comes to live here when I go back overseas. I can't cart a pregnant seventeen-year-old around the globe.*

His father had replied with venom. "I'll allow no such thing. In fact, if you don't dump the girl I'll disinherit you. You ungrateful little bastard. You're just as much a disgrace to this family as your brother was!"

Richard had responded with rage. But not the kind of rage Adelina would later evoke in him. No, it was a cold rage, a rage that resulted in a response that was worthy of his father. After a few phone calls, and the passing of a considerable amount of money, Cyrus Thompson III, the former shipping and manufacturing magnate, was declared incompetent and his affairs placed in the hands of his loving son.

No Last Will and Testament ever appeared to disinherit Richard Thompson. When he returned to Spain it was with a clear conscience and conviction that his father would be dead within a few weeks.

A terrible shame.

A few months later Richard installed his new young wife and daughter in the four-story house where his mother and brother had died. His mother's bedroom he turned over to Adelina. Perhaps the ghosts in there would haunt the superstitious bitch. He had the attic converted to a bedroom, which later became Julia's, and much later Sarah's.

Now, as he folded his hands in front of him and waited for the hearing to begin, Richard thanked whatever fates were out there that he'd made peace with Julia. He'd invested way too much time and energy over the years into ensuring her loyalty, and now it was paying off. That morning, before the hearing began, they'd discussed strategy. Finally, at one point, she looked dead across the table at him.

"Dad … I want you to level with me. I know it was the Cold War and bad stuff happened. I know people had to do things that look ugly in today's light. Did you do it? Did you give them the chemical weapons?"

Richard quickly calculated the correct response. Then concluded that he needed to tie Julia ever closer to him. The rest of his daughters would take their mother's side, he was sure of it. But his Julia had been too badly damaged by Adelina to *ever* take her side.

He had nodded. "I did. It was horrible. But also necessary."

She had closed her eyes and took a deep breath, her cheeks going a bit pale.

"Julia … you know better than anyone about foreign policy. You know how these things work. I didn't want to do it, and I certainly didn't know they would use it on innocent villagers. We actually provided the militia with satellite photos of the Russian training camp, as well as an advisor who was a Soviet defector. Vasily Karatygin—he'd converted to Islam and went over to the side of the mujahideen. But they didn't use it on the military … it was on civilians. I'd have done anything to prevent it."

She gave him a knowing look. "But since it did happen, you had to blame it on the Soviets. *Realpolitik.*"

He grimaced. "Sadly, yes."

She had taken the bait. So now he had at least one ally. Julia had promised to turn her attorneys loose on defeating the IRS—she'd met with them the previous day. And she promised to go after Maria Clawson. Richard, meanwhile, would take on Leslie Collins and the Senate Armed Services Committee.

His attention was jerked back to the front of the room when Senator Chuck Rainsley banged his gavel on the table.

"Mister Thompson, have you heard a single word I've said? I asked you a question." Rainsley's face was red.

Richard sighed. Then he did something that he thought might win over some of the media and the public, who looked at Rainsley as a giant blowhard.

"I'm sorry, Senator, I really hadn't noticed you were talking. What was that?"

A long moment of silence in the room was punctuated only by the clicking of digital cameras. First a titter in the back of the room, then a guffaw, and then a loud laugh from the audience.

Rainsley was infuriated. "Perhaps you'll hear better if you are declared in contempt of Congress."

Richard stared at Rainsley, knowing that at this point, the only thing that mattered was the court of public opinion and the grand jury. This Senate committee had no significant bite.

"I will repeat my question, Mister Thompson. You claim that CIA Deputy Director Collins was responsible for the massacre, and that you reported it. Do you have evidence? Copies of this report? Did you tell anyone, for example, during his confirmation hearings?"

"The information was classified. Of course I didn't keep copies of the report—keeping classified information is a felony."

Rainsley leaned forward, his face beginning to turn red. "Mister Thompson, isn't it true that you were one of the agents of the Central Intelligence Agency who aided and abetted the coup organizers in Spain in 1983?"

His face cold, Richard replied, "I cannot discuss classified information in an open hearing, Senator."

"Then tell me this!" Rainsley thundered. "You met your then sixteen-year-old wife in Spain during that coup. Why is it that she is now requesting political asylum in an allied country?"

Richard felt his face flush red. *That. Fucking. Whore.*

Anthony. May 7.

"This way," the aide said. He was clearly more than a servant or doorman. In his fifties, the man had the face of a pug and a thick Irish accent. "My name is Oswald O'Leary, I'm the Prince's chief aide. He's in his office upstairs."

Anthony followed the man up a set of marble stairs. "His chief aide? What does that job entail, if I might ask?"

O'Leary chuckled. "Whatever is necessary to preserve the standing of the crown, sir. I was actually assigned to the Queen's security escort many years ago, then seconded to Prince George-Phillip."

Something about O'Leary bothered Anthony. He tried to shut it out of his mind. Adelina's account of Oz disturbed him, but he could hardly suspect every man with an Irish accent.

On the other hand, O'Leary was close to the Prince.

"How did you meet the Prince?"

O'Leary said, smoothly, "His first real assignment with MI6, I was assigned to work with him. That would have been ... oh ... the spring of 1984. We were here in Washington, DC."

Anthony felt a chill. Carefully, he said, "And your assignment came from the Queen? Isn't that unusual?"

He asked the question as they reached the second floor and began walking down a long hallway.

O'Leary smirked. "Not really. My primary role was to protect the Crown from scandal. Those were rough years—Princess Margaret and Lord Snowden had nearly public affairs and divorced, Prince Andrew got involved with an American girl who turned out to be a porn star. There was concern the monarchy itself might be brought down. Here we are."

Anthony didn't have time to react as O'Leary opened the door. His mind was rushing over O'Leary's words. Concern the monarchy might be brought down? Assigned to watch over George-Phillip in the spring of 1984? That was when George-Phillip and Adelina first met.

That was when Oz made his first appearance.

Anthony looked back at O'Leary, keeping his face unnaturally still, tight, because he didn't want to give away what he'd realized. The pug-faced man looked back at him. Was this Oz? The man who had threatened Adelina? Who had entered her house? It would explain a great deal. Including the attack on Andrea which had taken place in the Embassy, where no one should have had access.

He had to jerk his attention away from O'Leary to Prince George-Phillip, who rose from his desk and approached, right hand out to shake.

"Anthony Walker. A pleasure to meet you again. I've followed your career with some interest since our first interview."

Anthony took George-Phillip's hand. The resemblance with Carrie and Andrea was startling. He wondered how no one had ever noticed before. "No doubt you know about my exile, then."

George-Phillip chuckled. "Indeed I do. I admire a man who risks all for his convictions. Have a seat, please. Carrie Sherman … well, I suppose you know she's my daughter … asked me to agree to meet with you. I'd like to hear what this is all about."

Anthony took the proffered seat, one of a pair of matching red leather Queen Anne chairs that faced each other by a side table. Tea had already been set on the table.

"Please … have some tea, Mister Walker."

Anthony smiled. "Anthony, please, Your Highness."

George-Phillip smiled. "Anthony, then. And you can call me George-Phillip."

Anthony glanced back at the door. O'Leary was gone. But what were the chances he was listening to whatever happened in this room?

Strong, Anthony thought. Very strong.

"Please," George-Phillip said. "Tell me more about your assignment."

Anthony nodded. "There are several layers to the story. The first thing you should know is, I was originally assigned to do a fluff piece on *Morbid Obesity*. Are you familiar with the rock band?"

"Not my style of music, but I know of them. Carrie's older sister runs a fairly large entertainment empire from what I understand."

"Correct. But the story quickly grew when the IRS and the grand jury opened their investigation into Secretary Thompson."

At the mention of Richard Thompson, George-Phillip's face soured. Not surprising. Anthony continued. "My interest here has expanded. You probably know I did a retrospective story on the Wakhan Corridor last year."

"I read it. You had most of it right."

Anthony scowled. "Except for the perpetrators, of course. Like everyone else, I thought it was the Soviets."

"I'll be frank with you, Anthony. I'm familiar in detail with what happened, *and* who was responsible."

Anthony nodded. "I thought so. Is *The Guardian's* story anywhere close to accurate?"

"Some of it," George-Phillip replied. "Although my recommendation at the time was that we go public. The Prime Minister and the then director of MI6 ordered that my investigation be squashed. Despite my distant royal status, I was very low on the bureaucratic food chain in those days. However, as of this morning, my investigation from 1984 has been declassified. I'm turning a copy over to you."

Anthony closed his eyes. That was more than he'd hoped for. "Thank you, sir. There's more."

George-Phillip raised his eyebrows. "Oh?"

Anthony swallowed. If he was wrong, and George-Phillip wasn't the man he thought he was—Anthony might be thrown out now and lose any possibility of doing this story.

He didn't think he was wrong. "Your Highness, yesterday morning I interviewed Adelina Thompson. Among other things, she told me how she came to marry Richard Thompson, and the nature of their thirty-year marriage. She also told me a great deal about your affair."

George-Phillip vaguely waved a hand. "I never liked that word. I loved Adelina as I have never loved another."

"Not even Lady Anne?"

George-Phillip closed his eyes. "Anne and I were comfortable together. And happy. But we did not have that … that passion. We shared a quiet and happy life, and a wonderful daughter."

"I'm sorry for your loss," Anthony said. "Your Highness, I'll be honest with you. I want to crucify Richard Thompson. I've got *almost* enough details to do it. I'm putting together a major story. But I need corroboration. I need details. Will you go public? Will you tell me your story?"

For the next three hours, Anthony sat across from George-Phillip, as the tea grew cold and they ignored the refreshments brought by Embassy employees. When George-Phillip produced the Wakhan file, they moved to the desk as George-Phillip spread out the contents, going over his conclusions.

Then they moved on. George-Phillip described his first meeting with Adelina. How swiftly they fell in love. As he spoke, his face took on a longing, wistful quality. He looked at Anthony and said, "I've never experienced anything quite like it. I would have done anything for her. Anything. But she didn't want it. She broke it off with me, without explanation."

"That must have been difficult," Anthony said, his tone noncommittal.

"It was devastating."

Anthony winced. Unlike, George-Phillip, Anthony knew exactly why she had broken it off. She'd told him of the shame of Richard's rape. The self-loathing she'd experienced. And then Oz.

He sighed. "Your Highness—"

"George-Phillip," the Prince corrected.

"Normally I wouldn't do this. But … I know why she broke it off with you. Then, and later in China."

"Dear God, man. Why?"

Anthony took a deep breath. Then he told George-Phillip what he'd learned from Adelina. The nocturnal visit and the note left in Julia's room. The assault that came much later. And now, the assassins hired to chase down Adelina, including the attack in the hospital in Abbotsford just a few hours before.

As he spoke, George-Phillip's face took on an expression of rage.

"Does she know who this person is?"

"We know he has an Irish accent. And … we know he's been involved in this affair for more than thirty years. Whoever it is, he wanted Adelina to stay far away from you, and he's become willing to kill to prevent that. And … we know he has access to this Embassy compound … to this residence?"

"*What?*" George-Phillip's tone was sharp. "Explain," he ordered.

"Andrea Thompson was attacked in her room here in the Embassy. That's why she ran. The man who attacked her said that he was giving her a gift from her father. Then he tried to smother her. She stabbed him with a pen and he ran."

George-Phillip's face paled in shock. Then he said, "O'Leary… he's was opposed to my involvement with Adelina from the beginning. And he's been the *only* person I've been around since the beginning. He was limping after she disappeared.…"

He picked up the phone at his desk and dialed a number. "Captain, this is Prince George-Phillip. I'm giving you an order which I expect to be carried out instantly and quietly. Detain Oswald O'Leary and bring him to me." George-Phillip was silent for a moment, listening. Then he said, "I'll explain later. It is imperative you detain him now."

He hung up the phone and turned to Anthony, rage on his face. "I only have two hours before my flight leaves for London. I'll bring O'Leary with me and we'll get to the bottom of this. There's no one else it could be."

CHAPTER TWENTY
Contingency plans

Leslie Collins. May 7.

Leslie Collins sat frozen in his seat, staring straight ahead and trying not to meet anyone's eyes. He held his right wrist in his left hand ... discreetly, but to take his own pulse as his doctor had taught him to do. Right now his pulse was nearly 160, dangerously high for a man his age and condition. The hearing would be over soon, thank God.

He'd received multiple messages from the office—first his secretary, several times. Then from the Director of Central Intelligence himself, which was not a call you ignored—but he had done so. Finally, the last call, twenty minutes before, came from the White House.

He'd ignored that one too.

As the hearing had progressed through the day, Collins had thought through everything he knew, everything he'd done. Soon enough the grand jury would be investigating him too. Somehow the investigators had gotten wind of Tyler Coleman's identity, which had led them back to Brennan Holdings, the shell company Leslie had operated for more than ten years to hide his own activities. Activities which were necessary for national security, but which politicians didn't have the stomach to approve of.

Soon enough Brennan Holdings would lead directly back to Collins. He'd be like Richard—pale and sweating in front of days long Senate hearings, followed by a trial and possibly incarceration. The investigation might even turn over his role in setting up the secret accounts in Thompson's name. If that happened then it might be the worst case: Thompson falsely exonerated while Collins took the fall for everything.

If he even survived that long. It wasn't lost on him that Ahmed al-Saud—Prince Roshan's eldest son—had also attended the hearing, sat down two seats from Leslie, then leaned over and said, "My father requested I inquire about your health, Mister Collins."

Everything was out of control. Collins had ordered Andrea Thompson's kidnapping in an effort to prevent the story from breaking, and yet his employees had fucked it up beyond all recognition. But now he'd realized that in no way was he the only player in this game. Who had tried to shoot Prince George-Phillip? Was it Thompson, because he'd found out the Prince had actually been the man screwing his wife? Was it Prince Roshan, trying to tie up loose ends, which might lead to him being identified as one of the Wakhan perpetrators?

For that matter, who had hunted down Adelina Thompson and tried to kill her not once, but *twice*? Had Thompson finally grown tired of her and decided to have her killed? Was it more sinister, and he was somehow trying to frame Collins?

Everything was falling apart. Collins stood, inevitably attracting the attention of the legion of reporters and photographers who were encamped on the floor between the dais and Richard Thompson.

It didn't matter anymore. He was shaking as he walked out of the hearing room. He needed to somehow get a grip on this situation. Maybe it was time to flush out Roshan. Or have him killed before he somehow dodged responsibility and tried to blame Collins for his activities.

Outside the hearing room, he was mobbed by reporters shouting unacceptable questions.

Were you responsible for the massacre at Wakhan?

Who kidnapped Andrea Thompson?

What was your role in the cover up, Director?

Collins pushed his way through. How dare they? No one understood. They didn't understand that you couldn't make an omelette without breaking some eggs. You can't defend a nation without doing some things that nice calm people in their living rooms couldn't stomach. Right after September 11, Americans had cried for blood. But they had no strength, and when they saw *actual* blood, they shied back.

It took men of Collins' stature, willing to do whatever it took, to keep the nation safe.

He left the crowd of reporters behind, making his way to the underground garage. He would go home and get some rest. He would plan. He would get through the rest of this awful week, and go forward with dignity.

But he would also start making contingency plans.

George-Phillip. May 7.

As the small twin-engine jet left the tarmac at Washington Reagan National Airport, brilliant red and orange light flooded through the small windows. The sun was setting over Washington, DC and the view from the air was amazing.

Jane was excited. She sat in a window seat this time, looking far down at the ground as the plane banked to the right, staying on a course over the Potomac River.

George-Phillip leaned forward next to her and pointed out the Washington Monument and the White House. Jane clapped her hands and bounced in her seat. Ahead of them, through the open door of the cockpit, he could see the crew managing the instruments.

Her pure joy in the view helped assuage some of the sting of O'Leary's betrayal and escape.

Less than ten minutes after he'd ordered O'Leary's detention, the captain of the Royal Marines guarding the Embassy returned with the news. Oswald O'Leary had driven out of the Embassy grounds less than one minute before George-Phillip placed the call. Where had he gone? And *why?* Why all of it? The story Anthony Walker had told, of secret phone calls and threats, attacks in the middle of the night—it was alarming in the extreme. He would never have suspected O'Leary, who he'd trusted for more than thirty years.

O'Leary had never hidden his disdain for her. As far back as 1984, he'd said, *You should stay away from that Thompson woman. The Queen would not be happy.* But disdain was a far cry from murder.

George-Phillip leaned toward the window again. He could see the heavy Washington traffic below, swollen like something alive. Clogged arteries, a disease-ridden old man.

The flight attendant, a young woman who likely had only recently graduated secondary school, approached their seat. "Please continue to keep your seat belts fastened until we reach cruising altitude. In the meantime, can I get you a drink, sir?"

"Orange juice for both of us, please."

"Why are *you* having juice, Daddy?" Jane asked.

"Because I want to," he replied, casually. Jane was at a stage where she asked a lot of nonsensical questions.

The flight attendant turned away and began walking toward the front of the plane when a sudden jerk of the jet seemed to lift her into the air for just a second, then she fell flat to the floor. George-Phillip felt intense G-forces pulling at his stomach as the plane banked hard to the right. Below, facing the window, George-Phillip could see Northern Virginia countryside spread out perpendicular to the plane. They were tilted up almost vertically. He twisted his neck, trying to see what was going on, and then caught sight of it.

Behind them, coming up fast. A bright light with a white contrail.

A *missile*.

Adriana and Jane screamed.

Dylan. May 7.

Dylan Paris looked up from the textbook he'd been studying when the Captain of the Royal Marines walked into the room. After four days basically hiding at the Embassy he'd grown restless, and despite all appearances to the contrary, he'd held out hope that he and Alex would make it back to Columbia in time for final exams.

That increasingly seemed less likely. All the same, yesterday she'd taken the metro out to Bethesda and picked up their textbooks and brought them back to the Embassy. For the time being, he was still in legal limbo. Not officially a refugee or asylum seeker—nor would he be willing to become one. He'd served his country in wartime, and all he'd done the previous Friday night was protect his family from attackers.

However, the fact was, one of those attackers was an armed federal agent. Never mind that Ralph Myers had been shot by a *defending* federal agent, Leah Simpson. Never mind that Dylan Paris had taken on the other two attackers— both criminals—with nothing more than a knife. The fact was, Dylan was a suspect in the killing of a federal agent, and when he walked out the doors of the Embassy—*if* he walked out—he was subject to arrest.

Alex had left an hour before, not long after Prince George-Phillip hastily made his exit for the airport. He knew she would be back later, but for now her trips outside the Embassy were their only real contact with the outside world.

I only expect to be in London for a few days. Just stay here until we manage to sort out what is happening. You're safe here.

But was he? A killer had attacked Adelina and three of her daughters as far away as Abbotsford, British Columbia just that morning. Only after that had he learned why Andrea had so abruptly—and secretly—fled the Embassy earlier in the week. She'd been attacked in her room by a man George-Phillip said was his longtime personal aide.

Why?

Dylan didn't know. But he knew he was restless. Being cooped up in the Embassy, with nothing to do and nowhere to go, was driving him over the edge.

Consequently, it was with more than a little interest that he looked up when the Marine Captain entered the room. Over the previous days Dylan had gotten to know some of the Royal Marines, several of whom had served in Afghanistan. They spoke the same language he did.

"Mister Paris," the Captain said.

"Hey," Dylan responded.

Visibly disturbed, the Captain said, "I'm afraid the Ambassador has ordered your eviction from the Embassy, sir. If you'll gather your things and accompany me, I would appreciate it."

George-Phillip. May 7.

When the obsolete Stinger missile hit the right engine of the jet, it felt as if a giant had grabbed hold of the plane in its fist like a toy, then slammed them into the ground. George-Phillip felt his neck wrench and his head hit the back of the seat hard and his vision went dark for a moment.

The engine, mounted on the right side of the tail of the plane, instantly exploded, sending hundreds of metal shards ripping through the rear cabin of the plane. George-Phillip grabbed for his daughter as a fragment of shrapnel punched a fist sized hole in the cabin no more than a foot in front of him. The screaming from Adriana and Jane didn't stop as the plane tipped over, the ground now above their heads, now below them, as the plane went into a dangerous spin and began to dive for the ground.

The flight attendant didn't scream. Thrown to the floor of the cabin by the intense G-forces, her neck was broken.

Air bellowed through the cabin, an animal cry of pain and rage as the plane strained to keep itself intact as it raced for the ground. George-Phillip floundered for breath. Next to him, Jane's head was canted forward and her hands were covering her face. She shrieked in short, extremely high-pitched bursts with gasps of air in between.

He leaned toward her, wrapping his arms around her and began to sing the first thing that popped into his mind, a lullaby his governess had once sung to soothe him.

Bah, Bah a black Sheep,
Have you any Wool?
Yes merry have I,
Three Bags full,

One for my master,
One for my Dame,
One for the little Boy
Who lives down the lane.

The words came out naturally and he sang them in a strong voice, desperate to overcome the terror that gripped Jane. Her shrieking continued, but it began to abate as he sang the lyrics as loud as he could.

Then the air masks popped out of the ceiling compartment and began flapping around in the air, buffeted by the terrible winds and crosswinds as the plane tilted this way and that. George-Phillip could see the ground getting closer and closer outside the plane, but it was no longer spinning around them. Rather, the plane had stabilized upright, more or less, pitching and yawing to the left and right drunkenly. Jane's shrieking subsided, though Adriana's hadn't.

But the ground was getting closer and closer, trees and houses and swimming pools and schools and shop racing by below, first on one side of the plane, then the other. George-Phillip thought he was going to vomit, but then a loud thump threw the cabin again.

Dylan. May 7.

Dylan was calm, though his mind raced, as he stuffed his books, cash and medication into a bag. The Captain had already informed him that federal agents were at the gate of the Embassy, ready to take custody of Dylan.

Once he finished packing his bag, he turned to the Captain.

"May I call my wife?"

"Of course." The Captain's expression wavered. He looked at the door, then to the window, then to Dylan. He met Dylan's eyes. "Do I have your word you won't try to escape? That you won't attempt to go out the window?"

Dylan met his eyes. Then nodded. "Yes."

"Then I'll leave you some privacy." He stepped outside into the hall, closing the door behind him.

Dylan took out his cell phone and dialed Alex's number. It went directly to voicemail. She must still be on the metro.

"Alex, it's Dylan. Listen to me carefully. The Embassy is turning me over to the feds. That's happening right now. I'll call you as soon as I know anything, but I don't know how long that will take. Have Carrie call Bear and Prince George-Phillip as soon as possible."

He paused, eyes darting to the window. He'd promised.

"I love you," he said. Then he hung up the phone and opened the door.

The Captain stood there, waiting for him. His face was unreadable, but Dylan was grateful he'd been given a chance to make a phone call.

"I'm ready," Dylan said.

He felt grim as he followed the Royal Marine out of the residence and toward the front of the ground, the reverse of the walk he'd made escorted by other Marines just a few days before.

Outside the Embassy gates, he saw a man and a woman, both in suits. On the left, the man was stout, his face almost chiseled, an unmistakably Irish face. Beside him a woman, taller, with almost-white hair.

"Dylan Paris?" the man said as the Marines opened the gate and escorted him outside.

Dylan said, "Yes."

"I'm Scott Kelly. Diplomatic Security Service. You're under arrest."

George-Phillip. May 7.

George-Phillip's teeth collided as the plane lurched up with a loud bump, and a rush of blood poured into his mouth. He'd bitten his tongue. Outside, the world swung wildly as the plane continued to swing left and right.

"We're going to attempt an emergency landing. Everybody make sure your belts are tight. Take the brace position, hands on your heads, lean forward and touch the seat in front of you, feet flat on the floor. Landing in seconds."

George-Phillip pushed Jane forward, helping her into the position, then leaned his own head against the back of the seat in front of him. The plane had leveled out, and outside he could see lights flashing by. The sky was still rose above them, but it was noticeably darker this close to the ground. Then the lights disappeared, and he could see water, racing underneath the jet.

He felt an inhuman thrust as the plane hit the water, nearly throwing him from his seat, belt or not. A crash, then another crash, the plane went skipping along the water like a flat stone thrown against the surface of the pond.

The plane hit the water again, tilting to the right as the nose swung left. A moment later the plane was stopped.

The pilot was in the doorway immediately. "Everybody to the front door!"

Ahead of him, Adriana unbuckled her seat and lurched toward him. "Jane!" she called.

George-Phillip had already unbuckled Jane's belt and swung her to his hip. "She's all right. We have to go before this thing sinks."

Water was already pouring into the cabin from a dozen or more holes in the aft of the cabin. The flight attendant's body was nearly covered with water now.

The pilot threw open the front door and a moment later a large yellow raft filled with air just below the door.

"Come on, then!" the pilot shouted. "Go! Go! Get on the boat!"

Adriana went first, then George-Phillip strained to pass Jane to her. Jane wasn't moving, she seemed almost catatonic, her eyes wide open, her face frozen. He leaned forward, holding the girl out the door of the plane to the life raft. A wave separated them for a moment, leaving a gap of black river water beneath Jane just as he began to lose his grip.

Then Adriana was there, her arms glued around the little girl. She sank to her knees in the center of the boat.

George-Phillip boarded next, followed by the navigator, two other crewmen, and finally the captain.

"Row, sir. Row." That was the captain, who was holding an oar out to George-Phillip. The Prince took the oar and began to paddle, opposite the crewmen across from him. Not far upriver, a huge bridge, and to their left George-Phillip could see emergency vehicles, lights flashing, along the edge of the water. The pilot had managed to maneuver them not only to the river, but back toward the airport.

Behind them, the plane sank into the river, marked only by a gush of bubbles as water rushed into the cabin of the plane.

CHAPTER TWENTY-ONE
He was the devil

Adelina. May 8.

Dreams.

Adelina knew she was asleep in the dead of night, even as she stared around her at the fog clouding her world. She hadn't slept well, nightmare visions of her daughters attacking an assassin from behind flashing repeatedly in her brain.

Andrea. Sarah. The two girls had acted instinctively and viciously to protect their mother and sister.

She tossed and turned, the painful crick in her neck taking on titanic proportions, a swollen red throbbing welt of rage flooding from her heart to her soul.

The rage would never dissipate. It would never scatter or melt away. Thirty years was too long to contain the lies. Thirty years was too long to hold that rage. Now was the time for her rage to become vengeance.

A flash of memory.

George-Phillip, twenty-one years old. A baby, younger than three of her daughters were now. He'd swept her up in his arms. They'd been stupidly reckless, stupidly open.

The Cherry Blossom Festival, spring of 1984. She'd worn a scarf over her hair and he'd worn sunglasses, but neither of them took any other steps to hide their identity. In a haze of drugged love they'd walked around the tidal basin near the Jefferson Memorial, hand in hand as the beautiful white and pink petals rained down around them. He'd pinned a flower in her hair, and they stood looking out to the water.

In her dream they lay down in the grass and he ran his fingers through her hair. She closed her eyes, a shiver of goose bumps running down the back of her neck as he kissed her.

Oblivious. *Stupid.*

Because it was an outing like that which had brought the attention of Oz.

George-Phillip was swept away, and she was walking barefoot along the cracked sidewalk in Bethesda, the condominium she'd hated so much towering above her. Her prison. The place she'd given in to despair. She walked up the stairs of the building, her feet moving through sludge and dirt, until she reached the penthouse floor. Walking down the hall, her footsteps left thick black footprints on the carpet.

The front door was open, and she walked into the condo like it was the gateway to hell. Julia was on the floor, two years old, her curly brown hair hanging in her eyes, wailing, and her face red. Above her, pinned to the wall with a steak knife, a note.

I told you to stay away from him!

Without transition she was in the formal dining room of the San Francisco home. Julia was older now, standing across from Adelina, her face twisted in rage, her teeth visible.

Yes, you do! You've treated me like dirt for the last eight years! Her shout was a dagger. *When I came home from that hideous abortion clinic in Beijing, you never even asked me what was wrong or where I'd been! Didn't you notice all the blood on the sheets, Mom? Didn't you notice how sick I got? I needed a mother and all I had was...*

Adelina wanted to cry, *I didn't know! I didn't know!*

Her eldest daughter, her first love, shook her head. *Nothing. Not once were you there when I needed you. When Lana sent that picture out, you didn't offer to help. You didn't hug me, and tell me it was going to get better. Someone in Bethesda Chevy Chase made copies and stuffed them in people's lockers at school. They tortured me, Mother. To the point where I couldn't see any way out but suicide. And what I've never understood, to this day, was why? Why wouldn't you help me? Why weren't you there when I needed you?*

Every word felt like another punch through her heart. Adelina stared at her daughter in shock. *Suicide?* She'd known all along that Julia was hurting, was isolated, but every time Adelina reached out to her, she jerked back. Her little girl had tried to commit suicide! Because of her. Because she was a failure. Because as hard as she'd tried to protect her daughters, she'd failed every single one of them.

Adelina started to cry. *I ...* she whispered. *I didn't know it was so bad for you. You're my daughter. I just wanted ... I wanted you to be better.*

Bitterly, Julia had replied, *You wanted to protect yourself.*

Adelina shook her head, clutching her hand to her chest, trying to soothe the pain that was radiating from her sternum. She couldn't tell Julia the truth. Richard would—no ... she couldn't even think of what he might do. What he might say. How he might hurt Adelina or one of the children. She remembered his horrible voice.

I'll take Carrie and sell her to the highest bidder.

Would you kill this baby to save that one?

She scrambled for words that would express part of the truth, but would protect the awful secrets at the heart of their marriage. *No ... that's not it at all. Your father and I ... we went through a really rough time in Belgium and in China. We thought ... we'd fallen out of love. And he had an affair in Belgium. And ... yes. I did in China.*

Julia's face twisted in disgust and contempt, and Adelina swayed on her feet. *So you were just too preoccupied.*

Julia ... what happened in China?

Then her daughter told the awful story, of getting involved with Harry Easton, the British Ambassador's son. That she'd been pushed into sex far too early, that she'd gotten pregnant. That the awful night she came home hours late, covered in snow, had been after an abortion. That the illness Adelina had believed was the flu had been the effects of too much bleeding. Adelina had kept her own secrets, and her daughter had learned to do the same.

It was hell, that they both could say so many words and at the same time obscure the real meaning behind them.

The blackness swept over Adelina. It swallowed everything, every thought and emotion and even her sight. Because Julia was right. No one had helped her. No one had been there for her. Her sociopath father had so effectively isolated Adelina from her own daughters that they *hated* her.

That was confirmed when Carrie, the daughter Adelina had always depended on, the one she knew she could count on no matter what, dismissively looked away from her.

Carrie murmured to Julia, "You've got family now. You've got me."

And that was right. Because, after all, it was Carrie who took care of Adelina's daughters. The grief she felt at that moment was greater than she'd ever felt before. Greater than the loss of her father. Greater than the loss of her own life when Richard so carelessly enslaved her. Because what she'd lost wasn't a *thing*, it was *her daughters*. The pain was so bad that she knew if she didn't get away *right then* she was never going to stop screaming.

So she ran. Adelina ran from her daughters because she could no longer face them. She ran into her room and locked the door and buried her face in a pillow and screamed her rage and pain and loss at God. God didn't answer. She'd lost the ability to feel Him, and even *that* loss didn't compare with the pain of losing her daughters.

In the dream, Richard somehow came *into her room*, he stood there above her, his face bright, his lips curled up in cruel amusement, as he said, *You see? None of them will ever believe you. You think they do, but they're mine. Just as you are.*

In the strange way dreams do, her room grew and lengthened. It became the ballroom at the Embassy in Beijing. Richard stood in front of her, hate and contempt in his eyes. Julia and Carrie were behind him, and they were tied up in a web of spit and lies, while George-Phillip pleaded with her. *Leave him, Adelina.*

Leave him!

I can't! Her daughters were behind Richard, and he would do anything to keep her enslaved, he would do anything to win. He turned to Julia and Carrie and began to whisper and croon in their ears, even as his hand behind his back crept forward, a wicked curved knife curling from his palm.

He was the devil. She was married to the devil. And she would never be free.

The violence of her screaming shook the walls and windows of the tiny motel in Abbotsford and awakened all three of her daughters. Jessica moved sluggishly, bringing her knees to her chest, her eyes wide as Adelina thrashed, terror in her eyes, as she scrambled back to the head of the bed, eyes searching everywhere for Richard.

It was Sarah who ran to her, followed shortly by Andrea. Then all three of them had their arms around her, and her screaming subsided into unfettered sobs.

Bear. May 8.

When Bear arrived at the house in suburban Virginia, he was, as always, startled by how neat the landscaping was, how precise the rows of flowers and rock beds were, how neatly the mulch surrounded the trees. Bear had never been suited for a life in the suburbs, and when he and Leah had lived together, their yard always had the ragged look of a bad haircut too many weeks in the past. Now, she lived in a home where the Kentucky bluegrass lawn was cut precisely two and a quarter inches long, where the flowers were nourished into a parade of colors.

It was days like this when Bear hated the man who had married his ex-wife.

He walked up the steps (which had obviously been swept that morning) and knocked on the door.

Gary Simpson answered. Of course. He looked much better than he had the last time they saw each other, a few hours after Leah was shot.

"Bear," Gary said.

"Gary. How is she?"

Gary said, "Come on in. The kids have been asking for you." He moved into the house, his huge frame surprisingly delicate.

Before Bear even made it in the door, a flash of brown hair and blue eyes raced to him, and then his daughter Rebecca's arms were around him. He lifted her up; arms wrapped around her, and breathed in the scent of her hair.

"Daddy," she whispered.

"Hey, sweetheart. How are things?"

He set her down. A few feet away, Jimmy, her fourteen-year-old younger brother, eyed Bear with a wary expression.

"I missed you," Rebecca said.

"Missed you too," Bear said. He blinked his eyes and rubbed them. Damn allergies. "How's your mom?"

"She's getting better," Jimmy said in a serious tone. "Have you caught the people who shot her?"

Bear walked in and sat down on the couch. "I'm working on it. Getting closer."

Jimmy frowned. "Why are you here, then?"

Bear sighed.

"Leave him alone, Jimmy." Rebecca's tone was contemptuous. "He came to check on us. And Mom."

"Shut up." Jimmy's tone was curt.

"*You* shut up."

Bear grimaced, then reached out and grabbed both of his surviving children and pulled them into a rough hug. "*Both* of you shut up. You don't need to fight."

Jimmy struggled for a moment, but Bear didn't relent. Finally the boy sighed and let his arms down. Only then did Bear let him go. He stood and said, "All right. Let me talk to your mother."

"She's in the back," Rebecca said. "I'll show you."

Bear felt distinctly uncomfortable as his daughter led him down the hall to the bedroom Leah shared with Gary. He didn't especially want to see the room. But he wanted to know she was okay. *Ex*-wife or not, he wanted her to be okay. It's not like they had parted in a wave of recrimination and rage. Their marriage just died, right alongside Leanna, their eldest daughter.

Rebecca knocked on the door and opened it at Leah's prompt.

Leah was sitting up on the bed, a pile of pillows propping her up. She had a book laying face down on the bed next to her, and a copy of *Guns and Ammo* was on the nightstand on her side of the bed.

"Hey, Leah. You've looked better."

She snorted. "I looked worse a few days ago. They let me out of the hospital yesterday. But it still doesn't feel good to have a hole in my side."

"When are you gonna be back at work?"

"Doctors say thirty days at least. I might have to do physical therapy. So light duty for the next few months."

Bear's face fixed on a large painting on the wall. It was three feet by four feet. Oil on stretched canvas. A mostly tan background, cloudy, as if up in the sky. Or in *heaven*. Because stretched across the canvas in a joyous pose was an angel, wings swept back. The angel bore the face of Leanne.

He choked a little and felt his eyes tear up. He looked away from the painting, then back to it. "Ahhh, *crap*," he muttered. "Where did that come from?"

Leah said in a near whisper, "Rebecca painted it for me. Sometimes it helps. You know. To remember she's happy now."

"Shit," Bear whispered. Then he did something no self-respecting lawman did. He choked back a sob. Suddenly he felt his younger daughter's arms around him.

"We miss her too, Dad," she whispered.

"You painted that?" he asked.

She nodded, her face sober. "Last year."

"Well." He took a deep breath, trying to get a hold of himself. He wiped the back of a fist against his eye, smashing the tear before it had a chance to roll down. He looked at Leah. "You know it's not too late to leave that scrawny accountant and come back."

Leah gave him a sad smile. "You know it is, Bear. Don't start that again."

He nodded. "Yeah I know. Joking."

"How's the case going?" she asked.

He shook his head. "You wouldn't believe it. You been watching the news?"

"A little. I watch it, but I don't understand it. Someone shot down Prince George-Phillip's plane last night? Fox News is going insane, they're talking about bombing Syria."

"Keep watching. And check the *Post*. Anthony Walker. I think the whole story's going to be out there soon. But I'll tell you this. It's nothing like we thought it was when that girl was kidnapped two weeks ago. And it sure isn't what the news thinks it is."

"You'll solve it if anyone can."

"I've got some help," he said. His voice was steadier now that they were talking work and cases. "Look ... I just wanted to check on you. I'm gonna get the sons of bitches who did this. I promise."

Her reply was a whisper. "Thanks."

He stood. Then awkwardly, he rested a hand on hers for a second. Then he jerked back. Rebecca was still near the door.

He said, "All right, kiddo, I'll catch you later. You take good care of your mom. And your brother."

"I always do," Rebecca said, her lips curling up in a grin.

Their goodbyes were brief and awkward, as always. Then he got back on the road, headed into the city. He still had a lot of work to do. But emblazoned on the back of his mind was the painting Rebecca had created, showing her older sister in heaven.

Richard. May 8.

The hearings had adjourned for a couple of days, though they were due to resume on Monday, with Leslie Collins testifying. In the meantime, Richard Thompson received a call from the White House, requesting his presence at a meeting at the State Department.

The White House Chief of Staff, Denis McCullough, had said to him, "Given the sensitivity of the situation, we'd like you to come in the back entrance at the loading dock. Be there at eleven and you'll be met."

Richard had nearly refused. You didn't ask a US Ambassador and former acting Secretary of Defense to meet at the back door like a criminal or servant. At the same time, a request from the White House wasn't a request; it was an order.

So at eleven that morning he'd approached the loading dock entrance of the State Department. A young man in a plain suit stood there next to the armed security guards. "Ambassador Thompson? I'm Rick Nabors, with Diplomatic Security. Please follow me."

Richard followed him. Down the ramp and into the cavernous garage at the back end of the Main State building. In the heat, he smelled the stench of garbage coming from a dumpster. Two delivery trucks were backed up against a filthy loading dock. Richard felt his rage building as he followed the arrogant young man up the stairs to the loading dock. They cleared another guard then he followed down the hall of the basement.

Despite his thirty-year diplomatic career, he'd only once been in the basement of this building. The bowels of the State Department were reserved for functionaries and mechanics, computer administrators and transportation functionaries. The cogs who made sure the organization functioned, but not the leaders, not the men and women who made the decisions.

Consequently, he was livid when Rick Nabors stopped at a bare door halfway down the hall. Richard could still smell the dumpster outside.

Nabors opened the door and said, "Please have a seat. You'll be joined in a few minutes. I'll be just outside the door if you need anything."

Richard stood and eyed the tiny conference room with a jaundiced eye. A *metal* conference table, painted steel grey, sat at the center of the room. Six cheap looking chairs with fabric cushions surrounded the table. Against the wall was a wall of metal shelving stacked with various kinds of equipment Richard had no name for. Circuit boards and boxes and wires. It was dusty in here.

A pitcher of water with ice sat in the center of the table with four glasses.

This was appalling. It was as if the meeting had been engineered solely to tell Richard that he was no longer in good graces. He took out his phone, ready to fire off an angry email to the Chief of Staff at the White House, when he realized he didn't even have a cell phone signal in here.

Then the door opened. He didn't need to call the Chief of Staff.

James Perry, the former Massachusetts Senator turned Secretary of State, entered the room first. Behind him was Denis McCullough, the White House Chief of Staff, responsible for the political survival of the President. Stout and grey haired, McCullough looked ridiculous standing next to the lanky James Perry. The third man to enter was Admiral Barry McFarlane, the National Security Advisor.

Richard came to his feet.

McCullough spoke first. His voice was jovial, friendly, despite the fact that they were meeting secretly in the basement of the State Department. "Richard! So nice you could make it."

The men shook hands and McCullough said, "Why don't we get started."

Interesting. Of the three men, McCullough technically had the lowest rank. The fact that he seemed to be leading the meeting made it clear that this was more political in nature than it was related to national security.

"All right," Richard answered.

McCullough leaned forward. "Ambassador Thompson—"

"Richard. Please." Richard tossed out the pleasantry automatically.

McCullough's face soured a little. "Ambassador Thompson—we've got a few issues we need to discuss with you. As I'm sure you can imagine, the President never imagined when he tapped you as Secretary of State that we'd be facing corruption investigations, kidnappings and murders."

Richard leaned forward and said, "Those are hardly my fault—"

McCullough said with a straight face, "Please do not interrupt me again." He picked an imaginary piece of lint from his coat sleeve.

Don't interrupt me again. Richard felt those words rush down his spine like poison. If a low level political functionary like Denis McCullough could speak to him like that, then he was sunk. It was over.

McCullough went on. "As I was saying, the President never imagined this series of events would take place. Fox News is having a field day. Afghanistan has lodged a complaint with the International Criminal Court. And the Chief of the SIS was *shot down* over American territory last night."

Good riddance, Richard thought.

"In short, Ambassador Thompson, you're embarrassing the President and the Administration. We're losing approval ratings in the polls. We need to find out how to put a stop to that bleeding. Now."

Perry looked at McCullough as if he'd discovered he was sitting next to a giant bug. His nostrils were flared and his eyes narrowed. He turned away from McCullough and leaned forward. "I have one question for you, Thompson. Were you responsible for procuring the chemical weapons which were used against the civilians in Afghanistan?"

"No. I was not."

Admiral McFarlane just sat there, not saying a word. It was disturbing.

Perry said, "Do you have any way of corroborating that? Any evidence? You told the Senate committee that you filed an official report. But there's no evidence of that."

"Collins probably destroyed it long ago. He's the deputy director of the CIA. If anyone could do it, he could."

McCullough interrupted. "We want you to fall on your own sword. The President will guarantee you'll never see the inside of a courtroom or jail cell. But this needs to end. We want you to take full responsibility, tell the world that you lied and that the President knew nothing."

Richard leaned forward and said, "And what about justice for those civilians? Does Leslie Collins walk away free?"

Perry shook his head. "You are the most cynical human being I've ever encountered, Thompson."

McCullough said, "Do it. We'll guarantee your immunity, Thompson."

Richard shook his head, then spoke, his voice rising in volume as he continued. "Never. Those banks accounts were frauds set up by Leslie Collins, and he's the one responsible for killing the civilians. I've been in government service for thirty years. I've been Ambassador to China and Russia and was President Bush's envoy to Iraq to try to stop the war from happening. I've been through a thousand background checks and there's never been a breath of scandal. How *dare* you?"

McCullough looked at Perry first, then the Admiral. Both shook their heads.

Then he looked back to Richard. "In that case, Ambassador, you can count on the President's opposition. You'll be crushed, and still held responsible for your crimes. We're done here."

The three men stood, and Perry led the way out. Richard sat in his seat, stunned at the sudden reversal. Unless he could get the Republican leadership to back him, then he had no hope. Right now, that didn't seem likely at all.

The door opened again, and the young Diplomatic Security Agent stuck his head in the room. "Ambassador? I'm to lead you out the back door."

CHAPTER TWENTY-TWO
Wear your seatbelt

Anthony. May 8.

In the ten years of Anthony's career as a reporter, he'd been through a lot of rundown and messy airports.

But Kabul International Airport took the crown. It was stifling hot inside the airport, where the air conditioning had apparently failed. Crowds of Afghani men competed for space with soldiers from half a dozen nations, most of them armed with automatic weapons, which they displayed with surprising casualness.

He cleared Customs surprisingly easily. He'd only brought one change of clothing, an audio recorder, his phone and laptop. He would wear the same clothes for the entire trip, which would, with any luck, see him departing again in less than twenty-four hours.

That's if he didn't get delayed in the war zone, held up by Customs or local officials. And assuming Karatygin would even meet with him. And if Karatygin did, assuming he let Anthony leave alive.

A lot of assumptions.

As he left the secured area and walked toward the baggage claim, he saw a man holding up a sign with his name. Soldier. Former soldier, rather, now with a private military contractor. His uniform was indistinguishable from the US Army Combat Uniform, although it bore no insignia. A pistol was holstered at his right hip and a rifle slung over his shoulder. The Kevlar vest he wore looked heavy.

"Anthony Walker? I'm Iggy Mann. You got any bags?" His voice was the thick molasses of northern Alabama.

Anthony lifted the bag on his shoulder, saying, "Nice to meet you. This is all I've got."

"All right. Let's get going. We want to get to Charikar fairly quickly if you want to see Karatygin. Word has it his people are pulling out tonight."

Anthony cursed under his breath. He waved Iggy onward then followed him.

A small convoy of vehicles sat in the sun outside the building. Black sports utility vehicles with wide wheelbases and shaded windows.

"We're in the middle vehicle. You get in the back."

Anthony followed. *The Washington Post* was paying a fortune for this escort. It was unusual, but then again, Afghanistan was a very dangerous country. He opened the back door of the SUV and tossed his bag in, then took one last look at the airport.

Several signs were above the doorways, the largest one reading WELCOME TO KABUL in English. Armored vehicles with large mounted machine guns were at each end of the terminal, and two tanks flanked the road.

"Get in," Iggy said from the front passenger seat. His tone was irritated. "I don't need you getting shot before we even get there."

Anthony nodded, sliding over the seat and pulling the door closed behind him. Immediately, all three vehicles in the small convoy started moving. The first one stayed fifty meters ahead of them, and as it left the airport, he saw a man pop up through the sunroof, assault rifle in hand.

"All right," Iggy said. "I don't know how much they briefed you before you left the States."

"Nothing. I don't know anything." Anthony's tone was nervous.

Iggy shook his head. "Great. Whatever. Here's the deal. If everything goes right, it's an hour drive. If it goes wrong, it might be tomorrow. Soon as we get out of the airport we go down Russia Road through the city. That's the most dangerous part, because parts of the drive, we don't have any distance view or open fields of fire. We'll be going balls to the walls, moving through traffic as fast as we can to clear the city. All right?"

"Yeah."

"Wear your seatbelt," Iggy said, a smirk on his face. "Once we clear the city, it's a straight shot up A76 until we get there."

"And Karatygin is still there?"

Iggy shrugged. "Last night he was. I hear they're getting restless. The Russians still got a price on Karatygin's head, and the US wouldn't mind seeing him die too. On the highway we've got to worry about the Taliban hitting us, but once we're in Karatygin's camp, it's US drones. Either way you end up dead. So every step of the way, you listen to me. Clear?"

Anthony nodded.

Iggy turned back to the front. "This must be a pretty big story for you to risk this much."

It was, Anthony thought. It was the biggest story.

The moment they pulled out of the airport, traffic was dense. Buildings crowded both sides of the street, both the streets and the sidewalks crowded with people. The overriding impression color wise wasn't that different from Baghdad—dun colored buildings surroundings dun colored streets and people with dun colored clothing. Colorful signs decorated many of the buildings, but the general impression was one of disrepair. Trash littered the street, in some places piled up deeply in corners of buildings. Clearly the city had little in the way of sanitation workers.

A white pickup truck pulled in between the front and middle vehicles of the column. Four men wearing turbans and sporting Kalashnikov rifles lounged in the back of the truck, which had no license plate.

"Mother fucker," Iggy said. He gripped his rifle and gave directions into the radio. "Casey, let the white truck mosey on by."

Moments later, the SUV ahead of them moved to the left side of the road—blocking oncoming traffic—and let the white pickup go by. Once it was gone, they sped up, racing through traffic.

At one point in the ride, they were caught in a square full of pedestrians. The truck in front inched forward, honking its horn, with the two behind pushing their way. Iggy squirmed around in his seat, trying to look in every direction at once. He spoke into the radio again. "Casey, you need to move it a little faster. We're sitting ducks right here."

Anthony didn't hear the response. But the brake lights were still showing on the vehicle in front of them. Until the man in the sunroof raised his rifle high in the air. He fired a short burst, the staccato sound echoing across the square. Immediately the crowd scattered, everyone running as quickly as they could away from the vehicles.

The tiny convoy sped up, the road ahead of them completely clear. Less and less buildings to the right, and then they were headed out of Kabul into the open countryside of Afghanistan.

"How dangerous is this road?"

Iggy looked back at Anthony and smirked in response to the question. "From one day to the next it's peaceful as a cow farm or deadly as a snake's nest. All depends on how the Taliban is feeling today."

Anthony nodded. "How are they feeling today?"

Iggy lit a cigarette, filling the cab with acrid smelling smoke. "Pretty cranky, I guess. With US troops withdrawing, it's a matter of time. Taliban's been probing, attacking new areas. Ganging up on the roads around Kabul. It's like they's a vulture hovering, waitin' to dive in the minute the mountain lion is gone." He winked at Anthony. "Kabul's the carcass."

Anthony shuddered. Iggy was almost certainly right. It wasn't hard to see what was happening in Afghanistan, and from what he'd seen, violent incidents were up nearly twice as much the year before. The main difference was the on-going withdrawal of US troops. Before long, Afghanistan might be a Taliban stronghold all over again.

"Anyways," Iggy continued, "we got a pretty good system. We don't like driving this highway if we can avoid it, but when we do, we usually make it without any losses. That's our job."

Usually. That was reassuring. Anthony decided to go over his notes for his story. If he could keep himself occupied, maybe he wouldn't have to think about the possibility of getting blown up in the Afghan countryside. The SUVs were moving quickly now, very quickly. But they didn't have to worry about traffic, because there wasn't any.

Anthony slid his laptop out of his bag. He had a lot of notes, and a lot of loose ends to track down.

George-Phillip's interview had lined up perfectly with Adelina Thompson's, which was incredibly valuable. What it gave him was a clear timeline of when Richard Thompson was out of the country and events surrounding her marriage and Carrie and Andrea's parentage. He had a copy of the police report, provided by Julia, and a scan of portions of Adelina's diary, also thanks to Julia. He had their brief interview with Nick Larsden before his death, naming Oz. He had George-Phillip's *suspicion* that Oz was Oswald O'Leary—his longtime aide and assistant.

He scanned over his notes. George-Phillip's original investigation report fingered Richard Thompson as the primary mover in the Wakhan massacre, aided by Prince Roshan, Leslie Collins and Vasily Karatygin. Roshan and Collins had everything to lose if the truth came out. But Karatygin might not. He'd once been a major in the Soviet *Spetznaz,* or Special Forces. He'd converted to Islam and joined the mujahideen in the early 1980s, and because of his knowledge of Soviet tactics, training, and equipment he'd quickly moved to the top of Ahmad Shah Massoud's militia.

Except now, Massoud was a provincial governor. And he'd long since disassociated from his former ally. Karatygin had surfaced after the US invasion in 2001. He now ran an "import-export" operation, which Anthony took to mean smuggling. Probably weapons and heroin. Anthony didn't think the odds were very good that Karatygin would be willing to talk. But it was a possibility. Maybe he'd been sitting in the desert for the last thirty years as Collins and Thompson and Roshan rose to the top of their nation's security organizations, while Karatygin hid out in caves from the Taliban. Maybe he was a little bit resentful. Or maybe he was worried about what would happen when and if the Taliban took over again.

Anthony didn't know *what* he might be worried about, but he hoped that by the time he asked Karatygin the operative questions, he'd have figured something out. Karatygin had agreed to meet, but he hadn't raised the issue of the Wakhan massacre—yet.

Some things just didn't make sense. Oswald O'Leary might be Oz, but *why?* He'd been George-Phillip's confidante for thirty years. Why would he betray George-Phillip? What possible reason did he have? Was he somehow linked to Richard Thompson? Or was it something even more insidious?

At the sound of a gunshot, Anthony looked up suddenly. The vehicle swerved, accelerating suddenly.

Iggy turned around, his rifle at the ready and his eyes scanning everywhere. "Sniper fire," he said. "Probably from the village off to the left. Don't worry about it; the odds of a hit are pretty slim. The bigger issue is making sure we don't slow down or panic."

To Anthony's eyes, the headlong rush down the twisting highway appeared to be panic. But he wasn't in a position to say anything at all. He knew little about the country and even less about current on-the-ground conditions.

A few minutes later they reached an indefinable moment where Iggy and the driver appeared to relax. In the distance, Anthony could see a cluster of buildings too small to be considered a town and too large to be a village. Buildings made from cinderblocks and tan stone abutted each other in a tangled and unrecognizable jumble. The only color were clotheslines scattered through the village, brilliant greens, reds and blues waving in the air, brightly colored pennants of resistance against the chaos and grim fundamentalism sweeping the nation once again.

Before they reached the village, the small convoy turned on a road slightly to the left then circled around. On a hill a quarter mile from the town was a walled compound.

Iggy pointed. "Karatygin's camp."

Anthony stared in fascination. Men—obviously armed—were positioned along the tops of the walls and in a tower overlooking the entire area. It wasn't a camp; it was a fortification. He felt a chill as he wondered if he'd leave this compound alive. The only thing protecting him was the GPS tracking device he carried and the fact that the *Post* knew exactly where he was.

The convoy pulled to a stop at the gate of the compound. Two guards armed with what appeared to be US military issue M16 rifles guarded the gate. But these men were clearly not Americans. They wore linen trousers and tunics, loosely fitting, with combat boots and no helmets. Both had long unkempt beards. Anthony watched helplessly as the guards questioned the men in the front vehicle of the convoy. There was nothing he could do to influence the situation right now other than sit tight and wait. And hope they didn't all get shot. There were six armed guards in the convoy, but Anthony didn't think they'd last long if Karatygin's compound was full of hostile people.

The gate opened, and the guards waved them in. The driver started the SUV moving, and Anthony stuffed his notebook away.

Iggy turned around in his seat. "Keep your mouth shut until I tell you it's okay. These guys are dangerous."

Coming from Iggy and his crew of armed veterans, that was saying something.

Inside the compound were half a dozen small buildings clustered around one larger building in the center. As they pulled to a stop, Anthony could see that armed guards were stationed all around the square, weapons at the ready. Iggy and the driver got out. Anthony followed suit. The ground was uneven rock.

The various guards stirred, then went silent, as a tall Afghani walked out of the center building. He was dressed in traditional Pashtun clothing, loose linen pants and a tunic that hung to his knees. Nothing about his clothing indicated anything unusual about his position. But the guards looked slightly more alert, held their weapons a little higher, and stood a little closer to the convoy.

"Which one of you is the reporter?" the man asked.

Anthony swallowed. "I am."

The man approached and looked him over. "Anthony Walker." The words were a statement.

"Yes."

"Come this way. Vasily would like to meet you."

This was it. Anthony shrugged his bag higher on his shoulder and followed the man into the darkness of the largest building. They moved through a darkened foyer, down the hall and into a brightly lit whitewashed room. A large window opened into a courtyard, lush with palms and other vegetation. The room had hardwood floors—highly unusual in Afghanistan—and lush Persian rugs. Colorful wall hangings in bright patterns hung from three walls.

A reupholstered couch was against the opposite wall, with two bare wooden chairs facing it. A man lay on the couch, his back propped up on pillows. He was pale and gaunt, with wispy white hair, and held a paperback book with bright red Cyrillic letters across the front. His eyes were sunken, with nearly black circles under them, and one eye was pale with a cataract.

Clearly this was Vasily Karatygin. And just as clearly, he was sick or dying. His obvious illness, however, didn't reduce the man's size—he was *extremely* large and muscular, with a lip swollen on one side and a crooked nose. Both clearly the result of a fight probably decades in the past.

The man looked up from his book as Anthony entered. He spoke some words—in Pashto, Anthony presumed—to the man escorting him inside, who answered in a subservient tone.

Finally Karatygin said, in English, "So, you're the reporter who wishes to question me about Richard Thompson. Have a seat."

Anthony was jolted by the words. Nowhere in his remote communication with Karatygin's representatives had he specified the reason for his visit. He swallowed nervously, hoping that Karatygin had no plans to have him murdered.

Then he took a seat and said, "Yes. I'm Anthony Walker with *The Washington Post*." Anthony took his recorder out of his bag and displayed it for Karatygin.

Karatygin smiled, curling his lower lip back, revealing a long black scar on his lip and several missing teeth. Anthony pressed *record*.

"I am Vasily Karatygin."

"I never mentioned Richard Thompson," Anthony said. "Why do you believe he's the reason I'm here?"

"You obviously would never make much of a spy, Mister Walker. It's obvious. Thompson is in the news a great deal these days—as is the massacre at Wakhan. I can only presume that you are here to ask me questions about both."

Anthony stared at Karatygin. Of course he was right, and in retrospect, it *was* obvious. He shrugged and said, "Yes. That's what I'm here for."

Karatygin stared at him for a moment. The smile was curving back into a menacing snarl. "At one time I would have simply had you killed for your presumption."

Anthony looked back. He didn't want to push right now.

Karatygin's face softened. "You are a lucky man, Walker. Lucky indeed."

Anthony didn't respond. Instead, he simply waited, not knowing what Karatygin was getting at.

He didn't have to wait long. Karatygin said, "When I was a boy, Walker, it was a different world. I was a good communist, raised in a good communist family. None of that drugged religion for me. But one day I was in a fistfight at school. I was fourteen years old."

Karatygin's face looked wistful as he spoke. "My mother was at work, and my father long dead. So when I arrived home our tiny flat was empty. I do not know what was in my head, but I took the opportunity to search through my mother's things. Perhaps I thought I would learn something of my father. Instead, I found the medal of my namesake."

Anthony raised an eyebrow. Karatygin immediately answered. "Vasily is a Russian form of Basil. She had a Saint Basil medallion in her dresser."

"I don't know much about religion," Anthony said.

Karatygin chuckled. "And you think I did, growing up in the Soviet Union? Hah. It was years before I found out anything. Basil was a father of the Church—a supporter of the Nicene Creed. A man who fed the poor and helped prostitutes and thieves. A saint. This was my mother's ambition for me."

"And what now?"

"Now I'm dying. I have a tumor in my lung, and more in my bones, and soon I'll be more tumor than man."

"Can you not seek treatment?"

Karatygin gave a short shake of his head. "It's far too late for that. My mother's God wishes me to come home, and I am afraid."

If half the things Anthony had heard about Vasily Karatygin were true, then he *should* be afraid. Anthony didn't say so, however. Instead, he said, "You had no religion, but you became a defector. How did that happen?"

"The invasion of Afghanistan was *durak* ... ehhh ... stupid. Criminal even. We killed civilians on a grand scale, we tortured and murdered. All in the name of winning the Cold War. I was disaffected well before I left. You see not long after I finished school, I found a biography of Basil in an antique store. Hidden. I bought it. I wanted to know what it was my mother had seen in my future. And the more I read, the more vicious the fighting became. The more I learned of this man of peace, the more I watched my country murder. But even *that* wasn't the end."

Anthony listened, fascinated. He nodded, encouraging Karatygin to go on.

"In 1979 I was a Major in the *Spetznaz*—what you would call Special Forces or commandos. We were ambushed not far from Fayzabad. I was wounded and left for dead. It took me *one year* to recover. *One year* to regain my health. I was brought back to help thanks to the hospitality of the villagers and the protection of Ahmad Massoud's *mujahideen*." Karatygin shrugged. "I regained my health. I converted to Islam. That didn't take. But it took long enough for me to become the enemy of my country. I fought against them until the Soviets withdrew."

"And now?"

Karatygin laughed. "Now I try to stay alive. I'm lucky this bunch does not abandon me. Instead, they keep nursing me back to health every time my illness worsens. They won't do that once your story is told."

"Why not?"

Karatygin smiled, the dark gaps in his teeth a nightmare. "Because in my zeal to carry the fight to my countrymen, I murdered. Not a few. Not a dozen. Hundreds."

Anthony swallowed. Then he said, "What was your role in the Wakhan massacre?"

Karatygin grimaced. Then he said, "I was the perpetrator. I organized it. I went to Thompson and asked him to help me procure the weapons."

"The sarin?"

Karatygin nodded. "They were Soviet stocks. A mujahideen raid near Kandahar captured them, and they ended up in CIA hands. Leslie Collins—I'm certain you are familiar with him—ran the CIA operation out of Pakistan. Thompson was his right hand man."

"Where does Prince Roshan fit into this?"

Karatygin smiled. "He was their confederate, of course. Roshan was highly interested in the effectiveness of the weapons. At the time, the three of them had the idea that they could use them on a large scale against Soviet troops. I was happy to help. But we had to test them first to assess the effectiveness."

Anthony shuddered. "The incident in Wakhan was a test?"

Karatygin nodded. His eyes were wide. Frightening. "It was. A successful one, wouldn't you say? Everyone in the village died. Even the dogs and the sheep died. When we realized how deadly it was, Collins and Thompson wanted to do it again, against a Soviet base. But by the time we returned back to our base, we realized we had a bigger problem."

"What?" Anthony asked.

"The weapons were stored in a cave in Badakhshan. After filling the tanks on the helicopters, the fumes slowly spread through the cave, and killed everyone. We abandoned the cave, and the men who were there."

"Jesus," Anthony said. "How many?"

"Twenty or so. Not as many as the civilians we murdered."

"And what happened to the cave?"

Karatygin gave Anthony a toothy smile. "It's still there. The barrels are still there, although the sarin is long since gone. Everything is still there. Even the skeletons."

Dear God, Anthony thought. He would have done almost anything to get a look at it. But the trip would take hours—or days really, given the road conditions and the violence. If he even survived the trip.

Karatygin leaned forward and said, "You want to see it. Don't you? I can tell."

Anthony nodded. Then he said, "I've been in the village. I did a story for *The Washington Post* about the massacre three years ago. It's ominous. Skeletons everywhere. Nobody even went back and buried the bodies. The skeletons of children, in the street."

Karatygin said, "Sometimes I think those children will come back. I see them coming at me in my sleep."

Anthony stared at the man across from him. This man, along with the others, had committed a truly evil act.

Anthony said, "Why are you telling me all of this now? I don't understand. Why?"

Karatygin looked away from Anthony. In a low voice he said, "I'm not fool enough to ever ask for forgiveness. Not for the people I've killed. But someone must speak the truth. Shouldn't they? How are Thompson and Roshan and Collins any different from the men who sent me to Afghanistan to die in the first place? How are they better?"

He looked at Anthony with naked rage in his eyes. "They aren't different *at all*. For them it is all about power and pride and position. Every one of them went on to become a man of power. It's time someone brought them down."

Karatygin shouted in Pashto. A moment later, one of his men appeared. A burst of words from each, then Karatygin began to struggle to stand. He reached for a cane then finally got to his feet, tottering.

He looked at Anthony and said, "The helicopter is on the way. I will show you. You must come."

Anthony stood. Then he nodded. "Let's go."

CHAPTER TWENTY-THREE
Big fish

Bear. May 8.

Bear's apartment looked much the same as it had for days. Tiny. Empty. Alone.

He slumped into the seat at the tiny table where he'd scanned through Richard Thompson's personnel file days before. The file had been stolen, and he still didn't know who had done it. Perhaps Thompson himself. Or Leslie Collins. Whoever it was, this case had moved on from there. Bear didn't even know where to go or what to do next.

Anthony had left for Afghanistan the previous evening, leaving only a message stating that he'd gotten what he wanted from his talk with George-Phillip. It might have been helpful to know what that was. Marky Lovecchio had been captured in Canada—Bear didn't know the details behind that, other than the fact that it happened during an attack against Adelina Thompson and her daughters. *Oz*—Oswald O'Leary—had gone missing. At Prince George-Phillip's request, the National Crime Information Center had issued an alert asking local law enforcement to be on the lookout for O'Leary.

Bear sighed, walked to the refrigerator, and looked inside. No beer. *Crap.*

That's when the phone rang. He walked back to the table and picked up his cell phone. It was an unfamiliar number.

"Bear Wyden."

"Mister Wyden—this is Wolfram Schmidt."

For almost a full second, Bear thought, *who the hell is Wolfram Schmidt?* But that didn't last long. All he had to think of was the humiliation of being *arrested* by the Internal Revenue Service.

"What can I do for you, Schmidt? Is this a friendly call?"

A grunt at the other end, and the fastidious IRS agent said, "It is, Wyden. Actually, I'm calling because I'm boarding a flight back to Washington in a few minutes and I'd like to meet with you this evening. I think we may have information that might be useful to each other. I presume you know Scott Kelly?"

"From DSS? Of course."

"At Agent Kelly's recommendation, we'd like to invite you back onto the investigation."

Bear's mouth ran away with him. "I'm not doing anything to railroad those girls. They've had enough."

Schmidt said, "I'm not either. It's clear to me that much more is going on here."

Bear took a breath. He'd been ready to say something nasty to the IRS agent and hang up the phone, but now he had to pause. "I'm listening," he said.

"The grand jury is ... broadening the scope of our investigation. We're preparing to offer immunity to Adelina and Andrea Thompson in return for their testimony."

"Oh yeah? Their testimony against who?"

"Richard Thompson and Leslie Collins."

"Big fish," Bear said. "Collins, in particular."

"Mister Wyden, there are no fish too big for the Internal Revenue Service."

Jesus. Bear could almost see the evil grin on Schmidt's face.

"Okay. So you offer them immunity. You're expanding the scope of the investigation. To what? Thompson raping Adelina when she was a kid? The Wakhan massacre? What's your plan here?"

"You've been paying attention," Schmidt said.

"I was wondering if you had been."

"At this point we don't have enough to make anything stick for Wakhan, at least not for Collins. But we've got solid evidence of Thompson's involvement."

"Yeah? What evidence?"

"Given that one of our suspects is deputy director of the CIA, I don't want to discuss that over the phone."

Bear didn't answer. Instead, he thought about his missing file. Then he said, "All right. Let's say he's listening right now. What would you tell him?"

"I'd tell him he's as good as convicted."

Bear grinned. "I like you, Schmidt. When does your flight get in?"

"Eight o'clock at National."

"I'll meet you. But I've got one other question. What about Julia Wilson? She's been hounded by you guys. And I don't believe for a minute that she did it."

Bear didn't like the uncomfortable pause that followed. Schmidt finally said, "If this goes where I think it will, Julia will probably be in the clear anyway. But I can't promise anything."

Bear sighed. "I guess that's the best I can ask for. But I gotta tell you. It seems thin."

"We'll talk more later."

Carrie. May 8.

"I don't know what to do, Carrie! You *know* what it was like when he got arrested in New York."

Carrie half-listened as Alexandra talked. Rachel was listless this afternoon, and her fever had stayed steady at one hundred and one degrees. She'd spoken on Wednesday with the pediatric nurse, who reassured Carrie that the low-grade fever wasn't that unusual.

"If there's a change, I want you to let me know," the nurse had said.

Carrie wanted to demand a battery of tests. She wanted to take her daughter to the hospital and make sure *everything possible* was being done. The nurse brushing Rachel's fever off had nearly enraged her. But she'd calmed herself and not said anything offensive.

On an intellectual level, Carrie knew the nurse was right. Children got fevers, chills, coughs and colds. They got rashes and stuffed up noses and diarrhea. You had to pay attention and focus on good nutrition and keeping them warm and hydrated and covered up. But not every fever was a sign of severe illness. And not every illness required hospitalization.

That's what Carrie knew intellectually. She was a scientist, after all.

But what she knew in her heart and in her gut was something else entirely. In her gut, she knew that a series of hideous circumstances had ripped her husband right out of her life before their daughter was born. Before she was even sure that she was pregnant.

She couldn't lose Rachel too.

So her thoughts were wound deeply around her daughter. She was listless, but was she *too* listless? She had a fever, but was it too high? Rachel had spots of color on her cheeks and hadn't nursed much.

All Carrie could see was the worst. What if the nurse was wrong? What if she had some horrible exotic disease and the nurse had misdiagnosed over the phone? After all, she hadn't *examined* Rachel, and what were her credentials to diagnose her daughter anyway? When she closed her eyes all she could see was Ray, his body pale, as with a snap and click, one after the other, the monitors turned off and he was taken from her forever. All she could see when she closed her eyes was losing her daughter.

She remembered talking with Ray, right before he passed. She'd made a lot of promises. *I promise I'll be a good mother to our child. I'll be there for her, and tell her the right things. I'll listen to her problems and sing her songs at night and I'll teach her to be strong. I'll tell her about you. I'll tell her that her father did the right thing, always. That when it really counted, you told the truth, and you inspired other people to do the right thing too.*

That wasn't all she'd promised him. She'd promised not to smother their daughter with her fears, because she knew that might happen. *And I promise I won't be like ... I won't make her miserable either. I'll teach her to love you and remember you but not to let it overshadow her life. Because I know you wouldn't do that. You'd want her to be strong.*

That was a lot easier to say than do. And Rachel was only six weeks old. How hard would it be when she was six? Or sixteen? How would she deal with it when her little girl got a *driver's license,* or started dating, or—

"Are you even listening to me?"

Alexandra's question made Carrie jerk. She hadn't been listening. She'd completely forgotten her sister was there. Alexandra looked—not quite offended—she looked ... hurt. Vulnerable and wounded.

"I'm sorry, Alexandra, I just ... I'm so worried..." The words didn't even make it out of her mouth before she started to sob. She choked it back viciously. But she couldn't force back the tears that had already escaped.

Alexandra sighed. "I'm sorry, Carrie. I'm sorry. I'm scared. I'm really scared. I've called the FBI and the IRS and the DC police and no one will tell me where he is, and he hasn't called and…" Her face looked broken.

Carrie closed her eyes. She needed to pull it together. She whispered, "Look. We'll figure it out. Maybe Bear knows. Or … or … *shit.*"

Alexandra whispered, "I don't know how much more I can take."

Dylan. May 8.

Dylan Paris ran his hands through his hair and looked around the room for what felt like the ten thousandth time.

No exits had magically appeared. Instead, he was waiting for the return of the two cops who had been questioning him. He didn't know what agency they were from—Justice Department or FBI or CIA or IRS or whatever—but he did know he'd answered the same questions over and over and over again.

At least it wasn't like that awful night he'd spent in a holding cell in the New York City jail, crammed in with drug dealers and rapists and God only knew who else. They'd let him take his anti-seizure meds, which was good, because no wanted to see him flopping around on the floor choking on his own vomit.

Dylan sighed. He needed to go home. Badly.

The door opened, and in walked two people. He instantly recognized one of them—the man who had arrested him the previous night. He looked like Crank's dad, Jack, Irish, with dark hair and a friendly countenance. His partner, though, she didn't look so friendly.

The man sat down across from Dylan. The woman, with her black suit and silver hair, stood slightly behind the man. Dylan thought she might be prematurely grey. Her skin was smooth, not flawless, but youthful.

"Dylan, how ya' doing? I'm Scott Kelly, with Diplomatic Security Services. This is my temporary boss, Emma Smith. She's from hell. I mean the IRS."

The woman frowned, but didn't respond otherwise to Kelly's joke.

Dylan didn't respond.

"You doing all right?" Kelly asked again.

Dylan shrugged. "I'm in a jail cell. How good do you expect me to be?"

Kelly nodded. "Yeah. I get it. But you gotta understand, when you kill a federal agent, there are some questions that have to be asked."

Dylan shook his head. "I thought the agent who died was in the hallway. And was shot by Leah Simpson."

Kelly nodded. "Smart guy. That's true, Leah was the one who took him down."

"She didn't like me much," Dylan said. "At least I didn't think so. What happened to her? Did she have kids?"

Kelly said, "She does. She'll survive the gunshot wounds. In fact, she's been sent home."

Dylan closed his eyes. Good. *Good.* He opened them. "That's a relief, I'm grateful to hear it."

Scott Kelly's face immediately softened. "Well, she's not out of the woods yet. But yeah. Anyway. We've got some questions for you."

Without inflection, Dylan said, "No, I didn't know the attackers. I don't know where the drugs or the money came from. It can't possibly be Andrea's, because everything she had was lost when she was kidnapped. I don't know where she is now, or why she left the Embassy. Does that answer your questions?"

The woman standing behind Kelly—Emma Smith—said, "Mister Paris, I suggest you cooperate."

Kelly's response was much more visceral. "Don't be a wiseass."

Dylan leaned forward. "I'm not being a wiseass. I've been asked all the same questions over and over again since late last night. What the hell is this? Why don't you go look at the recordings?"

Kelly said, "Because we need to know who the hell is trying to kill people in your wife's family, asshole."

That instantly deflated Dylan. He sighed and said, "All right. Sorry. Look, I'm just frustrated. I don't know why I'm locked up when all I did was try to protect my sister-in-law."

Kelly shrugged. "It is what it is. I don't have a lot of say about that."

Silence. Dylan's eyes flickered to Smith, still standing behind Kelly. She didn't respond or clarify, which meant that she *did* have some say about it. Whatever. He would cooperate.

"Ask your questions. I'll answer."

"Why did you take the money with you?"

"I took *some* of the money," Dylan corrected.

"Why?" Kelly demanded.

"People were trying to kill Andrea. By that time she'd been attacked three times. I knew we were in danger and it was clear Diplomatic Security couldn't protect us. So I grabbed as much of the money as I could, along with one of the guns, and I met Andrea where we had agreed to rendezvous."

"Why did she go over the side of the balcony? That was a stupid stunt out of the movies."

Dylan shrugged. "Isn't it better to die trying to survive? Instead of rolling over and letting them take you out?"

Kelly nodded, his expression showing a trace of approval. The boss lady from the IRS didn't like that.

She leaned forward and said, "Where did the money come from in the first place?"

Dylan shrugged. "I don't know. Not long before the attack, Andrea called me in and showed it to me. She was confused—she said it was in the same closet she'd gone in that morning. Which meant someone planted the stuff during the day."

"Where was she that day?" Smith demanded.

Dylan closed his eyes and thought back through events. He'd been in class in New York when Alex urgently texted him that Andrea had been kidnapped. They left for Washington that night. The attack in Bethesda later that week. Adelina's phone call. The assault on the condo. The hideous hotel they'd stayed in, and the days of running after.

He shook his head. "It's all a blur. Too much has happened in the last week, I honestly don't have a clue."

Kelly spoke. "Take me through the events of that night. Starting with the money and the drugs."

Dylan closed his eyes. He tried to remember the details. How the room looked. How it smelled. The fear on Andrea's face.

Dylan? Can you come here a second?

He'd walked down the hall and into the bedroom she'd been using. In the closet, underneath a pile of clothes was a cardboard box. Full of drugs and money.

Those weren't in here yesterday, or this morning. I know—I went through the closet before I left to get the blood test this morning. Who was in here?

After he finished telling that part of the story, he said, "Then the phone rang. The house phone."

"Who was it?" Smith asked.

"The girls' mom. Adelina Thompson. She said … she said that Andrea was in danger. She told me to get her out of the building. The shooting started seconds later."

Smith and Kelly looked at each other, then back at him. Kelly said, "Did you know the attackers?"

Dylan shook his head. Then he said, "I didn't get a chance to see them really. Lot of shooting. A *lot*. Andrea went over the side of the balcony, and I hid behind the door. Leah was shooting at the attackers, but then she went down. I had a couple of knives and..."

He closed his eyes. He didn't want to think about it. He didn't want to see it.

Smith asked in a harsh tone, "You had a couple of knives and what?"

"Take it easy, Smith," Kelly responded. "He's talking. Let him talk."

Dylan said, "I had a big heavy meat cleaver and a long kitchen knife. The first guy came in dumb and fast, not paying enough attention. I got his gun hand with the meat cleaver. The other one came in right behind him ... he was disoriented, and I stabbed him in the back. I'm pretty sure it severed his spine, he went down instantly."

Kelly nodded and said, "I understand you're a veteran. Afghanistan? Iraq?"

"Afghanistan."

"Purple heart? How bad was it?"

Dylan grimaced. "I nearly lost my leg. It took a long time before I was able to walk again."

"PTSD?" Kelly asked.

Dylan leaned forward and said, "Are you suggesting my mental state somehow made me hunt down these guys and kill them? I assure you I was fully conscious of what I was doing."

Kelly's mouth twitched up slightly on one side. "What exactly were you doing?"

"Defending my home and my sister-in-law. I'd do it all over again in a heartbeat."

Kelly said, "All right. Let's move on—"

"Wait," Smith ordered.

"What?" Kelly asked.

"You killed them both. What was next? Is that when you left?"

Dylan shook his head. "No. First I grabbed as much of the money as I could fit in a bag. My meds and phone and wallet and stuff. Then I ran. The balcony door was still open, and I could hear sirens coming."

Smith moved to Kelly's side and leaned on the table with two hands, forcing Dylan to look up at her. "What about the drugs? Did you take any of those?"

Dylan recoiled. "Hell, no."

"Come on, Dylan," Kelly said. "You can tell us. We know the VA had you heavily medicated for a long time. You weren't even tempted?"

Dylan leaned forward and spoke slowly and clearly. "No. I did not take any of the drugs."

"All right," Kelly said. "Which way did you go out?"

Dylan sighed. "Down the hall toward the elevators. Leah was out there—I thought she was dead. Along with two other guys."

"Did you know Ralph Myers?"

Dylan shook his head. "No."

"Did you know *any* of the people outside?"

"Leah, of course. I thought she was dead. The guy about halfway down the hall, I didn't know. And the one closest to the elevators was part of the guard detail."

"Did you take the elevator down?"

Dylan shook his head. "No. Stairs. I figured the cops would be coming up through the lobby and elevators, and the stairwell opens out to the alley instead of the lobby."

Smith and Kelly looked at each other. "How did you know that?" Smith asked.

"When Ray was still alive, we used to sneak out that way when there were reporters out front."

Kelly said, "Okay. That clears up some things. What happened—"

Dylan interrupted. "How long am I going to be in here?"

"As long as it takes," Smith responded.

"Look. I want to help you. I want to nail whoever it is hurting my family. But keeping me locked up isn't—"

"We'll decide when to let you go," Kelly said. "And it's not right now. Tell me what you know about Richard Thompson."

Dylan shifted uncomfortably. Then he said, "He's a complete bastard."

For the first time in the interview, Emma Smith half-smiled. She said, "Go on. When was the first time you met him?"

Dylan leaned back in his chair. "I guess … about four years ago. Before I joined the Army. Alex and I had met on a foreign exchange program my senior year in high school. Richard had a background check run on me. He called me into his office to make sure I knew how worthless I was. Then later on, when I was recovering in the hospital, he sent me an email. Told me to stay away from his daughter. To let her believe I'd died in Afghanistan."

Dylan thought back to those days. Recovering in the hospital, sometimes wishing he were dead, the pain was so bad. He'd gotten through it, but just barely. He said, "Without Alex I wouldn't be anything, you know. She was with me through most of my recovery. Running with me. Helping me train. She … she means everything to me. Her dad didn't give a flying fuck about any of that."

"What else?" Smith said. "What else do you know about him?"

"What? You mean like his career? I don't know shit about that. I watched the hearings on TV while I was cooped up in the Embassy, so I know he was really CIA. That's about it."

"What about Julia and Crank Wilson? How well do you know them?"

Dylan sighed. "Pretty well. They're family. I mean, they're always on the road, but for the last couple years it's been holidays … and disasters. When Ray was in the hospital Julia basically took charge, got everything managed. She helped organized my wedding too. Crank's a great guy. They stop by and have dinner with us every time they're in New York."

"What about money? Do you think she was hiding anything?"

"Hell, no," Dylan said. "Why would she need to? Every single album Crank's put out went platinum. They're rock stars. And she's invested the money from that all over the world. But it's not like ... not like being friends with a rock star. He's just my brother-in-law. We hang out and smoke and talk bullshit."

Kelly said, "All right. We're going to break and grab some lunch. We'll be back later to ask you some more questions."

Dylan sighed in relief. The two agents left, and he was escorted back to his cell.

George-Phillip. May 8.

"And you just turned him over to the US authorities?" George-Phillip shouted. "Why? And why wasn't I informed?"

Ambassador Stephen Easton backed up a step toward his desk. The corpulent old fool had spots of color on his cheeks as he said, "Your Highness, I am the Ambassador here. Not you. You don't determine what happens—"

"I made a promise, Ambassador. There was no reason at all for you to do that."

"Other than the law and for our relationship with the United States. If the boy is innocent then they'll let him go."

George-Phillip leaned closer to the Ambassador. "Don't you understand that the person orchestrating these attacks is a senior official in their government?"

Easton licked his upper lip. Then he turned away, without answering, and sat in the heavy leather chair behind his desk. He wheezed a little as he sat.

"Please have a seat, Your Highness. I understand you are upset, but there are things we must discuss. And the Prime Minister is expecting our call in less than five minutes."

George-Phillip wanted to shake the old fool. Instead, he calmly sat down in the chair.

"That's a serious accusation," Easton said.

"It's a serious situation."

"Please explain Oswald O'Leary's part in all of this."

George-Phillip sighed. "I'm not entirely clear on it. Apparently Adelina Thompson—"

"The woman you had an illicit affair with. The wife of an American diplomat."

George-Phillip starred back at Easton. Then he said, simply, "Yes."

Easton blinked several times. "Go on."

"Apparently O'Leary was opposed to my involvement with her..."

"No wonder," muttered Easton.

"Shall I continue without interruption?"

Easton frowned. Then he casually waved a hand. "Continue."

George-Phillip told the Ambassador what he had learned of the mysterious Oz. "I don't know what his motivation was."

The phone on Easton's desk rang, interrupting George-Phillip's narrative.

Easton pursed his lips. "It's the Prime Minister." He reached out and pressed a button on the phone.

"Hullo!" he nearly shouted. "Prime Minister? Ambassador Easton and Prince George-Phillip here, sir."

George-Phillip exchanged greetings with Duncan Howard, the Prime Minister of England. He'd never liked the man, a career politician who had climbed his way into his chair over the backs of his friends. But George-Phillip didn't have to like the Prime Minister. All he had to do was tolerate him and for now, work with him.

"George-Phillip, I was incredibly relieved to learn you survived the plane crash."

"Thank you, Prime Minister. Though I should correct you on a minor issue— it wasn't a crash. We were shot down, and lucky to survive."

On the other end of the line, the Prime Minister coughed. "I understood that is not firmly established as of yet."

"Prime Minister, believe me. It was a surface to air missile of some kind."

"It's quite interesting," the Prime Minister said. "I spoke with the Home Secretary not long ago. The National Crime Agency identified who fired at your home last week."

George-Phillip jerked forward in his seat, his attention suddenly riveted. The NCA, or National Crime Agency, was the national policing agency responsible for border policing, among other things. "I'm listening, Prime Minister."

"It seems that a Saudi national named ... let's see ... Hakim Silsilah. Odd name, that. The border police discovered a weapon secreted away in the trunk of his vehicle during a random inspection as he was heading to the Chunnel. The weapon matches the ballistics of the bullets we found in your house. So Silsilah was brought in and questioned. And you're going to be intrigued by what we found."

George-Phillip said, "Please, sir. My daughter's safety is at stake here. *What have you learned?*"

"Your Highness, Silsilah worked for the Saudi Intelligence Agency. In exchange for an asylum and immunity offer, he's divulged that he was ordered to assassinate you."

"By *whom?*"

"Prince Roshan of Saudi Arabia."

CHAPTER TWENTY-FOUR
God Stuff

Dylan. May 8.

After the lights were switched off, all Dylan could see was the faint emergency light down the hall, flooding through the square, barred hole in the door.

Dylan had once, as a teenager, spent a memorable night in a holding cell in the Fulton County Jail in Atlanta as a result of a series of stupid decisions by him and his friends. No charges had been filed. A few years later, he spent a nightmarish night in the New York City jail. In that case charges were filed: after a drunken ex-boyfriend sexually assaulted Alex, Dylan had attacked him.

In both cases, the jails were old. They smelled of oil and grease and sweat. The odor of men who paced like caged animals, mixed with urine and vomit.

This was different. For one thing it was clean. Before the lights had gone out, he'd seen clearly that the concrete floor and steel walls were without blemish, the walls painted a grayish white, and the floor dark grey. The bed actually had linens, though the blanket was rough wool, something close to an Army blanket. He could live with that.

At least he was alone and he'd been able to call Alex. They'd given him that. Predictably she'd been distraught, and he'd only had a few minutes to speak before he was told to get off the phone. He supposed that was better than nothing.

He was restless, raging that he wasn't out there to protect his wife and her sisters. By the end of the interviews, he had been sure that they were going to let him go. Kelly had become more and more friendly, his body language clear that he believed Dylan. Smith seemed to stay more on the fence, but even she didn't seem as menacing by the end of the interrogation.

He needed to get out of here. Dylan had paced the room. He'd walked back and forth until his feet were exhausted, then lay on the bed, tossing and turning.

It wasn't the jail on his mind, or even the danger.

Instead, his mind kept turning back to the conversation he'd had with Alex days ago.

Maybe you should consider AA like your mom?

I can't do all that God stuff. You know that.

He couldn't. Because Dylan wanted nothing to do with a God who would allow children to be slaughtered. A God who allowed war, who allowed terrorists to destroy buildings and kill thousands of people. Dylan didn't want the God of his parents. Capricious. Sometimes overly harsh, sometimes overly permissive. They were drunks, until his mom cleaned up her act. She'd thrown Dylan's dad out and never saw him again.

Occasionally—especially when he was recovering from his injuries after the war—Dylan wondered what had happened to his father. But he'd never wondered enough to do anything about it. He'd never sought him out. He'd never done much of anything to change it, because he knew that his dad was still sick.

As was Dylan.

He couldn't hide it anymore. He couldn't hide *from* it. Since Ray's death he had been slowly sliding off into oblivion. At first it was one drink, then two, then two weeks later he was drinking to quell his anxiety and pain. He didn't get *drunk.* He didn't lose his capacity or ability to function. But after six months, he'd started drinking occasionally even in the morning.

Dylan knew what that meant. He'd turned into a drunk. He'd turned into his father.

Maybe you should consider AA like your mom?

It wasn't that simple. He knew a little about AA. After all, his mother had joined when he was still a teenager. They'd gone to war more than once after she cleaned up—she knew he was still drinking then and pushed him hard to quit. Eventually he had. But he never joined AA. Their emphasis on spiritual development and belief in God seemed little more than a cult to Dylan. His mother and father—drunk and erratic as they were—had at one time regularly dragged Dylan to church, before they fell apart completely. He didn't remember much from those days—he'd been very young. But he did remember the talk about hell. *Lots* of talk about hell. You'll go to hell for this and go to hell for that. You'll go to hell if you don't believe, you'll go to hell if you don't believe *enough*, you'll go to hell if you lie or cheat or steal or have sex or touch yourself or drink or dance too much or vote Democrat or make friends with people with brown skin.

Dylan wasn't interested in that kind of a God, and when his mother started harping about *love* and how her "Higher Power" had set her free from the bondage of drink, he'd just turned away. He didn't want to hear it.

But Dylan was beginning to wonder. Because in recent weeks he'd found himself more and more often staring into the bottom of a bottle. And for the last two weeks, ever since he and Alex had boarded a train for Washington, he'd found himself constantly craving a drink. Or four. It wasn't the tension and stress. He'd learned how to handle that in the Army. You just buckle down and keep going, no matter how much it hurts.

No. It was something more. He'd spent his whole life wrestling with feelings that he wasn't worth anything. That he'd never amount to anything. Every time he came into contact with Alex's family, it underscored that inferiority. Her sisters were scientists and ran their own companies and even the youngest was brilliantly talented. No wonder Alex's parents looked down their noses at him.

His old therapist at the VA had taught him mindfulness exercises, meditations he could do when he sat still and focused inward. Dylan had struggled with that for months. He'd get deeper and deeper, last longer and longer, but finally he felt like he pierced through and saw right into his center.

He didn't like what he saw. Inside Dylan Paris was a gaping wound, a hole. He'd once filled that hole with alcohol, then with overwork when he went back to school. He'd filled it with his concentration on being a soldier. And, unfortunately, he'd filled it with another person. With Alex. When he lost her, or thought he had, while he was in Afghanistan, it felt like his world had ended.

He loved Alex, and he would have done anything for her. But he'd slowly come to realize that she couldn't fill that hole either. And so he'd begun drinking again. He knew it wouldn't heal that raw wound. Nothing could do that. But it served as an anesthetic, for at least a little while.

Maybe his mother and Alex were right. But he didn't see how he could do it. He'd had quite enough of shame and self-hate. An angry, vengeful God on top of that?

He lay back on the bed, staring up at the ceiling, barely illuminated from the hallway. In a day or two at most, maybe a week, he'd be out of here. He'd done nothing but defend his family, and once that sank in they would let him go.

Dylan was afraid of when that came. He was afraid of what he would do when he got out. Because for the last twenty-four hours since he was taken into custody outside the British Embassy, he'd thought far less about Alex than he had thought about getting his hands on a bottle.

Ray would be disgusted. He could almost imagine him, sitting across the cell from him, leaning forward, and saying, *Get up, Paris. Your girl loves you and deserves better.*

He was right. But Dylan didn't know how he was going to do it on his own. He *couldn't* do it on his own.

So Dylan Paris groaned as he got out of the bed. And for the first time in his life, he got on his knees. The floor was cold, the concrete unforgiving, and his knees and ankles hurt, especially the one that had sustained such heavy injures in Afghanistan.

Dylan closed his eyes and whispered, "I don't know what I'm doing here, but if you're really out there, and you really give a shit, then I … need … help." He began to shake. He felt a heaving in his stomach and the wound in his heart, the gaping hole felt exposed, naked. It felt *dirty.* It felt like *shame.*

"Please," he whispered. Then he slid down to the floor, overwhelmed with grief, grief for his childhood, grief for the violence he'd witnessed in Afghanistan, but most of all, grief for Roberts and Weber and even Hicks and above all, grief for Ray Sherman. His best friend and confidante and the only person other than Alex he'd ever trusted.

In truth, he'd trusted Ray more than Alex. And as the pain washed over him, he found himself, for the first time, weeping for the loss of his friend.

Sarah. May 9.

Sarah Thompson sat in a chair next to the window of the hotel, looking out at Vancouver Harbor.

Initially they'd had some difficulty getting the suite. None of them had any credit cards except Andrea, who had a pocket full of pre-paid gift cards. After another attack, they didn't want to be in a traceable location anyway. But after the credit card fiasco the immigration officer who had temporarily approved Adelina's asylum request, Liam Tremblay, stepped in. The hotel opened its doors wide after that.

They were staying in a spacious suite, with a common living area and two bedrooms. Sarah and Andrea slept in one room, Jessica and Adelina in the other.

Now, as the sun slowly rose, the sky pink above the harbor, the buildings reflected in the water below, Sarah waited impatiently for Eddie to wake up and text her. He'd worked third shift the night before, so it would likely be some hours. It wasn't even nine in the morning back in Washington.

While she waited, she scrolled on her phone, commenting on the Facebook and Instagram feeds of her friends from San Francisco; friends she'd effectively lost when the accident happened. Instead of going home for her senior year, she'd stayed on the East coast and home schooled. Even the homeschooling had fallen to the side when her mother went back to the West Coast after Christmas. Sarah didn't know if she was going to graduate high school this year or not. She might have to go back and spend another year in school.

That was fine. She'd still stay in Bethesda. She was eighteen now, and her parents couldn't say squat about it, and she sure as hell wasn't going to leave Carrie behind. Or Eddie. If she had to go back to school she'd do it at Bethesda Chevy Chase, where Julia had gone *her* senior year, and maybe she'd kick some ass for her sister.

The opening, then closing of a door alerted Sarah.

It was her mother. Adelina Thompson walked out of the bedroom with a worn and sad expression on her face. She looked around, saw Sarah, and approached.

"Coffee's made," Sarah whispered.

Her mother did a detour, pouring herself a cup of coffee, then sat down in the chair next to Sarah.

"Beautiful, isn't it?" her mother said.

"Yeah. It is."

They sat in silence for several minutes. It wasn't an uncomfortable silence, but for Sarah, it was a little weird. All her life, her mother had directed everything. Sit here. Stand there. Wear this. Play that instrument. Sometimes Sarah had resented her mother, raged against her. But that was all washed away when her mother sat in bed with her, holding her as Sarah cried out in savage pain from her knee to her shin, desperately waiting for the time to come when she could take her morphine again.

Sarah spoke first. "How is Jessica?"

"She's recovering. The doctors were going to release her yesterday anyway, even if we hadn't been attacked. She'll always be at risk for another stroke, but … she'll recover."

Sarah ran her fingers through her hair and said, "No … I mean … how is she *doing?*"

Adelina smiled. "You always get to the heart of things, don't you?"

Sarah shook her head. "Not always. I didn't know anything was wrong with Jessica. I didn't know … anything at all."

Adelina reached over and took her daughter's hand. "She's doing better. In her heart. In her head. She hates me, but not as much as she hates herself. She's grieving for her girlfriend. But she didn't have a chance to properly grieve, because she was all alone."

"I don't think she hates you."

Her mother grimaced. "That's sweet of you to say, but it's not true. It's okay. I did my best to protect you all. I failed. But I did everything I could."

"I know," Sarah said. She squeezed her mother's hand. "I *know*."

Adelina's eyes widened a little, and she blinked, hard.

Sarah spoke again. "What can I do? For her?"

The answer wasn't what she had hoped for. "We pray. We love her. I'm going to accept the immunity offer. Saturday we'll fly to Washington. Then we take her home and let her know how much she means to us."

Sarah said, "I hate what he did to you. I *hate* him."

Adelina whispered, "No. Don't hate … if it hadn't happened, I wouldn't have you."

CHAPTER TWENTY-FIVE

Hey, Dad

George-Phillip. May 9.

"**B**ut why do you have to go?" Jane asked. She was still in her Hello Kitty pajamas, eyes blurry from sleep. Adriana hovered near the door of the room. It was four in the morning, and George-Phillip was dressed in a badly fitting Royal Air Force flight suit.

"Because the Queen and Prime Minister have asked me to, and you don't tell the Queen no," George-Phillip replied. "I'll be back by Sunday evening at the latest."

"But I'm scared," Jane said. Her face contorted. She was about to start crying.

George-Phillip kneeled beside Jane and put his arms around her. "Adriana will take good care of you. And so will Captain Forrester. I'll be back very soon."

"Can we go see my sisters soon?"

George-Phillip smiled. "Of course. I'll speak with Carrie about it as soon as I get back to Washington."

"Carrie's sad about the baby."

"She is. Rachel's very sick and that makes her mother frightened."

Jane pouted. "Can't she get her some medicine?"

"Well, Rachel needs a special kind of medicine that comes from another person."

Jane looked confused and skeptical. "Medicine comes from bottles."

Adriana chuckled.

George-Phillip smiled. "Some medicine comes from bottles. But Rachel needs a bone marrow transplant. That's something that comes from deep inside your bones, and there aren't many people who can give her what she needs."

"Would they die? The people who give their bones?"

George-Phillip felt his eyes water. "No, Jane. They don't give their bones, just part of the insides of them. They wouldn't die. Jane, I really have to go."

"I could give her some of my bones."

He winced. "No, Jane, I don't know about all that." He looked at Adriana, then back at Jane. "I must go now. The plane will be waiting for me."

He leaned close and kissed her on the forehead.

Thirty minutes later, he arrived at Joint Base Andrews just outside Washington, DC. The entire drive he fretted about Jane's declaration. For one thing, it was unlikely that she was a donor match anyway. Rachel was his granddaughter, and Jane his daughter with another woman. They didn't share much genetics.

On the other hand, George-Phillip would ensure he had himself tested as soon as he returned to Washington. The driver pulled to a stop at the gate and conferred with the US Air Force guard. Moments later they were moving again, following the careful directions of the guard.

He hadn't wanted to make this flight at all. Certainly not without Jane. But he had little choice. He'd done the best he could to ensure her safety, including substantially increasing the security detail at the Embassy. Unlike the charter flight which he had previous taken to Washington—and the one which was shot down—this flight was being paid for out of public funds as a national security matter. The attempted assassination of the head of the Secret Intelligence Service was a security crisis. The fact that a foreign intelligence service had been responsible for that potentially made it an act of war.

As a result, the Prime Minister had called for an emergency cabinet meeting. He wanted George-Phillip there in person. A grim George-Phillip had extracted one concession—he would be flown back just as quickly as the trip over.

The car pulled to a stop in front of the main tower next to the runway. A military officer in fatigues stood there with a small escort. One of the men in the escort approached and opened the car door for George-Phillip. Fifty feet away, George-Phillip saw what was almost certainly his plane—a Tornado Air Defense Fighter, the long-range mainstay of the Royal Air Force.

"Prince George-Phillip? I'm General Hainey, US Air Force. I wanted to extend my welcome to Joint Base Andrews, I'm the base commander here."

"A pleasure to meet you, General. You didn't have to arise this early to meet me."

The general smiled. "I'm always up this early, Your Highness. Let me walk you to the plane."

"Of course."

George-Phillip turned toward the aircraft and walked beside the Air Force general, who began speaking. "We've been running a continuous combat air patrol since your flight was shot down the other night, and the FBI is trying to track down who did it. In the meantime, I want to let you know how grateful we all are that you survived the crash."

"Thank you," George-Phillip replied.

They reached the aircraft. A crew was running through a series of checks, and the pilot approached.

"Your Highness? I'm Captain Warfield. You'll be riding in the back here. Climb on up, we're just finishing pre-flight checks."

George-Phillip climbed the rickety ladder up to the top of the aircraft. He'd never been this close to one, and was surprised to find how large the aircraft was close up. He threw one leg over the side, then the other, and slid into the bucket seat. He started to puzzle out the tangle of straps.

"Here, Your Highness, let me help."

Captain Warfield leaned over the side and attached the harness, then tightened the straps.

"Put your helmet on, sir, and we'll get going. The oxygen mask is here."

The captain showed George-Phillip how to get the helmet and oxygen mask adjusted then cautioned him not to touch any of the buttons in the back. "Those are the weapons systems, sir, so that would be a bad thing."

"I wasn't planning to, Captain."

The pilot had the audacity to wink at him. "You never know with passengers, sir. Or civilians."

George-Phillip grumbled, "I'll thank you to remember that I was a Royal Marine."

"You weren't eligible for the Air Force? So sorry, sir, that must have been disappointing." The pilot said the words in a deadpan voice as he dropped into the front seat and lowered the canopy. Before George-Phillip could think of an appropriate reply, the pilot said, "Have you ever flown in one of these, sir?"

George-Phillip coughed then said, "No."

"Just hold on tight then, sir. It's a little like flying with a jet up your arse." With that, the twin engines fired up, starting with a low moan, then a loud screaming roar that vibrated the interior of the fighter. For just a second, George-Phillip felt some level of panic. He was going to cross the Atlantic *in this?*

It was too late. The pilot continued to monologue as they taxied to the runway. "The flight will be about two and a half hours sir, we'll be traveling at a little over one thousand four hundred miles per hour, except during the mid-air refueling."

George-Phillip swallowed. "Mid-air refueling?" He was familiar with the concept, but had never seen the execution.

"That's right, sir. The yanks have a carrier group in the Atlantic right now, and they're being right hospitable."

With that, George-Phillip heard the words over the radio. "Royal Air Force One-oh-five, you are cleared for takeoff."

"There we are, sir," Captain Warfield said.

Then George-Phillip felt his entire body sinking into the thick padding in the bucket seat as the plane seemed to leap forward, the ground suddenly racing by beneath them. The plane bounced crazily on the tarmac until, fifteen seconds later, it left the ground.

"We'll be going to altitude right quickly, sir. Just relax."

The angle of the aircraft leaned further and further back, until it was almost climbing at a sixty degree angle from the earth. George-Phillip looked out. Already, the ground was far below, and ahead he could see the Atlantic Ocean. In three hours, he would be in London.

Dylan. May 9.

Dylan placed his hand on the glass and spread his fingers out. On the other side of the window, Alex did the same.

"I think they're going to let me go soon," he said. "The questioning—they can't possibly believe I did anything wrong at this point."

Alex sniffed and said, "I miss you, Dylan."

"Hey ... it's gonna be fine. I promise. I won't let you down."

She smiled.

"Time!" The jail guard in the public area outside shouted the word.

Alex jerked a little, and a tear ran down her face. "I love you, Dylan."

"Love you too," he said.

She stood, then leaned forward and blew him a kiss. He gave her a wry smile.

After his breakdown the night before, he somehow felt better than he had in—months, really. He felt calm and at peace. And he knew what he had to do when he got out of here. He stretched and stood up to turn away from the seat.

"Paris, wait there. You've got another visitor."

Another visitor?

He couldn't imagine who it could be. Dylan had finally been allowed to call Alex that morning, but he hadn't expected her to show up, and didn't know the routines for visits yet. But she had made the trek to the FBI's temporary holding facility in Greenbelt, Maryland to see him. She told him that the newspapers had somehow learned of his incarceration, and several confused news reports discussed his connection to the Thompson clan and what, if anything, he might be guilty of.

He sank back into the seat, wondering who the visitor could possibly be.

Dylan's eyes widened when he got his answer.

He was five-nine and a half inches. Hair a little longer than was in style these days, and greying at the temples. His face was weathered from years of too much drinking and too much smoking, and his hands had the rough look of a manual laborer. His clothes were clean, but threadbare—either very old, or he had gotten them at a thrift store. A bushy mustache, shot with grey, hung over his upper lip like a big furry caterpillar.

He smiled uncomfortably, revealing a gap between two of his teeth. "Hey, Dylan."

It was Larry Paris. Dylan's father.

It took Dylan almost twenty seconds to croak out the words, "Hey, Dad ... what are you doing here?"

"That ain't the way to greet your dad, Dylan."

Dylan started to stand, "I don't know why you're here."

"Now wait one second—give me a chance, boy."

Dylan paused. He felt rage like he hadn't experienced since the night Randy Brewer had assaulted Alex. He took a deep breath. And another. His therapist at the VA had said over and over again, *slow down your breathing and think before you react.* He sighed, then turned and sat back down.

"What do you want, Dad? I haven't seen or heard from you in almost ten years. Why are you here now?"

His father's mustache twitched. He said, "I miss you, boy. I've missed you horribly. But I didn't know where you was."

Dylan said, "Bullshit. You never even sent a letter. You never called."

"That's cause your mother kicked me out. Look ... Dylan. You're my son. I'm sorry. I wish I'd gotten in touch. After your mom kicked me out, I was in jail for a while, and I've been knocking around for a bit. I'm working now, though, I got a job landscaping in Manassas. I'm trying to clean up my act. I ain't had a drink in a year."

Dylan snorted. He found that hard to believe. Visions of his father swept through his brain. Larry Paris had been a nasty drunk, a *mean* drunk. He'd casually and regularly hurt Dylan's mom and sometimes Dylan. Jabs and twisted arms and slaps across the face weren't uncommon in his home. Nor were the kind of words you couldn't take back.

I ain't had a drink in a year.

The words sounded hollow, but they also reminded Dylan of the words he'd said to Alex. That he *would* get help. Was Dylan any better than the man who sat on the other side of the glass?

"I'm listening," Dylan said. He crossed his arms over his chest.

"I hear you live in New York City now. That you're going to some fancy college. Columbia? And you're married. That was in the paper."

"Yeah, I'm married. I love her."

"Paper said she's from a rich family—she the one paying for college?"

"No, Dad. The Army's paying for it."

His father's face fell. "You got hit in the Army. Paper said you were injured real bad."

Dylan was intensely uncomfortable that anything in the news was about him. Somehow he'd avoided much in the way of media coverage during Ray's court martial. But now anything and everything related to the Thompson family was being picked over by the media.

"Yeah, Dad. Roadside bomb. I nearly lost the leg."

"Well, it's a blessing you didn't, son. It's a blessing."

Dylan just nodded, waiting for his father to get to the point of his visit.

Larry Paris looked down at the floor, then back up at his son. "Son, I'd like to come back into your life, if you'll have me. I know I don't live in New York, but you could visit sometimes. I'd like to meet your wife one of these days."

Dylan shrugged. "I don't expect to be in this jail much longer. It was self-defense. But when I get out, I'm probably headed back to New York right away. We've missed exams and we're going to have to go beg for a second chance from the university."

"Well. Will you give me a call when you get out? I'll leave my number with you."

Dylan swallowed. He was trying to figure out if he had any feelings for this man other than disdain.

Was this what he was headed for? Was he going to be like his father?

His father spoke again. "Son, I got one other question for you."

Dylan sighed. "What's that?"

"Well, you see, I'm not comfortable with this, but I know you're married into a rich family and all. I'm—in a tight financial spot. You see, I lost my driver's license last year when I had a DUI. And I haven't been able to work much—"

"I thought you had a job landscaping."

"Well, I did until I lost the job. Anyways, I'm just wondering it you can maybe help—"

Dylan stood up. "Dad—"

"Now hold on—"

"Dad—"

"Dylan, I'm just asking for—"

"Dad! Stop! First of all, we probably don't have any money. If you'd bothered reading more in the papers, you'd know the IRS has been busy seizing everything the family has. And second—you haven't seen me in ten years. And you show up here asking for money? When I'm in trouble? Why don't you ask me how I am, Dad? Why don't you ask me how Mom is? Why don't you show me you give just one shit?"

Dylan turned away. Behind him, he heard his father shout, "Son! I'm asking you to forgive me. That's all in the past!"

Dylan looked back over his shoulder. The man who had once seemed so large looked small now. The man who had taught Dylan he was worthless had diminished to the point of ridiculousness. The man who had beaten Dylan and his mother in his drunken meanness was asking for forgiveness.

"Of course I forgive you. You're my father. But ... that doesn't mean you get to screw up my life a second time." Dylan turned and walked away.

Anthony. May 9.

As Anthony sank into the backseat of the cab at Dulles International Airport in Northern Virginia, he closed his eyes. Everything was blurring together. It was nine o'clock at night in Washington, and he'd been on the flight for ... nineteen hours? He barely knew anymore.

"Where to?"

Anthony shook his head. "Sorry. Um ... Bethesda, please. Montgomery and Wisconsin."

The cab driver put the car in gear and sped away. It occurred to Anthony that he might not be welcome at Carrie's, at least not for a sudden drop-in. He wasn't thinking clearly. He'd been busy as hell Wednesday, including interviewing Prince George-Phillip, then flying halfway around the world for a twelve-hour visit in Afghanistan. Then he flew back. He'd been in the air for thirty-six out of the last forty-eight hours, and he was exhausted. He'd slept some on the flight, but it wasn't enough. And sleep hadn't come easily—the story was too much, too intense. He'd spent most of the flight outlining then writing. He'd emailed the story to Jackson Barlow, the executive editor, while on the plane.

Now he just wished he could go to sleep. But there was too much work to do. The story was shaping up—but he had an alarming number of open questions, and he had to have it together by Sunday morning. He badly wanted it to make the papers before the grand jury convened Monday morning.

He took out his phone to call Carrie. It was dead.

Damn it. He just had to hope she was there. He thought through his open questions. In the morning, he needed to talk to Bear and see if they could get at Wolfram Schmidt, the head of the investigation. From what little Anthony had been able to learn about the man—scrupulous to a fault—he wouldn't likely comment either on or off the record. But it was worth a try. He needed to ask Julia some questions, and Carrie.

His thoughts drifting over the questions, he didn't realize he'd fallen asleep until the driver shook him awake. Groggy, he paid the cab driver too much money and walked toward the high-rise condo.

Inside the lobby, building security was reinforced by armed guards hired by Julia Wilson. Anthony thought the other residents of the building couldn't be happy, because the guards were checking identification for everyone who entered the building.

Anthony identified himself, handed over his passport, and said, "I'm here to see Carrie Sherman."

"Please wait." The guard walked into the office behind the desk. Anthony could see him speaking into a phone, but couldn't hear what he said. When he returned, the guard said, "Arms out to your side, please."

Anthony swayed on his feet a little, then got his footing. The guards frisked him then searched his bag. Only then did one of them say, "I'll accompany you to the nineteenth floor, and Mrs. Sherman will step out and identify if you are who you say you are. If she gives the okay, you can go ahead. If not, then the Montgomery County Police will take you away."

"All right," Anthony said. He followed the guard to the elevator, then up. Carrie waved him in.

As he entered the condo, she gave him a curious look. "I thought you were in Afghanistan. Why didn't you call?" She led him in.

"I *was* in Afghanistan, but only for a few hours. I got what I needed. My phone was dead and I came straight from the airport." He swayed on his feet. "I've got a few more questions for you and Julia."

"You must be exhausted," Carrie said. She didn't mention Julia.

He nodded. "I am. After we're done, I'll head home and get some sleep."

She shook her head. "You should rest first."

He leaned forward. "Carrie, I can't. This story is huge. I just need verification from you about a couple of things. Please?"

She nodded. Her eyes were huge. "Yeah," she said.

"Okay. Um … let me get my notes." He sank into the couch and opened the bag he'd carried all the way around the world and opened his notebook.

As he was rummaging in the bag, Alexandra came down the hall, already talking. "Carrie, Dylan just called. You're not going to believe who showed up—" She stopped talking suddenly when she saw Anthony.

"It's okay," he said. "Don't mind me."

Alexandra said, "Hello." Then she looked away from him, toward Carrie. "Anyway … Dylan's *dad* showed up at the jail. It's the first time he's seen him in ten years and the first thing he did was ask for money." Her face twisted in distaste.

Carrie frowned. "Is Dylan okay?"

"Oddly enough—when I went to see him this morning, he looked better than he has in months. And he sounded better when I talked with him on the phone."

"Weird," Carrie replied. "We'll talk more about it in a bit, okay? Anthony's got some questions he wanted to ask."

Alexandra nodded. "I'm going to sit on the deck for a bit. It beautiful out tonight."

After fumbling a couple more minutes, Anthony said, "Okay. Here we go … first … I understand you met George-Phillip one time before."

"More than that, actually. But I didn't know he was my father. I met him a couple of times in China, in the mid and late nineties. I was a kid. And—he was kind of sneaky. He spoke at my graduation from Columbia."

Anthony grinned. "I kind of like that."

She met his smile with her own. "I do too. It … felt good to think of him … paying attention, even though he had to keep it all secret."

"Did you ever meet Leslie Collins?"

Carrie shook her head, slowly. "I probably did. Sometimes Dad or Mom had guests over, but they never actually introduced them. We would be paraded out, shown off for a moment then whisked away. Collins looks familiar though, so I think so."

"What about Prince Roshan?"

She nodded, more firmly this time. "I *do* remember him. He was here a few times. I was fascinated by his beard."

"You told me you remember your mother being sick on Valentine's of 1990."

"Just barely. I was really little. Julia remembered it though. She was … bruised. Badly. She stayed on the couch for days, I remember that."

"What was it like growing up with her as your mother?"

Carrie sighed and leaned back, then pulled one knee up to her chin. "It was … sometimes scary. Dad … *shit!* Richard … whatever … he was always remote. Stayed in his office, or at work. He showered me with things … lessons and instruments and tickets to the opera. Then when I was in college he gave me obscene amounts of money. I never really understood why, except—maybe it was to buy my loyalty. The one thing he had was calm. Mother was … distracted. Anxious. She would break down unpredictably. Scream at us. The worst was when I was … I don't know … seventeen?"

"What happened?"

"Okay, you know who Maria Clawson is?"

He nodded. "Yeah, she's making a comeback writing about Richard Thompson and Julia."

"Yeah, that's her. Well, back in 2002, when Julia and Crank met—there were sparks. They kissed, near the White House. And it turned out Maria had followed them. She got a photo that clearly showed Julia kissing Crank, and he was all spiked hair and leather jacket and torn up clothes. Mother went insane. See—Clawson was writing about our family for *years* at that point. *Richard's* nomination as Ambassador to Russia was held up, there were Senate hearings, it was ugly."

He nodded. "Go on."

"Anyway … when the photo ran on Clawson's blog, Mom blew up. I think … I think it was because of the pressure she was under. I don't know for sure, but I've been thinking over a lot of things. How he used to lean over and whisper in her ear, and she'd go pale. Anyway, that day she went nuts. Blew up, started throwing things. She came upstairs, and the twins were misbehaving—well, not really, but Sarah was a smartass—and she just lost it. She hit me. I hit her back. She ran off crying. It never happened again after that."

Anthony shook his head. The details matched up with what Adelina had told him. He took a deep breath and said, "All right. Almost there." He took a deep breath. He was struggling to keep his eyes open. But he had to finish this.

"Is Julia around?" he asked. "I had a couple more for her."

Carrie shook her head, a troubled expression on her face. "Julia's been in Boston the last couple of days. I think she's trying to straighten out the mess the IRS left her. I haven't heard from her at all."

"Is that unusual?"

She sighed. "We normally talk every day. But things are … different right now."

He nodded. "When will she be back?"

Pensive, she answered, "Sunday morning. You know it's Mother's Day, right? Crazy. Because we'll all be here."

"Adelina's coming back to Washington?"

She leaned forward and said, "You can run this, but *not* before Monday morning."

"Okay."

"She's been offered immunity. So has Andrea. They're going to testify for the grand jury."

Anthony smiled. "So she's coming back with Andrea, Jessica and Sarah."

Carrie nodded. Her eyes watered a little bit. "It'll be the first time we've all been together in a long time. Since Ray died."

He met her eyes. "It hurts, I know. I still miss my mom, badly."

"Your mom?"

Anthony murmured, "Yeah. Cancer. She passed last spring."

"I'm sorry. Well, you should just come here Sunday morning then. You can talk to Julia, and I'll be here."

"I wouldn't intrude..."

"No ... it's okay. Crank will be here too, and we're still holding out hope they'll release Dylan."

He said, "All right. That's it for now. Do you mind if I just email these quotes in from here? Then I'm going to catch a cab home."

Carrie said, "Go ahead. Of course."

He typed up his notes as quickly as possible, then inserted the quotes into his draft and emailed it to Jackson. They were small details, but made the story much stronger. The fact that Adelina, Julia, George-Phillip and Carrie's stories lined up so neatly helped a lot.

As he finished sending it, he leaned back and closed his eyes. For just a second, then he'd hit the road. In the morning he needed to track down Bear.

The moment his eyes closed, he was out. He didn't even feel when Carrie tucked a blanket around him and set his laptop on the coffee table.

CHAPTER TWENTY-SIX
Ulterior Motive

Anthony. May 10.

It was seven on Saturday morning when Anthony woke up to the smell of fresh coffee. He sat up, rubbing his eyes, and realized that he had fallen asleep in Carrie's condo. He was alert instantly—Anthony typically slept well, was an early riser and didn't drink a lot of coffee. But after the week he'd had, and the long distance travel, he was still exhausted.

The door to the balcony slid open and Anthony realized that Carrie was on the porch with Rachel in her arms. Alexandra had slid the door open. "There's coffee in the kitchen."

"Thanks," he said. He stumbled to his feet, then walked down the hall to the bathroom and washed his face. Only then did he return, make a cup of coffee, then step out onto the balcony to join the two sisters.

"Good morning," Carrie said as he came out.

Her face looked strained. Rachel was in her lap and looked pale and listless, and Carrie tucked her in a little tighter. Alexandra was sitting across from her, leaning back in her chair.

"Morning," Anthony said. He sank into one of the cast iron chairs. "I didn't mean to fall asleep here. Thanks for the blanket."

Carrie shook her head. Odd. She seemed to be avoiding his eyes. "It's fine. You were exhausted."

"I guess you'll be busy today prepping for everyone coming into town?"

She nodded. "Alexandra is picking them up at the airport late tonight. I'm … not taking Rachel out today, she's been running a low fever for a couple days."

"Is it serious?"

She shook her head. "No … the nurse just said keep her hydrated. But I don't like seeing her this listless."

"How long has it been since her transfusion?"

"Just a few days."

Alexandra said, "I'll take care of getting everyone here, Carrie. You just take care of Rachel."

Anthony said, "Is there anything I can get you?"

"No, I'm fine. What are your plans anyway?"

"I've got to put in a call to Bear. I've got questions for him, and if we can get in to see him, I want to talk to the guy running the investigation for the IRS."

She said, "You're welcome to work out of here until you meet them. We've got a lot of room, you know that."

Anthony smiled. "Thanks," he said. "I really do appreciate you letting me stay last night."

Carrie studiously looked away from him, instead choosing to fuss with Rachel's blanket for the fortieth time.

Anthony finished his coffee and awkwardly said, "Well, let me get to those calls."

He felt extremely self-conscious as he slid the door open again and stepped inside. He picked up his phone. *Damn it.* He'd forgotten to charge it. He dug in his bag for his USB charger and connected it to his laptop and waited while he checked his email.

He'd received one marked urgent from Jackson.

TO: Anthony Walker
FROM: Jackson Barlow
SUBJECT: Karatygin
Anthony,
Great job on the story. Got your updated notes. We're going to run this on the front page with a special report insert. The photographs are incredible.

That was good news. Anthony thought that this meant he was definitely out of the doghouse at work. Only a few more loose ends to tie up.

As his phone finally booted up, he saw he had half a dozen messages. He dialed into his voicemail.

Two messages from bill collectors. One from Carrie—that was interesting—wishing him luck in Afghanistan. Two more from Jackson Barlow, demanding to know when he was coming back from Afghanistan. A final message from Bear. It was terse, giving an address in Falls Church, Virginia and a time: nine o'clock.

It was eight now. He jumped to his feet and slid open the door again. "Hey Carrie—can I borrow your shower? And would it be possible to get the concierge to call a cab? I've got to get to Falls Church."

Carrie looked up and said, "Sure. Maybe one of us can drive you? A cab to Falls Church is going to cost a fortune."

Alexandra said, "I'll watch Rachel."

Carrie said, "I don't know."

"Carrie, I've got it. You go—you could use a break. And Rachel's fine. I'll call you if her fever goes up."

Carrie sighed. Then she looked at Anthony. "All right. I'll take you."

He hadn't participated at all in that exchange. But he nodded and said, "Thanks. I'll be ready in ten minutes."

Anthony was surprised to learn that Carrie drove a giant black Chevy Suburban, one of the biggest sports utility vehicles on the road. But when he thought about it, it made sense. After all, Ray Sherman had been killed in a car accident. It would stand to reason that she would have a lot of residual anxiety about cars.

Regardless of that, she expertly drove them out of the crowded streets of Bethesda and on to the Capitol Beltway. Rush hour wasn't over, and they sat in the car nearly twenty-five minutes before they made it across the bridge and into Virginia.

Anthony said, "I can't tell you how much I appreciate the ride."

She looked at him and said, "I have an ulterior motive."

For just a second Anthony's heart seemed to skip a beat. But he looked at her as calm as he could and said, "And that would be?"

Carrie didn't look at him. She said, "I want in on the meeting."

"I don't know if they'll let you—"

"Let me try to persuade them. I've certainly got as much a right as you. And I probably have information they need."

Anthony opened his mouth to speak, then thought. And closed it. Because she was right. She had *more* right than he did. After all, it was her family being ripped apart.

"All right. Just bear in mind that Schmidt—he's the head of the IRS investigation—hasn't even agreed to see me. He doesn't know I'm coming. So you showing up might make things even worse."

Carrie was no fool. She changed the subject. "What did you find out in Afghanistan?"

"Few things that really surprised me," he replied. "But I got hard corroboration, both witness testimony and physical evidence, that Richard Thompson was involved in the acquisition of the weapons."

"Jesus," she whispered. "I kept hoping it wasn't true."

"I don't blame you," he said. "You've had—a lot of tough realizations in the last few days."

She nodded. "Yes. That's true."

"I wish it hadn't been that way," he said. Not that his wishes made any difference, or could do anything to help Carrie. But it was true. He wished she'd not had such a tough time. "You're strong, you know. Most people would have buckled under the pressures you've faced."

She gave him a wry smile. "My mother taught me to stand up to all kinds of pressure."

Anthony's admiration of Carrie Sherman only grew at that statement.

Thirty minutes later, they finally arrived at a nondescript suburban house in Northern Virginia. The first thing Anthony noted about it was the precision of the bushes, which had been trimmed in perfectly even lines. Even the grass looked freshly cut, with not a blade out of place. Whoever took care of the landscaping here was a fanatic.

Carrie pulled the SUV to a stop. Three other cars were in the driveway, including one with federal government license plates. She took a deep breath.

"You ready for this?" he asked.

She nodded, once.

They simultaneously opened the doors of the Suburban and stepped down to the driveway. Moments later a large man who looked like a former linebacker opened the door.

"You must be Anthony Walker?"

"Yeah. And this is Carrie Sherman."

"Come on in. I'm Gary Simpson. This is my house, but I'm not in on the meeting. You're a little late."

"Traffic."

Anthony and Carrie walked forward to the door, and had an awkward moment where he stepped back to let her go first, and she did the same thing, causing them to collide.

She stifled a laugh and he said, "After you. Please."

He followed her in. Carrie stopped almost immediately on entering the foyer, her eyes on a large photograph that dominated the entry. Her eyes jerked to Gary. "You're married to Leah?"

"Yeah," he replied.

Tears appeared in Carrie's eyes. "She was shot protecting my sister. I'm so sorry."

Gary sucked in a breath, briefly speechless. Then he said, "Thanks. She's going to recover." He seemed to bite back tears, then waved them on. "In the dining room."

Anthony followed Carrie into the room. The first thing he saw was a wall which was almost completely windows, framing a view of woods with a small stream running through them on the far side of the backyard. The backyard was as carefully manicured as the front, including a gravel path leading to a small wooden bridge over the stream.

A dark, most likely antique table with eight chairs dominated the dining room.

At the head of the table was Wolfram Schmidt from the Internal Revenue Service. The last time Anthony had seen Schmidt, the IRS agents had tied zip ties around Anthony's wrists in a hotel room on the West Coast. Schmidt wore jeans and a button down white shirt, and stood beside a large whiteboard. Halfway down the table, Bear Wyden sat. Files were open in front of him. Next to him, a youngish looking woman in a suit, with nearly white hair and an annoyed expression.

Leah Simpson sat in a recliner in one corner of the room, looking pale with her feet up. Another man Anthony didn't recognize sat across from Bear, who stood up as Anthony and Carrie entered the room.

"Folks, I want to introduce you to Anthony Walker … and Carrie Sherman. Before you panic, Anthony is with *The Washington Post*, and I *asked* him to be here."

"Have you lost your mind?" the woman with white hair asked.

Bear grinned. "Anthony, let me introduce Emma Smith, from the Internal Revenue Service. Across from me is Scott Kelly, from Diplomatic Security. He's an old colleague of mine. In the corner nursing a grudge—and a bullet wound—is Leah Wy— um … Leah Simpson."

Leah made a sour face at Bear.

Schmidt said, "I don't know that bringing the press into this is a good idea."

"Just hear me out for five minutes," Anthony said. "If you want to throw us out then, feel free."

Schmidt looked at his watch, making him the first person Anthony had seen in a year who actually wore one anymore. "You have five minutes. Talk."

Anthony swallowed. "I have information you need for the grand jury. Information that will put Richard Thompson and Leslie Collins away for a very long time."

Schmidt didn't respond, but Emma Smith looked skeptical. Anthony continued. "First—in the last few days I've interviewed Adelina Thompson and most of her daughters."

Emma shrugged her shoulders. "We've done the same, and probably got the same information."

"I'm guessing you haven't gotten in to see Prince George-Phillip."

Emma sat forward, and Schmidt looked interested. "Tell me more," he said.

"The Prince's story lines up with Adelina's. He is Carrie's father. And—here's the kicker. George-Phillip was responsible for the British investigation into the Wakhan massacre, and his conclusions and recommendations were very different from what was made public at the time. I have a copy of that report. And ... I got back in from Afghanistan last night. I met with Vasily Karatygin."

Bear grinned at that news. Schmidt merely raised an eyebrow.

Anthony looked at the others in the room and said, "On Monday morning, the *Post* is going to run a special report which will crucify Thompson and Collins. I've got hard evidence of their involvement in the procurement of chemical weapons." Anthony went on to discuss what he had seen and learned in Afghanistan.

Schmidt said, "All right. What about her? Why is she here?"

Carrie said, "I'm the only person who can tell you anything about the inside of my parents' marriage."

"Plus," Anthony said, "if she doesn't stay, neither do I."

Emma Smith closed her eyes. "Wolfram, this is all—"

"Yes, I know. It's irregular. It's ... all mixed up. On the other hand, we're taking on the CIA here. I think we might need some unusual allies. Walker—I can't give you everything we have. It's an ongoing investigation, and there are things we know that I cannot and will not tell you. But I can give you some information, off the record. In return, you give me everything you've got."

Anthony said, "This is exclusive? I don't want to find my information on CNN."

"Of course. Have a seat." Schmidt paused for just a moment then said, "Both of you."

Anthony glanced at Carrie, who flashed him a smile. Both of them took seats at the table.

Bear leaned forward and said, "Before you came in, we were actually trying to figure out—a timeline, I guess. Who did what and when. We've had multiple parties involved in this."

Anthony nodded.

Schmidt wrote on the white board in large letters:

*Who kidnapped Andrea Thompson? Why?
*Who opened the accounts in the Caymans in Richard Thompson's name?
*Who murdered Mitch Filner and why?
*Who is Oz?
*Who did Ralph Myers work for?
*Who was involved in the shooting in Bethesda?
*Who attacked GP, the Bethesda condo and the house in San Francisco?

When he finished writing, Schmidt said, "And the biggest question is why?"

Bear said, "Well, we know the answers to some of these questions already."

Schmidt said, "Let's take them from the top?"

Bear Kelly said, "Our kidnappers were Tyler Coleman and Tariq Koury. Koury is a fairly well-known mercenary; he did a lot of work for CIA and SIS over the years in Iraq and Saudi Arabia. Coleman was a US Special Forces veteran who worked for a shell company until 2011. Brennan Holdings."

Emma said, "Brennan Holdings is a CIA shell company. Leslie Collins set it up in the mid-2000s."

Bear said, "We can prove that?"

Emma nodded. "Yes, we've got him cold on that. The only question is, was it Collins' personal operation, or did it have official sanction? We don't have any way of knowing at this point."

Anthony said, "In the end, it doesn't matter. The Agency will deny it no matter what the real answer is." Anthony thought it was interesting that none of the federal agents in the room disagreed with him. "Can I use that? Off the record?"

Schmidt looked at Bear, who shrugged. Then he looked back at Anthony. "All right. How do you guys usually write it? An *unidentified source close to the investigation*? I'll verify that the kidnappers worked for Brennan and that Collins founded that organization."

Scott Kelly said, "We also know Mitch Filner worked with Collins, *and* with Brennan, and turned up dead last week with a stab wound. We've got video evidence of Filner and Collins eating lunch together the day after the kidnapping."

Anthony's eyes widened. It was a lot of coincidences, but serious ones. He took out his notebook and began making notes.

Carrie leaned forward and said, "Why would Collins want to kidnap Andrea?"

Anthony said, "I actually have a theory about that."

Schmidt replied in a droll tone, "Please enlighten us."

"Okay. Number one—Andrea and Carrie's birth father is Prince George-Phillip. Number two—George-Phillip conducted the British investigation into Wakhan. He fingered Thompson, Collins and Prince Roshan as the key players behind the massacre. *And* he recommended going public with the findings of the investigation. I have a copy here, which he personally handed to me. Number three—Prime Minister Thatcher personally squashed the findings because of the Cold War. Both the British and US Administrations wanted maximum propaganda value out of blaming the Soviets for the attack. I think Collins ordered the kidnapping assuming that it would go off without a hitch, Andrea's body would have been disposed of and her parentage would never come up. He assumed—

correctly—that if it became public Thompson wasn't her father, then further examination of his life would end up exposing Wakhan."

Schmidt nodded. "So a public official ordered the kidnapping and murder of a US citizen—and a child—in order to preserve his own position."

Bear said, "It's consistent with everything we know."

"What about the accounts in the Caymans?" Schmidt said.

Emma leaned forward. "All right, what we know for sure is that Julia Wilson had nothing to do with it. After a lot of arm twisting, we obtained video from the banks in question. Yes, a woman opened the accounts, personally. No, it wasn't her. I'm guessing another contractor for Collins—the accounts were opened only a week after the White House settled on Thompson as the new SECDEF. Collins was laying the groundwork to discredit Thompson, in the event Thompson tried to blame Collins for Wakhan—which he did in the hearings this week."

"Some of the media's going along with it," Scott Kelly said.

"Exactly," Schmidt said. He looked at Anthony. "No offense. All of this is off the record until we say so, clear?"

"Yeah, I got you," Anthony said. "I'll clear anything I say with you guys unless it comes from somewhere else. Let's move on, we've been over that."

"All right. Next is—Mitch Filner. What happened to him?"

Emma said, "We know Filner worked for Collins in Southeast Asia, and lost his position with the CIA because of a rape accusation."

"That's ugly," Anthony said.

"It's fact, and at this point fairly widely known with the investigation team. You can go public with that. He lost his job and went to work for Brennan Holdings."

"Collins again," Schmidt said. "What if Collins was pissed off? Instead of a quiet kidnapping, a girl who just vanished, Collins ended up with a giant media fiasco and massive amounts of public scrutiny. Offing Filner was punishment."

Bear said, "Yeah, but is there anything we can make stick?"

Emma said, "Probably not with Filner."

Anthony continued to make notes. Carrie sat quietly next to him, listening, her eyes wide. This whole discussion must be a revelation for her. She'd been through the ringer—including dealing with media storm clouds. But this was an order of magnitude more difficult.

Bear said, "All right. What's the word from Joe Paretsky?"

Anthony perked up. He started to say something, but Carrie beat him to it. "Who's that?"

Bear said, "Your brother-in-law Dylan tackled him the other day. Paretsky shot a British guy named Charlie Frazier, who we are pretty sure is MI6. As in, he worked for your dad." The last words were said as he looked pointedly at Carrie.

"Why? I don't understand?" she said.

Leah interjected, "What I believe is that Prince George-Phillip assigned some agents to watch over you. They spied Paretsky and his now dead partner moving in on you and intervened. We didn't understand what was going down at the time because we didn't know the players. But my guess is, if Dylan hadn't jumped in, one of you might have been hit."

Carrie shivered.

Anthony shook his head. "If Collins didn't want a media fiasco, why blow up the house in San Francisco? Why attack the condo?"

Emma said, "He didn't."

"What do you mean?"

"Collins almost certainly blew up the townhouse. But we believe we found out who Ralph Myers was working for."

Bear sat up, his face intensely interested. "Who?"

"Saudi Arabia. Myers was badly in debt. College debt for his kid, then his wife got sick five years ago. Cancer. He was leveraged to the hilt. But about four years ago, his financial problems started getting better. Paid off his debts, got them under control, and everything's been fine since."

"Okay … he got recruited by somebody. Why do you believe it was Saudi Arabia?"

Schmidt replied, "EZ Pass records. Over the last four years, on eight different occasions Myers drove from his house in Arlington to Manassas. Each time, it was one day after Ahmed al-Saud made the same drive."

"Roshan's son," Anthony said. "A dead-drop."

"A what?" Carrie asked.

Bear grunted. "It's spy talk. One person drops something—cash, or documents, or something else, in an inconspicuous place. The other party then picks it up at a different time. That way the two are never seen together."

"But in this case, you've got the traffic records recording their movement."

"It wouldn't pass in court," Bear said. "Not without photos or some other corroboration. But we know at least their vehicles made that trip."

Anthony said, "That makes sense. Roshan probably got sick of seeing Collins screw everything up. So he decides to end the whole thing. Sends a team to kill the Thompson family—all of you—and another to take out George-Phillip. I wonder if he knows."

Carrie said, "He knows. While you were on your way to Afghanistan, someone shot a surface to air missile at his plane. It crashed into the Potomac. Yesterday he flew to London for an emergency cabinet meeting. They took him by jet fighter."

Schmidt said, "You know an awful lot about his movement."

She smiled at him. "He's my father. We've been communicating quite a bit since that revelation. He told me last night that the British government had arrested the man who had fired on his house and connected him somehow to Saudi Arabia."

"So who the hell stole my files?" Bear asked.

Schmidt, for the first time, looked sheepish. He said, quietly, "That would be me. At that point in time, since one person in DSS turned out to be a traitor, we weren't counting on trusting anyone. So we seized the records." He reached into his briefcase and passed across a file.

"Mother fucker," Bear said.

Schmidt merely smiled.

"So the last question," Bear said. "Who is Oz?"

Anthony answered that. "We know who it is now. Oswald O'Leary. Prince George-Phillip's assistant. What we don't know is why."

"Where is he now?" Schmidt asked.

Carrie said, "He got away. George-Phillip gave me photos and descriptive information to pass on to our security people. In case he shows up."

Schmidt said, "So what next? Adelina Thompson and our other key witness are testifying on Monday morning for the grand jury."

"I'm running my story Monday morning," Anthony said. "We've got everything we need. I'd love it if I could get some quotes from you, even if they are anonymously attributes. But the story's happening no matter what."

Schmidt said, "We'll give you some quotes. Thompson and Collins are guilty of mass murder, but you and I both know they may never go to jail."

Anthony said in a calm voice, "I can still publicly hang them."

"You're all forgetting one thing," Carrie said. "What about Dylan? He's sitting in jail for killing a man who was attacking his family."

Schmidt said, "Mrs. Sherman—just before you got here, we'd already determined to let Mr. Paris go and drop any charges."

Carrie closed her eyes. "Thank you," she whispered.

CHAPTER TWENTY-SEVEN
Time's a wasting

Dylan. May 10.

Dylan's release from the federal lockup happened quickly and later he would remember little of it. What he did remember was when the guard escorted him to the front door, back in his street clothes. Alexandra was waiting outside, along with Bear Wyden.

She flew to him, a flash of brown hair and green eyes and then he was enveloped in her arms and Dylan knew that at least for that moment, *right now*, everything was going to be okay.

"God, I missed you," he whispered, ignoring the people who walked past on the sidewalk, some of them less savory than others.

"Come on, kids. Time's a wasting." Bear's tone was gentle as he said the words.

Dylan and Alex pulled away from each other, and Dylan said, "Do I owe you for getting me out?"

Bear shrugged. "Nah, I'm just the delivery boy. You can thank the IRS."

"Oh, well that's weird. Bear—thanks."

Bear grinned. "Let's get going."

Five minutes later, they were driving on the Capitol Beltway back to Bethesda. In the car, Bear kept up a running patter about his opinion of DC cabbies (low), his opinion of the federal government owned car they were driving (even lower) and especially his opinion of the increasingly humid weather (lowest). Alex sat in the front passenger seat, and Dylan leaned forward in the seat behind her, keeping a hand on her shoulder.

When Bear came up for air, Dylan said, "So am I in the clear?"

Bear glanced over his shoulder at Dylan for just a second, and then his eyes were back on the road. "Yeah. You're not going to face any charges. You did the right thing after all. What you did was heroic, and almost certainly saved Andrea's life. Twice really, because when you took down that guy in Bethesda, he was almost certainly gunning for her or Carrie."

Dylan said in a low voice, "Thanks."

The ride was nearly thirty minutes. Dylan never took his hand off of Alex.

After a long period of quiet, Bear said, "You know, Alexandra—for what it's worth—I'm sorry that things came down the way they did. That you had to learn the things you did about your father."

Dylan felt Alex's muscles tense as Bear spoke. Then, just like that, she sagged into her seat. "It's okay," she said. "I always knew something was wrong. Sending Andrea away never made any sense until this."

Dylan squeezed her arm. Traffic was getting heavier as they approached the center of Bethesda. The sun was going down, the sky brilliant reds and oranges.

They came to a stop in the parking area at the base of the building Dylan had last seen when he was walking away, blood still on his hands and the bottom of his shoes. He stepped out of the car almost unconsciously, and reached for Alex's hand when she got out. He tilted his head back, looking up the side of the building, at the balconies, all the way to the nineteenth floor. He didn't want to go up there. He didn't want to walk into the place where he'd killed two men.

He closed his eyes, took a deep breath, and said, "Let's go."

They rode up the elevator in silence, but it was a heavy silence. Dylan knew what he needed to do, but he was afraid. He was afraid to admit weakness. He was afraid to admit he'd lost control. He was afraid to admit to Alex that he'd failed again. But if there was anyone in the world who would understand and be there for him, it was Alex. He *knew* that.

He gripped her hand a little tighter and said, "What's the plan tonight? Who is here?"

"Just us and Carrie and Rachel. Julia and Crank are flying down from Boston in the morning, and—Mother and the others will be here very late tonight. Why? What do you need?"

Dylan swallowed. Then he said, "I need to call my mom."

"Yeah?" she said. Her voice cracked a little.

He nodded. "I'm gonna find out where to get to an AA meeting around here."

Instantly, Alex's eyes went red. She pulled Dylan close to her, and spoke in a broken voice. "Dylan. I'm so proud of you."

Anthony. May 11.

After Anthony Walker handed the car keys to the valet at the entrance to the condominium, he turned around and stumbled face to face with Crank and Julia

Wilson. She was dressed in a white A-line dress with deep red flowers splashed across it. He wore jeans and a black T-shirt with the words, "Bullet for my Valentine" written in gothic red letters.

Her eyes narrowed a little. Something was off with her expression. "I wasn't expecting to find you here, Anthony. Don't you think you could leave the story alone for Mother's Day?"

He grinned. "I'm here by invitation, actually." Then he followed her and Crank into the building, ignoring the flashes of cameras and the shouted questions of other reporters. The security guards at the door cleared the three of them in.

The elevator ride up was awkward. Anthony swallowed uncomfortably, pursed his lips, and looked at the ceiling.

Crank clapped him hard on the shoulder. "No need to be awkward, Anthony. If Carrie invited you, that's all that matters."

Anthony coughed and said, "I think she felt sorry for me. My mom passed away a few years ago so I didn't have any plans this morning."

"My condolences," Crank said.

"Thanks."

The elevator doors opened. Anthony waited until Julia and Crank stepped out then followed them. Their identification was checked again by another guard and then they walked down the hallway.

Julia knocked. Anthony heard a shout, and moments later the door was opened.

It was unmistakably Sarah Thompson who answered the door, right down to the dyed streak in her hair. But instead of the black and grey she normally wore, today she was in a bright yellow taffeta dress.

Julia and Crank both looked stunned. Sarah ignored their expression and simply grabbed Julia and hugged her, then did the same with Crank. She gave Anthony a look he was unable to interpret—almost like she was keeping some sort of secret, then turned and walked into the condominium.

"Come on in, there's coffee and orange juice. Breakfast isn't ready yet, but will be soon."

The first impression Anthony had was of minor chaos. Jessica—still looking pale, but not as bad as she had when he met her in British Columbia a few days before—sat on the couch, with her feet up on a coffee table. Alexandra sat in another chair holding the baby, who giggled periodically but looked pale. Anthony was no expert on babies, but he'd seen enough to know that Rachel did not look well. Standing near Alexandra was a stocky man with broad shoulders, neatly shaven but with hair grown just over his collar. Anthony recognized Dylan Paris from the many photos he'd seen in the news. It would be a long time before Dylan would be anonymous again. Right now he nervously flipped a small white disk between his fingers.

Julia and Carrie immediately embraced. Carrie wore a turquoise dress that nearly matched Sarah's. Anthony didn't catch the words that passed between them, but Carrie almost immediately turned to Anthony and took his hand. "I'm glad you could make it," she said. "Please don't be too uncomfortable."

Anthony shrugged. Of course he was uncomfortable—who wouldn't be, attending someone else's family's Mother's Day celebration. Especially when it was *this* family, with *this* mother.

There were two conspicuously missing women. Andrea. And her mother.

Adelina. May 11.

Adelina's nerves were as taut as they'd ever been, the muscles in her neck stiff, her hands lightly shaking as she finished applying her mascara. The anxiety was a pit in her throat, slow burning and twisting like a rabbit on a spit. She was back in the same room she'd occupied off and on for more than thirty years. The room where she'd cried and wept. The room where she'd tried to nurture and protect her daughters, and the room where she gave up her dreams. The room where she'd waited all night after her 1 am arrival, tossing and turning, worried about what the morning would bring.

She sighed. She was afraid to go out there. Afraid to see all of her daughters. She was afraid of their judgment and their anger.

It didn't make any sense, really. She'd presided over a thousand family functions over the years. Birthdays and graduations, marriages, Christmas and Thanksgiving meals. She'd never been perfect, but she'd always done her best.

But inside, she was consumed by shame. Shame that she'd stayed married to Richard so long. Shame that she'd listened to his threats and his abuse. Shame that she'd let her daughters be exposed to such things.

Above all, shame that she had sent Andrea away. Even if it was to save her life.

So she stayed in her room and fretted. She prayed and wrote in the journal Julia had returned to her. She tried to build up the courage to face them.

And then, a knock on the door.

Adelina sat straight in her chair. "Yes?" she called. "I'll be ready in a moment."

Silence. Breathing outside the room. Then the words, "Mother, may I come in? It's Andrea."

Adelina sniffed. She looked at herself in the mirror. She was strong enough to do this. She could do it. She could do it.

"Come in," she said. Her voice cracked.

The door opened and Andrea slipped inside.

Andrea wore one of Carrie's dresses, a professional looking knee-length black affair with a wide belt.

She stepped into the room and said, "Won't you come out?"

Adelina swallowed. Then she whispered, "You know I didn't want to let you go. But I was afraid Richard would harm you. He told me he would, and I believed him."

Andrea nodded. "I know."

"Can you ever forgive me?"

Andrea walked close to her mother and rested her hands on her shoulders. Then she said, "Yes. I forgive you. You gave me my life. And my faith. Then you saved my life, and I didn't even know it. There's nothing to forgive, Mother. I'm your daughter and I always will be." As Andrea spoke, tears began to run down her face. Then she whispered, "I've always wanted to have my mother. And now I do. Now come out. The rest of your family is waiting for you."

Adelina whispered, "Okay."

Andrea turned and opened the bedroom door. Quivering with apprehension, Adelina followed. Out into the hallway, the hallway she'd walked through literally a thousand times. But never, not even during the worst of times with Richard, had she walked down the hallway with this much fear.

Her daughters were in the living room. As she entered, Julia came to her feet, followed by Carrie. Her two eldest daughters held hands and watched her with concern in their faces. Alexandra was close by, her husband's arm around her shoulders. Even Jessica came to her feet, Sarah beside her.

Carrie's eyes were wet. She reached out and took Adelina's hand. Julia said, "Mom ... welcome home."

CHAPTER TWENTY-EIGHT
Special Report

George-Phillip. May 12.

"**Welcome** back, Your Highness." The speaker was US Air Force General Hainey, who had arrived at Andrews Air Force Base once again to meet George-Phillip. This time, George-Phillip had just arrived on a return flight, which had raced the sun around the earth. He'd left London at 5 am—midnight in Washington—and arrived at Joint Air Base Andrews just before 3 am.

He shook hands with the General, the General's aids, and got in the car that had been provided by the Ambassador.

Inside the car was Linda Happer. Officially a translator with the Embassy, Linda was actually the MI6 Chief of Station in Washington, DC.

"Good morning, Chief," Linda said. "Nice flight suit."

"That's questionable," he replied. "What's the news?"

"That's the key question, sir. There's a lot—first this." She handed across a copy of *The Washington Post*. Splashed across the front page in two-inch high type was the headline: **GRAND JURY OPENS WAR CRIMES PROBE.** Beneath, the subheadline said: Richard Thompson, Leslie Collins implicated in poison gas massacre. Underneath the headline, taking up nearly half of the top half of the front page was a color photograph of the inside of a cave. Arm in arm, with wide grins on their faces, were a much younger Leslie Collins, Richard Thompson and Vasily Karatygin.

"Well. That's something," he said.

He scanned through the article, then flipped to the second page and his eyes widened. The headline on page two said, **Former headquarters of CIA officials became a crypt.** A photograph showed a cave scattered with bones and bodies. A cabinet was overturned, and papers were scattered about the room.

The cave had been sealed for thirty years following the massacre.

"We used dynamite to blast the opening to the cave," said Vasily Karatygin, the former Soviet defector and conspirator who is now dying. "It was the only way guaranteed to keep the secret. Everyone who assisted us died. But the documents, and the weapons, were all left behind. It was death to go back in that cave."

By the time I entered the cave last week, the sarin had long since dissipated, leaving behind a monument to monstrosity. Inside the cave were twenty-two bodies, both men and women, all of whom presumably worked for the conspirators. I also photographed and examined dozens of documents and papers, which are depicted in this report. The most damning: a letter from Adelina Thompson to her husband. The letter is terse and unemotional, consistent with the background of their marriage (see A Marriage Forged in Revolution, page A6), and demands that Thompson release sufficient funds to pay for renovations to the Thompsons' San Francisco home and for their daughter to attend day care. The letter (pictured below) is the clearest and most damning evidence placing Richard Thompson at the scene of one of the most notorious war crimes of the twentieth century.

"You're mentioned in the reporting, Your Highness. In the story about the Thompsons' marriage. You're discussed in there quite a bit. The Ambassador is livid."

George-Phillip murmured, "I'm sure he is." He felt at peace. If he had to resign his position today, he would be quite content.

She grinned.

"One more bit of news, sir."

"Yes?"

"The Virginia State Police caught up with Oswald O'Leary, sir. He's being held at a precinct in Alexandria for the time being. American Diplomatic Security is on their way to question them, but they gave me a courtesy call."

"I see. Are we invited, do you think?"

Linda nodded. "Yes, sir. If you'd like to question him, we can go right now."

"Let's go then. I have a meeting with the US Secretary of State at 10 am, so we'll need to make this quick and get back to the Embassy. I'm going to need a shower, that cockpit is cramped."

Leslie Collins. May 12.

This was a disaster.

Leslie Collins sat in his office, still in his bathrobe, reading the special report in *The Washington Post*, which had been delivered less than twenty minutes before.

A disaster. Bad enough that his photograph was splashed across the front page. The interior of the special report was much worse. Photographs of bodies. Their headquarters in the mountains of Afghanistan, bodies still scattered inside the cave, along with gear and personal property that clearly belonged to both Collins and Richard Thompson.

A timeline of Andrea Thompson's kidnapping. Links between Leslie's holding company and the kidnappers.

He was finished. Destroyed.

He turned the pages, growing more and more distressed with each word he read. This morning his colleagues would be reading this report. His *children* would be reading it. The news media would circle like sharks, searching for weaknesses, smelling the blood, and then they would attack, sawing their teeth into his hide, ripping him limb from limb until there was nothing left.

The article was so damning.

A senior source in the investigation told The Washington Post **that investigators now have strong evidence Collins ordered the kidnapping and murder of Andrea Thompson. Sources speculate that Collins was concerned that once it became public that Andrea Thompson was not related to Richard Thompson, the resulting questions would quickly lead to the exposure of their involvement in the Wakhan Massacre.**

Worried about that eventuality, Collins had a series of accounts opened in the Caymans in Richard Thompson's name. Initially, investigators believed the accounts were what they appeared to be, and opened an investigation into both Thompson and his eldest daughter Julia Wilson.

"The trail didn't make sense," said the Post's **source in the investigation. "Once we obtained Julia Wilson's cooperation, the story quickly unraveled."**

According to senior officials, Wilson will testify before the grand jury on Monday morning.

He leaned forward and placed his forehead on the desk. There had to be a way to survive this. There had to. He'd survived worse. He'd controlled lives. He'd run spies in a dozen countries; he'd protected his nation for a career spanning forty years. *Why?* This was terrible.

Collins jerked in his seat when the phone rang.

The secure line.

Hand shaking, he reached out and picked it up and put the receiver to his ear. "Collins."

"Leslie, it's Ralph Williams."

Collins closed his eyes. Ralph Williams was former Senator Williams, former head of the Select Committee on Intelligence, and now Director of Central Intelligence. Williams was the highest ranking Intelligence official in the United States, and Collins' boss.

"Yes, sir."

"Don't come in this morning. I'll be sending around a classified documents officer to collect anything you have in your safe at home."

"Sir?" Collins let a little outrage creep into his voice.

"Let me be clear, Collins. You aren't coming back. Now, or ever. You'll be lucky if you don't land in prison, but I guarantee you'll never work in public office again. I suggest you get started writing your memoirs if you have any hope of protecting your reputation."

Williams didn't even use common courtesy. He simply hung up the phone, leaving Collins with a clicking silence.

Collins put the phone down.

He took a deep breath. Thompson was equally implicated in the story, which detailed far too much of what had happened over the years. There would be congressional hearings, and if the newspaper story was accurate, the grand jury might well indict Collins. But that wasn't the biggest danger.

Prince Roshan was the biggest danger. Collins knew that if Roshan saw this article, he would likely send assassins immediately, lest Collins or Thompson implicate him. Roshan was ambitious—one day he hoped to be King. But there were more than 200 Royal Princes in Saudi Arabia—he was but one. A scandal would wipe out his chances for good.

Killers might already be on the way.

Christ. Swallowing the lump in his throat, Collins picked up the phone and dialed a number.

"Hello?" The answer at the other end of the line was terse.

Leslie coughed and his voice cracked when he spoke. "This is Mister Collins. I know it's late, but I'm hoping to get a ride to see my friend."

There was a long silence at the other end. The code phrase was simple enough. It was a panic signal, a signal designed long ago to allow for his quick departure from the country when and if needed. He'd had that insurance set aside for more than ten years. Now it was time to use it.

The man at the other end finally returned. "Ten am. Stafford."

Damn it. Stafford Regional Airport was forty miles south of Washington, and rush hour would be coming soon. They needed to get out of the house right away. He stood and walked out of his office, shouting, "Meredith! Meredith!"

He stomped down the hall to their room, still shouting her name. She let out a panicked shriek when he switched on the bedroom light, then she cried, "What? What is it?"

"Pack one bag with your most valuable possessions and get dressed in something comfortable. Comfortable shoes. You've got ten minutes and we're leaving."

"What?" she cried, sitting up in the bed.

He reached down and grasped her shoulders and leaned forward, nearly touching his nose to hers. "Pack. Bags. Get. Dressed. I'm leaving in ten minutes. With you or without you."

When he let go, she sagged back onto the bed, horror on her face. He didn't care. He marched into the walk-in closet and tore off his bathrobe, then began getting dressed. He rarely wore them, but today he put on a pair of tough jeans and a thick shirt. Then he took a backpack off the top shelf and began stuffing clothes into it.

"Leslie, you must explain right now!" Meredith cried out.

"No time. We're in danger. We're leaving."

"What about the twins? What about Susan?"

"The kids will be fine. But we won't, if we don't get out now. Get. Dressed."

She started moving, throwing clothes on—her gardening clothes. Good. No heels or dainty dresses. Then she started packing a bag.

George-Phillip. May 12.

"Prince George-Phillip? I'm Bear Wyden. Diplomatic Security Service."

The man who approached was of medium hight—considerably shorter than George-Phillip and stocky. George-Phillip suspected the *Bear* moniker came from the copious amount of hair the man seemed to have.

"Hello, Mister Wyden. I understand arrangements have been made for me to meet with O'Leary."

"Yes, sir. But—first—do you have a moment?"

George-Phillip raised his eyebrows. "Yes?"

"Sir, you should know I've been assigned to your daughter's case since the day she was kidnapped. Andrea's, that is. I've come to know her and Carrie pretty well, along with Adelina. I knew Adelina many years ago, too, in Belgium."

George-Phillip let out a sigh. "Yes ... I see. What can I do for you?"

Bear's mouth twisted a little. Then he said, "Those girls deserve a good father. They never had one. And Adelina Thompson has been tortured for decades. I don't trust anyone in the Intelligence business, but you seem like a decent sort. I just…"

George-Phillip let out a breath, then reached out and took Bear's shoulder. "I'll do my best, Mr. Wyden."

"Bear."

"I'll do my best. I promise."

"In that case, sir, I'll take you in to see O'Leary."

Minutes later, George-Phillip found himself in a room, accompanied by Wyden. O'Leary sat across from them. His feet were chained to a steel table. He had a serene expression on his face.

"Oswald," George-Phillip said.

O'Leary nodded. "Your Highness."

George-Phillip asked one question. "Why?"

O'Leary shook his head. "You still cannot see it? My job was to protect you and the Royal family, Your Highness. It always was."

"Protect me from what?"

"From scandal, sir. Surely you must realize. Prince Andrew was dating a porn star in 1982, and then that lunatic Fagan walked right into Buckingham Palace and sat down at the end of the Queen's bed. Princess Margaret and Lord Snowden divorced, and your own father died in a drunken accident. Is it any wonder the Queen wanted you protected?"

"The Queen?"

O'Leary nodded rapidly. "Of course, sir. I was detailed by the Queen herself to protect you from scandal."

George-Phillip sank into a chair across from O'Leary. *Oz.*

"You took it upon yourself, with this assignment, to break into Adelina's home. In 1983?"

"Of course, sir. To warn her away. I had no idea she was pregnant with your child sir, not then. But it wouldn't have made any difference."

"And you did it again in 1996, in China."

O'Leary nodded. "Yes, sir. For your own good."

"And you hired assassins to kill her. And her daughter."

O'Leary shrugged. "I'm loyal to the Crown, sir. Not to some whore you decided to sleep with."

Rage swept over George-Phillip. He stood and swept his hand back to strike O'Leary in the face, but Bear was quicker than he. Bear grabbed his wrist and said, "No, sir, I'm afraid you can't do that."

George-Phillip gasped. He took a deep breath, suddenly flooded with adrenalin. He couldn't believe the Queen would sanction murder. "O'Leary. When was the last time you spoke—with the Queen? Or anyone in her household? Anyone related to this … *assignment*."

O'Leary said, "Why … when you returned from Washington to London, sir. Officially the assignment was over then."

George-Phillip closed his eyes. Never in his life had he wanted to hurt someone as bad as he did right now. The betrayal shook him to his core.

He took a deep breath, his voice shaking, and said, "You are finished, O'Leary. I'll be speaking with the Home Office to have your diplomatic immunity revoked. You'll go to prison for hiring that assassin." He turned, still gasping for air.

"Your Highness! I only did what was right! What you didn't have the courage to do!" O'Leary's face was bright red. "I did everything to protect *you!*"

Without responding, George-Phillip stepped out into the hall, with Bear on his heels.

Outside, in the hallway, he saw Linda Happer. "Miss Happer. Please take me to the Embassy. I must get ready for my meeting with the Secretary of State."

Bear said, "I'm sorry about that, sir."

George-Phillip shook his head in disgust. "I—I'm appalled. And … incredibly disappointed. I've known O'Leary for thirty years."

Bear said nothing.

George-Phillip reached out and took his hand and shook. "Thank you, Mister Wyden."

"Yes, sir."

George-Phillip followed Happer out of the police station.

Leslie Collins. May 12.

Ten minutes after he'd awakened Meredith, Leslie Collins jerked opened the side door; backpack slung over one shoulder, and walked toward his car. It was dark, but a waxing gibbous moon low in the sky illuminated the driveway and side of the house. Collins could hear birds beginning to chirp, even though the sun hadn't begun to rise. It would be sunrise soon enough. He needed to be well on his way toward Stafford before the sun was up—otherwise traffic would delay them past the departure time for his flight.

The car chirped when he disabled the alarm and unlocked it, and then reached out for the door.

Meredith let out a shriek. Movement. A man, stepping away from the shadows of the unused garage.

"Mister Collins."

Collins jerked back. The man who faced him in the darkness was short. Short cropped hair. Unshaven, unkempt. He had dark skin. His accent was clearly Arabic.

"Mister Collins, I have a parting gift from a mutual friend. *Bit-tawfiq.*" Collins recognized the words. Arabic for *best of luck*. The man moved quickly, raising a pistol to Collins' forehead.

The man pulled the trigger and everything went black.

CHAPTER TWENTY-NINE
Big fat bullets

Richard. May 12.

Richard Thompson shook with the most powerful rage he'd ever felt as he continued reading the pages of the special report.

According to a source in the Special Prosecutor's office, Julia Wilson has been cooperating with the IRS investigation. She wore a wire to her last meeting with her father, capturing an audio recording where he admitted to procuring the weapons for the massacre. Mrs. Wilson is scheduled to testify before the grand jury Monday morning, followed by her mother.

How could she? Richard raged. His daughter. The one he'd cultivated. The only one he really loved. He felt a strange, twisted aching, an unfamiliar feeling; a feeling he hadn't really touched since his brother hung himself in the attic of their childhood home.

Grief.

He opened one of the cabinet doors and took out a glass. He hated this place. The President had given him two weeks to find a new place to live. He was being thrown out. Good riddance. These rat-infested quarters weren't fit for him.

The building, formerly Quarters 2 at Fort Myers, had been the home of a two-star General before Richard was here. A large white structure with southern colonnades and French windows, Richard hated it. *Hated* it. He took out a glass from the cabinet, turned it in the light, and flung it across the room.

It shattered against the wall, a curiously satisfying sound. He took out another glass and flung it. Glass flew across the room, and a tiny fragment hit his arm.

On the top shelf was a set of wine glasses. He flung them, one after another, each of them shattering. Glass was now scattered all across the kitchen floor.

It was Adelina's fault. He was losing everything. He'd even lost his favorite daughter. And it was that Spanish whore's fault. He slid a drawer open and eyed the kitchen knives greedily.

No. Not sure enough. He had a gun in his study, a .45 calibre Colt M1911A1 pistol. Big fat bullets to shoot through her big fat head. There was nothing else to be done. As his father would say (if the old bastard were still alive), he was *a disgrace. Just like his brother.*

Mrs. Wilson is scheduled to testify before the grand jury Monday morning, followed by her mother.

He stalked toward his office to get his gun. Poor Julia was going to be an orphan in a few hours.

Carrie. May 12.

"You're sure you're okay?" Carrie asked for the fifteenth time.

Alexandra nodded. "I'm *fine.* You stay with Julia and Mom, okay? They need you. I've got Andrea and the twins here, and I'm pretty sure Andrea can take on *anything.*"

Carrie's eyes darted to her mother's, then Andrea's. Andrea's lips held the barest of smiles. As if she were thinking she *could* take on anything. Carrie turned back to Alexandra and handed over Rachel. The baby didn't stir. Her fever had dropped back to normal overnight.

"She'll likely be awake in another two hours. There are four bottles of breast milk in the freezer and one in the fridge, you can warm—"

"Carrie!" Alexandra said. "I've got this!"

Dylan pulled his phone out and checked the time. "Mrs. Thompson ... Carrie and Julia. Time to go."

Carrie said, "I still don't think you need to come along, Dylan. We've got armed guards."

"Carrie," Alexandra said. "Shut up. Stop fretting."

She closed her eyes. "All right. In that case, let's go."

Dylan led the way out of the condominium, followed by Adelina and Julia. Carrie looked back at Alexandra and said, "Thank you. I don't know what's going on with you and him but ... it's better. It's better, isn't it?"

Alexandra nodded, her eyes glistening. "It is," she whispered.

Carrie smiled and walked out the door, following her mother and sister down to the elevator. They still had ninety minutes before they had to be at the Federal Courthouse, but traffic in Washington was unpredictable. The four of them rode down the elevator in silence, flanked by two armed guards. In the lobby different guards took over and escorted them outside. Pale light shone down from a purple sky.

They climbed into a large SUV, Adelina in the center, her daughters on either side, and Dylan in the front passenger seat next to the driver. Guards loaded up in another vehicle. They weren't taking any chances. The small convoy set out into traffic, which was heavily snarled. Rush hour.

Carrie sat staring out the window as Julia and their mother spoke quietly. She half paid attention to the words. Mother and daughter were catching up on events of the last two weeks. Jessica's health, the assassination attempts, the IRS investigation. Julia had kept it secret that she'd worn a wire and met with her father.

Carrie sighed. *Why* had she kept it secret? She looked over at her sister. Julia's hair was natural again; it had been some time. Shoulder length, the brown locks curling around her face. She looked sad.

Then it hit her. She thought about what she knew about her sister. About Julia's high school experiences, both in China and in Bethesda. The harassment and teasing. *Her suicide attempt.*

Julia hadn't said anything because she was *ashamed*. Ashamed that somehow her sisters would think less of her. Ashamed that she'd done the wrong thing.

Carrie took a deep breath. "You did the right thing, you know," she said.

Julia looked at her, eyes suddenly wide. "What?"

"You heard me. You did the right thing. I know he's your father. But you did the right thing."

Julia swallowed, her face swimming with emotion.

Adelina took Julia's hand in her left and Carrie's in her right and said, "This will all be over soon."

George-Phillip. May 12.

From the outside, Blair House consisted of four townhomes across the street from the White House, the central one of white brick and fronted with a columned portico. George-Phillip knew that inside, however, the four homes were seamlessly connected. With dozens of rooms and a large staff, the house served at the guesthouse of the President of the United States, and hosted visiting dignitaries and other events. George-Phillip had attended many events there over the decades.

This morning, he was met by a US Navy Commander.

"Your Highness. The Secretary is waiting for you in the dining room. Please follow me, sir."

George-Phillip was no longer in the flight suit he'd worn across the Atlantic and to the jail. He'd changed into a formal suit with highly polished shoes and cufflinks that had once been owned by his father. He'd had long enough while changing to have a very brief breakfast and a hand of Go Fish with Jane before he'd left again.

That wouldn't go on much longer. He'd handed his resignation to the Prime Minister while in London.

George-Phillip followed the Naval officer down the entry hall and to the small private dining room. As he entered, Secretary Perry stood. Both men were of similar height, though Perry, as always, looked dangerously gaunt.

Perry gestured to *The Washington Post*, spread out on the table amidst pitchers of orange juice and carafes of coffee.

"Have you seen this?" Perry asked.

"I have," George-Phillip said. "It's quite comprehensive."

"Have a seat, Your Highness. It's a pleasure seeing you this morning."

George-Phillip smiled. "And you, Secretary. Our mutual friend is on the way?"

"He is. But I asked him to be here a few minutes later so we could talk."

"Excellent," George-Phillip replied.

"I understand you're resigning."

George-Phillip smiled. "Word gets around fast, doesn't it? It's true. I need to spend more time with my children. Especially now that I have two more daughters I need to get to know. And several more ... surrogate daughters, I suppose. I feel equally responsible for them."

"Thompson was really a piece of work, wasn't he? I had no idea you were involved with Adelina, though. Is it true, what the article says?"

"That she was raped and basically held prisoner? Yes. Sadly, it is."

Perry grimaced and shook his head. "I always wondered. Have you seen her?"

George-Phillip shrugged. He felt an odd sort of pain at the question. "I don't know that she'd care to see me, Secretary."

Perry frowned. He looked at his watch, then said, "Prince Roshan will be here any minute ... Your Highness ... may I give you a bit of unsolicited personal advice?"

"Secretary?"

"Go see her. Not next week, or next year, or even tomorrow. Go see her today."

George-Phillip swallowed. He was saved from having to respond, however. The door opened, and the Navy Commander who had escorted him into the room opened the door.

"Mister Secretary? Prince George-Phillip? Prince Roshan has arrived."

The two men stood, and Perry said, "Please show him in, Commander."

Julia. May 12.

You heard me. You did the right thing. I know he's your father. But you did the right thing.

Carrie's voice rang through Julia's mind as she sat down at the end of the long conference table. Twenty-three men and women were arrayed up and down the table. Some wore suits, some wore button down shirts, and two of the men wore jeans and T-shirts. All of them had serious expressions on their faces.

At the opposite end of the table was a man she recognized. Rory Armitage. Armitage was a former Congressman from Georgia, later appointed to the federal circuit as a judge by President Bush. A stern, puritan man with tightly clipped hair and an austere expression, Armitage had been appointed several weeks earlier by the President to examine accusations of corruption in the defense department. The probe had rapidly broadened to include Richard Thompson and was now broadening even further.

To the side of the room, the court reporter, a mousy looking woman, sat at a small desk.

Armitage didn't stand. He merely sat at the opposite end of the table, barely taking his eyes off the papers in front of him.

To his right, a woman in a blue dress spoke. "Hi, I'm Mary Cooley, the foreperson of the grand jury. Can you please identify yourself, and your place of residence and occupation?"

"Julia Wilson. Boston, Massachusetts. I'm Chief Executive Officer of Morbid Enterprises, Inc."

"Mrs. Wilson, do you swear to tell the truth, the whole truth, and nothing but the truth, so help you God?"

"I do."

The woman waved to Armitage. "She's your witness."

Armitage didn't move. He looked up, blue eyes gazing at her over his reading glasses, and said, "Mrs. Wilson, I'm about to play a tape, labeled Prosecution Exhibit 332. Please listen carefully."

She sat back and listened as Armitage tapped on a keyboard. The room was flooded with sound. With her voice.

Dad … I want you to level with me. I know it was the Cold War and bad stuff happened. I know people had to do things that look ugly in today's light. Did you do it? Did you give them the chemical weapons?

There was a slight hiss in the background from the recording. Then she heard her father's voice. *I did. It was horrible. But also necessary.* A long pause, then, *Julia … you know better than anyone about foreign policy. You know how these things work. I didn't want to do it, and I certainly didn't know they would use it on innocent villagers. We actually provided the militia with satellite photos of the Russian training camp, as well as an advisor who was a Soviet defector. Vasily Karatygin—he'd converted to Islam and went over to the side of the mujahideen. But they didn't use it on the military … it was on civilians. I'd have done anything to prevent it.*

Her voice again. *But since it did happen, you had to blame it on the Soviets. Realpolitik.*

Her father: *Sadly, yes.*

Armitage typed something and the sound stopped. Then he spoke. "Mrs. Wilson, do you recognize the voices on that recording?"

"I do," she said. "Me. And my father."

"Please identify your father for the jury."

"Richard Thompson," she said. Inside, her stomach twisted. Her father had done—uncountable evil. But it still felt wrong.

You did the right thing. I know he's your father. But you did the right thing. Carrie's voice again.

"Mrs. Wilson, under what circumstances was this recording made?"

She looked down at the table. "In the days after my sister was kidnapped, I'd learned some horrible things. There was a police report, which showed my mother had been attacked, and that my father was the prime suspect. And my mother—she was missing at the time—had left a journal. I read some of it. It indicated she'd been—raped. By my father. She was sixteen when it happened. As my father became more embattled with the Administration, he reached out to me. In hopes of getting an ally. He talked about putting my mother away permanently, saying she was insane. And … I needed to know if what they were saying was true. About him being involved in that massacre."

"So you agreed to wear a wire for the federal investigators?"

She looked down. Then she said, "Yes."

She reminded herself of her sister's words. *I know he's your father. But you did the right thing.*

"Mrs. Wilson—were any offers of immunity made to you?"

She nodded. "Yes. The IRS made that offer. I didn't accept."

"Why not?"

She felt her temper flare. "I won't have it said that I turned against my father in order to stay out of jail. I didn't. I wore the wire because it was ... it was the right thing to do. Because there were innocent people hurt. And they deserve some kind of justice. I ... I can't have babies. But if I could, if I ever did have children, I would want them to know that I did the right thing."

Armitage's mouth pursed and he nodded. Then he said, "A couple more questions. Then we're done. Did you open any secret accounts in the Caymans on behalf of your father?"

"No."

"Did you assist him in laundering any drug money?"

"No."

"To the best of your knowledge, was your father involved in any drug money laundering?"

"Nothing that I'm aware of. I don't believe that's true. My father's guilty of many crimes. But I don't think simple greed is one of them."

Armitage turned to the foreperson, Mary Cooley. "Miss Cooley, your witness."

Cooley said, "I don't have any questions."

"Very well then," Armitage said. "Mrs. Wilson, thank you very much for your time, you may go." Then he said, "Please bring in the next witness. Mrs. Adelina Thompson."

Julia stood. Her arms and legs were shaking. She met the eyes of Mary Cooley for just a second. Then she turned to the door. As she approached it, it was opened, and her mother stepped in. Julia touched her mother on the arm as she brushed past her, and whispered, "Be strong."

George-Phillip. May 12.

Prince Roshan wore a conservative coal-grey business suit and a red keffiyeh. He smiled a broad toothy smile at the sight of George-Phillip.

"Prince George-Phillip. I wasn't expecting you this morning! What a pleasant surprise."

Somehow George-Phillip thought that Roshan wasn't at all pleasantly surprised.

"Come in, Your Highness," James Perry said. "Have a seat, please join us for breakfast. We have several *halal* dishes here."

Roshan eyed the plate of bacon and sausage and said, "You know my weaknesses, Mister Secretary. I hope Allah will forgive me for technical violations, but I must have a little of everything."

Perry waved for the servers to approach, and moments later the three of them were eating, with several minutes of companionable silence, punctuated only by the sounds of forks clinking against plates.

The silence was interrupted when Perry said, "Richard Thompson's grand jury meets today. You know he's sunk. So is Leslie Collins. Both of them have lost their careers, even if they don't find themselves imprisoned for war crimes."

"Yes," Roshan said. "It's a shame, really, I knew him once. I even had dinner with the two of them, many years ago. You remember, George."

George-Phillip grimaced. He didn't care for the familiarity. He said, "We know all about your role in the massacre, Prince Roshan. You should also know that we arrested your assassin in Britain. The one who shot at my home."

Roshan said, "Is this some strange British humor? You bring me here to insult me?"

Perry said, "Prince Roshan, yesterday the Virginia State Police found a Stinger missile casing not far from Great Falls Park. We've arrested your agent who fired it."

Roshan frowned, then wiped his lips with a linen napkin.

George-Phillip leaned forward. "The missile that you used to try to kill me and my daughter."

Perry said, "Prince Roshan, as I'm sure you are aware, shooting down a civilian aircraft bearing a cabinet member of the US ally could be considered an act of war. Britain and the United States are both members of NATO. We're allies. Did you really think we would stand by and allow you to fire missiles at airplanes in our country?"

Roshan said, "This is ludicrous. I object to this treatment."

Perry said, "If I could, I would see you in prison or executed for your crimes. As it is, I have to resort to diplomatic means. Go home, Roshan. You're no longer welcome in this country, or that of any of our allies. And please tell the King that if Saudi Arabia wishes to continue having the United States as an ally—as a *protector*—then you'll never serve in any official capacity again."

Roshan stood. "Arrogant Americans. You think you can tell us how to run our affairs?"

Perry said, "I'm sure you're aware of our armed drone program in the Middle East, Prince Roshan? If you don't do as I say, then I suggest you keep your eyes locked on the sky. Your days will be numbered."

Roshan threw his napkin down.

"Go home," George-Phillip said.

Prince Roshan marched out of the room.

"I wish we could do more," Perry said.

George-Phillip said, "MI6 is not as squeamish about assassinations as the United States is, James. Roshan's days *are* numbered. I've already spoken to the Prime Minister about it."

"Well, then. Your Highness … don't you have an appointment at the Federal Courthouse?"

Dylan. May 12.

When Adelina walked out of the chambers of the grand jury at nearly noon, she was pale and shaking. Dylan quickly moved to her side and took her arm. "You okay?" he murmured.

She smiled. "I'm not done for yet, Dylan."

Julia and Carrie both approached their mother. Julia's eyes were brimming with tears.

Adelina looked at them both, then said, "I'm proud of you both, you know."

Carrie said, "Will they indict him? Will he pay? I feel like he can never pay enough for what he did to you. Or what he did to those villagers."

Adelina put a hand on her daughter's shoulder. She whispered, "I wanted vengeance for the longest time. But … that's not up to me. Or you. We're called on to continue our lives … to forgive, if we can."

Jesus Christ, Dylan thought. We're called on to forgive? He thought about his father. His poor, weak and deluded father.

Carrie said, "Sometimes forgiveness is the hardest word in the world."

"You lost your husband. Then you lost your father." Adelina looked at her daughter with compassion in her eyes. "Of course it's hard. But I promise you … it will get easier."

Carrie grimaced. "Let's go, then. I might as well get started trying."

Adelina nodded, and the three women started walking toward the elevators. Dylan stayed ahead of them, watching for journalists, for threats of any kind. He'd spent the last three hours reading Anthony's reports in *The Washington Post* that morning, while Julia and then her mother testified. The report was—staggering. It revealed a level of corruption in the Central Intelligence Agency Dylan couldn't have imagined. Collins would go down, and so would Richard Thompson, but they wouldn't be the only ones.

The elevator opened and the four of them stepped inside.

"Probably going to be reporters downstairs," Dylan said. "The guards will be just outside waiting for us. Stay close until we get in the vehicles."

Adelina reached out and touched Dylan's hand. "Dylan. Thank you. For taking care of my daughters."

He gave her a sideways grin. "My pleasure, ma'am. I'd give my life for them."

He meant it. If he had to, he'd put himself between Alex and a bullet. Any of her sisters too. After all, that's what soldiers did. They put themselves in between their families and the desolation of war.

At least, that was the idea.

The elevator opened. The lobby of the courthouse was clear, armed guards and police everywhere. But outside, on the steps and blocking the street, were dozens of reporters and cameramen jostling for space. Beyond the reporters, hundreds of spectators, oddly drawn by the drama of a wife and daughter testifying against a former cabinet official.

"Here we go," Dylan said.

As they approached the doors, their security guards stepped inside. "This way, folks. This way!"

Out the revolving door they went. The crowd immediately pushed in toward them. Microphones shoved in their faces, reporters shouting and screaming. Their guards shoved the reporters back shouting, and Dylan joined in.

He yelled, "Give them some space!" while Julia called out, "No comment."

The gunshot came out of nowhere. Dylan heard it, his instincts suddenly kicking in as he swiveled on his feet and ducked down, searching out the source of the noise. One of their two guards fell to the ground, a giant hole in his face, and the other one suddenly screamed and fell backward, hitting Dylan, who tried to get out of the way.

He felt his reconstructed leg twist under him and he slipped, feeling the ankle snap. Dylan let out a scream of rage.

The crowd scattered, men and women, reporters and others screaming. As they ran, they revealed Richard Thompson, who had grabbed Carrie and was holding her by the neck. Richard's face was gaunt; dark circles under his eyes. He'd been awake for a long time. His face was unshaven, grey hair sprouting from his cheeks and neck. He had a pistol, a .45, trained on Adelina.

"I should have killed you long ago," he muttered. "I never should have let you live, you fucking whore."

"Let me *go!*" Carrie shouted, struggling.

"Shut up!" he shouted. He hit her with the butt of the pistol. "You aren't even my daughter. I'll kill you like a bug if you piss me off."

Carrie's eyes widened.

Dylan saw, running up the street, a tall man with dark hair. It was Prince George-Phillip. How did he know to come now? But he was too far away.

Julia strode forward, putting herself between her father and mother. In a low, cold voice, she said, "I am. I'm your daughter. And you're never hurting my mother again."

She reached out toward her disbelieving father and grasped the pistol, pulling it away from Carrie. "Now let her go," Julia ordered.

Dylan tried to struggle to his feet, but the shooting pain that lit up his leg like lightning told him he'd snapped something. *Goddamn it!* George-Phillip couldn't get here in time!

"Let her go," Julia said.

"You were my most beloved," Richard said. Almost casually, he let go of Carrie, who staggered away. His voice rose to a shout. "You were the one she hurt the most. *Her.* She's the one who called you names, and treated you like dirt, and … she made your life miserable. Don't you want vengeance? You can have it!"

"Father. It's time to give up," she said. "You've lost. It's not time for vengeance. It's time to forgive."

"No. No. I can't lose. I can't. I won't be a disgrace. I won't be." He took a step back then raised the gun. "Goodbye, Julia."

Dylan and Julia screamed at the same instant, but no one could move fast enough.

Richard Thompson pulled the trigger.

Epilogue

George-Phillip. May 12.

"**H**ave to let you off here, Your Highness. Street's blocked off by the Federal Courthouse."

George-Phillip leaned forward so he could see around the corner. The sidewalk and streets were packed with news vans and a large crowd of spectators and protesters.

"All right, then. Stay close. Go get a cup of coffee or something. I'll call you as soon as I'm finished."

The driver frowned. "Are you sure you want to get out here, Your Highness? That's a serious crowd, and you've already been attacked—"

"That threat's over. But thank you for your concern."

Without another word, George-Phillip opened the back door of the SUV and stepped out. A taxi driver, trapped behind the SUV, was laying on his horn continuously. What a snarled mess. Cars everywhere, pedestrians, reporters spilling all over the place. It wouldn't be surprising if he were mobbed by reporters—he'd been heavily profiled in that morning's article in the *Post*. But the unlikeliness of finding a British Royal Duke walking along the sidewalk in downtown DC probably protected him from that.

He began walking toward the crowd.

The crowd surged, as if a giant had swept a fist against them, and suddenly there was screaming—lots of it. People were pushing from the entrance of the federal building, fighting against the crowd. George-Phillip began to run toward the front of the courthouse, and caught a glimpse of his worst nightmare.

George-Phillip's eyes swept over the area even as he moved at a dead. What he saw was chaos. Richard Thompson, pistol in hand, holding Carrie by the throat.

Julia reaching for him. Adelina rushing in his direction to protect her daughter. Dylan Paris was on the ground, his foot bent at an unbearable angle.

George-Phillip ran faster at the unmistakable sound of a gunshot, even as his brain tried to interpret what he was seeing. Richard had released Carrie, who spun away, and then he shouted words George-Phillip couldn't make out over the screaming.

Richard raised his pistol, and George-Phillip shouted, "Stop!" as the man's finger tightened on the trigger.

George-Phillip collided with Adelina, arms around her and knocked her to the ground as the shot went off. The screaming continued around him. He heard another shot, then several more. George-Phillip's reddened gaze went to Richard, who twitched like a marionette once, twice, then fell face-first to the ground, blood blooming across his back.

"George-Phillip!" Adelina screamed, terror on her face. She sounded far away, and his side was beginning to hurt terribly.

"Hello, love," he said. "I've missed you terribly. Are you all right?"

Then Carrie was at his side, and Julia was helping Dylan, and he heard sirens approaching.

They, too, sounded far, far away. But her sudden kisses on his face, her breath against his, was as close as his own soul. He closed his eyes, flooded by the warmth of home.

The Washington Post. May 13, 2014.

Former Defense Secretary Charged With Attempted Murder of Britain's Prince George-Phillip

By Anthony Walker

Former Defense Secretary nominee Richard Thompson shot Great Britain's Prince George-Phillip in front of hundreds of witnesses Monday after an altercation with Thompson's wife and two of her daughters. Once US Ambassador to China and later Russia, Mister Thompson is under investigation for involvement in the delivery of chemical weapons to Afghan militia who used them on civilians. Additionally, his wife Adelina Thompson has accused the former Ambassador of raping her when she was sixteen years old. Thompson was shot by police after he fired on the Prince.

The shooting took place in front of Adelina Thompson and two of her daughters, Carrie Sherman and Julia Wilson. According to witnesses, Ambassador Thompson was attempting to murder his wife when Prince George-Phillip intervened.

The three women, with a brother-in-law, were taken with the Prince to Howard University Hospital Trauma Center. Ambassador Thompson was transported to George Washington University Hospital.

The embattled Ambassador faced Senate hearings only a week ago before the Senate Armed Services Committee, chaired by Senator Chuck Rainsley. During those hearings, it was revealed for the first time that Thompson was an active agent of the Central Intelligence Agency throughout his diplomatic career. Administration officials have refused to comment on Thompson's intelligence background.

White House spokesperson Kelly Daniels told *The Washington Post*, "We were distressed to learn of the very disturbing charges against Ambassador Thompson. As soon as the nature of those charges was revealed, his nomination was withdrawn. This Administration will not tolerate corruption or criminal activity. We wish a speedy recovery to the Prince, and the President asked me to convey his personal admiration for the Prince's heroism."

Ambassador Thompson is expected to recover, sources at George Washington University Medical Center told the *Post*, but it is likely he will never regain the use of his legs. Prince George-Phillip is expected to fully recover.

Rory Armitage, Justice Department Special Prosecutor, said, "Richard Thompson just added attempted murder of his wife to the long list of charges he faces. This investigation continues."

Accused co-conspirator and Deputy Director of Operations at CIA, Leslie Collins was murdered Monday morning while preparing to board a charter flight at Stafford Regional Airport. The pilot had registered a flight plan to Rio de Janeiro. Virginia State police are cooperating with the FBI to investigate the murder.

Carrie. May 26, 2014.

It was seventy-six degrees at eleven am when Carrie parked her black Suburban near Section 60 of Arlington National Cemetery. The grass seemed to go on forever, as did the endless rows of gravestones. Near this section of the cemetery more than any other, cars and trucks of all shapes and sizes were parked. Carrie blinked back tears when she saw how many. You weren't allowed to drive down the carefully maintained roads inside the cemetery unless you were a surviving spouse.

Carrie almost never used her military ID, which identified her as a widow of a soldier who died while on Active Duty. But the ID had allowed her onto the cemetery grounds, thus avoiding the busy public lots. She opened the door of the SUV and got out.

On the passenger side, Dylan was negotiating his way out of his seat. He'd been frustrated the last couple of weeks—a broken ankle had resulted in crutches and more physical therapy. But he and Alexandra had been able to return to New York in time to plead with Columbia to allow them to make up the missed time and exams. Alexandra got out of the backseat and slipped her hand around Dylan's arm. It was the first time Carrie had ever seen Dylan wear his uniform. But today he was in his dress blues: his beret positioned on his head, the bright yellow Private First Class stripe on his arm, the blue braid around his right shoulder indicating his service in the infantry. Carrie recognized the Combat Infantryman's Badge—Ray had worn the same badge—along with his Bronze Star and Purple Heart. He carried a wreath.

Carrie opened the passenger compartment door and unbuckled Rachel from her bulky car seat, then slipped the sleepy baby into a sling at her hip. Rachel nuzzled against her mother, then settled in the sling.

"When's her next transfusion?" Dylan asked.

"Next week," Carrie answered. "Although…"

She trailed off.

"What is it?" he asked.

"My father—George-Phillip—is having a blood test this week. There's … you know … a possibility."

He grunted. She was well aware how slim the odds were, especially since Andrea hadn't been a match.

The three of them walked into section 60. Neither Dylan, nor Carrie, made it more than twenty feet into the grounds before tears were streaming down their faces. They walked down the row between the stones, barely seeing the other families, the mothers and fathers and widows who were making their own way, quietly, to their lost loved ones.

In every direction, as far as they could see, were the gravestones.

Carrie saw the names and the dates and struggled to maintain her composure. But Dylan had given up. Tears were streaming down his face and he sobbed once then bit it back savagely. Alexandra took his hand.

The names. The *names*. Carrie looked around them, staggered by the enormity of it.

Scott Johnson. Sergeant. United States Army. March 2, 1987. July 12, 2005. Silver Star. Purple Heart. Operation Enduring Freedom.

Julie McIntosh. SSGT. United States Marine Corps. October 12, 1979. June 7, 2004. Purple Heart. Operation Iraqi Freedom.

Every single name represented someone's child, someone's brother or sister, someone's father or mother. Every single one represented a life cut short, a life ended with a period in a country halfway around the world. Every single stone was a broken heart.

Dylan continued to walk on his crutches, with Carrie holding one arm and Alexandra the other. Carrie couldn't see clearly anymore, and didn't even realize it when they arrived at their destination.

Raymond C. Sherman. SSGT. United States Army. April 13, 1986. August 19, 2013. Bronze Star. Purple Heart. Operation Enduring Freedom.

"I miss him," Alexandra said. "I didn't know him that well ... not like you two did. But he was a good man. And a good friend."

"Yeah," Dylan whispered. He handed a crutch to Alexandra then knelt in front of them both, setting the wreath in front of his best friend's grave. He whispered something—Carrie couldn't quite make it out. Then he stuck out a fist—as if he were fist-bumping Ray—and said, "Miss you, bruh."

Then Dylan came to his feet, clumsily, and saluted the grave.

Shit. The tears were streaming down Carrie's face, but she didn't care. She said, "Do you guys—do you mind—I mean..."

"You need some time alone," Dylan said. "It's okay. You ... you need it. We'll be over near the car."

Carrie hugged Dylan, hard, almost knocking him off his crutches. Rachel protested, but settled in when Carrie let go.

"Hey, don't knock me down, woman."

Carrie laughed. Then she looked Alexandra and Dylan in the eyes and nodded. The two of them walked away.

She turned and knelt beside the stone, and rubbed her fingers along his name, feeling the engraved letters.

"Hey babe," she whispered. "I need to introduce you to someone." Then she had to stop talking, because for a few moments all she could do was sob.

"This is our daughter. Isn't she beautiful? I'm sorry I couldn't bring her here before. It's just—it's been a really hard time without you. Even harder than I would have thought."

She rocked back on her heels. "Rachel is sick, but I'm praying that we'll find her a bone marrow donor soon. In the meantime, we're watching out for her. I promised you I'd take care of our daughter, and I will. I sort of named her after you, you know. As close as I could get. You can't name a girl Raymond, that would be weird."

She sniffed, hard. "You wouldn't believe what's gone on the last few weeks. Or maybe you would. Maybe you've been around paying attention. I don't know. I have a new father, and ... I don't know if I can trust him. But I think maybe I can.

He took a bullet for my mother—if that isn't the craziest thing I've ever heard. I'm going to try to get to know him, anyway. We'll see. Mom's ... well ... it's a long story. But I think she's going to be okay, and nothing in the world can make me happier."

She sniffed again, then muttered a curse, then took out a tissue and blew her nose, hard.

Rachel giggled. A loud baby giggle.

"What?" Carrie said. She blew her nose again.

Rachel laughed, louder this time. Her blue eyes shone wide and her little mouth was wide open. Baby laughs were the best in the world. This was Rachel's first.

Carrie blew her nose again, making a loud honking sound. Rachel cried out in delight, her little fists waving in the air.

"Do you see her, Ray? God, isn't she beautiful?"

He didn't answer, of course. She looked at his grave, and said, "I know ... I know somehow you can hear me. And I hope—I hope you can forgive me. No one can ever replace you Ray. No one. But ... I need to move on. I'm going to—I need you to let me go too. Because Rachel's going to need a dad." As she said the last few words, they came out faster and higher pitched and desperate.

She leaned close, her hands still rubbing the letters. She felt the smooth stone against her lips. "Baby, I'll miss you forever. I'll always, always love you. But I need to say goodbye now. I need to—I need to get on with my life, and with Rachel's. I don't know if anything's there with Anthony, but it ... it's worth a try, don't you think? I know you'd want me to be happy."

She paused, listening. She lay there for a long time, leaning against the grave. Then she said, "I love you, Ray. I'll be back to visit, and I'll bring Rachel back to visit. I hope ... I hope..." She sighed. "I love you, babe."

She slowly came to her feet. She kissed her hand, then pressed it against the gravestone and walked away.

Carrie. August 5, 2014.

When the phone rang, Carrie Sherman was startled awake. She often fell asleep after breastfeeding Rachel, and today wasn't much different. She was lying sideways on the couch, her feet up, Rachel lying in the sling on her chest. The baby slept peacefully.

The phone rang again. Carrie reached over and picked it up off the coffee table.

It was Doctor Gage. In a panic, she hit the accept button and put the phone to her ear.

"Hello? Hello?"

"Carrie? It's Doctor Gage."

"Hi ... is everything okay?"

"Carrie, I've got news."

Carrie waited, her heart suddenly beating a thousand times a second.

"Your father is a match, Carrie. We've got a donor."

The tears began running down Carrie's face before she could say a word. Her eyes dropped to the baby peacefully sleeping across her chest, tiny fists bunched.

"Carrie, are you there?"

Joyful tears in her voice, Carrie said, "Yes. Yes. Thank you so much."

Rachel, the tiny baby who had no idea what had gone into this moment, slept peacefully. Just as she should. Carrie closed her eyes and sent a prayer up to heaven in thanks for protecting her daughter.

Sarah. August 17, 2014.

Sarah sighed and leaned back in her chair. Carrie was out of the house, thank God, as was her mom. Right now it was just Jessica and Sarah, sitting on the balcony, a desk of cards between them. The breeze was nice, at a few degrees above seventy, making it the nicest day they'd experienced in a while.

Carrie had been restless that morning, fretting about Rachel's upcoming bone marrow transplant.

Prince George-Phillip was currently in London, but he would be flying to Washington next week for the painful bone marrow donation surgery. Sarah liked George-Phillip. She'd met him three times now, once at the Embassy, once at Blair House when the President had him stay as a guest there, and once for dinner at the condo. He was a funny man, and his ridiculous eyebrows made him even funnier. But his concern for his granddaughter was what won Sarah over.

Sarah stared out over the city and her eyes misted over.

"Do you remember how hot it was? Last year?"

Jessica nodded. It was August 17th the prior year, when they were in a car on the way to the zoo, that a jeep bearing death had come barreling through the intersection and cut Ray Sherman's life short and severely wounded Sarah. Indirectly, the accident had resulted in grave damage to Jessica as well.

"Yeah," Sarah said. "It was awful."

Jessica looked at Sarah and whispered, "I was awful to you. The year before the accident."

Sarah's mouth twitch to the right. She didn't say anything, except to slightly shake her head.

"No, really. I shouldn't have asked to change classes. We've been together all our lives. I should have talked to you."

Sarah closed her eyes, a cloud of emotion flooding through her. She whispered, "Why did you do it? I thought you hated me."

Jessica shook her head. "It was ... I was always in your shadow, you know? I was Plain Jane. And you—you had everybody's attention—from the time we were tiny kids. I was ... jealous. I wanted to strike out on my own. I'm sorry."

Sarah swallowed. "Jessica ... I love you ... and... you have to know ... I always felt that way about you. You were always Mom and Dad's favorite I thought. You were going to be the only one to follow Dad into the Foreign Service."

"I think I'll skip that now," Jessica said.

"True," Sarah said. She felt bleak.

"What are you going to do about school?"

Sarah shrugged. "I didn't finish. I was thinking about registering at BCC this year. They'll still let me go back and finish my senior year. I checked."

Jessica swallowed. Her eyes looked huge. Sarah thought Jessica was about to cry. She said, "Do you think ... I could come with you? Back to school? That we could finish together? We'd be class of 2015, I guess."

Sarah whispered, "I'd love that."

The Washington Post. September 20, 2015.

Ambassador Richard Thompson Convicted of Murder Under the 1996 War Crimes Act

By Bill Leiby

Former Defense Secretary nominee and Ambassador Richard Thompson was convicted Friday of 223 counts of murder under the provisions of the 1996 War Crimes Act. Thompson was sentenced to 223 consecutive life sentences. Thompson was acquitted of multiple charges of assault and rape.

The murder charges and life sentences were the result of a grand jury investigation last year which concluded that Thompson and Leslie Collins were primarily responsible for the acquisition of chemical weapons which were used in a village in remote Badakhshan province in the winter of 1982, resulting in the death of more than 200 civilians. Until last year, it was believed that the Soviets were responsible for the massacre.

The accusations of rape, along with the murder charges, were revealed in detail in the Pulitzer Prize winning series by Post reporter Anthony Walker last May. Collins was murdered the same day. His murder remains unsolved.

The rape charges were brought by Thompson's former wife, Adelina Ramos, who recently relocated to London with her youngest daughter, Andrea, who will be attending the exclusive Chelsea Independent College in preparation for University studies.

Family spokesperson Julia Wilson said in an official statement, "Our father is a complicated and disturbed man. The family will not be commenting on his conviction or imprisonment, except to extend our heartfelt and abject remorse and apologies to the victims of his actions."

Andrea. London.

"Mom!" Andrea called out as loud as she could when she entered the townhouse. Adelina had bought a stupidly expensive townhome in Chelsea—big enough that all of her daughters could visit when they wanted to. At one time or another they all had.

Now the size worked against her. Andrea shouted again. "Mom! Mom!"

She heard steps upstairs. Running. Adelina appeared at the top of the stairs, concern on her face. "Andrea, what is it?"

"I got accepted!"

Adelina screamed. "Oh my God!"

Andrea met her halfway up the stairs and threw her arms around her mother.

For the last nine months Andrea had been completing a final year of senior school to make up the deficiencies in her education. She didn't realize she *had* any deficiencies until she'd applied for college at King's College in London. The college had provisionally accepted her, but required her to take a year of preparatory school.

Now she was in.

Adelina followed her downstairs to the dining room and looked over the acceptance letter. She looked up at Andrea. "I'm so proud of you."

"I have to call Jessica and Sarah. And Julia. And … everyone. They'll scream!"

Jessica and Sarah had both decided to stay in Washington, DC after they graduated high school, both attending Georgetown University and living with Carrie and Rachel. Andrea didn't think that would last too much longer. Carrie seemed to be ready for them to move into their own place.

Of course, she'd see them all soon enough, when they arrived in London next week.

She took her mother's hand.

Adelina said, "You know … three years ago, I never could have imagined … this. All of it. Us being together like this. I'm so happy."

Andrea smiled. "I am too, Mom. You have no idea. Okay. I've got to call."

She picked up the phone, trying to decide which sister to talk to first.

Adelina. Calella, Spain.

When Adelina Ramos stepped out of the taxicab she took a deep, cleansing breath and closed her eyes and counted to twenty. Then, for good measure, she counted a little more before opening her eyes. It had been more than twenty years since she'd stood on this sidewalk, next to this building, and the last time she'd had a panic attack that resulted in a months' long hospitalization.

There would be no panic attack this time. She clutched her bag under her shoulder and walked through the crowd that spilled out of the bar at the base of the apartment building.

She knew the way.

Up three flights of stairs, then down a long hall. It was brighter in here than she remembered, and cleaner. But then, the few months she'd lived here with her mother, she'd been in a deep depression. Grief at the loss of her father and of her innocence.

Finally she reached the door. Number 32. She took a deep breath, bracing herself, then knocked on the door.

Inside, she heard shouts. Luis, she supposed. "Mamá. Someone's here!"

Seconds later, the door opened.

It was Luis. Older, *much* older than the last time she'd seen him. His face blanched, and he choked out a half strangled word she couldn't quite make out.

"Hola, Luis," she said.

He took her hand. "I … I didn't think you would come. Ever."

"Luis!" The shout came from the living room. "Who is it?"

Luis swallowed. "Come in," he said.

Adelina walked forward. She could feel her chest tightening; the beginnings of what could become a panic attack. She hadn't had one in a long time. But she'd never be wholly healed.

But she hadn't come here to be healed. She'd come here to see her mother. She followed Luis into the living room.

The apartment was different. Brighter, yet somehow smaller. The breeze blew the light cotton fabric of the drapes, and a television blared laughter in the corner. An old woman leaned on a recliner watching the television.

Adelina stared at her mother.

The years had not been kind to her. Her mother was at least seventy now. Her eyes seemed hollow, and deep trenches furrowed her skin. A cigarette burned in an ashtray next to her, the smoke lazily floating toward the window.

Then she turned her face toward Adelina. Her face seemed slack, her eyes unfocused, as if she were blind and couldn't quite make out what she was seeing.

"Who are you? What do you want?"

The words were knives in her stomach, and Adelina actually took a step back, gasping.

Luis moved to their mother's side and kneeled. He whispered, "Mother, it's your daughter. It's Adelina."

Her mother's eyes widened and she seemed to search the room. "Adelina?" Tears began to run down the old woman's face.

"Hello, Mother," Adelina said. She sighed, letting out a long breath, as her little brother, now in his forties, looked at her with worry in his eyes. Adelina had come to Calella daydreaming of confronting her mother. She'd imagined the scene, imagined telling her mother exactly how she felt about all those years of hurt.

She'd imagined herself saying, *You destroyed my life. You broke my heart.*

But now, tears were streaming down her mother's face. She was shaking, looking up at Adelina with fear in her eyes. She expected it. She expected the explosion, the accusations, the tirade. It was clear enough that so did Luis.

Adelina couldn't do it. Her daughters had once thought the same things of her.

Instead, Adelina slowly dropped to her knees beside her mother, and whispered, "Te extrañé, Mamá."

I missed you, Mommy.

Julia. London.

"This is insane," Alexandra said. "I thought *my* wedding was too complicated."

Julia laughed a little under her breath, then said, "Royal weddings are something else entirely, aren't they? I'm glad I didn't have to organize this one."

The crowds in London had been enormous. *Enormous.* Julia had never imagined anything quite on this scale. But they were away from the crowds now. Unlike the larger royal weddings, which were as much affairs of state as they were personal unions, this wedding was taking place at St. George's Chapel at Windsor Castle.

In *Windsor Castle*. Julia had been in a lot of places, including meals at the White House. But this was something else. From the room where they waited, she could see from the castle to the chapel itself. At any moment, Julia and her sisters would be summoned to the cathedral.

Meeting the Queen had been terrifying. George-Phillip had seemed as nervous as any of them when Adelina presented all six of her daughters, along with the spouses of those who were married. The wedding itself had only a few hundred guests. Or maybe a *thousand*. Most of the titled nobility of Europe were here, along with many of the senior members of the House of Commons, the Prime Minister, the US Ambassador, and the Archbishop of Canterbury, who was presiding over the ceremony itself.

In short—for one of the first times in her life, Julia found herself overwhelmed.

Julia, Carrie and Alexandra had walked through the cathedral yesterday afternoon, while their younger siblings had decided to go to an amusement park instead. The chapel was incredible. Vaulted ceilings with dozens of banners and flags above arched windows of stained glass. The walls, erected of stone hundreds of years ago, appeared so light that they could blow away, with tendrils of stone arches supporting the ceiling above them. The cathedral could seat hundreds, easily.

In this church were buried kings from hundreds of years ago: Edward IV, Henry VI and Henry VIII along with one of his wives, Jane Seymour. Later kings were buried in the Royal vault and the Memorial Chapel—including George-Phillip's grandfather. History Julia had only read about had taken place over hundreds of years in this room, and now her mother would be joining part of that history.

Julia, though, thought that did not account for her odd, maudlin mood. She was happy for her mother—incredibly so. Prince George-Phillip had been the man Adelina had lived and loved, even as she was a virtual prisoner, all those years. Julia had long since made her peace with her mother, and even her father, though it had taken more years of therapy to do so.

But there was one thing she'd never made peace with, and her encounter with Harry Easton had brought that screaming back to her mind.

Harry had been at an official reception in London two days before, which the sisters were invited to. She hadn't expected to see him, but in retrospect, there was no reason to be surprised. After all, he moved in these circles. They were polite—not quite friendly, but not unfriendly either.

Running into him, however, reminded Julia of the one thing in her life that *no* amount of money could buy. Now that she was in her mid-thirties, she'd accomplished everything she'd ever wanted in life. Except, in moments like this ...

moments when she watched Rachel laughing as she ran down the hallway chasing Jane, or watched Alexandra protectively curling her arms around her belly, when she watched Dylan and his joy at the prospect of being a father—Julia wished she could have that joy. She wished she could share that joy with her husband.

But it wasn't to be. Even the adoption agency they'd worked with had told her it might take a long time.

People will be reluctant to place a baby with a family in your situation.

By her situation, they meant, rock stars. Musicians. People who moved around too much. Never mind that Julia was chief executive officer of a major corporation.

She closed her eyes. The longing grew worse every year, but today wasn't hers, it was her mother's. She reached out and took Alexandra's hand. "Are you going to be okay?"

"Of course," Alexandra replied.

She was glowing. *Of course.* At six months pregnant, Alexandra was clearly showing, and was vividly happy. In a few months she'd begin her final year of law school. Dylan had graduated and was working in a social work internship at a Vet Center in the Bronx. His primary job there was counseling of war veterans with PTSD, and he'd never looked happier.

One of the protocol officers who worked for the Queen appeared in the doorway. "Ladies, please come join the bride."

Julia took a deep breath. She reached out and took Carrie and Alexandra's hands. They in turn, reached out to Jessica and Sarah. Andrea closed the circle. Julia said, "Let's go." She smiled, and broke the circle. The six women went down the stairs to meet their mother. They wore matching blue dresses with long flowing skirts. Julia thought that some of her sisters were more comfortable in these outfits than others. Sarah looked like she wished she'd been able to sneak in combat boots. She *was* probably the only woman in the cathedral with visible tattoos.

Adelina was ready when they arrived. She had dyed her hair back to its normal black—she'd been greying more and more in recent years. She wore a beautiful white gown, which glistened with tens of thousands of hand-sewn pearls. Julia knew exactly how much the dress, with its pearls, had cost. She'd commissioned it in China and had it flown to London for her mother.

Adelina reached out and took Julia's hand. She wore white gloves, and her skin was flushed. Her eyes were brimming with water.

"Please tell me that's waterproof mascara," Julia said.

Adelina blushed. She *blushed.* Julia swallowed. She'd often thought of her mother as a harridan, as old, as vicious. She'd never once thought of her as a *bride.*

"Oh, Mother, I'm so happy for you," Julia said.

Adelina leaned forward and gently kissed her eldest daughter's cheek. "I'm so grateful to have you here with me," she whispered.

The ceremony was planned to be informal. The state royal weddings were much more lavish, including, normally, the arrival of the bride in a horse-drawn glass carriage. George-Phillip and Adelina had made it clear early on they wanted a much smaller and more private ceremony, with family and friends only. Windsor Castle and Saint George's Chapel was selected as the site primarily due to its privacy.

The procession began with the pounding of drums outside, probably heard for miles around, followed by the sound of the band. Julia and her sisters slipped to the window to look out toward the chapel, but at the insistence of the protocol officer, Adelina stayed put.

Outside, the procession had begun. Julia watched as a team of horsemen crossed the courtyard, followed by Prince George-Phillip, and his cousin, the Prince of Wales, who walked on foot. George-Phillip wore the black uniform and white belt of the Royal Marines, with his medals from the Falklands War and his reserve service. Although he no longer served, he was an honorary Colonel and still wore his uniform on state occasions.

Behind the two Princes were the guests of honor. Adelina had insisted on breaking with tradition, and had six bridesmaids, all adults—her daughters. In order to balance out the wedding party, George-Phillip was accompanied by six other men, including a visibly uncomfortable Dylan Paris and Bear Wyden, both of whom seemed to squirm in their tuxedos.

Bear had almost violently resisted attending the wedding, but after Dylan personally went to his apartment and argued with him, he finally agreed. Now Director of the Joint Terrorism Task Force, Bear was based out of New York City, with frequent visits to Washington to see the kids. His ex-wife, Leah, had long since recovered from her injuries.

Julia turned back and walked to her mother. Adelina was breathing slowly and deeply, and wore a dreamy smile on her face.

Julia said, "I think it's almost time. They just went in."

A moment later, the protocol officer opened the door. Just outside the small chamber stood Crank's father, Jack Wilson, who had agreed to act in lieu of her father who had passed away many years before. Jack was a former Boston cop, sentimental and demonstrative, and when he saw Adelina in her dress his eyes watered. He held an arm out and she took it. He glanced back at Julia and she smiled at him. Of course. He had a tiny orange, white and green flag on his lapel—the national flag of Ireland. Julia suppressed a laugh. The papers in London would get play out of that for years.

The chamber orchestra just inside the entrance of the cathedral began playing. The walkway between the castle at the chapel was two hundred yards, guarded on both sides by a phalanx of Royal guards in bright red uniforms. On the grass on either side were hundreds—possible thousands—of spectators. Royal weddings in general got a lot of attention, Julia knew, but George-Phillip was so far removed from the throne it normally wouldn't have attracted much interest. But the media attention around the events following Andrea's kidnapping—and George-Phillip and Adelina's decades long love—had captured the attention of both countries. For days, news media on both sides of the Atlantic had replayed the video captured on the front steps of the federal courthouse in Washington, DC, when George-Phillip had saved Adelina's life.

Jack and Adelina began their slow walk across the courtyard. Adelina's daughters followed in pairs—Julia and Alexandra first, then Carrie and Andrea, followed by the twins. They were organized by height, rather than age. Behind them in the procession, Adriana Poole walked. She wore a blue dress, and held the hands of Jane and Rachel as she walked. Jane and Rachel were far apart in age, but wore matching green dresses. Rachel's face was rosy and chubby. Since the bone marrow transplant, she'd needed no further transfusions, and was as healthy and happy as any little girl on earth. She didn't listen very well though. She tugged on Adriana's hand, trying to pull away, then twisted in circles. Jane came around the other side and picked her up and the two girls giggled.

Julia took a deep breath as she stepped forward with Alexandra at her side. Julia hated that she was envious of her sisters. She didn't want to feel that way. But when she watched the beauty of Rachel's laughter, and the swell of Alexandra's belly, she ached inside to be a mother.

The music got louder as they approached the entrance to the cathedral. Though she'd been in there the day before, this was different, she realized, as they walked up the steps and entered.

The crowd hushed, hundreds of people standing on both sides of the aisle facing inward. Julia heard as Andrea, behind her, sucked in a breath as she saw the crowd inside the cathedral.

It was hard to really get a sense of the scale of a cathedral like this. But with hundreds of people in the cathedral, with *trees* extending down both sides of the church, overhanging the aisle and still not reaching the ceiling which was *way, way* up. The detailing on the ceiling was incredible; the windows were huge, making the entire structure feel light and tenuous.

The procession continued down the aisle. Enormously tall but slender columns stretched into the sky far above the people on each side, who wore colorful outfits, dresses of green and red and blue, the men in suits with far more variety of style and color than would happen in the United States, and the *hats*. So many hats, some of them crazy, some of them beautiful, some … better not mentioned at all.

As they moved further down the length of the cathedral, she saw Crank, sitting in the third row, not far from the Queen. Julia flashed him a smile, and he returned it, then winked at her. They'd been married for considerably more than a decade, but she still felt a flush down her face and body at his wink.

At the front of the cathedral, George-Phillip stood nervously, hands at his side. His eyebrows seemed to move of their own accord as he gazed on his approaching bride. He tried to look serious and royal, but he couldn't keep the tremendous smile off his face.

Finally, they reached the crossing. Jack, who had obvious tears on his face, passed Adelina's hand to George-Phillip. Then he bowed to the Prince and stepped to the side.

George-Phillip and Adelina joined hands.

As the ceremony continued, Julia's eyes moved from her mother to each of her sisters, standing in a line at the front of the cathedral. Carrie, who had lost a husband, but gained a beautiful little girl and a father. Rachel stood with Adriana Poole and Jane to the side of the cathedral, waving at the audience, a toothy smile on her face. Carrie stood straight and tall, a smile on her face as she watched their mother finally reaching for her own happiness.

Alexandra's face was flushed. The night before, Julia had felt her stomach, and felt the baby move. She'd visited Alexandra and Dylan several times during their pregnancy—all of the sisters were closer now than they had once been. Dylan and Alexandra were incredibly happy. When asked where she planned to work, she'd announced she was going to try for the American Civil Liberties Union. "Abuses like Dad's and Leslie Collins' shouldn't be allowed. I want to work for someone who can provide a counterbalance."

Sarah looked radiant. College agreed with her—as did her now long-term boyfriend. Her twin Jessica had a warm smile on her face. Jessica's recovery had been a long and difficult struggle. She and Dylan had become close as they occasionally attended 12-step meetings together, both in New York and Washington. He'd acted as a mentor to his younger sister-in-law.

And Andrea. The youngest sister, and arguably the one who had suffered the most because of Richard Thompson.

Julia had been to London half a dozen times since Andrea moved here with their mother. And every time she felt staggered by the joy she saw on her sister's face.

Julia looked back at her mother and the Prince, who were now facing each other as the Archbishop blessed their marriage. George-Phillip took her hands and bent down as Adelina lifted up on her toes and the newly married couple slowly and lovingly kissed.

Tears ran down her face as the Archbishop called in a loud voice, "I give you their Royal Highnesses, the Duke and Duchess of Kent."

Julia. Boston.

Like every other celebration, the wedding of Prince George-Phillip and his wife Adelina faded from memory. The couple now lived with Andrea at his town-house in Belgrave Square, and after a few days of celebration each of Adelina's daughters had returned to their own lives.

That meant Julia returned to Boston and her offices on Broadway in South Boston. She was there, preparing to convene a staff meeting, when her phone rang.

She stared dumbly at it for several seconds. The phone call was from United Methodist Family Services—the organization where she and Crank had applied to adopt. Fourteen months had passed since their home study with no word.

She scrambled. "Hello?"

"Julia? It's Renee Hunt."

"Yes?" Apprehension shot through Julia. She stood up, scanning the open work area and its fifteen employees. Crank was nowhere in sight. "What is it?"

She waved at her administrative assistant, then mouthed, *Find Crank!*

"Is Crank available?"

"Hold on, I'm not sure—wait, there he is. Hold on." She waved at him. Crank's eyes widened at her urgency, and he half jogged across the floor.

"What is it?" he whispered.

She put the phone on speaker, and said, "Renee, Crank is here. Now—what is it?"

On the other end of the line, Renee Hunt took a deep breath. Julia reached out and grabbed Crank's hand and squeezed, probably too hard. Then she heard the words.

"Are you guys busy tomorrow? I have good news. We have a baby for you."

Tears began to pour down Julia's face. Happy, joyous tears. "No. We'll cancel our plans, whatever they are."

She threw her arms around her husband.

Rachel. Bethesda, Maryland.

Mommy told me Daddy lives inside the rock at the big green park. I met him a bunch, at least three times. But he's dead inside the rock and can't play. I get sad for Daddy locked in the rock. Did you know that dead means you can't come out and play anymore? But Mommy says Daddy is with God and happy.

Maybe God plays with him. I'd be sad if I couldn't come out and play.

Mommy said we only go see Daddy on Memory Day. That's when everybody members their daddies and mommies if they don't have one. We have a picture of Daddy at home. Sometimes the picture makes Mommy sad, except when it makes her smile. I'm glad Daddy's happy with God. I wish I could meet him some day, and he could take me to the playground.

But now Mommy says I get to have another daddy for my birthday. When she kisses him she smiles. His beard is ticklish. That's why it makes me giggle.

When I giggle and my second daddy laughs, it makes Mommy smile. I like when she smiles. She says having a second daddy is like having two scoops of ice cream.

My birthday is tomorrow, and I get my second daddy.

I love him.

So does Mommy.

END

Author's Note

When writing a work of political fiction, sometimes the parallels to real life are inescapable.

Ronald Reagan, Eugene Jackson, Henry Kissenger and Margaret Thatcher and Queen Elizabeth II are all known historical personages. However, their roles in this story are completely fictional.

The Wakhan Corridor largely missed the violence of the Soviet invasion of Afghanistan, just as it has missed most of the violence of the current war in Afghanistan. However, the fighting has lasted 35 years, more than a generation--first with the Soviets, then the Taliban, and finally the United States. Much of the violence I described was typical, including massacres of civilians. There was no use of chemical weapons as described in this book.

Events in the Falkland Islands and the bombing of the Marine barracks in Beirut, Lebanon took place pretty much as I described them here. But virtually all of the details are left out.

Prince George-Phillip obviously does not exist. Some other members of the Royal family mentioned in this story, such as Princess Alexandra, do. However, everything described about the royal family is fiction.

I know little about the operations of the State Department's Diplomatic Security Service. Where I couldn't find the information on Google I just made it up.

www.ingramcontent.com/pod-product-compliance
Lightning Source LLC
Chambersburg PA
CBHW050117030726
47505CB00007B/1914